GEORGETTE

HEYER

GEORGETTE HEYER

ARABELLA • BATH TANGLE • THE NONESUCH

PEERAGE BOOKS

Arabella first published in 1949
by William Heinemann Limited

Bath Tangle first published in 1955
by William Heinemann Limited

The Nonesuch first published in 1962
by William Heinemann Limited

This edition first published in 1991 by
Peerage Books
an imprint of Reed International Books Limited
Michelin House
81 Fulham Road
London SW3 6RB

ISBN 1 85052 219 7

Printed and bound in the United Kingdom by The Bath Press

CONTENTS

ARABELLA

CHAPTER ONE

THE SCHOOLROOM in the Parsonage at Heythram was not a large apartment, but on a bleak January day, in a household where the consumption of coals was a consideration, this was not felt by its occupants to be a disadvantage. Quite a modest fire in the high, barred grate made it unnecessary for all but one of the four young ladies present to huddle shawls round their shoulders. But Elizabeth, the youngest of the Reverend Henry Tallant's handsome daughters, was suffering from the ear-ache, and, besides stuffing a roasted onion into the afflicted orifice, had swathed her head and neck in an old Cashmere shawl. She lay curled up on an aged sofa, with her head on a worn red cushion, and from time to time uttered a long-suffering sigh, to which none of her sisters paid any heed. Betsy was known to be sickly. It was thought that the climate of Yorkshire did not agree with her constitution, and since she spent the greater part of the winter suffering from a variety of minor ills her delicacy was regarded by all but her Mama as a commonplace.

There were abundant signs, littered over the table in the centre of the room, that the young ladies had retired to this cosy, shabby apartment to hem shirts, but only one of them, the eldest, was thus engaged. In a chair on one side of the fireplace, Miss Margaret Tallant, a buxom fifteen-year old, was devouring the serial story in a bound volume of *The Ladies' Monthly Museum*, with her fingers stuffed in her ears; and seated opposite to Miss Arabella, her stitchery lying neglected on the table before her, sat Miss Sophia, reading aloud from another volume of this instructive periodical.

"I must say, Bella," she remarked, momentarily lowering the book, "I find this most perplexing! Only listen to what it says here! *We have presented our subscribers with fashions of the newest pattern, not such as shall violate the laws of propriety and decorum, but such as shall assist the smile of good humour, and give an additional charm to the carriage of benevolence. Economy ought to be the order of the day* – And then, if you please, there is a picture of the most ravishing evening-gown – Do but look at it, Bella! – and it says that the Russian bodice is of blue satin, fastened in front with diamonds! *Well!*"

Her sister obediently raised her eyes from the wristband she was hemming, and critically scanned the willowy giantess depicted amongst the Fashion Notes. Then she sighed, and once more bent her dark head over her work. "Well, if that is their notion of economy, I am sure I couldn't go to London, even if my godmother invited me. And I know she won't," she said fatalistically.

"You must and you shall go!" declared Sophy, in accents of strong resolution. "Only think what it may mean to all of us if you do!"

"Yes, but I won't go looking like a dowd," objected Arabella, "and if I am obliged to have diamond fastenings to my bodices, you know very well -"

"Oh, stuff! I daresay that is the extreme of fashion, or perhaps they are made of paste! And in any event this is one of the older numbers. I know I saw in one of them that jewellery is no longer worn in the mornings, so very likely- Where is that volume? Margaret, you have it! Do, pray, give it to me! You are by far too young to be interested in such things!"

Margaret uncorked her ears to snatch the book out of her sister's reach. "No! I'm reading the serial story!"

"Well, you should not. You know Papa does not like us to read romances."

"If it comes to that," retorted Margaret, "he would be excessively grieved to find you reading nothing better than the latest modes!"

They looked at one another; Sophy's lip quivered. "Dear Meg, do pray give it to me, only for a *moment*!"

"Well, I will when I have finished the *Narrative of Augustus Waldstein*," said Margaret. "But *only* for a moment, mind!"

"Wait, I know there is something here to the purpose!" said Arabella, dropping her work to flick over the pages of the volume abandoned by Sophia. "*Method of Preserving Milk by Horse-Radish . . . White Wax for the Nails . . . Human Teeth placed to Stumps* . . . Yes, here it is! Now, listen, Meg! *Where a Female has in early life dedicated her attention to novel-reading she is unfit to become the companion of a man of sense, or to conduct a family with propriety and decorum*. There!" She looked up, the prim pursing of her lips enchantingly belied by her dancing eyes.

"I am sure Mama is not unfit to be the companion of a man of sense!" cried Margaret indignantly. "And *she* reads novels! And even Papa does not find *The Wanderer* objectionable, or Mrs Edgeworth's *Tales*!"

"No, but he did not like it when he found Bella reading *The Hungarian Brothers*, or *The Children of the Abbey*," said Sophia, seizing the opportunity to twitch *The Ladies' Monthly Museum* out of her sister's slackened grasp. "He said there was a great deal of nonsense in such books, and that the moral tone was sadly lacking."

"Moral tone is not lacking in the serial I am reading!" declared Margaret, quite ruffled. "Look what it says there, near the bottom of the page! 'Albert! be purity of character your duty!' I am sure he could not dislike that!"

Arabella rubbed the tip of her nose. "Well, I think he would say it was fustian," she remarked candidly. "But do give the book back to her, Sophy!"

"I will, when I have found what I'm looking for. Besides, it was I who had the happy notion to borrow the volumes from Mrs Caterham, so - Yes, here it is! It says that only jewellery of very plain workmanship is worn in the mornings nowadays." She added, on a note of doubt: "I daresay the fashions don't change so very fast, even in London. This number is only three years old."

The sufferer on the sofa sat up cautiously. "But Bella hasn't got any jewellery, has she?"

This observation, delivered with all the bluntness natural in a damsel of only nine summers, threw a blight over the company.

"I have the gold locket and chain with the locks of Papa's and Mama's hair in it," said Arabella defensively.

"If you had a tiara, and a . . . a cestus, and an armlet to match it, it might answer," said Sophy. "There is a toilet described here with just those ornaments."

Her three sisters gazed at her in astonishment. "What is a cestus?" they demanded.

Sophy shook her head. "I don't know," she confessed.

"Well, Bella hasn't got one at all events," said the Job's comforter on the sofa.

"If she were so poor-spirited as to refuse to go to London for such a trifling reason as that, I would never forgive her!" declared Sophy.

"Of course I would not!" exclaimed Arabella scornfully. "But I have not the least expectation that Lady Bridlington will invite me, for why should she, only because I am her god-daughter? I never saw her in my life!"

"She sent a very handsome shawl for your christening gift," said Margaret hopefully.

"Besides being Mama's dearest friend," added Sophy.

"But Mama has not seen her either – at least, not for years and years!"

"And she never sent Bella anything else, not even when she was confirmed," pointed out Betsy, gingerly removing the onion from her ear, and throwing it into the fire.

"If your ear-ache is better," said Sophia, eyeing her with disfavour, "you may hem this seam for me! I want to draw a pattern for a new flounce."

"Mama said I was to sit quietly by the fire," replied the invalid, disposing herself more comfortably. "Are there any acrostics in those fusty old books?"

"No, and if there were I would not give them to anyone so disobliging as you, Betsy!" said Sophy roundly.

Betsy began to cry, in an unconvincing way, but as Margaret was once more absorbed in her serial, and Arabella had drawn Sophia's attention to the picture of a velvet pelisse trimmed lavishly with ermine, no one paid any heed to her, and she presently relapsed into silence, merely sniffing from time to time, and staring resentfully at her two eldest sisters.

They presented a charming picture, as they sat poring over their book, their dark ringlets intermingled, and their arms round each other's waists. They were very plainly dressed, in gowns of blue kerseymere, made high to the throat, and with long tight sleeves; and they wore no other ornaments than a knot or two of ribbons; but the Vicar's numerous offspring were all remarkable for their good-looks and had very little need of embellishment. Although Arabella was unquestionably the Beauty of the family, it was pretty generally agreed in the neighbourhood that once Sophia had outgrown the over-plumpness of her sixteen years she might reasonably hope to rival her senior. Each had large, dark, and expressive eyes, little straight noses, and delicately moulded lips; each had complexions which were the envy of less fortunate young ladies, and which owed nothing to Denmark Lotion, Olympian Dew, Bloom of Ninon, or any other aid to beauty advertised in the society journals. Sophia was the taller of the two; Arabella had by far the better figure, and the neater ankle. Sophia looked to be the more robust; Arabella enchanted her admirers by a deceptive air of fragility, which inspired one romantically-minded young gentleman to liken her to a leaf blown by the wind; and another to address a very bad set of verses to her, apostrophizing her as the New Titania. Unfortunately, Harry had found this effusion, and had shown it to Bertram, and until Papa had said, with his gentle austerity, that he considered the jest to be outworn, they had insisted on hailing their sister by this exquisitely humorous appellation.

Betsy, brooding over her wrongs, found nothing to admire in either sister, and was weighing the advantage of cosseting from old Nurse against the possibility of being called upon to amuse Baby Jack, were she to remove herself to the nursery, when the door burst open, and a stout boy of eleven years, in nankeens and a frilled shirt, and with a mop of curly hair, precipitated himself into the room, exclaiming loudly: "Hallo! Such a kick-up! Mama is with Papa in the study, but I know what it's all about!"

"Why, what has happened?" exclaimed Sophia.

"Don't you wish you knew!" said Harry, drawing a piece of twine from his pocket, and beginning to tie it into a complicated knot. "Watch me tie this one, Meg! I know six of the chief knots now, and if Uncle James does not get Captain Bolton to take me on his next commission it will be the most infamous, swindling thing I ever heard of!"

"But you didn't come to tell us that!" said Arabella. "What is it?"

"Nothing but one of Harry's hums!" said Margaret.

"No such thing!" retorted her brother. "Joseph Eccles has been down to the White Hart, and brought back the post with him." He perceived that he had succeeded in riveting his sisters' attention on himself, and grinned at them. "Ay, you may stare! There's a letter from London, for Mama. Franked by some lord, too: I saw it."

Margaret's book slipped from her fingers to the floor; Sophia gave a gasp; and Arabella flew up out of her chair. "Harry! Not – oh, not from my godmother?"

"Oh, ain't it?" said Harry.

"If it comes from London, it must be from Lady Bridlington!" declared Sophia. "Arabella, I do believe our fortunes are in a way to being made!"

"I *dare* not suppose it to be possible!" said Arabella, quite faintly. "Depend upon it, she has written to say she cannot invite me!"

"Nonsense!" replied her practical sister. "If that were all, pray why should Mama take the letter to my father? I regard the matter as settled already. You are going to London for the Season."

"Oh, if it could be so indeed!" said Arabella, trembling.

Harry, who had abandoned knot-making in favour of trying to stand on his head, overbalanced at this moment, and fell in a heap on the floor, together with a chair, Sophia's work-box, and a hand-screen, which Margaret had been painting before succumbing to the superior attraction of *The Ladies' Monthly Museum*. Beyond begging him not to be such an ape, none of his sisters censured his clumsiness. He picked himself up, remarking scornfully that only a girl would make such a fuss about a mere visit to London. "The slowest thing!" he said. "I should like to know what you think you would do there!"

"Oh, Harry, how can you be so stupid? The balls! The theatres! Assemblies!" uttered Arabella, in choked accents.

"*I* thought you were going there to form an eligible connection," said Betsy. "That is what Mama said, for I heard her."

"Then you had no business to be listening!" said Sophia tartly.

"What's an eligible connection?" demanded Harry, beginning to juggle with several reels of sewing-silk, which had spilled out of the work-box on to the floor.

"I'm sure I don't know!"

"I do," offered the invalid. "It's a splendid marriage, of course. And *then* Bella will invite Sophy and Meg and me to stay with her in London, and we shall *all* find rich husbands!"

"That I shall certainly not do, miss!" declared Arabella. "Let me tell you that no one will invite you anywhere until you have a little more conduct!"

"Well, Mama *did* say it," argued Betsy, in a whining voice. "And you need not think I do not know about such things, because --"

Sophia interrupted her ruthlessly. "If, Betsy, you do not desire me to tell Papa of your shocking lack of delicacy, I advise you to take yourself off to the nursery where you belong!"

This terrible threat did not fail of its object. Complaining that her sisters were disagreeable cats, Betsy, went as slowly from the room as she dared, trailing her shawl behind her.

"She is very sickly," said Arabella, in an excusing tone.

"She is a precocious brat!" retorted Sophia. "One would have thought that she would have had more elegance of mind than to be thinking of such things! Oh, Bella, if only you were to be so fortunate as to make a Splendid Marriage! And if Lady Bridlington is to bring you out I am sure I do not see how you can fail to! For," she added nobly, "you are by far the prettiest girl *I* have ever seen!"

"Hoo!" interpolated Harry, adding his mite to the conversation.

"Yes," agreed Margaret, "but if she must have diamond buttons, and tiaras, and – and those things you spoke of, I don't see how it can be done!"

A damped silence greeted her words. Sophy was the first to recover herself. "Something," she announced resolutely, "will be contrived!"

No one answered her. Arabella and Margaret appeared to be dubiously weighing her pronouncement; and Harry, having discovered a pair of scissors, was pleasurably engaged in snipping short lengths off a skein of darning-wool. Into this pensive silence walked a young gentleman just emerging from adolescence into manhood. He was a handsome youth, fairer than his elder sister, but with something of her cast of countenance; and it was manifest, from the alarming height of his shirt collar, and the disorder of his chestnut locks, that he affected a certain modishness that bordered on dandyism. The Knaresborough tailor who enjoyed his patronage could not aspire to the height of art achieved by Weston or Stultz, but he had done his best, and had indeed been greatly assisted by the admirable proportions of his client. Mr Bertram Tallant set off a coat to advantage, and was blessed with a most elegant pair of legs. These were at the moment encased in a pair of buckskin breeches, but their owner cherished in one of his chests of drawers a pair of yellow pantaloons which he had not yet dared to display to his Papa, but which, he rather fancied, turned him into a veritable Tulip of Fashion. His top-boots, on which he expended much thought and labour, were as refulgent as could be expected of boots belonging to a gentleman whose parents were unhappily unable to supply their second son with the champagne indispensable for a really good blacking; and the points of his shirt-collars, thanks to the loving hands of his sisters, were so stiffly starched that it was only with great difficulty that he could turn his head. Like his elder brother James, at present up at Oxford, prior to taking Orders, he had been educated at Harrow, but he was at present domiciled at home, working under his father's guidance with a view to passing Smalls during the Easter Vacation. This task he had embarked on without enthusiasm, his whole ambition being to obtain a cornetcy in a Hussar regiment. But as this would cost not a penny less than eight hundred pounds, and the termination of the long war with Bonaparte had made promotion unlikely, unless by expensive purchase, Mr Tallant had decided, not unreasonably, that a civil occupation would prove less ruinous than a military career. He intended that Bertram, once provided with a respectable degree, should adorn the Home Office; and any doubts which the volatile disposition of his offspring might have engendered in his mind of his eligibility for that service, he was nearly able to allay by the reflection that Bertram was, after all, not yet eighteen, and that Oxford University, where he himself had passed three scholarly years, would exert a stabilizing influence on his character.

The future candidate for Parliament heralded his entrance into the schoolroom with a muted hunting-cry, followed immediately by the announcement that some people were unfairly favoured by fortune.

Arabella clasped both her hands at her breast, and raised a pair of speaking eyes to his face. "Bertram, is it *indeed* true? Now, don't try to roast me – pray don't!"

"Lord, yes! But who told you?"

"Harry, of course," replied Sophia. "The children know everything in this house!"

Mr Bertram Tallant nodded gloomily, and pulled up his sleeves a trifle. "You don't want him in here: shall I turn him out?" he enquired.

"Ho!" cried Harry, leaping to his feet, and squaring up to his senior in great good-humour. "A mill!"

"Not in here!" shrieked his sisters, with one accustomed voice.

But as they had no expectation of being attended to, each damsel made a dive to snatch her own particular property out of harm's way. This was just as well, since the room, besides being small, was crowded with knick-knacks. The brothers struggled and swayed together for a brief minute or two, but since Harry, though a lusty lad, was no match for Bertram, he was very soon thrust outside the room, and the door slammed against him. After dealing the scarred panels a few kicks, and threatening his senior with gruesome reprisals, he took himself off, whistling loudly through the convenient gap occasioned by the loss of one of his front teeth; and Bertram was able to remove his shoulders from the door, and to straighten his cravat.

"Well, you are to go," he informed Arabella. "I wish I had a rich godmother, that's all! Much old Mrs Calne ever did for me, except to give me a devilish book called the *Christian Comforter*, or some such thing, which was enough to send a fellow to the dogs directly!"

"I must say, I think it was excessively shabby of her," agreed Margaret.

"Even Papa said that if she had thought you had a taste for such literature, she might have supposed that you could find it upon his shelves."

"Well, my father knows I have no turn in that direction, and this I will say for him, he don't expect it of me." said Bertram handsomely. "He may be devilish straitlaced, and full of old-fashioned notions, but he's a right one at heart, and don't plague one with a pack of humbug."

"Yes, yes!" said Arabella impatiently, "but does he know of this letter? Will he let me go?"

"I fancy he don't like it above half, but he said he could not stand in your way, and must trust to your conducting yourself in Society with propriety, and not allowing your head to be turned by frivolity and admiration. And as to that," Bertram added, with brotherly candour, "I don't suppose they will think you anything out of the way amongst all the nobs, so there's precious little chance of its happening."

"No, I am sure they will not," said Arabella. "But tell me the whole! What did Lady Bridlington say in her letter?"

"Lord, I don't know! I was trying to make sense of a whole rigmarole of Greek when Mama came in, and I wasn't listening with more than half an ear. I daresay she'll tell it all to you. She sent me to say she wants you in her dressing-room."

"Good gracious, why could you not have told me that before?" cried Arabella, stuffing the half-finished shirt into a work-bag and flitting out of the room.

The Parsonage, although built on two storeys only, was a large, old-fashioned house, and to reach Mrs Tallant's dressing-room Arabella was obliged to traverse several corridors, all carpeted with a worn drugget, and all equally draughty.

The living of Heythram was respectable, being worth some three hundred pounds a year, in addition to which the present incumbent was possessed of a small independence; but the claims of a numerous family made the recarpeting of passages more a thing to be dreamed of than an allowable expense. The Vicar, himself the son of a landed gentleman, had married the beautiful Miss Theale, who might have been expected to have done better for herself than to have thrown her cap over the windmill for a mere younger son, however handsome he might be. Indeed, it had been commonly said at the time that she had married to disoblige her family, and might, if she had chosen, have caught a baronet on her hook. Instead she had fallen in love with Henry Tallant at first sight. Since his birth was genteel, and her parents had other daughters to dispose of, she had been permitted to have her way; and apart from wishing sometimes that the living were worth more, or that Henry would not put his hand in his pocket for every beggar who crossed his path, she had never given anyone reason to suppose that she regretted her choice. To be sure, she would have liked to have installed into the Parsonage one of the new water-closets, and a Patent Kitchen Range; or, like her brother-in-law up at the Hall, have been able, without feeling the pinch, to have burnt wax candles in all the rooms; but she was a sensible woman, and even when the open fire in the kitchen smoked, and the weather made a visit to the existing water-closet particularly disagreeable, she realized that she was a great deal happier with her Henry than ever she could have been with that almost forgotten baronet. She naturally concurred in his decision that whatever became of their daughters their sons at least must receive every advantage of education; but even while employing every shift of economy to ensure the respectable maintenance of James and Bertram at Harrow she was gradually building her ambitions more and more on the future of her eldest and most beautiful daughter. Without precisely regretting the circumstances which had made it impossible for herself to shine farther afield than York and Scarborough, she was determined that Arabella should not be similarly circumscribed. Perhaps it had been with this hope already at the back of her mind that she had invited her school-friend, Arabella Haverhill, who had contracted such a brilliant match, to stand as godmother to her infant daughter. Certainly her resolve to send the younger Arabella to make her début into society under the aegis of Lady Bridlington was of no very recent date. She had maintained throughout the years an infrequent but regular correspondence with her old friend, and was tolerably certain that fashionable life had in no way impaired the easy good-nature which had characterized the plump and cheerful Miss Haverhill. Lady Bridlington was not herself blessed with daughters she was, in fact, the mother of only one child, a son, some seven or eight years older than Mrs Tallant's daughter but from her friend's point of view this was a decided advantage. The mother of a family of hopeful girls, however good-natured, would not be in the least likely to take under her wing yet another young female in search of an eligible husband. But a widow in comfortable circumstances, with a strong inclination for all the amusements of fashion, and no daughters to launch upon the world, might reasonably be supposed to welcome the opportunity of chaperoning a young protégée to the balls, routs, and Assemblies she herself delighted in. Mrs Tallant could not conceive it to be otherwise. Nor was she disappointed. Lady Bridlington, crossing several sheets of gilt-edged notepaper with her sprawling pen, could not imagine why she should not have hit upon the notion herself. She was excessively dull, and liked nothing in the world so much as having young persons about her. It had long been a grief to her, she wrote, that she had no daughter of her own; and as she had no doubt that she would love her dearest Sophia's girl on sight she should await her arrival in the greatest impatience. Mrs Tallant had had no need to mention her object in sending Arabella to town: Henry Tallant might consider that Lady Bridlington's letters betrayed little but folly and frivolity, but her ladyship, however lacking in mental profundity, had plenty of worldly sense. Sophia might rest assured, she wrote, that she would leave no stone unturned to provide Arabella with a suitable husband. Already, she hinted, she had several eligible bachelors in her eye.

It was small wonder, then, that Arabella, peeping into her mother's dressing-room, should have found that admirable lady lost in a pleasant daydream.

"Mama?"

"Arabella! Come in, my love, and close the door! Your godmother has written, and in the kindest way! Dear, dear creature, I knew I might depend upon her!"

"It's true then? I am to go?" Arabella breathed.

"Yes, and she begs I will send you to her as soon as may be contrived, for it seems that Bridlington is travelling on the Continent, and she is quite moped to death, living in that great house all alone. I knew how it must be! She will treat you as her own daughter. And, oh, my dearest child, I never asked it of her, but she has offered to present you at one of the Drawing-rooms!"

This dizzy prospect took from Arabella all power of speech. She could only gaze at her mother, while that lady poured out a list of the delights in store for her.

"Everything I could wish for you! Almack's – I am sure she will be able to procure you a voucher, for she knows all the patronesses! Concerts! The theatre! All the *ton* parties – breakfasts, Assemblies, balls – my love, you will have such opportunities! you can have no notion! Why, she writes that – but never mind that! "

Arabella found her voice. "But Mama, how shall we contrive? The expense! I cannot I *cannot* go to London without any clothes to wear!"

"No, indeed!" said Mrs Tallant, laughing. "That would present a very odd appearance, my love!"

"Yes, Mama, but you know what I mean! I have only two ball dresses, and though they do very well for the Assemblies in Harrowgate, and country parties, I *know* they are not modish enough for Almack's! And Sophy has borrowed all Mrs Caterham's *Monthly Museums*, and I have been looking at the fashions in them, and it is too lowering ma'am! Everything must be trimmed with diamonds, or ermine, or point-lace!"

"My dear Arabella, don't put yourself in a taking! *That* has all been thought of, I assure you. You must know that I have had this scheme in my mind for many a long day." She saw her daughter's face of mystification, and laughed again. "Why, did you think I would send you into society looking like a rustic? I am not quite such a zany, I hope! I have been putting by for this very occasion since I don't know when."

"Mama!"

"I have a little money of my own, you know," explained Mrs Tallant. "Your dear Papa would never use it, but desired me to spend it only as I liked, because I used to be very fond of pretty things, and he never could bear to think I might not have them when I married him. That was all nonsense, of course, and I'm sure I very soon gave up thinking of such fripperies. But I was very glad to have it to spend on my children. And in spite of Margaret's drawing-lessons, and Sophy's music-master, and dearest Bertram's new coat, and those yellow pantaloons which he dare not let Papa see – my love, was there ever such a foolish boy? As though Papa did not know all along! and having to take poor Betsy to the doctor three times this year, I have quite a little nest-egg saved for you!"

"Oh, mama, no, no!" cried Arabella, distressed. "I would rather not go to London at all than that you should be put to such dreadful expense!"

"That is because you are sadly shatterbrained, my dear," replied her mother calmly. "I regard it as an investment, and I shall own myself extremely astonished if a great deal of good does not come of it." She hesitated, looked a little conscious, and said, picking her words: "I am sure I do not have to tell you that Papa is a Saint. Indeed, I don't suppose there is a better husband or father alive! But he is not at all practical, and when one has eight children to provide for, one must have a little worldly sense, or I don't know how one is to go on. One need have no anxiety about dear James, to be sure; and since Harry is set on going to sea, and his uncle is so obliging as to use his influence in his behalf, *his* future is settled. But I own I cannot be happy about poor Bertram; and where I am to find suitable husbands for all you girls in this restricted neighbourhood, I have not the least notion! Now, that is speaking more plainly than perhaps Papa would like, but you are a sensible puss, Arabella, and I have no scruple in being open with you. If I can but contrive to establish you respectably, you may bring out your sisters, and perhaps, even, if you should be so fortunate as to marry a gentleman of position, you might be able to help Bertram to buy his commission. I do not mean, of course, that your husband should purchase it precisely, but he might very likely have an interest at the Horse Guards, or – or something of the sort!"

Arabella nodded, for it was no news to her that she, as the eldest of four sisters, was expected to marry advantageously. She knew it to be her duty to do so. "Mama, I will *try* not to disappoint you!" she said earnestly.

CHAPTER TWO

IT WAS the candidly expressed opinion of the Vicar's children that Mama must have had a great work to prevail upon Papa to consent to Arabella's going to London. Few things were more reprehensible in his eyes than vanity and pleasure-seeking; and although he never raised any objection to Mama's chaperoning Arabella and Sophia to the Assemblies at Harrowgate, and had even been known to comment favourably upon their gowns, he always impressed upon them that such diversions, innocent in themselves, would, if indulged in to excess, inevitably ruin the character of the most virtuous female. He had himself no taste for society, and had frequently been heard to animadvert severely on the useless and frivolous lives led by ladies of fashion. Moreover, although he was not in the least above enjoying a good joke, he had the greatest dislike of levity, could never be brought to tolerate idle chatter, and if the conversation turned upon worldly trifles would never fail to give it a more proper direction.

But Lady Bridlington's invitation to Arabella did not take the Vicar by surprise. He knew that Mrs Tallant had written to her old friend, and however little he approved of the chief motive behind her resolve to launch her daughter into society, certain of the arguments she employed to persuade him could not but carry weight.

"My dear Mr Tallant," said his lady, "do not let us dispute about the merits of an advantageous match! But even you will allow that Arabella is an uncommonly handsome girl!"

Mr Tallant allowed it, adding reflectively that Arabella put him forcibly in mind of what her Mama was at the same age. Mrs Tallant was not impervious to this flattery: she blushed, and looked a little roguishly, but said that he need not try to bamboozle her (an expression she had picked up from her sons).

"All I wish to point out to you, Mr Tallant, is that Arabella is fit to move in the first circles!" she announced.

"My love," responded the Vicar, with one of his humorous looks, "if I believed you, I should perhaps consider it my duty to show you that an ambition to move in the first circles, as you call them, could never be an ideal I could wish any of my daughters to aspire to. But as I am persuaded that you have a great many other arguments to advance, I will hold my peace, and merely beg you to continue!"

"Well," said Mrs Tallant seriously, "I fancy – but you must tell me if I am mistaken – that you would not regard with any degree of complaisance an alliance with the Draytons of Knaresborough!"

The Vicar was plainly startled, and directed an enquiring look at his spouse.

"Young Joseph Drayton is growing extremely particular in his attentions," pronounced Mrs Tallant, in a voice of doom. She observed the effect of this, and continued in the blandest way: "Of course, I am aware that he is considered to be a great catch, for he will inherit all his father's wealth."

The Vicar was betrayed into an unchristian utterance. "I could not consent to it! He smells of the shop!"

"Exactly so!" agreed Mrs Tallant, well-satisfied. "But he has been dangling after Arabella these past six months."

"Do you tell me," demanded the Vicar, "that a daughter of mine encourages his attentions?"

"By no means!" promptly responded the lady. "Any more than she encourages the attentions of the curate, young Dewsbury, Alfred Hitchin, Humphrey Finchley, or a dozen others! Arabella, my dear sir, is by far the most sought-after belle of these parts!"

"Dear me!" said the Vicar, shaking his head in wonderment. "I must confess, my love, that none of these young gentlemen would be welcome to me as a son-in-law."

"Then, perhaps, Mr Tallant, you cherish hopes of seeing Arabella married to her cousin Tom?"

"Nothing," said the Vicar forcibly, "could be farther from my wishes!" He recollected himself, and added in a more moderate tone: "My brother is a very worthy man, according to his lights, and I wish his children nothing but good; but on several counts, which I need not enumerate, I should not desire to see any of my daughters marry their cousins. And, what is more, I am very sure that he has quite other designs for Tom and Algernon!"

"Indeed he has!" corroborated Mrs Tallant cordially. "He means them to marry heiresses."

The Vicar bent an incredulous gaze upon her. "Does my daughter affect any of these young men?" he demanded.

"I fancy not," replied Mrs Tallant. "That is to say, she does not show any marked preference for any one of them. But when a girl sees no other gentlemen than those who have been dangling after her ever since she left the schoolroom, what, my dear Mr Tallant, must be the end of it? And young Drayton," she added musingly, "is possessed of a considerable fortune. I do not mean that Arabella would consider *that*, but there is no denying that the man who drives a smart curricle, and can afford to be begging a female's acceptance of all the most elegant trifles imaginable, has a decided advantage over his rivals."

There was a pregnant silence, while all the implications of this speech sank into the Vicar's brain. He said at length, rather wistfully: "I had hoped that one day a suitable *parti* would present himself, to whom I might have given Arabella with a thankful heart."

Mrs Tallant threw him an indulgent glance. "Very likely, my dear, but it would be a great piece of nonsense to pretend that such things happen when one has made not the least push to bring them about! Eligible *partis* do not commonly appear as by magic in country villages: one must go out into the world to find them!" She saw that the Vicar was looking a little pained, and laughed. "Now, do not tell me that it was otherwise with us, Mr Tallant, for you know very well I met you first at a party in York! I own it was not in the expectation of my falling in love with you that my Mama took me there, but in your turn you will own that we should never have met if I had sat at home waiting for you!"

He smiled. "Your arguments are always unanswerable, my love. Yet I cannot entirely like it. I believe Arabella to be a well-behaved girl enough, but she is very young, after all, and I have thought sometimes that her spirits might, lacking wiser guidance, betray her into unbecoming conduct. Under Lady Bridlington's roof, she would, I fear, lead a life gay to dissipation, such as must make her unfit afterwards for rational society."

"Depend upon it," said Mrs Tallant soothingly, "she is by far too well-behaved a girl to occasion us a moment's anxiety. I am sure, too, that her principles are too sound to allow her to lose her head. To be sure, she can be a sad romp, and *that*, my dear sir, is because she has not yet enjoyed the advantages of town polish. I am hopeful of seeing her much improved by a season spent with Bella Bridlington. And if – mind, I only say if! – she were to contract a suitable alliance I am sure you would be as thankful as anyone could be!"

"Yes," agreed the Vicar, sighing. "I should certainly be glad to see her comfortably established, the wife of a respectable man."

"And *not* the wife of young Dewsbury!" interpolated Mrs Tallant.

"Indeed, no! I cannot suppose that any child of mine could attain happiness with a man whom I must – with reluctance – think a very vulgar fellow!"

"In that case, my dear," said Mrs Tallant, rising briskly to her feet, "I will write to accept Lady Bridlington's most obliging invitation."

"You must do as you think right," he said. "I have never interfered with what you considered proper for your daughters."

Thus it was that, at four o'clock on this momentous day, when the Vicar joined his family at the dinner-table, he surprised them by making a humorous reference to Arabella's projected trip. Not even Betsy would have ventured to have mentioned the scheme, for it was generally supposed that he must disapprove of it. But after grace had been said, and the family had disposed themselves about the long table, Arabella began, not very expeditiously, to carve one of the side-dishes, and the Vicar, looking up from his own labours in time to see her place a slightly mangled wing of chicken on a plate, remarked, with a twinkle: "I think Arabella must take lessons in carving before she goes into society, or she will disgrace us all by her unhandiness. It will not do, you know, my dear, to precipitate a dish into your neighbour's lap, as you seem to be in danger of doing at this moment!"

Arabella blushed, and protested. Sophia, the first to recover from the shock of hearing Papa speak with such good-humour of the London scheme, said: "Oh, but, Papa, I am sure it will not signify, for ten to one all the dishes are served by the footmen in grand houses!"

"I stand corrected, Sophia," said the Vicar, with dry meekness.

"Will Lady Bridlington have many footmen?" asked Betsy, dazzled by this vision of opulcnce.

"One to stand behind every chair," promptly replied Bertram. "And one to walk behind Arabella everytime she desires to take the air; and two to stand up behind my lady's carriage; and a round dozen, I daresay, to form an avenue in the front hall anytime her ladyship increases her covers for guests. When Arabella returns to us she will have forgotten how to pick up her own handkerchief, mark my words!"

"Well, I don't know how she will go on in such a house!" said Betsy, half-believing him.

"Nor I, indeed!" murmured Arabella.

"I trust she will go on, as you not very elegantly phrase it, my child, exactly as she would in her own home," said the Vicar.

Silence followed this rebuke. Bertram made a grimace at Arabella across the table, and Harry dug her surreptitiously in the ribs with his elbow. Margaret, who had been wrinkling her brow over her father's words, ventured at last to say: "Yes, Papa, but I do not precisely see how she can do so! It must be so very different to what we are accustomed to! I should not be surprised, for instance, if she found herself obliged to wear her party-gowns every evening, and I am sure she will not help with the baking, or starch shirts, or feed the chickens, or – or anything of that nature!"

"That was not quite what I meant, my dear," responded the Vicar repressively.

"Will she not be made to do any work at all?" exclaimed Betsy. "Oh, how much I wish *I* had a rich godmother!"

This ill-timed remark brought an expression of grave displeasure to the Vicar's face. It was evident to his family that the picture thus conjured up, of a daughter given over wholly to pleasure, was not one he could contemplate with anything but misgiving. Several darkling looks were cast at Betsy, which boded ill for one tactless enough to call down upon her sisters a lecture on the evils of idleness; but before the Vicar could speak, Mrs Tallant had intervened, calling Betsy to order for chattering, and saying cheerfully:

"Well, and I think Papa will agree that Arabella is a good girl, and deserves this indulgence more than any of you. I am sure I do not know how I shall manage without her, for whenever I want a task performed I know I may rely upon her to do it. And, what is a great deal to the point, let me tell you all! – she never shows me a pouting face, or complains that she is bored, or falls into a fit of the sullens because she is obliged to mend her old gown instead of purchasing a new one.

It could scarcely be expected that this masterly speech would please the three damsels to whom it was pointedly addressed, but it had the happy effect of softening the Vicar's countenance. He glanced at Arabella, who was furiously blushing and holding her head bent over her plate, and said gently: "Indeed, I am disposed to think that her character is well-established amongst us as one who wants neither sense nor feeling." Arabella looked up quickly, her eyes brightened by tears. He smiled at her, and said in a teasing voice: "If she will not let her tongue run like a fiddle-stick, nor express herself in terms which I might almost suppose she learns from her brothers, nor play pranks like a hoyden, I really believe I may indulge the hope that we shall not hear from Lady Bridlington that she is sunk quite beyond reproach in London!"

Such was the relief of his children at escaping one of Papa's homilies that this mild jest was received with a flattering degree of appreciation. Bertram seized the opportunity afforded by the general outcry of laughing protests to inform Betsy in a savage under-voice that if she opened her lips again he would most faithfully drop her in the middle of the duck-pond on the morrow, which promise so terrified her that she sat mumchance throughout the rest of the meal. Sophia, with real nobility of character, then asked Papa to explain something she had read in Sir John Malcolm's *History of Persia*, which the Vicar, whose only personal extravagance was his purchase of books, had lately added to his library. This was a happy inspiration: while her contemporaries gazed at Sophia in stupefaction, the Vicar, becoming quite animated, expounded at length on the subject, quite forgetting the immediate problems of the hour, and reducing his other offspring to a state of speechless indignation by saying, as he rose from the table, that he was glad to find that he had one daughter at least of a scholarly turn of mind.

"And Sophy never read a word of the book!" Bertram said bitterly, when, after enduring an evening in the parlour under the scourge of having passages from Sir John Malcolm's memorable work read aloud to them, he and his two elder sisters had escaped to the sanctuary of the girls' bedchamber.

"Oh, yes, I had!" retorted Sophia, sitting down on the end of her bed, and curling her legs under her in a way that, could her Mama but have seen it, would certainly have called down reproof upon her head.

Margaret, who was always sent up to bed before the appearance of the tea-tray, and thus had been spared the greater part of the evening's infliction, sat up, hugging her knees, and asked simply: "Why?"

"Well, it was that day that Mama was obliged to go out, and desired me to remain in the parlour in case old Mrs Farnham should call," explained Sophia. "I had nothing else to do!"

After regarding her fixedly for several moments, her brother and sisters apparently decided that the excuse was reasonable, for they abandoned the subject.

"I declare I was ready to sink when Papa said *that* about me!" remarked Arabella.

"Yes, but you know, Bella, he is very absent-minded," said Sophia, "and I fancy he had forgotten what you and Bertram did on Boxing Day, and what he said about your inclination for finery, when you pulled the feathers out of Uncle's peacocks to furbish up your old bonnet."

"Yes, perhaps he had," agreed Arabella, in a dampened tone. "But all the same," she added, her spirits reviving, "he never said I had no delicacy of principle, which he said to you when he discovered it was you, Sophy, who put one of Harry's trousers-buttons into the bag in Church that Sunday!"

This was so unanswerable that Sophia could think of no retort to make. Bertram said suddenly: "Well, since it is decided that you are to go to London, Bella, I'll tell you something!"

Seventeen years' intimate knowledge of her younger brother was not enough to restrain Arabella from demanding eagerly: "Oh, what, pray?"

"You may get a surprise when you are there!" said Bertram, in a voice of mystery. "Mind, I don't say you will, but you *may*!"

"What can you possibly mean? Tell me, Bertram! – *dearest* Bertram!"

"I'm not such a saphead! Girls always blab everything!"

"I would not! You know I would not! Oh, Bertram!"

"Don't heed him!" recommended Margaret, sinking back on to her pillow. "It's all humbug!"

"Well, it's not, miss!" said her brother, nettled. "But you needn't think I mean to tell you, for I don't! But don't be surprised, Bella, if you get a surprise before you have been in London very long!"

This ineptitude naturally threw his sisters into whoops. Unfortunately their mirth reached the ears of old Nurse, who promptly sailed into the room, and delivered herself of a shrill homily on the general impropriety of young gentlemen who sat on the ends of their sisters' beds. Since she was quite capable of reporting this shocking conduct to Mama, Bertram thought it prudent to remove himself, and the symposium came to an abrupt end. Nurse, blowing out the candles, said that if this came to Mama's ears there would be no London for Miss Arabella; but apparently it did not come to Mama's ears, for on the morrow, and indeed on all the succeeding days, nothing was talked of in the Parsonage (except in Papa's presence) but Arabella's entrance into the Polite World.

The first and most pressing consideration was the getting together of a wardrobe suitable for a young lady hopeful of making a successful début. Earnest perusal of the fashion journals had cast Arabella into a mood of despair, but Mama took a more cheerful view of the matter. She commanded the houseboy to summon the ubiquitous Joseph Eccles up to the Parsonage, and desired the pair of them to fetch down from one of the attics two formidable trunks. Joseph, who had been employed by the Vicar since the first year of his marriage as the farm-hand, considered himself the mainstay of the establishment, and was only too ready to oblige the ladies; and he lingered in the dressing-room, proffering counsel and encouragement in the broadest of Yorkshire dialects until kindly but firmly dismissed.

A pleasing aroma of camphor pervaded the air as soon as the lids were raised from the trunks, and the removal of a covering of silver paper disclosed treasures innumerable. The trunks contained the finery which Mama had worn (she said) when she was just such a giddy puss as Arabella. When she had married Papa she had had no occasion for such fripperies, but she had not been able to bring herself to give them away, and had packed them up and well-nigh forgotten all about them.

Three ecstatic gasps shuddered on the air as three rapt young ladies dropped down on their knees beside the trunks, and prepared to rummage to their hearts' content.

There were unimagined delights in the trunks: curled ostrich plumes of various colours; branches of artificial flowers; an ermine tippet (alas, turned sadly yellow with age, but it would serve to trim Sophy's old pelisse!); a loo-mask; a whole package of finest thread-lace; a tiffany cloak, which set Margaret peacocking round the room; several ells of ribbon of a shade which Mama said was called in her young days *opéra brulé*, and quite the rage; scarves of gauze, lace, and blonde, spangled and plain; a box containing intriguing knots of ribbon, whose names Mama could not quite remember, though she rather thought that that pale blue bunch was A Sign of Hope, and the pink bow A Sigh of Venus; point-lace tuckers, and lappet-heads; a feather muff; innumerable fans; sashes; a scarlet-flowered damask mantua petticoat – what a figure Mama must have looked in it! – and a velvet cloak, miraculously lined with sable, which had been a wedding-gift to Mama, but which she had scarcely worn, "because, my loves, it was finer than anything your aunt possessed, and, after all, she was the Squire's wife, and dreadfully inclined to take a pet, so that I always took care never to give her the least cause to be offended. But it is a beautiful fur, and will make a muff for Arabella, besides trimming a pelisse!"

It was fortunate that Mama was an indulgent parent, and so very fond of a joke, for the trunks contained, besides these treasures, such old-fashioned garments that the three Misses Tallant were obliged to laugh. Fashions had changed a great deal since Mama was a girl, and to a generation accustomed to high-waisted gowns of muslin and crape, with little puff-sleeves, and demure flounces round the hems, the stiff, voluminous silks and brocades Mama had worn, with their elaborate undergowns, and their pads, and their wired bodices, seemed not only archaic, but very ugly too. What was this funny jacket, with all the whalebone? A Caraco? Gracious! And this striped thing, for all the world like a dressing-gown? A lustring sack – well, it was certainly very like a sack, to be sure! Did Mama wear it in *company?* What was in this elegant box? *Poudre à la Maréchale*! But did Mama then powder her hair, like the picture of Grandmama Tallant, up at the Hall? Oh, *not* quite like that! A *gray* powder? Oh, Mama, no! and you without a gray hair to your head! How did you dress it? Not cut at *all*? Curls to the waist at the back? And all those rolls and puffs over the ears! How could Mama have had the patience to do it? So odd as it must have looked, too! But Mama, turning over half-forgotten dresses, grew quite sentimental, remembering that she had been wearing this very gown of green Italian taffeta, over a petticoat of satin, *soupir d'étouffe* (unaccountably missing), when she had first met Papa; remembering the pretty compliment paid to her by that rejected baronet when he had seen her in the white silk waist Sophia was holding up (it had had a book-muslin train, and there should be somewhere a pink silk coat, very smart, which she had worn with it); remembering how shocked her Mama had been when she had seen that rose-coloured Indian muslin underwear which Eliza – your Aunt Eliza, my loves – had brought her from London.

The girls did not know where to look when Mama sighed over a cherry-striped gown, and said how pretty it had been, for really it was quite hideous, and it made them feel almost uncomfortable to think of Mama's being seen abroad in such a garment. It was beyond laughter, so they sat respectfully silent, and were profoundly relieved when suddenly she shook off this unaccustomed mood, and smiled, and said in her own brisk way: "Well, I daresay you think I must have looked like a dowd, but I assure you I did not! However, none of these brocades is of any use to Arabella, so we will put them up again. But that straw-coloured satin will do famously for a ball-dress, and we may trim it with some of the point-lace."

There was a dressmaker in High Harrowgate, an elderly Frenchwoman, who had originally come to England as an émigrée from the Revolution. She had very often made dresses for Mrs Tallant and her daughters, and since she had excellent taste, and did not charge extortionate prices, except during the short season, it was decided that she should be entrusted with the task of making all Arabella's gowns. On the first day that the horses could be spared from the farm, Mrs Tallant and her two elder daughters drove to High Harrowgate, taking with them three bandboxes full of the silks, velvets, and laces which had finally been selected from Mrs Tallant's hoard.

Harrowgate, which was situated between Heythram and the large town of Knaresborough, was a watering-place renowned more for the excellent properties of its medicinal springs than for the modishness of its visitors. It consisted of two straggling villages, more than a mile apart, and enjoyed a summer season only. Since upwards of a thousand persons, mostly of valetudinarian habits, visited it then to drink the waters, both villages and their environs boasted more hotels and boarding-houses than private residences. From May till Michaelmas, public balls were held twice a week at the new Assembly Rooms; there was a Promenade, standing in the middle of an agreeable garden; a theatre; and a lending library, much patronized by Mrs Tallant and her daughters.

Mme Dupont was delighted to receive a client in the middle of January, and no sooner learned the reason for the bespeaking of such an extensive wardrobe than she entered into the spirit of the adventure with Gallic enthusiasm, fell into raptures over the silks and satins in the three bandboxes, and spread fashion-plates, and rolls of cambric and muslin and crape before the ladies' eyes. It would be a pleasure, she said, to make for a *demoiselle* with such a *taille* as Mademoiselle Tallant's; already she perceived how Madame's satin polonaise could be transformed into a ball-dress of the most ravishing, while as for the taffeta over-dress alas, that the elegant toilettes of the last century were no longer in vogue! – she could assure Madame that nothing could be more *comme il faut* than an opera cloak fashioned out of its ample widths, and trimmed with ruched velvet ribbon. As for the cost, that would be a matter for arrangement of the most amicable.

Arabella, who in general had a decided will of her own, as well as very definite ideas on the colour and style of her dresses, was so much shocked by the number of gowns Mama and Mme Dupont seemed to think indispensable for a sojourn in London that she scarcely opened her lips, except to agree in a faint voice with whatever was suggested to her. Even Sophia, who so often earned reproofs from Papa for chattering like a magpie, was awed into comparative silence. Not all her study of the fashion-plates in *The Ladies' Monthly Museum* had prepared her for the dazzling creations sketched in *La Belle Assemblée*. But Mama and Mme Dupont were agreed that only the simplest of these would be *convenable* for such a young lady. One or two ball-dresses of satin, or orange-blossom sarsnet, would be needed for grand occasions, but nothing could be prettier, said Madame, than crape or fine jaconet muslin for the Assemblies at Almack's. Some silver net drapery, perhaps – she had the very thing laid by – or a Norwich shawl, carried negligently across the elbows, would lend a *cachet* to the plainest gown. Then, for a morning half-dress, might she suggest a figured French muslin, with a demi-train? Or perhaps Mademoiselle would prefer a Berlin silk, trimmed with silk floss? For carriage dresses, she would recommend fine cambric, worn with a velvet mantle, and a Waterloo hat, or even a fur bonnet, ornamented – Mademoiselle's colouring made it permissible, even imperative! – with a bunch of cherries.

Morning dresses, afternoon dresses, carriage dresses, walking dresses, ball dresses it seemed to Arabella and Sophia that the list would never come to an end. "I cannot imagine how you will find time to wear the half of them!" whispered Sophia.

"Shoes, half-boots, reticules, gloves, stockings," murmured Mrs Tallant, conning her list. "Those will do for another day. You must take the greatest care of your silk stockings, my love, for I cannot afford to buy you many pairs! Hats – h'm, yes! What a fortunate thing it was that I kept all my old ostrich feathers! We shall see what we can contrive. I think that will do for today."

"Mama, what will Bella wear when she goes to the Drawing-room?" asked Sophia.

"Ah, *pour ça, alors, la grande parure*!" cried Madame, her eye brightening.

Mrs. Tallant crushed these budding hopes. "Full dress, to be sure, my dear: satin, I daresay. Feathers, of course. I do not know if hoops are still worn at Court. Lady Bridlington is to make your sister a present of the dress, and I know I may depend upon her to choose just what is right. Come, my dears! If we are to call upon your uncle on our way home it is high time we were off!"

"Call upon my uncle?" repeated Sophia, surprised.

Mrs Tallant coloured slightly, but replied in an airy way: "Certainly, my love: why should we not? Besides, one should never neglect the observances of civility, and I am sure he would think it very odd in me not to apprise him of Arabella's going to London."

Sophia knitted her brows a little over this, for although there had always been a good deal of coming and going between the two boys at the Hall, and their young cousins at the Vicarage, visits between their respective parents were rare. The Squire and his brother, while remaining on perfectly amicable terms, scarcely possessed a thought in common, each regarding the other with affectionate contempt; while the late Lady Tallant, besides labouring under all the disadvantages of a jealous temper, had been, even in her charitable brother-in-law's estimation, a very under-bred woman. There were two children of the marriage: Thomas, a bucolic young man of twenty-seven; and Algernon, who held a commission in the -th Regiment, stationed at present in Belgium.

The Hall, which was situated in a pretty little park, about a mile from the village of Heythram, was a commodious, unpretentious house built of the prevailing gray stone of the district. Comfort rather than elegance was the predominant note struck by its furniture and decorations, and it bore, in despite of the ministrations of an excellent housekeeper, the indefinable air of a residence that lacked a mistress. The Squire was more interested in his stables than in his house. He was generally thought to be a warm man, but careful; and although he was fond of his nephews and nieces, and always goodnaturedly mounted Bertram during the hunting-season, it was rarely that his affection led him to do more for them than to give them a guinea apiece every Christmas. But he was a hospitable man, and always seemed pleased to welcome his brother's family to his board.

He came bustling out of the house as soon as the Parsonage carriage drew up at his door, and exclaimed in a loud voice: "Well, well, if it's not Sophia, and the girls! Well, this is a pleasant circumstance! What, only the two of you? Never mind! Come in, and take a glass of wine! Bitter cold, ain't it? Ground's like iron: don't know when we shall get out again, damme if I do!"

Talking all the time, he led the ladies into a square parlour in the front of the house, breaking off his conversation only to shout to someone to bring refreshments into the parlour, and to be quick about it. He then ran his eye over his nieces, and said that they were prettier than ever, and demanded to be told how many beaux they could boast between them. They were spared the necessity of answering this jocular question by his instantly turning to Mrs Tallant, and saying: "Can't hold a candle to their Mama, though, I swear! I declare, it's an age since I've clapped eyes on you, Sophia! Can't think why you and poor Henry don't come up more often to eat your mutton with me! And how is Henry? Still poring over his books, I dare swear! I never knew such a fellow! But you shouldn't let him keep young Bertram's nose glued to 'em, my dear: that's a good lad – regular devil to go, nothing bookish about him!"

"Bertram is reading for Oxford, Sir John. You know he must do so!"

"Mark my words, he'll do no good there!" said the Squire. "Better make a soldier of him, as I did with my young rascal. But tell him to come up to the stables here, if he wants to see a rare piece of horseflesh: great rumps and hocks, grand shoulders! Don't mind the boy's trying him, if he likes to, but he's young yet: needs schooling. Does Bertram mean to come out when this frost breaks? Tell him the bay has a splint forming, or you may call me a Dutchman, but he may ride Thunderer, if he chooses."

"I think," said Mrs Tallant, with a faint sigh, "that his Papa does not wish him to hunt any more this season. It quite takes his mind off his book, poor boy!"

"Henry's an old woman," replied the Squire. "Ain't it enough for him to have James as bookish as he is himself? Where is that lad? Up at Oxford, eh? Ah well, each man to his taste! Now, that other young rascal of yours – what's his name? Harry! I like the cut of his jib, as he'd say himself. Going to sea, he tells me. How shall you manage it?"

Mrs Tallant explained that one of her brothers was to use his interest in Harry's favour. The Squire seemed satisfied with this, asked jovially after the health of his godson and namesake, and set about pressing cold meat and wine upon his guests. It was some time before any opportunity offered of breaking to him the reason of the visit, but when the spate of his conversation abated a little, Sophia, who could scarcely contain herself for impatience, said abruptly: "Sir, do you know that Arabella is going to London?"

He stared, first at her, and then at Arabella. "Eh? What's that you say? How comes this about?"

Mrs Tallant, frowning reprovingly at Sophia, explained the matter. He listened very intently, nodding, and pursing up his lips, as his habit was when he was interested; and after turning it over in his mind for several moments, began to perceive what an excellent thing it was, and to congratulate Arabella upon her good fortune. After he had wished her a great many town-beaux, envied the lucky one who should win her, and prophesied that she would shine down all the London beauties, Mrs Tallant brought his gallantry to an end by suggesting that her daughters would like to go to the housekeeper's room to visit good Mrs Paignton, who was always so kind to them. The style of the Squire's pleasantries was not just to her taste; moreover, she wished to have some private talk with him.

He had a great many questions to ask her, and comments to make. The more he thought about the scheme the better he liked it, for although he was fond of his niece, and considered her a remarkably handsome girl, he did not wish her to become his daughter-in-law. His understanding was not quick, nor had he much power of perception, but it had lately been borne in upon him that his heir had begun to dangle after his cousin in a marked manner. He did not suppose that Tom's affections were deeply engaged, and he was hopeful that if Arabella were removed from the neighbourhood he would soon recover from his mild infatuation, and make some more eligible lady the object of his gallantry. He had a suitable girl in his eye for Tom, but being a fairminded man he was obliged to own that Miss Maria was cast very much in the shade by Arabella. Nothing, therefore, that Mrs Tallant could have told him would have met with more approval from him. He gave the scheme his warmest approbation, and told her that she was a sensible woman.

"Ay, you need not tell me! this is your doing, Sophia! Poor Henry never had a particle of sense! A dear, good fellow, of course, but when a man has a quiverfill of children he needs to be a little sharper than Henry. But you have all your wits about you, my dear sister! You are doing just as you should: the girl's uncommon handsome, and should do well for herself. Ay, ay, you will be setting about the wedding preparations before the cat has time to lick her ear! Lady Bridlington, eh? One of the London nobs, I daresay: couldn't be better! But it will cost a great deal!"

"Indeed, you are right, Sir John," said Mrs Tallant. "It will cost a very great deal, but when such an opportunity is offered every effort should be made to take advantage of it, I believe."

"Ay, ay, you will be laying your money out to good purpose!" he nodded. "But can you trust this fine lady of yours to keep half-pay officers, and such-like, out of the girl's way? It won't do to have her running off with some penniless fellow, you know, and all your trouble wasted!"

The fact that the same thought had more than once crossed her mind did not make this piece of plain-speaking any more agreeable to Mrs Tallant. She considered it extremely vulgar, and replied in a repressive tone that she believed she might depend on Arabella's good sense.

"You had better drop a word of warning in your friend's ear," said Sir John bluntly. "You know, Sophia, if that girl of yours were to catch a man of property, and, damme, I don't see why she shouldn't! – it would be a great thing for her sisters! Ay, the more I think on it the better I like it! It is worth all the expense. When does she go? How do you mean to send her?"

"As to that, it is not yet decided, Sir John, but if Mrs Caterham holds by her original scheme, and lets Miss Blackburn go next month – you must know that she is the governess, I daresay – she could travel with Arabella. I believe her home is in Surrey, so she must go to London."

"But you won't send little Bella on the stage-coach!"

Mrs Tallant sighed. "My dear sir, the cost of posting is too great to be even thought of! I own, I do not like it, but beggars, you know, cannot be choosers!"

The Squire began to look very thoughtful. "Well, that won't do," he said presently. "No, no, we can't have that! Driving up to your grand friend's house in a hackney! We shall have to contrive a little, Sophia. Now, let me see!"

He sat staring into the fire for some minutes, while his sister-in-law pensively gazed out of the window, and tried not to let her mind dwell on what her sensitive husband's feelings must be, could he but have had the least idea of what she was doing.

"I'll tell you what, sister!" said the Squire suddenly. "I'll send Bella to London in my travelling-carriage, that's what I'll do! No sense in wasting money on posting: it don't matter to the girl if she spends some time on the road. What's more, those post-chaises can't take up all the baggage I'll be bound Bella will have with her. Ay, and this governess of yours will have a box as well, I daresay."

"Your travelling carriage!" exclaimed Mrs Tallant, rather startled.

"That's it. Never use it myself: it hasn't been out of the coachhouse since my poor Eliza died. I'll set the men on to furbish it up: it ain't one of these smart, newfangled barouches, but it's a handsome carriage – I bought it for Eliza, when we were first married, and it has my crest on the panel. You would not be comfortable, sending the girl off with strange post-boys, you know: much better to let my old coachman drive her, and I'll send one of the grooms along to sit up beside him, with a pistol in his pocket in case of highwaymen." He rubbed his hands together, well-pleased with the scheme, and began to estimate how many days it would take a strong pair of horses – or, at a pinch, even four – to reach London without getting knocked-up. He was inclined to think the plan would answer very well, and that Arabella would not at all object to resting the nags a day here or there upon the road. "Or she might travel by easy stages, you know!" he said.

Upon reflection, Mrs Tallant perceived that this plan had much to recommend it. Against the evils of lingering in the various posting-houses along the route, must be set the advantages of being driven by a steady, trustworthy coachman, and of being able, as the Squire had pointed out, to carry all the trunks and bandboxes in the carriage, instead of having to send them to town by carrier. She thanked him, therefore, and was still expressing the sense of her obligation to him when the young ladies came back into the room.

The Squire greeted Arabella with great joviality, pinching her cheek, and saying: "Well, puss, this is a new come-out for you, eh? I'll swear you're in high gig! Now, here's your mother and I have been putting our heads together, and the long and the short of it is you are to go to London in prime style, in your poor aunt's carriage, and Timothy-coachman to drive you. How will that be, my lass?"

Arabella, who had very pretty manners, thanked him, and said everything that was proper. He appeared pleased, told her she might give him a kiss, and he would be satisfied, and suddenly walked out of the room, adjuring her to wait, for he had a little something for her. When he came back, he found his visitors ready to take their leave of him. He shook hands warmly with them all, and pressed into Arabella's a folded banknote, saying: "There! that is to buy yourself some fripperies with, puss!"

She was quite overcome, for she had not expected anything of the sort; coloured, and stammered that he was by far too kind. He liked to be thanked, and beamed at her, and pinched her cheek again, very well satisfied with himself and her.

"But, Mama," said Sophia, when they were driving away from the Hall, "you will never let poor Arabella go to town in that antiquated carriage of my uncle's!"

"Nonsense!" replied her mother. "It is a very respectable carriage, and if it is old-fashioned I daresay it is none the worse for that. No doubt you would rather see her dash off in a chaise-and-four, but it would cost as much as fifty or sixty pounds, besides what one must give the postilions, and is not to be thought of. Why, even a pair of horses, so far as we are from London, would mean thirty pounds, and all for what? To be sure, it will be a little slow, but Miss Blackburn will be with your sister, and if they are obliged to stay a day in an inn – to rest the horses, you know – she will be able to look after her, and I may be comfortable in my mind."

"Mama!" said Arabella faintly. *"Mama!"*

"Good gracious, my love, what is it?"

Arabella dumbly proffered the Squire's banknote. Mrs Tallant took it from her, saying: "You would like me to take care of it for you, would you? Very well, I will do so, my dear, or you would be squandering it on presents for your brothers and sisters, perhaps!"

"Mama, it is a bill for *fifty pounds*!"

"No!" gasped Sophia.

"Well, that is certainly very generous of your uncle," said Mrs Tallant. "If I were you, Arabella, I would embroider a pair of slippers for him before you go away, for you will not like to be backward in any little attention."

"Oh, no! But I never dreamed – I am sure I did not thank him half enough! Mama, will you take it for my dresses, please?"

"Certainly not. *That* is all provided for. You will find it very much more comfortable in London to have this money by you – indeed, I had hoped your uncle might give you something to spend! There will be little things you may want to purchase, and vails to the servants, you know, and so on. And although your Papa would not like you to *gamble* precisely, there may be loo-parties, and naturally you would wish to play. In fact, it would be awkward if you did not."

Sophia opened her eyes at this. "Papa does not like any of us to play gambling games, ma'am, does he? He says that cards are to blame for many of the evils -"

"Yes, my dear, very likely! But a loo-party is quite a different thing!" said Mrs Tallant, somewhat obscurely. She fidgeted with her reticule for a moment, and then added, a little consciously: "I should not tease Papa with telling him the whole history of our doings today, girls. Gentlemen do not take the same interest in such things as we do, and I am sure he has very much more important things to think of."

Her daughters did not pretend to misunderstand her. "Oh, I would not breathe a word to him!" said Sophia.

"No," agreed Arabella. "And *particularly* not about the fifty pounds, for I am sure he would say it was too much, and I must give it back to my uncle! And I don't think I *could*!"

CHAPTER THREE

IN THE end, it was not until after the middle of February that Arabella set out to accomplish the long journey to London. Not only had Mme Dupont taken more time to make the necessary gowns than had been anticipated, but there had been many details to arrange besides; and Betsy had not failed to delay preparations by contracting a putrid sore throat, and low fever. It was felt to be typical of her. While Mrs Tallant still had her hands full, nursing her, Bertram, succumbing to temptation, took French leave of his books and his Papa, and enjoyed a splendid day with the hounds, which culminated in his return to the Parsonage on a farm wagon, with a broken collar-bone. A gloom was thrown over the house for quite a week by this mishap, because the Vicar was not only vexed, but deeply grieved as well. It was not the accident which upset him, for although he did not hunt himself now he had done so regularly in his youth, but (he said) the want of openness in Bertram which had led him to go off without asking permission, or, indeed, even telling his father what he meant to do. The Vicar could not understand such conduct at all, for surely he was not a harsh parent, and surely his sons must know that he did not wish to deprive them of rational enjoyment? He was bewildered, and disturbed, and begged Bertram to explain why he had behaved in such a manner. But it was quite impossible to explain to Papa why one chose rather to play truant, and afterwards take the consequences, than to ask his leave to do something of which one knew well he would not approve.

"How *can* you explain anything to my father?" Bertram demanded of his sisters, in a despairing tone. "He would only be more hurt than ever, and give one a thundering jaw, and make one feel like the greatest beast in nature!" "I know," said Arabella feelingly. "I think what makes him look so displeased and sad is that he believes you must be afraid of him, and so dared not ask his leave to go. And, of course, one *can't* explain that it isn't *that!*"

"He wouldn't understand if you did," remarked Sophia.

"Well, exactly so!" said Bertram. "Besides, you couldn't do it! A pretty botch I should make of telling him that I didn't ask leave because I knew he would look grave, and say I must decide for myself, but did I feel it to be right to go pleasuring when I have examinations to pass – oh, you know the way he talks! The end of it would be that I shouldn't have gone at all! I hate moralizing!"

"Yes," agreed Sophia, "but the worst of it is that whenever one of us vexes him he very likely falls into the most dreadful dejection, and worries himself with thinking that we are all of us heedless and spoilt, and himself much to blame. I wish he may not forbid you to go to London because of Bertram's wretched folly, Bella!"

"What a bag of moonshine!" exclaimed Bertram scornfully. "Why the deuce should he, pray?"

It certainly seemed a trifle unreasonable, but when his children next encountered the Vicar, which was at the dinner-table, his countenance wore an expression of settled melancholy, and it was plain that he derived no comfort from the young people's cheerful conversation. A somewhat thoughtless enquiry from Margaret about the exact colour of the ribbons chosen for Arabella's second-best ball dress provoked him to say that it seemed to him that amongst all his children only James was not wholly given over to levity and frivolity. Unsteadiness of character was what he perceived about him; when he considered that the mere prospect of a visit to London sent all his daughters fashion-mad he must ask himself whether he was not doing very wrong to permit Arabella to go. A moment's reflection would have convinced Arabella that this was the merest irritation of nerves, but her besetting sin, as her Mama had frequently told her, was the impetuosity which led her into so many scrapes. Alarm at the Vicar's words for an instant suspended every faculty; then she exclaimed hotly: "Papa! You are unjust! It is too bad!"

The Vicar had never been a severe parent; indeed, he was thought by some to allow his children a shocking degree of licence: but such a speech as this went beyond the bounds of what he would tolerate. His face stiffened to an expression of quelling austerity; he replied in a voice of ice: "The unwarrantable language you have used, Arabella; the uncontrolled violence of your manner; the want of respect you have shown me – all these betray clearly how unfit you are to be sent into the world!"

Under the table, Sophia's foot kicked Arabella's ankle; across it, Mama's eyes met hers in a warning, reproving look. The colour surged up into her cheeks; her eyes filled; and she stammered: "I beg your p-pardon, P-papa!"

He returned no answer. Mama broke the uneasy silence by calmly desiring Harry not to eat so fast; and then, just as though nothing untoward had occurred, began to talk to the Vicar about some parish business.

"What a dust you made!" Harry said presently, when the young people had fled to Mama's dressing-room, and poured out the whole story to Bertram, who had had his dinner brought to him there, on the sofa.

"I am *sick* with apprehension!" Arabella said tragically. "He means to forbid me!"

"Fudge! It was only one of his scolds! Girls are such fools!"

"Ought I to go down and beg his pardon? Oh, no, I dare not! He has shut himself up in the study! What shall I do?"

"Leave it to Mama!" said Bertram, yawning. "She's as shrewd as she can hold together, and if she means you to go to London, go you will!"

"I would not go to him now, if I were you," said Sophia. "You are in such an agitation of spirits that you would be bound to say something unbecoming, or start to cry. And you know how much he dislikes an excess of sensibility! Speak to him in the morning, after prayers!"

This course was decided on. And then, as Arabella afterwards confided to Bertram, it was more dreadful than all the rest! Mama had done her work too well: before the Vicar's erring daughter could utter a word of her carefully rehearsed apology, he had taken her hand, and said with his sweet, wistful smile: "My child, you must forgive your father. Indeed, I spoke to you with grave injustice yesterday! Alas, that I, who preach moderation to my children, should have so little control over my own temper!"

"Bertram, I had rather by far he had *beaten* me!" said Arabella earnestly.

"Lord, yes!" agreed Bertram, shuddering. "What a shocking thing! I'm glad I wasn't downstairs! It makes me feel like the devil when he gets to blaming himself. What did you say?"

"I could not utter a word! My voice was *wholly* suspended by tears, as you may imagine, and I was so afraid that he would be vexed with me for not being able to contain my feelings better! But he was not. Only fancy! he took me in his arms, and kissed me, and said I was his dear, good daughter, and oh, Bertram, I'm *not!*"

"Well, you need not put yourself in a pucker for that," recommended her matter-of-fact brother. "He won't think it above a day or two. The thing is that his dejected fit is at an end."

"Oh, yes! But it was much, much worse at breakfast! He would keep on talking to me about the London scheme – teasing me, you know, about the giddy life I should lead there, and saying that I must be sure to write very long letters home, even if I cannot get a frank for them, for he would be so much interested to hear of all my doings!"

Bertram stared at her in undisguised horror. "He did not!"

"But he did! And in the kindest way, only with that sad look in his eyes – *you* know! until I was ready to give up the whole scheme!"

"My God, I don't wonder at it!"

"No, and to crown all – as though I had not borne enough!" disclosed Arabella, hunting wildly for her handkerchief, "he said I should want something pretty to wear in London, and he would have a pearl pin he wore when he was a young man made into a ring for me!"

This staggering intelligence made Bertram's jaw drop. After a moment's stupefaction, he said resolutely: "That settles it! I shan't come downstairs today after all. Ten to one, if he saw me he would start to blame himself for my frisk, and I should be driven into running away to enlist, or something, because, you know, a fellow can't stand that kind of thing!"

"No, indeed! I am sure all *my* pleasure has been quite cut up!

Since Papa's tender mood of forbearance showed every sign of continuance, Arabella fell into such an abyss of despondency that she was only saved from renouncing the London scheme by the timely intervention of Mama, who gave her thoughts a more cheerful direction by calling her into her bedroom one morning, and saying with a smile: "I have something to show you, my love, which I think you will like."

There was a box lying open upon Mama's dressing-table. Arabella blinked at the flash of diamonds, and uttered a long-drawn: "Oh-h!"

"My father gave them to me," said Mrs Tallant, sighing faintly. "Of course I have never worn them of late years, for I have no occasion to. Besides, they are scarcely suitable for a clergyman's wife. But I have had them cleaned, and I mean to lend them to you to take with you to London. And I have asked Papa if he thinks I might give you Grandmama Tallant's pearl necklet, and he sees no objection to it. Your Papa has never cared for sparkling stones, you know, but he thinks pearls both modest and becoming to a female. However, if Lady Bridlington takes you to any dress-parties, which I am sure she will, the diamond set would be just the thing. You see, there is the crescent to set in your hair, and a brooch, and the bracelet as well. Nothing pretentious or vulgar, such as Papa would dislike, but I know the stones are of the finest water."

It was impossible to be dejected after this, or even to contemplate abandoning the London scheme. What with the trimming of hats, hemming of handkerchiefs, embroidering of slippers for the Squire, the arrival of her gowns from Harrowgate, and the knitting of a new purse for Papa, together with all the ordinary duties which fell to her lot, Arabella had no time to indulge in morbid reflections. Everything went on prosperously: the Caterhams' retiring governess expressed herself all willingness to chaperon Arabella on the journey; the Squire discovered that by driving only a few miles out of the way she could spend a day or two with her Aunt Emma, at Arksey, and so rest the horses; Bertram's collar-bone knit itself again; and even Betsy recovered from her sore throat. Not until the Squire's carriage actually stood at the Parsonage gate, waiting to take up the travellers, with all the trunks strapped securely behind it, and Mama's dressing-case (also lent for the occasion) placed tenderly within the vehicle, did the mood of depression again descend upon Arabella. Whether it was Mama's embrace, or Papa's blessing, or Baby Jack's fat little hand waving farewell which overcame her, it would have been hard to say, but her feelings were quite overset, and it was a lady dissolved into tears whom Bertram thrust forcibly into the carriage. It was long before she could be composed again, nor was her companion of much support to her, since an excessive sympathy, coupled, perhaps, with the natural melancholy of a female obliged by circumstances to seek a new post, caused her to weep quite as bitterly in her corner of the capacious carriage.

While familiar landmarks were still to be observed out of the windows, Arabella's tears continued to flow, but by the time the carriage had reached an unknown countryside they had ceased, and after sniffing cautiously at the vinaigrette, proffered in a trembling hand by Miss Blackburn, she was able to dry her wet cheeks, and even to derive a sensible degree of comfort from the opulence of the huge sealskin pillow-muff lying on her lap. This, with the tippet round her throat, had been sent to her with her Aunt Eliza's love – the same who had once given Mama a set of pink Indian muslin underwear. Even though one had never left one's home before, one could not be wholly given over to wretchedness when one's hands were tucked into a muff as large as any depicted in *La Belle Assemblée*. So large, indeed, was it, that Papa – But it would be wiser not to think of Papa, or any of the dear ones at home, perhaps. Better to fix one's attention on the countryside, and one's thoughts on the delights ahead.

To a young lady who had never been farther afield than to York – and that only when Papa had taken her and Sophia to be confirmed in the Minster – every new thing seen on the road was a matter for eager interest and exclamation. To those accustomed to the rapid mode of travel achieved by post-chaises, a journey in a somewhat ponderous carriage drawn by two horses, chosen more for their stamina than their speed, would have seemed slow beyond all bearing. To Arabella it was adventure, while to Miss Blackburn, inured by long custom to the horrors of the stage, it was unlooked-for comfort. Both ladies, therefore, soon settled down to enjoy themselves, thought the refreshments they were offered at the various halts excellent, found nothing to complain of in the beds at the posting-houses, and could not conceive of a more delightful way of undertaking a long journey. They were made very welcome at Arksey, where Aunt Emma received them with the greatest kindness, and the exclamation that Arabella was so like her dear Mama that she had nearly fainted away at the sight of her.

They spent two days at Arksey before taking the road again, and Arabella was quite sorry to leave the large, untidy house, so kind had Aunt Emma been, and so jolly all her cheerful cousins. But Timothy-coachman reported the horses to be quite fresh and ready for the road again, so there could be no lingering. They set forth once more, followed by the shouted good wishes and many hand-wavings of Aunt Emma's family.

After all the fun and the hospitality at Arksey, it did seem to be a little tedious to be sitting all day in a carriage, and once or twice, when a post-chaise-and-four dashed by, or some sporting curricle, with a pair of quick-goers harnessed to it, was encountered, Arabella found herself wishing that the Squire's carriage were not quite so large and unwieldy, and his horses less strengthy and rather more speedy beasts. It would have been pleasant, too, to have been able to have had a fresh pair poled-up when one of Uncle John's cast a shoe, instead of having to wait in a stuffy inn parlour while it was reshod; and Arabella, eating her dinner in the coffee-room of some posting-house, could not quite forbear a look of envy when some smart chaise drove into the courtyard, with horses sweating, and ostlers running out with a fresh team for the impatient traveller. Nor could she help wishing, once she had watched the mail-coach sweep through a turn-pike, that Uncle John had provided the groom not with a horse-pistol, for which there did not seem to be the slightest occasion, but with a yard of tin, that he might have blown up for the pike in that same lordly style.

The weather, which had been cold but bright in Yorkshire, worsened as they drove farther south. It was raining in Lincolnshire, and the landscape looked sodden. Not many people were to be seen on the road, and the prospect was so uninviting that Miss Blackburn said that it was a pity they had not had the forethought to provide themselves with a travelling chessboard, with which, in default of looking out of the windows, they might have whiled away the time. At Tuxford they were unlucky enough to find the New Castle Arms without a bed to spare, and were obliged to put up at a smaller and by far less genteel inn, where the sheets had been so ill-aired that Miss Blackburn not only lay and shivered in her bed all night, but arose in the morning with a sore throat, and a tickling at the back of her nose which presaged a cold in the head. Arabella, who, for all her air of fragility, rarely succumbed to minor ailments, was not a penny the worse for the experience, but her north-country soul had been offended by the dust she had seen under her bed, and she was beginning to think that it would be a relief to reach her journey's end. It was vexing to discover, just as she had packed Mama's dressing-case, and was ready to leave the inn, that one of the traces needed repair, for it had been arranged that they should spend the following night at Grantham, which, the guide-book informed her, lay some twenty-nine or thirty miles on from Tuxford. She hoped very much that the coachman would not decide that his horses could go no farther than to Newark, but since he was something of a despot, and had no opinion of fast travelling, it seemed more than likely that he would. However, the trace was mended in fairly good time, and they reached Newark in time to eat a late luncheon. Here, while he baited his horses, the coachman fell out with one of the ostlers, who asked him whether it was the King's state coach he had there; and this so much affronted him that he was quite as anxious as Arabella to reach Grantham that evening.

It was raining again when they left Newark, and the atmosphere was dank and chilly. Miss Blackburn wrapped herself up in a large shawl, and sniffed unhappily, as her cold gained on her. Even Arabella, who was largely impervious to climatic conditions, suffered a little from the many draughts that crept into the carriage, and wriggled numbed toes inside her half-boots of crimson jean.

The carriage bowled along at a sedate pace for several miles, the tedium being enlivened only at the Balderton turnpike, where, recognizing a Johnny Raw in the coachman, the pike-keeper made a spirited attempt to extort a fee from him. But although Timothy-coachman might never have set foot beyond the boundaries of Yorkshire before, he was harder-headed than any of these soft southern folk whom he despised so profoundly, and he knew very well that the ticket bought at the last toll-gate opened all the pikes to him until the next, south of Grantham, was reached. After an exchange of personalities which made Miss Blackburn utter little moans of dismay, and Arabella – regrettably – giggle, he won a signal victory over the pike-keeper, and drove through with a triumphant flourish of his whip.

"Oh, dear, I am becoming so tired of this journey!" confided Arabella. "I could almost wish to be held up by a highwayman!"

"My dear Miss Tallant, pray do not *think* of such a thing!" shuddered her companion. "I only hope we may be spared any sort of accident!"

Neither lady's wish was destined to be granted her. No such excitement as a hold-up awaited them, but a little way short of the Marston turnpike the perch of the carriage broke, and the body fell forward upon the box. The Squire's travelling carriage had stood too long in his coach-house.

After the coachman had delivered himself of a long, self-exculpatory monologue, the groom was sent off to take counsel of the pike-keeper, half a mile down the road. When he returned, it was with the pleasing intelligence that no adequate assistance was to be hoped for in the next village: it must be sought in Grantham, five or six miles farther on, where a conveyance could no doubt be hired to fetch the ladies in while the perch was mended, or replaced. The coachman then suggested that his passengers, both of whom were standing by the roadside, should climb up into the carriage again to await deliverance, while the groom took one of the horses and rode on to Grantham. Miss Blackburn was meekly ready to follow this advice, but her charge thought poorly of it.

"What! Sit in that horrid, draughty carriage all that time? I won't do it!" she declared.

"But we cannot continue to stand in the rain, dear Miss Tallant!" said Miss Blackburn.

"Of course we cannot! Either way I am persuaded you would catch your death! There must be a house hereabouts which would lend us shelter! What are those lights over there?"

They plainly shone from the windows of a residence set a little back from the road. The groom volunteered the information that he had noticed some lodge gates a few steps back.

"Good!" said Arabella briskly. "We will walk up to it, ma'am, and beg them to give us shelter for a little while."

Miss Blackburn, a timorous soul, protested feebly. "They would think it so strange of us!"

"No, why should they?" returned Arabella. "Why, when a carriage had an accident outside *our* gates last year, Papa sent Harry out at once to offer shelter to the travellers! We cannot shiver for an hour or more in that horrid carriage, ma'am, with nothing to do! Besides, I am shockingly hungry, and I should think they would be bound to offer us refreshment, would not you? I am sure it is dinner-time, and past!"

"Oh, I do not think we should!" was all Miss Blackburn had to say, and it seemed so stupid to Arabella that she paid no heed to it, but desired the groom to escort them to the lodge gates before riding off to Grantham. This he did, and the ladies, dismissing him there, trod up the short drive to the house, one of them murmuring disjointed protests, the other perceiving no reason in the world why she should not claim a hospitality anyone in Yorkshire would have been eager to offer.

CHAPTER FOUR

IT WAS at about this moment that that erratic young sprig of fashion, Lord Fleetwood, fixed his friend, and host, Mr Beaumaris, with a laughing eye, and demanded in a rallying tone: "Well! You promise me a rare day with the hounds tomorrow – by the by, where do we meet? but what – *what*, -- Robert, do you offer me for my entertainment this evening?"

"My cook," said Mr Beaumaris, "is generally thought to be an artist in his own line. A Frenchman: I think you will like his way of dressing a Davenport chicken, while some trick he has of flavouring a Benton sauce -"

"What, did you send Alphonse down, then, from London?" interrupted Lord Fleetwood, momentarily diverted.

"Alphonse?" repeated Mr Beaumaris, his finely chiselled brows lifting a little. "Oh, no! this is another. I don't think I know his name. But I like his way with fish."

Lord Fleetwood burst out laughing. "I expect if you discovered a cook with a way of serving game which you liked, you would send him off to that shooting-box of yours, and pay him a king's ransom, only to kick his heels for three parts of the year!"

"I expect I should," agreed Mr Beaumaris imperturbably.

"But," said his lordship severely, "I am not to be put off with a cook! I came here in the expectation of finding fair Paphians, let me tell you, and all manner of shocking orgies – wine out of skulls, y'know, and -"

"The lamentable influence of Lord Byron upon society!" interpolated Mr Beaumaris, with a faint, contemptuous smile.

"What? Oh, that poet-fellow that set up such a dust! Myself, I thought him devilish underbred, but of course it don't do to say so. But that's it! Where, Robert, are the fair Paphians?"

"If I had any Paphians in keeping here, you don't imagine, do you, Charles, that I would run the risk of being cut-out by a man of *your* address?" retorted Mr Beaumaris.

Lord Fleetwood grinned at him, but replied: "None of your gammon to me! It would take ten times my address to cut-out a – a – dash it, a Midas like you!"

"If my memory does not err, all that Midas touched turned to gold," said Mr Beaumaris. "I think you mean Croesus."

"No, I don't! Never heard of the fellow!"

"Well, most of the things I touch have a disheartening way of turning to dross," said Mr Beaumaris, lightly, but with a note of bitter self-mockery in his languid voice.

This was going a little too deep for his friend. "Humdudgeon, Robert! You can't bamboozle me! If there are to be no Paphians -"

"I can't conceive why you should have supposed there would be," interrupted his host.

"Well, I didn't, but I can tell you this, my boy! – that's the latest *on-dit*!"

"Good God! Why?"

"Lord, how should I know? Daresay it's because you won't throw your glove at any of the beauties who have been setting their caps at you any time these five years. What's more, your *chères-amies* are always such devilish high-flyers, dear boy, it puts notions into the heads of all the old tabbies! Think of the Faraglini!"

"I had rather not. The most rapacious female of my acquaintance."

"But what a face! what a figure!"

"And what a temper!"

"What became of her?" asked his lordship. "I haven't laid eyes on her since she left your protection."

"I think she went to Paris. Why? Had you a fancy to succeed me?"

"No, by Jove, I couldn't have stood the nonsense!" said his lordship frankly. "She'd have had me rolled-up within a month! What did you have to give for those match-grays she used to drive all over town?"

"I can't remember."

"To tell you the truth," confided Lord Fleetwood, "I shouldn't have thought it worth it myself – though I'm not denying she was a curst fine woman!"

"It wasn't."

Lord Fleetwood regarded him, half-curious, half-amused. "Is anything worth while to you, Robert?" he asked quizzically.

"Yes, my horses!" retorted Mr Beaumaris. "And, talking of horses, Charles, what the devil possessed you to buy one of Lichfield's breakdowns?"

"That bay? Now, there's a horse that fairly took my fancy!" said his lordship, his simple countenance lighting up with enthusiasm. "What a piece of blood and bone! No, really, Robert -!"

"If ever I find myself with a thoroughly unsound animal in my stables," said Mr Beaumaris ruthlessly, "I shall offer him to you in the happy certainty that he will take your fancy!"

Lord Fleetwood was still protesting with indignation and vehemence when the butler entered the room to inform his master, rather apologetically, that a carriage had broken down outside his gates, and the two ladies it bore were desirous of sheltering for a short time under his roof.

Mr Beaumaris's cool gray eyes betrayed no emotion, but his mouth seemed for an instant to harden. He said calmly: "Certainly. There should be a fire in the saloon. Tell Mrs Mersey to wait upon the ladies there."

The butler bowed, and would have withdrawn, but Lord Fleetwood checked him, exclaiming: "No, no, too shabby by half, Robert! I won't be fobbed off so! What do they look like, Brough? Old? Young? Pretty?"

The butler, inured to his lordship's free and easy ways, replied with unimpaired solemnity that one of the ladies was both young, and – he ventured to think – very pretty.

"I insist on your receiving these females with a proper degree of civility, Robert!" said his lordship firmly. "Saloon, indeed! Show 'em in, Brough!"

The butler glanced for guidance towards his master, as though he doubted whether the command would be endorsed, but Mr Beaumaris merely said with his usual indifference: "As you please, Charles."

"What an ungrateful dog you are!" said Lord Fleetwood, when Brough had left the room. "You don't deserve your fortune! This is the hand of Providence!"

"I should doubt of their being Paphians," was all Mr Beaumaris found to say. "I thought that was what you wanted?"

"Any diversion is better than none!" replied Lord Fleetwood.

"What a singularly infelicitous remark! I wonder why I invited you."

Lord Fleetwood grinned at him. "Now, Robert, did you think – *did* – you think – to come Tip Street over me? There may be plenty of toadies ready to jump out of their skins at the very thought of being invited to the Nonpareil's house – and no better entertainment offered than a rubber of piquet, I dare swear -"

"You are forgetting the cook."

"But," continued his lordship inexorably, "I ain't amongst 'em!"

Mr Beaumaris's habitual aspect was one of coldness, and reserve, but sometimes he could smile in a way that not only softened the austerity of his countenance but lit his eyes with a gleam of the purest amusement. It was not the smile he kept for social occasions – a faintly sardonic curl of the lips, that one – but those who were honoured by a glimpse of it generally revised their first impressions of him. Those who had never seen it were inclined to think him a proud, disagreeable sort of a man, though only the most daring would ever have uttered aloud such a criticism of one who, besides possessing all the advantages of birth and fortune, was an acknowledged leader of society. Lord Fleetwood, no stranger to that smile, saw it dawn now, and grinned more broadly than ever.

"How can you, Charles? When you must know that almost your only claim to fashion is being noticed by me!"

Arabella entered the room to find both its occupants laughing, and thus had the felicity of seeing Mr Beaumaris at his best. That she herself was looking remarkably pretty, with her dusky curls and charming complexion admirably set off by a high-crowned bonnet, with curled ostrich-feather tips, and crimson ribbons tied into a bow under one ear, never entered her head, since Mr Tallant's daughters had always been discouraged from thinking much about their appearance. She paused on the threshold, while the butler murmured her name and Miss Blackburn's, quite unselfconscious, but looking about her with a kind of wide-eyed, innocent interest. She was very much impressed by what she saw. The house was not a large one, but she perceived that it was furnished with a good taste which was as quiet as it was expensive. Her quick scrutiny took in Lord Fleetwood, who had put up an instinctive hand to straighten the Belcher necktie he affected, and passed on to Mr Beaumaris.

Arabella had one brother who aspired to dandyism, and she had thought that she had seen in Harrowgate gentlemen of decided fashion. She now perceived that she had much mistaken the matter. No one she had ever seen approached the elegance of Mr Beaumaris.

Lord Fleetwood, or any of his cronies, could have recognized the tailoring of that coat of olive-green superfine at a glance; Arabella, to whom the magic name of Weston was unknown, was merely aware of a garment so exquisitely cut that it presented all the appearance of having been moulded to its wearer's form. A very good form, too, she noted, with approval. No need of buckram wadding, such as that Knaresborough tailor had inserted into Bertram's new coat, to fill out those shoulders! And how envious Bertram would have been of Mr Beaumaris's fine legs, sheathed in tight pantaloons, with gleaming Hessian boots pulled over them! Mr Beaumaris's shirt-points were not as high as Bertram's, but his necktie commanded the respect of one who had more than once watched her brother's struggles with a far less complicated arrangement. Arabella was not perfectly sure that she admired his style of hairdressing – he affected a Stanhope crop – but she did think him a remarkably handsome man, as he stood there, laughter dying on his lips, and out of his gray eyes.

It was only a moment that he stood thus. She had the impression that he was scanning her critically; then he moved forward, and bowed slightly, and begged, in a rather colourless tone, to know in what way he could be of service to her.

"How do you do?" said Arabella politely. "I beg your pardon, but the thing is that there has been an accident to my carriage, and and it is raining, and horridly cold! The groom has rid in to Grantham, and I daresay will bring another carriage out directly, but – but Miss Blackburn has taken a chill, and we should be very much obliged if we might wait here in the warm!"

She was stammering and blushing by the time she came to the end of this speech. Outside, it had seemed the simplest thing in the world to solicit shelter; under Mr Beaumaris's eye, it all at once seemed as though the request were outrageous. To be sure, he was smiling, but it was a very different smile from the one his face had worn when she had entered the room. It was such a very slight curl of the lips, yet there was some quality in it which made her feel ruffled and uncomfortable.

But he said with perfect civility: "An unfortunate mishap. You must permit me to send you to Grantham in one of my carriages, ma'am."

Lord Fleetwood, who had been standing staring in the frankest admiration at Arabella, was jerked into action by this speech. Pulling a chair invitingly close to the fire, he exclaimed: "No, no, come and sit down, ma'am! I can see you are chilled to the bone! Shocking weather for travelling! You will have got your feet wet, I daresay, and *that* will never do, you know! Robert, where have your wits gone a-begging? Why don't you desire Brough to fetch some refreshment for Miss – er – Miss – for the ladies?"

With a look which Arabella was strongly inclined to construe as one of resignation, Mr. Beaumaris replied: "I trust he may be doing so. I beg you will be seated, ma'am!"

But it was Lord Fleetwood who handed Arabella to the chair he had placed, saying solicitously: "I am sure you are hungry, and will be glad of something to eat!"

"Well, yes, sir," confessed Arabella, who was very hungry indeed. "I own, I have been thinking of my dinner for several miles! And no wonder, for I see it is already past five o'clock!"

This naïve speech made his lordship, who never sat down to his dinner before half-past seven at the very earliest, swallow convulsively, but he recovered himself in an instant, and replied without a blink: "So it is, by Jupiter! You are famished, then! But never mind! Mr Beaumaris here was just saying that dinner would be served in a trice. Weren't you, Robert?"

"Was I?" said Mr Beaumaris. "I have the wretchedest of memories, but I am sure you are right. I beg you will do me the honour of dining with me, ma'am."

Arabella hesitated. She could see from her anguished expression that Miss Blackburn thought she should rather accept Mr Beaumaris's first offer; and not the most inveterate of optimists could have read into that languid gentleman's voice anything more than a reluctant civility. But this warm, comfortably furnished room was a most welcome change from the travelling carriage, and the aroma of cooking which had assailed her nostrils as she had crossed the hall had considerably whetted her appetite. She looked a little doubtfully at her host. Again it was Lord Fleetwood who, with his friendly smile and easy manners, clinched the matter. "Of course they will dine with us! Now, won't you, ma'am?"

"It would be giving too much trouble, sir!" said Miss Blackburn, in a sort of gasp.

"No trouble in the world, ma'am, I assure you! In fact, we are very much obliged to you, for we had been wishing that we were to have company, eh, Robert?"

"Certainly," agreed Mr Beaumaris. "Was I not just saying so?"

Miss Blackburn, having undergone a life-time of slights and snubs, was quick to catch the satirical inflexion. She cast him a scared, deprecating look, and coloured. His eyes met hers; he stood looking down at her for a moment, and then said in a much kinder tone: "I am afraid you are not quite comfortable there, ma'am. Will you not draw nearer to the fire?"

She was thrown into a flutter, and assured him rather disjointedly that she was perfectly comfortable, and himself too good, too obliging! Brough had come into the room with a tray of glasses and decanters, which he set down on a table, and Mr Beaumaris moved towards it, saying: "You will like to go upstairs with my housekeeper, I daresay, to take off your wet coat, but first you must let me give you a glass of wine." He began to pour out some Madeira. "Two extra covers for dinner, Brough – which you will serve immediately."

Brough thought of the Davenport fowls roasting on the spits in the kitchen, and of the artist in charge of them, and was visibly shaken. "Immediately, sir?" he said, in a failing voice.

"Let us say, within half-an-hour," amended Mr Beaumaris, carrying a glass of wine over to Miss Blackburn.

"Yes, sir," said Brough, and tottered from the room, a broken man.

Miss Blackburn accepted the wine gratefully, but when it was offered to Arabella she declined it. Papa did not like his daughters to taste anything stronger than porter, or the very mild claret-cup served at the Harrowgate Assembly Rooms, and she was a little doubtful of its possible effect on her. Mr Beaumaris did not press her in any way, but set the glass down again, poured out some sherry for himself and his friend, and returned to sit beside Miss Blackburn on the sofa.

Lord Fleetwood, meanwhile, had ensconced himself beside Arabella, and was chatting to her in his inconsequent, cheerful way, which set her quite at her ease. He was delighted to hear that she was on her way to London, hoped to have the pleasure of meeting her there – in the Park, possibly, or at Almack's. He had plenty of anecdotes of *ton* with which to entertain her, and rattled on in an agreeable fashion until the housekeeper came to escort the ladies upstairs.

They were taken to a guest-chamber on the first floor, and handed over there to a housemaid, who brought up hot water for them, and bore their damp coats away to be dried in the kitchen.

"Everything in the first style of elegance!" breathed Miss Blackburn. "But we should not be dining here! I feel sure we ought not, my dear Miss Tallant!"

Arabella was a little doubtful on this score herself, but as it was now too late to draw back she stifled her misgivings, and said stoutly that she was persuaded there could be no objection. Finding a brush and comb laid out on the dressing-table, she began to tidy her rather tumbled locks.

"They are *most* gentlemanlike," said Miss Blackburn, deriving comfort from this circumstance. "Of the first rank of fashion, I daresay. They will be here for the hunting, depend upon it: I collect this is a hunting-box."

"A hunting-box!" exclaimed Arabella, awed. "Is it not very large and grand, ma'am, to be that?"

"Oh, no, my dear! Quite a small house! The Tewkesburys, whose sweet children I was engaged to instruct before I removed to Mrs Caterham's establishment, had one much larger, I assure you. This is the Melton country, you must know."

"Good heavens, are they Melton men, then? Oh, how much I wish Bertram could be here! What I shall have to tell him! I think it is Mr Beaumaris who owns the house: I wonder who the other is? I thought when I first saw him he could not be quite the thing, for that striped waistcoat, you know, and that spotted handkerchief he wears instead of a cravat makes him look like a groom, or some such thing. But when he spoke, of course I knew he was not a vulgar person at all."

Miss Blackburn, feeling for once in her life pleasantly superior, gave a titter of laughter, and said pityingly: "Oh, dear me no, Miss Tallant! You will find a great many young gentlemen of fashion wearing much odder clothes than *that!* It is what Mr Geoffrey Tewkesbury – a very modish young man! – used to call *all the crack*!" She added pensively: "But I must confess that I do not care for it myself, and nor did dear Mrs Tewkesbury. My notion of a true gentleman is someone like Mr Beaumaris!"

Arabella dragged the comb ruthlessly through a tangle. "I thought him a very proud, reserved man!" she declared. "And not at all hospitable!" she added.

"Oh, no, how can you say so? How very kind and obliging it was of him to place me in the best place, so near the fire! Delightful manners! nothing high in them at all! I was quite overcome by his condescension!"

It was evident to Arabella that she and Miss Blackburn regarded their host through two very different pairs of spectacles. She preserved an unconvinced silence, and as soon as Miss Blackburn had finished prinking her crimped gray locks at the mirror, suggested that they should go downstairs again. Accordingly they left the room, and crossed the upper hall to the head of the stairway. Mr Beaumaris's fancy had led him to carpet his stairs, a luxury which Miss Blackburn indicated to her charge with one pointing finger and a most expressive glance.

Across the lower hall, the door into the library stood ajar. Lord Fleetwood's voice, speaking in rallying tones, assailed the ladies' ears. "I swear you are incorrigible!" said his lordship. "The loveliest of creatures drops into your lap, like a veritable honey-fall, and you behave as though a gull-groper had forced his way into your house!"

Mr Beaumaris replied with disastrous clarity: "My dear Charles, when you have been hunted by every trick known to the ingenuity of the female mind, you may more readily partake of my sentiments upon this occasion! I have had beauties hopeful of wedding my fortune swoon in my arms, break their bootlaces outside my London house, sprain their ankles when my arm is there to support them, and now it appears that I am to be pursued even into Leicestershire! An accident to her coach! Famous! What a green-horn she must believe me to be!"

A small hand closed like a vice about Miss Blackburn's wrist. Herself bridling indignantly, she saw Arabella's eyes sparkling, and her cheeks most becomingly flushed. Had she been better acquainted with Miss Tallant she might have taken fright at these signs. Arabella breathed into her ear: "Miss Blackburn, can I *trust* you?"

Miss Blackburn would have vigorously assured her that she could, but the hand released her wrist, and flew up to cover her mouth. Slightly startled, she nodded. To her amazement, Arabella then picked up her skirts, and fled lightly back to the top of the stairs. Turning there, she began to come slowly down again, saying in a clear, carrying voice: "Yes, indeed! I am sure I have said the same, dear ma'am, times out of mind! But do, pray, go before me!"

Miss Blackburn, turning to stare at her, with her mouth at half-cock, found a firm young hand in the small of her back, and was thrust irresistibly onward.

"But in spite of all," said Arabella, "I prefer to travel with my own horses!"

The awful scowl that accompanied these light words quite bewildered the poor little governess, but she understood that she was expected to reply in kind, and said in a quavering voice: "Very true, my dear!"

The scowl gave place to an encouraging smile. Any one of Arabella's brothers or sisters would have begged her at this point to consider all the consequences of impetuosity; Miss Blackburn, unaware of the eldest Miss Tallant's besetting fault, was merely glad that she had not disappointed her.

Arabella tripped across the hall to that half-open door, and entered the library again.

It was Lord Fleetwood who came forward to receive her. He eyed her with undisguised appreciation, and said: "Now you will be more comfortable! Devilish dangerous to sit about in a wet coat, y'know! But we are yet unacquainted, ma'am! The stupidest thing! – never can catch a name when it is spoken! That man of Beaumaris's mumbles so that no one can hear him! You must let me make myself known to you, too – Lord Fleetwood, very much at your service!"

"I," said Arabella, a most dangerous glitter in her eye, "am Miss Tallant!"

His lordship, murmuring polite gratification at being made the recipient of this information, was surprised to find his inanities quite misunderstood. Arabella fetched a world-weary sigh, and enunciated with a scornful curl of her lip: "Oh, yes! *The* Miss Tallant!"

"Th – *the* Miss Tallant?" stammered his lordship, all at sea.

"The rich Miss Tallant!" said Arabella.

His lordship rolled a anguished and an enquiring eye at his host, but Mr Beaumaris was not looking at him. Mr Beaumaris, his attention arrested, was regarding the rich Miss Tallant with a distinct gleam of curiosity, not unmixed with amusement, in his face.

"I had hoped that here at least I might be unknown!" said Arabella, seating herself in a chair a little withdrawn from the fire. "Ah, you must let me make you known to Miss Blackburn, my – my *dame de compagnie*!"

Lord Fleetwood sketched a bow; Miss Blackburn, her countenance wooden, dropped him a slight curtsy, and sat down on the nearest chair.

"Miss Tallant!" repeated Lord Fleetwood, searching his memory in vain for enlightenment. "Ah, yes! Of course! Er – I don't think I have ever had the honour of meeting you in town, have I, ma'am?"

Arabella directed an innocent look from him to Mr Beaumaris, and back again, and clapped her hands together with an assumption of mingled delight and dismay. "Oh, you *did* not know!" she exclaimed. "I need never have told you! But when you looked *so*, I made sure you were as bad as all the rest! Was anything ever so vexatious? I most particularly desire to be quite unknown in London!"

"My dear ma'am, you may rely on me!" promptly replied his lordship, who, like most rattles, thought himself the model of discretion. "And Mr Beaumaris, you know, is in the same case as yourself, and able to sympathize with you!"

Arabella glanced at her host, and found that he had raised his quizzing-glass, which hung round his neck on a long black riband, and was surveying her through it. She put up her chin a little, for she was by no means sure that she cared for this scrutiny. "Indeed?" she said.

It was not the practice of young ladies to put up their chins in just that style if Mr Beaumaris levelled his glass at them: they were more in the habit of simpering, or of trying to appear unconscious of his regard. But Mr Beaumaris saw that there was a decidedly militant sparkle in this lady's eye, and his interest, at first tickled, was now fairly caught. He let his glass fall, and said gravely: "Indeed! And you?"

"Alas!" said Arabella, "I am fabulously wealthy! It is the greatest mortification to me! You can have no notion!"

His lips twitched. "I have always found, however, that a large fortune carries with it certain advantages."

"Oh, you are a man! I shall not allow you to know anything of the matter!" she cried. "You cannot know what it means to be the object of every fortune-hunter, courted and odiously flattered only for your wealth, until you are ready to wish that you had not a penny in the world!"

Miss Blackburn, who had hitherto supposed her charge to be a modest, well-behaved girl, barely repressed a shudder. Mr Beaumaris, however, said: "I feel sure that you under-rate yourself, ma'am."

"Oh, dear me, no!" said Arabella. "I have too often heard myself pointed out as the rich Miss Tallant to be under any illusion, sir! And it is for this reason that I wish to be quite unknown in London."

Mr Beaumaris smiled, but as the butler came in just then to announce dinner, he said nothing, but merely offered his arm to Arabella.

The dinner, which consisted of two courses, seemed to Arabella sumptuous beyond her wildest imaginings. No suspicion crossed her mind that her host, after one swift glance at his board, had resigned himself to the knowledge that the reputations of himself and his cook had been placed in jeopardy; or that that artist in the kitchen, having, with strange Gallic imprecations which made his various assistants quake, rent limb from limb two half-roasted Davenport fowls, and flung them into a pan with a béchamel sauce and some tarragons, was even now, as he arranged a basket of pastry on a dish, undecided whether to leave this dishonoured house on the instant, or to cut his throat with the larger carving-knife. Soup à la Reine was removed with fillets of turbot with an Italian sauce; and the chickens à la Tarragon were flanked by a dish of spinach and croûtons, a glazed ham, two cold partridges, some broiled mushrooms, and a raised mutton pie. The second course presented Arabella with an even more bewildering choice, for there was, besides the baskets of pastry, a Rhenish cream, a jelly, a Savoy cake, a dish of salsify fried in butter, an omelette, and some anchovy toast. Mrs Tallant had always prided herself on her housekeeping, but such a repast as this, embellished as it was by elegant garnitures, and subtle sauces, was quite beyond the range of the Vicarage cook. Arabella could not help opening her eyes a little at the array of viands spread before her, but she managed to conceal her awe, and to partake of what was offered to her with a very creditable assumption of unconsciousness. Mr Beaumaris, perhaps loth to degrade his burgundy, or perhaps with a faint, despairing hope of adding piquancy to this commonplace meal, had instructed Brough to serve champagne. Arabella, having already cast discretion to the winds, allowed her glass to be filled, and sipped her way distastefully through it. It had a pleasantly exhilarating effect upon her. She informed Mr Beaumaris that she was bound for the town residence of Lady Bridlington; created several uncles for the simple purpose of endowing herself with their fortunes; and at one blow disposed of four brothers and three sisters who might have been supposed to have laid a claim to a share of all this wealth. She contrived, without precisely making so vulgar a boast, to convey the impression that she was escaping from courtships so persistent as to amount to persecution; and Mr Beaumaris, listening with intense pleasure, said that London was the very place for anyone desirous of escaping attention.

Arabella, embarking recklessly on her second glass of champagne, said that in a crowd one could more easily pass unnoticed than in the restricted society of the country.

"Very true," agreed Mr Beaumaris.

"*You* never did so!" remarked Lord Fleetwood, helping himself from the dish of mushrooms which Brough presented at his elbow. "You must know, ma'am, that you are in the presence of the Nonpareil – none other! quite the most noted figure in society since poor Brummell was done-up!"

"Indeed!" Arabella looked from him to Mr Beaumaris with a pretty air of innocent enquiry. "I did not know – I might not have heard the name quite correctly, perhaps?"

"My dear Miss Tallant!" exclaimed his lordship, in mock horror. "Not know the great Beaumaris! the Arbiter of Fashion! Robert, you are quite set down!"

Mr Beaumaris, whose almost imperceptibly lifted finger had brought the watchful Brough to his side, was murmuring some command into that attentive but astonished ear, and paid no heed. His command was passed on to the footman hovering by the side-table, who, being quite a young man, and as yet imperfectly in control of his emotions, betrayed in his startled look some measure of the incredulity which shook his trained soul. The coldly quelling eye of his superior recalled him speedily to a sense of his position, however, and he left the room to carry the stupefying command still farther.

Miss Tallant, meanwhile, had perceived an opportunity to gratify her most pressing desire, which was to snub her host beyond possibility of his recovery. "Arbiter of Fashion?" she said, in a blank voice. "You cannot, surely, mean one of the *dandy-set*? I had thought – Oh, I beg your pardon! I expect that in London that is quite as important as being a great soldier, or a statesman, or – or some such thing!"

Even Lord Fleetwood could scarcely mistake the tenor of this artless speech. He gave an audible gasp. Miss Blackburn, whose enjoyment of dinner had already been seriously impaired, refused the partridge, and tried unavailingly to catch her charge's eye. Only Mr Beaumaris, hugely enjoying himself, appeared unmoved. He replied coolly: "Oh, decidedly! One's influence is so far-reaching!"

"Oh?" said Arabella politely.

"Why, certainly, ma'am! One may blight a whole career by the mere raising of an eyebrow, or elevate a social aspirant to the ranks of the highest *ton* only by leaning on his arm for the length of a street."

Miss Tallant suspected that she was being quizzed, but the strange exhilaration had her in its grip, and she did not hesitate to cross swords with this expert fencer. "No doubt, sir, if I had ambitions to cut a figure in society *your* approval would be a necessity?"

Mr Beaumaris, famed for his sword-play, slipped under her guard with an unexpected thrust. "My dear Miss Tallant, *you* need no passport to admit you to the ranks of the most sought-after! Even I could not depress the claims of one endowed with – may I say it? your face, your figure, and your fortune!"

The colour flamed up into Arabella's cheeks; she choked over the last of her wine, tried to look arch, and only succeeded in looking adorably confused. Lord Fleetwood, realizing that his friend had embarked on yet another of his practised flirtations, directed an indignant glance at him, and did his best to engage the heiress's attention himself. He was succeeding quite well when he was thrown off his balance by the unprecedented behaviour of Brough, who, as the second course made its appearance, removed his champagne-glass, replacing it with a goblet, which he proceeded to fill with something out of a tall flagon which his lordship strongly suspected was iced lemonade. One sip was enough alike to confirm this hideous fear and to deprive his lordship momentarily of the power of speech. Mr Beaumaris, blandly swallowing some of the innocuous mixture, seized the opportunity to re-engage Miss Tallant in conversation.

Arabella had been rather relieved to see her wine-glass removed, for although she would have died rather than have owned to it she thought the champagne decidedly nasty, besides making her want to sneeze. She took a revivifying draught of lemonade, glad to discover that in really fashionable circles this mild beverage was apparently served with the second course. Miss Blackburn, better versed in the ways of the *haut ton*, now found herself unable to form a correct judgment of her host. To be plunged from a conviction that he was truly gentlemanlike to a shocked realization that he was nothing but a coxcomb, and then back again, quite overset the poor little lady. She knew not what to think, but could not forbear casting him a glance eloquent of the warmest gratitude. His eyes encountered hers, but for such a fleeting instant that she could never afterwards be sure whether she had caught the glimmer of an amused smile in them, or whether she had imagined it.

Brough, receiving a message at the door, announced that madam's groom had brought a hired coach to the house, and desired to know when she would wish to resume her journey to Grantham.

"It can wait," said Mr Beaumaris, replenishing Arabella's glass. "A little of the Rhenish cream, Miss Tallant?"

"How long," demanded Arabella, recalling Mr Beaumaris's odious words to his friend, "will it take them to mend my own carriage?"

"I understand, miss, that a new pole will be needed. I could not say how long it will be."

A faint clucking from Miss Blackburn indicated dismay at this intelligence. Mr Beaumaris said: "A tiresome accident, but I beg you will not distress yourselves! I will send my chaise to pick you up in Grantham at whatever hour tomorrow should be agreeable to you."

Arabella thanked him, but was resolute in refusing his offer, for which, she assured him, there was not the slightest occasion. If the wheelwright proved too dilatory for her patience she would finish her journey post. "It will be quite an experience!" she declared truthfully. "My friends assure me that I am a great deal too old-fashioned in my notions – that quite a respectable degree of comfort is to be found in hired chaises!"

"I perceive," said Mr Beaumaris, "that we have much in common, ma'am. But I shall not allow a distaste for hired vehicles to be old-fashioned. Let us rather say that we have a little more nicety than the general run of our fellow-creatures!" He turned his head towards the butler. "Let a message be conveyed to the wheelwright, Brough, that he will oblige me by repairing Miss Tallant's carriage with all possible expedition."

Miss Tallant had nothing to do but thank him for his kind offices, and finish her Rhenish cream. That done, she rose from the table, saying that she had trespassed too long on her host's hospitality, and must now take her leave of him, with renewed thanks for his kindness.

"The obligation, Miss Tallant, is all on my side," he replied. "I am grateful for the chance which has made us acquainted, and shall hope to have the pleasure of calling upon you in town before many days."

This promise threw Miss Blackburn into agitation. As she accompanied Arabella upstairs, she whispered: "My dear Miss Tallant, how *could* you? And now he means to call on you, and you have told him – oh dear, oh dear, what would your Mama say?"

"Pooh!" returned Arabella, brazening it out. "If he is indeed a rich man, he will not care a fig, or think of it again!"

"*If* he is – Good gracious, Miss Tallant, he must be one of the wealthiest men in the country! When I collected that he was in very truth Mr Beaumaris I nearly swooned where I stood!"

"Well," said the pot-valiant Arabella, "if he is so very grand and important you may depend upon it he has not the least intention of calling on me in town. And I am sure I hope he will not, for he is an odious person!"

She refused to be moved from this standpoint, or even to acknowledge that in Mr Beaumaris's person at least no fault could be found. She said that she did not think him handsome, and that she held dandies in abhorrence. Miss Blackburn, terrified that she might, in this alarming mood, betray her dislike of Mr Beaumaris at parting, begged her not to forget what the barest civility rendered obligatory. She added that one slighting word uttered by him would be sufficient to wither any young lady's career at the outset, and then wished that she had held her tongue, since this warning had the effect of bringing the militant sparkle back into Arabella's eyes. But when Mr Beaumaris handed her into the coach, and, with quite his most attractive smile, lightly kissed the tips of her fingers before letting her hand go, she bade him farewell in a shy little voice that gave no hint of her loathing of him.

The coach set off down the drive; Mr Beaumaris turned, and in a leisurely way walked back into his house. He was pounced on in the hall by his injured friend, who demanded to know what the devil he meant by inflicting lemonade upon his guests.

"I don't think Miss Tallant cared for my champagne," he replied imperturbably.

"Well, if she didn't, she could have refused it, couldn't she?" protested Lord Fleetwood. "Besides, it was no such thing! She drank two glasses of it!"

"Never mind, Charles, there is still the port," said Mr Beaumaris.

"Yes, by God!" said his lordship, brightening. "And, mind, now! I expect the very best in your cellar! A couple of bottles of that '75 of yours, or -"

"Bring it to the library, Brough – something off the wood!" said Mr Beaumaris.

Lord Fleetwood, always the easiest of preys, rose to the bait without a moment's hesitation. "Here, no, I say!" he cried, turning quite pale with horror. "Robert! No, really, Robert!"

Mr Beaumaris lifted his brows in the blandest astonishment, but Brough, taking pity on his lordship, said in a soothing tone: "We have nothing like that in our cellars, I assure your lordship!"

Lord Fleetwood, perceiving that he had once more been gulled, said with strong feeling: "You deserve I should plant you a facer for that, Robert!"

"Well, if you think you can -!"

"I don't," replied his lordship frankly, accompanying him into the library. "But that lemonade was a dog's trick to serve me, you know!" His brow puckered in an effort of thought. "Tallant! . . . Did you ever hear the name before, for I'll swear I never did?"

Mr Beaumaris looked at him for a moment. Then his eyes fell to the snuff-box he had drawn from his pocket. He flicked open the box, and took a delicate pinch between finger and thumb. "You have never heard of the Tallant fortune?" he said. "My *dear* Charles -!"

CHAPTER FIVE

THANKS TO Mr Beaumaris's message, which worked so powerfully on the wheelwright as to cause him to ignore the prior claims of three other owners of damaged vehicles, Arabella was only kept waiting for one day in Grantham. Since the Quorn met there on the morning following her encounter with Mr Beaumaris, she was able, from the window of a private parlour at the Angel and Royal Inn, to see just how he looked on horseback. She could have seen how Lord Fleetwood looked too, had she cared, but curiously enough she never even thought of his lordship. Mr Beaumaris looked remarkably well, astride a beautiful thoroughbred, with long, sloping pasterns, and shoulders well laid back. She decided that Mr Beaumaris's seat was as good as any she had ever seen. The tops to his hunting-boots were certainly whiter than a mere provincial would have deemed possible.

The Hunt having moved off, there was nothing for two delayed travellers to do for the rest of the day but stroll about the town, eat their meals, and yawn over the only books to be found in the inn. But by the following morning the Squire's carriage was brought round to the Angel, with a new pole affixed, and the horses well-rested, and the ladies were able to set forward betimes on the last half of their long journey.

Even Miss Blackburn was heartily sick of the road by the time the muddied carriage at last drew up outside Lady Bridlington's house in Park Street. She was sufficiently well acquainted with the metropolis to feel no interest in the various sounds and sights which had made Arabella forget her boredom and her fidgets from the moment that the carriage reached Islington. These, to a young lady who had never seen a larger town than York in her life, were at once enthralling and bewildering. The traffic made her feel giddy, and the noise of post-bells, of wheels on the cobbled streets, and the shrill cries of itinerant vendors of coals, brick-dust, door-mats, and rat-traps quite deafened her. All passed before her wide gaze in a whirl; she wondered how anyone could live in such a place and still retain her sanity. But as the carriage, stopping once or twice for the coachman to enquire the way of nasal and not always polite Cockneys, wound its ponderous way into the more modish part of the town, the din abated till Arabella began even to entertain hopes of being able to sleep in London.

The house in Park Street seemed overpoweringly tall to one accustomed to a rambling two-storeyed country-house; and the butler who admitted the ladies into a lofty hall, whence rose an imposing flight of stairs, was so majestic that Arabella felt almost inclined to apologize for putting him to the trouble of announcing her to her godmother. But she was relieved to find that he was supported by only one footman, and so was able to follow him up with tolerable composure to the drawing-room on the first floor.

Here her qualms were put to flight by the welcome she received. Lady Bridlington, whose plump, pink cheeks were wreathed in smiles, clasped her to an ample bosom, kissed her repeatedly, exclaimed, just as Aunt Emma had, on her likeness to her Mama, and seemed so unaffectedly glad to see her that all constraint was at an end. Lady Bridlington's good-nature extended even to the governess, to whom she spoke with kindness, and perfect civility.

When Mama had known Lady Bridlington, she had been a pretty girl, without more than commonsense, but with such a respectable portion, and with so much vivacity and good-humour, that it was no surprise to her friends when she contracted a very eligible match. Time had done more to enlarge her figure than her mind, and it was not many days before her young charge had discovered that under a superficial worldly wisdom there was little but a vast amount of silliness. Her ladyship read whatever new work of prose or verse was in fashion, understood one word in ten of it, and prattled of the whole; doted on the most admired singers at the Opera, but secretly preferred the ballet. vowed there had never been anything to equal Kean's *Hamlet* on the English stage, but derived considerably more enjoyment from the farce which followed this soul-stirring performance. She was incapable of humming a tune correctly, but never failed to patronize the Concerts of Ancient Music during the season, just as she never failed to visit the Royal Academy every year, at Somerset House, where, although her notion of a good picture was a painting that reminded her forcibly of some person or place with which she was familiar, she unerringly detected the hand of a master in all the most distinguished artists' canvasses. Her life seemed to a slightly shocked Arabella to consist wholly of pleasure; and the greatest exertion she ever put her mind to was the securing of her own comfort. But it would have been unjust to have called her a selfish woman. Her disposition was kindly; she liked the people round her to be as happy as she was herself, for that made them cheerful, and she disliked long faces; she paid her servants well, and always remembered to thank them for any extraordinary service they performed for her, such as walking her horses up and down Bond Street in the rain for an hour while she shopped, or sitting up till four or five in the morning to put her to bed after an evening-party; and, provided she was not expected to put herself out for them, or to do anything disagreeable, she was both kind and generous to her friends.

She expected nothing but pleasure from Arabella's visit, and although she knew that in launching the girl into society she was behaving in a very handsome way, she never dwelled on the reflection, except once or twice a day in the privacy of her dressing-room, and then not in any grudging spirit, but merely for the gratifying sensation it gave her of being a benevolent person. She was very fond of visiting, shopping, and spectacles; liked entertaining large gatherings in her own house; and was seldom bored by even the dullest Assembly. Naturally, since every woman of fashion did so, she complained of dreadful squeezes or sadly insipid evenings, but no one who had seen her at these functions, greeting a multitude of acquaintances, exchanging the latest *on-dits*, closely scanning the newest fashions, or taking eager part in a rubber of whist, could have doubted her real and simple enjoyment of them.

To be obliged, then, to chaperon a young lady making her début to a succession of balls, routs, Assemblies, Military Reviews, balloon ascensions, and every other diversion likely to be offered to society during the season, exactly suited her disposition. She spent the better part of Arabella's first evening in Park Street in describing to her all the delightful plans she had been making for her amusement, and could scarcely wait for Miss Blackburn's departure next day before ordering her carriage to be sent round, and taking Arabella on a tour of all the smartest shops in London.

These cast the shops of High Harrowgate into the shade. Arabella was obliged to exercise great self-restraint when she saw the alluring wares displayed in the windows. She was helped a little by her north-country shrewdness, which recoiled from trifles priced at five times their worth, and not at all by her cicerone who, having been blessed all her life with sufficient means to enable her to purchase whatever took her fancy, could not understand why Arabella would not buy a bronze-green velvet hat, trimmed with feathers and a broad fall of lace, and priced at a figure which would have covered the cost of all the hats so cleverly contrived by Mama's and Sophia's neat fingers. Lady Bridlington owned that it was an expensive hat, but she held that to buy what became one so admirably could not be termed an extravagance. But Arabella put it resolutely aside, saying that she had as many hats as she required, and explaining frankly that she must not spend her money too freely, since Papa and Mama could not afford to send her any more. Lady Bridlington was quite distressed to think that such a pretty girl should not be able to set her beauty off to the best advantage. It seemed so sad that she was moved to purchase a net stocking-purse, and a branch of artificial flowers, and to bestow them on Arabella. She hesitated for a few minutes over a handsome shawl of Norwich silk, but it was priced at twenty guineas, and although this could not be said to be a high price, she remembered that she had one herself, a much better one, for which she had paid fifty guineas, which she could very well lend to Arabella whenever she did not wish to wear it herself. Besides, there would be all the expense of

Arabella's Court dress to be borne later in the season, and even though a great deal might be found in her own wardrobe which could be converted to Arabella's needs, the cost was still certain to be heavy. A further inspection of the shawl convinced her that it was of poor quality, not at all the sort of thing she would like to give her young charge, so they left the shop without buying it. Arabella was profoundly relieved, for although she would naturally have liked to have possessed the shawl, it made her very uncomfortable to be in danger of costing her hostess so much money.

Her frankness in speaking of her circumstances made Lady Bridlington a little thoughtful. She did not immediately mention the matter, but when the two ladies sat before the fire in the small saloon that evening, drinking tea, she ventured to put into words some at least of the thoughts which were revolving in her head.

"You know, my dear," she said, "I have been considering the best way to set to work, and I have made up my mind to it that as soon as you have grown more used to London – and I am sure it will not be long, for you are such a bright, clever little puss! – I should introduce you, quietly, you know! The season has not yet begun, and London is still very thin of company. And I think that will suit us very well, for you are not used to the way we go on here, and a small Assembly – no dancing, just an evening-party, with music, perhaps, and cards – is the very thing for your first appearance! I mean to invite only a few of my friends, the very people who may be useful to you. You will become acquainted with some other young ladies, and of course with some gentlemen, and that will make it more comfortable, I assure you, when I take you to Almack's, or to some large ball. Nothing can be more disagreeable than to find oneself in a gathering where one does not recognize a single face!"

Arabella could readily believe it, and had nothing but approbation for this excellent scheme. "Oh, yes, if you please, ma'am! It is of all things what I should like, for I know I shall not know how to go on at first, though I mean to learn as fast as I can!"

"Exactly so!" beamed her ladyship. "You are a sensible girl, Arabella, and I am very hopeful of settling you respectably, just as I promised your Mama I would!" She saw that Arabella was blushing, and added: "You won't object to my speaking plain, my love, for I daresay you know how important it is that you should be creditably established. Eight children! I do not know how your poor Mama will ever contrive to get good husbands for your sisters! And boys are such a charge on one's purse! I am sure I do not care to think of what my dear Frederick cost his father and me from first to last! First it was one thing, and then another!"

A serious look came into Arabella's face, as she thought of the many and varied needs of her brothers and sisters. She said earnestly: "Indeed, ma'am, what you say is very just, and I mean to do my best not to disappoint Mama!"

Lady Bridlington leaned forward to lay her pudgy little hand over Arabella's, and to squeeze it fondly. "I knew you would feel just as you ought!" she said. "Which brings me to what I had in mind to say to you!" She sat back again in her chair, fidgeted for a moment with the fringe of her shawl, and then said without looking at Arabella: "You know, my love, everything depends on first impressions – at least, a great deal does! In society, with everyone trying to find eligible husbands for their daughters, and so many beautiful girls for the gentlemen to choose from, it is in the highest degree important that you should do and say exactly what is right. That is why I mean to bring you out quietly, and not at all until you feel yourself at home in London. For you must know, my dear, that only rustics appear amazed. I am sure I do not know why it should be so, but you may believe that innocent girls from the country are not at all what the gentlemen like!"

Arabella was surprised, for her reading had taught her otherwise. She ventured to say as much, but Lady Bridlington shook her head. "No, my love, it is not so at all! That sort of thing may do very well in a novel, and I am very fond of novels myself, but they have nothing to do with life, depend upon it! But that was not what I wished to say!" Again she played with the shawl-fringe, saying in a little burst of eloquence: "I would not, if I were you, my dear, be for ever talking about Heythram, and the Vicarage! You must remember that nothing is more wearisome than to be obliged to listen to stories about a set of persons one has never seen. And though of course you would not prevaricate in any way, it is quite unnecessary to tell everyone – or, indeed, anyone! – of your dear Papa's situation! I have said nothing to lead anyone to suppose that he is not in affluent circumstances, for nothing, I do assure you, Arabella, could be more fatal to your chances than to have it known that your expectations are very small!"

Arabella was about to reply rather more hotly than was civil when the recollection of her own conduct in Mr Beaumaris's house came into her mind with stunning effect. She hung her head, and sat silent, wondering whether she ought to make a clean breast of the regrettable affair to Lady Bridlington, and deciding that it was too bad to be spoken of.

Lady Bridlington, misunderstanding the reason for her evident confusion, said hastily: "If you should be fortunate enough to engage some gentleman's affection, dear Arabella, of course you will tell him just how you are placed, or I shall, and – and, depend upon it, he will not care a button! You must not be thinking that I wish you to practise the least deception, for it is no such thing! Merely, it would be foolish, and quite unnecessary, for you to be talking of your circumstances to every chance-met acquaintance!"

"Very well, ma'am," said Arabella, in a subdued tone.

"I knew you would be sensible! Well, now, I am sure there is no need for me to say anything more to you on this head, and we must decide whom I shall invite to my evening-party. I wonder, my love, if you would see if my tablets are on that little table. And a pencil, if you will be so good!"

These commodities having been found, the good lady settled down happily to plan her forthcoming party. Since the names she recited were all of them unknown to Arabella, the discussion resolved itself into a gentle monologue. Lady Bridlington ran through the greater part of her acquaintance, murmuring that it would be useless to invite the Farnworths, since they had no children; that Lady Kirkmichael gave the shabbiest entertainments, and could not be depended on to invite Arabella, even if she did decide to give a ball for that lanky daughter of hers; that the Accringtons must of course be sent a card, and also the Buxtons – delightful families, both, and bound to entertain largely this season! "And I mean to invite Lord Dewsbury, and Sir Geoffrey Morecambe, my dear, for there is no saying but what one of them might – And I am sure Mr Pocklington has been hanging out for a wife these two years, not but what he is perhaps a little old – However, we will ask him to come, for there can be no harm in that! Then, I must certainly prevail upon dear Lady Sefton to come, for she is one of the patronesses of Almack's, you know; and perhaps Emily Cowper might – And the Charnwoods, and Mr Catwick; and, if they are in town, the Garthorpes . . ."

She rambled on in this style, while Arabella tried to appear interested. But as she could do no more than agree with her hostess when she was appealed to, her attention soon wandered, to be recalled with a jerk when Lady Bridlington mentioned a name she did know.

"And I shall send Mr Beaumaris a card, because it would be such a splendid thing for you, my love, if it were known that he came to your début – for such we may call it! Why, if he were to come, and perhaps talk to you for a few minutes, and seem pleased with you, you would be *made*, my dear! Everyone follows his lead! And perhaps, as there are so few parties yet, he *might* come! I am sure I have been acquainted with him for years, and I knew his mother quite well! She was Lady Mary Caldicot, you know: a daughter of the late Duke of Wigan, and such a beautiful creature! And it is not as though Mr Beaumaris has never been to my house, for he once came to an Assembly here, and stayed for quite half-an-hour! Mind, we must not build upon his accepting, but we need not despair!"

She paused for breath, and Arabella, colouring in spite of herself, was able at last to say: "I – I am myself a little acquainted with Mr Beaumaris, ma'am."

Lady Bridlington was so much astonished that she dropped her pencil. "Acquainted with Mr Beaumaris?" she repeated. "My love, what can you be thinking about? When can you possibly have met him?"

"I – I quite forgot to tell you, ma'am," faltered Arabella unhappily, "that when the pole broke – I told you *that!* – Miss Blackburn and I sought shelter in his hunting-box, and – and he had Lord Fleetwood with him, and we stayed to dine!"

Lady Bridlington gasped. "Good God, Arabella, and you never told me! Mr Beaumaris's house! He actually asked you to dine, and you never breathed a word of it to me!"

Arabella found herself quite incapable of explaining why she had been shy of mentioning this episode. She stammered that it had slipped out of her mind in all the excitement of coming to London.

"Slipped out of your mind?" exclaimed Lady Bridlington. "You dine with Mr Beaumaris, and at his hunting-box, too, and then talk to me about the excitement of coming to London? Good gracious, child – But, there, you are such a country-mouse, my love, I daresay you did not know all it might mean to you! Did he seem pleased? Did he like you?"

This was a little too much, even for a young lady determined to be on her best behaviour. "I daresay he disliked me excessively, ma'am, for *I* thought *him* very proud and disagreeable, and I hope you won't ask him to your party on *my* account!"

"Not ask him to my party, when, if he came to it, everyone would say it was a success! You must be mad, Arabella, to talk so! And do let me beg of you, my dear, never to say such a thing of Mr Beaumaris in public! I daresay he may be a little stiff, but what is that to the purpose, pray? There is no one who counts for more in society, for setting aside his fortune, which is immense, my love, he is related to half the houses in England! The Beaumarises are one of the oldest of our families, while on his mother's side he is a grandson of the Duchess of Wigan – the Dowager Duchess, I mean, which of course makes him cousin to the present Duke, besides the Wainfleets, and – But you would not know!" she ended despairingly.

"I thought Lord Fleetwood most amiable, and gentlemanlike," offered Arabella, by way of palliative.

"Fleetwood! I can tell you this, Arabella: there is no use in your setting your cap at *him*, for all the world knows that he *must* marry money!"

"I hope, ma'am," cried Arabella, flaring up, "that you do not mean to suggest that I should *set my cap* at Mr Beaumaris, for nothing would prevail upon me to do so!"

"My love," responded Lady Bridlington frankly, "it would be quite useless for you to do so! Robert Beaumaris may have his pick of all the beauties in England, I daresay! And, what is more, he is the most accomplished flirt in London! But I do most earnestly implore you not to set him against you by treating him with the least incivility! You may think him what you please, but, believe me, Arabella, he could ruin your whole career and mine, too, if it came to that!" she added feelingly.

Arabella propped her chin in her hand, pondering an agreeable thought. "Or he could make everything easy for me, ma'am?" she enquired.

"Of course he could – if he chose to do it! He is the most unpredictable creature! It might amuse him to make you the rage of town – or he might take it into his head to say you were not quite in his style and if once he says *that*, my dear, what man will look twice at you, unless he has already fallen in love with you, which, after all, we *cannot* expect?"

"My dear ma'am," said Arabella, in dulcet accents, "I hope I should not be so ill-bred as to be uncivil to *anyone* – even Mr Beaumaris!"

"Well, my dear, I hope not, indeed!" said her ladyship doubtfully.

"I promise I will not be in the least degree uncivil to Mr Beaumaris, if he should come to your party," said Arabella.

"I am happy to hear you say so, my love, but ten to one he won't come," responded her ladyship pessimistically.

"He said to me at parting that he hoped to have the pleasure of calling on me in town before many days," said Arabella disinterestedly.

Lady Bridlington considered this, but in the end shook her head. "I do not think we should set any store by that," she said. "Very likely he said it for politeness' sake."

"Very likely," agreed Arabella. "But if you are acquainted with him, I wish you will send Lord Fleetwood a card for your party, ma'am, for he was excessively kind, and I liked him!"

"Of course I am acquainted with him!" declared Lady Bridlington, quite affronted. "But do not be setting your heart on him, Arabella, I beg of you! A delightful rattle, but the Fleetwoods are all to pieces, by what I hear, and however much he may flirt with you, I am persuaded he will never make you an offer!"

"Must every man I meet make me an offer?" asked Arabella, controlling her voice with an effort.

"No, my love, and you may depend upon it that they won't!" replied her ladyship candidly. "In fact, I have had it in mind to warn you against setting your ambitions *too* high! I mean to do all I can for you, but there is no denying that suitable husbands do not grow upon every bush! Particularly, my dear – and I know you will not fly into a miff with me for saying it! – when you have no portion to recommend you!"

In face of her ladyship's conviction, Arabella hardly liked to betray her feelings, so she bit her lip, and was silent. Fortunately, Lady Bridlington's mind was not of a tenacious nature, and as she just then recollected a very important lady whose name must be included amongst the list of invited persons, she forgot about Arabella's matrimonial chances in explaining why it would be folly to omit Lady Terrington from that list. Nothing more was said about Mr Beaumaris, her ladyship having been diverted, by some chance reference of her own, into describing to Arabella the various social treats she had in store for her. In spite of the fact that the season had not yet begun, these were so numerous that Arabella felt almost giddy, and wondered whether, in this round of gaiety, her hostess would find the time to accompany her to Church on Sunday. But in doubting whether Lady Bridlington would go to Church she wronged her: Lady Bridlington would have thought it a very odd thing not to be seen in her pew every Sunday morning, unless, as was very often the case, she chose to attend the service at the Chapel Royal, where, in addition to listening to an excellent sermon, she could be sure of seeing all her more distinguished friends, and even, very often, some member of the Royal Family. This good fortune was hers on Arabella's first Sunday in London, and the circumstance made fine reading for the interested brothers and sisters in Yorkshire, following, as it did (most artistically), descriptions of Hyde Park, and St. Paul's Cathedral, and a lively account of the racket and bustle of the London Streets.

"We attended Morning Service at the Chapel Royal, St James's on Sunday," wrote Arabella, in a fine, small hand, and on very thin paper, crossing her lines. *"We heard a very good sermon on a text from the Second Epistle to the Corinthians, pray tell dear Papa: He that had gathered much had nothing over; and he that had gathered little had no lack. London is still very thin of company"* – not for nothing had Arabella dutifully attended to her godmother's conversation! – *"but there were a great many fashionables present, and also the Duke of Clarence, who came up to us afterwards, and was very affable, with nothing high in his manner at all."* Arabella paused, nibbling the end of her pen, and considering the Duke of Clarence. Papa might not care to have his Royal Highness described, but Mama, and Sophy, and Margaret would most certainly wish to know just what he was like, and what he had said. She bent again over her page. *"I do not think one would say that he is precisely handsome,"* she wrote temperately, *"but his countenance is benevolent. His head is a queer shape, and he is inclined to corpulence. He made me think of my uncle, for he talks in just that way, and very loud, and he laughs a great deal. He did me the honour to say that I wore a vastly fetching hat: I hope Mama will be pleased, for it was the one with*

her pink feathers, which she made for me." There did not seem to be anything more to be said about the Duke of Clarence, except that he talked quite audibly in Church, and that was information scarcely likely to please the inhabitants of the Vicarage. She read over what she had written, and felt that it might disappoint Mama and the girls. She added a line. *"Lady Bridlington says that he is not near as fat as the Prince Regent, or the Duke of York."* On this heartening note she ended her paragraph, and embarked on a fresh one.

"I am growing quite accustomed to London, and begin to know my way about the streets, though of course I do not walk out by myself yet. Lady Bridlington sends a footman with me, just as Bertram said she would, but I see that young females do go alone nowadays, only perhaps they are not of the haut ton. *This is very* important,*and I am in constant dread that I shall do something improper, such as walking down St James's Street, where all the gentlemen's clubs are, and very* fast, *which of course I do not wish to be thought. Lady Bridlington gives an evening-party, to introduce me to her friends. I shall be all of a quake, for everyone is so grand and fashionable, though perfectly civil, and much kinder than I had looked for. Sophy will like to know that Lord Fleetwood, whom I met on the road, as I wrote to you from Grantham, paid us a morning-visit, to see how I did, which was very amiable and obliging of him. Also Mr Beaumaris, but we were out driving in the Park. He left his card. Lady Bridlington was in transports, and has placed it above all the rest, which I think nonsensical, but I find that that is the way of the World, and makes me reflect on all Papa has said on the subject of Folly, and the Hollowness of Fashionable Life."* That seemed to dispose satisfactorily of Mr Beaumaris. Arabella dipped her pen in the standish again. *"Lady Bridlington is everything that is kind, and I am persuaded that Lord Bridlington is a very respectable young man, and not at all abandoned to the Pursuit of Pleasure, as Papa feared. His name is Frederick. He is travelling in Germany, and has visited a great many of the battlefields. He writes very interesting letters to his Mama, with which I am sure Papa would be pleased, for he seems to feel just as he ought, and moralizes on all he sees in a truly elevating way, though rather long."* Arabella perceived that there was little room left on her sheet, and added in a cramped fist: *"I would write more only that I cannot get a frank for this, and do not wish to put Papa to the expense of paying some sixpences for the second sheet. With my love to my brothers and sisters, and my affectionate duty to dear Papa, I remain your loving daughter Arabella."*

Plenty of promising matter there for Mama and the girls to pore over, and to discuss, even though so much remained unwritten! One could not resist boasting a very little about the compliments paid to one by a Royal Duke, or just mentioning that a fashionable peer of the realm had called to see how one did – not to mention the great Mr Beaumaris, if one had happened to care a fig for that – but one felt quite shy of disclosing even to Mama how very gracious – how amazingly kind – everyone was being to an insignificant girl from Yorkshire.

For so it was. Shopping in Bond Street, driving on clement afternoons in Hyde Park, attending the service at the Chapel Royal, Lady Bridlington naturally encountered friends, and never failed to present Arabella to their notice. Some really forbidding dowagers who might have been expected to have paid scant heed to Arabella unbent in the most gratifying way, quite overpowering her by the kindness of their enquiries, and their insistence that Lady Bridlington should bring her to see them one day. Several introduced their daughters to Arabella, suggesting that she and they might walk in the Green Park some fine morning, so that in less than no time it seemed as though she had a host of acquaintances in London. The gentlemen were not more backward: it was quite a commonplace thing for some stroller in the Park to come up to Lady Bridlington's barouche, and stand chatting to her, and to her pretty protégée; while more than one sprig of fashion, with whom her ladyship was barely acquainted, paid her a morning visit on what seemed even to one so little given to speculation as Lady Bridlington the slenderest of excuses.

She was a little surprised, but after thinking about it for a few minutes she was as easily able to account for the ladies' civility as the gentlemen's. They were anxious to oblige her. This led her by natural stages to the reflection that she deserved a great deal of credit for having so well advertised Arabella's visit to town. As for the gentlemen, she had never doubted, from the moment of setting eyes on her god-daughter, that that fairy figure and charming countenance could fail to attract instant admiration. Arabella had, moreover, the most enchanting smile, which brought dimples leaping to her cheeks, and was at once mischievous and appealing. Any but the most case-hardened of men, thought Lady Bridlington enviously, would be more than likely, under its intoxicating influence, to behave in a rash manner, however much he might afterwards regret it.

But none of these conclusions quite explained the morning-visits of several high-nosed ladies of fashion, whose civilities towards Lady Bridlington had hitherto consisted of invitations to their larger Assemblies, and bows exchanged from their respective carriages. Lady Somercote was particularly puzzling. She called in Park Street when Arabella was out walking with the three charming daughters of Sir James and Lady Hornsea, and she sat for over an hour with her gratified hostess. She expressed the greatest admiration of Arabella, whom she had met at the theatre with her godmother. "A delightful girl!" she said graciously. "Very pretty-behaved, and without the least hint of pretension in her dress or bearing!"

Lady Bridlington agreed to it, and since her mind did not move rapidly it was not until her guest was well into her next observation that she wondered why Arabella should be supposed to show pretension.

"Of good family, I apprehend?" said Lady Somercote, carelessly, but looking rather searchingly at her hostess.

"Of course!" replied Lady Bridlington, with dignity. "A most respected Yorkshire family!"

Lady Somercote nodded. "I thought as much. Excellent manners, and conducts herself with perfect propriety! I was particularly pleased with the modesty of her bearing: not the least sign of wishing to put herself forward! And her dress too! Just what I like to see in a young female! Nothing vulgar, such as one too often sees nowadays! When every miss out of the schoolroom is decked out with jewellery, it is refreshing to see one with a simple wreath of flowers in her hair. Somercote was much struck. Indeed, he quite took one of his fancies to her! You must bring her to Grosvenor Square next week, dear Lady Bridlington! Nothing formal, you know: a few friends only, and perhaps the young people may find themselves with enough couples to get up a little dance."

She waited only for Lady Bridlington's acceptance of this flattering invitation before taking her leave. Lady Bridlington was left with her mind in a whirl. She was shrewd enough to know that more than a compliment to herself must lie behind this unexpected honour, and was at a loss to discover the lady's motive. She was the mother of five hopeful and expensive sons, and it was well known that the Somercote estates were heavily mortgaged. Advantageous marriages were a necessity to the Somercotes' progeny, and no one was more purposeful in her pursuit of a likely heiress than their Mama. For a dismayed instant Lady Bridlington wondered whether, in her anxiety to assist Arabella, she had concealed her circumstances too well. But she could not recall that she had ever so much as mentioned them: indeed, her recollection was that she had taken care never to do so.

The Honourable Mrs Penkridge, calling on her dear friend for the express purpose of bidding her and her protégée to a select Musical Soirée, and explaining, with apologies, how it was due to the stupidity of a secretary that her card of invitation had not reached her long since, spoke in even warmer terms of Arabella. "Charming! quite charming!" she declared, bestowing her frosted smile upon Lady Bridlington. "She will throw all our beauties into the shade! That simplicity is so particularly pleasing! You are to be congratulated!"

However perplexed Lady Bridlington might be by this speech, issuing, as it did, from the lips of one famed as much for her haughtiness as for her acid tongue, it seemed at least to dispose of the suspicion roused in her mind by Lady Somercote's visit. The Penkridges were a childless couple. Lady Bridlington, on whom Mrs Penkridge had more than once passed some contemptuous criticism, was not well-enough acquainted with her to know that almost the only sign of human emotion she had ever been seen to betray was her doting fondness for her nephew, Mr Horace Epworth.

This elegant gentleman, complete to a point as regards side-whiskers, fobs, seals, quizzing-glass, and scented handkerchief, had lately honoured his aunt with one of his infrequent visits. Surprised and delighted, she had begged to know in what way she could be of service to him. Mr Epworth had no hesitation in telling her. "You might put me in the way of meeting the new heiress, ma'am," he said frankly. "Dev'lish fine gal – regular Croesus, too!"

She had pricked up her ears at that, and exclaimed: "Whom can you be thinking of, my dear Horace? If you mean the Flint chit, I have it for a fact that –"

"Pooh! nothing of the sort!" interrupted Mr Epworth, waving the Flint chit away with one white and languid hand. "I daresay *she* has no more than thirty thousand pounds! This gal is so rich she puts 'em all in the shade. They call her the Lady Dives."

"Who calls her so?" demanded his incredulous relative.

Mr Epworth again waved his hand, this time in the direction which he vaguely judged to be northward. "Oh, up there somewhere, ma'am! Yorkshire, or some other of those dev'lish remote counties! Daresay she's a merchant's daughter: wool or cotton, or some such thing. Pity, but I shan't regard it: they tell me she's charming!"

"I have heard nothing of this! Who is she? Who told you she was charming?"

"Had it from Fleetwood last night, at the Great-Go," explained Mr Epworth negligently.

"That rattle! I wish you will not go so often to Watier's, Horace! I warn you, it is useless to apply to me! I have not a guinea left in the world, and I dare not ask Mr Penkridge to assist you again, until he has forgotten the last time!"

"Put me in the way of meeting this gal, and I'll kiss my fingers to Penkridge, ma'am," responded Mr Epworth, gracefully suiting the action to the word. "Acquainted with Lady Bridlington, ain't you? The gal's staying with her."

She stared at him. "If Arabella Bridlington had an heiress staying with her she would have boasted of it all over town!"

"No, she wouldn't. Fleetwood particularly told me the gal don't want it known. Don't like being courted for her fortune. Pretty gal, too, by what Fleetwood says. Name of Tallant."

"I never heard of a Tallant in my life!"

"Lord, ma'am, why should you? Keep telling you she comes from some dev'lish outlandish place in the north!"

"I would not set the least store by anything Fleetwood told me!"

"Oh, it ain't him!" said Mr Epworth cheerfully. "He don't know the gal's name either. It's the Nonpareil. Knows all about the family. Vouches for the gal."

Her expression changed; a still sharper look entered her eyes. She said quickly: "Beaumaris?" He nodded. "If *he* vouches for her – Is she presentable?"

He looked shocked, and answered in protesting accents: " 'Pon my soul, ma'am, you can't be in your senses to ask me such a demned silly question! Now, I put it to you, *would* Beaumaris vouch for a gal that wasn't slap up to the echo?"

"No. No, he would not," she said decidedly. "If it's true, and she has no vulgar connections, it would be the very thing for you, my dear Horace!"

"Just what I was thinking myself, ma'am," said her nephew.

"I will pay Lady Bridlington a morning-visit," said Mrs Penkridge.

"That's it: do the pretty!" Mr Epworth encouraged her.

"It is tiresome, for I have never been upon intimate terms with her! However, this alters the circumstances! Leave it to me!"

Thus it was that Lady Bridlington found herself the object of Mrs Penkridge's attentions. Since she had never before been honoured with an invitation to one of that lady's more exclusive parties, she was considerably elated, and at once seized the opportunity to invite Mrs Penkridge to her own evening-party. Mrs Penkridge accepted with another of her thin smiles, saying that she knew she could answer for her husband's pleasure in attending the party, and departed, thinking out rapidly some form of engagement for him which would at once spare him an insipid evening, and render it necessary for her to claim her nephew's escort.

CHAPTER SIX

Lady Bridlington did not expect Arabella's first party to be a failure, since she was a good hostess, and never offered her guests any but the best wines and refreshments, but that it should prove to be a wild success had not even entered her head. She had planned it more with the idea of bringing Arabella to the notice of other hostesses than as a brilliant social event; and although she had certainly invited a good many unattached gentlemen she had not held out the lure of dancing, or of cards, and so had little hope of seeing more than half of them in her spacious rooms. Her main pre-occupation was lest Arabella should not be looking her best, or should jeopardize her future by some unconventional action, or some unlucky reference to that regrettable Yorkshire Vicarage. In general, the child behaved very prettily, but once or twice she had seriously alarmed her patroness, either by a remark which betrayed all too clearly the modesty of her circumstances – as when she had asked, in front of the butler, whether she should help to prepare the rooms for the party, for all the world as though she expected to be given an apron and a duster! – or by some impulsive action so odd as to be positively outrageous. Not readily would Lady Bridlington forget the scene outside the Soho Bazaar, when she and Arabella, emerging from this mart, found a heavy wagon stationary in the road, with the one scraggy horse between its shafts straining under an unsparing lash to set it in motion. At one instant a demure young lady had been at Lady Bridlington's side; at the next a flaming fury was confronting the astonished wagoner, commanding him, with a stamp of one little foot to get down from the wagon at once – *at once!* – and not to *dare* to raise his whip again! He got down, quite bemused, and stood in front of the small fury, an ox of a man, towering above her while she berated him. When he had recovered his wits he attempted to justify himself, but failed signally to pacify the lady. He was a cruel wretch, unfit to be in charge of a horse, and a dolt, besides, not to perceive that one of the wheels was jammed, and through his own bad driving, no doubt! He began to be angry, and to shout Arabella down, but by this time a couple of chairmen, abandoning their empty vehicle, came across the square, expressing, in strong Hibernian accents, their willingness to champion the lady, and their desire to know whether the wagoner wanted to have his cork drawn. Lady Bridlington, all this time, had stood frozen with horror in the doorway of the Bazaar, unable to think of anything else to do than to be thankful that none of her acquaintances was present to witness this shocking affair. Arabella told the chairmen briskly that she would have no fighting, bade the wagoner observe the obstruction against which one of his rear wheels was jammed, herself went to the horse's head, and began to back him. The chairmen promptly lent their aid; Arabella addressed a short, pithy lecture to the wagoner on the folly and injustice of losing one's temper with animals, and rejoined her godmother, saying calmly: "It is mostly ignorance, you know!"

And although she did, when shown the impropriety of her behaviour, say she was sorry to have made a scene in public, it was evident that she was not in the least penitent. She said that Papa would have told her it was her duty to interfere in such a cause.

But no representations could induce her to say she was sorry for her quite unbecoming conduct two days later, when she entered her bedchamber to find a very junior housemaid, with a swollen face, lighting the fire. It appeared that the girl had the toothache. Now, Lady Bridlington had no desire that any of her servants should suffer the agonies of toothache, and had she been asked she would unquestionably have said that at the first convenient moment the girl should be sent off to have the tooth drawn. The mistress of a large household naturally had a duty to oversee the general well-being of her staff. Indeed, some years previously, when inoculation against cow-pox had been all the rage, she had with her own hands inoculated all the servants at Bridlington, and most of the tenants on the estate. Nearly every great lady had done so: it had been the accepted order of the day. But to bid the sufferer seat herself in the armchair in the best guest-chamber, to give her an Indian silk shawl to wrap round her head; and to disturb one's hostess during the sacred hour of her afternoon-nap by bursting in upon her with a demand for laudanum, was carrying benevolence to quite undesirable lengths. Lady Bridlington did her best to convey the sense of this to Arabella, but she spoke to deaf ears. "The poor girl is in the most dreadful pain, ma'am!"

"Nonsense, my love! You must not let yourself be imposed upon. Persons of her class always made a to-do about nothing. She had better have the tooth drawn tomorrow, if she can be spared from her work, and -"

"Dear madam, I assure you she is in no case to be toiling up and down all these stairs with coal-scuttles!" said Arabella earnestly. "She should cake some drops of laudanum, and lie down on her bed."

"Oh, very well!" said her ladyship, yielding to the stronger will. "But there is no occasion for you to be putting yourself into this state, my dear! And to be asking one of the under-housemaids to sit down in your bedroom, and giving her one of your best shawls -"

"No, no, I have only lent it to her!" Arabella said. "She is from the country, you know, ma'am, and I think the other servants have not used her as they ought. She was homesick, and so unhappy! And the toothache made it worse, of course. I do believe she wanted someone to be kind to her more than anything else! She has been telling me about her home, and her little sisters and brothers, and -"

"Arabella!" uttered Lady Bridlington. "Surely you have not been *gossiping with the servants?*" She saw her young guest stiffen, and added hastily: "You should never encourage persons of her sort to pour out the history of their lives into your ears. I expect you meant it for the best, my dear, but you have no notion how encroaching -"

"I hope, ma'am – indeed, I *know!*" said Arabella, her eyes very bright, and her small figure alarmingly rigid, "that not one of Papa's children would pass by a fellow-creature in distress!"

It was fast being borne in upon Lady Bridlington that the Reverend Henry Tallant was not only a grave handicap to his daughter's social advancement, but a growing menace to her own comfort. She was naturally unable to express this conviction to Arabella, so she sank back on her pillows, saying feebly: "Oh, very well, but if people were to hear of it they would think it excessively odd in you, my dear!"

Whatever anyone else might think, it soon became plain that the episode had given her ladyship's upper servants the poorest idea of Arabella's social standing. Her ladyship's personal maid, a sharp-faced spinster who had grown to middle-age in her service, and bullied her without compunction, ventured to hint, while she was dressing her mistress's hair that evening, that it was easy to see Miss was not accustomed to living in large and genteel households.

Lady Bridlington allowed Miss Clara Crowle a good deal of licence, but this was going too far. A pretty thing it would be if the servants, in that odious way they all had of talking about their betters, were to spread such a thing abroad! It would reach the ears of their employers in less than no time, and then the fat would indeed be in the fire! In a few dignified, well-chosen words Lady Bridlington gave her henchwoman to understand that Miss Tallant came from a mansion of awe-inspiring gentility, and was quite above considering appearances. She added, to clinch the matter, that very different customs obtained in the north from those common in London. Miss Crowle, a little cowed, but with a sting yet left in her tongue, sniffed, and said: "So I have always understood, my lady!" She then encountered her mistress's eyes in the mirror, and added obsequiously: "Not but what I am sure no one would ever suspicion Miss came from the north, my lady, so prettily as she speaks!"

"Certainly not," said Lady Bridlington coldly, and quite forgetful of the fact that she had experienced considerable relief, when Arabella had greeted her on her arrival, at finding that no ugly accent marred her soft voice. The dreadful possibility that she might speak with a Yorkshire burr had more than once occurred to her. Had she but known it, she had the Reverend Henry Tallant to thank for his daughter's pure accent. Papa was far too fastidious and cultured a man to permit his children to be slipshod in their speech, even frowning upon the excellent imitations of the farm-hand's conversation, achieved by Bertram and Harry in funning humour.

Miss Clara Crowle might be silenced, but Arabella's reprehensible conduct gave her hostess some serious qualms, and caused her to anticipate her evening-party with less than her usual placidity.

But nothing could have gone off better. To ensure that in appearance at least Arabella should do her credit, Lady Bridlington sent no less a personage than Miss Crowle herself to put the finishing touches to her toilet, rounding off the efforts of the housemaid detailed to wait on her. Miss Crowle was not best pleased when sent off to offer her services to Arabella, but it was many years since she had dressed a young and beautiful lady, and in spite of herself her enthusiasm awoke when she saw how delightfully Arabella's gown of jonquil crape became her, and how tasteful was the spangled scarf hanging over her arms. She saw at a glance that she could scarcely better the simple arrangement of those dark curls, twisted into a high knot on the top of her head, and with the short ringlets allowed to fall over her ears, but she begged Miss to permit her to place her flowers more becomingly. Her cunning hands deftly placed the faggot of artificial roses at just the right angle, and she was so well-satisfied with the result that she said Miss would be quite the belle of the evening, being as she was dark, and the fashion for fair beauties quite outdated.

Arabella, unaware of how greatly Miss Crowle was condescending to her, only laughed, a piece of unconcern that did her no harm in that critical maiden's eyes. Arabella was embarking on her first London party enormously heartened by the arrival, not an hour earlier, of her first London posy of flowers. The exciting box had been carried up to her room immediately, and, when opened, had been found to contain a charming bouquet, tied up – so fortunately! – with long yellow ribbons. Lord Fleetwood's card accompanied the tribute, and was even now propped up against the mirror. Miss Crowle saw it, and was impressed.

Lady Bridlington, presently setting eyes on Arabella just before dinner was announced, was delighted, and reflected that Sophia Theale had always had exquisite taste. Nothing could have set Arabella off to greater advantage than that delicate yellow robe, open down the front over a slip of white satin, and ornamented with clasps of tiny roses to match those in her hair. The only jewellery she wore was the ring Papa had had made for her, and Grandmama's necklet of pearls. Lady Bridlington was half inclined to ring for Clara to fetch down from her own jewel-case two bracelets of gold and pearls, and then decided that Arabella's pretty arms needed no embellishment. Besides, she would be wearing long gloves, so that the bracelets would be wasted.

"Very nice, my love!" she said approvingly. "I am glad I sent Clara to you. Dear me, where had you those flowers?"

"Lord Fleetwood sent them, ma'am," replied Arabella proudly.

Lady Bridlington received this information with disappointing composure. "Did he so? Then at all events we may be sure of seeing *him* here tonight. You know, my love, you must not be expecting a squeeze! I am sure I hope to see my drawing-rooms respectably filled, but it is early in the year still, so you must not be cast-down if you do not see as many people as you might have supposed you would."

She might have spared her breath. By half-past ten her drawing-rooms were crowded to overflowing, and she was still standing at the head of the stairs receiving late-comers. Nothing, she thought dizzily, had ever been like it! Even the Wainfleets, whom really she had not expected to see, were there; while the haughty Mrs Penkridge, escorted by her dandified nephew, had been amongst the earliest arrivals, unbending amazingly to Arabella, and begging leave to introduce Mr Epworth. Lord Fleetwood, and his crony, Mr Oswald Warkworth, were there, both hovering assiduously near Arabella, very full of gallantry and good spirits; Lady Somercote had brought two of her sons, and the Kirkmichaels their lanky daughter; Lord Dewsbury had failed, but Sir Geoffrey Morecambe was much in evidence, as were also the Accringtons, the Charnwoods, and the Seftons. Lady Sefton, dear creature that she was! had spoken with the greatest kindness to Arabella, and had promised later on to send her a voucher admitting her to Almack's Assembly Rooms. Lady Bridlington felt that her cup was full. It was to overflow. Last of all the guests, arriving after eleven o'clock, when her ladyship, having long since released Arabella from her place at her side, was on the point of abandoning her post and joining her guests in the drawing-rooms, Mr Beaumaris arrived, and came unhurriedly up the stairs. Her ladyship awaited him with a bosom swelling beneath its rich covering of purple satin, and her hand, clasping her fan, trembling slightly under the influence of the accumulated triumphs of this night. He greeted her with his cool civility, and she replied with tolerable composure, thanking him for his kind offices, in Leicestershire, towards her goddaughter.

"A pleasure, ma'am," said Mr. Beaumaris. "I trust Miss Tallant reached town without further mishap?"

"Oh, yes, indeed! So obliging of you to have called to enquire after her! We were sorry to have been out. You will find Miss Tallant in one of the rooms. Your cousin, Lady Wainfleet, too, is here."

He bowed, and followed her into the front drawing-room. A minute later, Arabella, enjoying the attentions of Lord Fleetwood, Mr Warkworth, and Mr Epworth, saw him coming towards her across the room, pausing once or twice on his way to exchange salutations with his friends. Until that moment she had thought Mr Epworth quite the best-dressed man present indeed, she had been quite dazzled by the exquisite nature of his raiment, and the profusion of rings, pins, fobs, chains, and seals which he wore; but no sooner had she clapped eyes on Mr Beaumaris's tall, manly figure than she realized that Mr Epworth's wadded shoulders, wasp-waist, and startling waistcoat were perfectly ridiculous. Nothing could have been in greater contrast to the extravagance of his attire than Mr Beaumaris's black coat and pantaloons, his plain white waistcoat, the single fob that hung to one side of it, the single pearl set chastely in the intricate folds of his necktie. Nothing he wore was designed to attract attention, but he made every other man in the room look either a trifle overdressed or a trifle shabby.

He reached her side, and smiled, and when she put out her hand raised it fleetingly to his lips. "How do you do, Miss Tallant?" he said. "I am happy indeed to have been granted this opportunity of renewing my acquaintance with you."

"Oh, it is too bad – a great deal too bad!" fluted Mr Epworth, rolling an arch eye at Arabella. "You and Fleetwood have stolen a march on the rest of us, you know – a shameful thing, 'pon my soul!"

Mr Beaumaris glanced down at him from his superior height, seemed to debate within himself whether this sally was worth the trouble of a reply, to decide that it was not, and turned back to Arabella. "You must tell me how you like London," he said. "It is abundantly plain that London likes you! May I procure you a glass of lemonade?"

This offer brought Arabella's chin up, and made her look at him with a distinct challenge in her eyes. She had had plenty of time to discover that it was not the common practice of hosts to sweep the wine from their tables at the end of the first course, and she strongly suspected Mr Beaumaris of quizzing her. He was looking perfectly grave, however, and met her eyes without a shadow of mockery in his own. Before she could answer him, Lord Fleetwood committed a strategical error, and exclaimed: "Of course! I'll swear you are parched with thirst, ma'am! I will get you a glass immediately!"

"Splendid, Charles!" said Mr Beaumaris cordially. "Do let me take you a little out of this crush, Miss Tallant!"

He seemed to take her acquiescence for granted, for he did not await a reply, but led her to where a sofa standing against one wall was momentarily unoccupied. How he contrived to find a way through the crowd of chattering guests was a mystery to Arabella, for he certainly did not force a passage. A touch on a man's shoulder, a bow and a smile to a lady, and the thing was done. He sat down beside her on the sofa, seated a little sideways, so that he could watch her face, one hand on the back of the sofa, the other playing idly with his quizzing-glass. "Does it come up to your expectations, ma'am?" he asked smilingly.

"London? Yes, indeed!" she responded. "I am sure I was never so happy in my life!"

"I am glad," he said.

Arabella remembered that Lady Bridlington had warned her against betraying too much enthusiasm: it was unfashionable to appear pleased. She remembered also that she had promised not to make a bad impression on Mr Beaumaris, so she added in a languid tone: "It is a shocking squeeze, of course, but it is always diverting to meet new people."

He looked amused, and said with a laugh in his voice: "No, don't spoil it! Your first answer was charming."

She eyed him doubtfully for a moment; then her irrepressible dimples peeped out. "But it is only rustics who own to enjoyment, sir!"

"Is it?" he returned.

"*You*, I am persuaded, do not enjoy such an Assembly as this!"

"You are mistaken: my enjoyment depends on the company in which I find myself."

"That," said Arabella naïvely, having thought it over, "is quite the prettiest thing that has been said to me tonight!"

"Then I can only suppose, Miss Tallant, that Fleetwood and Warkworth were unable to find words to express their appreciation of the exquisite picture you present. Strange! I formed the opinion that they were paying you all manner of compliments."

She laughed out at that. "Yes, but it was nonsense! I did not believe a word they said!"

"I hope you believe what *I* say, however, for I am very much in earnest."

The light tone he used seemed to belie his words. Arabella found him baffling, and directed another of her speculative glances at him. She decided that he must be answered in kind, and said daringly: "Are you being so obliging as to bring me into fashion, Mr Beaumaris?"

He let his eyes travel round the crowded room, his brows a little raised. "You do not appear to me to stand in any need of my assistance, ma'am." He perceived that Lord Fleetwood was edging his way past a knot of people, a glass in his hand, and waited for him to reach the sofa. "Thank you, Charles," he said coolly, taking the glass from his lordship, and presenting it to Arabella.

"You," said Lord Fleetwood, with deep feeling, "will receive a message from me in the morning, Robert! This is the most barefaced piracy I ever beheld in my life! Miss Tallant, I wish you will send this fellow about his business: his effrontery goes beyond what is allowable!"

"You must learn not to act on impulse," said Mr Beaumaris kindly. "A moment's reflection, the least touch of adroitness, and it would have been I who fetched the lemonade and you who had the privilege of sitting beside Miss Tallant on this sofa!"

"But it is Lord Fleetwood who earns my gratitude, for he is the more chivalrous!" said Arabella.

"Miss Tallant, I thank you!"

"You have certainly been amply rewarded, and have now nothing to do but to take yourself off," said Mr Beaumaris.

"Not for the world! " declared his lordship.

Mr Beaumaris sighed. "How often I have had to deplore your lack of tact!" he said.

Arabella, sparkling under the influence of all this exciting banter, raised her posy to her nose, and said, with a grateful look cast up at Fleetwood: "I stand *doubly* in Lord Fleetwood's debt!"

"No, no, it is I who stand in yours, ma'am, since you deigned to accept my poor tribute!"

Mr Beaumaris glanced at the posy, and smiled slightly, but said nothing. Arabella, catching sight of Mr Epworth, who was hovering hopefully in the vicinity, suddenly said: "Mr Beaumaris, who *is* that oddly dressed man?"

He looked round, but said: "There are so many oddly dressed men present, Miss Tallant, that I fear I am at a loss. You do not mean poor Fleetwood here?"

"Of course I do not!" exclaimed Arabella indignantly.

"Well, I am sure it would be difficult to find anything odder than that waistcoat he wears. It is very disheartening, for I have really expended a great deal of time in trying to reform his taste. Ah, I think I see whom you must mean! That, Miss Tallant, is Horace Epworth. In his own estimation, he undoubtedly personifies a set of creatures whom I have reason to believe you despise."

Blushing hotly, Arabella asked: "Is he a – a dandy?"

"He would certainly like you to think so."

"Well, if he is," said Arabella frankly, "I am sure you are no such thing, and I beg your pardon for saying it that evening!"

"Don't apologize to him, ma'am!" said Lord Fleetwood gaily. "It is time someone gave him a set-down, and *that*, I assure you, smote him with stunning effect! You must know that he thinks himself a notable Corinthian!"

"What is that, pray?" enquired Arabella.

"A Corinthian, ma'am, besides being a very Tulip of Fashion, is an amateur of sport, a master of sword-play, a deadly fellow with a pistol, a Nonpareil amongst whips, a -"

Mr Beaumaris interrupted this mock-solemn catalogue. "If you will be such a dead bore, Charles, you will provoke me to explain to Miss Tallant what the world means when it calls you a sad rattle."

"Well?" demanded Arabella mischievously.

"A fribble, ma'am, not worth your attention!" he replied, rising to his feet. "I see my cousin over there, and must pay my respects to her." He smiled, bowed, and moved away; stayed for a minute or two, talking to Lady Wainfleet; drank a glass of wine with Mr Warkworth; complimented his hostess on the success of her party; and departed, having done precisely what he had set out to do, which was to place Miss Tallant's feet securely on the ladder of fashion. The news would be all over town within twenty-four hours that the rich Miss Tallant was the Nonpareil's latest flirt.

"Did you see Beaumaris paying court to that dashed pretty girl?" asked Lord Wainfleet of his wife, as they drove away from Lady Bridlington's house.

"Of course I did!" replied his wife.

"Seemed very taken with her, didn't he? Not in his usual style, was she? I wonder if he means anything?"

"Robert?" said his wife, with something very like a snort. "If you knew him as well as I do, Wainfleet, you would have seen at one glance that he was amusing himself! I know how he looks in just that humour! Someone ought to warn the child to have nothing to do with him! It is too bad of him, for she is nothing but a baby, I'll swear!"

"They're saying in the clubs that she's as rich as a Nabob."

"So I have heard, but what that has to say to anything I don't know! Robert is quite odiously wealthy, and if ever he marries, which I begin to doubt, it will not be for a fortune, I can assure you!"

"No, I don't suppose it will," agreed his lordship. "Why did we go there tonight, Louisa? Devilish flat, that kind of an affair."

"Oh, shocking! Robert asked me to go. I own I was curious to see his heiress. He said he was going to make her the most sought-after female in London."

"Sounds like a hum to me," said his lordship. "Why should he do so?"

"Exactly what I asked him! He said it might be amusing. There are times, Wainfleet, when I would like to box Robert's ears!"

CHAPTER SEVEN

NOT ONLY in his cousin's bosom were vengeful thoughts nourished against Mr Beaumaris. Lady Somercote, not so doting a mother that she supposed any of her sons would be likely to prove more attractive to the heiress than the Nonpareil, could with pleasure have driven the long diamond pin she wore in her hair between his ribs; Mrs Kirkmichael thought bitterly that he might, considering the number of times she had gone out of her way to be agreeable to him, have bestowed a little of his attention upon her lanky daughter, a gesture which would have cost him nothing, and might have given poor Maria a start in the world; Mr Epworth, uneasily aware that for some inscrutable reason he was consistently cast in the shade by the Nonpareil, went the round of the clubs, saying that he had a very good mind to give Beaumaris a set-down at no very distant date; his aunt recalled that she had once quarrelled violently with Lady Mary Beaumaris, and said that it was from his mother Beaumaris had inherited his flirtatious disposition, adding that she was sorry for the woman he eventually married. Even Mr Warkworth and Lord Fleetwood said that it was rather too bad of the Nonpareil to trifle with the season's biggest catch; while several gentlemen who slavishly copied every detail of Mr Beaumaris's attire wished him safely underground.

There was one voice which was not raised to swell this chorus of disapprobation: Lady Bridlington was in raptures over Mr Beaumaris. She could talk of nothing else throughout the following day. While he sat beside Arabella, not a smile, not a gesture had escaped the good lady's anxious eye. He had paid no heed to any other girl in the room; he had plainly advertised to his world that he found Miss Tallant charming: there was no one in London more amiable, more truly polite, more condescending, or more in her ladyship's good graces! Over and over again she told Arabella that her success was now assured; it was not until her first transports had somewhat abated that she could be rational enough to drop a word of warning in Arabella's ear. But the more she thought of Mr Beaumaris's pronounced attentions to the girl, the more she remembered how many innocent maidens had fallen victims to his spear, the more she became convinced that it was necessary to put Arabella on her guard. So she said in an earnest voice, and with a slightly anxious look in her eye: "I am persuaded, my love, that you are too sensible a girl to be taken-in! But, you know, I stand to you in place of your Mama, and I think I should tell you that Mr Beaumaris is a most accomplished flirt! No one could be more delighted than I am that he should have singled you out, but it will never do, my dear, if you were to develop a *tendre* in *that* direction! I know I have only to drop a word in your ear, and you will not be offended by it! He is a confirmed bachelor. I could not tell you the number of hearts he has broken! Poor Theresa Howden – she married Lord Congleton some years later – went into a decline, and was the despair of her afflicted parents! They *did* think – and I am sure that nothing could have been more pronounced for all one season than – But no! Nothing came of it!"

Arabella had not been the reigning belle for twenty miles round Heythram without learning to distinguish between the flirt and the man who was in earnest, and she replied instantly: "I know very well that Mr Beaumaris means nothing by his compliments. Indeed, I am in no danger of being taken-in like a goose!"

"Well, my love, I *hope* you are not!"

"You may be sure I am not. If you do not see any objection, ma'am, I mean to encourage Mr Beaumaris's attentions, and make the best use I may of them! *He* believes himself to be amusing himself at my expense; I mean to turn him to very good account! But as for losing my heart – No, indeed!"

"Mind, we cannot depend upon his continuing to single you out!" said Lady Bridlington, with unwonted caution. "If he did, it would be beyond anything great, but there is no saying, after all! However, last night's work was enough to launch you, my dear, and I am *deeply* thankful!" She heaved an ecstatic sigh. "You will be invited everywhere, I daresay!"

She was quite right. Within one fortnight, she was in the happy position of finding herself with five engagements for the same evening, and Arabella had had to break into Sir John's fifty-pound bill to replenish her wardrobe. She had been seen at the fashionable hour of the Promenade in the Park, sitting beside the Nonpareil, in his high-perch phaeton; she had been almost mobbed at the theatre; she was on nodding terms with all manner of exalted persons; she had received two proposals of marriage; Lord Fleetwood, Mr Warkworth, Mr Epworth, Sir Geoffrey Morecambe, and Mr Alfred Somercote (to mention only the most notable of her suitors) had all entered the lists against Mr Beaumaris; and Lord Bridlington, travelling by fast post all the way, had returned from the Continent to discover what his mother meant by filling his house with unknown females in his absence.

He expressed himself, in measured terms, as being most dissatisfied with Lady Bridlington's explanation. He was a stocky, somewhat ponderous young man, with more sobriety than properly belonged to his twenty-six years. His understanding was not powerful, but he was bookish, and had early formed the habit of acquiring information by the perusal of authoritative tomes, so that by the time he had attained his present age his retentive memory was stocked with a quantity of facts which he was perhaps a little too ready to impart to his less well-read contemporaries. His father's death, while he was still at Eton, coupled with a conviction that his mother stood in constant need of superior male guidance, had added disastrously to his self-consequence. He prided himself on his judgment; was a careful steward of his fortune; had the greatest dislike of anything bordering on the unusual; and deplored the frivolity of those who might have been expected to have been his cronies. His mother's elation at not having spent one evening at home in ten days found no echo in his heart. He could neither understand why she should want to waste her time at social functions, nor why she should have been foolish enough to have invited a giddy girl to stay with her. He was afraid that the cost of all this mummery would be shocking; had Lady Bridlington asked for his counsel, which she might easily have done, he would have advised most strongly against Arabella's visit.

Lady Bridlington was a trifle cast-down by this severity, but since her late husband had left her to the enjoyment of a handsome jointure, out of which she always shared the expenses of the house in Park Street with Frederick, she was able to point out to him that the charge of entertaining Arabella fell upon her, and not upon him. He said that the wish to dictate to his Mama was far from him, but that he must persist in thinking the affair most ill-advised. Lady Bridlington was fond of her only son, but Arabella's success had quite gone to her head, and she was in no mood to listen to sober counsels. She retorted that he was talking a great deal of nonsense; upon which he bowed, compressed his lips, and bade her afterwards remember his words. He added that he washed his hands of the whole business. Lady Bridlington, who had no desire to see him fall a victim to Arabella's charms, was torn between exasperation, and relief that he showed no sign of succumbing to them.

"I will allow her to be a pretty-enough young female," said Frederick fairmindedly, "but there is a levity in her bearing which I cannot like, and all this gadding-about which she has led you into is not at all to my taste."

"Well, I can't conceive why you should have come running home in this foolish way!" retorted his mother.

"I thought it my duty, ma'am," said Frederick.

"It is a great piece of folly, and people will think it excessively odd in you! No one looked to see you in England again until July at the earliest!"

She was mistaken. No one thought it in the least odd of Lord Bridlington to have curtailed his tour. The opinion of society was pithily summed up by Mrs Penkridge, who said that she had guessed all along that that scheming Bridlington woman meant to marry the heiress to her own son. "Anyone could have seen how it would be!" she declared, with her mirthless jangle of laughter. "Such odious hypocrisy, too, to hold to it that she did not expect to see Bridlington in England until the summer! Mark my words, Horace, they will be married before the season is over!"

"Good gad, ma'am, I don't fear Bridlington's rivalry!" said her nephew, affronted.

"Then you are a goose!" said Mrs Penkridge. "Everything is in his favour! He is the possessor of an honoured name, and a title, which you may depend upon it the girl wants, and – what is a great deal to the point, let me tell you! – he has all the advantage of living in the same house, of being always at hand to minister to her wishes, squire her to parties, and – Oh, it puts me out of all patience!"

But Miss Tallant and Lord Bridlington, from the very moment of exchanging their first polite greetings. had conceived a mutual antipathy which was in no way mitigated by the necessity each was under to behave towards the other with complaisance and civility. Arabella would not for the fortune she was believed to possess have grieved her kind hostess by betraying dislike of her son; Frederick's sense of propriety, which was extremely nice, forbade him to neglect the performance of any attention due to his mother's guest. He could appreciate, and, indeed, since he had a provident mind, applaud Mrs Tallant's ambition to dispose of her daughters creditably; and since his own mother had undertaken the task of finding a husband for Arabella, he was prepared to lend his countenance to her schemes. What shocked and disturbed him profoundly was the discovery, within a week of his homecoming, that every gazetted fortune-hunter in London was dangling after Arabella.

"I am at a loss, ma'am, to guess what you can possibly have said to lead anyone to suppose that Miss Tallant is an heiress!" he announced.

Lady Bridlington, who had several times wondered much the same thing, replied uneasily: "I never said a word, Frederick! There is not the least reason why anyone should suppose such an absurdity! I own, I was a trifle surprised when – But she is a very pretty girl, you know, and Mr Beaumaris took one of his fancies to her!"

"I have never been intimate with Beaumaris," said Frederick. "I do not care for the set he leads, and must deplore his making any modest female the object of his gallantry. The influence he exerts, moreover, over persons whom I should have supposed to have had more -"

"Never mind that!" begged his mother hastily. "You told me yesterday, Frederick! You may think Beaumaris what you please, but even you will not deny that it lies in his power to bring whom he will into fashion!"

"Very likely, ma'am, but I have yet to learn that it lies in his power to prevail upon such men as Epworth, Morecambe, Carnaby, and – I must add! Fleetwood, to offer marriage to a female with nothing but her face to recommend her!"

"Not Fleetwood!" protested Lady Bridlington feebly.

"Fleetwood!" repeated Frederick in an inexorable tone. "I do not mean to say that he is precisely hanging out for a rich wife, but that he cannot afford to marry a penniless girl is common knowledge. Yet his attentions towards Miss Tallant are more marked even than those of Horace Epworth. And this is not all! From hints dropped in my presence, from remarks actually made to me, I am persuaded that the greater part of our acquaintance believes her to be in the possession of a handsome fortune! I repeat, ma'am: what can you have said to have given rise to this folly?"

"But I didn't!" cried poor Lady Bridlington almost tearfully. "Indeed, I took the greatest pains not to touch on the question of her expectations! It is false to call her penniless, because she is no such thing! With all those children, of course the Tallants can do very little for her upon her marriage, but when her father dies – and Sophia, too, for she has some money as well-"

"A thousand or so!" interrupted Frederick contemptuously. "I beg your pardon, ma'am, but nothing could be more plain to me than that something you have said – inadvertently, I daresay! has done all this mischief. For mischief I must deem it! A pretty state of affairs it will be if we are to have the world saying – as it will say, once the truth is known! – that you have foisted an impostress upon society!"

This terrible forecast temporarily outweighed in Lady Bridlington's mind the sense of strong injustice the rest of her son's remarks had aroused. She turned quite pale, and exclaimed: "What is to be done?"

"You may rely upon me, ma'am, to do what is necessary," replied Frederick. "Whenever the opportunity offers, I shall say that I have no notion how such a rumour came to be spread about."

"I suppose you must do so," agreed his mother dubiously. "But I do beg of you, Frederick, not to take the whole world into your confidence on the subject! There is not the least need for you to enter into all the details of the poor child's circumstances! "

"It would be quite improper for me to do so, ma'am," replied Frederick crushingly. "*I* am not responsible for her visit to London! I must point out to you, Mama, that it is *you* who have engaged yourself – unwisely, I consider – to establish her suitably. I am sure I have no desire to prejudice her chances of matrimony. Indeed, since I understand that you mean to keep her with you until some man offers for her, I shall be happy to see her married as soon as possible! "

"I think you are very disagreeable!" said Lady Bridlington, dissolving into tears.

Her peace of mind was quite cut up. When Arabella came into the room presently, she found her still dabbing at her eyes, and giving little sniffs. Quite dismayed, Arabella begged to be told the cause of this unhappiness. Lady Bridlington, glad of a sympathetic audience, squeezed her hand gratefully, and without reflection poured forth the sum of her grievances.

Kneeling beside her chair, Arabella listened in stricken silence, her hand lying slackly within Lady Bridlington's. "It is so unkind of Frederick!" Lady Bridlington complained. "And so unjust, for I assure you, my dear, I never said such a thing to a soul! How could he think I would do so? It would have been quite wicked to have told such lies, besides being so foolish, and vulgar, and everything that is dreadful! And why Frederick should think I could be so lost to all sense of propriety I am sure I don't know!"

Arabella's head sank; guilt and shame almost overpowered her; she could not speak. Lady Bridlington, misreading her confusion, felt a qualm of conscience at having so unguardedly taken her into her confidence, and said: "I should not have told you! It is all Frederick's fault, and I daresay he has exaggerated everything, just as he so often does! You must not let it distress you, my love, for even if it were true it would be absurd to suppose such a man as Mr Beaumaris, or young Charnwood, or a great many others I could name, care a button whether you are a rich woman or a pauper! And Frederick will make everything right!"

"How can he do so, ma'am?" Arabella managed to ask.

"Oh, when he sees the opportunity, he will say something to damp such ridiculous notions! Nothing very much, you know, but making light of the story! We need not concern ourselves, and I am sorry I spoke of it to you."

With all her heart Arabella longed for the courage to confess the whole. She could not. Already Lady Bridlington was rambling on, complaining fretfully of Frederick's unkindness, wondering what cause he had to suppose his mother ill-bred enough to have spread a false tale abroad, and wishing that his father were alive to give him one of his famous scolds. She said instead, in a subdued tone: "Is that why – why everyone has been so very polite to me, ma'am?"

"Certainly not!" said Lady Bridlington emphatically. "You must have perceived, my love, how many, many friends I have in London, and you may believe they accepted you out of compliment to me! Not that I mean to say – But before you were at all known, naturally it was my sponsorship that started you in the right way." She patted Arabella's hand consolingly. "Then, you know, you are so bright, and pretty, that I am sure it is no wonder that you are so much sought-after. And above all, Arabella, we must remember that the world always follows what is seen to be the mode, and Mr Beaumaris has made you the fashion by singling you out, even driving you in his phaeton, which is an honour indeed, I can tell you! "

Arabella's head was still bowed. "Does – does Lord Bridlington mean to tell everyone that I – that I have no fortune at all, ma'am?"

"Good gracious, no, child! That would be a fatal thing to do, and I hope he would have more sense! He will merely say it has been greatly exaggerated – enough to frighten away the fortune-hunters, but what will not weigh with an honest man! Do not give it another thought!"

Arabella was unable to obey this injunction. It was long before she could think of anything else. Her impulse was to fly from London, back to Heythram, but hardly had she reached the stage of calculating whether she still possessed enough money to pay her fare on the first coach than all the difficulties attached to such a precipitate retreat presented themselves to her. They were insuperable. She could not bring herself to confess to Lady Bridlington that her own was the wicked, ill-bred tongue accountable for the rumour, nor could she think of any excuse for returning to Yorkshire. Still less could she face the necessity of telling Papa and Mama of her shocking behaviour. She must remain in Park Street until the season came to an end, and if Mama was sadly disappointed at the failure of her schemes, at least Papa would never blame his daughter for returning to her home unbetrothed. She perceived clearly that unless something very wonderful were to happen this must be so, and felt herself guilty indeed.

Not for several hours did her mind recover its tone, but she was both young and optimistic, and after a hearty burst of tears, followed by a period of quiet reflection, she began insensibly to be more hopeful. Something would happen to unravel her difficulties; the odious Frederick would scotch the rumour; people would gradually grow to realize that they had been mistaken. Mr Beaumaris and Lord Fleetwood would no doubt write her down as a vulgar, boasting miss, but she must hope that they had not actually told everyone that it was she who had been responsible for the rumour. Meanwhile there was nothing to be done but to behave as though nothing were the matter. This, to a naturally buoyant spirit was not so hard a task as might have been supposed: London was offering too much to Arabella for her to be long cast-down. She might fancy all her pleasure destroyed, but she would have been a very extraordinary young woman who could have remembered her difficulties while cards and floral offerings were left every day at the house; while invitations poured in to every form of entertainment known to ingenious hostesses; while every gentleman was eager to claim her hand for the dance; while Mr Beaumaris took her driving in the Park behind his match-grays, and every other young lady gazed enviously after her. Whatever the cause, social success was sweet; and since Arabella was a very human girl she could not help enjoying every moment of it.

She expected to see some considerable diminution in her court once Lord Bridlington had let it be known that her fortune had been grossly exaggerated, and braced herself to bear this humiliation. But although she knew from Lady Bridlington that Frederick had faithfully performed his part, still the invitations came in, and still the unattached gentlemen clustered round her. She took fresh heart, glad to find that fashionable people were not, after all, so mercenary as she had been led to think. Neither she nor Frederick had the smallest inkling of the true state of affairs: she because she was too unsophisticated; Frederick because it had never yet occurred to him that anyone could doubt what he said. But he might as well have spared his breath on this occasion. Even Mr Warkworth, a charitably-minded gentleman, shook his head over it, and remarked to Sir Geoffrey Morecambe that Bridlington was doing it rather too brown.

"Just what I was thinking myself," agreed Sir Geoffrey, scrutinizing his neck-tie in the mirror with a dissatisfied eye. "Shabby, I call it. Do you think this way I have tied my cravat has something of the look of the Nonpareil's new style?"

Mr Warkworth directed a long, dispassionate stare at it. "No," he said simply.

"No, no more do I," said Sir Geoffrey, sad but unsurprised. "I wonder what he calls it? It ain't precisely a Mail-coach, and it certainly ain't an Osbaldeston, and though I did think it had something of the look of a *Trone d'amour*, it ain't that either. I can tie every one of *them*."

Mr Warkworth, whose mind had wandered from this vital subject, said, with a frown: "Damn it, it *is* shabby! You're right!"

Sir Geoffrey was a little hurt. "Would you say it was as bad as that, Oswald?"

"I would," stated Mr Warkworth. "In fact, the more I think of it the worse it appears to me!"

Sir Geoffrey looked intently at his own image, and sighed. "Yes, it does. I shall have to go home and change it."

"Eh?" said Mr. Warkworth, puzzled. "Change what? Good God, dear boy, I wasn't talking about your neck-tie! Wouldn't dream of saying such a thing to my worst enemy! Bridlington!"

"Oh, him!" said Sir Geoffrey, relieved. "He's a gudgeon!"

"Oughtn't to be gudgeon enough to think everyone else is one. Tell you what: wouldn't do him any good if he did hoax everybody with that bag of moonshine! She's a devilish fine girl the little Tallant, and if you ask me she wouldn't have him if he were the only man to offer for her."

"You can't expect him to know that," said Sir Geoffrey. "I shouldn't wonder if he hasn't a suspicion he's a dead bore: in fact, he can't have! Stands to reason: wouldn't prose on as he does, if he knew it!"

Mr Warkworth thought this over. "No," he pronounced at last. "You're wrong. If he don't know he's a dead bore, why does he want to frighten off everyone else? Havey-cavey sort of a business: don't like it! a man ought to fight fair."

"It ain't that," replied Sir Geoffrey. "Just remembered something: the little Tallant don't want it to be known she's as rich as a Nabob. Fleetwood told me: tired of being courted for her money. They were all after her in the north."

"Oh!" said Mr Warkworth. He asked with vague interest: "Where does she come from?"

"Somewhere up north: Yorkshire, I believe," said Sir Geoffrey, inserting a cautious finger into one of the folds of his neck-tie, and easing it a trifle. "I wonder if that's better?"

"Well, that's a queer thing. Saw Clayton the other day. *He* comes from Yorkshire, and he don't know the Tallant."

"No, and Withernsea don't either. Mind you, I won't swear it was Yorkshire! Might have been one of those other devilish rural places – Northumberland, or something. Know what I think?"

"No," said Mr. Warkworth.

"Shouldn't be surprised if she's the daughter of some merchant or other, which would account for it."

Mr Warkworth looked shocked. "No, really, dear old boy! Nothing of that sort about the girl! Never heard her utter a word that smelled of the shop!"

"Granddaughter, then," said Sir Geoffrey, stretching a point. "Pity, if I'm right, but I'll tell you one thing, Oswald! I wouldn't let it weigh with me."

Upon consideration, Mr Warkworth decided that he would not either.

Since these views were fairly representative, Arabella was not destined to suffer the mortification of seeing her usual gallants hang back when next she attended the Assembly at Almack's. Lord Bridlington was escorting his mother and her guest, for besides being very correct in such matters, he liked Almack's, and approved of the severity of the rules imposed on the club by its imperious hostesses. A number of his contemporaries said openly that an evening spent at Almack's was the flattest thing in town, but these were frippery fellows with whom Lord Bridlington had little to do.

His politeness led him to engage Miss Tallant for the first country dance, a circumstance which made the unsuccessful applicants for her hand exchange significant glances. They saw to it that he should have no further opportunity of standing up with her. Not one of them would have believed that he had no desire to do so, much preferring to stroll about the rooms, telling as many people as could be got to listen to him all about his travels abroad.

The waltz, which was still looked at askance by old-fashioned persons, had long since forced its way into Almack's, but it was still the unwritten law that no lady might venture to take part in it unless one of the patronesses had clearly indicated her approval. Lady Bridlington had taken care to impress this important convention upon Arabella's mind, so she refused all solicitations to take the floor when the fiddles struck up for the waltz. Papa would certainly not approve of the dance, she knew: she had never dared to tell him that she and Sophia had learnt the steps from their friends the Misses Caterham, a very dashing pair. So she retired to a chair against the wall, beside Lady Bridlington's, and sat fanning herself, and trying not to look as though she longed to be whirling round the floor. One or two more fortunate damsels, who had watched with disfavour her swift rise to popularity, cast her glances of such pitying superiority that she had to recollect a great many of Papa's maxims before she could subdue the very improper sentiments which entered her breast.

Mr Beaumaris, who had looked in midway through the evening – in fact, a bare ten minutes before the doors were relentlessly shut against late-comers – apparently for no other purpose than to entertain the wife of the Austrian Ambassador, saw Arabella, and was amused, guessing her emotions correctly. Suddenly he cast one of his quizzical looks at Princess Esterhazy, and said: "Shall I ask that chit to dance?"

She raised her delicate black brows, a faint smile flickering on her lips. "*Here*, my friend, you are not supreme! I think you dare not."

"I know I dare not," said Mr Beaumaris, disarming her promptly. "That is why I ask you, Princess, to present me to the lady as a desirable partner."

She hesitated, glancing from him to Arabella, and then laughed, and shrugged. "Well! She does not put herself forward, after all, and I find her style excellent. Come, then!"

Arabella, startled to find herself suddenly confronted by one of the most formidable patronesses, rose quickly.

"You do not dance, Miss Tallant. May I present Mr Beaumaris to you as a very desirable partner?" said the Princess, with a slightly malicious smile cast at Mr Beaumaris.

Arabella could only curtsy, and blush, and be sorry to find that she was so ill-natured as to be conscious of feelings of ignoble triumph over the ladies who had been kind enough to look pityingly at her.

Mr Beaumaris led her on to the floor, and encircled her waist with one arm, taking her right hand in a light clasp. Arabella was naturally a good dancer, but she felt extremely nervous, partly because she had never attempted the waltz, except in the Misses Caterham's old schoolroom, and partly because it was so strange to be held in such close proximity to a man. For several turns she answered Mr Beaumaris very much at random, being preoccupied with her feet. She was so much shorter than he that her head only just reached his shoulder, and since she felt shy she did not look up, but steadfastly regarded the top of his waistcoat. Mr Beaumaris, who was not in the habit of devoting himself to such very young ladies, found this bashfulness amusing, and not unattractive. After he thought she had had time to recover from it a little, he said: "It *is* a nice waistcoat, isn't it, Miss Tallant?"

That did make her look up, and quickly too, her face breaking into laughter. She looked so lovely, and her big eyes met his with such a frank, ingenuous expression in them, that he was aware of a stir of something in his heart that was not mere amusement. But he had no intention of going to dangerous lengths with this or any other pretty chit, and he said, in a bantering tone: "It is customary, you know, to exchange polite conversation during the dance. I have now addressed no fewer than three unexceptionable remarks to you without winning one answer!"

"You see, I am minding my steps," she confided seriously.

Decidedly this absurd child was a refreshing change from the generality of damsels! Had he been a younger man, he reflected, he might easily have succumbed to her charm. It was fortunate that he was thirty, and no longer to be caught by a pretty face and naïve ways, for he knew well that these would pall on him, and that he wanted something more in the lady whom he would one day marry. He had never yet found just what he was looking for, did not even know what it might prove to be, and was perfectly resigned to his bachelordom.

"It is not at all necessary," he said. "You dance delightfully. You do not mean to tell me that this is the first time you have waltzed?"

Miss Tallant certainly did not mean to tell him anything of the sort, and was already regretting her impulsive confidence. "Good gracious, no!" she said. "The first time at Almack's, however."

"I am happy to think, then, that mine was the honour of first leading you on to the floor. You will certainly be besieged by every man present now it is seen that you have no objection to the waltz."

She said nothing, but fell to studying his waistcoat again. He glanced down at her, a hint of mockery in the smile that hovered about his mouth. "How does it feel, Miss Tallant, to be the rage of town? Do you enjoy it, or have your northern triumphs given you a distaste for this sort of thing?"

She raised her eyes, and her chin too. "I am afraid, Mr Beaumaris, that you betrayed what I – what I begged you not to speak of!"

There was a distinctly sardonic look in his eye, but he replied coolly: "I assure you, ma'am, I have mentioned your circumstances to one person only: Lord Fleetwood."

"Then it is he who --" She broke off, flushing.

"Very probably," he agreed. "You must not blame him, however. Such things are bound to leak out."

Her lips parted, and then closed again. He wondered what she had so nearly said: whether he was to have been treated to her society manners, or whether she had been about to tell him the truth. On the whole, he was glad that she had thought better of it. If she took him into her confidence, he supposed he would be obliged, in mercy, to bring this game to a close, which would be a pity, since it was providing him with a great deal of entertainment. To have elevated an unknown provincial to the heights of society was an achievement which only one who had no illusions about the world he led could properly appreciate. He was deriving much enjoyment too from observing the efforts of his devoted copyists to win the provincial's hand. As for Arabella herself, Mr Beaumaris shrugged off a momentary compunction. She would no doubt retire in due course to her northern wilds, marry some red-faced squire, and talk for the rest of her life of her brilliant London season. He glanced down at her again, and thought that it would be a pity if she were to retire too soon. Probably, by the end of the London season he would be only too thankful to see her go, but for the present he was very well satisfied to gratify her by a little flirtation.

The music ceased, and he led her off the floor, to one of the adjoining rooms, where refreshments were served. These were of a very simple nature, the strongest drink offered being a mild claret-cup. Mr Beaumaris procured a glass of lemonade for Arabella, and said; "You must let me thank you for a delightful few minutes, Miss Tallant: I have seldom enjoyed a dance more." He received only a slight smile, and an inclination of the head in answer to this which were both so eloquent of incredulity that he was delighted. No fool, then, the little Tallant! He would have pursued this new form of sport, in the hope of teasing her into retort, but at that moment two purposeful gentlemen bore down upon them. Arabella yielded to the solicitations of Mr Warkworth, and went off on his arm. Sir Geoffrey Morecambe sighed in a languishing way, but turned his rebuff to good account by seizing the opportunity to ask Mr Beaumaris what he called the arrangement of his neck-cloth. He had to repeat the question, for Mr Beaumaris, watching Arabella walk away with Mr Warkworth, was not attending. He brought his gaze to bear on Sir Geoffrey's face, however, at the second time of asking, and raised his brows enquiringly.

"That style you have of tying your cravat!" said Sir Geoffrey. "I don't perfectly recognize it. Is it something new? Should you object to telling me what you call it?"

"Not in the least," replied Mr Beaumaris blandly. "I call it Variation on an Original Theme."

CHAPTER EIGHT

MR BEAUMARIS'S sudden realization that the little Tallant was no fool underwent no modification during the following days. It began to be borne in upon him that charm he never so wisely she was never within danger of losing her head over him. She treated him in the friendliest fashion, accepted his homage, and – he suspected – was bent upon making the fullest use of him. If he paid her compliments, she listened to them with the most innocent air in the world, but with a look in her candid gaze which gave him pause. The little Tallant valued his compliments not at all. Instead of being thrown into a flutter by the attentions of the biggest matrimonial prize in London, she plainly considered herself to be taking part in an agreeable game. If he flirted with her, she would generally respond in kind, but with so much the manner of one willing to indulge him that the hunter woke in him, and he was quite as much piqued as amused. He began to toy with the notion of making her fall in love with him in good earnest, just to teach her that the Nonpareil was not to be so treated with impunity. Once, when she was apparently not in the humour for gallantry, she actually had the effrontery to cut him short, saying: "Oh, never mind that! Who was that odd-looking man who waved to you just now? Why does he walk in that ridiculous way, and screw up his mouth so? Is he in pain?"

He was taken aback, for really he had paid her a compliment calculated to cast her into exquisite confusion. His lips twitched, for he had as few illusions about himself as had, to all appearances the lady beside him. "That," he replied, "is Golden Ball, Miss Tallant, one of our dandies, as no doubt you have been told. He is not in pain. That walk denotes his consequence."

"Good gracious! He looks as though he went upon stilts! Why does he think himself of such consequence?"

"He has never accustomed himself to the thought that he is worth not a penny less than forty thousand pounds a year," replied Mr Beaumaris gravely.

"What an odious person he must be!" she said scornfully. "To be consequential for such a reason as that is what I have no patience with!"

"Naturally you have not," he agreed smoothly.

Her colour rushed up. She said quickly: "Fortune cannot make the man: I am persuaded you agree with me, for they tell me you are even more wealthy, Mr Beaumaris, and I will say this! – you do not give yourself such airs as that!"

"Thank you," said Mr Beaumaris meekly. "I scarcely dared to hope to earn so great an encomium from you, ma'am."

"Was it rude of me to say it? I beg your pardon!"

"Not at all." He glanced down at her. "Tell me, Miss Tallant! – Just why do you grant me the pleasure of driving you out in my curricle?"

She responded with perfect composure, but with that sparkle in her eye which he had encountered several times before: "You must know that it does me a great deal of good socially to be seen in your company sir!"

He was so much surprised that momentarily he let his hands drop. The grays broke into a canter, and Miss Tallant kindly advised him to mind his horses. The most notable whip in the country thanked her for her reminder, and steadied his pair. Miss Tallant consoled him for the chagrin he might have been supposed to feel by saying that she thought he drove very well. After a stunned moment, laughter welled up within him. His voice shook perceptibly as he answered: "You are too good, Miss Tallant!"

"Oh, no!" she said politely. "Shall you be at the masquerade at the Argyll Rooms tonight?"

"I never attend such affairs, ma'am!" he retorted, putting her in her place.

"Oh, then I shall not see you there!" remarked Miss Tallant, with unimpaired cheerfulness.

She did not see him there, but, little though she might have known it, he was obliged to exercise considerable restraint not to cast to the four winds his famed fastidiousness, and to minister to her vanity by appearing at the ball. He did not do it, and hoped that she had missed him. She had, but this was something she would not acknowledge even to herself. Arabella, who had liked the Nonpareil on sight, was setting a strong guard over her sensibilities. He had seemed to her, when first her eyes had alighted on his handsome person, to be almost the embodiment of a dream. Then he had uttered such words to his friend as must shatter for ever her esteem, and had wickedly led her into vulgar prevarication. Now it pleased his fancy to single her out from all the beauties in town, for reasons better known to himself than to her, but which she darkly suspected to be mischievous. No fool, the little Tallant! Not for one moment would she permit herself to indulge the absurd fancy that his court was serious. He might intrude into her meditations, but whenever she was aware of his having done so she was resolute in banishing his image. Sometimes she was strongly of the opinion that he had not believed a word of her boasts on that never to be sufficiently regretted evening in Leicestershire; at others, it seemed as though she had deceived him as completely as she had deceived Lord Fleetwood. It was impossible to fathom the intricacies of his mind, but one thing was certain: the great Mr Beaumaris and the Vicar of Heythram's daughter could have nothing to do with one another, so that the less the Vicar's daughter thought about him the better it would be for her. One could not deny his address, or his handsome face, but one could – and one did – dwell on the many imperfections of his character. He was demonstrably indolent, a spoilt darling of society, with no thought for anything but his fleeting pleasure: a heartless, heedless leader of fashion, given over to selfishness, and every other vice which Papa's daughter had been taught to think reprehensible.

If she missed him at the masquerade, no one would have guessed it. She danced indefatigably the whole night through, refused an offer of marriage from a slightly intoxicated Mr Epworth, tumbled into bed at an advanced hour in the morning, and dropped instantly into untroubled sleep.

She was awakened at a most unseasonable hour by the sudden clatter of fire-irons in the cold hearth. Since the menial who crept into her chamber each morning to sweep the grate, and kindle a new fire there, performed her task with trained stealth, this noise was unusual enough to rouse Arabella with a start. A gasp and a whimper, proceeding from the direction of the fireplace, made her sit up with a jerk, blinking at the unexpected vision of a small, dirty, and tearstained little boy, almost cowering on the hearth-rug, and regarding her out of scared, dilating eyes.

"Good gracious!" gasped Arabella, staring at him. "Who are you?"

The child cringed at the sound of her voice, and returned no answer. The mists of sleep curled away from Arabella's brain; her eyes took in the soot lying on the floor, the grimed appearance of her strange visitant, and enlightenment dawned on her. "You must be a climbing-boy!" she exclaimed. "But what are you doing in my room?" Then she perceived the terror in the pinched, and grimed small face, and she said quickly: "Don't be afraid! Did you lose your way in those horrid chimneys?"

The urchin nodded, knuckling his eyes. He further volunteered the information that ole Grimsby would bash him for it. Arabella, who had had leisure to observe that one side of his face was swollen and discoloured, demanded: "Is that your master? Does he beat you?"

The urchin nodded again, and shivered.

"Well, he shan't beat you for this!" said Arabella, stretching out her hand for the dressing-gown that was chastely disposed across the chair beside her bed. "Wait! I am going to get up!"

The urchin looked very much alarmed by this intelligence, and shrank back against the wall, watching her defensively. She slid out of bed, thrust her feet into her slippers, fastened her dressing-gown, and advanced kindly upon her visitor. He flung up an instinctive arm, cringing before her. He was clad in disgraceful rags, and Arabella now saw that the ends of his frieze nether-garments were much charred, and that his skinny legs and his bare feet were badly burnt. She dropped to her knees, crying out pitifully: "Oh, poor little fellow! You have burnt yourself so dreadfully!"

He slightly lowered his protective arm, looking suspiciously at her over it. "Ole Grimsby done it," he said.

She caught her breath. "What!"

"I'm afeard of going up the chimbley," explained the urchin. "Sometimes there's rats – big, fierce 'uns!"

She shuddered. "And he forces you to do so – like that?"

"They most of 'em does," said the urchin, accepting life as he found it.

She held out her hand. "Let me see! I will not hurt you."

He looked wary, but after a moment appeared to consider that she might be speaking the truth, for he allowed her to take one of his feet in her hand. He was surprised when he saw that tears stood in her eyes, for in his experience the gentler sex was more apt to beat one with a broom-handle than to weep over one.

"Poor child, poor child!" Arabella said, a break in her voice. "You are so thin, too! I am sure you are half-starved! Are you hungry?"

"I'm allus hungry," he replied simply.

"And cold too!" she said. "No wonder, in those rags! It is wicked, *wicked*!" She jumped up, and, grasping the bell pull that hung beside the fireplace, tugged it violently.

The urchin uttered another of his frightened whimpers, and said: "Ole Grimsby 'll beat the daylights out of me! Lemme go!"

"He shan't lay a finger on you!" promised Arabella, her cheeks flushed, and her eyes sparkling through the tears they held.

The urchin came to the conclusion that she was soft in her head. "Ho!" he remarked bitterly, "you don' know ole Grimsby! Nor you don' know his ole woman! Broke one of me ribs he did, onct!"

"He shall never do so again, my dear," Arabella said, turning aside to pull open a drawer in one of the chests. She dragged out the soft shawl which had not so long since been swathed round the head of the sufferer from toothache, and put it round the boy, saying coaxingly: "There, let me wrap you up till we have had a fire lit! Is that more comfortable, my little man? Now sit down in this chair, and you shall have something to eat directly!"

He allowed himself to be lifted into the armchair, but his expression was so eloquent of suspicion and terror that it wrung Arabella's tender heart. She smoothed his cropped, sandy hair with one gentle hand, and said soothingly: "You must not be afraid of me: I promise you I will not hurt you, nor let your master either. What is your name, my dear?"

"Jemmy," he replied, clutching the shawl about him, and fixing her with a frightened stare.

"And how old are you?"

This he was unable to answer, being uninstructed in the matter. She judged him to be perhaps seven or eight years old, but he was so undernourished that he might have been older. While she waited for the summons of the bell to bring her maid to the room, she put more questions to the child. He seemed to have no knowledge of the existence of any parents, volunteering that he was an orphing, on the Parish. When he saw that this seemed to distress her, he tried to comfort her by stating that one Mrs Balham said he was love-begotten. It appeared that this lady had brought him up until the moment when he had passed into the hands of his present owner. An enquiry into Mrs Balham's disposition elicited the information that she was a rare one for jackey and could half-murder anyone when under the influence of this stimulant. Arabella had no idea what jackey might be, but she gathered that Jemmy's foster-mother was much addicted to strong drink. She questioned Jemmy more closely, and he, gaining confidence, imparted to her, in the most matter-of-fact way, some details of a climbing-boy's life which drove the blood from her cheeks. He told her, with a certain distorted pride, of the violence of one of ole Grimsby's associates, Mr Molys, a master-sweep, who, only a year before, had been sentenced to two years imprisonment for causing the death of his six-year old slave.

"Two years!" cried Arabella, sickened by the tale of cruelty so casually unfolded. "If he had stolen a yard of silk from a mercer's factory they would have deported him!"

Jemmy was not in a position to deny or to corroborate this statement, and preserved a wary silence. He saw that the young lady was very angry, and although her wrath did not seem to be directed against himself his experience had taught him to run no unnecessary risks of being suddenly knocked flying against the wall. He shrank into the corner of the chair therefore, and clutched the shawl more tightly round his person.

A discreet knock fell on the door, and a slightly flustered and considerably startled housemaid entered the room "Was it you rang, miss?" she asked, in astonished accents! Then her eye alighted on Arabella's visitor, and she uttered a genteel shriek. "Oh, miss! What a turn it gave me! The young varmint to give you such a fright! It's the chimney-sweep's boy, miss, and him looking for him all over! You come with me this instant, you wicked boy, you!"

Jemmy, recognizing a language he understood, whined that he had not meant to do it.

"Hush!" Arabella said, dropping her hand on one bony little shoulder. "I know very well it is the sweep's boy, Maria, and if you look at him you will see how he has been used! Go downstairs, if you please, and fetch me some food for him directly – and send someone up to kindle the fire here!"

Maria stared at her as though she thought she had taken leave of her senses. "Miss!" she managed to ejaculate. "A dirty little *climbing-boy*?"

"When he has been bathed," said Arabella quietly, "he will not be dirty. I shall need plenty of warm water, and the bath, if you please. But first a fire, and some milk and food for the poor child!"

The affronted handmaid bridled. "I hope, miss, you do not expect *me* to wash that nasty little creature! I'm sure I don't know what her ladyship would say to such goings-on!"

"No," said Arabella, "I expect nothing from you that I might expect from a girl with a more feeling heart than yours! Go and do what I have asked you to do, and desire Becky to come upstairs to me!"

"Becky?" gasped Maria.

"Yes, the girl who had the toothache. And when you have brought up food – some bread-and-butter, and some meat will do very well, but do not forget the milk! – you may send someone to tell Lord Bridlington that I wish to see him at once."

Maria gulped, and stammered: "But, miss, his lordship is abed and asleep!"

"Well, let him be wakened!" said Arabella impatiently.

"Miss, I dare not for my life! His orders were no one wasn't to disturb him till nine o'clock, and he won't come, not till he has shaved himself, and dressed, not his lordship!"

Arabella considered the question, and finally came to the conclusion that it might be wiser to dispense with his lordship's assistance for the time being. "Very well," she said. "I will dress immediately, then, and see the sweep myself. Tell him to wait!"

"See the sweep – dress – Miss, you won't never! With that boy watching you!" exclaimed the scandalized Maria.

"Don't be such a fool, girl!" snapped Arabella, stamping her foot. "He's scarcely older than my little brother at home! Go away before you put me out of all patience with you!"

This, however, Maria could not be persuaded to do until she had arranged a prim screen between the wondering Jemmy and his hostess. She then tottered away to spread the news through the house that Miss was raving mad, and likely to be taken off to Bedlam that very day. But since she did not dare to thwart a guest so much petted by her mistress, she delivered Arabella's message to Becky, and condescended to carry up a tray of food to her room.

Jemmy, still huddled in the big chair, was bewildered by the unprecedented turn of events, and understood nothing of what was intended towards him. But he perfectly understood the significance of a plate of cold beef, and half a loaf of bread, and his sharp eyes glistened. Arabella, who had flung on her clothes at random, and done up her hair in a careless knot, settled him down to the enjoyment of his meal, and sallied forth to do battle with the redoubtable Mr Grimsby, uneasily awaiting her in the front hall.

The scene, conducted under the open-mouthed stare of a footman in his shirt-sleeves, two astonished and giggling maids, and the kitchen-boy, was worthy of a better audience. Mr Beaumaris, for instance, would have enjoyed it immensely. Mr Grimsby, knowing that the sympathies of those members of the household he had so far encountered were with him, and seeing that his assailant was only a chit of a girl, tried at the outset to take a high line, rapidly cataloguing Jemmy's many vices, and adjuring Arabella not to believe a word the varmint uttered. He soon discovered that what Arabella lacked in inches she more than made up for in spirit. She tore his character to shreds, and warned him of his ultimate fate; she flung Jemmy's burns and bruises in his face, and bade him answer her if he dared. He did not dare. She assured him that never would she permit Jemmy to go back to him, and when he tried to point out his undoubted rights over the boy she looked so fierce that he backed before her. She said that if he wished to talk of his rights he might do so before a magistrate, and at these ominous words all vestige of fight went out of him. The misfortune which had overtaken his friend, Mr Molys, was still fresh in his mind, and he desired to have no dealings with an unjust Law. There was no doubt that a young lady living in a house of this style would have those at her back who could, if she urged them to it, make things very unpleasant for a poor chimney-sweep. The course for a prudent man to follow was retreat: climbing-boys were easily come by, and Jemmy had never been a success. Mr Grimsby, his back bent nearly double, edged himself out of the house, trying to assure Arabella in one breath that she might keep Jemmy and welcome, and that, whatever the ungrateful brat might say, he had been like a father to him.

Flushed with her triumph, Arabella returned to her room, where she found Jemmy, the plate of meat long since disposed of, eyeing with a good deal of apprehension the preparations for his ablutions. A capacious hip-bath stood before the fire, into which Becky was emptying the last of three large brass cans of hot water. Whatever Becky might think of climbing-boys, she had conceived a slavish adoration of Arabella, and she declared her willingness to do anything Miss might require of her.

"First," said Arabella briskly, "I must wash him, and put basilicum ointment on his poor little feet and legs. Then I must get him some clothes to wear. Becky, do you know where to procure suitable clothes for a child in London?"

Becky nodded vigorously, twisting her apron between her fingers. She ventured to say that she had sent home a suit for her brother Ben which Mother had been ever so pleased with.

"Have you little brothers? Then you will know just what to buy for this child!" Arabella said. "A warm jacket, and some smalls, and a shirt – oh, and some shoes and stockings! Wait! I will give you the money, and you shall go and procure the things immediately!"

"If you please, miss," said Becky firmly, "I think I ought to help you wash him first." She added sapiently: "Likely he'll struggle, miss not being used to it."

She was quite right. Jemmy fought like a tiger to defend his person from the intended rape, and was deaf alike to coaxings and to reassurances. But the two damsels before him had not helped to bring up their respective young brothers for nothing. They stripped Jemmy of his rags, heedless of his sobs and his protests, and they dumped him, wildly kicking, in the bath, and ruthlessly washed every inch of his emaciated small person.

It was not to be expected that Jemmy's howls would not be heard beyond the confines of the room. They were lusty, and they penetrated to Lady Bridlington's ears. It was inconceivable to the good lady that they could really be emanating from within her house, as they seemed to be, and she was just about to ring her bell, and desire Clara Crowle to send away whatever child it was who was screaming in the street, when the howls ceased (Jemmy had been lifted out of the bath, and wrapped in a warm towel), and she sank back again in her bed. Not long after this, Miss Crowle came softly in with her breakfast-tray, and the pleasing intelligence that Miss Arabella was out of her mind, and had got a dirty little boy in her room, and wouldn't let him go, not whatever anyone said. Hardly had her ladyship grasped the essential points of the story poured into her bemused ears than Arabella herself came in. Her visit made it necessary for Miss Crowle to revive her mistress with hartshorn-and-water, and to burn pastilles, for it brought on a nervous spasm of alarming intensity. Lady Bridlington now understood that she was expected not only to house a boy picked out of the gutter, but to pursue his late master by every means in her power. Arabella talked of the Law, and of magistrates; of cruelties which made it almost impossible for Lady Bridlington even to swallow her coffee; and of what Papa would say must be done in so shocking a case. Lady Bridlington moaned, and said faintly: "But you cannot! The boy must be given back to his master! You don't understand these things!"

"Cannot?" cried Arabella, her eyes flashing. "*Cannot* ma'am? I beg your pardon, but it is you who have not understood! When you have seen the dreadful marks on the poor little soul's back – and his ribs almost breaking through his skin! – you will not talk so!"

"No, no, Arabella, for heaven's sake -!" begged her godmother. "I won't have you bring him in here! Where is Frederick? My dear, of course it is all very dreadful, and we will see what can be done, but do, pray, wait until I am dressed! Clara, where is his lordship?"

"His lordship, my lady," responded Clara with relish, "having partaken of his breakfast, has gone riding in the Park, as is his custom. His lordship's gentleman happening to mention that Miss had a climbing-boy in her room, his lordship said as how he must be sent off at once."

"Well, he will not be!" said Arabella, not mincing matters.

Lady Bridlington, reflecting that it was just like Frederick to issue orders in this foolish style, and leave others to see them carried out, decided to postpone any further discussion until he should be present to lend her his support. She persuaded Arabella to go away, looked with distaste at her breakfast-tray, and begged Clara, in a failing voice, to give her her smelling-salts.

When Lord Bridlington returned from his morning exercise, he was displeased to learn that nothing had so far been done about the climbing-boy, except that Miss had sent one of the under-servants out to buy him a suit of clothes. He was still frowning over this when his Mama came downstairs, and almost fell upon his neck. "Thank heaven you are come at last!" she uttered. "What can have induced you to go out with the house in this uproar? I am driven nearly distracted! She wants me to employ the boy as a page!"

Frederick led her firmly into the saloon on the ground-floor, and shut the door upon the interested butler. He then demanded an explanation of an affair which he said he was at a loss to understand. His mother was in the middle of giving him one when Arabella came into the room, leading the washed and clothed Jemmy by the hand.

"Good-morning, Lord Bridlington!" she said calmly. "I am glad you are come home, for you will best be able to help me to decide what I ought to do with Jemmy here."

"I can certainly do so, Miss Tallant," he answered. "The boy must of course go back where he belongs. It was most improper of you, if you will permit me to say so, to interfere between him and his master."

He encountered a look which surprised him. "I do not permit anyone, Lord Bridlington, to tell me that in rescuing a helpless child from the brutality of a monster I am doing what is improper!" said Arabella.

"No, no, my dear, of course not!" hastily interposed Lady Bridlington.

"Frederick did not mean – But, you see, there is nothing one can do in these sad cases! That is – I am sure Frederick will speak to the man give him a good fright, you know!"

"Really, Mama -"

"And Jemmy?" demanded Arabella. "What will you do with him?"

His lordship looked distastefully at the candidate for his protection. Jemmy had been well scrubbed, but not the most thorough application of soap and water could turn him into a well-favoured child. He had a sharp little face, a wide mouth, from which a front tooth was missing, and a very snub nose. His short, ragged hair was perfectly straight, and his ears showed a tendency to stick out from his head.

"I do not know what you expect me to do!" said his lordship fretfully. "If you had any knowledge of the laws governing apprentices, my dear Miss Tallant, you would know that it is quite impossible to steal this boy away from his master!"

"When the master of an apprentice misuses a boy as this child has been misused," retorted Papa's daughter, "he renders himself liable to prosecution! What is more, this man knows it, and I assure you he does not expect to have Jemmy returned to him!"

"I suppose you think I should adopt the boy!" said Frederick, goaded.

"No, I do not think that," replied Arabella, her voice a little unsteady. "I only think that you might – show some compassion for one so wretchedly circumstanced!"

Frederick coloured hotly. "Well, of course I am excessively sorry, but -"

"Do you know that his master lights a fire in the grate beneath him, to force him up the chimney?" interrupted Arabella.

"Well, I don't suppose he would go up if – Yes, yes, shocking, I know, but chimneys must be swept, after all, or what would become of us all?"

"Oh, that Papa were here!" Arabella cried. "I see that it is useless to talk to you, for you are selfish and heartless, and you care for nothing but your own comfort!"

It was at this inopportune moment that the door was opened, and the butler announced two morning-callers. He afterwards explained this lapse, which he felt quite as acutely as his mistress, by saying that he had supposed Miss to be still upstairs with That Boy. Frederick made a hasty gesture indicative of his desire that the visitors should be excluded, but it was too late. Lord Fleetwood and Mr Beaumaris walked into the room.

Their reception was unusual. Lady Bridlington gave vent to an audible moan; her son stood rooted to the floor in the middle of the room, his face flushed, and his whole appearance that of a man who had been stuffed; and Miss Tallant, also very much flushed, bit her lip, and turned on her heel, leading a small urchin over to a chair by the wall, and bidding him gently to sit down on it, and to be a good boy.

Lord Fleetwood blinked upon this scene; Mr Beaumaris's brows went up, but he gave no other sign of surprise, merely bowing over Lady Bridlington's nerveless hand, and saying: "How do you do? I trust we don't intrude? I called in the hope of persuading Miss Tallant to drive to the Botanical Gardens with me. They tell me the spring flowers are quite a sight there."

"You are very obliging, sir," said Arabella curtly, "but I have more important affairs to attend to this morning."

Lady Bridlington pulled herself together. "My love, we can discuss all that later! I am sure it would do you good to take the air! Do but send that – that child down to the kitchen, and -"

"Thank you, ma'am, but I do not stir from the house until I have settled what is to be done with Jemmy."

Lord Fleetwood, who had been regarding Jemmy with frank curiosity, said: "Jemmy, eh? Er – friend of yours, Miss Tallant?"

"No. He is a climbing-boy who came by mistake down the chimney of my bedchamber," Arabella replied. "He has been most shamefully used, and he is only a child, as you may see – I daresay not more than seven or eight years old!"

The warmth of her feelings brought a distinct tremor into her voice. Mr Beaumaris looked curiously at her.

"No, really?" said Lord Fleetwood, with easy sympathy. "Well, that's a great deal too bad! Shocking brutes, some of these chimney-sweeps! Ought to be sent to gaol!"

She said impulsively: "Yes, that is what I have been telling Lord Bridlington, only he seems not to have the least understanding!"

"Arabella!" implored Lady Bridlington. "Lord Fleetwood can have no interest in such matters!"

"Oh, I assure you, ma'am!" said his lordship. "I am interested in anything that interests Miss Tallant! Rescued the child, did you? Well, upon my soul, I call it a devilish fine thing to do! Not as though he was a taking brat, either!"

"What does that signify?" said Arabella contemptuously. "I wonder how taking, my lord, you or I should be had we been brought up from infancy by a drunken foster-mother, sold while still only babies to a brutal master, and forced into a hateful trade!"

Mr Beaumaris moved quietly to a chair a little removed from the group in the centre of the room, and stood leaning his hands on the back of it, his eyes still fixed on Arabella's face.

"No, no! Exactly so!" hastily said Lord Fleetwood.

Lord Bridlington chose, unwisely, to intervene at this point. "No doubt it is just as you say, ma'am, but this is hardly a topic for my mother's sitting-room! Let me beg of you -"

Arabella turned on him like a flash, her eyes bright with tears, her voice unsteady with indignation. "I will not be silenced! It is a topic that should be discussed in every Christian lady's sitting-room! Oh, I mean no disrespect, ma'am! You have not thought – you cannot have thought! Had you seen the wounds on this child's body you could not refuse to help him! I wish I had made you come into my room when I had him naked in the bath! Your heart must have been touched!"

"Yes, but, Arabella, my heart *is* touched!" protested her afflicted godmother. "Only I don't want a page, and he is much too young, and such an ugly little thing! Besides, the sweep will very likely claim him, because, whatever you may think, if the boy is apprenticed to him, which he must be -"

"You may make your mind easy on that score, ma'am! His master will never dare to lay claim to him. He knows very well that he is in danger of being taken before a magistrate, for I told him so, and he did not doubt me!

Why, he cringed at the very word, and backed himself out of the house as fast as he could!"

Mr Beaumaris spoke at last. "Did you confront the sweep, Miss Tallant?" he asked, an odd little smile flickering on his lips.

"Certainly I did!" she replied, her glance resting on him for an indifferent moment.

Lady Bridlington was suddenly inspired. "He must go to the Parish, of course! Frederick, *you* will know how to set about it!"

"No, no, he must not!" Arabella declared. "That would be worse than anything, for what will they do with him, do you suppose, but set him to the only trade he knows? And he is afraid of those dreadful chimneys! If it were not so far away, I would send him to Papa, but how could such a little boy go all that way alone?"

"No, certainly not!" said Lord Fleetwood. "Not to be thought of!"

"Lord Bridlington, surely, surely you would not condemn a child to such a life as he has endured?" Arabella begged, her hands going out in a pleading gesture. "You have so *much*!"

"Of course he wouldn't!" declared Fleetwood rashly. "Now, come, Bridlington!"

"But why should I?" demanded Frederick. "Besides, what could I do with the brat? It is the greatest piece of nonsense I ever had to listen to!"

"Lord Fleetwood, will *you* take Jemmy?" asked Arabella, turning to him beseechingly.

His lordship was thrown into disorder. "Well, I don't think – You see, ma'am – Fact of the matter is – Dash it, Lady Bridlington's right! The Parish! That's the thing!"

"Unworthy, Charles!" said Mr Beaumaris.

The much goaded Lord Bridlington rounded on him. "Then, if that is what you think, Beaumaris, perhaps *you* will take the wretched brat!"

Then it was that Mr Beaumaris, looking across the room at Arabella, all flushed cheeks and heaving bosom, astonished the company, and himself as well. "Yes," he said. "I will."

CHAPTER NINE

THESE SIMPLE words struck the ears of his audience with stunning effect. Lord Fleetwood's jaw dropped; Lady Bridlington's and her son's rather protruberant eyes started at Mr Beaumaris; and Arabella stared at him in amazement. It was she who broke the silence. *"You?"* she said, the incredulity in her tone leaving him in no doubt of her opinion of his character.

A rather rueful smile twisted his lips. "Why not?" he said.

Her eyes searched his face. "What would you do with him?" she demanded.

"I haven't the smallest notion," he confessed. "I hope you may be going to tell me what I am to do with him, Miss Tallant."

"If I let you take him, you would throw him on the Parish, like Lord Fleetwood!" she said bitterly.

His lordship uttered an inarticulate protest.

"I have a great many faults," replied Mr Beaumaris, "but, believe me, you may trust my pledged word! I will neither throw him on the Parish, nor restore him to his master."

"You must be mad!" exclaimed Frederick.

"You would naturally think so," said Mr Beaumaris, flicking him with one of his disdainful glances.

"Have you considered what people would be bound to say?" Frederick said.

"No, nor do I propose to burden my head with anything that interests me so little!" retorted Mr Beaumaris.

Arabella said in a softened voice: "If you mean it indeed, sir, you will be doing the very kindest thing – perhaps the best thing you have ever done, and, oh, I *thank* you!"

"Certainly the best thing I have ever done, Miss Tallant," he said, with that wry smile.

"What will you do with him?" she asked again. "You must not be thinking that I mean you to adopt him as your own, or anything of that nature! He must be brought up to a respectable trade, only I do not know what would be the best for him!"

"Perhaps," suggested Mr Beaumaris, "he has views of his own on the subject. What, Jemmy, would you choose to do?"

"Yes, what would you like to do when you are a man?" said Arabella, turning to kneel beside Jemmy's chair, and speaking in a coaxing tone. "Tell me!"

Jemmy, who had been following all this with an intent look in his face, had no very clear idea of what it was about, but his quick, cockney mind had grasped that none of these swells, not even the stout, cross one, intended any harm to him. The scared expression in his eyes had given place to one of considerable acuteness. He answered his protectress without hesitation. "Give ole Grimsby a leveller!" he said.

"Yes, my dear, and so you shall, and I hope you will do the same by everyone like him!" said Arabella warmly. "But how would you choose to earn your living?"

Mr Beaumaris's lips twitched appreciatively. So the little Tallant had brothers, had she?

Lady Bridlington was looking bewildered, and her son disgusted. Lord Fleetwood, accepting Arabella's unconsciously betrayed knowledge of boxing-cant without question, looked Jemmy over critically, and gave it as his opinion that the boy was not the right build for a bruiser.

"Of course not!" said Arabella. "Think, Jemmy! What could you do, do you suppose?"

The urchin reflected, while the company awaited his pleasure. "Sweep a crossing," he pronounced at last.

"I could 'old the gen'lemen's 'orses, then."

"Hold the gentlemen's horses?" repeated Arabella. Her eye brightened. "Are you fond of horses, Jemmy?"

Jemmy nodded vigorously. Arabella looked round in triumph. "Then I know the very thing!" she said. "Particularly since it is you who are to take charge of him, Mr Beaumaris!"

Mr Beaumaris waited in deep foreboding for the blow to fall.

"He must learn to look after horses, and then, as soon as he is a little older, you may employ him as your Tiger!" said Arabella radiantly.

Mr Beaumaris, whose views on the folly of entrusting blood-cattle to the guardianship of small boys were as unequivocal as they were well-known, replied without a tremor: "To be sure I may. The future now being provided for --"

"But you never drive with a Tiger up behind you!" exclaimed Lord Bridlington. "You have said I know not how many times --"

"I do wish, Bridlington, that you would refrain from interrupting with these senseless comments," said Mr Beaumaris.

"But that child is far too young to be a Tiger!" pointed out Lady Bridlington.

Arabella's face fell. "Yes, he is," she said regretfully. "Yet it would be the very thing for him, if only we knew what to do with him in the meantime!"

"I think," said Mr Beaumaris, "that in the meantime I had better convey him to my own house, and place him in the charge of my housekeeper, pending further discussion between us, Miss Tallant."

He was rewarded with a glowing look. "I did not know you would be so kind!" said Arabella. "It is a splendid notion, for the poor little fellow needs plenty of good food, and I am sure he must get it in your house! Listen, Jemmy, you are to go with this gentleman, who is to be your new master, and be a good boy, and do as he bids you!"

Jemmy, clutching a fold of her dress was understood to say that he preferred to remain with her. She bent over him, patting his shoulder. "No, you cannot stay with me, my dear, and I am sure you would not like it half so well if you could, for you must know that he has a great many horses, and will very likely let you see them. Did you come here in your curricle, sir?" Mr Beaumaris bowed. "Well, there, do you hear that, Jemmy?" said Arabella, in a heartening tone. "You are to drive away in a carriage, behind a pair of beautiful gray horses!"

"I am driving my chestnuts today," said Mr Beaumaris apologetically. "I am so sorry, but I feel I should perhaps mention it!"

"You did very right," said Arabella approvingly. "One should never tell untruths to children! Chestnuts, Jemmy, glossy brown horses! How grand you will feel sitting up behind them!"

Apparently the urchin felt that there was much in what she said. He released her gown, and directed his sharp gaze upon his new owner. "Proper good 'uns?" he asked suspiciously.

"Proper good 'uns," corroborated Mr Beaumaris gravely.

Jemmy slid from the chair. "You ain't slumming me? You won't go a-givin' of me back to ole Grimsby?"

"No, I won't do that. Come and take a look at my horses!"

Jemmy hesitated, glancing up at Arabella, who at once took his hand, and said: "Yes, let us go and see them!"

When Jemmy beheld the equipage being led up and down the street, his eyes widened, and he drew a shuddering breath of ecstasy. "That's a bang-up set-out, that is!" he said. "Will I drive them 'orses, guv'nor?"

"You will not," said Mr Beaumaris. "You may sit up beside me, however."

"Yessir!" said Jemmy, recognizing the voice of authority.

"Up with you, then!" Mr Beaumaris said, lifting him into the curricle. He turned, and found that Arabella was holding her hand out to him. He took it in his, and held it for a moment.

"I wish I might find the words to thank you!" she said. "You will let me know how he goes on."

"You may rest easy on that head, Miss Tallant," he said, bowing. He took the reins in his hand, and mounted into the carriage, and looked down maliciously at Lord Fleetwood, who had accompanied them out of the house, and was just taking his leave of Arabella. "Come, Charles!"

Lord Fleetwood started, and said hurriedly: "No, no, I'll walk! No need to worry about me, my dear fellow!"

"Come, Charles!" repeated Mr Beaumaris gently.

Lord Fleetwood, aware of Arabella's eyes upon him, sighed, and said: "Oh, very well!" and climbed into the curricle, wedging Jemmy between himself and Mr. Beaumaris.

Mr Beaumaris nodded to his gaping groom, and steadied the chestnuts as they sprang forward. "Coward," he remarked.

"It ain't that I'm a coward!" protested his lordship. "But we shall have all the fools in London staring after us! I can't think what's come over you, Robert! You're never going to keep this brat in Mount Street! If it leaks out, and it's bound to, I suppose you know everyone will think it's a byblow of yours?"

"The possibility had crossed my mind," agreed Mr Beaumaris. "I am sure I ought not to let it weigh with me: Miss Tallant certainly would not."

"Well, damn it, I think that prosy fool, Bridlington, was right for once in his life! You've gone stark, staring mad!"

"Very true: I have known it this half-hour and more."

Lord Fleetwood looked at him in some concern. "You know, Robert, if you're not careful you'll find yourself walking to the altar before you're much older!" he said.

"No, she has the poorest opinion of me," replied Mr Beaumaris. "I perceive that my next step must be to pursue the individual known to us as 'ole Grimsby'."

"What?" gasped Fleetwood. "She never asked that of you!"

"No, but I feel she expects it of me." He saw that the mention of the sweep's name had made Jemmy look up at him in quick alarm, and said reassuringly: "No, I am not going to give you to him."

"Robert, never in all the years I've known you have I seen you make such a cake of yourself!" said his friend, with brutal frankness. "First you let the little Tallant bamboozle you into saddling yourself with this horrid brat, and now you talk of meddling with a chimney-sweep! *You!* Why, it's unheard of!"

"Yes, and, what is more, I have a shrewd suspicion that a benevolent career is going to prove extremely wearing," said Mr Beaumaris thoughtfully.

"I see what it is," said Fleetwood, after regarding his profile for a few moments. "You're so piqued she don't favour you you'll go to any lengths to fix your interest with the girl!"

"I will," said Mr Beaumaris cordially.

"Well, you'd better take care what you are about!" said his worldly-wise friend.

"I will," said Mr Beaumaris again.

Lord Fleetwood occupied himself during the rest of the short drive in delivering a severe lecture on the perfidy of those who, without having any serious intentions, attempted to cut out their friends with the season's most notable catch, adding, for good measure, a lofty condemnation of hardened rakes who tried to deceive innocent country maidens.

Mr Beaumaris listened to him with the utmost amiability, only interrupting to applaud this last flight of eloquence. "That's very good, Charles," he said approvingly. "Where did you pick it up?"

"Devil!" said his lordship, with feeling. "Well, I wash my hands of you – and I hope she will lead you a pretty dance!"

"I have a strong premonition," replied Mr Beaumaris, "that your hope is likely to be realized."

Lord Fleetwood gave it up, and as Mr Beaumaris saw no reason to take him into his confidence, what little time was left before Mount Street was reached was occupied in discussing the chances of the newest bruiser in his forthcoming fight with an acknowledged champion.

Mr Beaumaris, at this stage, would have been chary of confiding in anyone the precise nature of his intentions. He was by no means sure that he knew what they were himself, but that he had called in Park Street for precisely the reasons described by his friend, and, when confronted by the vision of Arabella fighting for the future of her unattractive protégé, had undergone an enlightenment so blinding as almost to deprive him of his senses, was certain. No consideration of the conduct to be expected of a delicately nurtured female had stopped her. She knew no discomfiture when two gentlemen of fashion had arrived to find her embroiled in the concerns of an urchin far beneath the notice of any aspirant to social heights. No, by God! thought Mr Beaumaris exultantly, she showed us what she thought of such frippery fellows as we are! We might have gone to the devil for all she cared. I might have made her a laughing-stock only by recounting the story – as I could! Lord, yes, as I *could*! Did she know it? Would she have cared? Not a farthing, the little Tallant! But I must stop Charles spreading this all over town.

Mr Beaumaris, hunting now in earnest, was by far too experienced a sportsman to pursue his quarry too closely. He let several days pass before making any attempt to approach Arabella. When next he encountered her it was at a ball given by the Charnwoods. He asked her to stand up with him for one of the country-dances, but when the moment for taking their places in the set came, led her to a sofa, saying: "Shall you object to sitting down with me instead? One can never converse in comfort while dancing, and I must consult you about our urchin."

"No, indeed!" she said warmly. "I have been so anxious to know how he goes on!" She seated herself, holding her fan in her clasped hands, and raised her eyes to his face in an enquiring look. "Is he well? Is he happy?"

"As far as I have been able to ascertain," replied Mr Beaumaris carefully, "he is not only fast recovering the enjoyment of excellent health, but is achieving no common degree of felicity by conduct likely to deprive me of the services of most of my existent staff."

Arabella considered this. Mr Beaumaris watched appreciatively the wrinkling of her thoughtful brow. "Is he very naughty?" she asked presently.

"According to the report of my housekeeper, Miss Tallant – but I daresay she is not to be at all believed! – he is the embodiment of too many vices for me to enumerate."

She seemed to accept this with unimpaired calm, for she nodded understandingly.

"Pray do not think that I should dream of burdening you with anything so unimportant as the complaints of a mere housekeeper!" begged Mr Beaumaris. "Nothing but the most urgent of exigencies could have prevailed upon me to open my lips to you upon this subject!" She looked startled, and enquiring: "You see," he said apologetically, "it is Alphonse!"

"Alphonse?"

"My chef," explained Mr Beaumaris. "Of course, if you say so, ma'am, he shall go! But I must own that his departure would cause me grave concern. I do not mean to say that my life would be shattered, precisely, for no doubt there *are* other chefs who have his way with a soufflé, and who do not take such violent exception to the raids of small boys upon the larder!"

"But this is quite absurd, Mr Beaumaris!" said Arabella severely. "You must have been indulging Jemmy beyond what is right! I daresay he is excessively ill-behaved: it is always so, unless their spirits are utterly broken, and we must be thankful that his are not!"

"Very true!" agreed Mr Beaumaris, entranced by this wisdom. "I will at once present this view of the matter to Alphonse."

Arabella shook her head. "Oh, no! it would not be of the least avail, I daresay! Foreigners," she said largely, "have no notion how to manage children! What is to be done?"

"I cannot help feeling," said Mr Beaumaris, "that Jemmy would benefit by country air."

This suggestion found favour. "Nothing could be better for him! " agreed Arabella. "Besides, there is no reason why he should tease you, I am sure! Only how may it be contrived?"

Much relieved at having so easily cleared this fence, Mr Beaumaris said: "The notion did just cross my mind, ma'am, that if I were to take him into Hampshire, where I have estates, no doubt some respectable household might be found for him.

"One of your tenants! The very thing!" exclaimed Arabella. "Quite a simple cottage, mind, and a sensible woman to take care of him! Only I am afraid she would have to be paid a small sum to do it."

Mr Beaumaris, who felt that no sum could be too large for the ridding of his house of one small imp who threatened to disrupt it, bore up nobly under the warning, and said that he had envisaged this possibility, and was prepared to meet it. It then occurred to Arabella that he might reasonably expect so great an heiress as herself to bear the charge of her protégé; and she embarked on a tangled explanation of why she could not at present do so. Mr Beaumaris interrupted her speech when it showed signs of becoming ravelled beyond hope. "No, no, Miss Tallant!" he said. "Do not deny me this opportunity to perform a charitable action, I beg of you!"

So Arabella very kindly refrained from doing so, and bestowed so grateful a smile upon him that he felt himself to have been amply rewarded.

"Are you quite in disgrace with Lady Bridlington?" he asked quizzically.

She laughed, but looked a little guilty. "I *was*," she owned. "But since she has seen that the story has not got about, she has forgiven me. She was persuaded that everyone would be laughing at me. As though I would care for such a thing as that, when I had but done my duty!"

"Certainly not!"

"Do you know, I had begun to believe that everyone in town – all the grand people, I mean – were quite heartless, and selfish?" she confided. "I am afraid I was not quite civil to you – indeed, Lady Bridlington assures me that I was shockingly rude! but then, you see, I had no notion that you were not like all the rest. I beg your pardon!"

Mr Beaumaris had the grace to acknowledge a twinge of conscience. It led him to say: "Miss Tallant, I did it in the hope of pleasing you."

Then he wished that he had curbed his tongue, for her confiding air left her, and although she talked easily for a few more minutes he was fully aware that she had withdrawn from him again.

He was able to retrieve his position a few days later, and took care not to jeopardize it again. When he returned from a visit to his estates he called in Park Street to give Arabella comfortable tidings of Jemmy, whom he had foisted on to a retired servant of his own. She was a little concerned lest the town-bred waif should feel lost and unhappy in the country, but when he informed her that the last news he had of Jemmy, before leaving Hampshire, was that he had let a herd of bullocks out of the field where they were confined, pulled the feathers from the cock's tail, tried to ride an indignant pig round the yard, and eaten a whole batch of cakes newly baked by his kind hostess, she perceived that Jemmy was made of resilient stuff, and laughed, and said that he would soon settle down, and learn to be a good boy.

Mr Beaumaris agreed to it, and then played his trump card. He thought Miss Tallant would like to know that he had taken steps to ensure the well-being of Mr Grimsby's future apprentices.

Arabella was delighted. "You have brought him to justice!"

"Well, not quite that," confessed Mr Beaumaris. He saw the disappointed look in her eye, and added hastily: "You know, I could not feel that to be appearing in a court of law was just what you would like. Then, too, when it is a question of apprentices one is apt to find oneself confronted with all manner of difficulties in the way of removing boys from their masters. It seemed best, therefore, to drop a word in Sir Nathaniel Conant's ear. He is the Chief Magistrate, and as I have some acquaintance with him the thing was easy. Mr Grimsby will take care how he disregards a warning from Bow Street, I assure you."

Arabella was a little sorry to think that Mr Grimsby was not to be cast into gaol, but being a sensible girl she readily appreciated the force of Mr Beaumaris's arguments, and told him that she was very much obliged to him. She sat pondering deeply for some moments, while he watched her, wondering what now was in her head. "It should be the business of people with interest and fortune to enquire into such things!" she said suddenly. "No one seems to care a button in a great city like this! I have seen such dreadful sights since I came to London – such beggary, and misery, and such countless ragged children who seem to have no parents and no homes! Lady Bridlington does not care to have anything of that nature spoken about, but, oh, I would like so much to be able to help such children as poor Jemmy!"

"Why don't you?" he asked coolly.

Her eyes flew to his; he knew that he had been too blunt: she would not tell him the truth about herself. Nor did she. After a tiny pause, she said: "Perhaps, one day, I shall."

He wondered whether her godmother had warned her against him, and when she excused herself from dancing with him at the next Assembly was sure of it.

But the warning came from Lord Bridlington. Mr Beaumaris's marked attentions to Arabella, including, as they had, so extraordinary a gesture as the adoption of Jemmy, had aroused the wildest hopes in Lady Bridlington's shallow brain. If any of his previous amatory adventures had led him to perform a comparable deed, she at least had never heard of it. She began to indulge the fancy that his intentions were serious, and had almost written to give Mrs Tallant a hint of it when Lord Bridlington dashed her hopes.

"You would do well, ma'am, to put your young friend a little on her guard with Beaumaris," he said weightily.

"My dear Frederick, and so I did, at the outset! But he has become so particular in his attentions, showing such a decided preference for her, and trying to fix his interest with her by every means in his power, that I really begin to think he has formed a lasting attachment! Only fancy if she were to form such a connexion, Frederick! I declare, I should feel it as much as if she were my own child! For it will be all due to me, you know!"

"You would be very unwise to put such a notion into the girl's head, Mama," he said, cutting short these rhapsodies. "I can tell you this: Beaumaris's intimates don't by any means regard his pursuit of Miss Tallant in that light!"

"No?" she said, in a faltering tone.

"Far otherwise, ma'am! They are saying that it is all pique, because she does not appear to favour him above any other. I must say, I should not have expected her to have shown such good sense! You must know that men of his type, accustomed as he is to being courted and flattered, are put very much on their mettle by a rebuff from any female who has not been so foolish as to pick up the handkerchief he has carelessly tossed towards them. It puts me out of all patience to see anyone so spoiled and caressed! But be that as it may, you should know, Mama, that bets are being laid and taken at White's against Miss Tallant's holding out against this siege!"

"How odious men are!" exclaimed Lady Bridlington indignantly.

Odious they might be, but if they were laying bets of that nature at the clubs there was nothing for a conscientious chaperon to do but warn her charge once more against lending too credulous an ear to an accomplished flirt. Arabella assured her that she had no intention of doing so.

"No, my dear, very likely not," replied her ladyship. "But there is no denying that he is a very attractive man: I am conscious of it myself! Such an air! such easy address! But it is of no use to think of that! I am sadly afraid that it is a kind of sport with him to make females fall in love with him.

"*I* shall not do so!" declared Arabella. "I like him very well, but, as I told you before, I am not such a goose as to be taken-in by him!"

Lady Bridlington looked at her rather doubtfully. "No, my love, I hope not indeed. To be sure, you have so many admirers that we need not consider Mr Beaumaris. I suppose – you will not be offended at my asking, I know! – I suppose no eligible gentleman has proposed to you?"

Quite a number of gentlemen, eligible and ineligible, had proposed to Arabella, but she shook her head. She might acquit some of her suitors of having designs on her supposed wealth, but two among them at least would never have offered for her hand, she was very sure, had they known her to be penniless; and the courtships of several notorious fortune-hunters made it impossible for her to believe that Lord Bridlington's well-meaning efforts had in any way scotched that dreadful rumour. She felt her situation to be unhappy indeed. Easter was almost upon them, and there had been plenty of time for her, with the opportunities which had been granted to her, to have fulfilled her Mama's ambitions. She felt guilty, for it had cost Mama so much money, which she could ill-afford, to send her to London, so that the least a grateful daughter could have done would have been to have repaid her by accepting some respectable offer of marriage. She could not do it. She cared for none of those who had proposed to her, and although that, she supposed, ought not to weigh too heavily in the scales when balanced against the benefits that would accrue to the dear brothers and sisters, she was resolved to accept no offer from anyone ignorant of her true circumstances. Perhaps there was still to come into her life some suitor to whom it would be possible to confess the whole, but he had not yet appeared, and, pending his arrival, it was with relief that Arabella turned to Mr Beaumaris, who, whatever his intentions might be, certainly coveted no fortune.

Mr Beaumaris offered her every facility to turn to him, but he could scarcely congratulate himself on the outcome. The smallest attempt at gallantry had the effect of transforming her from the confiding child he found so engaging into the society damsel who was ready enough to fence lightly with him, but who showed him quite clearly that she wanted none of his practised love-making. And when Lady Bridlington had repeated much of her son's warning, not omitting to mention the fact that Mr Beaumaris's friends knew him to be merely trifling, Mr Beaumaris found Miss Tallant even more elusive. He was reduced to employing an ignoble stratagem, and, having been obliged to visit his estates on a matter of business, sought Arabella out upon his return, and told her that he wished to consult her again about Jemmy's future. In this manner, he lured her to drive out with him in his curricle. He drove her to Richmond Park, and she raised no objection to this, though he had not previously taken her farther afield than Chelsea. It was a fine, warm afternoon, with the sun so brightly shining that Arabella ventured to wear a very becoming straw hat, and to carry a small sunshade with a very long handle, which she had seen in the Pantheon Bazaar, and had not been able to resist purchasing. She said, as Mr Beaumaris handed her up into the curricle, that it was very kind of him to drive her into the country, since she liked it of all things, and was able to think herself, while in that great park, many miles from town.

"Do you know Richmond Park, then?" he asked.

"Oh, yes!" replied Arabella cheerfully. "Lord Fleetwood drove me there last week; and then, you know, the Charnwoods got up a party, and we all went in three barouches. And tomorrow, if it is fine, Sir Geoffrey Morecambe is to take me to see the Florida Gardens."

"I must count myself fortunate, then, to have found you on a day when you had no other engagement," remarked Mr Beaumaris.

"Yes, I am out a great deal," agreed Arabella. She unfurled the sunshade, and said: "What was it that you wished to tell me about Jemmy, sir?"

"Ah, yes, Jemmy!" he said. "Subject to your consent, Miss Tallant, I am making – in fact, I have made – a trifling change in his upbringing. I fear he will never come to any good under Mrs Buxton's roof, and still more do I fear that if he remained there he would shortly be the death of her. At least, so she informed me when I went down to Hampshire the day before yesterday."

She gave him one of her warm looks. "How very kind that was of you! Did you go all that way on that naughty boy's account?"

Mr Beaumaris was sorely tempted. He glanced down at his companion, met her innocently enquiring gaze, hesitated, and then said: "Well, no, Miss Tallant! I had business there."

She laughed. "I thought it had been that."

"In that case," said Mr Beaumaris, "I am glad I did not lie to you."

"How can you be so absurd? As though I should wish you to put yourself to so much trouble! What has Jemmy been doing?"

"It would sadden you to know: Mrs Buxton is persuaded that he is possessed of a fiend. The language he employs, too, is not such as she is accustomed to. I regret to say that he has also alienated my keepers, who have quite failed to impress upon him the impropriety of disturbing my birds, or, I may add, of stealing pheasants' eggs. I cannot imagine what he can want with them."

"Of course he should be punished for doing so! I daresay he has not enough employment. One must remember that he has been used to work and should be made to do so now. It is not at all good for anyone to be perfectly idle."

"Very true, ma'am," agreed Mr Beaumaris meekly.

Miss Tallant was not deceived. She looked sharply up at him, and bit her lip, saying after a moment: "We are speaking of *Jemmy*!"

"I hoped we were," confessed Mr Beaumaris.

"You are being nonsensical," said Arabella, with some severity. "What is to be done with him?"

"I found, upon enquiry, that the only person who is inclined to regard him favourably is my head groom, who says that his way with the horses is quite remarkable. It appears that he has been for ever slipping off to the stables, where, for a wonder, he comports himself unexceptionably. Wrexham was so much impressed by finding him – er – hobnobbing with a bay stallion generally thought to be extremely dangerous, that he came up to represent to me the propriety of handing the boy over to him to train. He is a childless man, and since he expressed his willingness to house Jemmy, I thought it better to fall in with his schemes. I hardly think Jemmy's language will shock him, and I am encouraged to hope, from what I know of Wrexham, that he will know how to keep the boy in order."

Arabella approved so heartily of this arrangement, that he took the risk of saying in a melancholy tone: "Yes, but if it succeeds, I shall be at a loss to think of a pretext for getting you to drive out with me."

"Dear me, have I shown myself so reluctant?" said Arabella, raising her eyebrows. "I wonder why you will talk so absurdly, Mr Beaumaris? You may depend upon it that I shall take care to be seen every now and then in your company, for I cannot be so sure of my credit as to run the risk of having it said that the Nonpareil has begun to find me a dead bore!"

"You stand in no such danger, Miss Tallant, believe me." He drew in his horses for a sharp bend in the road, and did not speak again until the corner was negotiated. Then he said: "I am afraid that you deem me a very worthless creature, ma'am. What am I to do to convince you that I can be perfectly sensible?"

"There is not the least need: I am sure that you can," she replied amicably.

After that she became interested in the countryside, and from that passed to her forthcoming presentation. This event was to take place in the following week, and already her dress had been sent home from the skilful costumier who had altered an old gown of Lady Bridlington's to the present mode. Miss Tallant did not tell Mr Beaumaris that, naturally, but she did describe its magnificence to him, and found him both sympathetic and knowledgeable. He asked her what jewels she would wear with it, and she replied, in a very grand way: "Oh, nothing but diamonds!" and was promptly ashamed of herself for having said it, although it was perfectly true.

"Your taste is always excellent, Miss Tallant. Nothing could be more displeasing to a fastidious eye than a profusion of jewellery. I must congratulate you on having exerted so beneficial an influence over your contemporaries."

"I?" she gasped, quite startled, and half-suspecting him of quizzing her.

"Certainly. The total lack of ostentation which characterizes your appearance is much admired, I assure you, and is beginning to be copied."

"You cannot be serious!"

"But of course I am serious! Had you not noticed that Miss Accrington has left off that shocking collar of sapphires, and that Miss Kirkmichael no longer draws attention to the limitations of her figure by a profusion of chains, brooches, and necklaces which I should have supposed her to have chosen at random from an over-stocked jewel-box?"

There was something so irresistibly humorous to Arabella in the thought that her straitened circumstances had been at the root of a new mode that she began to giggle. But she would not tell Mr Beaumaris why she sat chuckling beside him. He did not press her for an explanation, but as they had by this time reached the Park, suggested that she might like to walk on the grass for a little way, while the groom took charge of the curricle. She assented readily, and while they strolled about, Mr Beaumaris told her something of that home of his in Hampshire. The bait failed. Miss Tallant confined her remarks on her own home to descriptions of the Yorkshire scene, and would not be lured into exchanging family reminiscences.

"I collect that your father is still alive, ma'am? You mentioned him, as I remember, on the day that you adopted Jemmy."

"Did I? Yes, indeed he is alive, and I wished for him very much that day, for he is the best man in the world, and he would have known just what was right to be done!"

"I shall hope to have the pleasure of making his acquaintance one day. Does he come to London at all?"

"No, never," replied Arabella firmly. She could not imagine that Mr Beaumaris and Papa would have the least pleasure in one another's acquaintance, thought that the conversation was getting on to dangerous ground, and reverted to her society manner.

This was maintained during most of the drive back to London, but when the open country was left behind, and the curricle was passing once more between rows of houses, it deserted her abruptly. In the middle of a narrow street, the grays took high-bred exception to a wagon with a tattered and flapping canvas roof, which was drawn up to one side of the road. There was barely room for the curricle to slip past this obstruction, and Mr Beaumaris, his attention all on his horses, failed to take notice of a group of youths bending over some object on the flag-way, or to heed the anguished yelp which made Arabella, casting aside the light rug which covered her legs, cry out: "Oh, stop!" and shut her sunshade with a snap.

The grays were mincing past the wagon; Mr Beaumaris did indeed pull them up, but Arabella did not wait for the curricle to come to a standstill, but sprang hazardously down from it. Mr Beaumaris holding his sidling, snorting pair in an iron hand, took one quick glance over his shoulder, saw that Arabella was dispersing the group on the flag-way by the vigorous use of her sunshade, and snapped: "Go to their heads, fool!"

His groom, still perched up behind, and apparently dumb-founded by Miss Tallant's strange conduct, came to himself with a start, jumped down, and ran round to hold the grays. Mr Beaumaris sprang down, and descended swiftly upon the battleground. Having scientifically knocked two louts' heads together, picked up the third lout by his collar and the seat of his frieze breeches, and thrown him into the road, he was able to see what had aroused Miss Tallant's wrath. Crouched, shivering and whimpering, on the flag-way, was a small, sandy-coated mongrel, with a curly tail, and one ear disreputably flying.

"Those wicked, brutal, *fiends*!" panted Miss Tallant, cheeks and eyes in a glow. "They were *torturing* the poor little thing!"

"Take care! He may snap at you!" Mr Beaumaris said quickly, seeing her about to kneel down beside the dog. "Shall I thrash them all soundly?"

At these words, the two smaller boys departed precipitately, the two whose heads were still ringing drew circumspectly out of range of Mr Beaumaris's long-lashed whip, and the bruised youth in the road, whined that they weren't doing any harm, and that all his ribs were busted.

"How badly have they hurt him?" Miss Tallant asked anxiously. "He cries when I touch him!"

Mr Beaumaris pulled off his gloves, and handed them to her, together with his whip, saying: "Hold those for me, and I'll see."

She obediently took them, and watched anxiously while he went over the mongrel. She saw with approval that he handled the little creature firmly and gently, in a way that showed he knew what he was about. The dog whined, and uttered little cries, and cowered, but he did not offer to snap. Indeed, he feebly wagged his disgraceful tail, and once licked Mr Beaumaris's hand.

"He is badly bruised, and has one or two nasty sores, but there are no bones broken," Mr Beaumaris said, straightening himself. He turned to where the two remaining youths were standing, poised on the edge of flight, and said sternly: "Whose dog is this?"

"It don't belong to no one," he was sullenly informed. "It goes all over, stealing things off of the rubbish-heaps: yes, *and* out of the butcher's shop!"

"I seen 'im in Chelsea onct with 'alf a loaf of bread," corroborated the other youth.

The accused crawled to Mr Beaumaris's elegantly shod feet, and pawed one gleaming Hessian appealingly.

"Oh, see how intelligent he is! cried Arabella, stooping to fondle the animal. "He knows he has you to thank for his rescue!"

"If he knows that, I think little of his intelligence, Miss Tallant," said Mr Beaumaris, glancing down at the dog. "He certainly owes his life to you!"

"Oh, no! I could never have managed without your help! Will you be so obliging as to hand him up to me, if you please?" said Arabella, prepared to climb into the curricle again.

Mr Beaumaris looked from her to the unkempt and filthy mongrel at his feet, and said: "Are you quite sure that you want to take him with you, ma'am?"

"Why, of course! You do not suppose that I would leave him here, for those wretches to torment as soon as we were out of sight! Besides, you heard what they said! He has no master – no one to feed him, or to take care of him! Please give him to me!"

Mr Beaumaris's lips twitched, but he said with perfect gravity: "Just as you wish, Miss Tallant!" and picked up the dog by the scruff of his neck. He saw Miss Tallant's arms held out to receive her new protégé, and hesitated. "He is very dirty, you know!"

"Oh, what does that signify? I have soiled my dress already, with kneeling on the flag-way!" said Arabella impatiently.

So Mr Beaumaris deposited the dog on her lap, received his whip and gloves from her again, and stood watching with a faint smile while she made the dog comfortable, and stroked its ears, and murmured soothingly to it. She looked up. "What do we wait for, sir?" she asked, surprised.

"Nothing at all, Miss Tallant!" he said, and got into the curricle.

Miss Tallant, continuing to fondle the dog, spoke her mind with some force on the subject of persons who were cruel to animals, and thanked Mr Beaumaris earnestly for his kindness in knocking the horrid boys' heads together, a violent proceeding which seemed to have met with her unqualified approval. She then occupied herself with talking to the dog, and informing him of the splendid dinner he should presently be given, and the warm bath which he would (she said) so much enjoy. But after a time she became a little pensive, and relapsed into meditative silence.

"What is it, Miss Tallant?" asked Mr Beaumaris, when she showed no sign of breaking the silence.

"Do you know," she said slowly, "I have just thought – Mr Beaumaris, something tells me that Lady Bridlington may not like this dear little dog!"

Mr Beaumaris waited in patient resignation for his certain fate to descend upon him.

Arabella turned impulsively towards him. "Mr Beaumaris, do you think – *would* you --?"

He looked down into her anxious, pleading eyes, a most rueful twinkle in his own. "Yes, Miss Tallant," he said. "I would."

Her face broke into smiles. "*Thank* you!" she said. "I knew I might depend upon you!" She turned the mongrel's head gently towards Mr Beaumaris. "There, sir! that is your new master, who will be very kind to you! Only see how intelligently he looks, Mr Beaumaris! I am sure he understands. I daresay he will grow to be quite devoted to you!"

Mr Beaumaris looked at the animal, and repressed a shudder. "Do you think so indeed?" he said.

"Oh, yes! He is not, perhaps, a very *beautiful* little dog, but mongrels are often the cleverest of all dogs." She smoothed the creature's rough head, and added innocently: "He will be company for you, you know. I wonder you do not have a dog already."

"I do – in the country," he replied.

"Oh, sporting dogs! They are not at all the same."

Mr Beaumaris, after another look at his prospective companion, found himself able to agree with this remark with heartfelt sincerity.

"When he has been groomed, and has put some flesh on his bones," pursued Arabella, serene in the conviction that her sentiments were being shared, "he will look very different. I am quite anxious to see him in a week or two!"

Mr Beaumaris drew up his horses outside Lady Bridlington's house. Arabella gave the dog a last pat, and set him on the seat beside his new owner, bidding him stay there. He seemed a little undecided at first, but being too bruised and battered to leap down into the road, he did stay, whining loudly. However, when Mr Beaumaris, having handed Arabella up to the door, and seen her admitted into the house, returned to his curricle, the dog stopped whining, and welcomed him with every sign of relief and affection.

"Your instinct is at fault," said Mr Beaumaris. "Left to myself, I should abandon you to your fate. That, or tie a brick round your neck, and drown you."

His canine admirer wagged a doubtful tail, and cocked an ear. "You are a disgraceful object!" Mr Beaumaris told him. "And what does she expect me to do with you?" A tentative paw was laid on his knee. "Possibly, but let me tell you that I know your sort! You are a toadeater, and I abominate toadeaters. I suppose, if I sent you into the country my own dogs would kill you on sight."

The severity in his tone made the dog cower a little, still looking up at him with the expression of a dog anxious to understand.

"Have no fear!" Mr Beaumaris assured him, laying a fleeting hand on his head. "She clearly wishes me to keep you in town. Did it occur to her, I wonder, that your manners, I have no doubt at all, leave much to be desired? Do your wanderings include the slightest experience of the conduct expected of those admitted into a gentleman's house? Of course they do not!" A choking sound from his groom, made him say over his shoulder: "I hope you like dogs, Clayton, for you are going to wash this specimen."

"Yes, sir," said his grinning attendant.

"Be very kind to him!" commanded Mr Beaumaris. "Who knows? he may take a liking to you."

But at ten o'clock that evening, Mr Beaumaris's butler, bearing a tray of suitable refreshments to the library, admitted into the room a washed, brushed, and fed mongrel, who came in with something as near a prance as could be expected of one in his emaciated condition. At sight of Mr Beaumaris, seeking solace from his favourite poet in a deep winged chair by the fire, he uttered a shrill bark of delight, and reared himself up on his hind legs, his paws on Mr Beaumaris's knees, his tail furiously wagging, and a look of beaming adoration in his eyes.

Mr. Beaumaris lowered his Horace. "Now, what the devil --?" he demanded.

"Clayton brought the little dog up, sir," said Brough. "He said as you would wish to see how he looked. It seems, sir, that the dog didn't take to Clayton, as you might say. Very restless, Clayton informs me, and whining all the evening." He watched the dog thrust his muzzle under Mr Beaumaris's hand, and said: "It's strange the way animals always go to you, sir. Quite happy now, isn't he?"

"Deplorable," said Mr Beaumaris. "Down, Ulysses! Learn that my pantaloons were not made to be pawed by such as you!"

"He'll learn quick enough, sir," remarked Brough, setting a glass and a decanter down on the table at his master's elbow. "You can see he's as sharp as he can stare. Would there be anything more, sir?"

"No, only give this animal back to Clayton, and tell him I am perfectly satisfied with his appearance."

"Clayton's gone off, sir. I don't think he can have understood that you wished him to take charge of the little dog," said Brough.

"I don't think he can have wanted to understand it," said Mr Beaumaris grimly.

"As to that, sir, I'm sure I couldn't say. I doubt whether the dog will settle down with Clayton, him not having a way with dogs like he has with horses.

I'm afraid he'll fret, sir."

"Oh, my God!" groaned Mr Beaumaris. "Then take him down to the kitchen!"

"Well, sir, of course – if you say so!" replied Brough doubtfully. "Only there's Alphonse." He met his master's eye, apparently had no difficulty in reading the question in it, and said: "Yes, sir. Very French he has been on the subject. Quite shocking, I'm sure, but one has to remember that foreigners are queer, and don't like animals."

"Very well," said Mr Beaumaris, with a resigned sigh. "Leave him, then!"

"Yes, sir," said Brough, and departed.

Ulysses, who had been thoroughly, if a little timidly, inspecting the room during this exchange, now advanced to the hearth-rug again, and paused there, suspiciously regarding the fire. He seemed to come to the conclusion that it was not actively hostile, for after a moment he curled himself up before it, heaved a sigh, laid his chin on Mr Beaumaris's crossed ankles, and disposed himself for sleep.

"I suppose you imagine you are being a companion to me," said Mr Beaumaris.

Ulysses flattened his ears, and gently stirred his tail.

"You know," said Mr Beaumaris, "a prudent man would draw back at this stage."

Ulysses raised his head to yawn, and then snuggled it back on Mr Beaumaris's ankles, and closed his eyes.

"You may be right," admitted Mr Beaumaris. "But I wonder what next she will saddle me with?"

CHAPTER TEN

WHEN ARABELLA had parted from Mr Beaumaris at the door of Lady Bridlington's house, the butler who had admitted her informed her that two gentlemen had called to see her, and were even now awaiting her in the smaller saloon. This seemed to her a trifle unusual, and she looked surprised. The butler explained the matter by saying that one of the young gentlemen was particularly anxious to see her, since he came from Yorkshire, and would not be unknown to her. A horrid fear gripped Arabella that she was now to be exposed to the whole of London, and it was with an almost shaking hand that she picked up the visiting-card from the salver the butler was holding out to her. But the name elegantly inscribed upon it was unknown to her: she could not recall ever having heard of, much less met, a

Mr Felix Scunthorpe.

"*Two* gentlemen?" she said.

"The other young gentleman, miss, did not disclose his name," replied the butler.

"Well, I suppose I must see them," Arabella decided. "Pray tell them that I shall be downstairs directly! Or is her ladyship in?"

"Her ladyship has not yet returned, miss."

Arabella hardly knew whether to be glad or sorry. She went up to her room to change her soiled gown, and came down again some few minutes later hoping that she had schooled her face not to betray her inward trepidation. She entered the saloon in a very stately way, and looked rather challengingly across it. There were, as the butler had warned her, two young gentlemen standing by the window. One was a slightly vacuous looking youth, dressed with extreme nicety, and holding, besides his tall hat, an ebony cane, and an elegant pair of gloves; the other was a tall, loose-limbed boy, with curly dark hair, and an aquiline cast of countenance. At sight of him, Arabella uttered a shriek, and ran across the room to cast herself upon his chest. "*Bertram!*"

"Here, I say, Bella!" expostulated Bertram, recoiling. "Mind what you are about, for the lord's sake! My neckcloth!"

"Oh, I beg your pardon, but I am so *glad* to see you! But how is this? Bertram, Papa is not in town?"

"Good God, no!"

"Thank heaven!" Arabella breathed, pressing her hands to her cheeks.

Her brother found nothing to wonder at in this exclamation. He looked her over critically, and said: "Just as well he ain't, for he'd be bound to give you one of his scolds for dressing-up as fine as fivepence! I must say, Bella, you're turned out in prime style! Slap up to the mark, ain't she, Felix?"

Mr Scunthorpe, much discomposed at being called upon to give an opinion, opened and shut his mouth once or twice, bowed, and looked despairing.

"He thinks you're complete to a shade," explained Bertram, interpreting these signs. "He ain't much of a dab with the petticoats, but he's a great gun, I can tell you! Up to every rig and row in town!"

Arabella looked at Mr Scunthorpe with interest. He presented the appearance of a very mild young man; and although his fancy waistcoat bespoke the man of fashion, he seemed to her to lack address. She bowed politely, which made him blush very much, and fall into a fit of stuttering. Bertram, feeling that some further introduction might be considered desirable by his sister, said: "You don't know him: he was at Harrow with me. He's older than I am, but he's got no brains, y'know: never could learn anything! I ran into him in the High."

"The High?" repeated Arabella.

"Oxford, you know!" said Bertram loftily. "Dash it, Bella, you can't have forgot I've been up to take my Smalls!"

"No, indeed!" she said. "Sophy wrote that you were gone there, and that poor James was unable to accompany you, because of the jaundice. I was so sorry! But how did you go on, Bertram? Do you think you have passed?"

"Lord, I don't know! There was one devilish paper – but never mind that now! The thing is that I met old Felix here, the very man I wanted!"

"Oh, yes?" Arabella said, adding with a civil smile: "Were you up for Smalls too, sir?"

Mr Scunthorpe appeared to shrink from such a suggestion, shaking his head, and making a sound in his throat which Arabella took to be a negative.

"Of course he wasn't!" said Bertram. "Don't I keep telling you he can't learn anything? He was visiting some friends in Oxford! He found it pretty dull work, too, didn't you, Felix? They would take him to blue-parties, all professors, and Bagwigs, and the poor fellow couldn't follow the stuff they talked. Shabby thing to do to him, for he was bound to make a cake of himself in that sort of company! However, that's not what I want to talk about. The thing is, Bella, that Felix is going to show me all the sights, because he's at home to a peg in London – been on the town ever since they threw him out of Harrow."

"And Papa gave his consent?" exclaimed Arabella.

"As a matter of fact," said Bertram airily, "he don't know I'm here."

"Doesn't know you're here?" cried Arabella.

Mr Scunthorpe cleared his throat. "Given him the bag," he explained. He added: "Only thing to do."

Arabella turned her eyes wonderingly towards her brother. He looked a little guilty, but said: "No, you can't say I've given him the bag!"

Mr Scunthorpe corrected himself "Hoaxed him."

Bertram seemed to be about to take exception to this too, but after beginning to refute it he broke off, and said: "Well, in a way I suppose I did."

"Bertram, you must be mad!" cried Arabella, pale with dismay. "When Papa knows you are in town, and without leave -"

"The thing is he won't know it," interrupted Bertram. "I wrote a letter to Mama, telling her I had met my friend Felix, and he had invited me to stay with him. So they won't be in a fret when I don't go back immediately, and they won't know where I am, because I didn't give my direction. And that brings me to what I particularly want to warn you about, Bella! I'm going by the name of Anstey while I'm in town, and while I don't mind if you tell this godmother of yours that I'm a friend of yours, you are not to say I'm your brother! She'd be bound to write and tell my mother, and then the fat would be in the fire!"

"But, Bertram, how can you *dare*?" asked Arabella, in an awed voice. "Papa will be so angry!"

"Yes, I know. I shall get a rare trimming, but I shall have had a bang-up time first, and I can stand a lick or two after," said Bertram cheerfully. "I made up my mind I'd do it, before you came to town. Do you remember my telling you that you might get a surprise? I'll swear you never thought *this* would be it!"

"No, indeed I did not!" Arabella said, sinking into a chair. "Oh, Bertram, I am quite in a quake! I cannot understand any of it! How can you afford to be staying in London? Are you Mr Scunthorpe's guest?"

"No, no, poor old Felix ain't standing the huff! I won a ticket in a lottery! Only think of it, Bella! A hundred pounds!"

"A lottery! Good God, what would Papa say if he knew *that*?"

"Oh, he would kick up no end of a bobbery, of course, but I shan't tell him.

And, you know, once I had won it the only thing to be done was to spend it, because you must see I had to get rid of it before Papa found I had it!" He saw that his sister was looking horrified, and said indignantly: "I must say, I don't see why you should grudge it to me! I daresay you are having a capital time yourself!"

"No, no, how could you think I would grudge you *anything*, Bertram? But to have you in town, and to be obliged to pretend I am not your sister, and to deceive Papa and Mama -" She stopped, remembering her own situation. "Oh, Bertram, how *wicked* we are!"

Mr Scunthorpe looked very much alarmed at this, but Bertram said: "Fudge! It's not telling lies precisely just not to mention that you have seen me when you write to Mama!"

" You do not know! It is worse than that!" whispered Arabella. "Bertram, I am in such a scrape!"

He stared at her. "You are? How is this?" He saw her glance towards his friend, and said: "You needn't mind Felix: he's no gabster!"

Arabella was easily able to believe this, but she not unnaturally felt reluctant to disclose her story to one who was a stranger to her, even though she had already realized that if he was not to betray her unwittingly he must be taken some way at least into her confidence. Mr Scunthorpe tweaked his friend's sleeve. "Must help your sister out of the scrape, dear boy. Happy to be of service!"

"I am very much obliged to you, sir, but no one can help me out of it!" said Arabella tragically. "If only you will be so kind as not to betray me!"

"Of course he won't betray you!" declared Bertram. "What in thunder have you been about, Bella?"

"Bertram, everyone believes me to be a great heiress." disclosed Arabella, in a stricken tone.

He stared at her for a moment, and then burst out laughing. "You goosecap! I'll wager they don't! Why, Lady Bridlington knows you are not! You don't mean that she put such a tale about?"

She shook her head. "I said it!" she confessed.

"*You* said it? What the devil made you do such a thing? However, I don't suppose anyone believed you!"

"They do believe it. Lord Bridlington says that every gazetted fortune-hunter in town is dangling after me – and, oh, Bertram, it is true! I have refused five offers already!"

The idea that there could be found five gentlemen ready to marry his sister struck Bertram as being exquisitely humorous, and he went off into another burst of laughter. Arabella was obliged to confess the whole, since he seemed so incredulous. Her narrative was rather disjointed, since he interpolated so many questions; and at one point a considerable digression was caused by Mr Scunthorpe, who, having regarded her fixedly for some moments, suddenly became loquacious, and said: "Beg pardon, ma'am, but did you say Mr Beaumaris?"

"Yes. He and Lord Fleetwood."

"The Nonpareil?"

"Yes."

Mr Scunthorpe drew a breath, and turned to address his friend. "You hear that, Bertram?"

"Well, of course I heard it!"

"Didn't think you could have. You see this coat of mine?"

Both Tallants stared at his coat in some bewilderment.

"Got my man to copy the lapels of one Weston made for the Nonpareil," said Mr Scunthorpe, with simple pride.

"Good God, what has that to say to anything?" demanded Bertram.

"Thought you might be interested," explained Mr Scunthorpe apologetically.

"Never mind him!" Bertram told his sister. "If it wasn't just like you, Bella, to fly into a miff, and go off into one of your crazy starts! Mind, I don't say I blame you! Did he spread the story over London?"

"I think it was Lord Fleetwood who did that. Mr Beaumaris told me once that he had not discussed the matter with anyone but Lord Fleetwood. Sometimes I have wondered whether – whether he had guessed the truth, but I cannot believe that he has, for he would despise me dreadfully, I am sure, if he knew how odiously I behaved, and certainly not stand up with me at all the balls – for he very seldom dances! – or take me out driving in his curricle."

Mr Scunthorpe looked very much impressed. "He does that?"

"Oh, yes!"

Mr Scunthorpe nodded portentously at Bertram. "You know what, dear boy? All the crack, your sister! Not a doubt of it. Knows all the best people. Drives out with the Nonpareil. Good thing she said she was an heiress."

"Oh, no, no, I wish I had never done so, for it has made everything so uncomfortable!"

"Now, Bella, that's gammon! I know you! Don't you try to tell me you don't like being all the go, because I wouldn't believe you if you did!" said Bertram, with brotherly candour.

Arabella thought it over. Then she gave a reluctant smile. "Well, yes, perhaps I do like it, but when I remember the cause of it I do indeed wish I had never said such a thing! Only consider what a fix I am in! If the truth were known now I should be utterly discredited! No one would even *bow* to me, I daresay, and I have the greatest dread that Lady Bridlington would send me home in disgrace! And then Papa would know, and – Bertram, I had almost rather throw myself into the river than have him know such a thing of me!"

"Lord, yes!" he agreed, with a shudder. "But it won't come to that! If anyone asks *me* any prying questions, I shall say you are well known to me, and so will Felix!"

"Yes, but that is not all!" Arabella pointed out. "I can never, never accept any offer made to me, and what Mama will think of such selfishness I dare not consider! For she so much hoped that I should form an eligible connection, and Lady Bridlington is bound to tell her that – that quite a number of very eligible gentlemen have paid me the most marked attentions!"

Bertram knit his brows over this. "Unless – No, you're right, Bella; devilish awkward fix! You would have to tell the truth, if you accepted an offer, and ten to one he'd cry off. What a tiresome girl you are, to be sure! Dashed if I see what's to be done! Do you, Felix?"

"Very difficult situation," responded Mr Scunthorpe, shaking his head. "Only one thing to be done."

"What's that?"

Mr Scunthorpe gave a diffident cough. "Just a little thing that occurred to me. Daresay you won't care about it: can't say I care about it myself, but can't hang back when a lady's in a fix."

"But what *is* it?"

"Mind, only a notion I had!" Mr Scunthorpe warned him. "You don't like it: you say so! I don't like it, but ought to offer." He perceived that the Tallants were quite mystified, blushed darkly, and uttered in a strangled voice: "Marriage!"

Arabella stared at him for a moment, and then went into a peal of mirth. Bertram said scornfully: "Of all the corkbrained notions! *You* don't want to marry Bella!"

"No," conceded Mr Scunthorpe. "Promised I would help her out of the scrape, though!"

"What's more," Bertram said severely, "those trustees of yours would never let you! You're not of age."

"Talk them over," said Mr Scunthorpe hopefully.

However, Arabella, thanking him for his kind offer, said that she did not think they would suit. He seemed grateful, and relapsed into the silence which appeared to be natural to him.

"I daresay I shall hit upon something," said Bertram. "I'll think about it, at all events. Should I stay to do the pretty to this godmother of yours, do you think?"

Arabella urged him strongly to do so. She was inclined to grieve over his necessary incognito, but he told her frankly that it would not at all suit him to be for ever gallanting her to the *ton* parties. "Very dull work!" he said. "I know you are gone civility-mad since you came to town, but it's not in my line." He then enumerated the sights he meant to see in London, and since these seemed to consist mostly of such innocuous entertainments as Astley's Amphitheatre, the Royal Menagerie at the Tower, Madame Tussaud's Waxworks, Napoleon's carriage, on view at Bullock's Museum, a look-in at Tattersall's, the departure of the Brighton coaches from the White Horse Cellar, and the forthcoming Military Review in Hyde Park, his anxious sister's worst qualms were allayed. At first sight he had seemed to her to have grown a great deal older, for he was wearing a sophisticated waistcoat, and had brushed his hair in a new style; but when he told her about the peep-show which had diverted him so much in Coventry Street, and expressed a purely youthful desire to witness that grand spectacle, *The Burning Of Moscow* (supported by Tight-rope Walking, and an Equestrian Display) she could feel that he was still boy enough not to hanker after the more sophisticated and by far more dangerous amusements to be found in London. But, then, as he confidentially informed Mr Scunthorpe, when they presently left Park Street together, females took such foolish notions into their heads that it would have been ridiculous to have disclosed to her that he had an equally ardent desire to see a bout of fisticuffs at the Fives-court, to blow a cloud with all the Corinthians at the Daffy Club, to penetrate the mysteries of the Royal Saloon, and the Peerless Pool, and certainly to put in an appearance at the Opera – not, he hastened to assure his friend, because he wanted to listen to music, but because he was credibly informed that to stroll in the Fops' Alley was famous sport, and all the go. Since he had decided, very prudently, to put up at one of the City inns, where, if he chose, he could be sure of a tolerable dinner at the Ordinary, which was very moderately priced, he entertained reasonable hopes of being able to afford all these diversions. But first, he perceived, it was necessary to buy a much higher-crowned and more curly-brimmed beaver to set on his head; a pair of Hessians with tassels; a fob, and perhaps a seal; and certainly a pair of natty yellow gloves. Without these adjuncts to a gentleman's costume he would look like a Johnny Raw. Mr Scunthorpe agreed, and ventured to point out that a driving-coat with only two shoulder-capes was thought, in well-dressed circles, to be a paltry affair. He said he would take Bertram along to his own man, a devilish clever tailor, even though he had not acquired the fame of a Weston or a Stultz. However, as the great advantage of patronizing this rising man lay in the assurance that he would be willing to rig out any friend of Mr Scunthorpe's on tick, Bertram raised no objection to jumping into a hackney at once, and telling the jarvey to drive with all speed to Clifford Street. Mr Scunthorpe vouched for it that Swindon's art would give his friend quite a new touch, and as this seemed extremely desirable to Bertram, he thought he could hardly lay out a substantial sum of money to better advantage. Mr Scunthorpe then imparted to him a few useful hints, particularly warning him against such extravagances of style as must give rise to the suspicion that he belonged to the extreme dandy-set frowned upon by the real Pinks of the *Ton*. Beyond question, the finest model for any aspiring gentleman to copy was the Nonpareil, that Go amongst the Goers. This put Bertram in mind of something which had been slightly troubling his mind, and he said: "I say, Felix, do you think my sister should be driving about the town with him? I don't mind telling you I don't like it above half!"

Here Mr Scunthorpe was able at once to allay his qualms: for a lady to drive in a curricle or a phaeton, with a groom riding behind, was unexceptionable. "Mind, it would not do for a female to go in a tilbury!" he said.

His brotherly concern relieved, Bertram abandoned the question, merely remarking that he would give a monkey to see his father's face if he knew how racketty Bella had become.

Arrived in Clifford Street, they obtained instant audience of Mr Swindon, who was so obliging as to bring out his pattern-card immediately, and to advise his new client on the respective merits of Superfine and Bath Suiting. He thought six capes would be sufficient for a light drab driving-coat, an opinion in which Mr Scunthorpe gravely concurred, explaining to Bertram that it would never do for him to ape the Goldfinches, with their row upon row of capes. Unless one was an acknowledged Nonesuch, capable of driving to an inch, or one of the Melton men, it was wiser, he said, to aim at neatness and propriety rather than the very height of fashion. He then bent his mind to the selection of a cloth for a coat, and although Bertram had not intended to order a new coat, he was persuaded to do so, as much by the assertion of Mr Swindon that a single-breasted garment of corbeau-coloured cloth, with wide lapels, and silver buttons, would set his person off to advantage, as by the whispered assurance of his friend that the snyder always gave his clients long credit. Indeed, Mr Scunthorpe was rarely troubled with his tailor's account, since that astute man of business was well aware that being a fatherless minor Mr Scunthorpe's considerable fortune was held in trust by tight-fisted guardians, who doled him out a beggarly allowance. Nothing so ungenteel as cost or payment was mentioned during the session in Clifford Street, so that Bertram left the premises torn between relief and a fear that he might have pledged his credit for a larger sum than he could afford to pay. But the novelty and excitement of a first visit to the Metropolis soon put such untimely thoughts to rout, while a lucky bet at the Fives-court clearly showed the novice the easiest way of raising the wind.

A close inspection of such sprigs of fashion as were to be seen at the Fives-court made Bertram very glad to think he had bespoken a new coat, and he confided to Mr Scunthorpe that he would not visit the haunts of fashion until his clothes had been sent home. Mr Scunthorpe thought this a wise decision, and, as it was of course absurd to suppose that Bertram should kick his heels at the City inn which enjoyed his patronage, he volunteered to show him how an evening full of fun and gig could be spent in less exalted circles. This entertainment, beginning as it did in the Westminster Pit, where it seemed to the staring Bertram that representatives of every class of society from the Corinthian to the dustman, had assembled to watch a contest between two dogs; and proceeding by way of the shops of Tothill Fields, where adventurous bucks tossed off noggins of Blue Ruin, or bumpers of heavy wet, in company with bruisers, prigs, coal-heavers, Nuns, Abbesses, and apple-women, to a coffee-shop, ended in the watch-house, Mr Scunthorpe having become bellicose under the influence of his potations. Bertram, quite unused to such quantities of liquor as he had imbibed, was too much fuddled to have any very clear notion of what circumstance it was that had excited his friend's wrath, though he had a vague idea that it was in some way connected with the advances being made by a gentleman in Petersham trousers towards a lady who had terrified him earlier in the proceedings by laying a palpable lure for him. But when a mill was in progress it was not his part to enquire into the cause of it, but to enter into the fray in support of his cicerone. Since he was by no means unlearned in the noble art of self-defence, he was able to render yeoman service to Mr Scunthorpe, no proficient, and was in a fair way to milling his way out of the shop when the watch, in the shape of several Charleys, all springing their rattles, burst in upon them and, after a spirited set-to, over-powered the two peacebreakers, and hailed them off to the watch-house. Here, after considerable parley, conducted for the defence by the experienced Mr Scunthorpe, they were admitted to bail, and warned to present themselves next day in Bow Street, not a moment later than twelve o'clock. The night-constable then packed them both into a hackney, and they drove to Mr Scunthorpe's lodging in Clarges Street, where Bertram passed what little was left of the night on the sofa in his friend's sitting-room. He awoke later with a splitting headache, no very clear recollection of the late happenings, but a lively dread of the possible consequences of what he feared had been a very bosky evening. However, when Mr Scunthorpe's man had revived his master, and he emerged from his bedchamber, he was soon able to allay any such misgivings. "Nothing to be in a fret for, dear boy!" he said. "Been piloted to the lighthouse scores of times! Watchman will produce broken lantern in evidence – they always do it! – you give false name, pay fine, and all's right!"

So, indeed, it proved, but the experience a little shocked the Vicar's son. This, coupled with the extremely unpleasant after-effects of drinking innumerable flashes of lightning, made him determine to be more circumspect in future. He spent several days in pursuing such harmless amusements as witnessing a badger drawn in a menagerie in Holborn, losing his heart to Miss O'Neill from a safe position in the pit, and being introduced by Mr Scunthorpe into Gentleman Jackson's exclusive Boxing School in Bond Street. Here he was much impressed by the manners and dignity of the proprietor (whose decision in all matters of sport, Mr Scunthorpe informed him, was accepted as final by patrician and plebeian alike), and was gratified by a glimpse of such notable amateurs as Mr Beaumaris, Lord Fleetwood, young Mr Terrington, and Lord Withernsea. He had a little practise with the single-stick with one of Jackson's assistants, felt himself honoured by receiving a smiling word of encouragement from the great Jackson himself, and envied the assurance of the Goes who strolled in, exchanged jests with Jackson, who treated them with the same degree of civility as he showed to his less exalted pupils, and actually enjoyed bouts with the ex-champion himself. He was quick to see that no consideration of rank or consequence was enough to induce Jackson to allow a client to plant a hit upon his person, unless his prowess deserved such a reward; and from having entered the saloon with a feeling of superiority he swiftly reached the realization that in the Corinthian world excellence counted for more than lineage. He heard Jackson say chidingly to the great Nonpareil himself (who stripped to remarkable advantage, he noticed) that he was out of training; and from that moment his highest ambition was to put on the gloves with this peerless master of the art.

At the end of a week, Mr Swindon, urged thereto by Mr Scunthorpe, delivered the new clothes, and, after purchasing such embellishments to his costume as a tall cane, a fob, and a Marseilles waistcoat, Bertram ventured to show himself in the Park, at the fashionable hour of five o'clock. Here he had the felicity of seeing Lord Coleraine, Georgy à Cockhorse, prancing down Rotten Row on his mettlesome steed; Lord Morton, on his long-tailed gray; and, amongst the carriages, Tommy Onslow's curricle; a number of dashing gigs and tilburies; the elegant barouches of the ladies; and Mr Beaumaris's yellow-winged phaeton-and-four, which he appeared to be able to turn within a space so small as to seem impossible to any mere whipster. Nothing would do for Bertram after that but to repair to the nearest jobmaster's stables, and to arrange for the hire of a showy chestnut hack. Whatever imperfections might attach to the bearing and style of a young gentleman from the country, Bertram knew himself to be a bruising rider, and in this guise determined to show himself to the society which his sister already adorned.

As luck would have it, he encountered her on the day when he first sallied forth, mounted upon his hired hack. She was sitting up beside Mr Beaumaris in his famous phaeton, animatedly describing to him the scene of the

Drawing-room in which she had taken humble part. This event had necessarily occupied her thoughts so much during the past week that she had been able to spare very few for the activities of her adventurous brother. But when she caught sight of him, trotting along on his chestnut hack, she exclaimed, and said impulsively: "Oh, it is – Mr Anstey! Do pray stop, Mr Beaumaris!"

He drew up his team obediently, while she waved to Bertram. He brought his hack up to the phaeton, and bowed politely, only slightly quizzing her with his eyes. Mr Beaumaris, glancing indifferently at him, caught this arch look, became aware of a slight tension in the trim figure beside him, and looked under his lazy eyelids from one to the other.

"How do you do? How do you go on?" said Arabella, stretching out her hand in its glove of white kid.

Bertram bowed over it very creditably, and replied: "Famously! I mean to come – I mean to visit you some morning, Miss Tallant!"

"Oh, yes, please do!" Arabella looked up at her escort, blushed, and stammered: "May I p-present Mr Anstey to you, Mr Beaumaris? He – he is a friend of mine!"

"How do you do?" responded Mr Beaumaris politely. "From Yorkshire, Mr Anstey?"

"Oh, yes! I have known Miss Tallant since I was in short coats!" grinned Bertram.

"You will certainly be much envied by Miss Tallant's numerous admirers," responded Mr Beaumaris. "Are you staying in town?"

"Just a short visit, you know!" Bertram's gaze reverted to the team harnessed to the phaeton, all four of them on the fret. "I say, sir, that's a bang-up team you have in hand!" he said, with all his sister's impulsiveness. "Oh, don't look at this hack of mine – showy, but I never crossed a greater slug in my life!"

"You hunt, Mr Anstey?"

"Yes, with my uncle's pack, in Yorkshire. Of course, it is not like the Quorn country, or the Pytchley, but we get some pretty good runs, I can tell you!" Bertram confided.

"Mr Anstey," interrupted Arabella, fixing him with a very compelling look, "I think Lady Bridlington has sent you a card for her ball: I hope you mean to come!"

"Well, you know, Bel – Miss Tallant!" said Bertram, with disastrous lack of gallantry, "that sort of mummery is not much in my line!" He perceived an anguished expression in her eyes, and added hastily: "That is, delighted, I am sure! Yes, yes, I shall be there! And I shall hope to have the honour of standing up with you!" he ended punctiliously.

Mr Beaumaris was obliged to pay attention to his team, but he did not miss the minatory note in Arabella's voice as she said: "I collect we are to have the pleasure of receiving a visit from you *tomorrow*, sir!"

"Oh!" said Bertram. "Yes, of course! As a matter of fact, I shall be taking a look-in at Tattersall's, but – Yes, to be sure! I'll come to visit you all right and tight!"

He then doffed his new hat, and bowed, and rode off at an easy canter. Arabella appeared to be conscious that some explanation was called for. She said airily: "You must know, sir, that we have been brought up almost as – as brother and sister!"

"I thought perhaps you had," responded Mr Beaumaris gravely.

She glanced sharply up at his profile. He seemed to be wholly absorbed in the task of manoeuvring the phaeton through a gap between a dowager's landaulet and a smart barouche with a crest on the panel. She reassured herself with the reflection that whereas she favoured her Mama, Bertram was said to be the image of what the Vicar had been at the same age, and said: "But I was telling you about the Drawing-room, and how graciously the Princess Mary smiled at me! She was wearing the most magnificent toilet I ever saw in my life! Lady Bridlington tells me that when she was young she was thought to be the most handsome of all the princesses. I thought she looked to be very good-natured."

Mr Beaumaris agreed to it, reserving to himself his enjoyment in hearing this innocent description of the Regent's most admired sister. Miss Tallant, entrancing him with one of her unguarded moments of na_vety, then told him of the elegant, gilt-edged card of invitation which had arrived that very day in Park Street from no less a personage than the Lord Chamberlain, who informed Lady Bridlington that he was commanded by his Royal Highness the Prince Regent to invite her, and Miss Tallant, to a Dress-party at Carlton House on Thursday next, to have the honour of meeting (in large capitals) Her Majesty The Queen. He said that he should be on the look-out for her at Carlton House, and refrained from observing that the Regent's parties, planned as they were on a magnificent scale which offended the taste of such arbiters of true elegance as himself, were amongst the worst squeezes in town, and had even been known to include such vulgarities as a fountain playing in the middle of the dinner-table to which he had himself been bidden.

He entered into her feelings upon this event with far more sympathy than did Bertram, when he presented himself in Park Street on the following afternoon. Lady Bridlington having retired, as she always did, to her couch, to recruit her energies for an evening to be spent at no fewer than four different parties, Arabella was able to enjoy the luxury of a tête-à-tête with her favourite brother. While acknowledging handsomely that he was glad to think of her being invited to Carlton House, he said that he supposed there would be a vast rout of fashionables present, and that for himself he preferred to spend his evenings in a simpler style. He further begged her not to favour him with a description of the gown she meant to wear. She perceived that he was not much interested in her social triumphs, and turned willingly enough to his own chosen amusements. He was slightly evasive on this subject, replying to her questions in general terms. His experience of the female sex had not led him to indulge his imagination with the belief that even an adoring sister would regard with favour such delights as a visit to Cribb's Parlour, where he had actually handled the Champion's famous silver cup, presented to him after his last fight, some years previously, against Molyneux, the Black; the blowing of a cloud at the Daffy Club, surrounded by young Bloods of the Fancy, veterans of the Ring, promising novices, and an array of portraits hanging round the walls of past champions whose very names filled him with awe; or a lounge through the famous

Saloon at Covent Garden, where the bold, ogling glances of the Cyprians who made this haunt their hunting-ground both shocked and terrified him. Nor did he tell her of an assignation he had made with a new acquaintance, encountered at Tattersall's that very morning. He had seen at a glance that Mr Jack Carnaby was quite the thing – almost a Tulip of Fashion, in fact, if dress and air were anything to judge by – but something warned him that Arabella would regard with horror his approaching introduction into a snug little gaming-house under the auspices of this gentleman. It would be of very little use to assure her that he was going merely for the experience, and had not the least intention of gaming away his precious blunt; even his knowledgeable cicerone had shaken his head over this new scheme, and had uttered cryptic warnings against ivory-turners and Greek banditti, adding that his uncle and principal trustee held that it was a good flat that was never down. He said that he had himself proved the truth of this excellent maxim, but since he owned, upon enquiry, that nothing was known to Mr Carnaby's discredit, Bertram paid scant heed to his advice. Mr Carnaby led him to a discreet house in Pall Mall, where, upon knocking in a certain fashion on the door, they were inspected through a grille, and finally admitted. Nothing could have been further removed from Bertram's expectations of what a gaming-hell would be like than the decorous house in which he found himself. The various servants were all very respectable men, with quiet manners, and it would have been hard to have found a more civil or obliging host than the proprietor. Never having indulged in any game more dashing than whist, Bertram spent some time in looking-on, but when he thought he had mastered the rules governing hazard, he ventured to join that table, armed with a modest rouleau. He soon perceived that Mr Scunthorpe had been quite at fault in his talk of Fulhams, and up-hills, for he enjoyed a run of astonishing luck, and came away at last with his pocket so full of guineas that he had no longer any need to worry over his growing expenses. A lucky bet at Tattersall's on the following day put him in a fair way to thinking himself at home on the Turf and at the Table, and it was not to be expected that he would lend any but an impatient ear to Mr. Scunthorpe's dark prophecy that having got into Tow Street he would end up in the clutch of a Bum-trap.

"Know what my uncle says?" Mr Scunthorpe demanded. "They always let a flat win the first time he goes to a hell. Hedge off, dear boy! they'll queer you on that suit!"

"Oh, fudge!" retorted Bertram. "I hope I'm not such a gudgeon as to dip too deeply! I'll tell you what, Felix, I *would* like to play just once at Watier's, if you could contrive it for me!"

"What?" gasped Mr Scunthorpe. "Dear old boy, they would never let you set foot inside the Great-Go, upon my honour they would not! Why, I've never played there myself! Much better go to Vauxhall! Might meet your sister there! See the Grand Cascade! Listen to the Pandean band! All the crack, you know!"

"Oh, dull work, when I might be trying my luck at faro!" said Bertram.

CHAPTER ELEVEN

FROM THE Daffy Club to Limmer's Hotel in Conduit Street was an inevitable step for any young gentleman interested in the Fancy to take. Here were to be found all the Pets of the Ring, and the Corinthians who patronized them. Bertram went there under the auspices of Mr Scunthorpe, who was anxious to turn his friend's thoughts away from more dangerous haunts. He had begun to acquire acquaintances in London, and was thus in the proud position of exchanging greetings with several of the men present. He and Mr Scunthorpe sat down in one of the boxes, and Mr Scunthorpe painstakingly pointed out to him all the notabilities he could see, including a very down-the-road looking man who, he whispered, could be trusted to tip a man the office what to back in any race. He then excused himself, and bore down upon this knowledgeable person, and became absorbed in conversation with him. While he was thus engaged, Bertram saw Mr Beaumaris stroll in with a party of friends, but as he had by this time fully grasped the exalted position occupied by the Nonpareil he was flattered beyond measure when, after raising his glass and regarding him through it for a moment, Mr Beaumaris walked across the sanded floor, and sat down at his table, saying with a slight smile: "Did I not meet you in the Park the other day? Mr – er – Anstey, I believe?"

Bertram acknowledged it, flushing shyly; but when Mr Beaumaris added casually: "You are related to Miss Tallant, I collect?" he made haste to deny any relationship, adding that Miss Tallant was quite above his touch. Mr Beaumaris accepted this without comment, and asked him where he was putting up in town. Bertram saw no harm in disclosing his direction, or even in telling Mr Beaumaris that this was his first visit to the Metropolis.

It was the expressed opinion of Mr Jack Carnaby that the Nonpareil was a haughty, disagreeable kind of man, but Bertram was unable to trace the least sign of haughtiness, or of reserve, in his manners. Mr Beaumaris's intimates could have informed Mr Tallant that while no one could be more snubbing, no one, on the other hand, could be – when he chose – more sympathetic. In less than no time, Bertram, forgetting his bashfulness, was confiding far more to his grand new acquaintance than he had the least idea of. Mr Beaumaris, himself a Melton man, complimented him on his seat on a horse, and any barrier Bertram might have raised between himself and the author of his sister's predicament crumbled at this touch. He was led on to describe the country over which he hunted, the exact locality of Heythram, and his own impossible ambitions, without having the smallest suspicion that all this information was being skilfully extracted from him. He told Mr Beaumaris about Smalls, and his hopes of adorning the Home Office, and when Mr Beaumaris said, with a humorous lift to one eyebrow, that he should not have supposed him to have had parliamentary ambitions, he blurted out his real ambition, ending by saying wistfully: "But it can't be, of course. Only I would have liked of all things to have been able to have joined a cavalry regiment!"

"I think you would do very well in a cavalry regiment," agreed Mr Beaumaris, rising, as Mr Scunthorpe came back to the table. "Meanwhile, do not draw the bustle with too much of a vengeance during this visit of yours to London!" He nodded to Mr Scunthorpe, and walked away, leaving that gentleman to explain to Bertram with the utmost earnestness just how greatly he had been honoured.

But Mr Beaumaris, quelling the ecstatic advances of his canine admirer, an hour or two later, said: "If you had any real regard for me, Ulysses, you would be greeting me with condolences rather than with these uncalled-for raptures."

Ulysses, considerably plumper, and with his flying ear more rebellious than ever, and his tail even more tightly curled over his back, stretched worshipfully before the god of his idolatry, and uttered an encouraging bark. After that he bustled to the door of the library, and plainly invited Mr Beaumaris to enter, and partake of refreshment there. Brough, tenderly relieving his master of his long cloak, and his hat and gloves, remarked that it was wonderful how knowing the little dog was.

"It is wonderful what encouragement he has received from my staff to continue to burden me with his unwanted presence in my house!" retorted Mr Beaumaris acidly.

Brough, who had dealt with Mr Beaumaris for many years, permitted himself to give what in a lesser personage would have been a grin, and to say: "Well, sir, if I had *known* you wanted him chased off, I'm sure I'd have done my best! Not but what he's so devoted to you that I doubt if he'd have gone, setting aside that it would go to my heart to chase off a dog that handles Alphonse like this one does."

"If that misbegotten animal has been upsetting Alphonse, I'll wring his neck!" promised Mr Beaumaris.

"Oh, no, sir, nothing of that sort! When you're out, and Ulysses comes downstairs (as come he does), he behaves to Alphonse as though he hadn't had a bite to eat in a month, nor wouldn't think of touching so much as a scrap of meat he found on the kitchen floor. Well, as I said to Mrs Preston, if ever a dog could speak, that one does, telling Alphonse as plain as a Christian that he's the only friend he's got in the world. Quite won Alphonse over, he has. In fact, when two nice loin chops was found to be missing, Alphonse would have it the undercook was accusing the dog of having stolen them only to cover up his own carelessness, and Ulysses sitting there looking as if he didn't know what a chop tasted like. He buried the bones under the rug in your study, sir, but I have removed them."

"You are not only an ill-favoured specimen," Mr Beaumaris informed Ulysses severely, "but you have all the faults of the under-bred: toadeating, duplicity, and impudence!"

Ulysses sat down to relieve the irritation of a healing wound by a hearty scratch. He was rebuked, and since he had heard that note in Mr Beaumaris's voice before – as when he had expressed a vociferous desire to share his bedchamber with him – he stopped scratching, and flattened his ears placatingly.

Mr Beaumaris poured himself out a glass of wine, and sat down with it in his favourite chair. Ulysses sat before him, and sighed deeply. "Yes, I daresay," said Mr Beaumaris, "but I have something better to do than to spend my time spreading ointment on your sores. You should remember, moreover, that you cannot be permitted to meet your benefactress again until you are entirely healed." Ulysses yawned at him, and lay down with his head on his paws, as one who found the conversation tedious. Mr Beaumaris stirred him with one foot. "I wonder if you are right?" he mused. "A month ago I should have been sure of it. Yet I let her saddle me with a foundling-brat, and a mongrel-cur – you will forgive my plain speaking, Ulysses! – and I am now reasonably certain that neither of you is destined to be the most tiresome of my responsibilities. Do you suppose that that wretched youth is masquerading under a false name for reasons of his own, or in support of her pretensions? Do not look at me like that! You may consider that experience should have taught me wisdom, but I do not believe that it was all a clever plot to inveigle me into declaring myself. I am not even sure that she regards me with more than tolerance. In fact, Ulysses, I am not very sure of anything – and I think I will pay my grandmother a long overdue visit."

In pursuance of this resolve, Mr Beaumaris sent for his curricle next morning. Ulysses, who had shared his breakfast, bundled ahead of him down the steps of his house, leaped into the curricle, and disposed himself on the passenger's seat with all the air of a dog born into the purple.

"No!" said Mr Beaumaris forcibly. Ulysses descended miserably from the curricle, and prostrated himself on the flag-way. "Let me tell you, my friend," said Mr Beaumaris, "that I have a certain reputation to maintain, which your disreputable appearance would seriously jeopardize! Do not be alarmed! I am not, alas, going out of your life for ever!" He climbed into the curricle, and said: "You may stop grinning, Clayton, and let 'em go!"

"Yes, sir!" said his groom, obeying both these behests, and swinging himself expertly up on to the curricle as it passed him. After a minute or two, having twice glanced over his shoulder, he ventured to inform Mr Beaumaris that the little dog was following him.

Mr Beaumaris uttered an oath, and reined in his reluctant pair. The faithful hound, plodding valiantly along, with heaving ribs, and several inches of tongue hanging from his parted jaws, came up with the curricle, and once more abased himself in the road. "Damn you!" said Mr. Beaumaris. "I suppose you are capable of following me all the way to Wimbledon! It now remains to be seen whether my credit is good enough to enable me to carry you off. Get up!"

Ulysses was very much out of breath, but at these words he mustered up enough strength to scramble into the curricle once more. He wagged a grateful tail, climbed on to the seat beside Mr Beaumaris, and sat there panting blissfully. Mr Beaumaris read him a short lecture on the evils of blackmail, which sorely tried the self-control of his groom, discouraged him peremptorily from hurling a challenge at a mere pedestrian dog in the gutter, and proceeded on his way to Wimbledon.

The Dowager Duchess of Wigan, who was the terror of four sons, three surviving daughters, numerous grand-children, her man of business, her lawyer, her physician, and a host of dependants, greeted her favourite grandson characteristically. He found her imbibing nourishment in the form of slices of toast dipped in tea, and bullying the unmarried daughter who lived with her. She had been a great belle in her day, and the ravages of her former beauty were still discernible in the delicate bones of her face. She had a way of looking at her visitors with an eagle-like stare, had never been known to waste politeness on anyone, and was scathingly contemptuous of everything modern. Her children were inordinately proud of her, and lived in dread of her periodical commands to them to present themselves at her house. Upon her butler's ushering Mr Beaumaris into her morning-room, she directed one of her piercing looks at him, and said: "Oh! So it's you, is it? Why haven't you been to see me since I don't know when?"

Mr Beaumaris, bowing deeply over her hand, replied imperturbably: "On the occasion of my last visit, ma'am, you told me you did not wish to see me again until I had mended my ways."

"Well, have you?" said the Duchess, conveying another slip of soaked toast to her mouth.

"Certainly, ma'am: I am in a fair way to becoming a philanthropist," he replied, turning to greet his aunt.

"I don't want any more of *them* about me," said her grace. "It turns my stomach enough already to have to sit here watching Caroline at her everlasting knitting for the poor. In *my* day, we gave 'em vails, and there was an end to it. Not that I believe you. Here, take this pap away, Caroline, and ring the bell! Maudling one's inside with tea never did any good to anyone yet, and never will. I'll tell Hadleigh to fetch up a bottle of Madeira – the lot your grandfather laid down, not that rubbish Wigan sent me t'other day!"

Lady Caroline removed the tray, but asked her parent in a shrinking tone if she thought that Dr Sudbury would approve.

"Sudbury's an old woman, and you're a fool, Caroline!" replied the Duchess. "You go away, and leave me to talk to Robert! I never could abide a pack of females hangin' round me!" She added, as Lady Caroline gathered up her knitting: "Tell Hadleigh the *good* Madeira! He knows. Well, sir, what have you to say for yourself now you *have* had the impudence to show your face here again?"

Mr Beaumaris, closing the door behind his aunt, came back into the room, and said with deceptive meekness that he was happy to find his grandmother in such excellent health and spirits.

"Graceless jackanapes!" retorted the Duchess with relish. She ran her eye over his handsome person. "You look very well – at least, you would if you didn't make such a figure of yourself in that rig! When I was a girl, no gentleman would have dreamed of paying a social call without powder, let me tell you! Enough to make your grandfather turn in his grave to see what you've all come to, with your skimpy coats, and your starched collars, and not a bit of lace to your neckcloth, or your wristbands! If you can sit down in those skin-tight breeches, or pantaloons, or whatever you call 'em, do so!"

"Oh, yes, I can sit down!" said Mr Beaumaris, disposing himself in a chair opposite to hers. "My pantaloons, like Aunt Caroline's gifts to the poor, are knitted, and so adapt themselves reasonably well to my wishes."

"Ha! Then I'll tell Caroline to knit you a pair for Christmas. That'll send her into hysterics, for a bigger prude I never met!"

"Very likely, ma'am, but as I am sure that my aunt would obey you, however much her modesty was offended, I must ask you to refrain. The embroidered slippers which reached me last Christmas tried me high enough. I wonder what she thought I should do with them?"

The Duchess gave a cackle of laughter. "Lord bless you, she don't *think!* You shouldn't send her handsome gifts."

"I send you very handsome gifts," murmured Mr Beaumaris, "but you never reciprocate!"

"No, and I never shall. You've got more than's good for you already. What have you brought me this time?"

"Nothing at all – unless you have a fancy for a mongrel-dog?"

"I can't abide dogs, or cats either. Fifty thousand a year if you've a penny, and you don't bring me as much as a posy! Out with it, Robert! what did you come for?"

"To ask you whether you think I should make a tolerable husband, ma'am."

"What?" exclaimed her grace, sitting bolt upright in her chair, and grasping the arms with her frail, jewelled hands. "You're never going to offer for the Dewsbury girl?"

"Good God, no!"

"Oh, so that's yet another idiot who's wearing the willow for you, is it?" said her grace, who had her own ways of discovering what was going on in the world from which she had retired. "Who is it now? One of these days you'll go a step too far, mark my words!"

"I think I have," said Mr Beaumaris.

She stared at him, but before she could speak her butler had entered the room, staggering under a specimen of the ducal plate which her grace had categorically refused to relinquish to the present Duke, on the twofold score that it was her personal property, and that he shouldn't have married anyone who gave his mother such a belly-ache as that die-away ninny he had set in her place. This impressive tray Hadleigh set down on the table, casting, as he did so, a very expressive look at Mr Beaumaris. Mr Beaumaris nodded his understanding, and rose, and went to pour out the wine. He handed his grandmother a modest half-glass, to which she instantly took exception, demanding to know whether he had the impertinence to suppose that she could not carry her wine.

"I daresay you can drink me under the table," replied Mr Beaumaris, "but you know very well it's extremely bad for your health, and also that you cannot bully me into pandering to your outrageous commands." He then lifted her disengaged hand to his lips, and said gently: "You are a rude and an overbearing old woman, ma'am, but I hope you may live to be a hundred, for I like you so much better than any other of my relatives!"

"I daresay that's not saying much," she remarked, rather pleased by this audacious speech. "Sit down again, and don't try to hoax me with any of your faradiddles! I can see you're going to make a fool of yourself, so you needn't wrap it up in clean linen! You haven't come here to tell me you're going to marry that brass-faced lightskirt you had in keeping when I last saw you?"

"I have not!" said Mr Beaumaris.

"Just as well, for laced mutton being brought into the family is what I won't put up with! Not that I think you're fool enough for that."

"Where *do* you learn your abominable expressions, ma'am?" demanded Mr Beaumaris.

"I don't belong to your mealy-mouthed generation, thank God! Who is she?"

"If I did not know from bitter experience, ma'am, that nothing occurs in London but what you are instantly aware of it, I should say that you had never heard of her. She is – or at any rate, she says she is – the latest heiress."

"Oh! Do you mean the chit that that silly Bridlington woman, has staying with her? I'm told she's a beauty."

"She *is* beautiful," acknowledged Mr Beaumaris. "But that's not it."

"Well, what is it?"

He reflected. "She is the most enchanting little wretch I ever encountered," he said. "When she is trying to convince me that she is up to every move in the social game, she contrives to appear much like any other female, but when, as happens all too often for my comfort, her compassion is stirred, she is ready to go to any lengths to succour the object of her pity. If I marry her, she will undoubtedly expect me to launch a campaign for the alleviation of the lot of climbing-boys, and will very likely turn my house into an asylum for stray curs."

"Oh, she will, will she?" said her grace, staring at him with knit brows. "Why?"

"Well, she has already foisted a specimen of each on to me," he explained. "No, perhaps I wrong her. Ulysses she certainly foisted on to me, but the unspeakable Jemmy I actually offered to take under my protection."

The Duchess brought her hand down on the arm of her chair. "Stop trying to gammon me!" she commanded. "Who is Ulysses, and who is Jemmy?"

"I have already offered to make you a present of Ulysses," Mr Beaumaris reminded her. "Jemmy is a small climbing-boy whose manifest wrongs Miss Tallant is determined to set right. I wish you might have heard her telling Bridlington that he cared for nothing but his own comfort, like all the rest of us; and asking poor Charles Fleetwood to imagine what his state might now be had he been reared by a drunken foster-mother, and sold into slavery to a sweep. Alas that I was not privileged to witness her encounter with the sweep! I understand that she drove him from the house with threats of prosecution. I am not at all surprised that he cowered before her: I have seen her disperse a group of louts."

"She sounds to me an odd sort of a gal," remarked her grace. "Is she a lady?"

"Unquestionably."

"Who's her father?"

"That, ma'am, is a mystery I have hopes that you may be able to unravel."

"I?" she exclaimed. "I don't know what you think I can tell you!"

"I have reason to believe that her home is within easy reach of Harrowgate, ma'am, and I recall that you visited that watering-place not so very long ago. You may have seen her at an Assembly – I suppose they do have Assemblies at Harrowgate? – or have heard her family spoken of."

"Well, I didn't!" replied her grace bitterly. "What's more I don't want to hear anything more about Harrowgate! A nasty, cold, shabby-genteel place, with the filthiest waters I ever tasted in my life! They did me no good at all, as anyone but a fool like that snivelling leech of mine would have known from the outset! Assemblies, indeed! It's no pleasure to me to watch a parcel of country-dowds dancing this shameless waltz of yours! Dancing! *I* could give you another name for it!"

"I have no doubt that you could, ma'am, but I must beg you to spare my blushes! Moreover, for one who is for ever railing against the squeamishness of the modern miss, your attitude towards the waltz seems a trifle inconsistent."

"I don't know anything about consistency," retorted her grace, with perfect truth, "but I do know indecency when I see it!"

"We are wandering from the point," said Mr Beaumaris firmly.

"Well, I never met any Tallants in Harrowgate, or anywhere else. When I wasn't trying to swallow something that no one is ever going to make me believe wasn't drained off from the kennels, I was sitting watching your aunt knot a fringe in the most uncomfortable hole of a lodging I've been in yet! Why, I had to take all my own bed-linen with me!"

"You always do, ma'am," said Mr Beaumaris, who had several times been privileged to see the start of one of the Duchess's impressive journeys. "Also your own plate, your favourite chair, your steward, your -"

"I don't want any of your impudence, Robert!" interrupted her grace. "I don't always *have* to take 'em!" She gave her shawl a twitch. "It's nothing to me whom you marry," she said. "But why you must needs dangle after a wealthy woman beats me!"

"Oh, I don't think she has any fortune at all!" replied Mr Beaumaris coolly. "She only said she had to put me in my place."

He came under her eagle-stare again. "Put you in your place? Are you going to tell me, sir, that she ain't tumbling over herself to catch you?"

"Far from it. She holds me at arm's length. I cannot even be sure that she has even the smallest *tendre* for me."

"Been seen in your company often enough, hasn't she?" said her grace sharply.

"Yes, she says it does her a great deal of good socially to be seen with me," said Mr Beaumaris pensively.

"Either she's a devilish deep 'un," said her grace, a gleam in her eye, "or she's a good gal! Lord, I didn't think there was one of these niminy-piminy modern gals alive that had enough spirit not to toadeat you! Should I like her?"

"Yes, I think you would, but to tell you the truth, ma'am, I don't care a button whether you like her or not."

Surprisingly, she took no exception to this, but nodded, and said: "You'd better marry her. Not if she ain't of gentle blood, though. You ain't a Caldicot of Wigan, but you come of good stock. I wouldn't have let your mother marry into your family if it hadn't been one of the best – not for five times the settlements your father made on her!"

She added reminiscently: "A fine gal, Maria: I liked her better than any other of my brats."

"So did I," agreed Mr Beaumaris, rising from his chair. "Shall I propose to Arabella, risking a rebuff, or shall I address myself to the task of convincing her that I am not the incorrigible flirt she has plainly been taught to think me?"

"It's no use asking me," said her grace unhelpfully. "It wouldn't do you any harm to get a good set-down, but I don't mind your bringing the gal to see me one day." She held out her hand to him, but when he had punctiliously kissed it, and would have released it, her talon-like fingers closed on his, and she said: "Out with it, sir! What's vexing you, eh?"

He smiled at her. "Not precisely that, ma'am – but I have the stupidest wish that she would tell me the truth!"

"Pooh, why should she?"

"I can think of only one reason, ma'am. That is what vexes me!" said Mr Beaumaris.

CHAPTER TWELVE

ON HIS way home from Wimbledon, Mr Beaumaris drove up Bond Street, and was so fortunate as to see Arabella, accompanied by a prim-looking maidservant, come out of Hookham's Library. He pulled up immediately, and she smiled, and walked up to the curricle, exclaiming: "Oh, how much better he looks! I told you he would! Well, you dear little dog, do you remember me, I wonder?"

Ulysses wagged his tail in a perfunctory manner, suffered her to stretch up a hand to caress him, but yawned.

"For heaven's sake, Ulysses, try to acquire a little polish!" Mr Beaumaris admonished him.

Arabella laughed. "Is that what you call him? Why?"

"Well, he seemed, on the evidence, to have led a roving life, and judging by the example we saw it must have been adventurous," explained Mr Beaumaris.

"Very true!" She watched Ulysses look up adoringly into his face, and said: "I knew he would grow to be attached to you: only see how he looks at you!"

"His affection, Miss Tallant, threatens to become a serious embarrassment."

"Nonsense! I am sure you must be fond of him, or you would not take him out with you!"

"If that is what you think, ma'am, you can have no idea of the depths to which he can sink to achieve his own ends. Blackmail is an open book to him. He is well aware that I dare not deny him, lest I should lose what little reputation I may have in your eyes."

"How absurd you are! I knew, as soon as I saw how well you handled him, that you know just how to use a dog. I am so glad you have kept him with you."

She gave Ulysses a last pat, and stepped back on to the flag-way. Mr Beaumaris said: "Will you not give me the pleasure of driving you to your door?"

"No, indeed, it is only a step!"

"No matter: send your maid home! Ulysses adds his entreaties to mine."

As Ulysses chose this moment to scratch one ear, this made her laugh.

"Mere bashfulness," explained Mr Beaumaris, stretching down his hand. "Come!"

"Very well – since Ulysses wishes it so much!" she said, taking his hand, and climbing into the curricle. "Mr Beaumaris will see me home, Maria."

He spread a light rug across her knees, and said over his shoulder: "I have recalled, Clayton, that I need something from the chemist's. Go and buy me a – a gum-plaster! You may walk home."

"Very good, sir," said the groom, at his most wooden, and sprang down into the road.

"A *gum-plaster*?" echoed Arabella, turning wide eyes of astonishment upon Mr Beaumaris. "What in the world can you want with such a thing, sir?"

"Rheumatism," said Mr Beaumaris defiantly, setting his horses in motion.

"*You*? Oh, no, you must be quizzing me!"

"Not at all. I was merely seeking an excuse to be rid of Clayton. I hope Ulysses will prove himself an adequate chaperon. I have something to say to you, Miss Tallant, for which I do not desire an audience."

She had been stroking the dog, but her hands were stilled at this, and the colour receded from her cheeks. Rather breathlessly, she asked: "What is it?"

"Will you do me the honour of becoming my wife?"

She was stunned, and for a moment could not utter a word. When she was able to control her voice a little, she said: "I think you must be quizzing me."

"You must know that I am not."

She trembled. "Yes, yes, let us say that that was all it was, if you please! I am very much obliged to you, but I cannot marry you!"

"May I know why you cannot, Miss Tallant?"

She was afraid that she was about to burst into tears, and answered in a shaken tone: "There are many reasons. Pray believe it is impossible!"

"Are you quite sure that these reasons are insuperable?" he asked.

"Quite, quite sure! Oh, please do not urge me further! I had never dreamed – it never entered my head – I would not for the world have given you cause to suppose – Oh, *please* say no more, sir!"

He bowed, and was silent. She sat staring down at her clasped hands in great agitation of spirit, her mind in a turmoil, tossed between surprise at such a declaration, coming from one whom she had believed to have been merely amusing himself, and the shock of realizing, for the first time, that there was no one she would rather marry than Mr Beaumaris.

After a slight pause, he said in his usual calm way: "I believe there is always a little awkwardness attached to such situations as this in which we now find ourselves. We must strive not to allow it to overcome us. Is Lady Bridlington's ball to rank amongst the season's greatest squeezes?"

She was grateful to him for easing the tension, and all the discomfort of the moment, and tried to reply naturally. "Yes, indeed, it is! I am sure quite three hundred cards of invitation have been sent out. Shall – shall you find time to look in, I wonder?"

"Yes, and shall hope that even though you will not *marry* me you may be persuaded to *dance* with me."

She replied she scarcely knew what: it was largely inaudible. He shot a quick look at her averted profile, hesitated, and then said nothing. They had reached Park Street by this time, and in another moment he had handed her down from the curricle.

"Do not come with me to the door! I know you do not like to leave your horses!" she said, in a hurried tone. "Good-bye! I shall see you at the ball."

He waited until he had seen her admitted into the house, and then got into the curricle again, and drove off. Ulysses nudged his nose under his arm. "Thank you," he said dryly. "Do you think I am unreasonable to wish that she would trust me enough to tell me the truth?"

Ulysses sighed heavily; he was rather sleepy after his day in the country.

"I suppose I shall end by telling her that I have known it all along. And yet – Yes, Ulysses, I am quite unreasonable. Did it seem to you that she was not as indifferent to me as she would have had me believe?"

Understanding that something was expected of him, his admirer uttered a sound between a yelp and a bark, and furiously wagged his tail.

"You feel that I should persevere?" said Mr Beaumaris. "I was, in fact, too precipitate. You may be right. But if she had cared at all, would she not have told me the truth?"

Ulysses sneezed.

"At all events," remarked Mr Beaumaris, "she was undoubtedly pleased with me for bringing you out with me."

Whether it was due to this circumstance, or to Ulysses' unshakeable conviction that he was born to be a carriage-dog, Mr Beaumaris continued to take him about. Those of his intimates who saw Ulysses, once they had recovered from the initial shock, were of the opinion that the Nonpareil was practising some mysterious jest on society, and only one earnest imitator went so far as to adopt an animal of mixed parentage to ride in his own carriage. He thought that if the Nonpareil was setting a new fashion it would become so much the rage that it might be difficult hereafter to acquire a suitable mongrel. But Mr Warkworth, a more profound thinker, censured this act as being rash and unconsidered. "Remember when the Nonpareil wore a dandelion in his buttonhole three days running?" he said darkly.

"Remember the kick-up there was, with every saphead in town running round to all the flower-women for dandelions, which they hadn't got, of course. Stands to reason you couldn't buy dandelions! Why, poor Geoffrey drove all the way to Esher looking for one, and Altringham went to the trouble of rooting up half-a-dozen out of Richmond Park, and having a set-to with the keeper over it, and then planting 'em in his window-boxes. Good idea, if they *had* become the mode: clever fellow, Altringham! – but of course the Nonpareil was only hoaxing us! Once he had the whole lot of us decked out with them, he never wore one again, and a precious set of gudgeons we looked! Playing the same trick again, if you ask me!"

Only in one quarter did unhappy results arise from the elevation of Ulysses. The Honourable Frederick Byng, who had for years been known by the sobriquet of Poodle Byng from his habit of driving everywhere with a very highly-bred and exquisitely shaved poodle sitting up beside him, encountered Mr Beaumaris in Piccadilly one afternoon, and no sooner clapped eyes on his disreputable companion than he pulled up his horses all standing, and spluttered out: "What the devil –?"

Mr Beaumaris reined in his own pair, and looked enquiringly over his shoulder. Mr Byng, his florid countenance suffused by an angry flush, was engaged in backing his curricle, jabbing at his horses' mouths in a way that showed how greatly moved he was. Once alongside the other curricle, he glared at Mr Beaumaris, and demanded an explanation.

"Explanation of what?" said Mr Beaumaris. "If you don't take care, you'll go off in an apoplexy one of these days, Poodle! What's the matter?"

Mr Byng pointed a trembling finger at Ulysses. "What's the meaning of *that*?" he asked belligerently. "If you think I'll swallow any such damned insult --!

He was interrupted. The two dogs, who had been eyeing one another measuringly from their respective vehicles, suddenly succumbed to a mutual hatred, uttered two simultaneous snarls, and leaped for one another's throats. Since the curricles were too far apart to allow them to come to grips, they were obliged to vent their feelings in a series of hysterical objurgations, threats, and abuse, which drowned the rest of Mr Byng's furious speech.

Mr Beaumaris, holding Ulysses by the scruff of his neck, laughed so much that he could hardly speak: a circumstance which did nothing to mollify the outraged Mr Byng. He began to say that he should know how to answer an attempt to make him ridiculous, but was obliged to break off in order to command his dog to be quiet.

"No, no, Poodle, don't call me out!" said Mr Beaumaris, his shoulders still shaking. "Really, I had no such intention! Besides, we should only make fools of ourselves, going out to Paddington in the cold dawn to exchange shots over a pair of dogs!"

Mr Byng hesitated. There was much in what Mr Beaumaris said; moreover Mr Beaumaris was acknowledged to be one of the finest shots in England, and to call him out for a mere trifle would be an act of sheer foolhardiness. He said suspiciously: "If you're not doing it to make a laughing-stock of me, why *are* you doing it?"

"Hush, Poodle, hush! You are treading on delicate ground!" said Mr Beaumaris. "I cannot bandy a lady's name about in the open street!"

"What lady? I don't believe a word of it! Why can't you make that damned mongrel be quiet?"

In lamentable contrast to his well-trained adversary, who was now seated virtuously beside his master again, and affecting a maddening deafness, Ulysses, convinced that he had cowed the contemptible dandy, was hurling extremely ignoble taunts at him. Mr Beaumaris cuffed him, but although he cowered under the avenging hand he was quite unrepentant, and resumed his threats with unabated fervour.

"It is all jealousy, Poodle!" Mr Beaumaris said soothingly. "The hatred of the vulgar for the aristocrat! I think we had better part, don't you?"

Mr Byng gave an angry snort, and drove off. Mr Beaumaris released Ulysses, who shook himself, sighed his satisfaction, and looked up for approbation. "Yes, you will, I perceive, ruin me yet," said Mr Beaumaris severely. "If I am any judge of the matter, you picked your language up in the back-slums, and have probably been the associate of dustmen, coal-heavers, bruisers, and other such low persons! You are quite unfit for polite circles."

Ulysses lolled his tongue out, and grinned cheerfully.

"At the same time," said Mr Beaumaris, relenting, "I daresay you would have made mincemeat of the creature, and I must own that I am not entirely out of sympathy with you. But poor Poodle will certainly cut me for a week at least."

However, at the end of five days Mr Byng unbent, adopting a tolerant attitude towards Ulysses. It had been borne in upon him that to drive past the Nonpareil's curricle, staring rigidly ahead, was provocative of just the amusement amongst his acquaintances which he particularly wished to discourage.

Mr Beaumaris and Miss Tallant met again in the dazzling splendour of the Circular Room at Carlton House, on the night of the Regent's Dress-party. Arabella was so much impressed by the elegance of the sky-blue draperies, and the almost intolerable glare of a huge cut-glass chandelier, reflected, with its myriads of candles, in four large pier-glasses, that she momentarily forgot her last meeting with Mr Beaumaris, and greeted him by saying impulsively: "How do you do? I have never seen anything like it in my life! Each room is more magnificent than the last!"

He smiled. "Ah, but have you yet penetrated to the Conservatory, Miss Tallant? Our Royal host's *chef d'oeuvre*, believe me! Let me take you there!"

By this time she had recollected under what circumstances they had parted, so short a time previously, and her colour had risen. Many tears had been shed over the unhappy circumstance which had made it impossible for her to accept Mr Beaumaris's suit, and it had required all the excitement of a party at Carlton House to make her forget for one evening that she was the most miserable girl alive. She hesitated now, but Lady Bridlington was nodding and beaming, so she placed her hand on Mr Beaumaris's arm, and went with him through a bewildering number of apartments, all full of people, up the grand stairway, and through several saloons and antechambers. In the intervals of bowing to acquaintances, and occasionally exchanging a word of greeting, Mr Beaumaris entertained her with an account of Ulysses' quarrel with Mr Byng's poodle, and this made her laugh so much that a good deal of her constraint vanished. The Conservatory made her open her eyes very wide indeed, as well it might. Mr Beaumaris watched her, a look of amusement in his face, while she gazed silently round the extraordinary structure. Finally, she drew a breath, and uttered one of her unexpectedly candid remarks. "Well, I don't know why he should call it a Conservatory, for it is a great deal more like a cathedral, and a very bad one too!" she said.

He was delighted. "I thought you would be pleased with it," he said, with deceptive gravity.

"I am not at all pleased with it," replied Arabella severely. "Why is there a veil over that statue?"

Mr Beaumaris levelled his glass at Venus Asleep, under a shroud of light gauze. "I can't imagine," he confessed. "No doubt one of Prinny's flashes of taste. Would you like to ask him? Shall I take you to find him?"

Arabella declined the offer hastily. The Regent, an excellent host, had already managed to spend a minute or two in chat with nearly every one of his guests, and although Arabella was storing up the gracious words he had uttered to her, and meant to send home to the Vicarage an exact account of his amiability, she found conversation with such an exalted personage rather overpowering. So Mr Beaumaris took her back to Lady Bridlington, and after staying beside her for a few minutes was buttonholed by a gentleman in very tight satin knee-breeches, who lisped that the Duchess of Edgeware commanded his instant attendance. He bowed, therefore, to Arabella, and moved away, and although she several times afterwards caught a glimpse of him, he was always engaged with friends, and did not again approach her. The rooms began to seem hot, and overcrowded; the company the most boring set of people imaginable; and the vivacious, restless, and scintillating Lady Jersey, who flirted with Mr Beaumaris for quite twenty minutes, an odious creature.

Lady Bridlington's ball was the next social event of importance. This promised to be an event of more than ordinary brilliance, and although the late Lord Bridlington, to gratify an ambitious bride, had added a ballroom and a conservatory to the back of the house, it seemed unlikely that all the guests who had accepted her ladyship's invitation could be accommodated without a degree of over-crowding so uncomfortable as to mark the evening as an outstanding success. An excellent band had been engaged for the dancing, Pandean pipes were to play during supper, extra servants were hired, police-officers and link-boys warned to make Park Street their special objective, and refreshments to supplement the efforts of Lady Bridlington's distracted cook ordered from Gunter's. For days before the event, housemaids were busy moving furniture, polishing the crystal chandeliers, washing the hundreds of spare glasses unearthed from a storeroom in the basement, counting and recounting plates and cutlery, and generally creating an atmosphere of bustle and unrest in the house. Lord Bridlington, who combined an inclination for ceremonious hospitality with a naturally frugal mind, was torn between complacency at having drawn to his house all the most fashionable persons who adorned the *ton,* and a growing conviction that the cost of the party would be enormous. The bill for wax candles alone threatened to rise to astronomical heights, and not his most optimistic calculations of the number of glasses of champagne likely to be drunk reduced the magnums that must be ordered to a total he could contemplate with anything but gloom. But his self-esteem was too great to allow of his contemplating for more than a very few minutes the expedient of ekeing out the precious liquor by making it into an iced cup. Cups there must certainly be, as well as lemonade, orgeat, and such milder beverages as would please the ladies, but unless the party were to fall under the stigma of having been but a shabby affair after all the best champagne must flow throughout the evening in unlimited quantities. His mind not being of an order to question his own consequence, his gratification on the whole outweighed his misgivings, and if a suspicion did enter his head that he had Arabella to thank for the flattering number of acceptances which poured into the house, he was easily able to banish it. His mother, rather shrewder than he, gave honour where it was due, and, in a fit of reckless extravagance, was moved to order a new gown for Arabella from her own expensive dressmaker. But she was not, after all, so sadly out of pocket over the transaction, since a very few words whispered into the ear of Mme Dumaine were enough to convince that astute woman of business that the réclame of designing a toilette for the great Miss Tallant would fully justify her in making a substantial reduction in the price of a gown of figured lace over a white satin robe, with short, full, plaited sleeves, fastened down the front with pearl buttons to match the edging of pearls to the overdress. Arabella, ruefully surveying the depredations caused by a succession of parties to her glove-drawer, was obliged to purchase a new pair of long white gloves, as well as new satin sandals, and a length of silver net to drape round her shoulders in the style known as à l'Ariane. There was not very much left, by this time, of the Squire's handsome present to her; and when she considered how impossible her own folly had made it for her to requite her family's generosity in the only way open to a personable young female, she was overcome by feelings of guilt and remorse, and could not refrain from shedding tears. Nor could she refrain from indulging her fancy with the contemplation of the happiness which might even now have been hers, had she not allowed her temper to lead her so grossly to deceive Mr Beaumaris. This was a thought more bitter than all the rest, and it was only by the resolute exercise of her commonsense that she was able to regain some degree of calm. It was not to be supposed that the haughty Mr Beaumaris, related as he was to so many noble houses, so distinguished in his bearing, so much courted, and so much pursued, would ever have looked twice at a girl from a country Vicarage, with neither fortune nor connection to recommend her to his notice.

It was therefore with mixed feelings that Arabella awaited the arrival of the first guests on the appointed night. Lady Bridlington, thinking that she looked a little hagged (as well she might, after a week of such nerve-racking preparation) had tried to persuade her to allow Miss Crowle to rub a little – a very little! – rouge into her cheeks, but after one look at the result of this delicate operation Arabella had washed it away, declaring that never would she employ such aids to beauty as must, could he but see them, destroy for ever Papa's affection for his eldest daughter. Lady Bridlington pointed out, very reasonably, that there could be no fear of Papa's seeing them, but as

Arabella remained adamant, and showed alarming signs of being about to burst into tears, she pressed her no more, consoling herself with the reflection that even without her usual blooming colour her goddaughter could not fail to appear lovely in the exquisite gown of Mme Dumaine's making.

One cause at least for satisfaction was granted to Arabella: although some guests might arrive early, and leave betimes to attend another function; others walk in past two o'clock, having relegated Lady Bridlington's ball to the third place on their list of the evening's engagements, so that the ball was rendered chaotic by the constant comings and goings, and Park Street echoed hideously for hours to the shouts of My lord's carriage! or My lady's chair! and heated police-officers quarrelled with vociferous link-boys, and chairmen exchanged insults with coachmen, Bertram arrived punctually at ten o'clock, and nobly remained throughout the proceedings.

He had recklessly ordered an evening dress from the obliging Mr Swindon, rightly deeming the simple garments he had brought with him from Heythram quite inadequate to the occasion. Mr Swindon had done well by him, and when Arabella saw him mount the stairway between the banks of flowers which she had helped all day to revive by frequent sprinklings of water, her heart swelled with pride in his appearance. His dark blue coat set admirably across his shoulders; his satin knee-breeches showed scarcely a crease; and nothing could have been more chaste than his stockings or his waistcoat. With his dark, curly locks rigorously brushed into the fashionable Brutus, his handsome, aquiline countenance interestingly pale from the nervousness natural to a young gentlemen attending his first *ton* party, he looked almost as distinguished as the Nonpareil himself. Arabella, fleetingly clasping his hand, bestowed on him so speaking a look of admiration that he was betrayed into a grin so boyish and attractive as to cause another early arrival to demand of her companion, who was that handsome boy?

Emboldened by the intensive coaching of a noted French dancing-master, whom he had found the time to visit, he claimed his sister's hand for the first waltz, and, being a graceful youth, taught by the athletic sports at Harrow to move with precision and a complete control over his limbs, acquitted himself so well that Arabella was moved to exclaim: "Oh, Bertram, how elegantly you dance! Do, pray, let us make up a set for the quadrille, and dance together in it!"

This, however, he did not feel himself capable of doing. It was true that he had acquired the rudiments of the more simple steps, but he doubted his ability to go through the *grande monde* or the *pas de zéphyr* without muffing these figures. Gazing up into his face, it occurred to Arabella that he too was looking a trifle hagged. She anxiously asked him if he were quite well, and he assured her that he had never been better in his life, very creditably refraining from confiding to her that his adventurous career had made so deep a hole in his purse that the question of how he was to meet his liabilities had been causing him some sleepless nights. Since she had not seen him since a furtive assignation in the Mall one morning, under the vague chaperonage of the nursemaids who aired their charges there, and bought glasses of milk for them, fresh from the cows that lent so rural an air to the scene, she could not but feel uneasy about him. The faint rakishness that now hung about him did nothing to allay her fears, and she rather unjustly blamed Mr Scunthorpe for setting his feet upon a path Papa would certainly not have wished him to tread. She had formed no very favourable opinion of Mr Scunthorpe, and, with the praiseworthy notion of introducing Bertram into better company, made him known to one of the most disinterested of her admirers, young Lord Wivenhoe, heir to an affluent Earldom, and known to the greater part of London as Chuffy Wivenhoe, an affectionate sobriquet earned for him by his round, good-humoured countenance. This lively young nobleman, although he had not so far offered for her hand, formed one of Arabella's court, and was one of her favourites, being blessed with ingenuous manners, and an overflowing friendliness. She introduced Bertram to him with the best of intentions, but had she known that the engaging Chuffy had been reared by a misguided parent according to the principles laid down by the late Mr Fox's father, she might have refrained from so doing. In spite of every evidence to disprove them, the Earl of Chalgrove held Lord Holland's maxims in high esteem, and blandly encouraged his heir to indulge in every extravagance that captured his erratic fancy, discharging his gaming-debts as cheerfully as he discharged the bills that poured in from his tailor, his coachbuilder, his hatter, and a host of other tradesmen who enjoyed his patronage.

The two young gentlemen took an instant liking to one another. Lord Wivenhoe was some years Bertram's senior, but his mind was as youthful as his countenance, whereas Bertram's aquiline features, and superiority of intellectual attainment, added several years to his true age. They found themselves with much in common, and before they had enjoyed one another's society for more than a very few minutes had arranged to go together to a forthcoming race-meeting.

Meanwhile, Miss Tallant's pleasure in dancing with her young friend from Yorkshire had not passed unnoticed. Gloom was struck into several hearts that had cherished hopes of winning the heiress, for not the most sanguine amongst her suitors could persuade himself that she had ever smiled up into his face with such unshadowed affection as she bestowed upon Bertram, or had talked so much or so confidentially to him. It struck that acute observer, Mr Warkworth, that there was an elusive resemblance between the pair. He mentioned the matter to Lord Fleetwood, who had been so fortunate as to secure the promise of Arabella's hand for the quadrille, and was being incorrigibly blind to the claims of the less well-favoured damsels who had not been solicited to waltz, and were consequently chatting animatedly together in gilt chairs placed round the walls of the ballroom.

Lord Fleetwood stared hard at the Tallants for a minute or two, but could perceive no likeness, which, indeed, existed more in an occasional expression than in their lineaments. "No, dash it!" he said. "The little Tallant ain't got a beak of a nose!"

Mr Warkworth acknowledged it, and excused his lapse by explaining that it was only a sudden notion he had taken into his head.

Mr Beaumaris did not arrive until after midnight, and consequently failed to secure a waltz with Arabella. He seemed to be in one of his more inaccessible moods, and, having exerted himself to say a few civil things to his hostess, to dance once with a lady to whom she presented him, and once with his cousin, Lady Wainfleet, occupied himself in strolling through the various saloons, talking languidly to acquaintances, and surveying the company through his quizzing-glass with a faintly bored air. After about half-an-hour, when two sets were forming for a country-dance, he went in search of Arabella, who had disappeared from the ballroom in the direction of the conservatory, at the end of the last dance, accompanied by Mr Epworth, who protested that there had never been such a jam in the history of London balls, and offered to procure her a cooling glass of lemonade. Whether he redeemed this promise or not, Mr Beaumaris never knew, but when he walked into the conservatory a few minutes later, it was to find Arabella shrinking back in a chair in a state of the greatest discomfort, and trying to disengage her hands from the fervent clasp of Mr Epworth, romantically on his knees before her. Everyone else having left the conservatory to take their places in the new sets, the enterprising Mr Epworth, fortified by liberal doses of Lord Bridlington's champagne, had seized the opportunity once more to press his suit upon the heiress. Mr Beaumaris entered in time to hear her utter in a tone of distress: "Oh, pray do not! Mr Epworth, I implore you, get up! I am very much obliged to you, but I shall never, never change my mind! It is ungentlemanly of you to tease me like this!"

"Do try not to be such a dead bore, Epworth!" said Mr Beaumaris, with all his usual sangfroid. "I came to ask you if you would stand up with me for the next dance, Miss Tallant."

She was blushing furiously, and returned rather an incoherent answer. Mr Epworth, considerably mortified at having been found in such a posture by one whose contempt he dreaded, got to his feet, muttered something about taking his leave, and left the conservatory. Mr Beaumaris, taking her fan from Arabella's hand, unfurled it, and began gently to wave it beside her heated countenance. "How many times has he proposed to you?" he enquired conversably. "How very ridiculous he looked, to be sure!"

She was obliged to laugh, but said warmly: "He is the most odious little man, and seems to think he has only to persevere to make me receive his advances with complaisance!"

"You must make allowances for him," said Mr Beaumaris. "If he did not believe you to be a wealthy woman he would cease to trouble you."

Her bosom swelled; she said in a low, shaking voice: "Had it not been for *you* sir, he would never have known it!"

He was silent, as much from disappointment as from the rueful knowledge that although Fleetwood's had been the tongue which had spread the rumour, it had been his own idly malicious words which had convinced Fleetwood of the truth of Arabella's claim.

After a moment, she said in a subdued tone: "Shall we take our places in the set?"

"No, the numbers must by now be made up," he replied, continuing to fan her.

"Oh! Well – well, perhaps we should go back into the ballroom, at all events!"

"Don't be alarmed!" said Mr Beaumaris, with a touch of asperity. "I have not the smallest intention of embarrassing you by kneeling at your feet!"

Her colour rushed up again; she turned away her head in confusion, her lip slightly trembling. Mr Beaumaris shut the fan, and gave it back to her. He said gently: "I am not, I hope, such a coxcomb as to distress you by repeated solicitations, Miss Tallant, but you may believe that I am still of the same mind as I was when I made you an offer. If your sentiments should undergo a change, one word – one look! – would be sufficient to apprise me of it." She lifted her hand in a gesture imploring his silence. "Very well," he said. "I shall say no more on that head. But if you should stand in need of a friend at any time, let me assure you that you may depend upon me."

These words, delivered, as they were, in a more earnest tone than she had yet heard him use, almost made her heart stand still. She was tempted to take the risk of confessing the truth; hesitated, as the dread of seeing his expression change from admiration to disgust took possession of her; turned her eyes towards him; and then hurriedly rose to her feet, as another couple entered the conservatory. The moment was lost; she had time not only to recollect what might be the consequences if Mr Beaumaris treated her second confidence with no more respect than he had treated her first; but also to recall every warning she had received of the danger of trusting him too far. Her heart told her that she might do so, but her scared brain recoiled from the taking of any step that might lead to exposure, and to disgrace.

She went back into the ballroom with him; he relinquished her to Sir Geoffrey Morecambe, who came up to claim her; and within a very few minutes had taken leave of his hostess, and left the party.

CHAPTER THIRTEEN

BERTRAM'S ACQUAINTANCE with Lord Wivenhoe prospered rapidly. After a day spent together at the races, each was so well pleased with the other that further assignations were made. Lord Wivenhoe did not trouble to enquire into his new friend's age, and Bertram naturally did not confess that he was only just eighteen years old. Wivenhoe drove him to Epsom in his curricle, with a pair of dashing bays harnessed in the bar, and finding that Bertram was knowledgeable on the subject of horseflesh, good-naturedly offered to hand over the ribbons to him. So well did Bertram handle the pair, and at such a spanking pace did he drive them, showing excellent judgment in the feathering of his corners, and catching the thong of his whip just as the Squire had taught him, that he needed no other passport to Wivenhoe's favour. Any man who could control the kind of prime cattle his lordship liked must be a capital fellow. When he could do so without abating his cheerful conversation, he was clearly a right 'un, at home to a peg, and worthy of the highest regard. After some very interesting exchanges of reminiscences about incurable millers, roarers, lungers, half-bred blood-cattle, gingers, and slugs, which led inevitably to still more interesting stories of the chase, during the course of which both gentlemen found themselves perfectly in accord in their contempt of such ignoble persons as roadsters and skirters, and their conviction that the soundest of all maxims was, Get over the ground if it breaks your neck, formality was at an end between them, and his lordship was not only begging Bertram to call him Chuffy, as everyone else did, but promising to show him some of the rarer sights in town.

Bertram's fortunes, ever since he had come to London, had fluctuated in a bewildering manner. His first lucky evening with what he had swiftly learnt to refer to as St Hugh's Bones had started him off on a career that seriously alarmed his staider friend, Mr Scunthorpe. He had been encouraged by his luck to order a great many things from the various shops and warehouses where Mr Scunthorpe was known, and although a hat from Baxter's, a pair of boots from Hoby's, a seal from Rundell and Bridge, and a number of trifling purchases, such as a walking cane, a pair of gloves, some neckcloths, and some pomade for his hair were none of them really expensive, he had discovered, with a slight shock, that when added together they reached rather an alarming total. There was also his bill at the inn to be taken into account, but since this had not so far been presented he was able to relegate it to the very back of his mind.

The success of that first evening's play had not been repeated: in fact, upon the occasion of his second visit to the discreet house in Pall Mall he had been a substantial loser, and had been obliged to acknowledge that there might have been some truth in Mr Scunthorpe's dark warning. He was quite shrewd enough to realize that he had been a pigeon amongst hawks, but he was inclined to think that the experience would prove of immense value to him, since he was not one to be twice caught with the same lure. Playing billiards with Mr Scunthorpe at the Royal Saloon, he was approached by an affable Irishman, who applauded his play, offered to set him a main or two, or to accompany him to a snug little ken where a penchant for faro, or rouge-et-noir could be enjoyed. It was quite unnecessary for Mr Scunthorpe to whisper in his ear that this was a nibble from an ivory-turner: Bertram had no intention of going with the plausible Irishman, had scented a decoy the moment he saw him, and was very well pleased with himself for being no longer a flat, but, on the contrary, a damned knowing one. A pleasantly convivial evening at Mr Scunthorpe's lodging, with several rubbers of whist to follow an excellent dinner, convinced him that he had a natural aptitude for cards, a belief that was by no means shaken by the vicissitudes of fortune which followed this initiation. It would be foolish, of course, to frequent gaming-hells, but once a man had made friends in town there were plenty of unexceptionable places where he could enjoy every form of gaming, from whist to roulette. On the whole, he rather thought he was lucky at the tables. He was quite sure that he was lucky on the Turf, for he had several very good days. It began to be a regular habit with him to look in at Tattersall's, to watch how the sporting men bet their money there, and sometimes to copy them, in his modest way, or at others to back his own choice. When he became intimate with Chuffy Wivenhoe, he accompanied him often, either to advise him on the purchase of a prad, to watch some ruined man's breakdowns being sold, or to lay out his blunt on a forthcoming race. Once he had fallen into the way of going with Wivenhoe it was impossible to resist spending a guinea for the privilege of being made free of the subscription-room; and once the very safe man whom his lordship patronized saw the company he kept it was no longer necessary for him to do more than record his bets, just as the Bloods did, and wait for settling-day either to receive his gains, or to pay his losses. It was all so pleasant, and every day was so full of excitement, that it went to his head, and if he was sometimes seized by panic, and felt himself to be careering along at a pace he could no longer control, such frightening moments could not endure when Chuffy was summoning him to come and try the paces of a capital goer, or Jack Carnaby carrying him off to the theatre, or the Fives-court, or the Daffy Club. None of his new friends seemed to allow pecuniary considerations to trouble them, and since they all appeared to be constantly on the brink of ruin, and yet contrived, by some fortunate bet, or throw of the dice, to come about again, he began to fall insensibly into the same way of life, and to think that it was rustic to treat a temporary insolvency as more than a matter for jest. It did not occur to him that the tradesmen who apparently gave Wivenhoe and Scunthorpe unlimited credit would not extend the same consideration to a young man whose circumstances were unknown to them. The first hint he received of the different light in which he was regarded came in the form of a horrifying bill from Mr Swindon. He could not believe at first that he could possibly have spent so much money on two suits of clothes and an overcoat, but there did not seem to be any disputing Mr Swindon's figures. He asked Mr Scunthorpe, in an airy way, what he did if he could not meet his tailor's account. Mr Scunthorpe replied simply that he instantly ordered a new rig-out, but however much Bertram had been swept off his feet he retained enough native shrewdness to know that this expedient would not answer in his case. He tried to get rid of a very unpleasant feeling at the pit of his stomach by telling himself that no tailor expected to be paid immediately, but Mr. Swindon did not seem to be conversant with this rule. After a week he presented his bill a second time, accompanied by a courteous letter indicating that he would be much obliged by an early settlement of his account. And then, as though they had been in collusion with Mr Swindon, other tradesmen began to send in their bills, so that in less than no time one of the drawers in the dressing-table in Bertram's bedroom was stuffed with them. He managed to pay some of them, which made him feel much easier, but just as he was convincing himself that with the aid of a judicious bet, or a short run of luck, he would be able to clear himself from debt altogether, a polite but implacable gentleman called to see him, waited a good hour for him to come in from a ride in the Park, and then presented him with a bill which he said he knew had been overlooked. Bertram managed to get rid of him, but only by giving him some money on account, which he could ill-spare, and after an argument which he suspected was being listened to by the waiter hovering round the coffee-room door. This fear was shortly confirmed by the landlord's sending up his account with the Red Lion next morning. Matters were becoming desperate, and only one way of averting disaster suggested itself to Bertram. It was all very well for Mr Scunthorpe to advise against racing and gaming: what Mr Scunthorpe did not understand was that merely to abstain from these pastimes would in no way solve the difficulty. If Mr Scunthorpe found himself at Point Non Plus he had trustees who, however much they might rate him, would certainly come to his rescue. It was quite unthinkable that Bertram should appeal to his father for assistance: he would rather, he thought, cut his throat, for not only did the very thought of laying such a collection of bills before the Vicar appal him, but he knew very well that the settlement of them must seriously embarrass his father. Nor would it any longer be of any use to sell his watch, or that seal he had bought, or the fob that hung beside it from his waistband: in some inexplicable way his expenses seemed to have been growing ever larger since he had begun to frequent the company of men of fashion. A vague, and rather dubious notion of visiting a moneylender was vetoed by Mr Scunthorpe, who told him that since the penalties attached to the lending of money at interest to minors were severe, not even Jew King could be induced to advance the smallest sum to a distressed client under age. He added that he had once tried that himself, but that the cents-per-cent were all as sharp as needles, and seemed to smell out a fellow's age the moment they clapped eyes on him. He was concerned, though not surprised, to learn of Bertram's having got into Queer Street, and had the quarter not been so far advanced that he himself was at a standstill, he would undoubtedly have offered his friend instant relief, for he was one, his intimates asserted, who dropped his blunt like a generous fellow. Unfortunately he had no blunt to drop, and knew from past experience that an application to his trustees would result in nothing but unfeeling advice to him to rusticate at his house in Berkshire, where his Mama would welcome him with open arms. To do him justice, Bertram would have been exceedingly reluctant to have accepted pecuniary assistance from any of his friends, since he saw no prospect, once he had returned to Yorkshire, of being able to reimburse them. There was only one way of getting clear, and that was the way of the Turf and the Table. He knew it to be hazardous, but as he could not see that it was possible for him to be in a worse case than he was already, it was worth the risk. Once he had paid his debts he rather thought that he should bring his visit to London to an end, for although he had enjoyed certain aspects of it enormously, he by no means enjoyed insolvency, and was beginning to realize that to stand continually on the edge of a financial precipice would very soon reduce him to a nervous wreck. An interview with a creditor who was not polite at all, but, on the contrary, extremely threatening, had shaken him badly: unless he made a speedy recovery it could only be a matter of days before the tipstaffs would be on his heels, even as Mr Scunthorpe had prophesied.

It was at this stage in his career that two circumstances occurred which seemed to hold out hopes of delivery. A fortunate evening playing faro for modest stakes encouraged him to think that his luck had turned again; and Chuffy Wivenhoe, earwigged by a jockey at Tattersall's, passed on to him the name of the certain bet thus disclosed. It really seemed as though Providence was at last aiding Bertram. It would be madness not to bet a substantial amount on the horse, for if it won he would have solved all his difficulties at one blow, and would have enough money left over to pay for his fare back to Yorkshire on the stage-coach. When Wivenhoe laid his own bet, he followed suit, and tried not to think of the predicament he would be in on settling-day if that infallible jockey had for once in his life been mistaken in his judgment.

"I'll tell you what, Bertram," said Wivenhoe, as they strolled out of the subscription-room together, "if you should care for it, I'll take you along with me to the Nonesuch Club tonight: all the go, y'know, and devilish exclusive, but they'll let you in if you come with me."

"What is it?" Bertram asked.

"Oh, faro and hazard, for the most part! It was started by some of the great guns only this year, because Watier's is becoming damned flat: they say it won't last much longer – never been the same since Brummell had to run for it! The Nonesuch is devilish good sport, I can tell you. There ain't many rules, for one thing, and though most of the men bet pretty heavily, the patrons fixed the minimum stake at twenty guineas, and there's only one faro-table. What's more, it ain't a shabby business enterprise, like half the gaming-clubs, and if you want to play hazard you appoint the croupier from amongst your set, and someone will always volunteer to call the odds. None of these paid croupiers and groom-porters, which make the Great Go more like a hotel than a social club. The whole idea is to make it a friendly affair, keep out the scaff and raff, and do away with all the rules and regulations which get to be such a dead bore! For instance, there's no damned syndicate running the faro-bank: they take it in turns, the well-breeched swells, like Beaumaris, and Long Wellesley Pole, and Golden Ball, and Petersham, and the rest of that set. Oh, it's the Pink of the Mode, I can tell you top-of-the-trees!"

"I'd like to go with you," Bertram said, "only – Well, the fact is I'm none too plump in the pocket just now! Had a shocking run of luck!"

"Oh, no need to fret over that!" said his insouciant friend. "I keep telling you it ain't like Watier's! No one cares whether you bet twenty guineas or a hundred! You come: a man's luck is bound to change if he sticks to it – one of the things my governor told me, and *he* should know!"

Bertram was undecided, but since he was already engaged to dine at Long's Hotel with Lord Wivenhoe there was no need for him to return a definite answer to the invitation until he had thought it over rather more carefully. His lordship said that he should depend upon him, and there the matter for the moment rested.

It was not to be supposed that Bertram's protracted sojourn in London was causing his sister no anxiety. Arabella was very anxious indeed, for although she was not taken into his confidence she could not doubt, from his appearance, that he was spending money far more lavishly than the winning of a hundred pounds in a lottery justified him in doing. She seldom set eyes on him, and when they did meet she could not think that he was looking well. Late nights, unaccustomed potations, and worry, were taking their toll. But when she told him that he was looking fagged to death, and implored him to return to Yorkshire, he was able to retort with a good deal of truth that she was not particularly blooming herself. It was true. Her bright colour had faded a little, and her eyes had begun to seem a trifle large for her face, etched in, as they were, with shadows. Lord Bridlington, observing this, ascribed it to the absurd exigencies of a London season, and moralized on the folly of females with social ambitions. His mother, who had not failed to take note of the fact that her charge was no longer driving in the Park so frequently with Mr Beaumaris, and had developed a habit of evading his visits to the house, drew more correct conclusions, but failed signally to induce Arabella to confide in her. Whatever Frederick chose to say, Lady Bridlington was by this time convinced that the Nonpareil was very much in earnest, and she could not imagine what could be holding Arabella back from encouraging his advances. Divining that her reasons would be quite inexplicable to the good lady, Arabella preferred to keep her own counsel.

It had not escaped the notice of the Nonpareil that his tiresome love was not enjoying her customary good-looks and spirits, nor was it unknown to him that she had lately refused three advantageous offers of marriage, since the rejected suitors made no secret of the fact that their hopes were quite cut-up. She had excused herself from dancing with him at Almack's, but three times during the course of the evening he had been aware that her eyes were following him.

Mr Beaumaris, rhythmically drawing Ulysses' flying ear through his hand – a process which reduced Ulysses to a state of blissful idiocy – said meditatively: "It is a melancholy reflection, is it not, that at my age I can be such a fool?"

Ulysses, his eyes half-closed, his senses swooning in ecstasy, gave a sigh which his god might, if he chose, interpret as one of sympathy.

"What if she proves to be the daughter of a tradesman?" said Mr Beaumaris. "I do owe something to my name, you know. It might even be worse, and surely I am too old to be losing my head for a pretty face!"

Since his hand was still, Ulysses nudged him. Mr Beaumaris resumed his steady pulling of that shameful ear, but said: "You are quite right: it is not her pretty face. Do you believe her to be entirely indifferent to me? Is she really afraid to confess the truth to me? She must not be – no, Ulysses, she must not be! Let us look on the darker side! Is she ambitious to acquire a title? If that is so, why, then, has she sent poor Charles to the rightabout? You believe her to be aiming higher? But she cannot suppose that Witney will come up to scratch! Nor do I think that your suspicions are correct, Ulysses."

Ulysses, catching the note of severity in his voice, cocked an anxious eye at him. Mr Beaumaris took his muzzle in his hand, and gently shook it. "What do you advise me to do?" he asked. "It appears to me that I have reached Point Non Plus. Should I -" He broke off, and rose suddenly to his feet, and took a turn about the room. "What a saphead I am!" he said. "Of course! Ulysses, your master is a fool!" Ulysses jumped up to place his forepaws against those elegant pantaloons, and uttered a protesting bark. All this walking about the room, when Mr Beaumaris might have been better employed, was not at all to his taste. "Down!" commanded Mr Beaumaris. "How many more times am I to request you not to sully the purity of my garments by scrabbling at them with your ignoble, and probably dirty, paws? Ulysses, I shall be leaving you for a space!"

Ulysses might find this a little beyond him, but he fully understood that his hour of bliss was at an end, and so lay down in an attitude of resignation. Mr Beaumaris's subsequent actions filled him with vague disquiet, for although he was unacquainted with the significance of portmanteaux, some instinct warned him that they boded no good to little dogs. But these inchoate fears were as nothing when compared to the astonishment, chagrin, and dismay suffered by that peerless gentleman's gentleman, Mr Painswick, when he apprehended that his employer proposed to leave town without the support and expert ministration of a valet whom every Tulip of Fashion had at one time or another attempted to suborn from his service. He had accepted with equanimity the information that his master was going out of town for perhaps as much as a week, and was already laying out, in his mind, the raiment suitable for a sojourn at Wigan Park, or Woburn Abbey, or Belvoir, or perhaps Cheveley, when the full horror of the event burst upon him. "Put up enough shirts and neckcloths to last me for seven days," said Mr Beaumaris. "I'll travel in riding-dress, but you may as well pack the clothes I have on, in case I should need them. I shan't take you with me."

It took a full minute for the sense of this pronouncement to penetrate to the mind of his valet. He was shocked, and could only gaze at Mr Beaumaris in stupefaction.

"Tell 'em to have my travelling-chaise, and the bays, at the door by six o'clock," said Mr Beaumaris. "Clayton can accompany me for the first couple of stages, and bring the horses home."

Mr Painswick found his voice. "Did I understand you to say, sir, that you would not be requiring Me?" he asked.

"You did," responded Mr Beaumaris.

"May I enquire, sir, who then is to wait upon you?" demanded Mr Painswick, in a voice of ominous quiet.

"I am going to wait upon myself," replied Mr Beaumaris.

Mr Painswick accorded this attempt at humour the perfunctory smile it deserved. "Indeed, sir? And who, if you please, will press your coat for you?"

"I suppose they are accustomed to pressing coats at the posting-houses," said Mr Beaumaris indifferently.

"If you can call it pressing," said Mr Painswick darkly. "whether you will be pleased with the result, sir, is, if I may be permitted to say so, Another Matter."

Mr Beaumaris then said something so shocking that it gave his henchman, as he afterwards reported to Brough, a Very Nasty Spasm. "I daresay I shan't," he said, "but it won't signify."

Mr Painswick looked searchingly at him. He did not bear the appearance of one bordering on delirium, but there could be little doubt that his case was serious. Mr Painswick spoke in the tone of one soothing a refractory patient. "I think, sir, it will be best for me to accompany you."

"I have already told you that I don't need you. You may have a holiday."

"I should not, sir, have the Heart to enjoy it," returned Mr Painswick, who invariably spent his holidays in indulging nightmareish visions of his understudy's sending Mr Beaumaris forth with his clothes improperly brushed, his boots dulled by neglect, or, worst of all, a speck of mud on the skirts of his driving-coat. "If I may say so without offence, sir, you cannot Go Alone!"

"And if *I* may say so without offence, Painswick," retorted Mr Beaumaris, "you are being foolish beyond permission! I will readily own that you keep my clothes in excellent order – I should not continue to bear with you, if you did not – and that the secret of imparting a gloss to my Hessians, which you so jealously guard, makes you not wholly undeserving of the extortionate wage I pay you; but if you imagine that I am unable to dress myself creditably without your assistance, your powers of self-deception must be greater than even I was aware of! Upon occasion – and merely to reward you! – I have permitted you to shave me; I allow you to help me into my coats, and to hand me my neckcloth. But at no time, Painswick, have I allowed you to dictate to me what I should wear, to brush my hair, or to utter a word – a sound! while I am engaged in arranging that neckcloth! I shall do very well without you. But you must put up enough neckcloths to allow for some failures."

Mr Painswick swallowed these insults, but tried one last, desperate throw. "Your Boots, sir! You will never use a jack!"

"Certainly not," said Mr Beaumaris. "Some menial shall pull them off for me."

Mr Painswick gave a groan. "With greasy hands, sir! And only I know what it means to get a thumb-mark off your Hessians!"

"He shall handle them through gloves," promised Mr Beaumaris. "You need not lay out my knee-breeches: I am going to the Nonesuch Club tonight." He added, possibly to atone for his harshness: "Don't wait up for me, but call me at five o'clock tomorrow morning!"

Mr Painswick responded in a voice trembling with suppressed passion: "If, sir, you choose to dispense with my services upon your journey, I am sure it is not for me to utter a word of criticism, nor would I so far demean myself as to remonstrate with you, whatever my feelings may be. But retire from my post before I have put you to bed, sir, and removed your raiment for proper attention, nothing will prevail upon me to do!"

"As you please," said Mr. Beaumaris, unmoved. "Far be it from me to interfere in your determination to become a martyr in my cause!"

Mr Painswick could only throw him a look of searing reproach, being, as he afterwards confided to Brough, unable to trust himself to say more. It had been Touch and Go with him, he said, whether he remained another day in the service of one so lost to the sense of what was due to himself and his valet. Brough, who was perfectly well-aware that wild horses would not have parted his colleague from Mr Beaumaris, sympathized in suitable terms, and produced a bottle of Mr Beaumaris's second-best port. The healing properties of port, when mixed with a judicious quantity of gin, soon exercised a beneficial effect upon Mr Painswick's wounded feelings, and remarking that there was nothing like a glass of flesh-and-blood for setting a man up, he settled down to discuss with his crony and rival all the possible reasons that might be supposed to underlie Mr Beaumaris's rash and unbecoming conduct.

Mr Beaumaris, meanwhile, after dining at Brooks's, strolled across St James's Street towards Ryder Street, where the Nonesuch Club was established. Thus it was that when, rather later in the evening, Bertram Tallant entered the faro-room under the protective chaperonage of Lord Wivenhoe, Mr Beaumaris was afforded an excellent opportunity of estimating in just what manner Miss Tallant's enterprising young relative had been spending his time in London.

Two circumstances had decided Bertram in favour of visiting the Nonesuch Club. The first was the news that that sure winner, Fear-not-Victorious, had been unplaced in his race; the second the discovery of a twenty-pound bill amongst the tangle of accounts in the dressing-table. Bertram had sat staring at it quite numbly for some minutes, not even wondering how he had come to mislay it. He had suffered a terrible shock, for he had argued himself into believing that Fear-not-Victorious was bound to win, and had not seriously considered how he was to meet his creditor at Tattersall's on Monday if the animal were unplaced. The utter impossibility of meeting him at all burst upon him with shattering effect, so that he felt sick with apprehension, and could see nothing but a hideous vision of the Fleet Prison, where he would no doubt languish for the rest of his days, since it did not appear to him that his father could be expected to do more for so depraved a son than to expunge his name from the family tree, and forbid all mention of him at the Vicarage.

Rendered reckless by this last and most crushing blow, he rang the bell for the waiter, and demanded a bottle of brandy. It was then borne in upon him that orders had been issued in the tap not to supply him with any liquor for which he did not put down his blunt. Flushing darkly, he drove his hand into his breeches' pocket, and dragged out his last remaining handful of coins. Throwing one of these on the table, he said: "Fetch it, damn you! – and you may keep the change!"

This gesture a little relieved his feelings, and the first glass of brandy, tossed at one gulp down his throat, had a still more heartening effect upon him. He looked again at the twenty-pound bill, still clasped between his fingers. He remembered that Chuffy had named twenty pounds as the minimum stake permitted to punters at the Nonesuch. Such a coincidence was surely too marked to be ignored. The second glass of brandy convinced him that here in his hand lay his last chance of saving himself from irretrievable ruin and disgrace.

Not being accustomed to drinking neat brandy, he was obliged before setting out for Long's Hotel to swallow a damper in the form of a glass of porter. This had a sobering effect, and the walk through the streets to Long's put him in tolerable shape to do justice to *maintenon* cutlets, and the hotel's famed Queensberry hock. He had made up his mind to be guided by Fate. He would lay down his twenty guineas upon a card chosen at random from the livret: if it turned up, he would take it for a sign that his luck had changed at last, and play on until he had covered all his debts; if it lost, he would be very little worse off than he was already, and could, at the worst, cut his throat, he supposed.

When he and Lord Wivenhoe entered the faro-room at the Nonesuch, Mr Beaumaris, holding the bank, had just completed a deal, and had tossed the pack on to the floor. He raised his eyes, as a waiter laid a fresh pack before him, and looked straight across to the door. The lure of hazard had drawn all but one other of the club's doyens from the room, and that one, Lord Petersham, was lost in one of his fits of deep abstraction.

Damn Petersham! thought Mr Beaumaris, on the horns of a dilemma. Why must he choose this of all moments to dream of tea?

That amiable but vague peer, perceiving Lord Wivenhoe, smiled upon him with the doubtful air of one who seemed to recollect seeing his face before. If he took notice of a youthful stranger within the sacred precincts of the club, he gave no sign of it. Mr. Warkworth stared very hard at Bertram, and then glanced towards the head of the table. Lord Fleetwood, filling his glass, frowned, and also looked to the Nonpareil.

Mr Beaumaris gave an order to the waiter to bring him another bottle of burgundy. One blighting word from him, and the stranger would have nothing to do but bow himself out with what dignity he could muster. There was the rub: the boy would be unbearably humiliated, and one could not trust that young fool, Wivenhoe, to smooth over the rebuff. He would be far more likely to kick up a dust over the exclusion of one of his friends, placing the unhappy Bertram in a still more intolerable position.

Lord Wivenhoe, finding places for himself and Bertram at the table, was casually making Bertram known to his neighbours. One of these was Fleetwood, who favoured Bertram with a curt nod, and again looked under his brows at the Nonpareil; the other, like most of the men in the room, was content to accept any friend of Chuffy's without question. One of the older men said something under his breath about babes and sucklings, but not loudly enough to be overheard.

Mr Beaumaris glanced round the table. "Stakes, gentlemen," he said calmly.

Bertram, who had changed his bill for one modest rouleau, thrust it in a quick movement towards the queen in the livret. Other men were placing their bets; someone said something which made his neighbour laugh; Lord Petersham sighed deeply, and deliberately pushed forward several large rouleaus, and ranged them about his chosen cards; then he drew a delicately enamelled snuff-box from his pocket, and helped himself to a pinch of his latest blend. A pulse was beating so hard in Bertram's throat that it almost hurt him; he swallowed, and fixed his eyes on Mr Beaumaris's hand, poised above the pack before him.

The boy has been having some deep doings, thought Mr Beaumaris. Shouldn't wonder if he's rolled-up! What the devil possessed Chuffy Wivenhoe to bring him here?

The bets were all placed; Mr Beaumaris turned up the first card, and placed it to the right of the pack.

"Scorched again!" remarked Fleetwood, one of whose bets stood by the card's counterpart.

Mr Beaumaris turned up the Carte Anglaise, and laid it down to the left of the pack. The Queen of Diamonds danced before Bertram's eyes. For a dizzy moment he could only stare at the card; then he looked up, and met Mr Beaumaris's cool gaze, and smiled waveringly. That smile told Mr Beaumaris quite as much as he had need to know, and did nothing to increase his enjoyment of the evening ahead of him. He picked up the rake beside him, and pushed two twenty-guinea rouleaus across the table. Lord Wivenhoe called for wine for himself and his friend, and settled down to plunge with his usual recklessness.

For half-an-hour the luck ran decidedly in Bertram's favour, and Mr

Beaumaris was encouraged to hope that he would rise from the table a winner. He was drinking fairly steadily, a flush of excitement in his cheeks, his eyes, glittering a little in the candlelight, fixed on the cards. Lord Wivenhoe sat cheerfully losing beside him. He was soon punting on tick, scrawling his vowels, and tossing them over to the bank. Other men, Bertram noticed, did the same. There was quite a pile of paper before Mr Beaumaris.

The luck veered. Three times did Bertram bet heavily on the bank's card. He was left with only two rouleaus, and staked them both, sure that the bank could not win his money four times in succession. It could. To his own annoyance, Mr Beaumaris turned up the identical card.

From then on, he accepted, with an unmoved countenance, vowel upon vowel from Bertram. It was quite impossible to tell the boy either that he would not take his vouchers, or that he would be well-advised to go home. It was even doubtful whether Bertram would have listened to him. He was in the grip of a gamester's madness, betting recklessly, persuaded by one lucky chance that the luck smiled upon him again, convinced when he lost that ill-fortune could not last. That he had the least idea of the sum he already owed the bank, Mr Beaumaris cynically doubted.

The evening broke up rather earlier than usual, Mr Beaumaris having warned the company that he did not sit after two o'clock, and Lord Petersham sighing that he did not think he should take the bank over tonight. Wivenhoe, undaunted by his losses, said cheerfully: "In the basket again! What do I owe, Beaumaris?"

Mr Beaumaris silently handed his vowels to him. While his lordship did rapid sums in mental addition, Bertram, the flush dying out of his cheeks, sat staring at the paper still lying in front of Mr Beaumaris. He said jerkily: "And I?" and stretched out his hand.

"Dipped, badly dipped!" said Wivenhoe, shaking his head. "I'll send you a draught on my bank, Beaumaris. The devil was in it tonight!"

Other men were totting up their losses; there was a noise of lighthearted conversation dinning in Bertram's ears; he found that his vowels totalled six hundred pounds, a sum that seemed vast to him, almost incredible. He pulled himself together, pride coming to his rescue, and rose. He looked very white now, and ridiculously boyish, but he held his head well up, and spoke to Mr Beaumaris perfectly calmly. "I may have to keep you waiting for a few days, sir," he said. "I-I have no banking accommodation in London, and must send to Yorkshire for funds!"

What do I do now? wondered Mr Beaumaris. Tell the boy the only use I have for his vowels is as shaving-papers? No: he would enact me a Cheltenham tragedy. Besides, the fright may do him a world of good. He said: "There is no hurry, Mr Anstey. I am going out of town tomorrow for a week, or five days. Come and see me at my house – let us say, next Thursday. Anyone will tell you my direction. Where are you putting up?"

Bertram replied mechanically: "At the Red Lion, in the City, sir."

"Robert!" called Fleetwood, from the other side of the room, where he was engaged in a lively argument with Mr Warkworth. "Robert, come and bear me out! *Robert!*"

"Yes, in a moment!" Mr Beaumaris returned. He detained Bertram a moment longer. "Don't fail!" he said. "I shall expect to see you on

Thursday."

He judged it to be impossible to say more, for there were people all round them, and it was plain that the boy's pride would not brook a suggestion that his gaming-debts should be consigned to the flames.

But he was still frowning when he reached his house, some time later. Ulysses, gambolling and squirming before him, found that his welcome was not receiving acknowledgment, and barked at him. Mr Beaumaris bent, and patted him absentmindedly. "Hush! I am not in the mood for these transports!" he said. "I was right when I told you that you were not destined to be the worst of my responsibilities, was I not? I think I ought to have set the boy's mind at ease: one never knows, with boys of that age – and I didn't like the look in his face. All to pieces, I have little doubt. At the same time, I'll be damned if I'll go out again at this hour of night. A night's reflection won't hurt him."

He picked up the branch of candles that stood upon the hall-table, and carried it into his study, and to his desk by the window. Seeing him sit down, and open the ink-standish, Ulysses indicated his sentiments by yawning loudly. "Don't let me keep you up!" said Mr Beaumaris, dipping a pen in the standish, and drawing a sheet of paper towards himself.

Ulysses cast himself on the floor with a flop, gave one or two whines, bethought him of a task left undone, and began zealously to clean his forepaws.

Mr Beaumaris wrote a few rapid lines, dusted his sheet, shook off the sand, and was just about to fold the missive, when he paused. Ulysses looked up hopefully. "Yes, in a minute," said Mr Beaumaris. "If he has quite outrun the constable -" He laid down the paper, drew out a fat pocket-book from his inner pocket, and extracted from it a bill for a hundred pounds. This he folded up in his letter, sealed the whole with a wafer, and directed it. Then he rose, and to Ulysses' relief indicated that he was now ready to go to bed. Ulysses, who slept every night on the mat outside his door, and regularly, as a matter of form, challenged Painswick's right to enter that sacred apartment each morning, scampered ahead of him up the stairs. Mr Beaumaris found his valet awaiting him, his expression a nice mixture of wounded sensibility, devotion to duty, and long-suffering. He gave the sealed letter into his hand. "See that that is delivered to a Mr Anstey, at the Red Lion, somewhere in the City, tomorrow morning," he said curtly. "In person!" he added.

CHAPTER FOURTEEN

NOT FOR three days did any news of the disaster which had overtaken Bertram reach his sister. She had written to beg him to meet her by the Bath Gate in the Green Park, and had sent the letter by the Penny Post. When he neither appeared at the rendezvous, nor replied to her letter, she began to be seriously alarmed, and was trying to think of a way of visiting the Red Lion without her godmother's knowledge when Mr Scunthorpe sent up his card, at three o'clock one afternoon. She desired the butler to show him into the drawing-room, and went down immediately from her bedchamber to receive him.

It did not at once strike her that he was looking preternaturally solemn; she was too eager to learn tidings of Bertram, and went impetuously towards him with her hand held out, exclaiming: "I am so very glad you have called to see me, sir! I have been so much worried about my brother! Have you news of him? Oh, do not tell me he is ill?"

Mr Scunthorpe bowed, cleared his throat, and grasped her hand spasmodically. In a somewhat throaty voice he replied: "No, ma'am. Oh, no! Not *ill*, precisely!"

Her eyes eagerly scanned his face. She now perceived that his countenance wore an expression of deep melancholy, and felt immediately sick with apprehension. She managed to say: "Not – not *dead*?"

"Well, no, he ain't dead," replied Mr Scunthorpe, but hardly in reassuring tones. "I suppose you might say it ain't as bad as that. Though, mind you, I wouldn't say he won't be dead, if we don't take care, because when a fellow takes to – But never mind that!"

"Never mind it?" cried Arabella, pale with alarm. "Oh, what can be the matter? Pray, pray tell me instantly!"

Mr Scunthorpe looked at her uneasily. "Better have some smelling-salts," he suggested. "No wish to upset a lady. Nasty shock. Daresay you'd like a glass of hartshorn and water. Ring for a servant!"

"No, no, I need nothing! Pray do not! Only put me out of this agony of suspense!" Arabella implored him, clinging with both hands to the back of a chair.

Mr Scunthorpe cleared his throat again. "Thought it best to come to you," he said. "Sister. Happy to be of service myself, but at a standstill. Temporary, of course, but there it is. Must tow poor Bertram out of the River Tick!"

"River?" gasped Arabella.

Mr Scunthorpe perceived that he had been misunderstood. He made haste to rectify this. "No, no, not drowned!" he assured her. "Swallowed a spider!"

"Bertram has swallowed a spider?" Arabella repeated, in a dazed voice.

Mr Scunthorpe nodded. "That's it," he said. "Blown up at Point Non Plus. Poor fellow knocked into horse-nails!"

Arabella's head was by this time in such a whirl that she was uncertain whether her unfortunate brother had fallen into the river, or had been injured in some explosion, or was, more mildly, suffering from an internal disorder. Her pulse was tumultuous; the most agitating reflections made it impossible for her to speak above a whisper. She managed to utter: "Is he dreadfully hurt? Have they taken him to a hospital?"

"Not a case for a hospital, ma'am," said Mr Scunthorpe. "More likely to be screwed up."

This pronouncement, conjuring up the most horrid vision of a coffin, almost deprived Arabella of her senses. Her eyes started at Mr Scunthorpe in a look of painful enquiry. "Screwed up?" she repeated faintly.

"The Fleet," corroborated Mr Scunthorpe, sadly shaking his head. "Told him how it would be. Wouldn't listen. Mind, if the thing had come off right, he could have paid down his dust, and no harm done. Trouble was, it didn't. Very rarely does, if you ask me."

The gist of this speech, gradually penetrating to Arabella's understanding, brought some of the colour back to her face. She sank into a chair, her legs trembling violently, and said. "Do you mean he is in *debt*?"

Mr Scunthorpe looked at her in mild surprise. "Told you so, ma'am!" he pointed out.

"Good God, how could I possibly guess –? Oh, I have been so afraid that something of the sort must happen! Thank you for coming to me, sir! You did very right!"

Mr Scunthorpe blushed. "Always happy to be of service!"

"I must go to him!" Arabella said. "Will you be so kind as to escort me? I do not care to take my maid on such an errand, and I think perhaps I should not go alone."

"No, wouldn't do at all," Mr Scunthorpe agreed. But better not go, ma'am! Not the thing for you. Delicate female – shabby neighbourhood! Take a message."

"Nonsense! Do you think I have never been to the City? Only wait until I have fetched a bonnet, and a shawl! We may take a hackney, and be there before Lady Bridlington comes downstairs."

"Yes, but – Fact is, ma'am, he ain't at the Red Lion!" said Mr Scunthorpe, much disturbed.

She had sprung up from her chair, but at this she paused. "Not? But how is this? Why has he left the inn?"

"Couldn't pay his shot," explained Mr Scunthorpe apologetically. "Left his watch. Silly thing to do. Might have come in useful."

"Oh!" she cried out, horror in her voice. "Is it as bad as *that*?"

"Worse!" said Mr Scunthorpe gloomily. "Got queered sporting his blunt on the table. Only hadn't enough blunt. Took to signing vowels, and ran aground."

"*Gaming!*" Arabella breathed, in a shocked voice.

"Faro," said Mr Scunthorpe. "Mind, no question of any Greeking transactions! No fuzzing, or handling the concave-suit! Not but what it makes it worse, because a fellow has to be dashed particular in all matters of play and pay, if he goes to the Nonesuch. All the go, I assure you: Corinthian club – best of good *ton*! They play devilish high there – above my touch!"

"Then it was not you who took him to such a place!"

"Couldn't have been," said Mr Scunthorpe simply. "Not a member. Chuffy Wivenhoe."

"Lord Wivenhoe! Oh, what a fool I have been!" cried Arabella. "It was I who made him known to Lord Wivenhoe!"

"Pity," said Mr Scunthorpe, shaking his head.

"But how wicked of him to have led Bertram to such a place! Oh, how could he have done so? I had no suspicion – I thought him so agreeable, and gentlemanlike –!"

"Polite to a point," agreed Mr Scunthorpe. "Very good sort of a man: very well-liked. Daresay he did it for the best."

"How could he think so?" Arabella said hotly.

"Very exclusive club," he pointed out.

She said impatiently. "It is of no use for us to argue on that head. Where is Bertram?"

"Don't think you'd know the place, ma'am. It's – it's near Westminster!"

"Very well, let us go there at once!"

In considerable agitation, Mr Scunthorpe said: "No, dash it! Can't take a lady to Willow Walk! You don't quite understand, ma'am! Poor Bertram – couldn't pay his shot – not a meg on him – duns in his pocket – tipstaffs after him – had to give 'em all the bag! Can't quite make out exactly how it was, but think he must have gone back to the Red Lion when he left the Nonesuch, because he has his portmanteau with him. Seems to have bolted for it to Tothill Fields. Very low back-slum, ma'am. Silly fellow ought to have come and knocked me up – happy to have given him my sofa!"

"Good God, why did he not?"

He coughed in an embarrassed way. "Might have been a little bit on the go," he said diffidently. "Scared of being pounded by the tipstaffs, too. Come to think of it, might easily be if he stayed with me. Dashed tradesmen know he's a friend of mine! At all events, he ain't with me – didn't send me word where he was till this morning – feeling too blue-devilled, I daresay. Don't blame him: would myself!"

"Oh, poor Bertram, poor Bertram!" she cried, wringing her hands. "I do not care where he is, see him I must, if I have to go to this Willow Walk alone!"

"Good God, ma'am, mustn't do that!" he exclaimed, appalled. "Very rough set of coves in Willow Walk! Besides –" He paused, looking acutely uncomfortable. "Not quite himself!"

"Oh, he must be ill with worry, and despair! Nothing would keep me from him at such a time! I will fetch my bonnet, and we may be off directly!"

"Ma'am, he won't like it!" Mr Scunthorpe said desperately. "Very likely be ready to murder me only for telling you! You *can't* see him!"

"Why can I not?"

"He's been in the sun a trifle! You see – very understandable thing to do! –

shot the cat!"

"Shot the cat?"

"Can't blame him!" Mr Scunthorpe pleaded. "Wouldn't have told you, if you hadn't been so set on seeing him! Felt desperate – shot the cat – felt better – kept on swallowing balls of fire – result, looking as queer as Dick's hatband, when I saw him!"

"Do you mean that he has been drinking?" demanded Arabella. "What, in heaven's name, is a ball of fire?"

"Brandy," said Mr Scunthorpe. "Devilish bad brandy too. Told him to make Blue Ruin the preferred suit. Safer."

"Every word you say makes me the more determined to go to him!" declared Arabella.

"Assure you much better to send him some blunt, ma'am!"

"I will take him all I have, but oh, it is so little! I cannot think yet what is to be done!"

Mr Scunthorpe pointed significantly to the ceiling. "You don't think the old lady -?" he suggested delicately.

She shook her head. "Oh, no, no! Impossible!"

Mr Scunthorpe looked a little thoughtful. "In that case, ma'am, better take you to him. Talking very wildly this morning. No saying what he might do."

She almost ran to the door. "We have not a moment to waste, then!"

"No, no!" he assured her. "No need to be on the fret! Won't cut his throat today! Told the girl to hide his razor."

"What girl?"

He became very much confused, blushed, and uttered: "Girl he sent to my lodging with a message. Been looking after him."

"Oh, God bless her!" Arabella cried fervently. "What is her name? How much I must owe her!"

As the lady in question had introduced herself to Mr Scunthorpe as Leaky Peg, he was obliged to take refuge in prevarication, and to hope devoutly that they would not encounter her in Willow Walk. He said that he had not caught her name. Arabella seemed a little disappointed, but since this was no time for wasting over trifles she said no more, but ran out of the room to fetch her bonnet and shawl.

It was impossible for her to leave the house without the butler's being aware of it, but although he looked surprised, he made no comment, and in a few minutes' time she and Mr Scunthorpe were seated in a ramshackle hackney coach, which seemed as though, many years before, it had formed part of a nobleman's equipage, but which had fallen into sad decay. The coverings to the seats and the squabs were tattered and dirty, and the vehicle smelled strongly of beer and old leather. These evils Arabella scarcely noticed, in such a turmoil was her mind. It was a struggle to support her spirits at all; she felt ready to sink; and was unable, while in such a state of agitation, to form any plan for Bertram's relief. The only solution which had so far presented itself to her mind was an instinctive impulse, no sooner thought of than recoiled from, to send off an express to Heythram. Mr Scunthorpe's suggestion of applying to Lady Bridlington she well knew to be useless, nor would her pride tolerate the putting of herself under such added obligation to her godmother. Wild notions of selling Mama's diamonds, and the pearl necklet that had belonged to Grandmama Tallant, could not, she knew, be entertained, for these trinkets were not hers to dispose of at will.

Beside her, Mr Scunthorpe, feeling vaguely that her spirits required support, tried to entertain her by pointing out, conscientiously, the various places of interest the hackney drove past. She scarcely heeded him, but when they reached Westminster, began to look about her a little, insensibly cheered by the respectability of the neighbourhood. But the hackney lumbered on, and in a surprisingly short space of time it was hard to realize that she must be within a stone's throw of the Abbey, so squalid were her surroundings. An unlucky attempt made by Mr Scunthorpe to divert her, by pointing out an ugly brick structure which he said was the Tothill Fields Bridewell, made her shudder so alarmingly that he hastily informed her that it was so crammed to overflowing with felons that there was no room for another soul behind its walls. A row of squat almshouses was the next object of interest to be seen. This was followed by a charity school, but the district seemed to Arabella to be largely composed of wretched hovels, ancient mansions, fallen into depressing decay, and a superfluity of taverns. Frowsy looking women stood in the doorways of some of the hovels; half-naked urchins turned cartwheels on the dirty cobbles, in the hope of gaining largesse from persons well-breeched enough to travel in hackney coaches; at one corner, a fat woman, seated behind an iron cauldron appeared to be dispensing tea to a curiously ill-assorted crowd of persons, ranging from bricklayers to bedizened young women; various street-cries echoed in the narrow streets, from offers of coal to entreaties for old iron; and the male population seemed to consist entirely of scavengers, sweeps, and unidentifiable persons with blue jowls, and mufflers round their necks in place of collars.

After passing the entrances to several noisome alleys, the hackney turned into Willow Walk, and proceeded down it for some way before drawing up outside a dingy house, whose windows showed, besides fluttering oddments of washing hung out to dry, several broken panes of glass. In the open doorway, an old woman sat in a rocking-chair, puffing at a clay pipe, and engaged in conversation with a younger female, who held a squalling infant on one arm, which she from time to time shook, or refreshed from a black bottle, from which she herself took frequent pulls. Arabella had no positive knowledge of what was in that black bottle, but that it must contain strong liquor she felt convinced. The thought of Bertram was momentarily banished from her head; as Mr Scunthorpe handed her down from the hackney, and punctiliously brushed off the straws that clung to the flounce of her simple cambric dress, she opened her reticule, hunted in it for a shilling, and astonished the mother of the infant by pressing it into her hand, and saying earnestly: "Pray buy the baby some milk! Oh, pray do not give it that horrid stuff!

Both women stared at her with fallen jaws. The old Irishwoman, the first to regain command over her faculties, burst into a cackle of mirth, and informed her that she was talking to no less a personage than Quartern Sue. This conveyed little to Arabella, but while she was still puzzling over the appellation, Quartern Sue, recovering from her stupefaction, had launched forth into a catalogue of her embarrassments, and was holding her hand cupped suggestively. Mr Scunthorpe, beads of sweat standing upon his brow, took it upon himself to hustle his charge into the house, whispering to her that she must not get into talk with such ill-famed women. Quartern Sue, never one to let slip an opportunity, followed them, her beggar's whine rising to a crescendo, but was repulsed at the foot of a rickety, uncarpeted stairway by a strapping young woman, with a tousle of greasy yellow hair, a countenance which not all the ravages of gin had entirely deprived of comeliness, and a tawdry dress, stained in various places, and with the bodice cut so low as to reveal glimpses of a dirty shift. This lady, having driven Quartern Sue forth by a series of remarks, not one of which was intelligible to Arabella, turned and confronted the genteel visitors with a belligerent look on her face, and her arms set widely akimbo. She demanded of Mr Scunthorpe, with whom she appeared to be acquainted, what he meant by bringing a flash mort to the ken. Mr Scunthorpe uttered the one word, Sister! in strangled accents, upon which the blonde beauty turned a pair of fierce, bloodshot eyes upon Arabella, and ejaculated: "Ho! Sister, is it?"

"Girl who brought me the message!" explained Mr Scunthorpe in a blushful aside to Arabella.

The blonde beauty needed no other passport to Arabella's favour. If she was conscious – as she could hardly have failed to have been – of the strong aroma of daffy which hung about the person of Leaky Peg, she gave no sign of it, but started forward, with her hands held out, and impulsive words on her lips. "Oh, are you the girl who has been kind to my brother? You must let me thank you! I can never, never repay you! Mr Scunthorpe here has been telling me that it was you who took care of him when he – when he came to this place!"

Leaky Peg stared very hard at her for a moment, and then said pugnaciously: "I found the covey on the mop, blue as megrim, see? and him no more than a mouth! Half flash and half foolish, that's him. Strike me, I don't know what I see in the hick!"

"Miss Tallant, better come upstairs!" said the anguished Mr Scunthorpe, to whom Leaky Peg's vocabulary was rather more intelligible than to Arabella.

"You dub your mummer, you death's head on a mopstick!" Leaky Peg advised him. "Leave me and the swell mort be!" She turned back to Arabella, and said roughly: "Lurched, ain't he? He tells me there's a fastener out after him. He hadn't so much as a meg in his truss when I come up with him in the boozing-ken. I took him along with me – strike me if I know why!" She jerked her thumb towards the stairs. "You want to take him away: this ain't his lay, nor it ain't mine neither! Spouting a kid's mish all to buy him mutton and smash, which he don't eat! Me! You take him off; you're welcome!"

Gathering from these words that Leaky Peg had been keeping Bertram supplied with food, Arabella, tears standing in her eyes, seized one of her hands, and pressed it fervently between both her own, saying: "How good you are! Indeed, I thank you! He is only a boy, you know, and what must have become of him without you I dare not think!"

"Well, it's little enough I got from it!" remarked Leaky Peg caustically. "You and him with your breakteeth words! You get up them dancers, you and that moulder alongside you that looks like a toothdrawer! First door on the right: stale-drunk, he is, but he ain't backt yet!"

With these heartening words she turned on her heel, and strode out of the house, driving before her Quartern Sue, who had had the temerity to venture on to the threshold again. Mr Scunthorpe made haste to usher Arabella up the stairs, saying reproachfully: "Shouldn't talk to her, ma'am! Not at all the thing! Assure you!"

"The thing!" she exclaimed scornfully. "She has a kind heart, sir!"

Abashed, Mr Scunthorpe begged pardon, and tapped at a door at the head of the stairs.

Bertram's voice sounded from within the room, and without waiting for her escort to usher her in Arabella lifted the latch and quickly entered.

The apartment, which looked out on to a filthy yard, where lean cats prowled amongst garbage-heaps, was small, rather dark, and furnished with a sagging bed pushed up against one wall, a deal table, two wooden chairs, and a strip of threadbare carpet. The remains of a loaf of bread, a heel of cheese, together with a glass, a jug, and an empty bottle stood on the table; and on the mantelshelf, presumably placed there by Leaky Peg, was a cracked mug containing a wilting bunch of flowers. Bertram, who was stretched on the bed, raised himself on his elbow as the door opened, an apprehensive look in his face. He was fully dressed, but was wearing a handkerchief knotted round his neck, and looked both ill and unkempt. When he saw Arabella, he uttered something like a sob, and struggled up, and to his feet. "Bella!"

She was in his arms on the word, unable to prevent herself from bursting into tears, but passionately clasping him to her. His breath reeked of spirits, but although this shocked her, she did not recoil from him, but hugged him more tightly still.

"You should not have come!" he said unsteadily. "Felix, how *could* you have brought her here?"

"Warned her she wouldn't like it," Mr Scunthorpe excused himself. "Very set on seeing you!"

Bertram gave a groan. "I did not mean you to know!"

She disengaged herself, wiped her tears away, and sat down on one of the chairs. "Bertram, you know that is nonsense!" she said. "Whom should you turn to if not to me? I am so sorry! What you must have suffered in this dreadful house!"

"Pretty, ain't it?" he said jeeringly. "I don't know how I came here: Leaky Peg brought me. You may as well know, Bella, I was so foxed I don't remember anything that happened after I bolted from the Red Lion!"

"No, I quite see," she said. "But, Bertram, pray do not go on drinking! It is all so bad, and that makes it worse! You look sadly out of sorts, and no wonder! Have you a sore throat, dearest?"

He flushed, his hand going instinctively to the handkerchief round his neck. "This! Oh, no! Gammoning the draper, my dear!" He saw her look of bewilderment, and added, with a short laugh: "You would be surprised at the cant I have learnt from my hosts here! I've become a spouter – at least Peg manages the business for me! Pawned, Bella, pawned! Shan't have a rag to my back soon – not that that will signify!"

Mr Scunthorpe, seated on the edge of the bed, exchanged a meaning look with Arabella. She said briskly: "It would signify very much! We must think what is to be done. Only tell me what you owe!"

He was reluctant to divulge the sum, but she insisted, and after a little while he blurted out: "It comes to more than seven hundred pounds! There is no possibility of my being able to get clear!"

She was aghast, for she had not supposed that he could owe nearly so much. The sum seemed vast beyond belief, so that she could not be surprised when Bertram, casting himself into the other chair, began to talk in a wild way of putting a period to his existence. She let him run on, guessing that his despair needed the relief of just such mad outpourings, and having no very real fear that he would put his violent threats into execution. While he talked she cudgelled her brains for a solution to his difficulties, only lending half an ear to him, but patting his hand soothingly from time to time. Mr Scunthorpe intervened at last, saying with great commonsense: "Don't think you ought to jump into the river, dear old boy. Sister wouldn't like it. Bound to leak out. Your governor might not like it either: never can tell!"

"No, indeed!" Arabella said. "You must not talk of it any more, Bertram. You know how wicked it would be!"

"Well, I suppose I shan't kill myself," Bertram said, a shade sulkily. "Only, I can tell you this: I'll never face my father with *this*!"

"No, no!" she agreed. "Seven hundred pounds! Bertram, how has it been possible?"

"I lost six hundred at faro," he said, dropping his head in his hands. "The rest – Well, there was the tailor, and the horse I hired, and what I owe at Tatt's, and my shot at the inn – oh, a dozen things! Bella, what am I to do?"

He sounded much more like the younger brother she knew when he spoke like that, a scared look in his face, and in his voice an unreasoning dependence on her ability to help him out of a scrape.

"Bills don't signify," pronounced Mr Scunthorpe. "Leave town: won't be followed. Not been living under your own name. Gaming debts another matter. Got to raise the wind for that. Debt of honour."

"I know it, curse you!"

"But all debts are debts of honour!" Arabella said. "Indeed, you should pay your bills first of all!"

A glance passed between the two gentlemen, indicative of their mutual agreement not to waste breath in arguing with a female on a subject she would clearly never understand. Bertram passed his hand over his brow, heaving a short sigh, and saying: "There's only one thing to be done. I have thought it all over, Bella, and I mean to enlist, under a false name. If they won't have me as a trooper, I'll join a line regiment. I should have done it yesterday, when I first thought of it, only that there's something I must do first. Affair of honour. I shall write to my father, of course, and I daresay he will utterly cast me off, but that can't be helped!"

"How can you think so?" Arabella cried hotly. "Grieved he must be – oh, I dare not even think of it! – but you must know that never, never would he do such an unchristian thing as to cast you off! Oh, do not write to him yet! Only give me time to think what I can do! If Papa knew that you owed all that money, I am very sure he would pay every penny of it, though it ruined him!"

"How can you suppose I would be such a gudgeon as to tell him *that*? No! I shall tell him that my whole mind is set on the army, and I had as lief start in the ranks as not!"

This speech struck far more dismay into Arabella's heart than his previous talk of committing suicide, for to take the King's shilling seemed to her a likely thing for him to do. She uttered, hardly above a whisper: "No, no!"

"It must be, Bella," he said. "I'm sure the army is all I'm fit for, and I cannot show my face again with a load of debt hanging over me. Particularly a debt of honour! O God, I think I must have been mad!" His voice broke, and he could not speak for a moment. In the end he contrived to summon up the travesty of a smile, and to say: "Pretty pair, ain't we? Not that *you* did anything as wrong as I have."

"Oh, I have behaved so dreadfully!" she exclaimed. "It is even my fault that you are reduced to these straits! Had I never presented you to Lord Wivenhoe -"

"That's fudge!" he said quickly. "I had been to gaming-houses before I met him. He was not to know I wasn't as well-blunted as that set of his! I ought not to have gone with him to the Nonesuch. Only I had lost money on a race, and I thought – I hoped – Oh, talking pays no toll! But to say it was your fault is all gammon!"

"Bertram, who won your money at the Nonesuch?" she asked.

"The bank. It was faro."

"Yes, but someone holds the bank!"

"The Nonpareil."

She stared at him. "Mr Beaumaris?" she gasped. He nodded. "Oh, no, do not say so! How could he have let you – No, no, Bertram!"

She sounded so much distressed that he was puzzled. "Why the devil shouldn't he?"

"You are only a boy! He must have known! And to accept notes of hand from you! Surely he might have refused to do so much at least!"

"You don't understand!" he said impatiently. "I went there with Chuffy, so why should he refuse to let me play?"

Mr Scunthorpe nodded. "Very awkward situation, ma'am. Devilish insulting to refuse a man's vowels."

She could not appreciate the niceties of the code evidently shared by both gentlemen, but she could accept that they must obtain in male circles. "I must think it wrong of him," she said. "But never mind! The thing is that he is – that I am particularly acquainted with him! Don't be in despair, Bertram! I am persuaded that if I were to go to him, explain that you are not of age, and not a rich man's son, he will forgive the debt!"

She broke off, for there was no mistaking the expressions of shocked disapprobation in both Bertram's and Mr Scunthorpe's faces.

"Good God, Bella, what will you say next!"

"But, Bertram, indeed he is not proud and disagreeable, as so many people think him! I – I have found him particularly kind, and obliging!"

"Bella, this is a *debt of honour*! If it takes me my life long to do it, I must pay it, and so I shall tell him!"

Mr Scunthorpe nodded judicial approval of this decision.

"Spend your life paying six hundred pounds to a man who is so wealthy that I daresay he regards it no more than you would a shilling?" cried Arabella. "Why, it is absurd!"

Bertram looked despairingly at his friend. Mr Scunthorpe said painstakingly: "Nothing to do with it, ma'am. Debt of honour is a debt of honour. No getting away from that."

"I cannot agree! I own, I do not like to do it, but I *could* do it, and I know he would never refuse me!"

Bertram grasped her wrist. "Listen, Bella! I daresay you don't understand – in fact, I can see that you don't! – but if you dared to do such a thing I swear you'd never see my face again! Besides, even if he did tear up my vowels I should still think myself under an obligation to redeem them! Next you will be suggesting that you should ask him to pay those damned tradesmen's bills for me!"

She coloured guiltily, for some such idea had just crossed her mind. Suddenly, Mr Scunthorpe, whose face a moment before had assumed a cataleptic expression, uttered three pregnant words. "Got a notion!"

The Tallants looked anxiously at him, Bertram with hope, his sister more than a little doubtfully.

"Know what they say?" Mr Scunthorpe demanded. "Bank always wins!"

"I know that," said Bertram bitterly. "If that's all you have to say -"

"Wait!" said Mr Scunthorpe. "Start one!" He saw blank bewilderment in the two faces confronting him, and added, with a touch of impatience: "Faro!"

"Start a faro-bank?" said Bertram incredulously. "You must be mad! Why, even if it were not the craziest thing I ever heard of, you can't run a faro-bank without capital!"

"Thought of that," said Mr Scunthorpe, not without pride. "Go to my trustees. Go at once. Not a moment to be lost."

"Good God, you don't suppose they would let you touch your capital for such a cause as that?"

"Don't see why not!" argued Mr Scunthorpe. "Always trying to add to it. Preaching at me for ever about improving the estate! Very good way of doing it: wonder they haven't thought of it for themselves. Better go and see my uncle at once."

"Felix, you're a gudgeon!" said Bertram irritably. "No trustee would let you do such a thing! And even if they would, good God, we neither of us want to spend our lives running a faro-bank!"

"Shouldn't have to," said Mr Scunthorpe, sticking obstinately by his guns. "Only want to clear you of debt! One good night's run would do it. Close the bank then."

He was so much enamoured of this scheme that it was some time before he could be dissuaded from trying to promote it. Arabella, paying very little heed to the argument, sat wrapped in her own thoughts. That these were by no means pleasant would have been apparent, even to Mr Scunthorpe, had he been less engrossed in the championing of his own plans, for not only did her hands clench and unclench in her lap, but her face, always very expressive, betrayed her. But by the time Bertram had convinced Mr Scunthorpe that a faro-bank would not answer, she was sufficiently mistress of herself again to excite no suspicion in either gentleman's breast.

She turned her eyes towards Bertram, who had sunk back, after his animated argument, into a state of hopeless gloom. "I shall think of something," she said. "I *know* I shall contrive to help you! Only please, please do not enlist, Bertram! Not yet! Only if I should fail!"

"What do you mean to do?" he demanded. "I shan't enlist until I have seen Mr Beaumaris, and and explained to him how it is! That I *must* do. I-I told him I had no funds in London, and should be obliged to send into Yorkshire for them, so he asked me to call at his house on Thursday. It is of no use to look at me like that, Bella! I couldn't tell him I was done-up, and had no means of paying him, with them all there, listening to what we were saying! I would have died rather! Bella, have you any money? Could you spare me enough to get my shirt back? I can't go to see the Nonpareil like this!"

She thrust her purse into his hand. "Yes, yes, of course! If only I had not bought those gloves, and the shoes, and the new scarf! There are only ten guineas left, but it will be enough to make you more comfortable until I have thought how to help you, won't it? Do, do remove from this dreadful house! I saw quite a number of inns on our way, and one or two of them looked to be respectable!"

It was plain that Bertram would be only too ready to change his quarters, and after a brief dispute, in which he was very glad to be worsted, he took the purse, gave her a hug, and said that she was the best sister in the world. He asked wistfully whether she thought Lady Bridlington might be induced to advance him seven hundred pounds, on a promise of repayment over a protracted period, but although she replied cheerfully that she had no doubt that she could arrange something of the sort, he could not deceive himself into thinking it possible, and sighed. Mr Scunthorpe, prefixing his remark with one of his deprecating coughs, suggested that as the hackney had been told to wait for them, he and Miss Tallant ought, perhaps, to be taking their leave. Arabella was much inclined to go at once in search of a suitable hostelry for Bertram, but was earnestly dissuaded, Mr Scunthorpe promising to attend to this matter himself, and also to redeem Bertram's raiment from the pawnbroker's shop. The brother and sister then parted, clinging to one another in such a moving way that Mr Scunthorpe was much affected by the sight, and had to blow his nose with great violence.

Arabella's first action on reaching Park Street again was to run up to her bedchamber, and without pausing to remove her bonnet to sit down at the little table in the window, and prepare to write a letter. But in spite of the evident urgency of the matter she had no sooner written her opening words than all inspiration appeared to desert her, and she sat staring out of the window, while the ink dried on her pen. At last she drew a breath, dipped the pen in the standish again, and resolutely wrote two lines. Then she stopped, read them over, tore up the paper, and drew a fresh sheet towards her.

It was some time before she had achieved a result that satisfied her, but it was done at last, and the letter sealed up with a wafer. She then rang the bell-pull, and upon a housemaid's coming in answer to the summons desired the girl to send Becky to her, if she could be spared from her duties. When Becky presently appeared, shyly smiling and twisting her hands together in her apron, Arabella held out the letter, and said: "If you please, Becky, do you think you could contrive to slip out, and – and carry that to Mr Beaumaris's house? You might say that I have asked you to go on an errand for me, but – but I shall be very much obliged to you if you will not disclose to anyone what it is!"

"Oh, miss!" breathed the handmaid, scenting a romance. "As though I would say a word to a living soul!"

"Thank you! If – if Mr Beaumaris should be at home, I should be glad if you would wait for an answer to the letter!"

Becky nodded her profound understanding of this, assured Arabella that she might trust her through fire and water, and departed.

Nothing could have been more conspiratorial than her manner of entering Arabella's room half-an-hour later, but she brought bad news: Mr Beaumaris had gone into the country three days ago, and had said that he might be away from London for a week.

CHAPTER FIFTEEN

MR BEAUMARIS returned to his London house in time to partake of a late breakfast on Tuesday morning, having been absent for six days. It had been considered probable by his dependants that he would be away for a full week, but as he rarely gave any positive information on his movements, counted no cost, and had accustomed his highly-paid servants to live in a constant state of expectation of being obliged, at a moment's notice, to provide suitable entertainment for himself, or for a score of guests, his premature arrival caused no one any dismay. It caused one member of his household a degree of joy bordering on delirium. A ragged little mongrel, whose jauntily curled tail had been clipped unhappily between his legs for six interminable days, and who had spent the major part of this time curled into a ball on the rug outside is master's door, refusing all sustenance, including plates of choice viands prepared by the hands of the great M. Alphonse himself, came tumbling down the stairs, uttering canine shrieks, and summoned up enough strength to career madly round in circles before collapsing in an exhausted, panting heap at Mr Beaumaris's feet. It spoke volumes for the light in which Mr Beaumaris's whims were regarded by his retainers that the condition to which his disreputable protégé had wilfully reduced himself brought every member of the household who might have been considered in some way responsible into the hall to exonerate himself from all blame. Even M. Alphonse mounted the stairs from his basement kingdom to describe to Mr Beaumaris in detail the chicken-broth, the ragout of rabbit, the shin of beef, and the marrow-bone with which he had tried to tempt Ulysses' vanished appetite. Brough broke in on his Gallic monologue to assure Mr Beaumaris that he for one had left nothing undone to restore Ulysses' interest in life, even going to the lengths of importing a stray cat into the house, in the hope that this outrage would galvanize one notoriously unsympathetic towards all felines to activity. Painswick, with a smug air that rendered him instantly odious to his colleagues, drew attention to the fact that it had been his superior understanding of Ulysses' processes of thought which Mr Beaumaris had to thank for his finding himself still in possession of his low-born companion: he had conceived the happy notion of giving Ulysses one of Mr Beaumaris's gloves to guard.

Mr Beaumaris, who had picked Ulysses up, paid no heed to all these attempts at self-justification, but addressed himself to his adorer. "What a fool you are!" he observed. "No, I have the greatest dislike of having my face licked, and must request you to refrain. Quiet, Ulysses! quiet! I am grateful to you for your solicitude, but you must perceive that I am in the enjoyment of my customary good health. I would I could say the same of you. You have once more reduced yourself to skin and bone, my friend, a process which I shall take leave to inform you I consider as unjust as it is ridiculous. Anyone setting eyes on you would suppose that I grudged you even the scraps from my table!" He added, without the slightest change of voice, and without raising his eyes from the creature in his arms: "You would also appear to have bereft my household of its senses, so that the greater part of it, instead of providing me with the breakfast I stand in need of, is engaged in excusing itself from any suspicion of blame and – I may add – doing itself no good thereby."

Ulysses, to whom the mere sound of Mr Beaumaris's voice was ecstasy, looked adoringly up into his face, and contrived to lick the hand that was caressing him. On his servants, Mr Beaumaris's voice operated in quite another fashion: they dispersed rapidly, Painswick to lay out a complete change of raiments; Brough to set the table in the breakfast-parlour; Alphonse to carve at lightning speed several slices of a fine York ham, and to cast eggs and herbs into a pan; and various underlings to grind coffee-beans, cut bread, and set kettles on to boil. Mr Beaumaris tucked Ulysses under one arm, picked up the pile of letters from the table in the hall, and strolled with them into his library. To the zealous young footman who hastened to fling open the door for him, he said: "Food for this abominable animal!" – a command which, relayed swiftly to the kitchen, caused M. Alphonse to command his chief assistant instantly to abandon his allotted task, and to prepare a dish calculated to revive the flagging appetite of a Cambacérès.

Mr Beaumaris, tossing a pile of invitations and bills aside, came upon a billet which had not been delivered through the medium of the Penny Post, and which was superscribed, *Urgent*. The writing, certainly feminine, was unknown to him. "Now, what have we here, Ulysses?" he said, breaking the wafer.

They had not very much. *"Dear Mr Beaumaris,"* ran the missive, *"I should be* very much obliged to you *if you would do me the honour of calling in Park Street* as soon as may be convenient to you, *and requesting the butler to inform* me *of the event. I remain, Ever yours most sincerely, Arabella Tallant."*

This model of the epistolary art, which had caused Miss Tallant so much heart-searching, and so many ruined sheets of hot-pressed notepaper, did not fail of its effect. Mr Beaumaris cast aside the rest of his correspondence, set Ulysses down on the floor, and bent his powerful mind to the correct interpretation of these few, heavily underlined, words. He was still engaged on this task when Brough entered the room to announce that his breakfast awaited him. He carried the letter into the parlour, and propped it against the coffee-pot, feeling that he had not yet got to the bottom of it. At his feet, Ulysses, repairing with enthusiasm the ravages of his protracted fast, was rapidly consuming a meal which might have been judged excessive for the satisfaction of the appetite of a boa-constrictor.

"This," said Mr Beaumaris, "was delivered here three days ago, Ulysses!"

Ulysses, whose keen olfactory sense had discovered the chicken giblets cunningly hidden in the middle of his plate, could spare no more than a perfunctory wag of the tail for this speech; and to Mr Beaumaris's subsequent demand to know what could be in the wind he returned no answer at all. Mr Beaumaris pushed away the remains of his breakfast, a gesture which was shortly to operate alarmingly on the sensibilities of the artist belowstairs, and waved aside his valet, who had just entered the room. "My town dress!" he said.

"I have it ready, sir," responded Painswick, with dignity. "There was just one matter which I should perhaps mention."

"Not now," said Mr Beaumaris, his eyes still bent upon Miss Tallant's tantalizing communication.

Painswick bowed, and withdrew. The matter was not, in his fastidious estimation, of sufficient importance to justify him in intruding upon his employer's evident preoccupation; nor did he broach it when Mr Beaumaris presently came upstairs to change his riding-dress for the blue coat, yellow pantaloons, chaste waistcoat, and gleaming Hessians with which he was wont to gratify the eyes of beholders in the Metropolis. This further abstention was due, however, more to the sense of irretrievable loss which had invaded his soul on the discovery that a shirt was missing from Mr Beaumaris's execrably packed portmanteau than from a respect for his master's abstraction. He confined his conversation to bitter animadversions on the morals of inn-servants, and the depths of depravity to which some unknown boots had sunk in treating Mr Beaumaris's second-best pair of Hessians with a blacking fit only to be used on the footwear of country squires. He could hardly flatter himself that Mr Beaumaris, swiftly and skilfully arranging the folds of his neckcloth in the mirror, or delicately paring his well-cared for finger-nails, paid the least heed to his discourse, but it served in some measure to relieve his lacerated feelings.

Leaving his valet to repair the damage to his wardrobe, and his faithful admirer to sleep off the effects of a Gargantuan meal, Mr Beaumaris left the house, and walked to Park Street. Here he was met by the intelligence that my lord, my lady, and Miss Tallant had gone out in the barouche to the British Museum, where Lord Elgin's much disputed marbles were now being exhibited, in a wooden shed built for their accommodation. Mr Beaumaris thanked the butler for this information, called up a passing hackney, and directed the jarvey to drive him to Great Russell Street.

He found Miss Tallant, her disinterested gaze fixed upon a sculptured slab from the Temple of Nike Apteros, enduring a lecture from Lord Bridlington, quite in his element. It was Lady Bridlington who first perceived his tall, graceful figure advancing across the saloon, for since she had naturally seen the collection of antiquities when it was on view at Lord Elgin's residence in Park Lane, and again when it was removed to Burlington House, she felt herself to be under no obligation to look at it a third time, and was more profitably engaged in keeping a weather eye cocked for any of her acquaintances who might have elected to visit the British Museum that morning. Upon perceiving Mr Beaumaris, she exclaimed in accents of delight: "Mr Beaumaris! What a lucky chance, to be sure! How do you do? How came you not to be at the Kirkmichael's Venetian Breakfast yesterday? Such a charming party! I am persuaded you must have enjoyed it! Six hundred guests – only fancy!"

"Amongst so many, ma'am, I am flattered to know that you remarked my absence," responded Mr Beaumaris, shaking hands. "I have been out of town for some days, and only returned this morning. Miss Tallant! 'Servant, Bridlington!"

Arabella, who had started violently upon hearing his name uttered, and quickly turned her head, took his hand in a clasp which seemed to him slightly convulsive, and raised a pair of strained, enquiring eyes to his face. He smiled reassuringly down into them, and bent a courteous ear to Lady Bridlington, who was making haste to assure him that she had come to the Museum merely to show the Grecian treasures to Arabella, who had not been privileged to see them on their *first* showing. Lord Bridlington, not averse from any aggrandizement to his audience, began in his consequential way to expound his views on the probable artistic value of the fragments, a recreation which would no doubt have occupied him for a considerable period of time had Mr Beaumaris not cut him short by saying, in his most languid way: "The pronouncements of West, and of Sir Thomas Lawrence, must, I imagine, have established the aesthetic worth of these antiquities. As to the *propriety* of their acquisition, we may, each one of us, hold to our own opinion."

"Mr Beaumaris, do you care to visit Somerset House with us?" interrupted Lady Bridlington. "I do not know how it comes about that we were not there upon Opening Day, but such a rush of engagements have we been swept up in that I am sure it is a wonder we have time to turn round! Arabella, my love, I daresay you are quite tired of staring at all these sadly damaged bits of frieze, or whatever it may be called – not but what I declare I could feast my eyes on it for ever! – and will be glad to look at pictures for a change!"

Arabella assented to it, throwing so beseeching a look at Mr Beaumaris that he was induced to accept a seat in the barouche.

During the drive to the Strand, Lady Bridlington was too much occupied in catching the eyes of chance acquaintances, and drawing their attention to the distinguished occupant of one of the back seats by bowing and waving to them, to have much time for conversation. Arabella sat with her eyes downcast, and her hand fidgeting with the ribands tied round the handle of her sunshade; and Mr Beaumaris was content to watch her, taking due note of her pallor, and the dark shadows beneath her eyes. It was left to Lord Bridlington to entertain the company, which he did very willingly, prosing uninterruptedly until the carriage turned into the courtyard of Somerset House.

Once inside the building, Lady Bridlington, whose ambitions had for some time been centred on promoting a match between Arabella and the Nonpareil, seized the first opportunity that offered of drawing Frederick away from the interesting pair. She stated her fervent desire to see the latest example of Sir Thomas Lawrence's art, and dragged him away from a minute inspection of the President's latest enormous canvas to search for this fashionable masterpiece.

"In what way can I serve you, Miss Tallant?" said Mr Beaumaris quietly.

"You–you had my letter?" faltered Arabella, glancing fleetingly up into his face.

"This morning. I went instantly to Park Street, and, apprehending that the matter was of some urgency, followed you to Bloomsbury."

"How kind – how *very* kind you are!" uttered Arabella, in accents which could scarcely have been more mournful had she discovered him to have been a monster of cruelty.

"What is it, Miss Tallant?"

Bearing all the appearance of one rapt in admiration of the canvas before her, she said: "I daresay you may have forgot all about it, sir, but – but you told me once – that is, you were so obliging as to say – that if my sentiments underwent a change -"

Mr Beaumaris mercifully intervened to put an end to her embarrassment. "I have certainly not forgotten it," he said. "I perceive Lady Charnwood to be approaching, so let us move on! Am I to understand, ma'am, that your sentiments *have* undergone a change?"

Miss Tallant, obediently walking on to stare at one of the new Associates' *Probationary Pictures* (described in her catalogue as "An Old Man soliciting a Mother for Her Daughter who was shewn Unwilling to consent to so disproportionate a match") said baldly: "Yes."

"My surroundings," said Mr Beaumaris, "make it impossible for me to do more than assure you that you have made me the happiest man in England, ma'am."

"Thank you," said Arabella, in a stifled tone. "I shall try to be a – to be a conformable wife, sir!"

Mr Beaumaris's lips twitched, but he replied with perfect gravity: "For my part, I shall try to be an unexceptionable husband, ma'am!"

"Oh, yes, I am sure you will be!" said Arabella naïvely. "If only -"

"If only – ?" prompted Mr Beaumaris, as she broke off.

"Nothing!" she said hastily. "Oh, dear, there is Mr Epworth!"

"A common bow in passing will be enough to damp his pretensions," said Mr Beaumaris. If that does not suffice, I will look at him through my glass."

This made her give an involuntary gurgle of laughter, but an instant later she was serious again, and evidently struggling to find the words with which to express herself.

"What very awkward places we do choose in which to propose to one another!" remarked Mr Beaumaris, guiding her gently towards a red-plush couch. "Let us hope that if we sit down, and appear to be engrossed in conversation no one will have the bad manners to interrupt us!"

"I do not know what you must think of me!" said Arabella.

"I expect I had better not tell you until we find ourselves in a more retired situation," he replied. "You always blush so delightfully when I pay you compliments that it might attract attention to ourselves."

She hesitated, and then turned resolutely towards him, tightly gripping her sunshade, and saying: "Mr Beaumaris, you do *indeed* wish to marry me?"

"Miss Tallant, I do *indeed* wish to marry you!" he asserted.

"And–and you are so wealthy that my–my fortune can mean nothing to you?"

"Nothing at all, Miss Tallant."

She drew an audible breath. "Then – will you marry me at once?" she asked.

Now, what the devil's the meaning of this? thought Mr Beaumaris, startled. Can that damned young cub have been getting up to more mischief since I left town?

"At once?" he repeated, voice and countenance quite impassive.

"Yes!" said Arabella desperately. "You must know that I have the greatest dislike of–of all *formality*, and–and the nonsense that always accompanies the announcement of an engagement! I–I should wish to be married very quietly – in fact, in the strictest secrecy – and before anyone has guessed – that I have accepted your very obliging offer!"

The wretched youth must have been deeper under the hatches than I guessed, thought Mr Beaumaris, and still she dare not tell me the truth! Does she really mean to carry out this outrageous suggestion, or does she only think that she means it? A virtuous man would undoubtedly, at this juncture, disclose that there is not the smallest need for these measures. What very unamusing lives virtuous men must lead!

"You may think it odd of me, but I have always thought it would be so very romantic to elope!" pronounced Papa's daughter defiantly.

Mr Beaumaris, whose besetting sin was thought by many to be his exquisite enjoyment of the ridiculous, turned a deaf ear to the promptings of his better self, and replied instantly. "How right you are! I wonder I should not have thought of an elopement myself! The announcement of the engagement of two such notable figures as ourselves must provoke a degree of comment and congratulation which would not be at all to our taste!"

"Exactly so!" nodded Arabella, relieved to find that he saw the matter in so reasonable a light.

"Consider, too, the chagrin of such as Horace Epworth!" said Mr Beaumaris, growing momently more enamoured of the scheme. "You would be driven to distraction by their ravings!"

"Well, I do think I might be," said Arabella.

"There is not a doubt of it. Moreover, the formality of making application to your father for permission to address you is quite antiquated, and we shall do well to dispense with it. If some little feeling still exists in the minds of old-fashioned persons against marrying minors out of hand, it need not concern us, after all."

"N–no," agreed Arabella, rather doubtfully. "Do you think people will–will be very much shocked, sir?"

"No," said Mr Beaumaris, with perfect truth. "No one will be in the least shocked. When would you like to elope?"

"Would tomorrow be too soon?" asked Arabella anxiously.

Mr Beaumaris might wish that his love would give him her confidence, but it would have been idle to have denied that he was hugely enjoying himself. Life with Arabella would contain few dull moments; and although her estimate of his morals was unflattering enough to have discomposed any man of sensibility it left his withers unwrung, since he was well-aware that her assumption of his readiness to behave in so improper a fashion sprang from an innocence which he found enchanting. He replied with great promptness: "Not a moment too soon! But for the recollection that there are one or two preparations which perhaps I should make I should have suggested that we should leave this building together at once."

"No, that would be impossible," said Arabella seriously. "In fact – I do not know very much about such things, but I cannot but feel that it will be excessively difficult for me to escape from Park Street without anyone's knowing! For I must carry a valise with me, at least, besides my dressing-case, and how may it be contrived? Unless I crept out at dead of night, of course, but it would have to be very late indeed, for the porter always waits up for Lord Bridlington to come in. And I might fall asleep," she added candidly.

"I have a constitutional dislike of eloping at dead of night," said Mr Beaumaris firmly. "Such exploits entail the use of rope-ladders, I am credibly informed, and the thought of being surprised perhaps by the Watch in the very act of throwing this up to your window I find singularly unnerving."

"Nothing," said Arabella, "would prevail upon me to climb down a rope-ladder! Besides, my bedroom is at the back of the house."

"Perhaps," said Mr Beaumaris, "you had better leave me to make the necessary arrangements."

"Oh, yes!" responded Arabella gratefully. "I am sure you will know just how it should be contrived!"

This reflection upon his past career Mr Beaumaris bore with an unmoved countenance. "Just so, Miss Tallant," he said gravely. "Now, it occurs to me that, tomorrow being Wednesday, there will be a gala night at Vauxhall Gardens."

"Yes, Lady Bridlington thought at one time of taking me to it," agreed Arabella. "But then, you know, she recalled that it is the night of the party at Uxbridge House."

"A very dull affair, I have no doubt. I shall invite Lady Bridlington – and Bridlington, I suppose – to do me the honour of joining *my* party at Vauxhall. You will naturally be included in this invitation, and at a convenient moment during the course of the evening, we shall slip away together to the street entrance, where my chaise will be awaiting us."

Arabella considered this proposition, and discovered two objections to it. "Yes, but how very odd it would seem to Lady Bridlington if you were to go away in the middle of your own party!"

The reflection that Lady Bridlington might well deem this eccentricity the least odd feature of the affair Mr Beaumaris kept to himself. He said: "Very true. A note shall be delivered to her after our departure."

"Well, I suppose that would be better than nothing," Arabella conceded. "Oh, will she ever forgive me for treating her so?" This involuntary exclamation seemed to escape her without her knowledge. She raised the second of her objections. "And in any event it will not answer, because I cannot take a valise to Vauxhall!"

"That you will also leave to me," said Mr Beaumaris.

"But you cannot call in Park Street to fetch it!" she pointed out.

"Certainly not."

"And I will *not* elope without a change of clothes, or my hairbrushes, or my tooth-powder!" declared Arabella.

"Most improper," agreed Mr Beaumaris. "All these things shall be forthcoming."

"You cannot buy such things for me!" gasped Arabella, shocked.

"I assure you I should enjoy doing it."

She stared at him, and then exclaimed wretchedly: "How dreadful it all is! I never, never thought I should come to this! I daresay it seems the merest commonplace to you, but to me – But I see that it is of no use to cavil!"

The tell-tale muscle at the corner of Mr Beaumaris's mouth quivered, and was sternly repressed. "Well, perhaps not precisely commonplace," he said. "It so happens that I have not previously eloped with anyone. However, to a man of ordinary ingenuity the affair should not prove impossible to achieve creditably, I trust. I perceive Mrs Penkridge, who is hoping to catch either your eye or mine. We shall permit her to do so, and while she asks you to say if you do not think Nollekens's bust over there most like, I shall go in search of Lady Bridlington, and engage her to bring you to Vauxhall tomorrow evening."

"Oh, pray do not! I dislike Mrs Penkridge excessively!" she whispered.

"Yes, an odious woman, but impossible to avoid," he returned.

Seeing him rise to his feet, Mrs Penkridge bore down upon him, her acidulated smile on her lips. Mr Beaumaris greeted her with his smooth civility, stayed for perhaps a minute, and then, to Arabella's indignation, made his bow, and went off in the direction of the next room.

Either Lady Bridlington proved hard to find, or he must have fallen a victim to her garrulity, Arabella thought, for it seemed a very long time before she set eyes on him again. When he did reappear, Lady Bridlington was walking beside him, wreathed in smiles. Arabella made her excuses to Mrs Penkridge, and went across to her godmother, who greeted her with the cheerful intelligence that Mr Beaumaris had formed the most delightful scheme for an evening at Vauxhall. "I did not scruple to accept, my love, for I knew you would like it of all things!" she said.

"Yes," said Arabella, feeling that she was now committed to an irrevocable and reprehensible course which she would no doubt regret her life long. "I mean, oh, yes! how very agreeable!"

CHAPTER SIXTEEN

UPON LEAVING Somerset House, Mr Beaumaris got into a hackney, and drove to the Red Lion inn. What he learned at that hostelry threw abundant light on to Arabella's conduct. Since he had his own reasons for believing Arabella's heart to have been won long since, he was not in the least wounded by the discovery that she proposed to marry him as a means of rescuing her brother from debt, but, on the contrary, considerably amused. Having paid Bertram's bill at the inn, and received his watch back from the landlord, he returned to his own house in yet another hackney.

The same delight in the ridiculous which had made him wear a dandelion in his button-hole for three consecutive days for no better purpose than to enjoy the discomfiture of his misguided friends and copyists made him deeply appreciative of the situation in which he now found himself; and he beguiled the tedium of the drive to Mount Street in wondering when it would cross his absurd love's mind that the disclosure, following hard upon the wedding-ceremony, that she required a large sum of money from him without a moment's loss of time, might be productive of a little awkwardness. He could not resist picturing the scene, and was still laughing softly when he reached his house, a circumstance which considerably surprised his butler.

"Send round to the stables for my tilbury, will you, Brough?" he said. "And desire Painswick – oh, you're there, are you?" he added, as his valet descended the stairs. "I want to hear no more about missing shirts, on which excessively boring subject I can see from your expression you are prepared to discourse at length, but you may tell me this! Where is the letter I gave into your hands to be delivered at the Red Lion, to a Mr Anstey, and why did you not tell me that it had not been so delivered?"

"You may perhaps recall, sir," said Painswick reproachfully, "that I mentioned to you while you sat at breakfast that there was a matter which I deemed it my duty to bring to your notice. Upon which, sir, you said, Not now."

"Did I? I had no idea you could be so easily silenced. Where is the letter?"

"I placed it, sir, at the bottom of the pile that was awaiting you on the table here," replied Painswick, tacitly disclaiming further responsibility.

"In that case it is in the library. Thank you: that is all."

Ulysses, who had been lying stretched out in the library, enjoying the sleep of the replete, awoke at Mr Beaumaris's entrance, yawned, got up, shook himself, sneezed several times, stretched, and indicated by his cocked ears and wagging tail that he was now ready for any adventure.

"I am glad to see you restored to your usual self," said Mr Beaumaris, running through the mass of his neglected correspondence, and picking up his own letter to Bertram. "You know, you should not have dissuaded me from going out again that evening! Just look what has come of it! And yet I don't know. I would not have missed this morning's interview for a thousand pounds! I suppose you think that I am behaving very badly? I am, of course, but do me the justice to own that she deserves it for being such an adorable little fool!"

Ulysses wagged his tail. He was not only willing to do Mr Beaumaris justice, but presently indicated his readiness to accompany him on whatever expedition he had in mind.

"It would be useless to suggest, I suppose, that you are occupying Clayton's seat?" said Mr Beaumaris, mounting into his tilbury.

Clayton, grinning, expressed himself as being agreeable to taking the little dog on his knees, but Mr Beaumaris shook his head.

"No, no, I fear he would not like it. I shan't need you," he said, and drove off, remarking to his alert companion: "We are now faced with the wearing task of tracking down that foolish young man's inarticulate friend, Felix Scunthorpe. I wonder whether, in the general medley, there is any bloodhound strain in you?"

He drew blank at Mr Scunthorpe's lodging, but on being informed that Mr Scunthorpe had mentioned that he was going to Boodle's, drove at once to St James's Street, and was so fortunate as to catch sight of his quarry, walking up the flag-way. He reined in, and called imperatively: "Scunthorpe!"

Mr Scunthorpe had naturally perceived who was driving a spanking chestnut between the shafts of the tilbury, but as he had no expectation of being recognized by the Nonpareil this summons surprised him very much. He was even a little doubtful, and said cautiously: "Me, sir?"

"Yes, you. Where is young Tallant?" He saw an expression of great wariness descend upon Mr Scunthorpe's face, and added impatiently: "Come, don't be more of a fool than you can help! You don't suppose I am going to hand him over to the tipstaffs, do you?"

"Well, he's at the Cock," disclosed Mr Scunthorpe reluctantly. "That is to say," he corrected himself, suddenly recalling his friend's incognito, "he is, if you mean Mr Anstey."

"Have you any brothers?" demanded Mr Beaumaris.

"No," said Mr Scunthorpe, blinking at him. "Only child."

"You relieve my mind. Offer my congratulations to your parents!"

Mr Scunthorpe thought this over, with knit brow, but could make nothing of it. He put Mr Beaumaris right on one point. "Only one parent," he said. "Father died three months after I was born."

"Very understandable," said Mr Beaumaris. "I am astonished that he lingered on for so long. Where is this Cock you speak of?"

"Thing is – not sure I ought to tell you!" said Mr Scunthorpe.

"Take my word for it, you will be doing your misguided friend an extremely ill-turn if you don't tell me!"

"Well, it's at the corner of Duck Lane, Tothill Fields," confided Mr

Scunthorpe, capitulating.

"Good God!" said Mr Beaumaris, and drove off.

The Cock inn, however, though a small, squat building, proved to be more respectable than its situation had led Mr Beaumaris to suppose. Duck Lane might abound in filth of every description, left to rot in the road, but the Cock seemed to be moderately clean, and well-kept. It even boasted an ostler, who emerged from the stable to gape at the tilbury. When he understood that the swell handling the ribbons had not merely stopped to enquire the way, but really did desire him to take charge of his horse and carriage, a vision of enormous largesse danced before his eyes, and he hastened to assure this noble client that he was ready to bestow his undivided attention on the equipage.

Mr Beaumaris then descended from the tilbury, and walked into the tap of the inn, where his appearance caused a waterman, a jarvey off duty, two bricklayer's labourers, a scavenger, and the landlord to break off their conversation in mid-sentence to stare at him.

"Good-morning!" said Mr Beaumaris. "You have a Mr Anstey putting up here, I think?"

The landlord, recovering from his surprise, came forward, bowing several times. "Yes, your honour! Oh, yes, indeed, your honour! – Chase that cur out of here, Joe! – If your honour will -"

"Do nothing of the sort, Joe!" interrupted Mr Beaumaris.

"Is he *yours*, sir?" gasped the landlord.

"Certainly he is mine. A rare specimen: his family tree would surprise you! Is Mr Anstey in?"

"He'll be up in his room, sir. Keeps hisself *to* hisself, in a manner of speaking. If your honour would care to step into the parlour, I'll run up and fetch him down before the cat can lick her ear."

"No, take me up to him," said Mr Beaumaris. "Ulysses, do stop hunting for rats! We have no time to waste on sport this morning! Come to heel!"

Ulysses, who had found a promising hole in one corner of the tap, and was snuffing at it in a manner calculated to keep its occupant cowering inside it for the next twenty-four hours at least, regretfully obeyed this command, and followed Mr Beaumaris up a steep, narrow stairway. The landlord scratched on one of the three doors at the top of this stair, a voice bade him come in, and Mr Beaumaris, nodding dismissal to his guide, walked in, shut the door behind him, and said cheerfully: "How do you do? I hope you don't object to my dog?"

Bertram, who had been sitting at a small table, trying for the hundredth time to hit upon some method of solving his difficulties, jerked up his head, and sprang to his feet, as white as his shirt. "*Sir!*" he uttered, grasping the back of his chair with one shaking hand.

Ulysses, misliking his tone, growled at him, but was called to order. "How many more times am I to speak to you about your total lack of polish, Ulysses?" said Mr Beaumaris severely. "Never try to pick a quarrel with a man under his own roof! Lie down at once!" He drew off his gloves, and tossed them on to the bed. "What a very tiresome young man you are!" he told Bertram amiably.

Bertram, his face now as red as a beetroot, said in a choked voice: "I was coming to your house on Thursday, as you bade me!"

"I'm sure you were. But if you hadn't been so foolish as to leave the Red Lion so – er – hurriedly, there would not have been the slightest need for this rustication of yours. *You* would not have worried yourself half-way to Bedlam, and *I* should not have been obliged to bring Ulysses to a locality you can see he does not care for."

Bertram glanced in a bewildered way towards Ulysses, who was sitting suggestively by the door, and said: "You don't understand, sir. I–I was rolled-up! It was that, or–or prison, I suppose!"

"Yes, I rather thought you were," agreed Mr Beaumaris. "I sent a hundred pound banknote to you the next morning, together with my assurance that I had no intention of claiming from you the vast sums you lost to me. Of course, I should have done very much better to have told you so at the time – and better still to have ordered you out of the Nonesuch at the outset! But you will agree that the situation was a trifle awkward."

"Mr Beaumaris," said Bertram, with considerable difficulty, "I c-can't redeem my vowels now, but I pledge you my word that I *will* redeem them! I was coming to see you on Thursday, to tell you the whole, and–and to beg your indulgence!"

"Very proper," approved Mr Beaumaris. "But it is not my practice to win large sums of money from schoolboys, and you cannot expect me to change my habits only to accommodate your conscience, you know. Shall we sit down, or don't you trust the chairs here?"

"Oh, I beg pardon!" Bertram stammered, flushing vividly. "Of course! I don't know what I was thinking about! Pray, will you take this chair, sir? But it will not do! I must and I will – Oh, can I offer you any refreshment? They haven't anything much here, except beer and porter, and gin, but if you would care for some gin -"

"Certainly not, and if that is how you have been spending your time since last I saw you I am not surprised that you are looking burned to the socket."

"I haven't been – at least, I did at first, only it was brandy but not–not lately," Bertram muttered, very shamefaced.

"If you drank the brandy sold in this district, you must have a constitution of iron to be still alive," remarked Mr Beaumaris. "What's the sum total of your debts? Or don't you know?"

"Yes, but – *You* are not going to pay my debts, sir!" A dreadful thought occurred to him; he stared very hard at his visitor, and demanded: "Who told you where I was?"

"Your amiable but cork-brained friend, of course."

"*Scunthorpe?*" Bertram said incredulously. "It was not – it was not someone else?"

"No, it was not someone else. I have not so far discussed the matter with your sister, if that is what you mean."

"How do you know she is my sister?" Bertram said, staring at him harder than ever. "Do you say that Scunthorpe told you that too?"

"No, I guessed it from the start. Have you kept your bills? Let me have them!"

"Nothing would induce me to!" cried Bertram hotly. "I mean, I am very much obliged to you, sir, and it's curst good of you, but you must *see* that I couldn't accept such generosity! Why, we are almost strangers! I cannot conceive why you should think of doing such a thing for me!"

"Ah, but we are not destined to remain strangers!" explained Mr Beaumaris. "I am going to marry your sister."

"Going to marry *Bella*?" Bertram said.

"Certainly. You perceive that that puts the whole matter on quite a different footing. You can hardly expect me either to win money from my wife's brother at faro, or to bear the odium of having a relative in the Fleet. You really must consider *my* position a little, my dear boy."

Bertram's lip quivered. "I see what it is! She *did* go to you, and *that* is why – But if you think, sir, that I have sunk so low I would let Bella sacrifice herself only to save me from disgrace -"

Ulysses, taking instant exception to the raised voice, sprang to Mr Beaumaris's side, and barked a challenge at Bertram. Mr Beaumaris dropped a hand on his head. "Yes, very rude, Ulysses," he agreed. "But never mind! Bear in mind that it is not everyone who holds me in such high esteem as you do!"

Much confused, Bertram stammered; "I didn't mean – I beg your pardon! I only meant – She never said a word of this to me!"

"Didn't she? How secretive females are, to be sure! Perhaps she felt that her parents should be the first persons to learn the news."

"Well, I suppose she *might*," Bertram said doubtfully. "But considering she said she couldn't marry anyone, because she made 'em all think she was an heiress -"

"She didn't make me think anything of the sort," said Mr Beaumaris.

"Oh, I *see*!" said Bertram, his brow clearing. "Well, I must say, sir, I'm dashed glad, because I had a notion she liked you more than all the rest! I – I wish you very happy! And, of course, I do see that it makes a difference to my debt to *you*, only I don't think I should let you pay the other debts, because it is not in the least your affair, and -"

"Now, don't let us go into all that again!" begged Mr Beaumaris. "Just tell me what you propose to do if I don't pay your debts!"

"I thought of enlisting in a cavalry regiment, if they would take me," confessed Bertram. "Under an assumed name, of course!"

"I should think that a cavalry regiment would suit you very well," said Mr Beaumaris. "But it will be very much more comfortable for you, and for all of us, if you join it under your own name, and as a cornet. What do you want? a Hussar regiment?"

These incredible words made Bertram turn first red, and then white, swallow convulsively, and finally blurt out: "You *c-couldn't* mean that! After *this*! I – Oh, sir, *do* you mean it?"

"Yes, of course, but give me your bills!"

"I don't deserve anyone should do anything for me!" Bertram said, overcome.

"The bills!"

Bertram, already floating in some beatific dream, started, and said: "The bills? Oh! Oh, yes, I have them all here – only you will be very much shocked to see how much I have spent, and -"

"Nothing ever shocks me," replied Mr Beaumaris, holding out a hand. He stuffed the sheaf of crumpled papers into the pocket of his driving-coat, and said: "I will settle all these so that none of your creditors will know that it was not you who paid them. Do you owe anything in this neighbourhood beyond your shot here?"

Bertram shook his head. "No, for Bella gave me all the money she had, when she came to see me. I am afraid you would not have liked her doing so, sir, and nor did I, but Felix brought her, like the saphead he is! It – it was a horrid place, and I think I ought to tell you that it was all my fault that she ever went to such a back-slum!"

"You fill me with dismay," said Mr Beaumaris. "I do trust she did not set eyes on any destitute person whom she may feel it to be her duty to befriend?"

"Well, I don't *think* she did," Bertram replied. "Felix did say that she told a woman they all call Quartern Sue not to give her baby gin to drink, and gave her a shilling to buy it some milk. And I am excessively sorry, sir, and I would not have had it happen for the world, but Felix says that they walked smash into Leaky Peg, who–who took me to the place when I was so castaway I didn't know even where I was, or how I came there. She–she *was* very good to me, in her way, you know, and Bella got it into her head she owed her a debt of gratitude for looking after me! But that's all right, because I gave Peg five pounds out of the money Bella left for me!"

"Heaven help me!" said Mr Beaumaris. "She will undoubtedly expect me to house this doxy! *Leaky Peg*, did you say? Good God!"

"No, no, sir, of course she won't!" exclaimed Bertram. "Why *should* she?"

"Because that is her invariable practice," said Mr Beaumaris bitterly. "You don't suppose, do you, that I voluntarily adopted that animal over there?"

"You don't mean Bella gave him to you? Well, that's a great deal too bad of her! I must say, I thought it was a queer sort of a dog for *you* to have, sir!"

"The whole of London thinks it is a queer sort of a dog for me to have. Even the landlord of this tavern tried to chase him from the taproom!" He drew out his pocketbook, and extracted from it several banknotes, and pushed them across the table. "There you are: pay your shot here, redeem whatever lies in pawn, and book yourself the box-seat on the first stage to Harrowgate. I believe the northern-bound coaches leave at some godless hour of the morning, so you had better spend tonight at whatever inn they set out from. A few days in the fresh air will, I trust, repair the ravages of all the brandy you imbibed, and make it possible for you to meet your father without arousing suspicion."

Bertram tried to speak, failed, tried once more, and managed to say in a very gruff voice: "I c-can't thank you as I should, and of course I know it is for Bella's sake! But I *can* do one thing, and I will! I shall confess the whole to my father, sir, and–and if he says I may not join a Hussar regiment, after behaving so badly, well–well it will serve me right!"

"Yes," said Mr Beaumaris, "that is very noble of you, of course, but I have always found it to be an excellent plan, before one indulges in an orgy of expiation, to consider whether the recipient of the sort of confession you have in mind may not be made to suffer a great deal of quite unnecessary pain."

Bertram was silent for a moment, as this sank into his brain. "You don't think I should tell my father, sir?"

"I not only don't think you should: I utterly forbid you to mention the matter to him."

"I don't quite like to deceive him," Bertram said shyly. "You see -"

"I am sure you don't, so if your mind is set on doing penance, that will serve your turn excellently. You have been staying in Berkshire with Scunthorpe. Just bear that in mind, and forget that you have ever been within ten miles of London!" He rose, and held out his hand. "Now I must go. Don't harrow yourself with thinking that you have broken all the ten commandments! You have only done what four out of five young fools do, if set loose upon the town. Incidentally, you have acquired a deal of valuable experience, and when next you come to London you will do much better."

"I shall never be able to show my face in London again, sir," said Bertram wistfully. "But thank you!"

"Nonsense! A few years' service, and you will become a dashing Captain, I daresay, with a fine pair of military whiskers. No one will recognize you. By the way, don't call to take leave of your sister: she is very much occupied today. I will tell her that you are safely despatched to Yorkshire. Ulysses, stop scratching! Do try to be a little more worthy of me! Yes, we are now going, but it is quite unnecessary, and, indeed, extremely uncivil, to caper about in that joyful fashion!" He picked up his gloves, shook hands, and walked to the door, but bethought him of something, and put a hand into his inner pocket. "Association with that hound – the boon companion of every prig in town, I have not a shadow of doubt – is fast undermining my morals. Your watch, Bertram!"

CHAPTER SEVENTEEN

MR BEAUMARIS'S subsequent proceedings, during the short space of time that elapsed before his elopement, were many and varied, but although they included precise instructions to his coachman and his postilion, and a drive out of London, there was one curious omission: he took no steps to procure a special licence, so that it was to be inferred that he contemplated a flight to the Border, and a ceremony performed across the anvil at Gretna Green: a departure from the canons of good taste which would have staggered any of his associates who had had the least suspicion of his clandestine intentions. But as no one who met him detected anything out of the ordinary in his demeanour no one except his prospective bride speculated at all on the course of action he meant to pursue.

Arabella, naturally enough, employed every moment that was unoccupied by social engagements in a great deal of speculation, but as she was wholly ignorant of the rules governing hasty marriages the need of a special licence did not occur to her. She certainly supposed that she would be driven to Gretna Green, and, having once accepted this hateful necessity, resolutely turned her thoughts away from it. Romantic though such an adventure might be, no young lady, reared, as she had been, in the strictest propriety, could embark on it without feeling herself to have sunk to irreclaimable depths of depravity. How she was ever to explain such conduct to the satisfaction of Papa was an unanswerable question. Only the thought of Bertram's predicament in any way sustained her. She snatched ten minutes between seeing a balloon-ascent and dressing for a more than ordinarily splendid ball, in scribbling a letter to Bertram, assuring him that he need only wait patiently at the Cock for a few more days before he should infallibly be rescued from all his embarrassments.

Of Mr Beaumaris she saw nothing until she met him at Vauxhall Gardens. He was not present at the ball on the night previous to their assignation, a circumstance of which she hardly knew whether to be glad or sorry.

Perhaps it was fortunate that Lady Bridlington's plans for their amusement left her with so little time for reflection. The indulgence of a quiet hour or two in her own bedchamber was not granted her. Try as she would she was unable to stay awake after that splendid ball, and only awoke next morning when Maria drew back her window-blinds. The day was full to overflowing with engagements: she was dressing for Mr Beaumaris's Vauxhall Gardens party, before, as it seemed to her, she well realized what she was about.

It so happened that through the press of invitations which had showered down upon the house in Park Street Arabella had never before visited the famous gardens. They took sculls across the river, to enter by the water-gate, and at any other time she must have been transported by the sight which met her eyes. The gardens, which were laid out in groves and colonnades, were lit (as Lord Bridlington instructively informed her) by no fewer than thirty-seven thousand lamps, some of them suspended in graceful festoons between the pillars of the colonnades. The orchestra, detected across the principal grove, was established in a giant kiosk, glittering all over with coloured lights; there was a spacious Pavilion, lined with mirrors, which formed the principal supper-room for those who did not care to go to the expense of hiring one of the boges which opened on to the various colonnades; a Rotunda, where excellent concerts were held throughout the season; several magnificent fountains; and innumerable walks where lovers could lose themselves at will.

Mr Beaumaris met his guests at the water-entrance, and conducted them to the Rotunda, where, since it was past eight o'clock, the concert was already in progress. Arabella could scarcely meet his eyes, but forced herself to look up once, very fleetingly, into his face. He smiled at her, but no private speech passed between them.

After the first act of the concert, at about ten o'clock, a bell rang, and those who had no ear for music poured into the Rotunda to witness the marvels of the Grand Cascade. Even though feelings of guilt were in danger of overcoming her, Arabella could not help uttering an exclamation of delight when a dark curtain arose to reveal a rural scene, done in miniature, but amazingly life-like, of a cascade, a watermill, a bridge, and a succession of coaches, wagons, and other vehicles passing with every appearance of verisimilitude across the stage. Even the sound of the wheels, and the rush of the waters was ingeniously counterfeited, so that she thought it no matter for wonder that people should visit Vauxhall three and four times only to see this marvel.

When the curtain descended again, Mr Beaumaris suggested that his guests might like to partake of supper instead of waiting to hear the second part of the concert. This being agreed to, they edged their way out of the row where they were sitting and strolled down one of the colonnades to the supper-box which had been hired for their accommodation. This was in an excellent position, not too close to the orchestra in the kiosk to make conversation a labour, and commanding a splendid view of the principal grove. No one, of course, could visit Vauxhall without eating the wafer-thin slices of ham for which the suppers were famous, or tasting the rack-punch; but in addition to these delicacies Mr Beaumaris had ordered a meal so excellently chosen as to tempt the most fugitive appetite. Even Arabella, whose appetite had deserted her several days before, could enjoy the chicken, cooked before her eyes in a chafing-dish; and was persuaded to toy with a trifle. Mr Beaumaris prepared a peach for her with his own hands, and since an imminent elopement was no excuse, she believed, for a present lapse of good manners, she ate this too, smiling shyly and gratefully at him. She found little to say beyond the merest commonplace throughout supper, but this silence passed unnoticed in the spate of Lord Bridlington's discourse. He kindly explained to the ladies the mechanism which produced the wonders of the Grand Cascade; sketched the history of the Gardens; extensively examined their claim to be considered a development of the old Spring Gardens; and disposed of the tradition which linked the district with the name of Guy Fawkes. He was only interrupted when it became necessary to exchange greetings with some acquaintance who happened to walk past the box; and since his mother murmured encouraging remarks every now and then, and Mr Beaumaris, with great self-control, forbore to utter one of his blighting snubs, he enjoyed himself very much, and was sorry when his host suggested that Miss Tallant would like to see the Fireworks.

He was allowed to take Arabella on his arm on their way to the part of the grounds whence these could best be seen, while Mr Beaumaris followed beside Lady Bridlington, but just as he had secured two excellent places he found himself, quite how he did not know, supplanted, and was obliged to attend to his Mama, who did not like her situation, and insisted on his finding her a place where her view of the set-pieces would not be obscured by the head-dress of a lady who favoured immensely tall ostrich plumes.

Arabella momentarily forgot her troubles in enchantment, and clapped her hands when the rockets soared skywards, and burst into stars. Mr Beaumaris, inured to fireworks, derived even more entertainment through watching her round-eyed delight; but after the first of the set-pieces had burnt itself out, he consulted his watch, and said gently: "Shall we go, Miss Tallant?"

These words brought her to earth with a shock. An impulse to tell him that she had changed her mind had to be sternly repressed, and all the miseries poor Bertram must be enduring recalled. She clutched her taffeta cloak round her, and said nervously: "Oh, yes! Is it already time? Yes, let us go at once!"

There was not the least difficulty in detaching themselves unnoticed from a crowd of persons all intent upon the evolutions of a giant Catherine-wheel; Arabella laid a cold hand on Mr Beaumaris's arm, and went with him down an alley, past the Fountain of Neptune, most tastefully illuminated, along one of the colonnades, and so to the land-entrance. Several carriages were awaiting their owners here, and amongst them Mr Beaumaris's travelling chaise, with a pair of horses harnessed to it, and his head-coachman, and one postilion in attendance. Neither of these individuals betrayed the smallest surprise at seeing a lady on his master's arm, and although Arabella was too much embarrassed to raise her eyes she was aware that they were conducting themselves as though this elopement were an everyday occurrence in their lives. They sprang to well-trained activity as soon as they saw their master; the cloths were swept from the back of Mr Beaumaris's highly-bred horses; the steps of the chaise were let down, the doors opened, and Mr Beaumaris handed his bride tenderly up into the luxurious vehicle. So little time had she been kept waiting in the road that she did not even look to see whether any baggage was strapped to the back of the chaise. Mr Beaumaris paused only to exchange a word with the coachman, and then sprang up, and took his place beside Arabella on the comfortably cushioned seat; the doors were shut on them; the postilion swung himself into the saddle, and the equipage moved forward.

Mr Beaumaris spread a soft rug over Arabella's legs, and said: "I have a warmer cloak here: may I put it round your shoulders?"

"Oh, no, thank you! I am quite warm!" Arabella said nervously.

He took her hand, and kissed it. After a moment she drew it away, and sought desperately for something to say to relieve the tension of the moment.

"How very well-sprung your chaise is, sir!" she achieved.

"I am glad you are pleased with it," he responded, in the same polite tone which she had used. "I remembered, of course, that we are alike in detesting hired vehicles."

"Are – are we?" she said doubtfully. "I mean, of course -"

"We exchanged opinions, the first time we met, on the only tolerable way of travel," Mr Beaumaris reminded her.

This recollection not unnaturally deprived her of speech. Mr Beaumaris, most obligingly, forbore to press her for an answer, but talked agreeably about the concert they had heard that night. Arabella, who had experienced a few moments' panic on finding herself shut up with her bridegroom in a chaise, travelling to an unknown but probably remote destination, was overwhelmingly grateful to him for behaving precisely as though he were escorting her home from some place of entertainment. She had been much afraid that he would perhaps have tried to make love to her. She had not much experience in such matters, but it had occurred to her that a gentleman starting on an elopement might expect some demonstration of affection from his beloved. A week earlier, safe in the darkness of her bedchamber, her cheek on a damp pillow, Arabella had owned to herself that life could hold no greater happiness for her than for Mr Beaumaris to take her in his arms; now, miserably conscious of her duplicity, she could imagine nothing more unnerving. But Mr Beaumaris, surely the calmest of runaway-bridegrooms, showed no desire to succumb to his ardour. Finding that he was being answered in monosyllables, he presently gave up trying to engage Arabella in genteel conversation, and leaned back in his corner of the chaise, his head a little turned against the squabs behind it towards her, so that he could watch her face in the dim moonlight that penetrated into the vehicle. Arabella was scarcely aware that he had stopped talking to her. She was lost in her own thoughts, seated bolt upright, and clinging with one hand to the strap that hung from the wall of the chaise beside her. She could see the postilion bobbing up and down before her, and, when the cobbles were left behind, was vaguely conscious of having left the streets and to be driving through the countryside. In what direction they were travelling, or where she would find herself at the first halt, she had no idea, nor were these the questions that troubled her mind. The impropriety of her conduct she had from the start known to be unforgiveable; what now filled her with repugnance was the sudden realization that in marrying Mr Beaumaris while he still laboured under a misapprehension she was treating him so shabbily that it was doubtful if he would ever pardon her, much less continue to regard her with even a shred of affection. At this melancholy reflection a small sob escaped her, which had the effect of making Mr Beaumaris say: "What is it, my love?"

"Nothing! Nothing!" whispered Arabella, much agitated.

To her relief, he appeared to accept this, for he said no more. She decided, in a wave of remorse, that he was the greatest gentleman of her acquaintance, with the best manners, the most delicate forbearance, and quite the kindest disposition. It was at this point that the moment for which Mr Beaumaris had been waiting arrived. All at once Arabella wondered how soon after the wedding-ceremony she could break the news to him that she required him not only to forgive her brother's debt to him, but also to bestow a hundred pounds on him for the settlement of all his other liabilities; and what words she could find with which most unexceptionably to express this urgent necessity. There were no such words, as a very little cudgelling of her brain sufficed to convince her. She could not imagine how she could ever have been foolish enough to have supposed that the thing could be done, or that such a confession could be made without afterwards rendering it impossible for her to convince him that she did indeed love him.

These, and still more disagreeable thoughts, were jostling one another in Arabella's frightened mind when the pace at which they were travelling seemed sensibly to slacken. The chaise swung round at so sharp an angle that only her clutch on the strap saved Arabella from being thrown on to Mr Beaumaris's shoulder. It proceeded for a very little way, and then drew up. Arabella turned towards the dupe beside her, and said breathlessly: "I cannot! I cannot! Mr Beaumaris, I am *very* sorry, but it was all a mistake! Please take me back to London at once! Oh, please take me back!"

Mr Beaumaris received this daunting request with a remarkable degree of composure, merely replying, as the door of the chaise was opened: "Shall we discuss this matter in a more private spot? Let me assist you to alight, my love!"

"Please take me back! I–I don't want to elope, after all!" said Arabella, in an urgent whisper.

"Then we won't elope," returned Mr Beaumaris reassuringly. "I must own that I think it quite unnecessary for us to do so. Come!"

Arabella hesitated, but since he seemed determined that she should descend from the chaise, and perhaps wanted to rest his horses, she allowed him to hand her down. They seemed to be standing before a large building, but it showed none of the welcoming lights to be expected of a posting-inn, nor had the chaise driven into a courtyard. At the top of a flight of broad, shallow stone steps a large door opened, and a beam of light from the interior of the building showed Arabella neat flower-beds flanking the entrance. Before she had recovered from the surprise of finding herself at what was plainly a private residence, Mr Beaumaris had led her up the steps, and into a lofty hall, furnished in a massive style, and lit by candles in wall-chandeliers. An elderly butler bowed them in, and said: "Good-evening sir." One powdered and liveried footman divested Mr Beaumaris of his cloak, another relieved him of his hat and gloves.

Arabella stood turned to stone as all the implications of her surroundings burst upon her. Mr Beaumaris's soothing assurance to her that they would not elope now became invested with the most sinister significance, and it was a pathetically white and frightened face which she turned towards him. He smiled at her, but before either of them had time to speak, the butler had informed Mr Beaumaris that he would find the Yellow Saloon in readiness; and a most respectable-looking housekeeper, with neat white hair under a starched cap, had appeared upon the scene, and was dropping a curtsy to Arabella.

"Good-evening, miss! Good-evening, Mr Robert! Please to take Miss into the saloon, while I see that the maids unpack her trunk! You will find a nice fire, for I am sure Miss must be chilled after the drive, so late as it is. Let me take your cloak, miss! I shall bring you up a glass of hot milk directly: I am sure you will be glad of it."

The promise of a glass of hot milk, which hardly seemed to be in keeping with the hideous vision of seduction and rape which had leapt to her mind, a little reassured Arabella. One of the footmen had thrown open a door at the back of the hall; Mr Beaumaris possessed himself of a trembling, icy little hand, and said: "I want to make you known to Mrs Watchet, my love, who is a very old friend of mine. Indeed, one of my earliest allies!"

"Now, Master Robert! I'm sure I am very happy to see you here, miss – and mind, now, don't let Master Robert keep you out of your bed till all hours!"

The fear that Master Robert had quite different intentions receded still farther. Arabella summoned up a smile, said something in a shy little voice, and allowed herself to be led into a saloon, fitted up in the first style of elegance, and offering her all the comfort of a small fire, burning in a brightly polished grate.

The door was softly closed behind them; Mr Beaumaris drew a chair invitingly forward, and said: "Come and sit down, Miss Tallant! You know, I cannot but be glad that you have decided after all not to elope with me. To tell you the truth, there is one circumstance at least that makes me reluctant to proceed with you to Scotland – a journey that would occupy six or seven days, I daresay, before we found ourselves back in London."

"Oh!" said Arabella, sitting down primly on the edge of the chair, and regarding him out of scared, doubtful eyes.

"Yes," said Mr Beaumaris. "Ulysses!"

Her eyes widened. "Ulysses?" she repeated blankly.

"The animal you were so obliging as to bestow upon me," he explained. "Most unfortunately, he has developed so marked a predilection for my society that he frets himself to skin and bone if I am absent from him for more than a night. I did not quite like to bring him with me upon our elopement, for I can discover no precedent for taking a dog with one upon such an occasion, and one scarcely cares to violate the conventions at such a moment."

The door opened just then to admit Mrs Watchet, who came in, carrying a glass of steaming milk on a silver tray. This, with a plate of macaroons, she set down on a small table at Arabella's elbow, telling her that when she had drunk it, and said goodnight to Master Robert, she should be escorted upstairs to her bed-chamber. With a slightly severe injunction to Mr Beaumaris not to keep Miss talking to him too long, she then curtsied herself out of the room.

"Sir!" said Arabella desperately, as soon as they were alone again: "What is this house to which you have brought me?"

"I have brought you to my grandmother's house, at Wimbledon," he replied. "She is a very old lady, and keeps early hours, so you must forgive her for not being downstairs to receive you. You will meet her tomorrow morning. My aunt, who lives with her, would undoubtedly have sat up to receive you had she not gone a few days ago to stay with one of her sisters for a short time."

"Your grandmother's house?" exclaimed Arabella, almost starting from her chair. "Good God, why have you brought me to such a place, Mr Beaumaris?"

"Well, you know," he explained, "I could not but feel that it was possible you might think better of that notion of eloping. Of course, if, after a night's repose, you still believe we should go to Gretna Green, I assure you I shall escort you there, whatever Ulysses' claims upon me may be. For myself, the more I consider the matter, the more I am convinced that we should do better to steel ourselves to meet the felicitations of our friends, and announce our betrothal in the columns of the society journals in the accepted manner."

"Mr Beaumaris," interrupted Arabella, pale but resolute, "I cannot marry you!" She added, on another of her small sobs: "I don't know why you should ever have wanted to marry me, but -"

"I have lost my entire fortune on 'Change, and must instantly repair it," he interrupted promptly.

Arabella rose jerkily, and confronted him. "I have not a penny in the world!" she announced.

"In that case," responded Mr Beaumaris, maintaining his calm, "you really have no choice in the matter: you must obviously marry me. Since we are being frank with one another, I will confess that my fortune is still intact."

"I deceived you! I am not an heiress!" Arabella said, feeling that he could not have understood her words.

"You never deceived me for a moment," said Mr Beaumaris, smiling at her in a way which made her tremble still more violently.

"I *lied* to you!" cried Arabella, determined to bring him to a sense of her iniquities.

"Most understandable," agreed Mr Beaumaris. "But I am really quite uninterested in heiresses."

"Mr Beaumaris," said Arabella earnestly, "the whole of London believes me to be a wealthy woman!"

"Yes, and since the whole of London must certainly continue in that belief, you have, as I have already pointed out to you, no choice but to marry me," he said. "My fortune, happily, is so large that *your* lack of fortune need never be suspected."

"Oh, why didn't you tell me you knew the truth?" she cried, wringing her hands.

He possessed himself of them, and held them lightly. "My dearest goose, why didn't you trust me, when I assured you that you might?" he countered. "I have cherished throughout the belief that you would confide in me, and you see I was quite right. So certain was I that you would not, when the time actually came, run off with me in this absurd fashion, that I visited my grandmother yesterday, and told her the whole story. She was very much diverted, and commanded me to bring you to stay for a few days with her. I hope you will not object to this: she frightens half the world, but you will have me to support you through the ordeal."

Arabella pulled her hands resolutely away, and turned from him to hide her quivering lips, and suffused eyes. "It is worse than you know!" she said, in a stifled tone. "When you know all the truth, you will not wish to marry me! I have been worse than untruthful: I have been shameless! I can never marry you, Mr Beaumaris!"

"This is most disturbing," he said. "Not only have I sent the notice of our betrothal to the *Gazette*, and the *Morning Post*, but I have obtained your father's consent to our marriage."

At this, she spun round to face him again, a look of utter astonishment in her face. "*My Father's consent?*" she repeated incredulously.

"It is usual, you know," explained Mr Beaumaris apologetically.

"But you do not know my father!"

"On the contrary. I made his acquaintance last week, and spent two most agreeable nights at Heythram," he said.

"But – Did Lady Bridlington tell you?"

"No, not Lady Bridlington. Your brother let slip the name of his home once, and I have an excellent memory. I am sorry, by the way, that Bertram should have been having such an uncomfortable time during my absence from town. That was quite my fault: I should have sought him out, and settled his difficulties before I left for Yorkshire. I did write to him, but he had unfortunately departed from the Red Lion before the delivery of my letter. However, you won't find that the experience has harmed him, so I must hope to be forgiven."

Her cheeks were now very much flushed. "You know it all then! Oh, what must you think of me? I asked you to marry me because – because I wanted you to give me seven hundred pounds to save poor Bertram from a debtor's prison!"

"I know you did," said Mr Beaumaris cordially. "I don't know how I contrived to keep my countenance. When did it occur to you, my ridiculous little love, that to demand a large sum of money from your bridegroom as soon as the ring was on your finger might be a trifle awkward?"

"Just now – in your chaise!" she confessed, covering her face with her hands. "I couldn't do it! I have behaved very, very badly, but when I realized what I was about – oh, indeed, I knew I could never do it!"

"We have both behaved very badly," he agreed. "I encouraged Fleetwood to spread the news that you were a great heiress: I even allowed him to suppose that I knew all about your family. I thought it would be amusing to see whether I could make you the rage of London – and I blush to confess it, my darling: it *was* amusing! Nor do I really regret it in the least, for if I had not set out on this most reprehensible course we might never have come much in one another's way again, after our first meeting, and I might never have discovered that I had found the very girl I had been looking for for so long."

"No, no, how can you say so?" she exclaimed, large tears standing on the ends of her lashes. "I came to London in the hope of – of contracting an eligible marriage, and I asked you to marry me because you are so very rich! You *could* not wish to marry such an odious creature!"

"No, perhaps I couldn't," he replied. "But although you may have forgotten that when I first addressed myself to you, you declined my offer, I have not. If wealth was all your object, I can't conceive what should have induced you to do so! It seemed to me that you were not entirely indifferent to me. All things considered, I decided that my proper course was to present myself to your parents without further loss of time. And I am very glad I did so, for not only did I spend a very pleasant time at the Vicarage, but I also enjoyed a long talk with your mother – By the way, do you know how much you resemble her? more, I think, than any of your brothers and sisters, though they are all remarkably handsome. But, as I say, I enjoyed a long talk with her, and was encouraged to hope, from what she told me, that I had not been mistaken in thinking you were not indifferent to me."

"I never wrote a word to Mama, or even to Sophy, about – about – not being indifferent to you!" Arabella said involuntarily.

"Well, I do not know how that may be," said Mr Beaumaris, "but Mama and Sophy were not at all surprised to receive a visit from me. Perhaps you may have mentioned me rather frequently in your letters, or perhaps Lady Bridlington gave Mama a hint that I was the most determined of your suitors."

The mention of her godmother made Arabella start, and exclaim: "Lady Bridlington! Good God, I left a letter for her on the table in the hall, telling her of the dreadful thing I had done, and begging her to forgive me!"

"Don't disturb yourself, my love: Lady Bridlington knows very well where you are. Indeed, I found her most helpful, particularly when it came to packing what you would need for a brief sojourn at my grandmother's house. She promised that her own maid should attend to the matter while we were listening to that tedious concert. I daresay she has long since told that son of hers that he may look for the notice of our engagement in tomorrow's *Gazette*, together with the intelligence that we have both of us gone out of town to stay with the Dowager Duchess of Wigan. By the time we reappear in London, we must hope that our various acquaintances will have grown so accustomed to the news that we shall not be quite overwhelmed by their astonishment, their chagrin, or their felicitations. But I am strongly of the opinion that you should permit me to escort you home to Heythram as soon as possible: *you* will naturally wish your father to marry us, and I am extremely impatient to carry off my wife without any loss of time. My darling, what in the world have I said to make you cry?"

"Oh, nothing, nothing!" sobbed Arabella. "Only that I don't deserve to be so happy, and I n-never was indifferent to you, though I t-tried very hard to be, when I thought you were only trifling with m-me!"

Mr Beaumaris then took her firmly into his arms, and kissed her; after which she derived much comfort from clutching the lapel of his elegant coat, and weeping into his shoulder. None of the very gratifying things which Mr Beaumaris murmured into the curls that were tickling his chin had any other effect on her than to make her sob more bitterly than ever, so he presently told her that even his love for her could not prevail upon him to allow her to ruin his favourite coat. This changed her tears to laughter, and after he had dried her face, and kissed her again, she became tolerably composed, and was able to sit down on the sofa beside him, and to accept from him the glass of tepid milk which he told her she must drink if she did not wish to incur Mrs Watchet's displeasure. She smiled mistily, and sipped the milk, saying after a moment: "And Papa gave his consent! Oh, what will he say when he knows the whole? What did you tell him?"

"I told him the truth," replied Mr Beaumaris.

Arabella nearly dropped the glass. "All the truth?" she faltered, dismay in her face.

"All of it – oh, not the truth about Bertram! His name did not enter into our conversation, and I strictly charged him, when I sent him off to Yorkshire, not to divulge one word of his adventures. Much as I like and esteem your father, I cannot feel that any good purpose would be served by distressing him with *that* story. I told him the truth about you and me."

"Was he dreadfully displeased with me?" asked Arabella, in a small, apprehensive voice.

"He was, I fear, a little grieved," owned Mr Beaumaris. "But when he understood that you would never have announced yourself to have been an heiress had you not overheard me talking like a coxcomb to Charles Fleetwood, he was soon brought to perceive that I was even more to blame for the deception than you."

"*Was* he?" said Arabella doubtfully.

"Drink your milk, my love! Certainly he was. Between us, your Mama and I were able to show him that without my prompting Charles would never have spread the rumour abroad, and that once the rumour had been so spread it was impossible for you to deny it, since naturally no one ever asked you if it were true. I daresay he may give you a little scold, but I am quite sure you are already forgiven."

"Did he forgive you too?" asked Arabella, awed.

"*I* had all the merit of making the confession," Mr Beaumaris pointed out virtuously. "He forgave me freely. I cannot imagine why you should look so much surprised: I found him in every way delightful, and have seldom enjoyed an evening more than the one I spent conversing with him in his study, after your Mama and Sophy had gone to bed. Indeed, we sat talking until the candles guttered in their sockets."

Arabella's awed expression became even more marked. "Dear sir, what – what did you talk *about*?" she enquired, quite unable to visualize Papa and the Nonpareil hobnobbing together.

"We discussed certain aspects of Wolf's *Prolegomena ad Homerum*, a copy of which work I chanced to see upon his bookshelf," replied Mr Beaumaris calmly. "I myself picked up a copy when I was in Vienna last year, and was much interested in Wolf's theory that more than one hand was employed in the writing of the *Iliad* and the *Odyssey*."

"Is – is *that* what the book is about?" asked Arabella.

He smiled, but replied gravely: "Yes, that is what it is about – though your father, a far more profound scholar than I am, found the opening chapter, which treats of the proper methods to be used in the recension of ancient manuscripts, of even more interest. He took me a little out of my depth there, but I hope I may have profited by his very just observations."

"Did you *enjoy* that?" demanded Arabella, much impressed.

"Very much. In spite of my frippery ways, you know, I do occasionally enjoy rational conversation, just as I can spend a very agreeable evening playing at lottery-tickets with Mama, and Sophy, and the children."

"You did not do *that!*" she cried. "Oh, you are quizzing me! You must have been shockingly bored!"

"Nothing of the sort! The man who could be bored in the midst of such a lively family as yours must be an insufferable fellow, above being pleased by anything. By the by, if that uncle of yours does not come up to scratch, we must do something towards helping Harry to achieve his burning ambition to become a second Nelson. Not the eccentric uncle who died, and left you his entire fortune, but the one who still lives."

"Oh, pray don't speak of that dreadful fortune ever again!" begged Arabella, hanging down her head.

"But I must speak of it!" objected Mr Beaumaris. "Since I presume that we shall frequently be inviting the various members of your family to stay with us, and can hardly pass them all off as heirs and heiresses, *some* explanation of your superior circumstances must be forthcoming! Your Mama – an admirable woman! – and I decided that the eccentric uncle would serve our turn very well. We were further agreed, quite tacitly, you know, that it will be unnecessary, and, indeed, quite undesirable, to mention the matter to Papa."

"Oh, no it would never do to tell him that!" she said quickly. "He would not like it at all, and when he is grieved with any of us – Oh, if only he does not discover the scrape Bertram fell into, and if only Bertram didn't fail to pass that examination at Oxford, which I am much afraid he may have, because it did not sound to me as though -"

"It is not of the slightest consequence," he interrupted. "Bertram – though Papa does not yet know it is not going to Oxford: he is going to join a good cavalry regiment, where he will feel very much more at home, and, I daresay, become a great credit to us all."

At this, Arabella caught his hand in her free one, and kissed it, exclaiming, with a sob in her voice: "How good you are! How much, much *too* good you are, my *dear* Mr Beaumaris!"

"Never," said Mr Beaumaris, snatching his hand away, and taking Arabella into his arms so ungently that the rest of the milk in the glass was spilt over her gown, *"Never*, Arabella, dare to do such a thing again! And don't talk such fustian to me, or persist in calling me Mr Beaumaris!"

"Oh, I must!" protested Arabella, into his shoulder. "I can't call you – I can't call you – Robert!"

"You have called me Robert very prettily, and you will find, if you persevere, that it will rise quite easily to your lips in a very short space of time."

"Well, if it will please you, I will *try* to say it," said Arabella. She sat up suddenly, as a thought occurred to her, and said in her impulsive way: "Oh, Mr Beau – I mean, dear Robert! -- there was an unfortunate female, called Leaky Peg, in that horrid house where I went to see poor Bertram, and she was so very kind to him! Do you think --?"

"No, Arabella!" said Mr Beaumaris firmly. "I do not!"

She was disappointed, but docile. "No?" she said.

"No," said Mr Beaumaris, drawing her back into his arm.

"I thought we might have taken her away from that dreadful place," suggested Arabella, smoothing his coat-lapel with a coaxing hand.

"I am quite sure you did, my love, but while I am prepared to receive into my household climbing-boys and stray curs, I must draw the line at a lady rejoicing in the name of Leaky Peg."

"You don't think she might learn to become a housemaid, or something of that sort? You know -"

"I only know two things," interrupted Mr Beaumaris. "The first is that she is not going to make the attempt in any house of mine; and the second, and by far the more important, is that I adore you, Arabella!"

Arabella was so much pleased by this disclosure that she lost interest in Leaky Peg, and confined herself to the far more agreeable task of convincing Mr Beaumaris that his very obliging sentiments were entirely reciprocated.

BATH TANGLE

CHAPTER ONE

TWO LADIES were seated in the library at Milverley Park, the younger, whose cap and superabundance of crape proclaimed the widow, beside a table upon which reposed a Prayer Book; the elder, a Titian-haired beauty of some twenty-five summers, in one of the deep window-embrasures that overlooked the park. The Funeral Service had been read aloud, in a pretty, reverent voice, by the widow; but the Prayer Book had been closed and laid aside for some time, the silence being broken only by desultory remarks, uttered by one or other of the ladies, and the ticking of the clock upon the mantelpiece.

The library, whose curiously carved bookshelves and gilded and painted ceiling had earned it honourable mention in every Guide Book to Gloucestershire, was a handsome apartment, situated upon the ground floor of the mansion, and furnished with sombre elegance. It had been used, until so short a time previously, almost exclusively by the late Earl of Spenborough: a faint aroma of cigars hung about it, and every now and then the widow's blue eyes rested on the big mahogany desk, as though she expected to see the Earl seated behind it. An air of gentle sorrow clung about he, and there was a bewildered expression on her charming countenance, as though she could scarcely realize her loss.

It had indeed been as sudden as it was unexpected. No one, least of all himself, could have supposed that the Earl, a fine, robust man in his fiftieth year, would owe his death to so paltry a cause as a chill, contracted when salmon fishing on the Wye. Not all the solicitations of his host and hostess had prevailed upon him to cosset this trifling ailment; he had enjoyed another day's fishing; and had returned to Milverley, testily making light of his condition, but so very far from well that his daughter had had no hesitation in overriding his prohibition, and had sent immediately for a physician. A severe inflammation of both lungs was diagnosed, and within a week he was dead, leaving a wife and a daughter to mourn him, and a cousin, some fifteen years his junior, to succeed to his dignities. He had no other child, a circumstance generally held to account for his startling marriage, three years earlier, to the pretty girl who had not then attained the dignity of her twentieth year. Only the most forbearing of his friends could think the match allowable. Neither his splendid physique nor his handsome face could disguise the fact that he was older than his bride's father, for his birth-date could be read in any *Peerage*, and his daughter had been the mistress of his establishment for four years. When no heir to the Earldom resulted from the unequal match, those who most deprecated the Earl's many eccentricities pronounced it to be a judgment upon him, his sister, Lady Theresa Eaglesham, adding obscurely, but with conviction, that it would teach Serena a lesson. Any girl who dismissed her chaperon at the age of twenty-one, refused two flattering offers of marriage, and cried off from an engagement to the most brilliant prize in the Marriage Mart was well served when her father brought home a young bride to supplant her, said Lady Theresa. And all to no purpose, as she for one had foretold from the outset!

Some such reflection seemed to be in the widow's mind. She said mournfully: "If I could have been more dutiful! I have been so very conscious of it, and *now* the thought quite oppresses me!"

Her stepdaughter, who had been leaning her chin on her hand, and gazing out at the trees in the park, just touched with autumn gold, turned her head at this, and said bracingly: "Nonsense!"

"Your Aunt Theresa -"

"Let us be thankful that my Aunt Theresa's dislike of me has kept her away from us at this moment!" interrupted Serena.

"Oh, don't say so! If she had not been indisposed -"

"She was never so in her life. Wretched work my Uncle Eaglesham made of her excuses." He is a poor creature."

"Perhaps she has stayed away, then, because she does not like me," said the widow unhappily.

"No such thing! Now, Fanny, don't be absurd! As though anyone could help liking you! For my part, I am excessively obliged to her for remaining in Sussex. We can never meet without rubbing one another, and although I think her the most Gothic woman alive, I own she had something to bear when I spent my first Season under her roof. Poor woman! She brought two eligible suitors up to scratch, and I liked neither. My character was retrieved only when I was stupid enough to become engaged to Ivo Rotherham, and lost beyond recovery when I put an end to that most abominable episode of my life!"

"How dreadful it must have been for you! Within a month of the wedding!"

"Not in the least! We quarrelled more royally than ever before, and I positively enjoyed crying-off. You will allow, too, that there is a distinction in having given the odious Marquis a set-down!"

"I should never have dared to do so. His manners are so – so very unconciliating, and he looks at one as though he held one in contempt, which throws me into confusion, try as I will to overcome such folly."

"Detestable man!"

"Oh, Serena, hush! You cannot always have thought so!"

Her stepdaughter threw her a quizzing glance. "Are you in one of your romantical flights? Goose! I became engaged to Ivo because I thought it would suit me to be a Marchioness, because Papa made the match, because I have known him for ever, because we have some tastes in common, because – oh, for a number of excellent reasons! Or so they seemed, until I discovered him to be unendurable."

"Indeed, I don't wonder at it that you could not love him, but have you never – have you never met anyone for whom you felt a – a decided partiality, Serena?" asked Fanny, with a wondering look.

"Yes, indeed! Does that set me up in your esteem!" Serena replied, laughing. "I fancied myself very much in love when I was just nineteen years old. The most handsome creature, and with such engaging manners! You would have been in raptures! Alas, he had no fortune, and Papa would not countenance the match. I believe I cried for a week, but at this length of time I cannot be sure."

"Oh, you are funning!" Fanny said reproachfully.

"No, upon my honour! I did like him very much, but I have not laid eyes on him in six years, my dear, and the melancholy truth is that Papa was quite right when he assured me that I should recover from the disappointment."

The widow looked as if she thought this melancholy indeed. "Who was he, Serena if you don't dislike telling me?"

"Not in the least. His name was Hector Kirkby."

"And you have never met him again?"

"Never! But he was a soldier, and his regiment had just been ordered to Portugal, so that that cannot be considered wonderful."

"But now that the War is over -"

"Fanny, you are incorrigible!" exclaimed Serena, a good deal of affectionate amusement in her face. "Now that the War is over, I am no longer a green girl, and Hector if he is alive, which I am sure I hope he may be – is in all likelihood married, and the father of a hopeful family, and would be hard put to it to recall my name!"

"Oh, no! *You* have not forgotten!"

"Well, no," acknowledged Serena, "but, to own the truth, until you put me in mind of him I had not thought of him for years! I am afraid I am a coldhearted sort of a female after all!"

Fanny, who had seen her flirt with and rebuff several eligible suitors, was almost inclined to believe that it must be so. But no one could look upon that beautiful face, with its lovely, wilful mouth, its lustrous eyes, brilliant under rather heavy, smiling lids, and think its owner coldhearted. In fact, it was quite the last epithet anyone could have found to bestow upon such a vital, passionate creature as Serena, thought Fanny. She was headstrong, and obstinate, some times quite dreadfully mannish, as eccentric as her father, quick-tempered, impulsive, impatient of restraint, and careless of appearances; but with all these faults, and a great many more, she had a wealth of kindness and of generosity, and a chivalry which made her beloved amongst her father's dependants.

"You are putting me out of countenance! Why do you stare so?"

Recalled by the sound of that low-pitched, musical voice, Fanny gave a little start, coloured up, and said: "As though anything could! I beg your pardon: my wits were wandering! Oh, Serena, how *very* kind you have been to me!"

"Good gracious!" The brows which Serena did not scruple to darken, shot up; the eyes, gleaming more green than hazel, mocked, but gently. "My poor dear! This dismal occasion has put the most sickly thoughts into your head! Or is it rather my cousin Hartley? I am sure I do not blame you, if that is the case!"

Diverted, the widow exclaimed involuntarily: "How much *you* must blame *me* for having disappointed all your hopes of keeping him out of the succession!"

"Fudge! I never had any! No, indeed! I am much in your debt, for not having given me a half-brother young enough to have been my son. How ridiculous I must then have appeared! It does not bear thinking of."

"Too generous!" Fanny said into the folds of a black-bordered handkerchief. "And your Papa -! Never one word of reproach to me, but I know how much he disliked the thought of Hartley's succeeding him!"

"Dear Fanny, pray don't cry! We shall have my uncles, and your father, and Mr Perrott upon us at any moment, to say nothing nothing of Hartley himself! To be sure, one would not have *wished* him to have stepped into Papa's shoes, but it is no such great matter, after all! If you know any harm of him, it is more than I do."

"Your Papa said that he would have liked him better if he *had* known any harm of him," said Fanny dolefully.

This made Serena laugh, but she said: "Very true! He is virtuous and a dead bore! I am sure, the first Carlow to be so. However, my father had known it any time these dozen years, and might, had the matter seriously troubled him, have married again long before you were out of the school room. To suppose that he married you only for the sake of an heir shows you to be a great simpleton. Heavens, will they never bring this carouse to an end? It is a full hour since the carriages returned!"

"Serena! Not a *carouse*!" Fanny protested. "How can you talk so?"

"To hold a feast over the remains of the departed is a custom that can only disgust any person of sensibility!"

"But, indeed it is only a cold collation!" Fanny said anxiously.

The doors at one end of the room opened softly, and the butler came in, with the intelligence that the funeral party was breaking up, carriages being called for, and Mr Perrott, his late lordship's attorney, desiring him to carry his respects to my lady, and to ask if it would be convenient to her to receive him presently. Addressing himself to Serena, he volunteered the information that the funeral had been so well attended that several of the humbler mourners had found it impossible to force their way into the church, a circumstance which appeared to afford him consolation. Receiving from Fanny an assurance that she was ready to see Mr Perrott, he withdrew again.

The minutes lagged past. Fanny said faintly: "I don't know why it should affect one so. The Will must be read, I know, but I wish it were over!"

"For my part, I think it a great piece of work to make!" said Serena. "Such a parade, such stupid formality, which there is not the least occasion for! The only persons who might wish to hear it read are those to whom my father has left private bequests, and they are not invited to be present! It can contain no surprises for you, or for me, or, indeed, for my cousin.

"Oh, no! It is all my folly – and fearing to vex Papa! From what he said to me, I collect that he and Mama expect me to return home – to Hartland, I mean. He spoke as though it were certain. I said nothing, for there was no time – or perhaps I had not the courage," she added, with a pitiful little smile.

"Tell me what you wish to do!"

"If it were my duty to return, I would do so," the widow faltered.

"*That* does not answer my question! At Hartland, your wishes are of no account; *here*, surely, it has been other wise!"

"Yes, indeed it has!" Fanny said, her eyes filling with tears. "It is that which makes me wonder whether it is perhaps naughtiness and self-will which prompts me to think that my first duty *now* is to you, and not to Papa!"

"If you can't be comfortable without the assurance that you are doing your duty, let me tell you that my whole dependance is upon you – Mama!" Serena said, her voice prim, but irrepressible humour gleaming in her eyes. "If you are not to take me in charge, what is to become of me? I give you fair warning I won't live with my Aunt Theresa, or with my Aunt Susan! And even I should hesitate to set up my own establishment without a respectable female to bear me company. Depend upon it, *that* would mean Cousin Florence! The Carlows and the Dorringtons would be as one in agreeing that the poor creature must be sacrificed."

Fanny smiled, but said in a serious tone: "I can't take you in charge, but I *can* be your chaperon, and although I am very silly I do think it would answer better than for you to be obliged to live with Lady Theresa, or even with Lady Dorrington. And if it is what *you* would like, dearest Serena, I cannot doubt that it is what your Papa would desire me to do, for he was fonder of you than of anyone."

"Fanny, *no*!" Serena said, stretching out her hand impulsively.

"But it is not at all to be wondered at! You are so very like him. So I have quite made up my mind what I ought to do. Only I do hope that Papa will not order me, for it would be so very shocking to be obliged to disobey him!"

"He won't do so. *He* must realize, though you do not, that you are Lady Spenborough, not Miss Claypole! Moreover -" She stopped, but, upon receiving a look of enquiry, continued bluntly: "Forgive me, but I am persuaded neither he nor Lady Claypole will press you to return to them! With such a numerous family, and your elder sister still unwed – oh, no, they cannot wish for your return!"

"No! Oh, how very right you are!" exclaimed Fanny, her brow clearing. "Agnes, too, would so particularly dislike it, I daresay!"

There was no time for more. The doors were again opened, and a number of funereally clad gentlemen were ushered into the room.

The procession was led by the eldest, and certainly the most impressive of these. Lord Dorrington, whose girth had upon more than one occasion caused him to be mistaken for the Duke of York, was brother to the first Lady Spenborough and from having a great notion of his own importance, and a strong disposition to meddle in other persons' affairs, had appointed himself to the position of doyen to the party. He came ponderously into the room, his corsets slightly creaking, his massive jowl supported by swathe upon swathe of neckcloth, and, having bowed to the widow, uttering a few words of condolence in a wheezing voice, at once assumed the task of directing the company to various chairs. "I shall desire our good Mr Perrott to seat himself at the desk. Serena, my love, I fancy you and Lady Spenborough will be comfortable upon the sofa. Spenborough, will you take this place? Eaglesham, my dear fellow, if you, and ah – Sir – William, will sit here, I shall invite Rotherham to take the wing-chair."

Since only Mr Eaglesham attended to this speech, only he was irritated by it. Precedency having been cast overboard, he had entered the library in Lord Dorrington's ample wake. He was as spare as his lordship was corpulent, and wore the harassed expression which, the unkind asserted, was natural to Lady Theresa Carlow's consort. Having married the late Earl's sister, he considered that he had a better right than Dorrington to assume the direction of affairs, but he knew no way of asserting it, and was obliged to content himself with moving towards a chair as far distant as possible to that one indicated by Dorrington, and by muttering animadversions against pretentious and encroaching old popinjays, which were as soothing to himself as they were inaudible to everyone else.

The first in consequence was the last to enter the room, the Marquis of Rotherham, saying: "Oh, go on, man, go on!" thrusting the attorney before him, and strolling into the library behind him.

His entrance might have been said to have banished constraint. The Lady Serena, never remarkable for propriety, stared incredulously, and exclaimed: "What in the world brings *you* here, I should like to know?"

"So should I!" retorted his lordship. "How well we should have suited, Serena! So many ideas as we have in common!"

Fanny, well accustomed to such exchanges, merely cast an imploring look at Serena; Mr Eaglesham uttered a short laugh; Sir William Claypole was plainly startled; Mr Perrott, who had drawn up the original marriage settlements, seemed to be suddenly afflicted with deafness; and Lord Dorrington, perceiving an opportunity for further meddling, said, in what was meant to be an authoritative tone: "Now, now! We must not forget upon what a sad occasion we are gathered together! No doubt there is a little awkwardness attached to Rotherham's unavoidable presence here. Indeed, when I learned from our good Perrott -"

"*Awkwardness?*" cried Serena, her colour heightened, and her eyes flashing. "I promise you, I feel none, my dear sir! If Rotherham is conscious of it, I can only say that I am astonished he should choose to intrude upon a matter which can only concern the family!"

"No, I am not conscious of it," responded the Marquis. "Only of intolerable boredom!"

Several pairs of eyes turned apprehensively towards Serena, but she was never a fighter who resented a knock in exchange. This one seemed rather to assuage than to exacerbate her wrath. She smiled reluctantly, and said in a milder tone: "Well! But what made you come, then?"

Mr Perrott, who had been engaged in spreading some documents over the desk, gave a little, dry cough, and said: "Your ladyship must know that the late Earl appointed my Lord Rotherham to be one of the Executors of his Will."

That this intelligence was as unexpected as it was unwelcome was made plain by the widening of Serena's eyes, as she turned them, in a look compound of doubt and disgust, from Rotherham to the attorney. "I might have guessed that that was how it would be!" she said, turning aside in mortification, and walking back to her seat in the window embrasure.

"Then it is a great pity you did not guess!" said Rotherham acidly. "I might then have been warned in time to have declined the office, for which I daresay there could be no one more unsuited!"

She deigned no reply, but averted her face, fixing her gaze once more upon the prospect outside. Her cousin, wearing his new dignities uneasily, was inspired by his evil genius to assume an air of authority, saying in a tone of reproof: "Such conduct as this is quite unbecoming, Serena! Now that the late unhappy event has made me head of the family I do not scruple to say so. I am sure I do not know what Lord Rotherham must be thinking of such manners."

He brought himself under the fire of two pairs of eyes, the one filled with wrathful astonishment, the other with cruel mockery.

"Well, you can certainly be sure of that!" said Rotherham.

"For my part," said Dorrington, in a peevish voice, "I consider it very odd in my poor brother, very odd indeed! One would have supposed – however, so it has always been! Eccentric! I can find no other word for it."

This provoked Mr Eaglesham, swelling with annoyance, to point out to his lordship the very remote nature of his connection with the late Earl. There were others, he took leave to tell him, whose claims to have been appointed Executor of the Will were very much nearer than his. Lord Dorrington's empurpled cheeks then became so alarmingly suffused that Spenborough said hastily that the appointment of Lord Rotherham was perfectly agreeable to him, whatever it might be to others.

"Obliging of you!" said Rotherham, over his shoulder, as he crossed the room to where Fanny was still standing nervously beside her chair. "Come! Why do you not sit down?" he said in his abrupt, rather rough way. "You must be as anxious as any of us, I daresay, to be done with this business!"

"Oh, yes! Thank you!" she murmured. She glanced fleetingly up at him, as she seated herself, faltering: "I am very sorry, if you dislike it. Indeed, I am afraid it may be troublesome to you!"

"Unlikely: Perrott will no doubt attend to everything." He hesitated, and then added, in a still brusquer manner: "I should be making you speeches of condolence. Excuse me on that head, if you please! I am no great hand at polite insincerities, and give you credit for believing you cannot wish to figure as inconsolable."

She was left feeling crushed; he walked away to a chair near the window in which Serena sat, and she, taking advantage of Sir William Claypole's claiming his daughter's attention at that moment, said: "You might give her credit for some natural sorrow!"

"Dutiful!"

"She was most sincerely attached to my father."

"Very well: I give her credit for it. She will soon recover from such sentiments, and must be less than honest if she does not feel herself to have been released from a most unnatural tie." He looked at her from under the heavy bar of his black brows, a satirical gleam in his eyes. "Yes, you find yourself in agreement with me, and don't mean to admit it. If sympathizing speeches are expected of me, I will address mine to you. I am sorry for you, Serena: this bears hard on you."

There was no softening either in voice or expression, but she knew him well enough to believe that he meant what he said.

"Thank you. I expect I shall go along very tolerably when I have become –

a little more accustomed."

"Yes, if you don't commit some folly. On that chance, however, I would not wager a groat. Don't shoot daggerlooks at me! I'm impervious to 'em."

"On this occasion at least you might spare me your taunts!" she said, in a low, indignant voice.

"Not at all. To spar with me will save you from falling into a green melancholy."

She disdained to answer this, but turned again to look out of the window; and he, as indifferent to the snub as to her anger, took up a lounging position in his chair, and sardonically surveyed the rest of the company.

Of the six men present he gave the least impression of being a mourner at a funeral. His black coat, which he wore buttoned high across his chest, was at odd variance with a neckcloth tied in a sporting fashion peculiarly his own; and his demeanour lacked the solemnity which characterized the elder members of the party. From his appearance, he might have been almost any age, and was, in fact, in the late thirties. Of medium height only, he was very powerfully built, with big shoulders, a deep chest, and thighs by far too muscular to appear to advantage in the prevailing fashion of skin tight pantaloons. He was seldom seen in such attire, but generally wore top-boots and breeches. His coats were well-cut, but made so that he could shrug himself into them without assistance; and he wore no other jewellery than his heavy gold signet-ring. He had few graces, his manners being blunt to a fault, made as many enemies as friends, and, had he not been endowed with birth, rank, and fortune, would possibly have been ostracized from polite circles. But these magical attributes were his, and they acted like a talisman upon his world. His Belcher neckties and his unconventional manners might be deplored but must be accepted: he was Rotherham.

He was not a handsome man, but his countenance was a striking one, his eyes, which were of a curiously light gray, having a great deal of hard brilliance, and being set under straight brows which almost met. His hair was as black as a crow's wing, his complexion swarthy; and the lines of his face were harsh, the brow a little craggy, the chin deeply cleft, and the masterful nose jutting between lean cheeks. His hands were his only beauty, for they combined strength with shapeliness. Any of the dandy set would have used all manner of arts to show them off: my Lord Rotherham dug them into his pockets.

Since Lord Dorrington and Mr Eaglesham showed no disposition to bring their acrimonious dialogue to an end, and Lord Spenborough's polite attempts to recall them to a sense of their surroundings were not attended to, Rotherham intervened, saying impatiently: "Do you mean to continue arguing all day, or are we to hear the Will read?"

Both gentlemen glared at him; and Mr Perrott, taking advantage of the sudden silence, spread open a crackling document, and in severe accents announced it to be the last Will and Testament of George Henry Vernon Carlow, Fifth Earl of Spenborough.

As Serena had foretold, it contained little of interest to its auditors. Neither Rotherham nor Dorrington had expectations; Sir William Claypole knew his daughter's jointure to be secure: and once Mr Eaglesham was satisfied that the various keepsakes promised to his wife had been duly bequeathed to her he too lost interest in the reading, and occupied himself in thinking of some pretty cutting things to say to Lord Dorrington.

Serena herself still sat with her face turned away, and her eyes on the prospect outside. Shock had at first left no room for any other emotion than grief for the loss of her father, but with the arrival of his successor the evils of her present situation were more thoroughly brought to her mind. Milverley, which had been her home for the twenty-five years of her life, was hers no longer. She who had been its mistress would henceforth visit it only as a guest. She was not much given to sentimental reflection, nor, during her father's lifetime, had she been conscious of any deep attachment to the place. She had taken it for granted, serving it as a matter of duty and tradition. Only now, when it was passing from her, did she realize her double loss.

Her spirits sank; it was an effort to keep her countenance, and impossible to chain her attention to the attorney, reciting in a toneless voice and with a wealth of incomprehensible legalities a long list of small personal bequests. All were known to her, many had been discussed with her. She knew the sources of Fanny's jointure, and which of the estates would furnish her own portion: there could be no surprises, nothing to divert her mind from its melancholy reflections.

She was mistaken. Mr Perrott paused, and cleared his throat. After a moment, he resumed his reading, his dry voice more expressionless than before. The words: ". . . all my estates at Hernesley and at Ibshaw" intruded upon Serena's wandering thoughts, and informed her that her share of the bequests had been reached at last. The next words brought her head round with a jerk.

". . . to the use of Ivo Spencer Barrasford, the Most Noble the Marquis of Rotherham -"

"*What?*" gasped Serena.

". . . in trust for my daughter, Serena Mary," continued Mr Perrott, slightly raising his voice, "to the intent that he shall allow her during her spinsterhood such sums of money by way of pin-money as she has heretofore enjoyed, and upon her marriage, conditional upon such marriage being with his consent and approval, to her use absolutely."

An astonished silence succeeded these words. Fanny was looking bewildered, and Serena stunned. Suddenly the silence was shattered. The Most Noble the Marquis of Rotherham had succumbed to uncontrollable laughter.

CHAPTER TWO

SERENA WAS on her feet. "Was my father out of his senses?" she cried. "*Rotherham* to allow -! *Rotherham* to consent to my marriage! Oh, *infamous*, abominable!"

Her feelings choked her; she began to stride about the room, panting for breath, striking her clenched fist into the palm of her other hand, fiercely thrusting her uncle Dorrington aside when he attempted ponderously to check her.

"Pray, Serena -! Pray, my dear child, be calm! Abominable indeed, but try to compose yourself!" he besought her. "Upon my word! To appoint a trustee outside the family! It passes the bounds of belief! I suppose I am not nobody! Your uncle! What more proper person could have been found to appoint? God bless my soul, I was never more provoked!"

"Certainly one may say that eccentricity has been carried pretty far!" observed Mr Eaglesham. "Very improper! I venture to say that Theresa will most strongly disapprove of it."

"It must be shocking to any person of sensibility!" declared Spenborough. "My dear cousin, everyone must enter into your feelings upon this occasion! No one can wonder at your very just displeasure, but, depend upon it, there can be found a remedy! Such a whimsical clause might, I daresay, be upset: Perrott will advise us!" He paused, looking towards the attorney, who, however, preserved an unencouraging silence. "Well, we shall see! At all events, the Will cannot be binding to Rotherham. It must be within his power to refuse such a Trusteeship, surely!"

"*He!*" The word burst from Serena's lips. She swept round, and bore down upon the Marquis, as lithe as a wild cat, and as dangerous. "Was it your doing? *Was* it?"

"Good God, no!" he said contemptuously. "A pretty charge to saddle myself with!"

"How could he do such a thing? How *could* he?" she demanded. "And without your knowledge and consent? No! No! I don't believe it!"

"When you have come to the end of all this fretting and fuming, perhaps you may! Your father desired nothing so much as our marriage, and this is his way of bringing it about. It's a cock that won't fight, however!"

"No!" she said, cheeks and eyes flaming. "I will never be so enforced!"

"Nor I!" he said brutally. "Why, you featherheaded termagant, do you imagine that *I* wish for a wife upon such terms? You mistake the matter, my girl, believe me!"

"Then release me from so intolerable a situation! To be obliged to beg *your* consent -! *Something* must be done! It *must* be possible! My whole fortune tied up – pin-money – Good God, how could Papa treat me so? Will you assign the Trust to my cousin? Will you do that?"

"Poor devil, no! If I could, I would not! You would bully him into giving his consent to your marriage to the first wastrel that offered, only to break the Trust! Well, you won't bully me, so make up your mind to that, Serena!"

She flung away from him, and resumed her restless pacing, tears of rage running down her face. Fanny went to her, laying a hand on her arm, saying, in a beseeching tone: "Serena! Dearest Serena!"

She stood rigidly, her throat working. "Fanny, don't touch me! I am not *safe!*"

Fanny found herself being pushed unceremoniously aside. Rotherham, who had come up behind her, seized Serena's wrists, and held them in a hard grasp. "You have edified us enough!" he said harshly. "A little more conduct would be becoming in you! No, you will neither hit me, nor claw my eyes out! Be still, Serena, and think what a figure you make of yourself!"

There was a pause. Fanny trembled for the issue, herself a good deal distressed. The stormy eyes, shifting from Rotherham's dark face, found hers. The glare went out of them. A shuddering sigh broke from Serena; she said: "Oh, Fanny, I beg your pardon! I didn't hurt you, did I?"

"No, no, never!" Fanny cried.

Serena began unconsciously to rub the wrists which Rotherham had released. She glanced round the room, and gave a rather hysterical little laugh. "Indeed, I am very sorry! I am behaving so badly, and have thrown you all into embarrassment. Pray excuse me! Rotherham, I must see you before you leave Milverley: will you come to me, if you please, in the Little Drawing-room?"

"At once, if you wish it."

"Oh, no! My senses are quite disordered still. You must give me time to mend my temper if I am not to be betrayed again into unbecoming warmth!"

She hurried out of the room, repulsing Fanny, who would have accompanied her, with a gesture, and a quick shake of her head.

Her departure unleashed the tongues of her relations, Mr Eaglesham deploring so passionate a disposition, and recalling his wife's various pronouncements on the subject; Fanny firing up in defence; Dorrington ascribing the outbreak to Rotherham's provoking manners; and Spenborough reiterating his determination to overset the clause. This at once led to further disputation, for Dorrington, while agreeing that the clause should be overset, resented Spenborough's assumption of authority; and Mr Eaglesham, on general grounds, was opposed to any scheme of Dorrington's. Even Claypole was drawn, though reluctantly, into expressing an opinion; but Mr Perrott, waiting with gelid calm for the discussion to end, met all appeals with noncommittal repressiveness; and Rotherham, his shoulders to the door, his arms folded across his chest, and one leg crossed negligently over the other, appeared to consider himself the audience to a farce which at once bored and slightly diverted him. It lasted too long for his patience, however, and he put a ruthless end to it, interrupting Dorrington to say: "You will none of you overset it, and you are none of you concerned in it, so you may as well stop making gudgeons of yourselves!"

"Sir, you are offensive!" declared Mr Eaglesham, glaring at him. "I do not hesitate to tell you so!"

"Why should you? I don't hesitate to tell you that you're a muttonhead! I collect that you think her aunt the properest person to control Serena's hand and fortune. You'd look mighty blue if you could succeed in foisting that charge on to Lady Theresa! What a trimming she would give you, by God!"

Lord Dorrington burst into a rumbling laugh which immediately set him coughing and wheezing. Mr Eaglesham, much incensed, opened his mouth to retaliate, and then, as the appalling truth of Rotherham's words came home to him, shut it again, and seethed in silence. After regarding him sardonically for a moment or two, Rotherham nodded at the attorney, and said: "You may now read us the rest of this original document!"

Mr Perrott bowed, and replaced the spectacles on his nose. The Will contained no further surprises, and was listened to without comment. Only at the end of the reading did Rotherham unfold his arms, and stroll over to the desk, holding out an imperative hand. Mr Perrott put the Will into it; the stiff sheets were flicked over; in frowning silence the Marquis studied the fatal clause. He then tossed the document on to the desk, saying: "Ramshackle!" and walked out of the room.

His departure was the signal for the break-up of the party. Mr Perrott, declining Fanny's civil offer of hospitality, was the first to take leave. He was accompanied out of the library by the new Earl, who desired information on several points, and followed almost immediately by Mr Eaglesham, who was engaged to spend the night with friends in Gloucester; and by Lord Dorrington, who had had the forethought to bespeak dinner at one of his favourite posting-houses, and was anxious lest it should spoil. Fanny soon found herself alone with her father, who, with Spenborough, was remaining at Milverley until the morrow.

She awaited his first words with a fast-beating heart, but these, not surprisingly, were devoted not to her affairs but to Serena's. "An awkward business!" Sir William said. "Quite unaccountable! A strange man, Spenborough!"

She agreed to it, but faintly.

"One cannot wonder at your daughter-in-law's vexation, but I should be sorry to see any daughter of mine in such a passion!"

"Oh, pray do not regard it, Papa! In general, she is so good! But this, coming as it does at *such* a moment, when she is in so much affliction and behaving so beautifully –! The distressing circumstances, too – her previous connection with Rotherham – the most ungentlemanly language he used. She must be pardoned! She is so good!"

"You astonish me! Your Mama was much inclined to think her not at all the thing. She has some odd ways! But there, these great ladies think they may behave as they please! I daresay she would tie her garter in public, as the saying goes!"

"Oh, no, no! Indeed, you misjudge her, Papa! If she is an unusual girl, recollect that to dear Lord Spenborough she was more a son than a daughter!"

"Ay! It is an unhappy thing for a girl to lose her mother! No more than twelve years of age, was she? Well, well! You are very right, my dear:

allowances must be made for her. I am very sensible to it, particularly now, when I should have wished above all things that I could have brought your mother to you!"

Fanny was too much astonished at having her opinion deferred to by him to do more than murmur a confused assent.

"It is an unfortunate circumstance that she should be lying-in when her presence must have been a comfort to you."

"Oh, yes! I mean – that is, It was so kind of her to have spared you to me!"

"No question of that! I never knew your Mama to give way to crotchets of that kind. Besides, you know, a tenth lying-in is by no means the same thing as a first. One does not make a piece of work over it! She will be sadly disappointed, however, not to receive better news of you than I can carry to her. Not that *my* hopes were high. After three years, it was scarcely to be expected. A sad pity, upon all counts!" She hung her head, blushing deeply, and he made haste to add: "I don't mean to reproach you, my dear, how ever much I must wish it had been otherwise. I daresay Spenborough felt it?"

She replied in so suffocated a voice that only the words "always so considerate" could be distinguished.

"I am glad to hear you say so. It is no very pleasant thing to know that one's possessions must pass into the hands of some trumpery cousin – no great thing, the new Earl, is he? – but I hold him to be as much to blame as you. What a freak, to contract inflammation of the lungs while the succession was still unsure! I never knew such improvidence!" He sounded indignant, but recollected immediately to whom he spoke, and begged pardon. "There is no sense in dwelling upon the matter, to be sure. For *your* sake, it is a great deal to be regretted. Your rank must always command respect, but had you been the mother of a son your consequence would have been enhanced beyond anything, and your future decided. As things have fallen out, it is otherwise. I don't know, Fanny, if you have any thoughts on this head?"

She gathered her forces together, and replied with tolerable firmness: "Yes, Papa. I have the intention of removing to the Dower House, with dear Serena."

He was taken aback. "With Lady Serena!"

"I am persuaded it is what Lord Spenborough would have desired me to do. She must not be deserted!"

"I imagine there can be no question of that! She has her uncle, and that aunt who brought her out, after all! Spenborough, too, was saying to me this morning that he and my lady hoped she would continue to make this her home. I own, I thought it handsome of him. To be taking a firebrand into one's family is not what *I* should choose!"

"Hartley and Jane – Lord and Lady Spenborough, I mean, have been everything that is kind: Serena is fully conscious of it, but she knows it would not do. If you please, Papa, I believe it to be my duty to take care of Serena!"

"*You* take care of *her*!" he ejaculated, laughing. "I wish I may see it!"

She coloured, but said: "Indeed, it is she who has taken care of me, but I am her mother-in-law, and the most proper person to act as her chaperon, sir."

He considered this, and yielded a reluctant assent. "It might be thought so indeed, but at your age – I don't know what your Mama will say to it! Besides, the young lady, with that fortune at her back, will very soon be snapped up, temper and all!"

"She has too strong a mind to be taken-in. I don't fancy she will be married for a little while yet, Papa."

"Very true! Nothing of that nature can be contemplated for a year at least. You will keep strict mourning, of course. Your Mama was inclined to think that you should return to Hartland for that period, for however much you may be known as the Dowager Countess, my dear, it cannot be denied that you are by far too young to live alone. We had some notion that when you put off your mourning, and will no doubt be thinking of setting up an establishment of your own, you might take one of your sisters to live with you. But that is to look some way ahead, and I don't mean to dictate to you! There is something to be said for this scheme of yours, after all. You have been used to be the mistress of a great house, my dear, and you would not like to be living at Hartland again, in the old way. No, I am much disposed to think that you have hit upon the very thing to make all straight! That is, if you believe that you can be comfortable with Lady Serena?"

"Oh. yes! So *very* comfortable!"

"Well, I should never have thought it! I only hope she may not get into a scrape. *You* will be blamed for it, if she does! Her character is unsteady: *that* was plain when she made herself the talk of the town by jilting Rotherham! You were still in the schoolroom, but I well remember what an uproar it caused! I believe the wedding-cards had actually been sent out!"

"It was very bad, but, indeed, Papa, I honour her for her resolution in drawing back before it was too late! Dear Lord Spenborough wished the match to take place, but nothing, I am persuaded, could have been more ineligible! *He* liked Rotherham because he is such a great sportsman, and such a splendid rider to hounds, and he could never be brought to see that he would be a dreadfully harsh and disagreeable husband! He would have made Serena so unhappy! He is the most hateful man, and takes a delight in vexing her! You must have heard the way he speaks to her – the things he doesn't scruple to say!"

"Ay! And I heard her too! A very improper style she uses towards him! Let me tell you, Fanny, that there is something very displeasing in that bold manner of hers! She expresses herself with a freedom I would not tolerate in one of *my* daughters."

"She has known him since she was a child – has never stood upon ceremony with him! If she is sometimes betrayed into unbecoming warmth, it is his fault, for so unkindly provoking her! And as for temper, I am sure he has a worse one than hers could ever be!"

"Well, it's plain you have a fondness for her, my dear," he said indulgently. "For my part, I would not be in Rotherham's shoes at this moment for something! He may think himself fortunate if he comes off without a scratched face, I daresay!"

But when he joined her in the Little Drawing-room, Rotherham found Serena quite composed. He said, as he closed the door: "What now? Am I here to be entreated, or abused?"

She bit her lip, but said: "You would not be moved by either, I suppose."

"Not in the least, but I am quite at your disposal if you wish to continue quarrelling with me."

"I am determined not to do so."

He smiled. "*That* resolution will be broken soon enough! What *do* you want, Serena?"

"I wish you will sit down! Ivo, what is to be done?"

"Nothing."

"You cannot mean to accept the Trust!"

"Why not?"

"Good God, one moment's reflection must be enough to make you see how intolerable it would be! For both of us!"

"I can see why you should think it intolerable, but why should I find it so?"

"You don't want for sense, so I suppose you are trying to provoke me! Can you doubt that the story will be one of the *on-dits* of the town within a week? My Uncle Dorrington will take care of that! Everyone will be talking about it, and laughing at it!"

"This is a new come-out for you, Serena!" he said admiringly. "You were never used to give a straw for what anyone might say of you!"

She flushed, and looked away. "You are mistaken. In any event, to have everyone watching us would be detestable!"

"Let 'em watch! They will be tired of it by the time you are out of black gloves, and in the meanwhile it won't worry me."

"To have everyone conjecturing?"

"Lord, Serena, I've been food for conjecture any time these dozen years! There have been some very good stories made up about me, too."

She looked despairingly at him. "I know this humour too well to suppose it is of the least use to continue talking. You mean to fob me off by pretending not to understand me."

"No, I don't. I understand you very well, but you're refining too much upon it. There's nothing remarkable in my being appointed to be your Trustee: everyone knows I was one of your father's closest friends, and no one will be surprised that he chose to name me rather than that old fool, Dorrington, or the rasher of wind your aunt married!"

"No – if it had not been for that wretched engagement!" she said frankly. "*That* is what makes it so intolerable! Papa's intention is – is *blatant*!"

"You can console yourself with the reflection that it is I, and not you, who will be a laughing-stock for the vulgar," he said grimly.

"How can you talk so? I promise you, I don't wish you to be put into such a position!"

"Don't waste a thought on it! I'm inured!"

"Oh, how *odious* you are!" she exclaimed, with suppressed violence.

"*That* sounds more like you!" he said cordially. "I thought it would not be long!"

She controlled herself with a strong effort, not lost on him, tightly gripping her hands together in her lap, and clenching her teeth on her lower lip.

"Take care, Serena! you will go into strong convulsions if you bottle up so much spleen!"

She was always quick to perceive the ridiculous, and gave a gasp. Her eyes did indeed flash a challenge, but her sense of humour got the better of her temper, and she burst out laughing. "Oh -! At least own that you would provoke a saint!"

"I never tried to. *You* are no saint!"

"No, alas!" she sighed. "Come! don't tease me, Ivo, *pray*! Is there *no* way of upsetting that infamous Will?"

"I should imagine not. I'm no lawyer, however. Consult your father's attorney! I warn you, he returned no very encouraging answers to your uncles, when they appealed to him. I daresay it might be upset if I were to contravene the Trust, but I shan't."

"If you were to refuse to act -?"

"I shan't do that either. You wouldn't get control of your fortune if I did, and that's what you chiefly want, isn't it?"

"Of course it is! My father gave me £250 pounds a year for pin-money, and that was very well while he lived, but how the *deuce* am I to support myself on such a sum?"

"Don't try to bamboozle me, my girl! Your mother's fortune was settled on you."

"Ten thousand pounds, invested in the Funds! The whole of my income will be less than £700! Good God, Ivo, I daresay Papa must have spent as much on my hunters alone!"

"Oh, more! He gave a thousand guineas for that flea-bitten gray which carried you so well last season. But you will hardly hunt this year!"

"This year! No! But am I to be reduced to penury all the days of my life?" she demanded. "What if I should remain a spinster? Has any provision been made for that contingency?"

"No, none. I looked particularly at the Will to be sure of it," he replied. "A damned, ill-managed business – but I suppose he thought there was no fear the point would arise."

"He has certainly done his best to thrust me into marriage with the first man who is so obliging as to offer for me!" she said bitterly.

"You are forgetting something, my love!"

She looked mistrustfully at him. "No! *Your* consent must be obtained!"

"Just so! But make yourself easy! I shan't withhold it unreasonably."

"You would do anything to spite me!"

"Well, if I do, you will have a very good case against me, and will no doubt be able to break the Trust. Meanwhile, let me give you a piece of advice! If you don't wish to afford the world matter for gossip, assume the appearance at least of complaisance! How you came to make such a ninnyhammer of yourself, for all those fools to gape at, I know not! Rail at me in private if you choose, but in public behave so that the interested may believe you to be very well-satisfied with the arrangement, and see nothing in it but what is natural and comfortable."

She was obliged to acknowledge the good sense of this advice. "But for the rest -! How shall I do? *Can* I support myself on so little, Ivo?"

"You *might* do so on much less, but from what I know of you you would not. But what is all this talk of supporting yourself? You don't mean to set up your establishment, do you? *That* your father never intended!"

"No, I don't – but if I did you could not prevent me! At least I don't have to win your odious consent for anything but marriage!"

"You don't, but if you indulged in any such folly your debts would very soon teach you the unwisdom of flouting my advice," he retorted.

Her bosom swelled, but she said nothing.

"Well, what *do* you mean to do?" he asked.

"I shall remain with Lady Spenborough," she answered coldly. She discovered that he was frowning, and raised her brows. "Pray, have you any objection?"

"No. No, I've no objection. You won't feel yourself straitened, at all events, while you live under her roof, and *she* has been so handsomely provided for that she may well support you. But – here?"

"At the Dower House. I perceive that that displeases you! You must be ingenious indeed if you can hit upon a plausible reason to account for your disapproval!"

"I am not displeased, I don't disapprove, and if you show hackle again without cause, you may expect to have your ears boxed as they never have been yet – more's the pity!" he said savagely. "Live where you choose! It's all one to me. Have you anything more to say?"

"No, I have not, and I should be very happy to think I need never say another word to you for as long as I live – and of all things in the world there is nothing – *nothing* – so abominable, and contemptible, and cowardly, and ungentlemanly as persons who walk out of the room when one is addressing them!"

He had opened the door, but at that he burst out laughing, and shut it again. "Very well! But I warn you I shall give as good as I get!"

"You need not tell me that! If you don't disapprove, why did you scowl so?"

"My habitual expression, possibly. It was unintentional, I assure you. The thought in my mind was merely that it would be better for you to remove from this vicinity. To be situated at the Dower House cannot be anything but painful to you, Serena, believe me!"

She said impulsively: "Oh, I *beg* your pardon! But how could I guess you meant nothing but kindness?"

"A home-thrust!" he interjected.

"No, no! I didn't mean it so! Only, in general – but never mind that! I know it must be painful to remain here, but I think that is the kind of sensibility I ought to overcome. And, you know, Ivo, my cousin is not quite up to the trick!"

"So I should imagine."

"He is a very good sort of a man in his way, and he wishes to do just as he ought, but although he has always been the heir-at-law he was not *bred* to succeed Papa, and I fancy he never expected that it would come to that, so what with that, and Papa's not liking him above half, he has never been put in the way of things here, and the truth is that he's not *fit to go*!"

"What is that to the purpose?"

"Why, don't you see? I shall be able to help him in a thousand ways, and to school him a little, and to see that all goes on as it should!"

"Good God! Serena, take my word for it, you would be very ill advised to undertake anything of the sort!"

"No, you mistake, Ivo! It was my cousin's own suggestion! He told me that he hoped I would remain at Milverley, and put him in the way of things. Of course I would never do *that,* but I was a good deal touched, and I don't doubt I can be just as useful to him if I live with Fanny, at the Dower House."

"Nor do I!" he said, with the flash of a wry grin. "If your cousin wants information, let him seek it of your father's agent!"

"I daresay he will, but although Mr Morley is an excellent person, he was not bred here, as I was! It is not a *part* of him! Oh -! I express myself so clumsily, but *you* must surely know what I mean!"

"I do!" he said. "It is precisely what *I* meant when I counselled you to remove from this neighbourhood!"

CHAPTER THREE

IT HAD been the wish of both Fanny and Serena to have removed themselves from the great house as soon possible after the funeral; but in the event several weeks elapsed before they at last found themselves installed at the Dower House. This house, which stood on the fringe of the park, and at no great distance from the little town of Quenbury, was a pretty, old-fashioned building, which had been inhabited until some fifteen months earlier by Serena's elder, widowed aunt. Upon the death of this lady, it had been lived in by an old servant only, the various schemes for its occupation by this or that distant relative having all of them, from one cause or another, fallen through. It was discovered that some repairs and renovations were needed to make it properly habitable. Serena ordered these to be set in hand immediately, forgetting her altered status at Milverley. Her cousin found her in conference with the estate carpenter in the dismantled drawing room at the Dower House, and when they rode back to Milverley together startled her by saying: "I am glad you have given your orders to Staines. If I had not been so much occupied yesterday, I should have desired him to come up to see you, and to do whatever you may require of him."

She felt as though she had received a slap in the face, and gasped. "I beg your pardon!"

He assured her very kindly that there was not the least need of apology, but she was deeply mortified, knowing herself to have erred in a way that was most likely to cause resentment. She tried to make further amends; he said that he perfectly understood; reiterated his wish that she would always look upon Milverley as her home; and left her with a strong desire to hasten the preparations for her departure.

But even had the Dower House been ready for instant occupation, it would scarcely have been possible for her to have left Milverley. The task of assembling all her own and Fanny's personal belongings proved to be a far more difficult and protracted one than she had anticipated. A thousand unforeseen difficulties arose; and she was constantly being applied to by her cousin for information and advice. She could not but pity him. He was a shy, unassuming man, more painstaking than able, who plainly found the unexpected change in his circumstances overwhelming. That he might succeed his cousin he had never regarded as more than a remote possibility; and since the Earl had shared this view, he had never been granted the opportunity to become familiar with all the details of a great estate. He came to it from a far more modest establishment, where he had been living in quiet content with his wife, and his youthful family, and for many weeks felt crushed by the appalling weight of fortune, lands, and title. In Serena's presence, he had the uncomfortable sensation of being a nonentity, but he was really very grateful to her, and knew that he would have found himself in a worse case without her, since she could always explain the meaning of the mysteries uttered by such persons as agents and bailiffs. With these he had not learnt to be at ease. He knew himself to be under close observation; they assumed that he had knowledge which he lacked; he was afraid to appear contemptible by confessing ignorance; and relied on Serena to make all plain. She thought he would do better when he had his wife beside him, for it appeared, from the many references to Jane's capabilities, that hers was the stronger character. But the new Countess was not coming to Milverley until their London house had been disposed of. She seemed to be very busy, and scarcely a day passed without her writing to know whether she should sell some piece of furniture, or send it to Milverley; what he wished her to do about the new barouche; whether she should employ Pickford's to convey all their heavy cases to Milverley; and a dozen other problems of the same nature.

Serena found that she was obliged to spend several days in London. The preparation of the house in Grosvenor Square for its new owner could not be wholly entrusted to servants. Fanny, whom travel always made unwell, shrank from the journey; so Serena, undertaking to execute all her commissions, set out with no other escort than her maid, and in a hired post-chaise. It was a novel experience, all her previous journeys having been made either in her father's company, or under the direction of a courier, but she was in no way daunted, finding it rather amusing to be paying her own shot at the posting-house in which she spent the night, contracting for the hire of horses and postilions, and ordering her own dinner. But Lady Theresa, whose guest she was, was shocked beyond measure, dared not guess what her father would have said, ascribed it all to her having cried off from her engagement to Rotherham, and recalled with approval her own girlhood, when she had never done so much as walk in the park at Milverley without having her footman in attendance.

It was painful to visit the house in Grosvenor Square under such altered circumstances, and disagreeable to discover that Lady Spenborough had already inspected it from cellars to attics. Serena was thunderstruck when this news was divulged to her by the housekeeper: she had not believed such conduct to be possible. There could be no denying that her ladyship had every right to go to the house, but there was a want of delicacy about the proceeding which gave a disagreeable impression, hard to shake off. It was excused by the Countess herself, who paid a morning-visit at Lady Theresa's house in Park Street for the express purpose of explaining to Serena the peculiar exigency which had made it necessary for her to go to Grosvenor Square. All was glossed over, in a speech beginning with the words: "I dare say you must have wondered a little . . ." but although Serena forgave she was unable to forget, and had never been in such sympathy with her aunt as when that lady later described the Countess's behaviour as encroaching, and such as sank her below reproach. But Lady Theresa was not astonished, for she had never liked Jane. From the outset she had detected beneath the insipid formality of her manners a sort of shabby gentility which had quite given her a disgust of the young woman. She dressed badly, too, had no countenance, and grossly indulged her children.

It was not until November that Fanny and Serena were at last installed at the Dower House. So much preparation and bustle had been attached to the arrival at Milverley of Lady Spenborough and her hopeful family, and so many pinpricks had had to be endured, that Serena was able to agree wholeheartedly with Fanny, when she exclaimed, as they sat down to their first dinner in their new home: "Oh, how comfortable this is!" Wearied out by all the exertions of the past weeks, she believed that she could be happy in her new surroundings, and looked forward with confidence to the future. The sensation of being uncomfortably cooped-up would pass when she grew more accustomed to living in small rooms; it would be amusing to mingle freely with such neighbours as she had previously received only on Public Days; she was sure she should find plenty to do and to be interested in.

Alas for such sanguine hopes! There were more trials to be endured than she had suspected. She had foreseen that the loss of her father's companionship would be hard to bear, but not that she would find herself pining for things she would have voted, a year earlier, a great bore. In her world, winters were enlivened by visits: one expected to spend a week at Badminton, another at Woburn; one presided over shooting-parties, rode to hounds, and entertained a succession of guests. All this was at an end: she had never dreamed that she could miss it so intolerably. She recalled the many occasions on which she had inveighed against the necessity of inviting this or that person to stay at Milverley, but it would not do: that was the life to which she had been bred, and she could not easily relinquish it. Nor could she cross the threshold of Milverley without suffering a pang. Its occupation by her cousins seemed scarcely less deplorable than the invasion of Rome by the Goths. She knew herself to be unreasonable, and for a long time never confided even to Fanny the burning resentment that consumed her every time the new owners departed from some trivial but time-honoured custom. "We think," and "We prefer," were words too often heard on Jane's tongue, uttered with a calm complacency which was in itself an offence. As for Hartley, it required a real effort for her to maintain friendly relations with anyone so unworthy to succeed her father. She acknowledged his wish to do right, she was aware of the difficulties that confronted him, but when he confessed himself to be no racing man, and divulged that he meant to dispose of his predecessor's string, she could not have been more shocked if he had declared himself to have become a follower of Mahomet. She was not mollified by his considering it to be his duty to hunt a little: his horsemanship, judged by her standards, did him little credit.

Fanny saw how much she was chafed, and grieved over it, but could not enter into her sentiments. Her changed circumstances exactly suited Fanny. She had never felt herself at home at Milverley; the Dower House was just what she liked. A dining room suitable for the entertainment of no more than six persons, a pretty drawing-room, and a cosy breakfast parlour were infinitely preferable to her than half a dozen huge saloons, leading one out of the other; and the exchange of endless, echoing galleries for two neat halls, one over the other, was to her a gain. To consult with her housekeeper on such questions as how the mutton should be dressed for dinner, or pippins best preserved in jelly; to spend the morning in the stillroom, or in overlooking her linen, was exactly what she liked, and what Serena was no hand at at all. Indeed, Serena knew nothing of such matters. It was natural to her to command; she had reigned over her father's household to admiration, triumphantly confuting the older ladies who had considered her too young to succeed in such a charge; but her notion of housekeeping was to summon the steward, or the groom of the chambers, and to give him a general direction. Had an ill-chosen dinner ever been sent to table, she would have taken instant steps to ensure that such an accident should not be repeated; but had she been required to compose a menu she would have been as hard put to it to do so as to boil an egg, or make up her own bed. As Fanny had been thankful to leave the reins of government at Milverley in her hands, so was she now content to let Fanny manage all the domestic affairs at the Dower House. She could only marvel that she should enjoy the task, and find so much to interest her in such restricted surroundings. But the more brilliant the parties at Milverley had been the more Fanny had dreaded them. Her disposition was retiring, her understanding not powerful, and her marriage had followed so swiftly on her emergence from the schoolroom that she had come to it with little knowledge of her husband's world, and none at all of its personalities. Her grace and gentle dignity had supported her through many ordeals, and only she knew what nerve-racking work it had been, during the first months of marriage, to take part in conversations which bristled with elliptical references to events of which she was ignorant, or to persons whom she had never met. To receive a visit from Mrs Aylsham, from the Grange, or to listen to Jane's anecdotes about her children, suited her very well. Serena could imagine nothing more insipid, and hardly knew how to sit through such sessions without yawning.

The Milverley ladies, though acquainted with most of the neighbouring gentry, had never been intimate with any. The gulf that lay between Milverley and more modest establishments was too great to allow of anything approaching a free exchange of hospitality; and although the 5th Earl had been affable to his neighbours, and Serena meticulous in the observances of civility, it was generally felt that a dinner or an evening party at Milverley called for no reciprocal invitation. On hunting days, if the last point had carried him far from Milverley, it was not unusual for his lordship to take his pot-luck in the house of some hunting-acquaintance. As often as not, he would have his daughter with him, the pair of them muddied to the eyebrows; and no guests, it was agreed, could have been less haughty, or easier to entertain. But after being passed from footman to footman on the way up the Grand Stairway at Milverley, traversing several saloons, being received in the Long Drawing-room by the Lady Serena, and sitting down to his lordship's notion (genially expressed) of "just a neat, plain dinner," there were few ladies with minds of so lofty an order that they could contemplate without an inward shudder any formal return of such hospitality.

When the stepmother and daughter took up their residence at the Dower House, a good deal of diffidence was felt by the well-bred; and all but pushing persons of no sensibility waited to see what attitude they would assume towards their neighbours before thrusting upon them civilities which might be unwelcome.

"With the result," said Serena, fully alive to the scruples operating on the minds of the delicate, "that we are left to the mercy of the Ibsleys, and that odious Laleham-woman, my dear Fanny! Oh, I must tell you that I came smash up against Mrs Orrell in Quenbury this morning, and taxed her openly with neglect! You know that unaffected way she has! She told me, with *such* a twinkle, that old Lady Orrell had said to her that she hoped she would not be in a hurry to leave cards on us, for *that* would be lowering herself to Lady Laleham's level! You may imagine how I roared!"

"Oh, did you tell her how happy we should be to receive her?"

"To be sure I did! But you would have been shocked, Fanny! We enjoyed a delightful gossip, and made out between us that Lady Laleham's beginnings must have been wholly vulgar! Don't eat me! I know how much you affect her society!"

"Now, Serena -! You know very well -! But what is one to do? Sir Walter Laleham's having been a friend of your dear Papa's makes it so impossible for us to snub her! I can't conceive how he came to marry her!"

"Oh, he was all to pieces, and she had a great fortune, or was a great heiress, or some such thing! I pity her daughters: she has them in complete subjection, and, depend upon it, she means them all to contract brilliant marriages! She may succeed with Emily, but I defy her to foist the freckled one on to anything better than a baronet."

"How can you, Serena?" protested Fanny.

"I'm sure I could *not*!"

"No, pray be serious! I daresay Anne will be quite as pretty as Emily in a year or two, and I do think Emily quite delightfully pretty, don't you? Only I do hope she may not be persuaded into doing anything she doesn't quite like."

"I'll tell you what, Fanny: I shouldn't wonder at it if all this toad-eating is directed to that end! Lady Laleham hopes to jockey you into sponsoring Emily!"

"Oh, no, surely she could not? Besides, there is no need! She seems to know everyone, and to go everywhere!"

"Franked by the Lalehams! Yes, but she's as shrewd as she can hold together, and knows very well she is only tolerated. She is the kind of person one is obliged to invite to a rout-party, but never to a dinner for one's friends!"

Fanny admitted the truth of this, but said: "Yet her manners are not at all vulgar, and she doesn't precisely toad-eat one."

"Her manners have all the tiresome formality of those who dare not unbend for fear of appearing not quite the thing, and her toad-eating is of the most unendurable order of that ancient art! I swear I prefer the truckler to that ridiculous parade of grandeur! 'You and I, dear Lady Spenborough....' 'A woman of quality's laugh, as we know, Lady Serena....' Ugh!"

"Oh, yes, very bad! quite absurd! But I like Emily, do not you? She is such a lively girl, with such natural, confiding manners!"

"Too easily quelled! It is a study to see her guilt-stricken countenance when Mama's basilisk eyes admonish her! I will allow her to be both natural and beautiful, but if you have discovered more wit in her than may be stowed in your thimble, and leave room to spare, you have remarkable powers of discernment, my dear!"

"Ah, but you are so clever, Serena!" Fanny said simply.

"I?" exclaimed Serena incredulously.

"Oh, yes! Everyone says so, and indeed it is true!"

"My dear Fanny, what in the world are you at? I have not the smallest pretensions to anything more than commonsense!"

"But you have! You have a well-informed mind, and you always know what to say to people. Why, when the Castlereaghs were staying with us last year, I was quite lost in admiration at the way you contrived to talk to him! When I could think of nothing to say but the merest commonplace!"

"Good gracious, what nonsense! *That* style of thing, I promise you, is nothing but a trick! You forget how long I have been knocking about the world. When you are as old as I am you will be doing the same."

"Oh, no! I never shall be able to," Fanny said, shaking her head. "I am quite as stupid as Emily Laleham, and I'm sure you must often be quite provoked by me."

"Never till this moment!" Serena declared, with a slightly heightened colour, but in a rallying tone. "Good God, if ever I have another suitor I'll take good care to keep him out of your way! You would make him believe me a blue-stocking, and after that, farewell to my chance of contracting even a respectable marriage!"

That made Fanny laugh, and no more was said. But Serena was shocked to realize how truly she had spoken. Much as she loved the gentle creature, she was sometimes provoked by her simplicity, and often longed for the companionship of someone with wits to match her own.

It was hard, too, to accustom herself to what she thought a dawdling way of living, and harder still to abandon her hunting. That, while she was in deep mourning, she must always have done, but she might, had either Fanny or her cousin shared her passion, have enjoyed some gallops. But Fanny was a very nervous horsewoman, willing to amble with her along the lanes, but cast into an agony of apprehension at the mere suggestion of jumping the smallest obstacle; and Hartley regarded horses as nothing more than a means of getting from one place to another.

She had felt herself obliged to send her hunters to Tattersall's, retaining only one little spirting thoroughbred mare, which could be stabled at the Dower House. The stables there had not been built to accommodate more than six horses, and although Hartley had politely begged her to consider the

Milverley stables as much her own as they had ever been her pride would not allow her to be so much beholden to him. Fanny, knowing what a grief it must be to her, was aghast, but Serena, who could not bear to have a wound touched, or even noticed, said lightly: "Oh, fiddle! What's the use of keeping hunters one can't ride? I can't afford to have them eating their heads off, and I know of no reason why my cousin should!"

Shortly before Christmas, they received a visit from Lord Rotherham. One of his estates, not his principal seat, which was situated in quite another part of the country, but a smaller and more favoured residence, was Claycross Abbey, which lay some ten miles beyond Quenbury. He rode over on a damp, cheerless day, and was ushered into the drawing-room to find Serena alone there, engaged, not very expertly, in knotting a fringe. "Good God, Serena!" he ejaculated, checking on the threshold.

She had never been more glad to see him. Every grudge was forgotten in delight at this visit from one who represented at that moment a lost world. "Rotherham!" she cried, jumping up, and going to him with her hand held out. "Of all the charming surprises!"

"My poor girl, you *must* be bored!" he said.

She laughed. "Witness my occupation! To tears, I assure you! I was so extravagant as to send to London for a parcel of new books, thinking to be kept well entertained for at least a month. But having been so improvident as to swallow *Guy Mannering* almost at one gulp – has it come in your way? I like it better, I think, than *Waverley* – I am left with *The Pastor's Fireside*, which seems sadly flat; a *History of New England*, for which I am not in the correct humour; a most tedious *Life of Napoleon*, written in verse, if you please! and, of all imaginable things, an *Enquiry into Rent*! Fanny has failed miserably to teach me to do tambour-work that doesn't shame the pair of us, so, in desperation, I am knotting a fringe. But sit down, and tell me what has been going on in the world all this time!"

"Nothing that I know of. You must have seen that Wellington and Castlereagh carried it against old Blucher. For the rest, the only *on-dits* which have come in my way are that Sir Hudson Lowe has his eye on a handsome widow, and that the Princess of Wales has now taken to driving about the Italian countryside in a resplendent carriage drawn by cream-coloured ponies. Rehearsing an appearance at Astley's, no doubt. Tell me how you go on!"

"Oh – tolerably well! What has brought you into Gloucestershire? Do you mean to spend your Christmas at Claycross?"

"Yes: an unwilling sacrifice on the altar of duty. My sister comes tomorrow, bringing with her I know not how many of her offspring; and my cousin Cordelia, labouring, apparently, under the mistaken belief that I must be pining for a sight of my wards, brings the whole pack down upon me on Thursday."

"Good heavens, what a houseful! I wonder you should not rather invite them to Delford!"

"I invited them nowhere. Augusta informed me that I should be delighted to receive them all, and as for taking Cordelia's eldest cub into Leicestershire at this season, no, I thank you! I have more regard for my horses, and should certainly prefer Gerard not to break his neck while under my aegis."

She frowned, and said, with a touch of asperity: "It is a pity you cannot be kinder to that boy!"

"I might be, if his mother were less so," he responded coolly.

"I think it is not in your nature. You have neither patience nor compunction, Ivo."

"On *your* tongue the stricture sits oddly, my dear Serena!"

She flushed. "I hope that at least I have compunction."

"So do I, but I have not seen it!"

Her eyes flashed, but she choked back a retort, saying, after a moment's struggle: "I beg your pardon! You remind me – very properly! – that your conduct towards your wards is no concern of mine."

"Good science, Serena!" he said approvingly. "I am now thrown in the close, and shall make no attempt to come up to time. You are at liberty to censure my conduct towards my wards as much as you please, but why waste these remarks on me? Cordelia will certainly drive over to pay you a visit, and will be delighted to learn your opinion of me: it is identical with her own!"

Fanny entered the room as Serena exclaimed: "Oh, can we never be for ten minutes together without quarrelling?"

"I believe it has been rather longer than that, so we may plume ourselves upon the improvement," he replied, rising, and shaking hands with Fanny. "How do you do? You have no occasion to look dismayed: I came only to pay my respects, and have already stayed too long. I hope you are well?"

She had never known how to reply to such speeches as this, and coloured hotly, stammering that she was so glad – hoped he would stay to dine – they had not expected....

"Thank you, no! I have no business with Spenborough, and paused here only on my way to Milverley."

"You need not vent your anger on poor Fanny!" Serena said indignantly.

"I have no compunction!" he flung at her. "My sister spends Christmas at Claycross, Lady Spenborough, and has charged me to discover from you whether you are yet receiving visitors."

"Oh, yes! We shall be very happy to see Lady Silchester. Pray, assure her -! It is most kind!"

He bowed, and took his leave of them. Fanny gave a sigh of relief, and said: "I am so thankful! Mrs Stowe tells me that the turbot had to be thrown away, and to have been obliged to have set an indifferent dinner before Lord Rotherham would have made me feel ready to sink! *How* he would have looked! What has put him out of temper?"

"Must you ask? I did, of course!"

"Dearest Serena, indeed you should not!"

"No, I did mean not to quarrel, only I said something severe – Well! it was true enough, but I never thought it would touch him on the raw! I'm sorry for it, but I daresay if we had not quarrelled over that we should have done so over something else."

"Oh, dear! But perhaps he won't visit us again!" said Fanny hopefully.

CHAPTER FOUR

FANNY'S HOPE was soon proved to be ill-founded. Two days later, Serena, who had been walking in the park, returned to the Dower House to find a strange carriage standing in the stableyard. Even as she recognized the crest on the panel, Rotherham came out of the stable, and, after the curtest of greetings, said abruptly: "That mare of yours is too short in the back."

"Nonsense!" she replied.

"I never talk nonsense about horseflesh."

She laughed, putting back the hood from her bright hair. "I have a wager with myself that I will *once* meet you without quarrelling, so let us agree that the mare is by far too short in the back, has weak hocks as well, and very likely a spavin forming."

A smile glimmered; he said, in a milder voice: "Where have you been walking? I should have thought it too dirty a day to lure you out for any other exercise than hunting."

She stifled a sigh. "Don't speak of hunting! I believe they met today at Normansholt, and have been thinking that the scent must be running breast-high. How comes it that you are not out?"

"Augusta commanded me to escort her here instead."

"I pity you! Is she with Fanny? I must go in."

He began to walk with her towards the house, the long skirt of his driving-coat of white drab brushing his ankles. "Do you continue to stable your other horses at Milverley?" he demanded.

She hesitated. "I might have done so, but no!"

"Where, then?"

"Why, the truth is I've sold 'em!" she said lightly.

He looked thunderstruck. "Sold them! Good God, am I to understand that your cousin would not house them for you?"

"By no means! He was perfectly willing to do so, but it would be a great piece of nonsense for me to be keeping half a dozen hunters I can't use eating their heads off in the stable; and since Jane doesn't ride I thought it best to be rid of them. Besides, were we not agreed – such an event you cannot have forgotten! – that I cannot, in my present circumstances, afford to maintain a string of hunters?"

He was very much vexed, and said roughly: "Don't talk that stuff to me! Why the devil didn't you apply to me? If you need money for such a reason as that, you may have it!"

"Out of *your* pocket, Ivo?"

"Nonsense! You are a rich woman!"

She was surprised, and a good deal touched. "My dear Ivo, I know as well as you do that it is not in your power to contravene the Trust! I am not so bird-witted as you must think me! I had all that out with Mr Perrott long since."

"Let me tell you, Serena, that these independent ways of yours are not at all becoming!" he said angrily. "Consulting Perrott -! There was not the least need!"

She smiled. "You have convinced me that there was every need! Thank you, Ivo, but I am persuaded you must perceive how improper it would be for you to be franking me!"

"No such thing! If I lend you money, be sure I shall keep strict account of it, and expect to be repaid in due course!"

"Ah, but Papa warned me never to get into the hands of moneylenders!" she retorted, laughing at him. "No, no! Say no more! Indeed, I am not ungrateful, but I don't care to be behindhand with the world! As for my horses – why, yes! it cost me a pang to part with them, but that is all done with now, and I promise you I don't repine any more. Pray go in, and tell Lady Silchester that I shall be with her directly! I must not appear in all my dirt!"

She vanished into the house as she spoke; after a scowling moment, he followed her, cast his driving coat and hat on to a chair, and joined his sister and Fanny in the drawing room.

When Serena presently entered the room, she had changed her walking-dress for a robe of clinging black crape, made high to the throat, and relieved only by a little ruff of goffered lawn. The sombre hue seemed to enhance the whiteness of her skin; if Fanny, in her weeds, was ethereally fair, she, with her flaming locks and creamy complexion appeared magnificent.

Lady Silchester, already, though only two years older than her brother, a formidable matron, stared, and exclaimed: "Upon my word, Serena, I never saw you looking better!"

"Do we take that for praise, or censure?" demanded Rotherham.

"Oh, you need not try to frown me down! Serena knows I always speak my mind! How do you do, Serena? I am glad to find you and Lady Spenborough so comfortable. Though I daresay you are a trifle cramped. How do your cousins go on at Milverley? I suppose I shall be obliged to call. I fancy I never met Hartley's wife. Lady Theresa warns me I shall find her to be no great thing. However, I should not wish to be uncivil!"

"My dear Lady Silchester, if you do not know enough of my aunt at this date -! Jane is perfectly amiable, I assure you."

"Well, I am happy to hear you say so. It would be excessively disagreeable for you to be living so close if she were not. Not that I mean to say it is not the horridest thing, whatever she may be like. I shan't enlarge on that head, but I feel for you most sincerely, Serena."

"Thank you."

"The stupid way things have been left, too!" pursued the lady. "Most thoughtless and awkward! I can't think what Spenborough could have been about! If I have been asked once, I have been asked a dozen times if you and Rotherham mean to make it up. You need not fear! I have told everyone there is no question of that. People are so impertinent!"

"As you say!" Rotherham struck in.

"Oh, you mean *I* am, I suppose!" she said, quite unmoved. "You need not glare at me in that murdering way: I hope I know Serena well enough not to stand on ceremony with her."

"Certainly you do!" replied Serena, amused. "Do scotch the rumour! There's not a word of truth in it."

"So Rotherham has been telling me. I'm very glad to know it. Not that I'm not fond of you, my dear, but it would never have done! You have a great deal too much spirit for Rotherham. Lady Spenborough and I were saying only a few minutes ago that nothing but a meek little mouse will do for him."

"I am obliged to you both!" said Rotherham.

Scarlet with confusion, Fanny said, "Oh, no! I didn't – that is, it was Lady Silchester who -"

She was mercifully interrupted by the entrance of a servant, and got up, saying: "Oh, to be sure -! Lady Silchester, you'll take a nuncheon! Shall we remove into the breakfast-parlour?"

Serena, who was shaking with laughter, said, as the embarrassing guest was shepherded out of the room: "I should be sorry for the mouse!"

He grinned ruefully. "So should I, indeed! Augusta is abominable!"

They joined the other two in the breakfast-parlour, where a noonday repast of cold meat and fruit had been set on the table; but they had hardly taken their seats when the sound of carriage wheels was heard; and in another few minutes the butler came in to inform Fanny that Lady Laleham and Miss Laleham were in the drawing-room.

Fanny was obliged to excuse herself to her guests. She was surprised that Lybster, in general fully to be relied on, should not have denied her; and when he had closed the parlour door behind her, administered a gentle reproof. But it seemed that he had done his best to exclude the unwanted visitors, saying that he believed my lady to be engaged. He had been overborne. Lady Laleham had begged that a message might be carried to my lady: she would not detain her above a minute. With a sinking heart, Fanny entered the drawing-room.

It was as she had foreseen it would be. Lady Laleham, a handsome, fashionably dressed woman, with very correct manners, and an air of great assurance, had plainly no intention of making her visit a brief one. She came forward, full of apologies and protestations. There was a recipe for pickling pears which she had promised quite a fortnight ago to give to dear Lady Spenborough's housekeeper. She dared not guess what Lady Spenborough must have been thinking of her. "Only, from one cause and another, it went out of my head. I believe you desired to have it immediately, too, which quite covers me with shame! I have it with me here, but felt that a word of explanation was due to you."

Fanny had no recollection of having expressed a desire to be given the recipe; but she accepted it, with a civil thank-you.

"I so much dislike persons who make promises only to break them. But I must not keep you! I collect you have friends with you. Did I not see the Rotherham carriage in your yard?"

There was nothing for it but to admit it, and to invite the two ladies to join the party in the breakfast parlour. With only a little show of reluctance, Lady Laleham allowed herself to be persuaded. Fanny believed she had come for no other purpose.

Nothing could have exceeded the lady's aplomb when she reached the parlour. It was quite unnecessary for Fanny to introduce her.

"Yes, indeed I am acquainted with Lady Silchester! How do you do? I believe the last time we met was at the Ormesbys' ball: such a crush, was it not? Ah, Lord Rotherham! Don't disturb yourself, I beg! It is quite shocking to be invading your party in this unconscionable way, but Lady Spenborough *would* have it so! To own the truth, it falls out very fortunately that I should find you here, for I have been wanting to see you."

"Indeed!" he said, a strong inflexion of surprise in his voice.

"Yes, for my eldest son informs me that Gerard Monksleigh is quite a particular friend of his, and will be staying with you for Christmas. Nothing will do but that I must get up a little party for these flighty young people! I should like so much to ask Mrs Monksleigh if she will not bring her daughters to it, but how this may be done when I have not the pleasure of her acquaintance I know not, unless you will come to my aid, Lord Rotherham!"

He returned a civil answer, but could not take it upon himself to commit his cousin. Lady Silchester said: "The girls want to go to the Assembly at Quenbury. I don't know how Cordelia Monksleigh likes it for Susan and Margaret, but I'm by no means sure I care to let Caroline go. Serena! What do you think of the scheme? Would you advise it?"

Serena, who had placed Emily Laleham in a chair between her own and Rotherham's, saw the sparkle in the girl's big, pansy-soft eyes as they were turned anxiously towards her, and smiled, saying: "I never attended the Quenbury Assemblies myself, but I should think there could be no harm in them."

"A dead bore," said Rotherham. "You will meet no one there whom you know, and, unless you have a taste for being toad-eaten, will do better to remain at home."

"You are too severe," interposed Serena, with a good deal of meaning in her voice.

"Well, so I would," said his sister, "but now the girls have taken the notion into their heads it is very hard to know what to do. It is a great pity they can't dance at Claycross, but with only Elphin and Gerard between the three of them, that won't answer. As long as there are no waltzes or quadrilles I daresay Silchester would not object to Caroline's going. Elphin will be there, after all, and if the company should be too mixed he must dance with his sister."

"An evening of rare pleasure for both," commented Rotherham.

A stifled giggle made him glance down at the enchanting face beside him. A look, half of mischief, half of consternation was cast up at him. "Oh, I beg your pardon!" gasped Emily, in a frightened undervoice.

"Not at all! When I choose to be witty I like to receive just acknowledgment. Do you mean to go to this Assembly?"

"Oh, I don't know! I do *hope* – but I'm not precisely out yet, and perhaps Mama won't permit me."

"What is the significance of being *precisely* out?"

"Don't quiz her!" said Serena, perceiving that she was at a loss to know how to answer. "She will be precisely out when she has been presented. When is it to be, Emily?"

"In the spring. Mama will give a ball!" she said, in an awed tone. "At least," she added naïvely, "it is Grandmama really, only she won't come to it, which I think is a great shame. "

Rotherham looked amused, but before he could probe into the mystery of this speech, which Serena feared was his intention, his notice was claimed by Lady Laleham, seated on his left hand.

"What do you say, Lord Rotherham? Your sister and I find that we share the same scruples, but I fancy I have hit on a scheme to make it unobjectionable for our giddy young people to attend the Assembly. Do you not agree that if we make up our own party between us it will solve the problem?"

"Certainly," he replied.

With this unenthusiastic assent she was satisfied, and began at once to engage Lady Silchester's co-operation.

Rotherham turned again to Emily, and found her face upturned, quite pink with excitement, her eyes sparkling. "Oh, *thank* you!" she breathed.

"Are you so fond of Assemblies?"

"Yes, indeed! That is to say, I don't know, for I was never at one before."

"Not being precisely out. Do you live in Quenbury?"

"Oh, no! At Cherrifield Place! Don't you know it? You came by it this morning!"

"Did I?"

"Yes, and Mama knew it must be you, because of the crest. We were at the gate, meaning only to walk into the village, but Mama said we would come here instead, because there was a recipe she wished to give Lady Spenborough."

"Providential!"

She was puzzled, and, scared by the satirical note in his voice, was stricken to silence. Serena, a trifle unsteadily, said: "Well, I hope you will enjoy the Assembly, and have a great many partners."

"Within the limits of exclusiveness," interpolated Rotherham, meeting her eye.

She frowned at him, knowing him to be quite capable of saying something outrageous enough to be understood by his innocent neighbour. Fortunately, since he met the frown with a bland look she knew well, Lady Laleham, having achieved her object, now judged it to be good tactics to take her leave. Her carriage was called for, and she bore her daughter off, well pleased with the success of her morning's campaign.

"I never meet that woman but I smell the shop," observed Lady Silchester calmly. "I wish I may not be her dear Augusta Silchester hereafter!"

"You are well served for having been fool enough to have mentioned the Assembly," said her brother.

"Very true. I shall have the headache, and send Caroline with Cordelia."

"I believe she knew you were here, and that is why she came!" declared Fanny, very much ruffled.

"She did!" Serena said, her eyes dancing. "That absurd child let the secret out in the most innocent fashion imaginable! How I contrived to keep my face I don't know! Well for her Mama was not attending!"

"A pretty little dab of a girl," said Lady Silchester. "Not enough countenance, but she'll take very well, I daresay. Dark girls are being much admired just now. Depend upon it, her mother means her to go to the highest bidder. They say Laleham is pretty well at a standstill."

"What I want to know," said Rotherham, "is why Grandmama won't be at the ball which she is to give."

"I was in dread that you would ask her!" Serena said.

"I shall discover it at the Assembly, when you are not there to spoil sport."

"You will not go to the Assembly!" she exclaimed incredulously.

"Certainly I shall."

"Having a taste for being toad-eaten?" she quizzed him.

"No, for Miss Laleham's artless conversation!"

"Ah, she won't gratify you! You have frightened her away!"

"She must be lured back to hand."

"No, no, it would be too bad of you! You might wake expectations in Mama's bosom, moreover!"

"Irresistible! I shall come out on the side of my niece and my wards, and you will hear next that I am not by half as disagreeable as they had supposed."

She laughed, but could not believe him to be serious. However, the next visitor to the Dower House was Mrs Monksleigh, who drove over from Claycross on Christmas Eve, and disclosed that the Assembly scheme was now a settled thing. "I own, I thought it would come to nothing, and so I warned the girls. I'm sure I was never more astonished than when Rotherham said he saw no harm in it, and as for Susan, she was ready to drop! I expected he would have given her one of his set-downs, but he was perfectly amiable!"

Mrs Monksleigh was the relict of a military man, who had left her with six children and a competence judged by his family to be respectable, and by her, inadequate. She was a very goodnatured woman, but having, unfortunately, less than common sense, she had never been able to teach herself habits of economy. There was a want of management in her house which led to a succession of financial crises driving her quite distracted, and never failing to exasperate Rotherham. He was not her cousin, but her husband's; and, in addition to being her Trustee, was joined with her in the guardianship of her children. She could neither understand why her poor husband had made such a choice, nor cease to bewail it. No one could have been more unacceptable to her! He was a man of no sensibility, and impatient temper, and had so little affection for his cousin's children that it was a question whether he knew them apart. His decrees were imperious, and issued without the smallest regard for her wishes; himself a man of huge fortune, he had no comprehension of the difficulties confronting those left to maintain the elegances of life upon a mere pittance. He always thought she should have been able to manage better! It was he who had insisted on Gerard's being sent to school, although her own dear Dr Ryde had pronounced the poor little fellow's constitution to be too delicate for the rigours of Eton. She could not believe that he would have cared if Gerard had died of it. Miraculously, Gerard had survived; and Charlie, of course, had always been very stout, so that she had no fears for him; but now Rotherham was saying that it was time poor little Tom was sent to join his brother. Do as she would, she could not make him understand the shocking expense of having two sons at Eton. There was no end to the calls on her purse: she was sure the fees were the least part of the whole. As for the girls, beyond saying that he saw no reason why Susan should be presented at a Drawing-room, and annihilating Margaret by telling her that when she could address him without prefixing her remarks with a giggle he might attend to her, he never noticed them. Very likely he had forgotten that little Lizzie even existed: he could certainly never remember her name.

The Carlow ladies listened, and sympathized, and agreed that it was a hard case, Fanny rather more sincerely than Serena. Serena could perceive that there might be something to be said in Rotherham's defence. He made too little allowance, she believed, for the difficulties besetting a woman left with six children on her hands; but she, like him, was intolerant of folly, and Mrs Monksleigh was so very foolish! But she thought him less than kind to Gerard, of whom he was contemptuous; and quite indifferent to the younger members of the family. This opinion was shared by Lady Silchester, who excused it, however, by saying that gentlemen always disliked to be plagued by children, and that no one could expect such a thorough sportsman as Rotherham to take to Gerard, who had no taste for sport, a very bad seat, and far too little spirit. But even she could not pretend that her brother had shown the smallest sign of approval when the more robust Charlie, upon the occasion of his only visit to Delford, had given evidence of such spirited behaviour as led him into the performance of every kind of prank, from trying to bestride his guardian's more unmanageable horses to falling off the stable-roof, and breaking his collar-bone. All he had said was that Charlie might think himself fortunate that he had broken his collar-bone, and that he would be damned if ever he saddled himself with the whelp again.

"So Augusta quite mistakes the matter when she says he would like poor Gerard better if he were bolder, and didn't stand so much in awe of him," complained Mrs Monksleigh. "I'm sure no boy could be bolder than Charlie, for he is for ever in a scrape, and he never minds a word anyone says to him, but *that* doesn't please Rotherham either! I assure you, Lady Serena, I live in dread of his making Rotherham angry while we are at Claycross, for I know he wouldn't hesitate to use the poor boy with dreadful harshness, which I have told him I utterly forbid. Indeed, I thought all was lost yesterday, when that most disagreeable keeper made such a commotion about Charlie's putting a charge of shot into his leg. Just as though it had not been an accident! Of course, it was wrong of Charlie to take the gun without leave, but the man was only very little hurt, after all! Rotherham said in the most *menacing* way that he would teach Charlie a lesson, and I could feel one of my spasms coming on, only Augusta told Rotherham he was a great fool not to have locked up the gunroom when he had an imp like Charlie to stay, and said surely he could not wish me to fall into strong hysterics, and so it passed off, and I was truly grateful to Augusta."

Even Fanny could not help laughing at this ingenuous history, although she did not appreciate, as Serena instantly did, the masterly nature of Lady Silchester's strategy. She wondered at Mrs Monksleigh's having dared to leave Charlie to his own devices while she came to the Dower House; but it appeared that Mrs Monksleigh had not dared. She had brought him with her, but she had not wished Fanny to be troubled with him, and had prevailed upon Gerard to take charge of him. The carriage had set them both down at Cherrifield Place. Gerard Monksleigh and Edgar Laleham were up at Cambridge together, in the same year and at the same college. Mrs Monksleigh hoped that Lady Laleham would not object to her having sent Charlie with his brother. Serena did not think that she would object to anything that strengthened the connection with Claycross.

They saw no more of the Claycross party until the night of the Assembly, when, to their surprise, Rotherham walked in on them midway through the evening. His satin knee-breeches and silk stockings made Serena exclaim: "Then you did go to the Assembly!"

"I did, and am there now, in the card-room – or so I hope Cordelia may believe!"

She raised her brows. "The bird would not come to hand?"

"On the contrary! But a driven bird, scared into the model of insipid propriety. I stood up for the two first dances with her, and all the conversation I could get out of her was 'Oh, Lord Rotherham!' and 'Oh, yes, Lord Rotherham!' and once, by way of a change, 'Exactly so, Lord Rotherham!' So I tried the effect of telling her she was taking the shine out of all the local beauties, but as that elicited nothing more encouraging than 'How can you, Lord Rotherham?' I drew no more coverts, but came instead to take formal leave of you and Lady Spenborough. My party breaks up tomorrow, and I must be in London by the end of the week."

"Good God, Ivo, do you mean to tell me that Emily is the only girl you have honoured with an invitation to dance? Not even your niece, or Susan, or Margaret?" cried Serena, scandalized.

"They would thank you for that suggestion as little as I do."

"But it was most improper – quite abominable!" she said hotly. "Just what sets people's backs up! It would have been bad enough to have danced only with the ladies of your own party. That would have made everyone say merely that you were disagreeably haughty! But to single out one girl, and she not of your own party – Ivo, it is the height of insolence, and a great piece of unkindness to Emily besides!"

"Not at all!" he retorted, with a curling lip. "Her mother did not think so, I promise you!"

"That is worse than all the rest! You know very well what she is! There are no bounds to her ambition! Depend upon it, you have now raised the most absurd expectations in her breast, turned that unfortunate child into an object of envy and speculation, all for sport! No, Fanny, I will *not* be hushed! There is something so particularly displeasing in the whole business! You may argue it as you will, Rotherham, but it was very ill done! I could name you a dozen girls, all, I daresay, at the Assembly tonight, as worthy of your notice as Emily Laleham! But no! You have been playing the great man, condescending to grace a country Assembly – for anything I can tell, though I should be sorry to think it of you, amused to see what a flutter was caused by your mere presence!"

"You need not think it!" he struck in, his cheeks whitened, and a pulse throbbing beside his thinned mouth.

"Indeed, I believe it to be a kind of unthinking arrogance, but it does you no credit, Rotherham! If you went to a public Assembly, you had no choice but to behave with civility towards all! You might have danced with no one, since your excuse for going there was only to indulge your young guests with a ball, but for a whim to single out one girl and she by far the loveliest! – and then to stroll away, as though you thought yourself above the rest of the company – oh, no, Ivo, how could you? Every feeling is offended!"

"I thank you! You have quite a turn for the high dramatic! No doubt you expect me now to return for the express purpose of conferring upon two or three other damsels the singular honour – if such you do indeed consider it! – of standing up with me!"

"It is what my father would have done in such a situation, for he was most truly the gentleman!" she said, a sob rising in her throat. "I should think the better of you!"

"I care nothing for your opinion of me!" he snapped. "Lady Spenborough, have you any commissions for me to execute in London? I shall be most happy!"

"Oh, none, thank you!" she said faintly.

"Then I will take my leave! Your most obedient servant, ma'am!"

A formal bow, one scorching glance thrown at Serena, and he was gone.

"Oh, dear!" said Fanny, pressing her hands to her temples. "I feel quite sick! And, oh, *Serena*, we never thought to offer him so much as a glass of ratafia!"

CHAPTER FIVE

IT WAS hardly to be expected, Serena thought, that the several ladies of their acquaintance in the neighbouring district would spare her a description of the Boxing Day Assembly, and greatly did she dread being obliged to listen either to animadversions on Rotherham's manners, or to bitter criticisms of Lady Laleham's encroaching ways. But the weather saved her. A week of incessant rain made quagmires of all the roads, and rendered the paying of morning-calls ineligible. They were undisturbed by visitors at the Dower House until Spenborough had himself driven there one afternoon to announce to the ladies Jane's safe delivery of a son.

He was a fond and an excellent father, and could scarcely have been more delighted if the child had been his first son, instead of his fourth. Fanny and

Serena tried to say all that was expected of them, and succeeded so well that he found himself very much in charity with them both, and confided to them that the happy event had relieved his mind of considerable anxiety. "For, you know, with the shock of my cousin's sad death, and all the exertion of disposing of the house, and the bringing of the children to Milverley, there is no saying what might have happened. But Jane is equal to anything!"

They reiterated their congratulations; he beamed, and thanked, and said: "Extremely obliging! I knew you would be glad, and determined you should be the first to be informed of the event. We mean the child to be given the name of Francis, and we hope, Lady Spenborough, that you will consent to be one of his sponsors!"

Fanny, quite pink with pleasure, said that she would be most happy; and Serena, seeing that she was really gratified, determined to forgive Jane for cutting up the South Lawn into a formal flower-garden, and even suggested that Hartley should stay to dine at the Dower House. He needed no persuasion; a message was sent to the stables; another to the kitchen; and he sat down in a wing-chair beside the fire to discuss, over several glasses of sherry, the doctor's opinion of Jane's constitution, the midwife's admiration of her fortitude, and the very diverting things the elder children had said upon being informed that God had sent them a new brother.

It was some time before these topics had been talked out, but at last he could think of no more to say on them. He said that he must not go boring on, complimented Fanny on her cook's way of dressing a haunch of venison, and suddenly remarked: "So Rotherham took his guests to the Assembly on Boxing Day! I wouldn't believe it when Dr Cliffe told me so, but it seems to be true enough. I saw Orrell the other day, and he vouched for it. A queer start, wasn't it?"

"It was a scheme got up for the entertainment of the young people," said Fanny calmly.

"Ay, so I understand. No harm, of course, but I shouldn't have thought Rotherham the man to condescend so far. I am not particularly acquainted with him, but he has always seemed to me pretty high in the instep: one of your haughty care-for-nobodies! However, Orrell assures me he was very civil and amiable. That Laleham woman was mightily set up by his standing up with her daughter, and not seeming to care for anyone else, but walking off to the card room immediately. Orrell says it was a study to look at the faces of the other mamas! But he came back at tea time, took in his cousin, and afterwards solicited some girl that had no partner to stand up with him, which was thought to be very goodnatured in him, and lowered the Laleham crest a trifle! This Rhenish cream is most excellent, Lady Spenborough: a capital dinner! I shall tell Jane I get nothing so good at Milverley!"

Fanny could not help glancing across the table to see whether Serena partook of her own astonishment. She could detect nothing in her face but a look of approval; and when, after Spenborough had left them, she ventured to ask her if she had not been very much surprised, she received a decided negative.

"You were not? I own, I could hardly credit my ears. I had no notion that he cared so much for your opinion!"

"No, indeed, and nor does he!" Serena answered. "The outcome would have been the same whoever had taken him to task. When he does such things as that it is not from any *conscious* idea of his own consequence, or a contempt for persons of inferior rank, but from a sort of heedless arrogance, as I told him. He had the misfortune to lose his father when he was still a schoolboy: a most estimable man, I believe. Papa was used to say that everyone stood in great awe of him, because he was such a *grand seigneur*, but that pride in *him* didn't lead him to offend people by any careless manners, but to treat everyone with the same punctilious courtesy. *We* should have thought him very stiff, I daresay, for he was held to be oldfashioned even when Papa was a young man. But Lady Rotherham was insufferably proud! You never knew her: I assure you, she was so puffed-up with conceit and consequence that there was no bearing it! She brought up all three of her children, and in particular, of course, Ivo, to believe themselves so superior that they might behave as they chose, since a Barrasford must be beyond the reach of censure! As for considering the feelings of others, such a notion can never have entered her head! Her selfishness was beyond anything, too! Everything, she thought, must give way to *her* whims. One cannot wonder at Ivo's arrogance: the only wonder is that it should be unconscious – not rooted, as it was with her, in conceit! He was never taught to think of anything but his own pleasure, but his disposition is not bad, nor does he mean to offend the sensibilities of others. It is all heedlessness! If he can but be made to see that he has behaved badly, he is sorry for it at once."

"Oh, Serena! When I am sure he was ready to murder you for having presumed to tell him his conduct was not gentlemanly -!"

"No, no, you are mistaken, Fanny!" Serena said, laughing a little. "He didn't wish to murder me, but himself! Oh, well, perhaps me, but much more himself! He knew what I said to be true, and that is what wounded his pride, and made him smart so."

"Do you think so?" Fanny said doubtfully.

"I know it! Don't imagine that he instantly set about mending the matter because his conduct had given *me* an ill opinion of him! He did it because it gave *him* that ill opinion. He has the faults of his mother's temper, but at the bottom he is more his father's son than hers. Papa always held to it that with *that* upbringing, and all the toad-eating and nonsense that surrounded him when he was by far too young to perceive the folly of it, it said a great deal for his character that he grew up to care so little for pomp and dignity, and of all creatures to dislike most those that flatter him. You will never see Ivo in company with any of the odious hangers-on who fawn on great men, administering all the time to their vanity, you know. He holds such stuff in utter contempt. It was otherwise with his brother. If you had but seen Captain Lord Talbot Barrasford – in all the magnificence of silver lace, for he was a Hussar! – plainly thinking how much his regiment was honoured by his having joined it -! I used to wonder how he contrived to maintain his precious dignity when compelled to quarter himself in some Spanish hovel. Oh, I should not be saying so *now*, I know! He fell in action, very gallantly, I believe, and if he was not much mourned, at least he must be respected. People say that Augusta was very like him, as a girl. But she had the good fortune to marry Silchester, who is a sensible man, and by the time I was old enough to become acquainted with her she was much as you see her today – with a good deal of Ivo's unconcern with what people may be thinking, and quite unaffected. I don't mean to say she does not know her own worth, but it is something she takes for granted, and scarcely thinks about."

"Oh, yes! She quite frightened me, at first, with her odd, blunt way of talking, but I have always found her perfectly kind, and have never doubted that *she* has a heart!"

Serena smiled. "None of the Barrasfords has what is generally meant when people speak of *warmheartedness*. If you mean, as I collect you do, that Rotherham's nature is cold, I think I had rather say that it is fiery! He is a hard man, certainly. I shouldn't turn to him for sympathy, but I have known him to be kind."

"I suppose, when you were betrothed, he must have been, but -"

"Oh, no, not when he fancied himself to be in love with me! Far from it!" Serena interrupted, laughing. "He would like to be much kinder in the execution of his duty as my Trustee than I could permit!"

"Why, what can you mean? You yourself suspected that the arrangement was made at his instigation!"

"Well, yes, while I was in such a rage, I did," admitted Serena. "Only, of course, I soon saw that it could not have been. I'm afraid it was poor Papa's notion of a clever stroke. The match was so much of his making that he could not bear to abandon it."

"I know it was a splendid one, but did he care for that? It was not like him!"

"Well, I suppose he must have cared a little, but the thing was that he liked Rotherham, and believed we should suit, because he was an honest man, and there was no flummery about either of us! You know what Papa was, when he had taken a notion firmly into his head! I don't think anything could have brought him to believe that Ivo was as thankful to be out of a scrape as I was. I never supposed that the pair of them concerted this infamous scheme because Ivo wished to win me back, and as soon as I was cooler, I knew, of course, that Papa would not have done it to give Ivo an opportunity to be revenged on me."

"Revenged!"

"Well," said Serena, reflectively wrinkling her nose, "he has not a forgiving nature, and there's no denying I did deal his pride the most wounding blow when I cried off. So, when I heard Papa's Will read, I thought – oh, I don't know *what* I thought! I was too angry to think at all. And then I believed that he wouldn't refuse to act because he meant to punish me for that old slight by using the power he had been given in a malicious way. To own the truth, I thought he would be pleased when he discovered that I had been obliged to sell my horses, but I was quite out! He was very much vexed, and tried to make me believe he could increase my allowance. But I had gone into that with Perrott, and I knew better – which vexed him more than ever! He would certainly have given me a larger allowance, and never told me it was his own money, and you will agree that however improper that may have been it was very kind!"

Fanny said in a wondering tone: "Perhaps he *is* fond of you, Serena!"

"Yes, when he is not disliking me excessively. I never doubted it," said

Serena coolly. "It is the sort of fondness one has for an old acquaintance, who shares many of one's ideas and tastes. At the moment, however, I expect dislike has the upper hand. He will come about!"

Nothing was heard of Rotherham until the end of January. The weather continued to be dull, and wet, one leaden day succeeding the last, and exercising a depressive influence on the spirits. Fanny contracted a severe chill, and seemed unable wholly to shake off its effects. She continued very languid, complained of rheumatic pains, and found the days intolerably long. The novelty – for such she had felt it to be – of being mistress of her own house had worn off; and the monotony of the life she was leading made her fretful. The only variations that offered were the occasional visits of neighbours with whom she had nothing in common; and her only amusements were playing cribbage or backgammon with Serena, or going up to the great house to play with Jane's children. The Countess always had a kind welcome for her, and she could be merry with the children; but a fatal flaw attached to her visits, and caused them to become less and less frequent. She could never be in Jane's company without being obliged to listen to her complaints of Serena. She knew no way of silencing Jane. "I wish that you would drop Serena a hint," were words that always made her heart sink. It was not that Jane undervalued Serena, or was not sincerely attached to her, or was unsympathetic. No one, Jane was careful to assure her, in the calm voice of infallibility which so much exasperated Serena, had a greater regard for her, no one could be more certain of her wish to be of use to her cousin, or could more thoroughly appreciate the painful nature of her feelings, *but* -! Gentle though she was, Fanny would have leapt to Serena's defence, had she not felt, too often, that Jane had right on her side. As Hartley grew in self-confidence, he naturally depended on his cousin less and less. He inaugurated new customs without consulting her and, since he was inclined to be consequential he contrived – unwittingly, Fanny believed – to convey the impression that he thought his innovations a vast improvement on anything that had been done by his predecessor. Fanny tried to convince Serena that he did not mean to seem to slight her father, but her attempts at peace-making only drew down the vials of Serena's wrath upon her own head. Serena, fretting quite as much as Fanny at the boredom of her days, found an outlet for her curbed energy in riding about Milverley, detecting changes (none of them acceptable to her), discovering omissions, and chatting with tenants, or discussing improvements with the bailiff just as she had always done, and so rubbing up against her cousin half a dozen times in a week. To make matters worse, she was far more often right than he; and whereas he, lacking the late Earl's geniality, was not much liked, she, inheriting it, was loved.

Serena, having more strength of character than Fanny, did not wilt under the trials that beset her, but tried to overcome boredom by throwing herself even more energetically, and much to her cousin's dismay, into the Milverley affairs. Could she but have found a congenial companion with whom to exchange ideas, she might have refrained, but no such person seemed to exist in the immediate neighbourhood. She became increasingly impatient with Fanny; and the very fact that she seldom allowed her exasperation to appear exacerbated it. There were even days when she felt that she and

Fanny conversed in different languages, and that she might almost have preferred to have been cooped up with her aunt. She would have found herself opposed to nearly every one of Lady Theresa's opinions; but Fanny had no opinions. When Lady Theresa, an accomplished and conscientious correspondent, wrote that Lady Waldegrave was dying of water on the chest, Fanny could be interested, and would discuss the sad news at far greater length than Serena thought necessary; but when Lady Theresa informed her niece that retrenchment was all the cry now, and that it was an open secret the Opposition meant to launch an attack on the tax on income which the nation had endured for ten years, some saying that it would be proposed that the two shillings in the pound now exacted should be reduced by as much as half, Fanny had nothing to say beyond a vague: "Oh!" As for Lavallette's rescue by three British subjects, which, Lady Theresa asserted, was at the moment the only topic to be hotly discussed, she thought an escape very exciting, but never reached the smallest understanding of the wider aspects of the case.

Serena was beginning to think that she could even welcome Rotherham in his most quarrelsome mood when the post brought her a letter from him. It informed her in the curtest terms that Probate having at last been obtained, he should call at the Dower House some time during the following week, when he expected to be at Claycross, to explain to her the arrangements which had been made to enable her to draw her allowance as and when she should require it. He was hers, etc., Rotherham.

"Oh, good God, still in the sullens!" exclaimed Serena disgustedly tossing the single sheet on to the fire. "And what does he mean by saying coolly that he will call here *some* time next week? If he comes without having the civility first to discover when it will be convenient for us to receive him, Lybster shall say that we are neither of us at home! I will *not* endure his high-handed ways!"

Fanny looked alarmed, but, fortunately for her peace of mind, circumstances made it impossible for this amiable plan to be put into execution. Rotherham drove himself over from Claycross in his curricle, reaching the entrance to the grounds of the Dower House just as Serena, mounted on her mare, approached it from the opposite direction.

Rotherham reined in, and waited for her to come up. She was looking extremely handsome, in a severe black beaver hat of masculine style, with a high crown and a stiffly curled brim, but the expression on her face was decidedly stormy. Perceiving it, Rotherham instantly said: "Good-morning, Serena. Who is the latest unfortunate to have incurred your displeasure?"

"My cousin," she replied curtly. "It is apparently enough for him to discover that some practice has been the custom at Milverley for years for him to overset it!"

"I pity him!" he said.

Her smouldering eyes, which had been running over the points of the two well-matched bays harnessed to his curricle, lifted to his face, and narrowed. "Is Lady Spenborough expecting you?" she demanded. "She has not told me so, and *I* have had no letter from you since the one you wrote to inform me that you were coming to Claycross."

"You could hardly have done so, since I have not written another to you."

"It would have been more civil in you to have discovered when it would be convenient for us to receive you!"

"Accept my apologies! It had not occurred to me that you would so soon be filling your days with engagements."

"Of course I am not! But -"

"Have no fear! I do not expect to take up many minutes of your time."

"I hope not, indeed, but I am afraid you will be detained for longer than you may have bargained for. I must change out of my habit before I can attend to you. No doubt Lady Spenborough will be found in the drawing room."

She wheeled the mare, and rode through the gateway. He followed her at his leisure, and within a few minutes was shaking hands with Fanny. She said something about sending to find Serena, and he interrupted her, saying: "I met her outside the gate, and the fiend's own temper she was in. I don't envy you!"

She replied, with dignity: "I am very much attached to Serena, Lord Rotherham."

"And resent my sympathy?"

"I cannot think that you know – or have ever known – how to value her," she said, almost trembling at her own boldness.

"Oh, I know her virtues!" he responded. "She would have been well enough had she ever been broke to bridle."

She could not trust herself to answer him. A slight pause ensued; he then said, with the abruptness which always disconcerted her: "Is she at loggerheads with Spenborough?"

She hesitated. He had picked up a book that lay on the table, and was idly flicking over the pages, but he raised his eyes from it, directing a piercing look at her. "Well?"

She was a little flustered by this compelling glance, and the imperative note in his voice. "It is often very painful to her. Lord Spenborough means to do right, but he is not always – does not always know how to tell her what he means to do – in in a way that won't offend her!"

"I can guess! Spenborough's a fool, and has the misfortune to succeed an excellent landlord."

"Indeed, he is fully conscious of that, and also I fear that his people do not like him as they like her!"

"Inevitable. I told her at the outset to remove from this neighbourhood."

"Perhaps she should have done so," Fanny said sadly. "She is made to feel sometimes that he holds her Papa's notions cheap. But I am sure he does not mean any such thing!"

"Pretty well for a man who never came to Milverley but as a guest on sufferance! But it won't do to bolster Serena up in such ideas as that!"

"Oh, no, no! Nor would she ever say such a thing to him, or to anyone, except perhaps me! She is most loyal to him. Even when she disapproves of something he has done, and – and is told of it by one of our people – one of *his* people, I should say -"

"Ay, there's the rub, eh? You need not tell me she gives 'em no encouragement! I know Serena!"

"Perhaps," said Fanny wistfully, "she will grow more accustomed to it, in time."

"She will never do so," he replied bluntly. "How do *you* go on with Hartley and his wife, Lady Spenborough?"

"They are always very kind and civil, I assure you."

"It falls to your lot to keep the peace, does it? You will not succeed, and, I repeat – I don't envy you!"

She said nothing, wishing that Serena would come in, and wondering how to entertain this uncomfortable guest. No topic of conversation occurred to her; after another pause, she said: "Perhaps I should send someone to find Serena. I am afraid something has detained her, or – or"

He laughed suddenly. "No, don't do that, I beg! Having fallen into her black books for not having craved her permission to call here today, I plunged rather deeper by assuring her that my business would not take up more than a few minutes of her time. This, I fancy, led her to suppose that I was in haste, and so she warned me that I should be kept waiting while she changed out of her habit. Do you care to wager any sum on the length of time she will take over that operation? I will lay handsome odds against the chance of her appearing under half an hour."

"Oh, dear!" she exclaimed, looking more dismayed than amused. "Oh, *pray* do not quarrel again!"

"Against that chance, I lay no odds at all. Are you moped to death here?"

She jumped nervously, startled by the sudden question. "Oh -! No, no! Sometimes, perhaps – the weather has been so inclement! When the spring comes we mean to do great things with the garden. It had been sadly neglected, you know.

He complimented her upon her show of snowdrops, saying they were more forward than those at Claycross; she was encouraged to pursue the topic; and in the safe discussion of horticulture twenty minutes were successfully spent. The butler then came in to announce that a nuncheon awaited my lady's pleasure; and Fanny, desiring him to have a message carried to Lady Serena, conducted Rotherham to the breakfast-parlour. He continued to converse amiably with her: she thought she had seldom seen him so affably inclined, and was considerably astonished, since nothing, she felt, could have been more calculated to put him out of temper than Serena's continued absence. When Serena did at last sweep into the room, she waited, with a fast-thudding heart, for the expected explosion. But Rotherham, rising, and setting a chair for Serena, said, in the voice of a man agreeably surprised: "Why, Serena, already? I had thought it would have taken you longer! You should not have hurried: there was not the least need!"

One look at Serena's face had been enough to tell Fanny that she was in a dangerous mood. She quaked; but after a moment, while the issue trembled in the balance, Serena burst out laughing, and exclaimed: "Detestable man! Very well! if you are not in quarrelling humour, so be it! What's the news in town?"

The rest of the visit passed without untoward incident: even, Fanny thought, pleasantly. Serena was lively; Rotherham conversable; and neither said anything to provoke the other. They parted on good terms; and Fanny, perceiving how much good the visit had done to Serena's spirits, was even sorry that it would not soon be repeated. Rotherham was returning immediately to London, for the opening of Parliament, and was unlikely to be in Gloucestershire again for some time.

The ladies settled down again to the uneventful existence which was their lot, almost the only alleviation to the monotony being the frequent visits of Emily Laleham. Little though she had known it, Serena had for long been the object of Miss Laleham's awed admiration. As a schoolroom miss, she had had glimpses of her, riding with her father, and had thought that surely no one had ever been more beautiful, or more dashing. She worshipped from afar, wove wonderful stories around her, in which she rescued the goddess from extremely unlikely perils, but never, in her wildest flights, had she imagined herself on terms of quite ordinary friendship with her. But Serena, amused by her ingenuousness, had encouraged her to repeat her visit to the Dower House. She needed no pressing, but thereafter was always finding excuses to call there.

But by the end of February even the mild diversion provided by Emily's visits came to an end, for the Lalehams removed to London, Lady Laleham being quite unable to endure more than three months in the country. Only the schoolroom party remained in Gloucestershire, a house in the best part of town having been hired by Sir Walter for the season. "For my coming-out!" said Emily proudly.

"Very kind of Papa!" smiled Serena.

"Oh, yes! At least, it is Grandmama's, of course. I wish she could be there to see me in my Court dress!"

"Your grandmama doesn't live in London, I collect?"

"Oh, no, she lives in Bath! And I love her *dearly!*" said Emily, in an oddly defiant voice.

March, coming in like a lion, saw Fanny the victim of neuralgia. Jane came to visit her, but this attention was marred by an air of graciousness which conveyed a strong impression of a great lady condescending to her humbler relations. Jane was beginning to assume consequential manners, and was unwise enough to tell Serena that she did not think it quite the thing for her to ride "all over the country" with only a groom for companion. Spenborough could not like it. "I told him I would certainly drop a hint in your ear."

"Drop one from me in his!" flashed Serena. "That I am not an attorney's daughter on my preferment!"

The encounter was one of many. Uneasy tension lay between the two houses; there were frequent quarrels; Serena's temper grew brittle, and several times she snapped at Fanny. Then, one wet afternoon, she found Fanny weeping softly beside the fire in her bedroom, and was aghast.

"Fanny! Dearest Fanny, what is it?"

"Oh, nothing, nothing!" Fanny sobbed, trying to hide her face. "Pray, do not -! I didn't mean – It is just that I am a little low!"

Serena was on her knees before her, holding her hands comfortingly. "It is not like you! I'm sure there must be some reason – Oh, Fanny, it is not because I was cross?"

"Oh, no! I never meant to vex you, only I am so stupid!"

Filled with remorse, Serena soothed and petted her back to tranquillity. "I am the most hateful wretch alive! To turn on you, merely because Hartley had enraged me! I don't know what I deserve!"

Fanny dried her eyes. "It was silly of me. I know how hard it is for you to endure Hartley. And Jane is growing so conceited! Even I feel it, and it is much worse for you to have her behaving as though she had lived at Milverley all her life! Rotherham told me you ought not to live here, and he is quite right."

"Much he knows!" said Serena scornfully.

"But he does know, Serena. I have seen how much it rubs you, and it's no wonder! I wish it were possible for us both to go away!"

"But -" Serena stopped suddenly. "Good God, what a pair of goosecaps we are!" she exclaimed. "Why – oh, why the *devil* don't we go away? It has been intolerable here ever since Christmas. *You* have been unwell, *I* have been cross, and the plain truth is that we are finding life a dead bore. We *will* go away!"

"But we could not!" gasped Fanny. "Not to London, while we are in mourning! I know Mama would say I ought not!"

"Not to London, no! We could very well go to Bath, however."

Fanny's eyes widened. "Bath?"

"Yes! And not even your mama will think it improper, because you will go there on the advice of Dr Cliffe, to drink the waters! We will hire a house for six months or so, and if we cannot go to the Assemblies, at least there will be the libraries, and the Pump Room, and -"

"Serena!" breathed Fanny, awed.

Serena laughed at her. "Well? Shall we do it?"

"Oh, Serena, *yes!* Milsom Street – the shops – the London coach coming in – the Sydney Gardens -!"

"And some faces other than our own to look at!"

"Yes, indeed! Oh, what a delightful scheme! Now, *where*," said Fanny, her woes forgotten, "should you like to hire a house? And how must we set about it?"

CHAPTER SIX

THE REMOVAL to Bath having been decided upon, nothing remained but to choose between lodgings there, or a furnished house. Fanny, unaccustomed to arranging such matters, would have wasted weeks in indecision, but it was otherwise with Serena. It was she who entered into all the negotiations, she who knew what would best suit them. Fanny had nothing to do but to agree; and if asked what were her own inclinations she could only say that she would like to do whatever Serena thought most proper. So Serena, remarking that to keep five indoor servants in idleness for several months would be a false economy, discarded all ideas of renting lodgings, and dispatched Lybster to Bath to inspect the various houses recommended by the agent. This resulted in Fanny's signing a contract to hire, for six months, a house in Laura Place, which Lybster pronounced to be the most eligible of all he had seen. By the middle of March all the furniture at the Dower House was shrouded in holland covers, and Spenborough, who had spared no pains to assist the ladies in all the troublesome details of removal (even lending the late Earl's enormous and antiquated travelling coach for the transport of servants and baggage), was able to heave a sigh of rather guilty relief.

Since Milverley lay only some twenty-five miles from Bath, the ladies accomplished the journey in the barouche. Fanny, fortified on the road by smelling-salts, declared that she had never made a journey more comfortably, and, instead of retiring instantly to bed to nurse a sick headache, was able, on their arrival in Laura Place, not only to inspect the house, but to change her dress for dinner, and to discuss with Serena the exciting news contained in a letter from Lady Theresa, which was found awaiting her. The Princess Charlotte was engaged to Leopold of Saxe-Coburg!

This was just the kind of news which Fanny enjoyed. Nothing could be more interesting than the approaching nuptials of the heiress presumptive to the throne; and when the heiress had already made a considerable stir by breaking her engagement to the Prince of Orange the new contract could not but provide food for a good deal of speculation. Fanny was not acquainted with the Princess, who had been kept very close; but she had met Prince Leopold during the rather premature Peace Celebrations in 1814: indeed, she was sure he had been present at the great rout-party they had given at Spenborough House for so many of the foreign notables. Did not Serena recall a handsome young man in that alarming Grandduchess's train? She was persuaded he must be all that was most amiable; it was no wonder that the Princess should have preferred him to the Prince of Orange. Did not Serena agree that it must be a love-match?

"So my aunt informs us," said Serena. "It seems not to be a match of the Prince Regent's seeking, at all events. Indeed, it would be wonderful if it were! It may be very romantic – though I thought the young man a trifle dull, myself! – but a Saxe-Coburg can't be considered any great thing for *such* an heiress! A younger son, too!"

But Fanny insisted that this was even an advantage, since a Prince without a principality would be content to live in England, instead, like the Prince of Orange, of insisting on taking the Princess Charlotte to live for some part of the year in his own domains. As for his being dull, she thought Serena judged too harshly. For her part, she liked his dignified manners, his air of grave reflection; and had felt, on the only occasion when she had met him, that the young Prince of Orange was nothing more than a rattle. And with such an undistinguished face and figure!

To read all the information about Prince Leopold's career and his manifold perfections which was printed in the various newspapers and journals became one of each day's first objects for Fanny. However little she might have to say on the subject of Brougham's extraordinary attack on the Prince Regent, with its disastrous consequences to his Party, she had plenty to say on the shabby nature of the dukedom conferred on Prince Leopold, and perused with painstaking thoroughness all seven Articles of the proposed Marriage Settlement.

Bath was well provided with libraries, and these were considered to be amongst its most agreeable lounges. Most of them provided their subscribers with all the new English and French publications, monthly reviews, and other magazines, all the London papers, and some of the French ones. Fanny divided her patronage between Duffield's, in Milsom Street, and Meyler & Sons, which conveniently adjoined the Great Pump Room. Here, every morning, she dutifully drank the waters, declaring that she derived immense benefit from them. Serena agreed to this, with suitable gravity, but thought privately that the orchestra, which discoursed music there, the shops in the more modish streets, and the constant procession of new faces, were of even greater benefit to her spirits.

Apart from one or two elderly persons, who had been acquainted either with the first Lady Spenborough, or with Lady Claypole, they had no acquaintance in the town. It was no longer a resort of high fashion, though still a very prosperous and genteel watering-place; and the most notable person to be encountered was Madame D'Arblay, who had been residing there all the winter. Fanny once found herself standing beside her at the ribbon counter in a shop on Gay Street, and was very much awed. The celebrated authoress had bought nothing more uncommon than an ell of black sarsenet ribbon; and nobody, Fanny assured Serena, could have supposed from her manners or her appearance that she had ever done anything out of the common way. Fanny had longed for the courage to introduce herself. "For *Evelina*, you know, was quite my favourite book, and I'm sure I was persuaded I could never love any gentleman one tenth as much as I loved Lord Orville!"

"What a pity you did not tell her so! I daresay she would have been very much pleased," Serena said.

"Yes, but I thought she might have wished me rather to have spoken about her last book," said Fanny naïvely. "Do you recall that author who dined with us once, and was affronted because your dear papa praised his *first* book, and never said a word about his others? And I couldn't have talked to Miss Burney about *The Wanderer*, because it was so tedious I gave it up after the first volume!"

Upon their first coming to Bath, Serena had written both their names in the subscription-books at the Lower and the New Assembly Rooms. Fanny was doubtful of the propriety of this, but the worldly-wise Serena said: "Depend upon it, my dear, it would be foolish to do otherwise! In such a place as this it never does to offend the susceptibilities of the Masters of Ceremonies. We shan't, of course, go to the balls, or even to the Card Assemblies, but after we have been in mourning for six months we might, I think, go to the concerts, if we wished."

Fanny submitted, and soon found that her comfort was increased by the good-will of Mr Guynette of the Lower Rooms, and Mr King of the Upper. Neither of these gentlemen delayed to pay a call of ceremony upon the distinguished ladies in Laura Place, and each rivalled the other in civility. Had the Dowager Countess been as old as Mrs Piozzi, Bath's latest resident, the visits would have been made; but the zealous gentlemen might not have felt it to be so incumbent upon them to render her so many little attentions, or to keep her so meticulously informed of any item of Bath news. Any Dowager Countess must command respect: one so touchingly youthful, so angelically fair, and with such gentle, unassuming manners might command devotion.

"Fanny!" said Serena, much amused by the frequent visits of the rival Masters, "if there should be a Mrs King or a Mrs Guynette, which I'm sure I hope there may not be, I shudder to think of the evil passions you must be arousing in their bosoms!"

"I?" exclaimed Fanny, startled. "Good God, what can you mean?"

Serena laughed at her. "Well, how many times have these assiduous gentlemen found it necessary to call in Laura Place? I swear I've lost count! There was Mr King, coming to promise you a secluded place if only you could be brought to attend some lecture or other at the Upper Rooms; there was Mr Guynette, bethinking himself that you might not know which are the best stables for your carriage-horses; there was the occasion when -"

"Serena! Oh, *hush*!" Fanny cried, blushing and aghast. "I'm sure they have both been very kind, but -"

"Excessively kind! And *so* attentive! When Mr Guynette ran out of the Pump Room to summon a chair for you on Tuesday, only because three drops of rain had fallen, I began to think that it is you who need a chaperon, not I!"

"Oh, I know you are funning, but indeed I wish you will not!" Fanny said, distressed. "It would be so very unbecoming in me, and in them, too! And it is all nonsense! They feel it to be their duty to do everything in their power to make *any* visitor's stay in Bath agreeable!" A dreadful thought occurred to her; she fixed her innocent blue eyes on Serena's face, and gasped: "Serena! I have not – I have not appeared *fast*?"

"No, no!" Serena said soothingly. "Just pathetic!" She perceived that Fanny was seriously discomposed, and added: "Goose! I was only quizzing you!"

"If I thought that I had seemed to be encouraging any gentleman to pay me undue attentions, it would be the most shocking thing, and would destroy all my pleasure in being in Bath!"

Serena reassured her, reflecting, not for the first time, that it was seldom wise to employ a rallying tone with her. The tone of her mind was serious, and she was more prone to be shocked than amused by encounters with more lively spirits. There could be no doubt that her air of youthful helplessness, coupled, as it was, with an ethereal beauty, had awakened chivalry in two middle-aged gentlemen, but Serena refrained from telling her so. Not the most severe critic could suspect her of flirtatiousness; and not for worlds would Serena have destroyed her pleasure in being in Bath.

This was very real. Looking at the shop windows, listening to the orchestra in the Pump Room, walking, on fine days in Sydney Gardens, noting each new face that appeared, speculating on the relationships and identities of the various *habitués* of the Pump Room, seemed to be just what she liked. She was sure the man who always wore a pink flower in his buttonhole must be the brother, and *not* the husband, of the fat woman with the yellow wig. There was a pronounced likeness: did not Serena agree? And had Serena noticed the bonnet with the green feathers which that odd-looking woman who dressed in such an antiquated style was wearing? She had seen it displayed in the window of that milliner's in Milsom Street only last week, and with the most *shocking* price attached! Serena always returned satisfactory answers, but had she told the truth she would have said that she had never noticed the fat woman in the yellow wig, or the odd-looking woman either.

The fact was that the dawdling life in Bath suited Serena no better than life at the Dower House. Mingled with the ache in her heart for the loss of one who had been more a companion than a father, was a restlessness, a yearning for she scarcely knew what, which found its only relief in gallops over the surrounding countryside. Owing to the steepness of its streets, carriages were not much used in Bath, chairmen supplanting coachmen in the task of conveying ladies to balls and concerts. Fanny had entertained serious thoughts of sending home her barouche, and could not understand the impulse which prompted Serena, morning after morning, to escape from Bath, attended only by her devoted but critical groom, Fobbing, to the surrounding hills. She knew that Serena had a great deal of uncomfortable energy, but she never realized that her more protracted expeditions coincided with the arrival in Laura Place of one of Lady Theresa Eaglesham's punctual letters; and certainly never suspected that these letters, which seemed to her to be tiresomely full of dull political news, made Serena feel that she had slipped out of the world. To Fanny, the loss of London dinner-parties where little was talked of but a Government crisis, or a victory over the Opposition, was a gain; and she could not conceive what there was to excite interest in the news that the Grenvilles and the Foxites were splitting, in consequence of Brougham's speech. The fortunes of Whig and Tory were of far less moment to Fanny than the fear that her mama might send her sister Agnes to Bath, to bear her company.

This dread seriously impaired Fanny's peace of mind, until it became apparent that Lady Claypole's anxiety for the well-being of her married daughter was not of so urgent a nature as to prompt her either to go to Bath herself at the beginning of the London season, or to send thither a second daughter of rather more than marriageable age. Lady Claypole, with a third daughter straining at the schoolroom leash, would let no consideration interfere with her determination to achieve a respectable alliance for Agnes. She seemed to have abandoned all thought of a brilliant one, but hinted, in a crossed and double-crossed letter, that she cherished hopes of bringing a very worthy man of tolerable substance up to scratch. Fanny sighed over the letter, but was thankful to be spared Agnes's companionship. An elder and jealous sister, who made up in learning what she lacked in beauty, and might be trusted to keep a censorious eye on her junior, could not add to her comfort. She infinitely preferred the society of her daughter-in-law, however little dependence Mama might place on dear Serena's discretion. Mama could not approve of Serena. She said that she conducted herself as though the protection of a wedding-ring were hers, and had, at once, too great and too little a notion of her own consequence. Mama had seen her hob-nobbing with quite unworthy persons, as though she thought her rank absolved her from the necessity (indispensable to *every* unmarried female) of behaving with reserve. Mama sincerely trusted she might not draw Fanny into some scrape, and ended her letter with an earnest adjuration to her daughter not to forget what her own situation now was, or what respect was due to the relict of an Earl.

Fanny replied dutifully to this missive, but even as her pen assured Lady Claypole that she misjudged dearest Serena, a feeling of guilt made it tremble into a blot. Something told her that Mama would deeply disapprove of Serena's latest friendship. Indeed, it could not be denied that Serena was hob-nobbing with a very ungenteel person.

The acquaintance had been struck up in the Pump Room, and in the oddest way. Upon several occasions, both she and Fanny had been diverted by the startling appearance presented by an elderly female of little height but astonishing girth, who, while she adhered, perhaps wisely, to the fashions of her youth, was not wise enough to resist the lure of bright colours. She had a jolly, masterful countenance, with three chins beneath it, and a profusion of improbable black ringlets above it, imperfectly confined by caps of various designs, worn under hats of amazing opulence. Serena drew giggling protests from Fanny by asserting that she had counted five ostrich plumes, one bunch of grapes, two of cherries, three large roses, and two rosettes on one of these creations. An enquiry elicited from Mr King the information that the lady was the widow of a rich merchant of Bristol – or he might have been a shipowner: Mr King could not take it upon himself to say. No doubt a very good sort of a woman in her way, but (her la'ship would agree) sadly out of place in such a select place as Bath. She was a resident, he was sorry to say, but he had never been more than distantly civil to her. Fabulously wealthy, he believed: for his part he deeply deplored the degeneracy of the times, and was happy to think he could remember the days when mere vulgar wealth would not have made it possible for a Mrs Floore to rub shoulders with my Lady Spenborough.

It might have been this speech, which she listened to with a contemptuous shrug, that inclined Serena to look with an indulgent eye upon Mrs Floore. The widow was a regular visitor to the Pump Room, and often, when not engaged in hailing her acquaintance, and laughing and chatting with them in cheerful but unrefined accents, would sit staring at Serena, in an approving but slightly embarrassing way. Serena, conscious of the fixed regard, at last returned it, her brows a little lifted, and was surprised to see the old lady nodding and smiling at her encouragingly. Considerably amused, she moved gracefully towards her. "I beg your pardon, ma'am, but I think you wish to speak to me?"

"That's a fact, for so I did!" said Mrs Floore. "Though whether your ladyship would condescend to speak to me was more than I could tell! Not but what I've been watching you close, and for all you're so tall and high-stepping, my lady, you've a friendly way with you, and you don't look to me to be so haughty you hold your nose up at ordinary folk!"

"Indeed, I hope not!" said Serena, laughing.

Mrs Floore poked a finger into the ribs of a mild-looking man seated in a chair beside her, and said: "I don't know where *your* wits have gone a-begging, Tom Ramford! Get up, and offer your place to Lady Serena, man!"

In great confusion, Mr Ramford hastily obeyed this sharp command. His apologies and protestations were cut short, Mrs Floore saying kindly, but with decision: "There, that'll do! You take yourself off now!"

"Poor man!" said Serena, as she seated herself. "You are very severe, ma'am! Pray, how do you come to know my name?"

"Lord, my dear, everyone knows who *you* are! I'll wager you don't know who I am, though!"

"You would lose, ma'am. You are Mrs Floore, a resident, I believe, of Bath," Serena retorted.

The old lady chuckled richly, all her chins quivering. "Ay, so I am, and I'll be bound you know it because you asked someone who the deuce that old fright could be, dressed in a gown with panniers!"

"I did ask who you might be, but I did *not* so describe you!" instantly responded Serena.

"Lord, I wouldn't blame you! I'd look a worse fright if I was to stuff myself into one of these newfangled gowns you all wear nowadays, with a waist under my armpits and a skirt as straight as a candle! All very well for you, my lady, with the lovely slim figure you have, but I'll tell you what I'd look like, and that's a sack of meal, with a string tied round it! Ay, that makes you laugh, and I see that it's quite true about your eyelids, though I thought it a piece of girl's nonsense when I was told about it: they *do* smile!"

"Good God, who can have told you anything so ridiculous, ma'am?" demanded Serena, colouring faintly.

"Ah, that's just it!" said Mrs Floore. "I daresay you've been wondering what made me wishful to become acquainted with you. Well, I've got a granddaughter that thinks the world of your ladyship, and by all accounts you've been mighty kind to her."

"A granddaughter?" Serena repeated, stiffening suddenly in her chair. "You cannot mean that you are – But, no! Surely Lady Lale – the person who springs to my mind – was a Miss Sebden?"

"So she was," agreed Mrs Floore affably. "Sebden was my first, and Sukey's papa. I've had two good husbands, and buried 'em both, which is more than Sukey can boast of, for all the airs she gives herself!"

"Good gracious!" Serena exclaimed, wishing with all her heart that Rotherham could have been present, to share (as he certainly would) her own enjoyment. "Well, then, I am very happy to know you, Mrs Floore, for I have a sincere regard for little Emily Laleham. She has often taken pity on our dullness this winter, you know. We – Lady Spenborough and I – missed her sadly when she went to London."

Mrs Floore looked gratified, but said: "That's just your kindness, my lady, that makes you say so. I don't deny I'm uncommonly partial to Emma, but I ain't a fool, and I can see who it was that took pity, even if Emma hadn't talked so much about you I was in a fair way to hating the sound of your name! Sukey – for Sukey she's always been to me, and always will be, let her say what she likes! – sent her to spend the New Year with me, and it was Lady Serena this, and Lady Serena that till I'd very likely have had a fit of the vapours, if I'd been a fine lady, which I thank God I'm not, nor ever could be!"

"What an infliction!" Serena said, smiling. "I am astonished you should have wished to become acquainted with me, ma'am! I think, you know, that when she was only a child Emily thought me a very *dashing* female, because I was used to hunt with my father, and do all manner of things which seemed very romantical to her! I hope she may be wiser now that she knows me better. I fear I'm no model for a young female to copy."

"Well, *that*, begging your pardon, is where you're out, my dear!" said Mrs Floore shrewdly. "You've done Emma a great deal of good, and I don't scruple to tell you so! She's a good little soul, and as pretty as she can stare, but she hasn't a ha'porth of common sense, and between the pair of them, Sukey, and that piece of walking gentility which calls herself a governess and looks to me more like a dried herring in petticoats, were in a fair way to ruining the poor child! But Emma, admiring your ladyship like she did, had the wit to see the difference between your manners and the ones her ma and that Miss Prawle was trying to teach her! Prawle! *I'd* Prawle her! 'Grandma,' Emma said to me, 'Lady Serena is always quite unaffected, and she is as civil to her servants as to Dukes and Marquises and all, and I mean to behave exactly like her, because she came over with the Conqueror, and is a great lady!' Which," concluded Mrs Floore, "I can see for myself, though what this Conqueror has to say to anything I'm sure I don't know!"

"Oh, no! Nor anyone else!" uttered Serena, quite convulsed.

"I promise you, I took no account of *him*," said Mrs Floore. "The Quality have their ways, and we have ours, and what may be all very well for high-born ladies don't do for the parson's daughter, as you may say. All I know is that Emma will do better to copy the manners of an Earl's daughter than her ma's, and so I told her!"

Serena could only say: "Indeed, she need copy no one's manners, ma'am! Her own are very pleasing, and unaffected."

"Well, to be sure, *I* think so," said Mrs Floore, beaming upon her, "but I'm no judge, though I did marry a gentleman! Oh, yes! Mr Sebden was quite above my touch, and married me in the teeth of his grand relations, as you may say. You might not think it to look at me now, but I was very much admired when I was a girl. Dear me, yes! Such suitors as I had! Only I took a fancy to poor George, and though my Pa didn't like the match above half, George being too idle and gentlemanly for his taste, he never could deny me anything I'd set my heart on, and so we were married, and very happily, too. Of course, his family pretty well cast him off, but he didn't care a button for that, *nor* for turning me into a grand lady. Mind you, when Pa died, and left his whole fortune to me, the Sebdens began to pay me a lot of civilities, which was only to be expected, and which I was glad of, on account of Sukey. Yes, I thought nothing was too good for my Sukey, so pretty as she was, and with her Pa's genteel ways and all! Ah, well! I often think now that her brother wouldn't have grown up to despise his ma, however much money had been spent on sending him to a fashionable school!"

A gusty sigh prompted Serena to say: "Indeed, I didn't know you had had a son that died! I am so sorry!"

"Well, I didn't, not exactly," said Mrs Floore. "Not but what I sometimes feel it just as much as if he had died, for I'm sure he'd have been a good, affectionate boy. The thing was I always longed for a son, but the Lord never blessed us with more than the one child. No. There was only Sukey, and everything that money could buy she had. She went to a grand school in London, and made all manner of fine friends there, I warrant you! So, when poor George died, and the Sebdens offered to bring Sukey out, I let them do it, and the next thing I knew was she was engaged to marry Sir Walter Laleham. Between you and me, my lady, he never seemed to me any great thing, though I'm bound to say I didn't know then what he was going to cost me, first and last! Not that I grudge it, because this I will say: he may be a gamester and he may drink a deal too much, but he ain't ashamed of his ma-in-law, and if it weren't for Sukey I might go to his house, and welcome!"

Staggered by these extremely frank confidences, Serena could think of nothing better to say than: "I believe Sir Walter is generally very well liked. My father and he were at Eton together, and afterwards at Oxford."

"Ay, were they so? Oh, well, it's a fine thing for a man to be of the first rank, but it's a better thing to have a bit of sense, if you'll pardon my saying so! And what with offering for Sukey, who, he might ha' known, would rule the roast, even if he'd been a Duke, and never having the wit to back the right horse, he's my notion of a silly noddy! But, there! I shouldn't be saying so, and no more I would have, only that there's something about your ladyship I like, besides knowing you was kind to Emma. What's more, says I to myself, if you've been living in the same place as Sukey it's not likely I could tell you anything you didn't know about her, because it's my belief those airs of hers wouldn't deceive a new-born baby! Now, *would* they?"

"I assure you, ma'am, Lady Laleham is – is everywhere received!"

"I know that well enough, my dear, and many's the time I've enjoyed a laugh over it. For though I don't deny it was marrying Sir Walter that took her into the first circles, it's me that keeps her there!"

Meeting frankness with frankness, Serena said: "I don't doubt it, ma'am. Even had I not guessed as much from things Emily has said, it is common knowledge that Sir Walter – as the saying goes married money."

Mrs Floore chuckled. "I'll go bail it is! Ah, well! If it weren't for the silly fellow getting knocked into horsenails so often, and him and Sukey not daring to provoke me for fear I might leave my fortune away from them, let alone providing for Emma's coming-out, I daresay I should never see anything of either of 'em, nor my grandchildren neither, so maybe it's all for the best. It suited Sukey very well when I married Ned Floore, because who's to know I'm her ma, unless I tell 'em, which in the general way I don't? What's more, Floore was a very warm man, with never a chick nor child of his own, and every penny he had he left to me, and no strings tied to 'em! So whenever I feel low I tell Sukey I've taken a fancy to pay her a visit in her fine London house. It's as good as a play to see how many excuses she'll make up to put me off, never dreaming that I do it only to tease her! I never had any taste for grand company myself, but Sukey has, and you can say that's my doing, for having sent her to a smart school. So she needn't be afraid! I can't help laughing at her, but I've got no notion of embarrassing her: no, nor Emma either!"

"I am very sure, ma'am, that Emma at least you could not embarrass. She speaks of you with so much affection!"

"Bless her heart!" said Mrs Floore. "All the same, my lady, it wouldn't do her a bit of good if I was to go around telling everyone I'm her grandma, so I beg you won't mention it. I've been letting my tongue run away with me, like I shouldn't, but you're one of those that can be trusted, *that's* certain!"

"Thank you! If you wish it, I will not mention the relationship to anyone but Lady Spenborough, and her you may also trust."

"Poor young thing!" remarked Mrs Floore. "Such a sweet face as she has! It quite goes to my heart to see her in her weeds, and she no more than a baby. There! The General is taking his leave of her, and she'll be looking to see what's become of you. You'd best go, my lady, for I daresay she wouldn't think it a proper thing for you to be sitting chatting to me."

"Not at all," said Serena calmly, making a sign to Fanny. "If you will allow me, I should like to make you known to her, ma'am." She smiled at Fanny, as she came up, and said: "Fanny, I wish to introduce Mrs Floore to you, who is Emily's grandmama."

Fanny, however astonished she might be, was far too well-bred to betray any other emotions than civil complaisance. She bowed, and held out her hand, which, after heaving herself on to her feet, Mrs Floore shook with great heartiness, saying that she was honoured, and only wished Sukey could see her.

"Which, however, it's just as well she can't. And if ever you should find yourselves in Beaufort Square, that's where I live, and a warm welcome you'd have from me – and no offence taken if you don't choose to come!"

"Thank you, we should like very much to visit you," replied Serena.

"So kind!" murmured Fanny.

Mrs Floore beamed all over her face. "Then I'll tell you what you should do, my dears: just you send your footman round to tell me you mean to pay me a call, and if it should happen that there's company with me I'll send 'em packing, because for one thing it wouldn't be seemly for you to be going to parties, and for another my friends ain't just in your style, any more than I am myself, the only difference between us being that I shan't holler at you across the street, or go prating about you all over Bath, which one or two I know *might*!"

With these reassuring words, she shook hands again, blessed Serena's lovely face, and waddled away.

"Serena!" breathed Fanny. "What an *extraordinary* creature!"

"Yes, but quite delightful, I promise you!"

"But, Serena, she is dreadfully vulgar! You cannot really mean to visit her!"

"Certainly I mean to, and I shall think very poorly of you if you don't accompany me!"

"But, dearest, do you – do you think your papa would have permitted it?" Fanny ventured to say.

That made Serena laugh. "My dear Fanny, you know very well Papa never interfered with me, or thought himself too grand to rub shoulders with the rest of the world!"

"Oh, no, no, I never meant – only I can't help feeling that everyone would say I ought not to let you become acquainted with vulgar persons, and in particular your Aunt Theresa, though how she thinks I can prevent you from doing exactly as you choose when *she* could not, I'm sure I don't know!" said Fanny despairingly.

CHAPTER SEVEN

THE CALL was paid, though without the suggested prelude; and the welcome accorded to the ladies was so good-natured and unaffected that Fanny was brought to acknowledge that however vulgar Mrs Floore might be she had a great deal of drollery, and was certainly no toad-eater. She declined a civil invitation to return the visit, saying, with paralysing candour, that it was one thing for their ladyships to visit in Beaufort Square whenever they felt so inclined, and quite another for them to be entertaining her in Laura Place, and very likely making all their acquaintance wonder what kind of company they had got into.

Since this was very much what Fanny had been thinking she instantly turned scarlet, and stammered an inarticulate protest, which made her hostess tell her very kindly that there was no need for her to flush up, because facts were facts, and no getting round them, and in any event she was grown so stout that it was as much as she cared to do to walk to the Pump Room and back. "And as for calling a chair, I give you my word I never do so without I expect the poor fellows carrying me to drop down dead between the shafts, which would be a very disconcerting thing to happen," she added.

Serena laughed. "Very well, ma'am, it shall be as you wish! But pray believe we should be happy to see you in Laura Place!"

This won her a glance of decided approval from their fellow-guest, a gentlemanly-looking young man of some thirty years of age, who had been sitting with Mrs Floore when they were announced. It was to be inferred, since he had not been sent packing, that Mrs Floore considered him worthy to meet her distinguished visitors. She introduced him as Ned Goring, the son of her late husband's business partner, who had ridden over from Bristol to pay his respects to her; and it soon transpired that the redoubtable old lady had inherited, besides two fortunes, considerable interest in her father's soap factory, and her husband's shipyard. Young Mr Goring, a junior partner in the latter, evidently regarded her with respect and affection; and when, in the course of conversation with him, Serena said something about her liking Mrs Floore so much, he replied in his blunt way: "Everyone must who knows her, I think. I never knew anyone with a kinder heart, or a sounder understanding."

She warmed to him, knowing the world well enough to realize how many men in his position, having achieved through education a greater gentility than was aspired to by their fathers, would have found it necessary to have excused a friendship with one so frankly vulgar as Mrs Floore. That lady being fully occupied with Fanny, Serena took pains to draw Mr Goring out. She very soon discovered that he had been educated at Rugby and at Cambridge, and liked him the better when he replied, in answer to an enquiry: "Yes, I am pretty well acquainted with George Alplington, but since I entered my father's business our ways have lain apart. How does he go on? He is an excellent fellow!"

"Very expensively!"

He laughed. "Ah, I was used to tell him he would end up a Bond Street beau! Then, of course, he would make some opprobrious mention of tar, that being the only commodity to be used in my trade which he knew of, and it was a chance if either of us emerged from the argument without a black eye!"

At this point, Fanny rose to take leave, and the party broke up, Serena shaking hands with her new acquaintance, and expressing the friendly hope that they might meet again. As she walked back to Laura Place beside Fanny, she observed: "I liked that young man, did not you? There was something particularly pleasing about his manners, which I thought very easy and frank. He has an air of honest manliness, too, which, in these days of fribbles and counter-coxcombs, I own I find refreshing!"

A new terror reared itself in Fanny's head; the weekly letter to Mama was painstakingly inscribed, and contained no reference to Beaufort Square.

However, nothing more was heard of Mr Goring. Serena's friendship with Mrs Floore prospered, but in a mild way that resolved itself into an occasional call, and frequent meetings in the Pump Room, when sometimes conversation was exchanged, and sometimes no more than cordial greetings. The next occurrence to enliven the routine of Bath life was an unexpected visit from Rotherham. Fanny and Serena, coming in one sunny afternoon in April, after walking for an hour in the Sydney Gardens, were greeted with the intelligence that his lordship had been awaiting them in the drawing-room for some twenty minutes or more. Fanny went to take off her bonnet and pelisse, but Serena chose to go immediately to the drawing-room, and entered it, saying: "Well! This is a surprise! What brings you to Bath, Rotherham?"

He was standing before the small wood-fire, glancing through a newspaper, but he cast this aside, and came forward to shake hands. His expression was forbidding, and the tone in which he answered her decidedly acid. "I shall be grateful to you, Serena, if you will in future be so good as to inform me of it when you intend to change your habitation. I learned of this start by the merest chance."

"Good gracious, why should I?" she exclaimed. "I suppose I need not apply to you for permission to come to Bath."

"You need not! Responsibility for your movements was spared me. You are free to do as you please, but since I am your Trustee you would save me annoyance, and yourself inconvenience, if you will advertize me when you wish new arrangements made for the payment of your allowance! I imagine it would not suit you to be obliged to send all the way to Gloucester for any monies you might need!"

"No, to be sure it would not!" she agreed. "It was stupid of me not to have recollected that!"

"Quite featherheaded!"

"Yes, but the thing is that I have a considerable sum by me, and that is how I came to forget the matter. What a fortunate circumstance that you should have put me in mind of it! I must write to ask Mr Perrott to make a new arrangement too, or who knows when I may find myself in the basket?"

"As it is he who collects the larger part of your income, it would certainly be as well."

"Could you find no one in town with whom to pick a quarrel?" she asked solicitously. "Poor Ivo! It is too bad!"

"I am not picking a quarrel. It would surprise you, I daresay, if I told you that I rarely quarrel with anyone but yourself. "

"Ah, that's because very few people have the courage to pick up your gauntlet!" she said, smiling.

"An amiable portrait you draw!"

"But a speaking likeness!" she countered, a laughing challenge in her eye.

He shook his head. "No: I choose rather to prove you wrong. We won't quarrel this time, Serena."

"As you wish! Will you alter the arrangement for my tiresome allowance, if you please?"

"I have already done so. There is the direction," he replied, handing her a piece of paper.

"Thank you! That was kind of you. I am sorry to have been so troublesome. Did you come all the way from town just for that?"

"I had business at Claycross," he said curtly. "You seem to be comfortably established here. How do you go on?"

"Very prosperously. It was a relief to escape from Milverley."

He nodded, but made no comment, merely saying, after a brief, keen scrutiny of her face: "Are you well? You look a trifle peaked."

"If I do, it is because black doesn't become me. I mean to lighten my mourning, and have ordered a charming gray gown.

"You are mistaken."

"What, in going into half-mourning?"

"No, in thinking black does not become you. Are you sure that Bath agrees with your constitution?"

"Yes, indeed! Now, don't, I beg of you, Rotherham, put it into Fanny's head that I am looking hagged! I think I did become a little out of sorts, but Bath will soon set me to rights." She glanced at him, and added, with difficulty: "I have not learned yet not to miss Papa. Don't let us speak of that! You know how it is with me! I don't care to talk of what so much affects me, and making a parade of grief is of all things the most repugnant to me."

"Yes, I know," he replied. "You need not be afraid. I have nothing to say on that subject, for there *is* nothing to be said. Your aunt, by the by, charged me with all manner of messages to you. I met her at the Irebys' party a couple of nights ago. It is wonderful, Serena, how much she likes you when a hundred miles or so separate you from her!"

She laughed. "Very true! My love to her, if you please, and tell her that I quite depend upon her letters for the latest *on-dits*. Where are you putting up, Ivo? Do you make a long stay in Bath?"

"At the York House. I return to town tomorrow."

"How shabby! You will stay to dine with us at least! We keep unmodishly early hours here, I warn you."

He hesitated. "I can hardly sit down to dinner with you in my riding-dress, and I brought no other."

"Ah, so you did mean to pick a quarrel with me!" she rallied him. "Fanny will pardon your top-boots, and I hope you don't mean to stand on ceremony with *me*!" She turned her head, as Fanny came into the room, and said: "Here is Rotherham, so full of punctilio he will not dine with us in his riding-dress! Persuade him, Fanny, while I make myself tidy!"

She returned presently to find them apparently in perfect charity with one another, Rotherham having been so obliging as to furnish Fanny with all the latest news of the Royal Marriage preparations. Since it was rarely that he had been known to pander to such feminine curiosity, Serena could only suppose that he was determined on amiability. Nothing occurred during the evening to make her change her mind. He indulged Fanny's taste for gossip, without betraying too much contempt for it; and entertained Serena with a pungent description of what he described as the flutter in the Whig dovecot. Both ladies were pleased, and if an elliptical reference, which made Serena's eyes dance, was incomprehensible to Fanny, or the conversation turned on Mr Canning's journey home from Lisbon, she had her embroidery-frame to occupy her, and was merely glad to see Serena in such spirits. Such phrases as: "Pretty well to be employing a frigate for one's pleasure!" and: "Never was there such a job! " put her forcibly in mind of agonizing evenings at Milverley, or in Grosvenor Square, when she had been obliged to strain every nerve in the effort to follow just such conversations. It was no longer her duty to do so, and she could only be thankful.

Her wandering thoughts were reclaimed presently, for the talk seemed to have switched from the despotic behaviour of someone called Ferdinand, to a subject of more interest. Rotherham was asking Serena who was at present visiting Bath.

"My dear Ivo! At the start of the London season? None but dowdies!"

Fanny protested that she was too severe, but Serena laughed, and shook her head. "General Creake, old Lady Skene, Mrs Piozzi, Madame D'Arblay and her set: Mrs Holroyd, Mrs Frances, Miss Bowdler – need I continue?"

"You need not, indeed! I had hoped you might have found some more enlivening company."

"I have!" Serena said.

"I mistrust that smile," Rotherham said dryly. "Who is it?"

"I'll tell you one day. At present my lips are sealed!" she replied, with an air of mock solemnity.

"That means, I imagine, that you know well I should disapprove."

"I daresay you might, but very likely you would not, and in any event it doesn't concern you." She glanced mischievously at Fanny, and added: "I find the acquaintance excessively enlivening!"

"But Lady Spenborough does not?"

"Fanny has such grand notions! Besides, she is my mama-in-law, and feels it to be her duty to chaperon me very strictly!"

"Now, Serena!"

"I don't envy her *that* task. I shan't gratify you by trying to discover the mystery, but I wish you will take care what you are about."

"I will. It is not precisely a mystery, only, although I dare say I might safely tell you about it, I believe I ought not, at this present."

He looked frowningly at her, but said nothing. She began to talk of something else, and the subject was not again mentioned until Rotherham took his leave. Serena having run out of the room to fetch a letter which she desired him to frank, he said abruptly: "Don't let her run into some scrape! You could not prevent her, I suppose: I know that headstrong temper!"

"Indeed, you are mistaken!" Fanny assured him.

He looked sceptical, but was prevented from saying more by Serena's coming back into the room with her letter.

"There it is," she said, laying it upon the writing-table, and opening the lid of the standish. "Cousin Florence will be very much obliged to you for saving her at least sixpence."

He took the pen she was holding out to him, and dipped it in the ink. "Shall I carry it to London, and post it there?"

"If you please. I wish you might have stayed longer in Bath, though."

"Why? To have made the acquaintance of the Unknown?" he said, scrawling his name across the corner of her letter.

She laughed. "No – though I want very much to present you to the Unknown! To ride with me, merely. You never think a fence too high for me, or beg me to have a care!"

"In the *saddle* I think you very well able to take care of yourself."

"This is praise indeed!"

He smiled. "I never denied your horsemanship, Serena. I wish it were possible for me to stay, but it is not. This curst ball looms ahead of me!"

"What ball?"

"Oh, did I not tell you? I am assured it is my duty to lend Rotherham House to Cordelia, so that she may launch Sarah, or Susan, or whatever the girl's name may be, upon the world with as much pomp as possible. I am unconvinced, but when it comes to Augusta adding her trenchant accents to Cordelia's plaintive ones I am against the ropes, and would give a dozen balls only to silence the pair of them."

"Good God! Upon my word, I think it is amazingly good-natured of you, Ivo!" Serena said, quite astonished.

"Yes, so do I!" he replied.

He departed, and the ladies were left to marvel over this new and unexpected turn, Fanny declaring that she would never have believed he could be brought to do so much for his unfortunate wards, and Serena saying: "I certainly never thought of his giving a ball for Susan, but I have sometimes suspected that he does a great deal more for them than he chooses to divulge."

"I'm sure I never thought so! What put it into *your* head?"

"Well, it crossed my mind, when Mrs Monksleigh was complaining of his having insisted on her sending the boys to Eton because it was where their father was educated, that he could not have *compelled* her to do so, which she vows he did, unless it was he, and not she, who was to bear the cost of it. Only consider what that must be! Three of them, Fanny, and Gerard now at Cambridge! I am persuaded Mrs Monksleigh could not have contrived it, even had she had the least notion of management, which she has not!"

Fanny was much struck, and could only say: *"Well!"*

"It is not so wonderful," Serena said, amused. 'Nor need it make you feel, as I see it does, that you have grievously misjudged him! He is so rich that I daresay he would not notice it if he were paying the school-fees of a dozen children. *I* shall feel I have misjudged him when I see him showing his wards a little kindness."

"Well, if he is giving a grand ball for Susan, I call it a great deal of kindness!" said Fanny, with spirit.

Except for various formal notices in the London papers, they heard nothing more of the ball until the arrival of Lady Theresa's next letter to her niece. Lady Theresa had taken her third daughter to the function, but it did not seem as though she had enjoyed it, in spite of the many compliments she had received on Clarissa's beauty, and the gratifying circumstance of her never having lacked a partner. Any pleasure Lady Theresa might have derived from the ball had been destroyed by the sight of Cordelia Monksleigh, in a hideous puce gown, standing at the head of the great stairway to receive the guests. She had been unable to banish the reflection that there, but for her own folly, might have stood Serena, though not, she trusted, in puce. Moreover, had Serena been the hostess it was to be hoped that the company would have been more exclusive. What could have induced Rotherham to have given Cordelia Monksleigh *carte blanche*, as there was no doubt he had done, was a matter passing Lady Theresa's comprehension. Had anyone told her that she would live to see That Laleham Creature storming Rotherham House (heavily underscored), she would have laughed in his face. But so it had been; and if Serena had seen her positively flinging her chit of a daughter at all the eligible bachelors, besides forcing herself on the notice of every distinguished person present, she might, at last, have regretted her own folly, wilfulness, and improvidence.

"Well, well, well!" commented Serena, much appreciating this impassioned missive. "I wonder what Mrs Floore will have to say about it? For my part, I can't but admire the Laleham-woman's generalship! To have stormed the Rotherham stronghold is something indeed! How angry Lady Silchester must have been! I wish I had been present!"

Mrs Floore, encountered on the following morning in the Pump Room, echoed these sentiments. "To think of my granddaughter at a party like that, for I've read all the notices, my dear, and there was never anything like it! Lord, Sukey will be as proud as an apothecary and I'm sure I don't blame her! Say what you will, she gets what she's set her heart on, my Sukey! And Emma being solicited to stand up with lords and honourables and I don't know what besides! Depend upon it, Sukey will have got a lord in her eye for Emma already! Well, and if he's a nice, handsome young fellow I hope she may catch him!"

"I expect she will, ma'am," said Serena, laughing.

"Yes, but I don't trust her," said Mrs Floore. "She's a hard, ambitious woman, my dear. Mark my words, if a Duke with one foot in the grave, and cross eyes, and no teeth, was to offer for that child, Sukey would make her accept him!"

"Oh, no!" protested Serena.

"No," said Mrs Floore. "She wouldn't, because I should have something to say to it!"

"Very rightly! But I don't think there is such a Duke, ma'am."

"It'll be as well for him if there isn't," said Mrs Floore darkly.

Serena left her brooding vengefully, and went off to change a book at Duffield's Library, on Milsom Street. This accomplished, she left the library, almost colliding on the doorstep with a tall man, who fell back instantly, saying: "I *beg* your pardon!"

Even as she looked quickly up at him he caught his breath on a gasp. She stood gazing almost incredulously into a face she had thought forgotten.

"Serena!" he said, his voice shaking. "*Serena!*"

More than six years slid from her; she put out her hand, saying as unsteadily as he: "Oh, can it be possible? *Hector!*"

CHAPTER EIGHT

THEY STOOD handfasted, the gentleman very pale, the lady most delicately flushed, hazel eyes lifted wonderingly to steady blue ones, neither tongue able to utter a word until a testy: "By your leave, sir! by your leave!" recalled them to a sense of their surroundings, and made Major Kirkby drop the hand he was holding so tightly, and step aside, stammering a confused apology to the impatient citizen whose way he had been blocking.

As though released from a spell, Serena said: "After all these years! You have not altered in the least! Yes, you have, though: those tiny lines at the corners of your eyes were not there before, I think, and your cheeks were not so lean – but I swear you are as handsome as ever, my dear Hector!"

He smiled at the rallying note in her voice, but his own was perfectly serious as he answered, in a low tone: "And you are more beautiful even than my memories of you! Serena, Serena –! Forgive me! I hardly know what I am saying, or where I am!"

She gave an uncertain little laugh, trying for a more commonplace note. "You are in Milsom Street, sir, wholly blocking the way into Duffield's excellent library! And the spectacle of a gentleman of military aspect, standing petrified with his hat in his hand, is attracting a great deal of attention, let me tell you! Shall we remove from this too public locality?"

He cast a startled glance about him, coloured up, laughed, and set his high-crowned beaver on his fair head again. "Oh, by God, yes! I am so bemused –! May I escort you? – Your maid – footman –?"

"I am alone. You may give me your arm, if you will be so good, but were you not about to go into the library?"

"No – yes! What can that signify? Alone? How comes this about? Surely–"

"My dear Hector, my next birthday, which is not so far distant, will be my twenty-sixth!" she said, placing her hand in his arm, and drawing him gently away from the entrance to the library. "Did I never go out without a footman in attendance when you knew me before? Perhaps I did not, since I was in my Aunt Theresa's charge! She has the most antiquated notions! How long ago it seems! I was barely nineteen, and you were so proud of your first regimentals! To what exalted heights have you risen? Tell me how I should address you!"

His free hand came up to press her gloved fingers, lying so lightly in the crook of his left arm. "As you do! The sound of *Hector* on your lips is such music as I never hoped to hear again! There were no exalted heights: I have no more imposing title than that of Major."

"It sounds very well, I promise you. Are you on furlough? You do not wear regimentals."

"I sold out at the end of last year. You might not be aware – my elder brother has been dead these three years. I succeeded to the property at the time of Bonaparte's escape from Elba, and but for that circumstance must have sold out two years ago."

"I did not know – pray forgive me!"

"How should you?" he said simply. "I never dreamed that I could hold a place in your memory!"

She was struck to the heart, realizing how small a place had been held by him, and said haltingly: "Or I – that you should recall so clearly – after so – long !"

"You have never been absent from my thoughts. Your face, your smiling eyes, have been with me through every campaign!"

"No, no, how can you be so romantical?" she exclaimed, at once startled and touched.

"It is true! When I read of your engagement to Lord Rotherham – how can I describe to you what I suffered?"

"You saw that notice!"

"I saw it." He smiled ruefully. "I was used, whenever a London newspaper came in my way, to search the social columns for the sight of your name! Absurd of me, was it not? The *Morning Post* that included *that* announcement was sent to me by my sister. She knew I had been acquainted with you, and thought I should be interested to learn of your engagement. She little guessed what passions were roused in me! I had prepared myself for your marriage to another; I could have borne it, I hope, with better command over my own sensations had it been any other than Rotherham!"

She looked up in surprise. "Did you dislike him so much? I had thought you scarcely knew him!"

"It was true: I met him perhaps three times only." He paused, and she saw his well-moulded lips tighten. After a moment, he said: "I have always believed that it was *he* who separated us."

She was startled. "Oh, no! Indeed, it wasn't so! Why, how could it have been possible?"

"His influence over your father was brought to bear. I knew him for my enemy, Serena, from the outset."

"No! Recollect how young you were! His manners are not conciliating, and that abrupt way he has, and the frowning look, made you think he disliked you. My father would not countenance the match from worldly reasons. He thought us, besides, too young, and – oh, I suppose he had even then set his heart on my marrying Rotherham!"

"Had he not allowed Rotherham to persuade him into the belief that we were not suited to one another, I cannot think he would have been so adamant! His affection for you was too great to admit of his sacrificing you to mere worldly ambition. "

"Perhaps he did think that, but that Ivo put it into his head I will not allow! Good God, Hector, why should he have done so?"

"When I read the notice of your engagement, I knew the answer to that enigma!"

"Nonsense! That came three years later! Ivo had no thought of marrying me *then*!" She flushed, and added: "I jilted him, you know."

"I did know it. For you, it must have been painful indeed; for me – a relief I cannot describe to you! I knew then that your *heart* had not been engaged, that the match was made by your father, *de convenance*!"

She was silent for a moment, but said presently: "I hardly know how to answer you. Papa most earnestly desired it. He *promoted* it, but no more than that! There was no compulsion no pressure exerted to make me – Hector, if it distresses you, I am sorry for it, but I should be sorrier still to deceive you! I was very willing: I fancied myself in love with Ivo. There! It is out, and you know now that I was not as constant as you."

He said, in a moved tone: "It is what I always loved in you – your honesty! that fearless look in your eyes, a frankness so engaging -! But you *did* not love Rotherham!"

"No – a brief, bitterly fought campaign, that engagement of ours! I behaved shockingly, of course, but you may believe he was as well rid of me as I of him!"

Again he pressed her hand. "I couldn't believe that. That you were well rid of him, yes! His temper, so peremptory and overbearing -"

"Oh, yes, but my own temper, you know, is very bad!" she said ruefully.

He smiled. "It is like you say to so, but it is not true, Serena. "

"I'm afraid you don't know me."

"Don't I? If ever it was bad, there must have been great provocation! "

"I thought so, at all events," she said, a gleam of fun in her eyes. "I always think so, whenever I lose it! That was one of the questions on which Rotherham and I could never agree!"

"I cannot bear to think of you subjected, even for so short a time, to that imperious, tyrannical disposition!"

She could not help laughing. "I wish he might be privileged to hear you! He would think it a gross injustice that you should have no pity for *his* sufferings!"

"I can believe it! Do you ever meet him now?"

"Frequently. There was no estrangement. We are very good friends, except when we are sworn foes! Indeed, he is my Trustee."

"Your Trustee!" he said, looking as though he found the information shocking. "I knew how much attached to him Lord Spenborough was, but that he should have placed you in a position of such embarrassment – Forgive me! I should not be speaking to you so!"

"You mistake: I don't find it embarrassing! To be sure, I was in such a passion when I first discovered how it was to be – But there were circumstances enough to enrage me! Never mind that! As for meeting Ivo, in the old way, neither of us has been aware of any awkwardness. It is the popular notion that I should be cast into blushes in Ivo's presence, but either that's a great piece of nonsense, or I am a creature sadly lacking in sensibility! I can't be shy of a man I've known all my life! Since my father's death, too, he seems sometimes to me like a link with -" She broke off. "But, come! We have talked enough of *me*! Tell me of yourself! I long to hear of all your doings in Spain!"

"I don't think I could ever hear enough of you," he said seriously. "Nothing of any consequence has befallen me. Nothing until today! When I saw you, it was as though these six years and more had never been!"

"Oh, hush! I too was conscious of just that feeling, but it is nonsensical! Much has happened to both of us!"

"To *you*! I know well how great a tragedy your father's death must have been to you. To have written to you would have been presumption: I could only *wish* that I had the right to comfort you!"

As always, she was rendered uncomfortable by spoken sympathy. She said: "Thank you. The shock was severe, and the sense of loss must remain with me for long and long, but you must not think me borne down by it, or out of spirits. I go on very well."

"I know your indomitable courage!"

Her impulse was to check him. She subdued it, afraid of wounding him, and walked on beside him with downcast eyes while he continued talking of her father. That he truly understood the extent of her loss, and most sincerely entered into her feelings, she could not doubt. He spoke well, and with great tenderness: she would rather he had been silent.

He seemed to realize it, and broke off, saying: "It is painful for you to talk of it. I will say no more: what I feel – all that I cannot express – you must know!"

"Yes, I – You are very good, very kind! How glad I am I should have chosen to go to Duffield's this very morning! Do you make a long stay in Bath?"

"I came to visit my mother, and arrived only yesterday. There are no calls upon my time, and I had meant to remain with her for a few weeks. Since my father's death, she has resided here. The climate agrees with her constitution, and she derives benefit from the baths. She is a sad invalid, and seldom goes out, or – But are you living here too, Serena!"

"For a few months only, with my mother-in-law."

"Ah! I knew that Lord Spenborough had married again, and feared that you must have been made unhappy."

"No, indeed!"

"You live with Lady Spenborough? You like her? She is kind to you?" he said anxiously.

"Very!"

"I am very much relieved to hear you say so. I was afraid it might not be so. To have had a mama thrust upon you at your age cannot have been agreeable. Too often one hears of mamas-in-law domineering over the children of a previous marriage! But if she is *truly* motherly to you I can believe that you may be glad *now* that the marriage took place. Her protection must be a comfort to you."

Her eyes began to dance, but she said demurely: "Very true! I look forward to presenting you to her. I hope you will not think her *very* formidable!"

"Will you let me call on you?" he said eagerly. "She will not object to it?"

"I am sure she will receive you most graciously!"

"There is something quelling in the very word!" he said, smiling. "As for *dowager*, that conjures up such a picture as might terrify the boldest! If she should wear a turban, I shall shake in my shoes, for it will remind me of a great-aunt of whom, as a boy, I lived in dread! When may I call on her? Where is your direction?"

"In Laura Place." She looked round her suddenly, and burst out laughing. "Good God, do you know how far we have walked? Unless my eyes deceive me, we have reached nearly to the end of Great Pulteney Street! If I have at least led you in the right way it must have been by instinct! I have no recollection even of crossing the bridge!"

"Nor I," he admitted, turning, and beginning to retrace his steps beside her. "I have been walking in a dream, I think. I could wish we were at the other end of the town, so that I need not part from you so soon. My fear is that when you leave me I shall wake up."

"Major Kirkby, I begin to think you are turned into an accomplished flirt!"

"I? Ah, you are quizzing me! I never flirted, I think, in my life."

"Good gracious, will you tell me that there is not *one* beautiful Spaniard left mourning your departure?"

He shook his head. "Not one, upon my honour!"

"I had no notion life was so dull in Spain!"

"I never saw one whom I thought beautiful," he said simply.

They walked on, and were soon in Laura Place again. He parted from her at her door, lingering, with her hand in his, to say: "Tell me when I may call on you!"

"When you wish," she replied, smiling at him.

His clasp on her hand tightened; he bent to kiss it; and at last released it, and went striding away, as though he dared not trust himself to look back.

A minute later, Fanny was greeting Serena with relief. "Oh, I am so glad you are come in! I feared some accident had befallen, for you have been away this age and more! Good God, dearest! What has happened? You look as if a fortune had dropped on you from the sky!"

"Not a fortune!" Serena said, her eyes very bright and sparkling, and a smile hovering about her mouth. "Better than that, and by far more unexpected! I have met – an old acquaintance!"

"*That* would not make you look *so*! Now, be serious, love, I do beg of you!"

"Oh, I cannot be! You must hold me excused! Did you ever feel yourself a girl again, in your first season? It is the most delightful thing imaginable! I have told him he may call on us: pray be so obliging as to like him! It will be a study to see his face when I present him to you: he pictures you in a turban, Fanny!"

Fanny let her embroidery frame drop. *"He?"* Her face brightened suddenly. "Not – Oh, Serena, you don't mean you have met that young man again? the man you told me you had loved – the *only* man you had loved?"

"Did I tell you so? Yes, it is he!"

"Oh, *Serena*!" sighed Fanny ecstatically. "How *very* glad I am! It is exactly like a romance! At least – is he still *single*, dearest?"

"Yes, of course he is! That is to say, I never asked him! But there is no doubt! I wonder how soon he will think it proper to call on us? I fancy it will not be long!"

It was not long. Major Kirkby, in fact, paid his visit of ceremony upon the following day, arriving in Laura Place on the heels of a heavy thunderstorm. Lybster, relieving him of his dripping cloak and hat, sent Fanny's page running to fetch a leather to rub over the Major's smart Hessians, and permitted himself to scrutinize with unusual interest this visitor who was not deterred by inclement weather from paying morning visits. He had been informed that her ladyship was expecting a Major Kirkby to call sometime, but no suspicion had been aroused in his mind that the unknown Major might prove to be a visitor quite out of the common. If he had thought about the matter at all, the picture in his mind's eye would have been of some middle-aged Bath resident; and when he opened the door to a tall, handsome gentleman, nattily attired, and not a day above thirty, if as old, he suffered a severe shock, and instantly drew his own perfectly correct conclusions. While the page wiped the mud from those well-cut boots, and the Major straightened his starched neckcloth, Lybster took a rapid and expert survey, contriving in a matter of seconds to ascertain that the long-tailed blue coat of superfine had come from the hands of one of the first tailors, that the Major had a nice taste in waistcoats, and knew how to arrange a neckcloth with modish precision. He had a fine pair of shoulders on him, and an excellent leg for a skin-tight pantaloon. His countenance, a relatively unimportant matter, came in for no more than a cursory glance, but the butler noted with approval that the features were regular, and the Major's air distinguished. He led the way upstairs to the drawing-room, the Major following him in happy ignorance of the ferment of conjecture his appearance had set up.

A door was opened, his name announced, and he trod into an elegantly furnished apartment, whose sole occupant was a slender little lady, dressed all in black, and seated at the writing-table.

Taken by surprise, Fanny looked up quickly, the pen still held between her fingers. The Major checked on the threshold, staring at her. He beheld a charming countenance, with very large, soft blue eyes, and a mouth trembling into a shy smile, golden ringlets peeping from under a lace cap, and a general air of youth and fragility. Wild thoughts of having entered the wrong house crossed his mind; considerably disconcerted, he stammered: "I beg your pardon! I thought – I came – I must have mistaken the direction! But I asked your butler if Lady Spenborough – and he led me upstairs!"

Fanny laid the pen down, and rose to her feet, and came forward, blushing and laughing. "I am Lady Spenborough. How do you do?"

He took her hand, but exclaimed involuntarily: "The *Dowager* Lady Spenborough? But you cannot be -" He stopped in confusion, began to laugh also, and said: "Forgive me! I had pictured – well, a very different lady!"

"In a turban! Serena told me so. It is very naughty of her to roast you, Major Kirkby. Do, pray, be seated! Serena will be down directly. She was caught in that dreadful storm, and was obliged to change her dress, which was quite soaked."

"Walking in this weather! I hope she may not have taken a chill! It was very imprudent."

"Oh, no! She never does so," responded Fanny placidly. "She was used to ride with her Papa in all weathers, you know. She is a famous horsewoman – quite intrepid!"

"Yes, so I believe. I never saw her in the saddle, however. Our – our former acquaintance was in London. You and she now reside here? Or, no! I think she told me you were here only for a visit."

"Oh, yes! We have been living since Lord Spenborough's death in my Dower House, at Milverley."

"Ah, then, she has not been obliged quite to leave her home! I remember that she was much attached to it." He smiled warmly at her. "When I read of Lord Spenborough's death, I was afraid she might be obliged to live with Lady – with someone, perhaps, not agreeable to her! I am sure she must be happy with you, ma'am!"

"Oh, yes! That is, *I* am very happy," said Fanny naïvely. "She is so kind to me! I don't know how I should go on without her."

At that moment, Serena came into the room, her copper ringlets still damp, and curling wildly. As she closed the door, she said mischievously: "Now, what an infamous thing it is that you should have come when I wasn't here to present you to my mama-in-law, sir! She has not terrified you, I trust?"

He had jumped up, and strode to meet her, taking her hand, and holding it for a minute. "What an infamous thing it was that you should have taken me in!" he retorted, smiling down at her with so glowing a look in his eyes that her own sank, and she felt her colour rising.

"It was irresistible! Are you satisfied that she is truly motherly?"

"Serena! You never said so!" cried Fanny indignantly.

"No, not I! It was Major Kirkby's hope!"

He drew her forward to a chair beside the small fire, and placed a cushion behind her as she seated herself. She looked up, to thank him, and he said: "Do you know that your hair is quite wet?"

"It will soon dry beside this fire."

"Are you always so reckless? I wish you will take care!"

She smiled. "Why, do I seem to you invalidish? It's well you didn't see me when I came in, for I don't think there was a dry stitch on me!"

"Then perhaps it is as well. I should certainly have been anxious."

"Fanny will tell you that I am never ill. Do *you* take cold every time you are caught in the rain?"

"No, indeed! I should not long have survived in Portugal! But that is another matter: you are not a soldier!"

She saw that he would not readily be persuaded that her constitution was not delicate, and was a little amused. It was not unpleasant to find herself an object of solicitude, so she said no more, leading him instead to talk of his experiences in the Peninsula. He stayed for half-an-hour, and then, very correctly, rose to take his leave. Fanny, as she shook hands with him, said, in her pretty, soft voice: "You know we cannot entertain in any formal style, Major Kirkby, but if you will not think it a bore to dine quietly with us one evening, we should be happy to welcome you."

"A bore! I should like it of all things!" he said. "May I indeed do that?"

The engagement was made, and Fanny's hand kissed. "Thank you!" the Major said, with a twinkle.

There was a good deal of meaning in his voice. Fanny gave a little choke of laughter, and tried to look demure.

He turned from her to Serena. "I think you are very fortunate in your mama-in-law! Shall I see you, perhaps, in the Pump Room tomorrow? Do you go there?"

"Very frequently – to watch Fanny screwing up her face, and most heroically drinking the water!"

"Ah! Then I shall meet you there!" he said, and pressed her hand, and went away.

Serena glanced almost shyly at Fanny. "Well?"

"Oh Serena, how *very* charming he is! You did not tell me the half! I think I never saw such kind eyes! He is so much in love with you, too!"

"He does not know me."

"My dear!"

Serena shook her head. "Do you think he does? I am so much afraid – You see, he believes me to be – oh, so many excellent things which I am not! He has no notion of my shocking temper, or my obstinacy, or -"

"Serena, you goose!" Fanny cried, embracing her. "He loves you! Oh, and he will take such care of you, and value you as he should, and think nothing too good for you! He is the very man to make you happy!"

"Fanny, Fanny!" Serena protested. "He has not offered for me yet!"

"How absurd you are! When he can barely take his eyes off you! He will offer for you before the week is out!"

CHAPTER NINE

FANNY WAS disappointed. It was ten days later before the Major declared himself, and he did it then at her instigation.

That he was head over ears in love no one could doubt. He went about like a man dazzled by strong sunshine, so oblivious of his surroundings or any worldly care that his anxious mother was thrown into great disquiet, convinced at one moment that he no longer held her in affection, and at the next that his restlessness and absence of mind must have its root in some deepseated disorder. Since the state of her health made her shrink from social intercourse, and her only expeditions from her eyrie in Lansdown Crescent down into the town were to the Abbey Baths, she remained in ignorance of the true state of affairs. Fashionable Bath could have enlightened her, for although the Major retained just enough sense not to haunt Laura Place it seemed not to occur to him that the spectacle of a tall and handsome young man searching the Pump Room every morning for the Lady Serena Carlow might possibly attract attention. The *habitués* of the Pump Room derived considerable entertainment from it, one gentleman asserting that it was now his custom to set his watch by the Major's arrival; and old General Hendy, whose own practice was to steer a gouty and determined course to Fanny's side, saying indignantly that he never saw such a silly, moonstruck fellow, and had a good mind to tell him what a cake he was making of himself. Whenever the Major came bearing down upon Serena, he scowled at him awfully; but as the Major had no eyes for anyone but Serena, this strong hint from a senior officer went unnoticed. General Hendy was not the only person hostile to the courtship. High sticklers viewed it with disapproval, some maintaining that it was improper for the Lady Serena to be encouraging any gentleman to pay his addresses to her while she was in mourning for her father, others considering that such a match would be scandalously unequal.

Had the Major been less besotted he must have perceived the glances, curious, amused, or condemnatory, and have realized that his goddess had become the most talked-of woman in Bath. He would have been aghast. Serena realized it, and laughed. Fanny did not realize it until Mrs Floore shocked her by saying: "A very pretty beau your daughter-in-law has got for herself, my lady, I do declare! Lord, it's as good as a play to watch him! Morning after morning, in he comes, and if Lady Serena is here he goes plunging across the room to her, never noticing another soul, and if she ain't he goes off like a dog that's lost its tail!"

Dismayed, Fanny exclaimed: "Oh, how could I be so thoughtless? I never dreamed that people would notice – talk about Lady Serena -!"

"Lord, ma'am, who cares for a bit of gossip?" said Mrs Floore comfortably. "There's no harm that ever I heard of in a beautiful girl being courted, and if people choose to talk, let 'em!"

Serena said the same. "My dear Fanny, don't tease yourself! The world began to talk about me when I drove a high-perch phaeton in Hyde Park! I was eighteen then, and much Papa cared for the exclamations of the censorious! When I declared I would no longer be burdened with a duenna hands were upflung in horror; when I jilted Rotherham I was known to be past reclaim! Add to these all my other iniquities, and you must perceive that I've given people so much to talk about that had I cared for their whisperings I must have retired to a nunnery! What's more, didn't my aunt warn you that I am an acknowledged flirt?"

"Serena, do not say so!"

"Well, it's quite true, you know," said Serena candidly. "How often have *you* accused me of trifling with some ridiculous creature's sensibilities?"

"Oh, no, no! I never said that! Only that you have so much liveliness, dearest, and so much beauty, that – that gentlemen can't help but fall in love with you, and you are so heedless of your beauty that you don't quite realize it!"

"Fanny, you're a goose!" Serena told her severely. "Of course I do! If a personable man does me the honour to think me beautiful alas, that there should not be more of them! But my red hair, you know, is a sad blemish! – well, if he *does* admire me, what should I do but reward him with a little elegant dalliance?"

"How can you talk so? If I believed you to be *flirting* with Major Kirkby – Oh, no, Serena, you could not!"

"You are very right! It would be a feat beyond my power. He would be incapable of it!"

"I wish you will be serious!" Fanny said despairingly.

"I can't be! No, no, don't pester me with questions, or lecture me on the proprieties, Fanny! Very likely I have taken leave of my senses – indeed, I sometimes fear I have! – but either I shall come about, or – or – I shall not! And as for the rest of the world, it may go to the devil!"

Fanny could only conclude that she was as much in love as the Major, and wished that he would come to the point. Why he did not do so she was at a loss to understand, and was beginning to wonder if some impediment perhaps existed, when, to her surprise, he was ushered into the drawing-room in Laura Place one afternoon, and said, as he grasped her hand: "I hoped I might find you at home! Serena is out, I know: it is you I particularly wish to see! You are her guardian – the properest person to be consulted! You know her – I believe you must be aware of the nature of the feelings which I – Lady Spenborough, in the joy of seeing her again, hearing her voice, touching her hand, all other considerations were forgotten! I allowed myself -" He broke off, trying to collect himself, and took a few hasty steps about the room.

Filled with trepidation, she said, after a moment: "You allowed yourself, Major Kirkby -?"

"To be happy in a dream! A dream of years, which seemed suddenly to have turned to reality!"

"A dream! I beg your pardon, but why do you call it so?" she asked anxiously.

He turned, and came back to the fireside. "Should I not? Lady Spenborough, I ask myself that question again and again! I tell myself it could be reality, but I cannot silence the doubt – the scruple – that warns me it *should* not!"

His agitation, the strong emotion under which he was evidently labouring, the oppressed look upon his brow, all awoke her ready compassion. Her disposition was timid; she was always very shy with anyone whom she did not know well; but she felt no shyness upon this occasion. She said, with her pretty smile: Will you not be seated, and tell me what it is that is troubling you? You know, I am very stupid, and I don't at all understand what you mean!"

He threw her a grateful look, saying: "You are so very kind! I am talking like a fool, I suppose! I came to ask you – Lady Spenborough, should I be the most presumptuous dog alive to beg Serena to marry me?"

Astonishment widened her eyes. "Presumptuous? But – but why?"

"You don't think so? But have you considered? You know, I fancy, that the feelings I entertain are not – are not of recent birth! It is nearly seven years since I first saw her, and from that day those feelings have remained unchanged! She appeared to me then like some heavenly creature descended to earth to make every other woman seem commonplace! Her beauty, her grace, the very music of her voice, I could never forget! They have remained with me, haunted all my dreams -" He stopped, reddening, and tried to laugh. "I am talking like a fool again!"

"No, no!" she breathed. "Pray do not think so! Go on, if you please!"

He stared down at his hands, lying clasped between his knees. "Well! You are aware, I daresay, that I had the temerity to raise my eyes – too high!"

"You should not say so," she interpolated gently.

"It was true! *Then* I thought otherwise. I was very young! Rank and fortune seemed to me to be of no account when set in the scales against such an attachment as I believed ours to be! I think I never forgave those that parted us until now, when the treasure I had believed unattainable seems to be within my reach, and I see – as any man of honour must! – all the force of the arguments which were advanced against me, seven years ago!"

Again she interrupted him. "Forgive me! But seven years ago *she* was just come out, and *you* were a younger son, with no prospects! She is her own mistress now, and you are not a boy, just joined, and proud, as Serena once told me, of your first regimentals. *Then,* had she been permitted to marry you, she must have followed the drum; today, it is otherwise, is it not?"

He looked up, fixing his eyes upon her intently. "I have come into the property which I never thought to inherit, but it is not large. Indeed, in *her* eyes the estate must seem a small one, and brings me what I should rather call an easy competence than a handsome fortune. The *elegances* of life I can command, but not its luxuries! The house to which I should take her, though I have been used to hear it spoken of as commodious, cannot compare with Milverley. I was never at Milverley, but I have visited such places. I have even stayed in one or two, and I know that beside the size and style of such an establishment my poor little manor must be dwarfed indeed. I could afford, I think, to hire a house in town for the Season, but it could not be a mansion, like Spenborough House."

"Oh!" she cried involuntarily. "Can you suppose that such considerations as that would weigh with Serena?"

"No! Her mind is too lofty – her disposition too generous ! If she gave her heart, she would, I think, be ready to live in a cottage! It is with me that those considerations weigh! They must do so – and the more heavily because *she* would laugh them aside!"

"I don't know what any woman could want more than what you can offer her," Fanny said wistfully.

"Lady Spenborough, are you sincere? You don't think it would be wrong in me to ask her to be my wife?"

"No, indeed! To be sure, I cannot feel that a *cottage* would do for Serena," said Fanny, quite unable to picture Serena in such a setting, "because she doesn't like to feel herself cooped-up. Besides, you could scarcely keep servants in a cottage, and, with all the will in the world, Major Kirkby, she could never manage without!"

He could not help laughing. "I should think not indeed!"

"You see," Fanny explained, "she has always had so many servants to wait upon her that she has never been obliged to attend very much to domestic matters. But I daresay you have a good housekeeper?"

"Of course! I didn't mean that she would have to sweep floors, or cook the dinner, or even tell the maids what they must do. My mother was used to direct the servants, but since she has lived in Bath Mrs Harbury has attended to all such matters, and could very well continue to do so, if Serena wished it."

"I expect she would wish it," said Fanny, with lively memories of Serena's unconcern with the domestic arrangements at the Dower House. She added reflectively: "It is the oddest thing! I am sure Serena never groomed a horse in her life, or swept out a stall, but she would manage a stable far more easily than a house!"

These words brought another scruple to his mind. He said: "Her hunting! Could she bear to give that up? Even if I could endure to let her risk her neck, my home is in Kent, and that is poor hunting-country – humbug country, I expect she would call it! There are several packs, but I have never been much addicted to the sport. I could become a subscriber, but I doubt – She told me once that she thought nothing equal to the Cottesmore country!"

"Yes," said Fanny. "She and her papa were used to visit Lord Lonsdale every year, at Lowther Hall. But for the most part, of course, they hunted with the Duke of Beaufort's pack. I believe – but I have never hunted myself! – that that is very good country too." She smiled at him, as something very like a groan burst from him. "Major Kirkby, you are too despondent! It would be a very poor creature who would set such considerations as *that* in the balance!"

"I know she would not! But I should wish her to have everything she desired!"

"Well, if she desired it so very much, perhaps it could be contrived. You might purchase a lodge in the Shires, or -"

"*That* I might do, but maintain a dozen or so first-rate hunters I could not!"

"But Serena has a very large fortune of her own!" said Fanny.

He sprang up, and began to walk about the room again. "Yes! I have no knowledge – but it was bound to be so! I wish to God it were not! You will understand me, Lady Spenborough, when I say that I had rather by far she were penniless than that there should be so great a disparity – as I fear there must be – between our fortunes!"

"I do understand you," she replied warmly. "Such a sentiment cannot but do you honour, but, believe me, it would be most wrong, most foolish, to let such a scruple stand in the way of – perhaps – the happiness of you both!"

He came striding back to her, and caught her hand to his lips. "I have no words with which to thank you! If I have *your* consent, I care for no other! You know Serena – you love her – and you tell me to go forward!"

"Oh, yes, but I am not her guardian, you know! She is quite her own mistress ! At least -" She paused, suddenly struck by an unwelcome thought. "I had forgot! Oh, dear!"

"She has a guardian? Someone to whom I should apply before approaching her?"

"No, no! Only her fortune is – is strangely tied-up, and perhaps – But I should not be talking of her affairs!"

He pressed her hand slightly. "Do not! I hope it may be so securely tied-up that I could not touch it if I would! I must go. If I could express to you my gratitude for your kindness, your understanding -!" He smiled down at her with a good deal of archness. "The word *dowager* will never again have the power to terrify me!"

She laughed, and blushed. He again kissed her hand, and turned to go away, just as the door opened, and Serena, in her walking-dress, came into the room.

"I thought I recognized the modish hat reposing on the table in the hall!" she remarked, drawing off her gloves, and tossing them aside. "How do you do, Hector?" Her eyes went from him to Fanny, and the smile in them deepened. "Now, what conspiracy have you been hatching to make you both look so guilty?"

"No conspiracy," the Major said, going to her, and helping her to take off her pelisse. "Did you find your very odd acquaintance – Mrs Floore, is it not? – at home? I should think she was very much obliged to you for your visit!"

"I believe you are quite as high in the instep as Fanny, and disapprove of Mrs Floore as heartily!" Serena exclaimed.

"I own I cannot think her a proper friend for you," he admitted.

"Stuff! I found her at home, and *I* was very much obliged to *her* for the welcome she was kind enough to give me. I must say, Fanny, I wish we were in London, just that we might see with our own eyes the Laleham-woman's triumph!"

"You don't mean to say that she has made up a brilliant match for poor little Emily already?" cried Fanny.

"No, she hasn't done *that,* but, if she's to be believed, she might have her pick of a dozen eligible partis tomorrow, if she chose! Flying at higher game, I conclude! So does Mrs Floore. *She* still holds by her cross-eyed Duke! I am very sceptical about him, but there seems to be no doubt that the Rotherham ball has worked like a charm. I daresay it might help to open *some* doors, but what tactics the Laleham-woman employed to force open some others, and which of the Patronesses she outgeneralled into surrendering vouchers for Almack's, I would give a fortune to know. One can't but admire her!"

"*Odious* woman!" Fanny said. "I am sorry for Emily."

"Nonsense! She will be in high feather, enjoying a truly magnificent season."

"But who is this lady?" asked the Major.

"She is Mrs Floore's daughter, not as engaging as her mama, but quite as redoubtable."

"She is a hateful, scheming creature!" said Fanny, with unusual asperity. "Excuse me! – I must speak to Lybster! – Something I forgot to tell him he must do! No, no, pray don't pull the bell, dearest!"

"Good gracious, Fanny, what in the world?" Serena stopped, for the door had closed softly behind Fanny.

"Serena!"

She turned her head, struck by the urgent note in the Major's voice. One look at his face was enough to explain Fanny's surprising behaviour. She felt suddenly breathless, and absurdly shy.

He came towards her, and took her hands. "It was not conspiracy. I came to ask her, as one who is in some sort your guardian, if I might ask you to marry me."

"Oh, Hector, how could you be so foolish?" she said, her voice catching on something between a laugh and a sob. "What has poor Fanny to say to anything? Did she tell you that you might? Must I ask her what I should reply?"

"Not that! But I am aware now, as I never was seven years ago, of the gulf that lies between us!"

She pulled one of her hands away, and pressed her fingers against his mouth. "Don't say such things! I *forbid* you! Don't think yourself unworthy of me! If you only knew – But you don't, my poor Hector, you don't! It's I who am unworthy! You've no notion how detestable I can be, how headstrong, how obstinate, how *shrewish*!"

He caught her into his arms, saying thickly: "Do not *you* say such things! My goddess, my queen!"

"Oh, no, no, no!"

He raised his head, smiling a little crookedly down at her. "Do you dislike to hear yourself called so? There is nothing I would not do to please you, but you cannot help but be my goddess! You have been so these seven years!"

"Only a goddess could dislike it! You see by that how wretchedly short of the mark I fall. I have a little honesty – enough to tell you *now* that you must not worship me."

He only laughed, and kissed her again. She protested no more, too much a woman not to be deeply moved by such idolatry, and awed by the constancy which, though it might have been to a false image, could not be doubted.

It was not long before he was saying to her much of what he had previously said to Fanny, anxiously laying his circumstances before her, and dwelling so particularly on the disparity between them of rank and fortune, that she interrupted presently to say with mingled amusement and impatience: "My dearest Hector, I wish you will not talk such nonsense!

Why do you set so much store by rank? You are a gentleman, and I hope I am a gentlewoman, and as for fortune, we shall do very well!"

His expression changed; he said: "I wish to God you had no fortune!"

It was not to be expected that she should understand such a point of view, nor did she. In her world, a poorly dowered girl was an object for compassion. Even a love-match must depend upon the marriage-settlements, and wealthy and besotted indeed must be the suitor who allied himself to a portionless damsel. She looked her astonishment, and repeated, in a blank voice: "Wish I had no fortune?"

"Yes! I had rather by far you were penniless, than – I daresay – so rich that my own fortune must seem the veriest pittance beside yours!"

Laughter sprang to her eyes. "Oh, you goose! Do you fear to be taken for a fortune-hunter? Of all the crack-brained ideas to take into your head! No, indeed, Hector, this is being foolish beyond permission!"

"I don't know that I care so much for that – though it is what people will say! – but I must support my wife, not live upon *her* fortune! Serena, surely you must understand this!"

It seemed to her absurdly romantic, but she only said quizzingly: "Was this thought in your head seven years ago?"

"Seven years ago," he replied gravely, "your father was alive, and you were not sole mistress of your fortune. If I thought about the matter at all – but you must remember that I was *then* no more than a green boy! – I imagine I must have supposed that Lord Spenborough, if he countenanced the match, would settle on you a sum comparable to my own means.

"Or have cut me off without a penny?" she enquired, amused.

"Or have done that," he agreed, perfectly seriously.

She perceived that he was in earnest, but she could not help saying, with a gurgle of laughter: "It is too bad that you cannot enact the rôle of Cophetua! I must always possess an independence, which cannot be wrested from me. But take heart! It is by no means certain that I shall ever have more than that. Are you prepared to take me with my wretched seven hundred pounds a year, my ridiculous fortune-hunter? I warn you, it may well be no more!"

"Are you in earnest?" he asked, his brow lightening. "Lady Spenborough said something about your fortune's being oddly tied-up, but no more than that. Tell me!"

"I will, but if you mean to take it as a piece of excellent good news we are likely to fall out!" she warned him. "Nothing was ever more infamous! My dear but misguided papa left my fortune – all but what I have from my mother – to Rotherham, in trust for me, with the proviso that he was to allow me no more than the pin-money I had always been given, until I was married – with, mark you! his lordship's consent and approval! In the event of my marrying without that august approval, I may, I suppose, kiss my fingers to my inheritance!"

He was staggered, and his first thoughts agreed exactly with her own. "*What*? You must win Rotherham's consent? Good God, I never in my life heard of anything so iniquitous!"

"Just so!" said Serena, with immense cordiality. "I hope you will perceive that I was not to be blamed for flying into the worst passion of my career when *that* clause was read to me!"

"I do not wonder at it! Rotherham, of all men alive! Pardon me, but the indelicacy of such a provision, the – But I must be silent on that head!"

"Abominable, wasn't it? I am heartily of your opinion!"

He sat for a moment or two, with his lips tightly compressed, but as other thoughts came into his mind, his face relaxed, and he presently exclaimed: "Then if he should refuse his consent, you will have no more than will serve for your gowns, and – and such fripperies!"

"Very true but you need not say it as though you were glad of it!"

"I am glad of it!"

"Well, so am not I!" retorted Serena tartly.

"Serena, all I have is yours to do with as you please!" he said imploringly.

She was touched, but a strong vein of common sense made her say: "I am very much obliged to you, but what if I should please to spend all you have upon my gowns and such fripperies? My dear, that is very fine talking, but it won't do! Besides, the very thought of Ivo's holding *my* pursestrings to the day of his death, or mine, is enough to send me into strong convulsions! He shall not do it! And now I come to think of it, I believe he will not be able to. He told me himself that if he withheld his consent unreasonably I might be able to break the Trust. Hector, if you do not instantly wipe from your face that disappointed look, you will have a taste of my temper, and so I warn you!"

He smiled, but said with quiet confidence: "Rotherham will never give his consent to your marrying *me*!"

"We shall see!"

"And nothing – *nothing!* would prevail upon me to seek it!" said the Major, with suppressed violence.

"Oh, you need not! That at least was not stipulated in Papa's Will! I shall inform him myself of my betrothal – but that will not be until I am out of mourning, in the autumn."

"The autumn!" He sounded dismayed, but recollected himself immediately, and said: "You are very right! My own feelings – But it would be quite improper for such an announcement to be made until you are out of black gloves!"

She stretched out her hand to lay it upon one of his. "Well, I think it would, Hector. In general, I set little store by the proprieties, but in such a case as this – oh, every feeling would be offended! In private we are engaged, but the world shall not know it until October."

He lifted the hand to his lips. "You are the only judge: I shall be ruled entirely by your wishes, my queen!"

CHAPTER TEN

THE ENGAGED couple, neither of whom wasted a moment's thought on what must be the inevitable conclusions arrived at by the interested, admitted only two persons into the secret. One was Fanny, and the other Mrs Kirkby. The Major could not be happy until he had made Serena known to his mother; and since she was reluctant to appear in any way neglectful, it was not long before she was climbing the hill to Lansdown Crescent, escorted by her handsome cavalier.

Had the expedition been left to the Major's management, Serena would have been carried in a sedan-chair, his rooted conviction that no female was capable of exertion making it quite shocking to him to think of her undertaking so strenuous a walk. But Serena had other ideas. "What, stuff myself into a chair in such bright May weather? Not for the world!" she declared.

"Your carriage, then? My mother goes out so seldom that she has not thought it worth while to keep hers in Bath, or I would -"

"My dear Hector," she interrupted him, "you cannot in all seriousness suppose that I would have my own or your mother's horses put to merely to struggle up that steep hill!"

"No, which is why I suggested you should hire a chair. I am afraid you will be tired."

"On the contrary, I shall enjoy the walk. I feel in Bath as though I were hobbled. Only tell me the exact direction of Mrs Kirkby's house, and I will engage to present myself punctually, and in no need of hartshorn to revive me!"

He smiled, but said: "I shall fetch you, of course."

"Well, that will be very agreeable, but I beg you won't put yourself to the trouble if your reason is that you fear for my safety in this excessively respectable town!"

"Not your *safety*, precisely, but I know that you won't take your maid, and I own I cannot like you to go out alone."

"You would be surprised if you guessed how very well able I am to take care of myself. I was done with young ladyhood some years ago. What is more, my dear, times have changed a trifle since you lived in England before. In London, I might gratify you by taking my maid with me – though it is much more likely that I should prefer to go in my carriage, and alone! – but in Bath it is quite unnecessary."

"Nevertheless I hope you will allow me to be your escort."

"Indeed, I shall be glad of your company," she responded, not choosing to argue the point further, and trusting that time would dull the edge of a solicitude she found a little oppressive.

Certainly the pace she set when they walked up to Lansdown Crescent did not encourage him to suppose that she was less healthy than she looked. She had never lost the rather mannish stride she had acquired in youth, when, to the disapproval of most of her relations, she had been reared more as a boy than as a girl, and she could never shorten it to suit Fanny's demure steps. A walk with Fanny was to Serena a form of dawdling, which she detested; it was a real pleasure to her to be pacing along beside a man again. She would not take the Major's arm, but went up the hill at a swinging rate, and exclaimed, when she was obliged to hold her hat on against the wind: "Ah, this is famous! One can breathe up here! I wished we might have found a house in Camden Place, or the Royal Crescent, but there were none to be hired that Lybster thought eligible."

"I myself prefer the heights," he admitted, "but there's no doubt Laura Place is a more convenient situation."

"Oh, yes! And Fanny would not have liked the hill," she agreed cheerfully.

A few minutes later she was making the acquaintance of her future mother-in-law.

Mrs Kirkby, a valetudinarian of retiring habits, and a timid disposition, was quite overpowered by her visitor. She had been flustered at the outset by the intelligence that her only remaining son was betrothed to a lady of title whose various exploits were known even to her. An inveterate reader of the social columns in the journals, she could have told the Major how many parties the Lady Serena had graced with her presence, what was the colour of her dashing phaeton, how many times she had been seen in Hyde Park, mounted on her long-tailed gray, what she had worn at various Drawing-rooms, in whose company she had visited the paddock at Doncaster, and a great many other items of similar interest. Nor was she ignorant of the Lady Serena's predilection for waltzing, and quadrilles; while as for the Lady Serena's previous engagement, so scandalously terminated within so short a distance from the wedding-day, she had marvelled at it, and shaken her head at it, and moralized over it to all her acquaintance. It had therefore come as a severe shock to her to learn that her son was proposing to ally himself to a lady demonstrably unsuited to a quiet Kentish manor and she had not been able to forbear asking him, in a quavering voice: "Oh, Hector, but is she not very *fast*?"

"She is an angel!" he had replied radiantly.

Mrs Kirkby did not think that Serena looked like an angel. Angels, in her view, were ethereal creatures, and there was nothing at all ethereal about Serena. She was a tall and beautiful young woman of fashion, the picture of vigorous health, and so full of vitality that half an hour in her company left the invalid a prey to headache, palpitations, and nervous spasms. It was not, as Mrs Kirkby faintly assured her elderly companion, that she was loud-voiced, for her voice was particularly musical. It was not that she was talkative, or assertive, or fidgety, for she was none of these things. In fact, Mrs Kirkby had been unable to detect faults; what had prostrated her were the Lady Serena's virtues. "Anyone can see," she said, between sniffs at her vinaigrette, "that she has never moved in any but the first circles! Her manners have that well-bred ease that *shows* she has been used to act as hostess to every sort of person, from Royalty, I daresay, to commoners!

Nothing could have been more perfect than her bearing towards me, and what I have ever done to deserve to have such a daughter-in-law thrust upon me I'm sure I don't know!"

Happily, the Major was far too dazzled by his goddess's brilliant good-looks to notice any lack of enthusiasm in his mother's demeanour. It seemed to him that Serena brought light into a sunless room, and it never occurred to him that anyone could find it too strong. So great was his certainty that no one could set eyes on Serena without being captivated, and so complete was his absorption, that he accepted at face value all his mother's acquiescent answers to the eager questions he later put to her. Had she ever seen such striking beauty? No, indeed, she had not. So much countenance, such a complexion! Yes, indeed! Those eyes, too! he had known she could not choose but to be fascinated by them. So changeable, and expressive, and the curve of the lids above them giving them that smiling look! Very true: most remarkable! She must have been pleased, he dared swear, with the perfection of her manners, so easy, so polished, and yet so unaffected! Exactly so! And the grace of her every movement! Oh, yes! most graceful! He did not know how it was, for she never tried to dominate her company, but when she came into a room, her personality seemed to fill it: had his mother been conscious of it! Most conscious of it! Would she think him fanciful if he told her that it seemed to him as though those glorious eyes had some power of witchcraft? He thought they cast a spell over any one on whom they rested! Yes, indeed! Mrs Kirkby (in a failing voice) thought so too.

So the Major was able to tell Serena, in all good faith, that his mother was in transports over her; and such was his infatuation that he would have found nothing to cavil at in Mrs Kirkby's subsequent assertion, to the sympathetic Miss Murthly, that the Lady Serena had bewitched her son.

In his saner moments, slight doubts of his mother's approval of all Serena's actions did cross the Major's mind; and, without being precisely aware of it, he was glad that the seclusion in which she lived made it unlikely that certain freaks would come to her ears. Although herself of respectable lineage, she had never moved in the highest circle of society, and possibly might not appreciate that the code of conduct obtaining there was less strict than any to which she had been accustomed. Great ladies permitted themselves more licence than was the rule amongst the lesser gentry. Their manners were more free; they expressed themselves in language shocking to the old-fashioned; secure in birth and rank, they cared little for appearances, and were far less concerned with the proprieties than were more obscure persons. When he had first encountered Serena, the Major had been struck by the marked difference which existed between her relations with the elders of her family, and those that were the rule in his own family. That she should have lived on terms of unceremonious equality with an indulgent father was not perhaps surprising; but the extremely frank style of her conversations with her formidable aunt had never ceased to astonish him. There was no lack of ceremony about the Lady Theresa Eaglesham, but while, on the one hand, she had not hesitated to censure conduct which she considered unbecoming in her niece, on the other, she had not scrupled to gossip with her, as with a contemporary. Young Hector Kirkby, seven years earlier, had been quite unable to picture any of his aunts informing his sister that Lady M... was big with child, and the wits laying bets on the probable paternity of the unborn infant. Major Hector Kirkby, no longer a green boy, devoutly trusted that Serena would never, in the future, regale these prim spinsters with extracts from Lady Theresa's singularly unrestricted letters. He even refrained from repeating to his mother a very good story Lady Theresa had sent her niece about the Royal Wedding. *"Rumour has it,"* wrote Lady Theresa, *"that the ceremony went off well, except for an* entrave *at the end, when the P. Charlotte was kept waiting for half an hour in the carriage, while Leopold hunted high and low for his greatcoat, which no one could find. The P. Regent,* très benin *until then, hearing the cause of the delay, burst out with 'D... his greatcoat!' It is now believed, by the by, that he is* not *dropsical . . . "*

No: decidedly that was not a story for Mrs Kirkby, quite as inveterate an admirer of Royalty as Fanny.

Nor did the Major inform his parent that her future daughter in-law, riding out of Bath in his company before breakfast, dispensed with a chaperon on these expeditions. Mrs Kirkby would have been profoundly shocked, and he was himself doubtful of the propriety of it. But Serena laughed at him, accusing him of being frightened of all the quizzy people in Bath, and he stifled his qualms. It was a delight to be alone with her, an agony to be powerless to check her intrepidity. She would brook no hand upon her bridle: he had learnt that, when, in actual fact, he had caught it above the bit, instinctively, when her mare had reared. The white fury in her face had startled him; her eyes were daggers, and the virago-note sounded in her voice when she shot at him, from between clenched teeth: "Take your hand from my rein!" The dangerous moment passed; his hand had dropped; she got the mare under control, and said quite gently: "You must never do so again, Hector. Yes, yes, I understand, but when I cannot manage my horses I will sell them, and take to tatting instead!"

He thought her often reckless in the fences she would ride at; all she said, when he expostulated, was: "Don't be afraid! I never overface my horses. The last time I did so I was twelve, and Papa laid his hunting-crop across my shoulders: an effective cure!"

He said ruefully: "Can't you tell me some other way I might be able to check your mad career?"

"Alas, none!" she laughed.

He had nightmarish visions of seeing her lying with a broken neck beside some rasper; and, to make it worse, Fanny said to him, with a trustful smile: "It is so comfortable to know you are with Serena, when she rides out, Major Kirkby! I know she is a splendid horsewoman, but I can never be easy when she has only Fobbing with her, because she is what the hunting people call a *bruising* rider, and for all Fobbing has been her groom since she was a little girl she never will mind him!"

"I wish to God I might induce her to mind *me*!" he ejaculated. "But she will not, Lady Spenborough, and when I begged her to consider what must be *my* position if she should take a bad toss when in my care, she would do nothing but laugh, and advise me to ride off the instant I saw her fall, and swear I was never with her!"

"Oh, dear!" she sighed. She saw that he was really worried, and added soothingly: "Never mind! I daresay we are both of us too anxious. Lord

Spenborough, you know, was used to tell me there was no need for me to tease myself over her. *He* never did so! If he thought she had been reckless, he sometimes swore at her, but I don't think he was ever really *alarmed*!"

"That, ma'am, I could not do!"

"Oh, no! I know you never would! Though I daresay she would not be in the least offended if you did," said Fanny reflectively.

The bright May weather was making Serena increasingly impatient of the quiet life she was obliged to lead. At this time, in any other year, she would have been in the thick of the London season, cramming a dozen engagements into a single day. She did not wish herself in London, and would have recoiled from the thought of breakfasts and balls, but Bath provided no outlet for her overflowing energy. Fanny was content to visit the Pump Room each weekday and the Laura Chapel each Sunday, and found a stroll along the fashionable promenades exercise enough for her constitution; Serena could scarcely endure the unvarying pattern of her days, and felt herself caged in so small a town. She said that Bath was stifling in warm weather, sent to Milverley for her phaeton, and commanded the Major to escort her on a tour of the livery stables of Bath, in search of a pair of job horses fit for her to drive.

He was very willing, fully sympathizing with her desire to escape from the confinement of the town, and realizing that to be driven in a barouche by Fanny's staid coachman could only bore her. He thought that the phaeton would provide both ladies with an agreeable and unexceptionable amusement. That was before he saw it. But the vehicle which arrived in Bath was not the safe and comfortable phaeton he had expected to see. Serena had omitted to mention the fact that hers was a high-perch phaeton; and when he set eyes on it, and saw the frail body hung directly over the front axle, its bottom fully five feet from the ground, he gave an exclamation of dismay. "Serena! You don't mean to drive yourself in *that*?"

"Yes, most certainly I do! But, oh, how much I wish I still had the pair I was used to drive! Match grays, Hector, and such beautiful steppers!"

"Serena – my dearest! I beg you won't! I know you are an excellent whip, but you could not have a more dangerous carriage!"

"No – if I were not an excellent whip!"

"Even nonpareils have been known to overturn these high perch phaetons!"

"To be sure they have!" she agreed, with a mischievous smile. "The difficulty of driving them is what lends a spice!"

"Yes, but – My love, *you* are the only judge of what it is proper for you to do, but to be driving the most sporting of all carriages – Dearest, do females commonly do so?"

"By no means! Only very dashing females!"

"No, don't joke me about it! Perhaps, in Hyde Park though I own I should have thought – But in Bath -! You can't have considered! You would set the whole town talking!"

She looked at him with surprise. "Should I? Yes, very likely! – there is no knowing what people will talk of! But you can't – *surely* you can't expect me to pay the least heed to what they may choose to say of me?"

He was silenced, startled to discover that he did expect this. After a moment, she said coaxingly: "Will you go with me, and see whether I am to be trusted not to overturn myself? I must try these job horses of mine. From what I can see of them I fancy there can be no fear that they will have the smallest desire to bolt with me!"

"You will give Bath enough to stare at without that!" he replied, in a mortified tone, and left her.

It was as well he did so, for quick anger flashed in her eyes, and he might otherwise have had another taste of her temper. His solicitude for her safety, though it might fret her independent spirit, she could understand, and make a push to bear with patience. Criticism of her conduct was an impertinence she would tolerate no better from him than from her cousin Hartley. She had almost uttered a blistering set-down, when he turned on his heel, and was shocked to realize that she had been within an ace of telling him that whatever might be the creed governing the behaviour of the ladies of his set, *she* was Spenborough's daughter, and profoundly indifferent to the opinion such persons might hold of her.

It was not to be expected that she would, in this instance, think herself at fault. An easy-going father, famed for his eccentricities, had sanctioned, even encouraged, her sporting proclivities. In much the same spirit as he had told her, facing her first jump, to throw her heart over, he had taught her to handle all the most mettlesome teams in his stables. This very high-perch phaeton had been built for her to his order: disapproval of it was disapproval of him. "Whatever else you may do, my girl," had said the late Earl, "don't you be missish!"

The Major having removed himself, Serena's wrath was vented, in some sort, on Fanny. "Intolerable!" she declared, striding up and down the drawing-room, in her mannishly cut driving-dress. "*I* to pander to the prejudices of a parcel of Bath dowds and prudes! If that is what he thinks I must do when we are married the sooner he learns that I shall not the better it will be for him! Pretty well for Major Kirkby to tell a Carlow that her behaviour is unseemly!"

"Surely, dearest, he cannot have said that!" expostulated Fanny mildly.

"Implied it! What, does he think my credit to stand upon so insecure a footing that to be seen driving a sporting carriage must demolish it?"

"You know he does not. Don't be vexed with me, Serena, but it is not only a parcel of Bath dowds who think it a *fast* thing for you to do!" She added hastily, as the blazing eyes turned towards her: "Yes, yes, it is all nonsense, of course! *You* need not care for it, but I am persuaded that no man could endure to have his wife thought fast!"

"What Papa countenanced need not offend Hector!"

"I am sure it does not. Now, do, *do*, Serena, be calm! Did not what your papa countenanced very frequently offend his own sister?" She saw the irrepressible smile leap to those stormy eyes, the lips quiver ruefully, and was emboldened to continue: "What *he* permitted must have been right – indeed, how could *I* feel otherwise? – but, you know, he was not precisely the same as other people!"

"No! The eccentric Lord Spenborough, eh?"

"Do you think that it vexed him to be called that?" asked Fanny, fearing that she had offended.

"On the contrary! He liked it! As I do! Anyone who chooses to say that I am as eccentric as my father may do so with my good will! I don't seek the title, any more than he did: it is what hum-drum, insipid provincials say of anyone who does not heed all their tiresome shibboleths! I do what I do because it is what I wish to do, not, believe me, my dear Fanny, to court the notice of the world!"

"I know – oh, I know!"

"You may, but it appears that Hector does not!" Serena flashed. "His look – the tone in which he spoke his final words to me -! Intolerable! Upon my word, I am singularly unfortunate in my *prétendants*! First Rotherham -"

"Serena!" Fanny cried, with a heightened colour. "How can you speak of Rotherham and Major Kirkby in the same breath?"

"Well, at least Rotherham never lectured me on the proprieties!" said Serena pettishly. "He doesn't give a button for appearances either."

"It is not to his credit! I know you don't mean what you say when you put yourself into a passion, but to be comparing those two is outrageous - now, isn't it? The one so arrogant, his temper harsh, his disposition tyrannical, his manners abrupt to the point of incivility; and the other so kind, so solicitous for your comfort, loving you so deeply – Oh, Serena, I beg your pardon, but I am quite shocked that you could talk so!"

"So I apprehend! There is indeed no comparison between them. My opinion of Rotherham you know well. But I must be allowed to give the devil his due, if you please, and credit him with *one* virtue! I collect you don't count it a virtue! We won't argue on that head. My scandalous carriage awaits me, and if we are not to *aborder* one another I'd best leave you, my dear!"

She went away, still simmering with vexation, a circumstance which caused her groom, a privileged person, to say that it was as well she was not driving her famous grays.

"Fobbing, hold your tongue!" she commanded angrily.

He paid no more attention to this than he had paid to the furies of a seven year old termagant, but delivered himself of a grumbling monologue, animadverting severely on her headstrong ways and faults of temper; recalling a great many discreditable incidents, embellished with what he had said to his lordship and what his lordship had said to him; and drawing a picture of himself as an ill-used and browbeaten serf, which must have made her laugh, had she been listening to a word he said.

Her rages were never sullen, and by the time she had discovered the peculiarities of her hired horses, this one had quite vanished. Remorse swiftly took its place, and the truth of Fanny's words struck home to her. She saw again the Major's face, as much hurt as mortified, remembered his long devotion, and without knowing that she spoke aloud, exclaimed: "Oh, I am the greatest beast in nature!"

"Now, that, my lady," said her henchman, surprised and gratified, "I never said, nor wouldn't. What I *do* say and, mind, it's what his lordship has told you time and again! – is that to be handling a high-spirited pair when you're in one of your tantrums -"

"Are you scolding still?" interrupted Serena. "Well, if these commoners are your notion of a high-spirited pair, they are not mine!"

"No, my lady, and it wouldn't make a bit of difference to you if they was prime 'uns on the fret!" said Fobbing, with asperity.

"It would make a great deal of difference to me," she sighed. "I wonder who has my grays now?"

"Now, we don't want to have a fit of the dismals!" he said gruffly. "If you was driving a pair of stumblers, you'd still take the shine out of any other lady on the road, my lady, that I *will* say! It's time you was thinking of turning them, if you don't want to be late back them not being what you might call sixteen mile an hour tits."

"Yes, we must go back," she agreed.

He relapsed into silence, and she was free to pursue her own uncomfortable reflections. By the time they had reached Laura Place again, she had beaten herself into a state of repentance which had to find instant expression. Without pausing to divest herself of her hat or her driving-coat, she hurried into the parlour behind the dining-room, stripping off her gloves, and saying over her shoulder to the butler: "I shall be wanting Thomas almost immediately, to deliver a letter for me in Lansdown Crescent."

She was affixing a wafer to an impetuous and wildly scrawled apology when she heard the knocker on the front door. A few moments later, she heard the Major's voice saying: "You need not announce me!" and sprang to her feet just as he came quickly into the room.

He was looking pale, and anxious. He shut the door with a backward thrust of his hand, and spoke her name, in a tense way that showed him to be labouring under strong emotion.

"Oh, Hector, I have been writing to you!" she cried.

He seemed to grow paler. "Writing to me! Serena, I beg of you – only listen to me!"

She went towards him, saying penitently: "I was odious! a wretch! Oh, pray forgive me!"

"Forgive you! *I?* Serena, my darling, I came to beg you to forgive me! That I should have presumed to criticize your actions! That I should -"

"No, no, I used you monstrously. Do not you beg my pardon! If you wish me not to drive my phaeton in Bath, I won't! There! Am I forgiven?"

But this, she found, would not do for him at all. His remorse for having presumed to remonstrate with his goddess would be soothed by nothing less than her promising to do exactly as she chose upon all occasions. An attempt to joke him out of his mood of exaggerated self-blame failed to draw a smile from him; and the quarrel ended with his passionately kissing Serena's hands, and engaging himself to drive out with her in the phaeton on the very next day.

CHAPTER ELEVEN

THE MAJOR, reconciled to his goddess, could not be satisfied with setting her back on the pedestal he had built for her: the idealistic trend of his mind demanded that he should convince himself that she had never slipped from it. To have parted with the romantic vision he had himself created would have been so repugnant to him that the instant his vexation had abated, which it very swiftly did, he had set himself to prove to his own satisfaction that not her judgment but his had been faulty. It was impossible that the lady of his dreams could err. What had seemed to him intractability was constancy of purpose; her flouting of convention sprang from loftiness of mind; the levity, which had more than once shocked him, was a social mask concealing more serious thoughts. Even her flashes of impatience, and the dagger-look he had twice seen in her eyes, could be excused. Neither rose from any fault of temper: the one was merely the sign of nerves disordered by the shock of her father's death; the other had been provoked by his own unwarrantable interference.

Not every difference that existed between imagination and reality could be explained away. The Major's character was responsible; he had been an excellent regimental officer, steady in command, always careful of the welfare of his men, and ready to help junior officers seeking his advice in any of the private difficulties besetting young gentlemen fresh from school. His instinct was to serve and to protect, and it could not be other than disconcerting to him to find that the one being above all others whom he wished to guide, comfort, serve, and protect showed as little disposition to lean on him as to confide her anxieties to him. So far from seeking guidance, she was much more prone to impose her will upon her entire entourage. She was as accustomed to command as he, and, from having been motherless from an early age, she had acquired an unusual degree of independence. This, joined as it was to a deep-seated reserve, made the very thought of disclosing grief to another repellent to her. When she felt most she was at her most flippant; any attempt to lavish sympathy upon her made her stiffen, and interpose the shield of her raillery. As for needing protection, it was her boast that she was very well able to take care of herself; and when it came to serving her the chances were that she would say, gratefully, but with decision: "Thank you! You are a great deal too good to me – but, you know, I always like to attend to such things myself!"

He had not known it. Fanny, understanding his perplexity, tried to explain Serena to him. "Serena has so much strength of mind, Major Kirkby," she said gently. "I think her mind is as strong as her body, and that is very strong indeed. It used to amaze me that I never saw her exhausted by all the things she would do, for it is quite otherwise with me. But nothing is too much for her! It was the same with Lord Spenborough. Not the hardest day's hunting ever made them anything but sleepy, and excessively hungry; and in London I have often marvelled how they could contrive not to be in the least tired by all the parties, and the noise, and the expeditions." She smiled, and said apologetically: "I don't know how it is, but if I am obliged to give a breakfast, perhaps, and to attend a ball as well, there is nothing for it but for me to rest all the afternoon."

He looked as if he did not wonder at it. "But not Serena?" he asked.

"Oh, no! She never rests during the daytime. That is what makes it so particularly irksome to her to be leading this dawdling life. In London, she would ride in the Park before breakfast, and perhaps do some shopping as well. Then, very often we might give a breakfast, or attend one in the house of one of Lord Spenborough's numerous acquaintances. Then there would be visits to pay, and perhaps a race-meeting, or a picnic, or some such thing. And, in general, a dinner-party in the evening, or the theatre, and three or four balls or assemblies to go to afterwards."

"Was this your life?" he asked, rather appalled.

"Oh, no! I can't keep it up, you see. I did try very hard to grow accustomed to it, because it was my duty to go with Serena, you know. But when she saw how tired I was, and how often I had the headache, she declared she would not drag me out, or permit my lord to do so either. You can have no notion how kind she has been to me, Major Kirkby! My best, my dearest friend!"

Her eyes filled with tears; he slightly pressed her hand, saying in a moved tone: "*That* I could not doubt!"

"She has a heart of gold!" she told him earnestly. "If you knew what care she takes of me, how patient she is with me, you would be astonished!"

"Indeed, I should not!" he said, smiling. "I cannot conceive of anyone's being out of patience with you!"

"Oh, yes!" she assured him. "Mama and my sisters were often so, for I am quite the stupidest of my family, besides being shy of strange persons, and not liking excessively to go to parties, and a great many other nonsensical things. But Serena, who does everything so well, was never vexed with me! Major Kirkby, if it had not been for her I don't know what I should have done!"

He could readily believe that to such a child as she must have been at the time of her marriage, life in the great Spenborough household must have been bewildering and alarming. He said sympathetically: "Was it very bad?"

Her reply was involuntary. "Oh, if I had not had Serena I could not have borne it!" The colour rushed up into her face; she said quickly: "I mean – I mean – having to entertain so many people – talk to them – be the mistress of that huge house! The political parties, too! They were the worst, for I have not the least understanding of politics, and if Serena had not taken care to tell me what was likely to be talked about at dinner I must have been all at sea! The dreadful way, too, the people of the highest *ton* have of always being related to one another, so that one is for ever getting into a scrape!"

He could not help laughing, but he said: "I know exactly what you mean!"

"Yes, but, you see, Serena used to explain everybody to me, and so I was able to go on quite prosperously. And it was she who managed everything.

She had always done so." She paused, and then said diffidently: "When – when perhaps you might sometimes think her wilful, or – or overconfident, you must remember that she has been the mistress of her papa's houses, and his hostess, and that he relied on her to attend to all the things which, in general, an unmarried lady knows nothing about."

"Yes," he said heavily. "He must have been a strange man!" He caught himself up. "I beg pardon! I should not say that to you!"

"Well, I don't think he was just in the common way," she agreed. "He was very goodnatured, and easy-going, and so kind that it was no wonder everyone liked him. He was quite as kind to me as Serena, you know."

"Oh! Yes, of – I mean, I'm sure he must have been!" he stammered, considerably taken aback.

She went on with her stitchery, in sweet unconsciousness of having said anything to make him think her marriage deplorable. She would have been very much shocked could she have read his mind; quite horrified had she guessed the effect on him of what she had told him of Serena's life and character. Her words bore out too clearly much that he had begun to realize; and with increasing anxiety he wondered whether Serena could ever be content with the life he had to offer her. But when he spoke of this to her, she looked surprised, and said: "Bored? Dear Hector, what absurdity is in your head now? Depend upon it, I shall find plenty to do in Kent!"

An item of news in the *Courier* made her ask him one day if he had ever had any thoughts of standing for election to Parliament. He assured her that he had not, but before he well knew where he was she was discussing the matter, making plans, sketching a possible career, and reckoning up the various interests at her command. In laughing dismay, he interrupted her, to say: "But I should dislike it of all things!"

He was relieved to find that she was not, apparently, disappointed, for he had had the sensation of being swept irresistibly down a path of her choosing. "Would you? Really? Then, of course, you won't stand," she said cheerfully.

When she talked of her life while he had been in the Peninsula, he was often reminded of Fanny's words: Serena seemed to be related to so many people. "Some sort of a fifth cousin of mine," she would say, until it seemed to him that England must be littered with her cousins. He quizzed her about it once, and she replied perfectly seriously: "Yes, and what a dead bore it is! One has to remember to write on anniversaries, and to ask them to dine, and some of them, I assure you, are the most shocking figures! Only wait until I introduce you to my cousin Speen! Fanny will tell you she sat, *bouche béante*, the first time she ever saw him, at one of our turtle-dinners! He arrived drunk, which, however, he was aware of, and begged her to pardon, informing her as a great secret that he was a jerry-sneak – which the world knows! – and might never be decently bosky when my lady was at home, so that he had determined while she was away never to be less than well to live!"

"An *odious* little man!" said Fanny, with a shudder. "For shame, Serena! As though you had not better relations than Speen!"

"True! If Hector should not be cast into transports by Speen, I shall take him to stay at Osmansthorpe!" Serena said mischievously. "Have you a taste for the ceremonious, my love? *There*, his lordship lives *en prince*, and since his disposition is morose and his opinion of his own importance immense, the dinner-table is enlivened only by such conversations as he chooses to inaugurate. The groom of the chambers will warn you before you leave your room, however, what subject his lordship wishes to hear discussed."

"Serena!" expostulated Fanny. "Don't heed her, Major Kirkby! It is very formal and dull at Osmansthorpe, but not as bad as that!"

"If it is *half* as bad as that, I would infinitely prefer to make the acquaintance of Cousin Speen!" he retorted. "Must we really set out on a series of visits to all your relations, Serena?"

"By no means!" she answered promptly. "Order me to set them all at a distance, and you will be astonished to see with what a good grace I shall obey you! I should not care a button if I never saw most of them again."

He laughed, but at the back of his mind lurked the fear that these people, deplorable or dull, formed an integral part of the only life she understood, or, perhaps, could be happy in. When he called in Laura Place one day, expecting to find her fretting at the rain, which had been falling steadily since dawn, and discovered her instead to be revelling in a scandalous novel, the conviction grew on him that the placid existence he had planned for them both would never satisfy her.

She gave him her hand, and one of her enchanting smiles, but said: "Don't expect to hear a word from my lips, love! I have here the most diverting book that ever was written! Have you seen it? The chief characters in it are for the most part easily recognizable, and it is no great task to guess at the identities of the rest. I have not laughed so much for weeks!"

He picked up one of the small, gilt-edged volumes. "What is it? *Glenarvon* – and by an anonymous writer. Is it so excellent?"

"Good God, no! It is the most absurd farrago of nonsense! But I prophesy it will run through a dozen editions, because none of us will be able to resist searching either for ourselves or our acquaintance in it. Could you have believed it? – Lady Caroline Lamb is the author? The Lambs are all in it, and Lady Holland – very well hit off, I imagine, from all I have ever heard of her, but Papa disliked that set, so that I was never at Holland House – and Lady Oxford, and Lady Jersey, and poor Mr Rogers, whom she calls a yellow hyena! I must say, I think it unjust, don't you? Glenarvon, of course, is Byron, and the whole thing is designed as a sort of vengeance on him for having cried off from his *affaire* with her."

"Good God!" he exclaimed. "She must be mad to have done such a thing!"

"I think she is, poor soul! Never more so than when she tumbled head over ears in love with Byron! For my part, I was so unfashionable as to take him in instant aversion. How she could have borne with his insufferable conceit, and the airs he put on to be interesting, I know not – though I daresay if one could bear that dreadful Lamb laugh nothing would daunt one! Not but what I am extremely sorry for William Lamb, laugh as he may! If it is true that he stands by her, I do most sincerely honour him. I fancy she meant to portray him in a kindly way, but some of the things she writes of him may well make him writhe. She is so very obliging as to favour the world with what one can only take to be a description of her own honeymoon – so *warm* as to make poor Fanny blush to the ears! It can't be *pleasant* for William Lamb, but it won't harm him. For she portrays herself, in the character of Calantha, as an innocent child quite dazzled by the world, quite ignorant, wholly trusting in the virtue of every soul she met! Pretty well for a girl brought up in Devonshire House!"

"It sounds to be unedifying, to say the least of it," the Major said. "Do you like such stuff?"

"It is the horridest book imaginable!" Fanny broke in. "And although I never did more than exchange bows with Lord Byron, I am persuaded he never murdered a poor little baby in his life! As for Clara St. Everarde, who followed Glenarvon about, dressed as a page, if *she* is a real person too, and did anything so *grossly* improper, I think it a very good thing she rode over a cliff into the sea – though I am excessively sorry for the horse!"

"Observe!" said Serena, much entertained. "It is the horridest book imaginable – but she has read all three volumes!"

"Only because you would keep asking me if I did not think Lady Augusta must be meant for Lady Cahir (and I'm sure I don't know!) and laughing so much that I was bound to continue, only to see what amused you so!"

The Major, who had been glancing through the volume he held, laid it down distastefully. "I think you have wasted your money, Serena."

"Oh, I did not! Rotherham sent it to me in a parcel by the mail! I never thought to be so much obliged to him! He says nothing else is being talked of in town, which I can well believe."

"*Rotherham* sent it to you?" he ejaculated, as much astonished as displeased.

"Yes, why not? Oh, are you vexed because he has written me a letter?" Serena rallied him. "You need not be! Not the most jealous lover, which I hope you are not, could take exception to this single sheet! He is the worst of letterwriters, for this is all he can find to say to me: *My dear Serena, In case it has not come in your way I send you Lady C. Lamb's latest attempt to set Society by the ears. She succeeds* à merveille. *Nothing else is talked of. The Lambs hoped to be rid of her at last, but W. Lamb stands firm. By the by, if Glenarvon's final letter in this singular effusion is a copy of the original, you will agree I am eclipsed in incivility. I have some thoughts of visiting Claycross, and may possibly come to Bath next week. Yours, etc. Rotherham.* You will agree that there is nothing to rouse your ire in *that*!" Serena said, tossing the letter on to the table. "Except," she added thoughtfully, "that I had as lief he did not come to Bath. He would be bound to discover our secret, my love, and if he should be in one of his disagreeable fits there's no saying how awkward he might not choose to make it for us. I'll fob him off."

"I could wish that you would not!" he replied. "For my part, I would choose to admit him into our confidence, if only that I might have the right to inform him that *I* am *not* very much obliged to him for sending you a novel which you describe as 'rather warm'!"

"Good God, if that is the humour you are in, I will most certainly fob him off!" she cried. "How can you be so absurd, Hector? Do you believe *me* to be an innocent Calantha? Rotherham knows better!"

"*What?*" he demanded sharply.

"No, no, pray -!" Fanny interposed, in an imploring tone. "Major Kirkby, you quite mistake – Serena, consider what you say, dearest! Indeed, your vivacity carries you too far!"

"Very likely! But it will be well if Hector learns not to place the worst construction upon what I say!" Serena retorted, her colour considerably heightened.

He said quickly: "I beg your pardon! I did not mean – Good God, how could I possibly -? If you were *not* an innocent Calantha, as you put it – now, don't eat me! – I am persuaded you would feel as strongly as I do the impropriety of *anyone's* sending you such a book to read! Throw it away, and let us forget it! You cannot like to see your friends libelled, surely!"

"Now, this goes beyond the bounds of what may be tolerated!" declared Serena, between vexation and amusement. "*My* friends? The Melbourne House set! Do you take me for a *Whig*? Oh, I was never so insulted! I don't know what you deserve I should do to you!"

A playful rejoinder would have restored harmony, but the Major's strong sense of propriety had been too much offended for him to make it. He took her up in all seriousness, endeavouring to make her enter into his sentiments. She grew impatient, thinking him prudish, and only the entrance of Lybster, bringing in the letters which had been fetched from the receiving-office, averted a lively quarrel. Serena broke off short, saying coolly: "Ah! Now, if my aunt has written to me, Fanny, we may learn whether Lord Poulett marries Lady Smith Burgess, or whether it was nothing but an *on-dit*! Good gracious! Between us, we have seven letters, no less!" She handed several of them to Fanny, and glanced at the superscriptions on her own. A gleam of mischief shot into her eyes; she cast a provocative glance at the Major. "I can guess the subject of most of *my* correspondence! It will be as well if I don't break the wafers until you are gone, I daresay! You will not object, however, to my seeing what my aunt has to say. A great deal, apparently: I'm glad she was able to get a frank, for I should have been ruined else!"

He made no reply, but walked away to the window, looking very much displeased. Suddenly Serena uttered a little crow of laughter. "Oh, Hector, you are utterly confounded! No, no, don't look so stiff! It is the funniest thing! My aunt writes to tell me that *she* is sending me *Glenarvon*! She says I shall be *aux anges* over it!"

It was too absurd. In spite of himself, he laughed. She stretched out her hand to him, smiling, and he kissed it, muttering: "Forgive me!"

Her fingers pressed his. "Oh, fudge! Such a foolish *tracasserie* as it was! Now, let us see what my aunt has to say to me! Lady Cowper looking hagged and frightened: I don't wonder at it, and shall shed no tears! I believe she has been Lady Caroline's enemy from the start, and think her a false, malicious woman behind those smiles and protestations of hers. Oh, she has been so obliging as to send me a key to the book! Fanny, she thinks Lady Morganet is not wholly a portrait of Lady Bessborough, but has a good deal of the Duchess of Devonshire mixed in it. Well! if one puts one's husband in a novel, I suppose it would be over-nice to exclude one's mama and one's aunt – even if the aunt be dead, and unable to protest!" Her eye ran down the closely written sheets; she gave a gurgle, but folded the letter, and laid it aside. "The rest is mere town-gossip, and will keep. Hector, where is Stanton-drew? I am told I should not neglect to visit it. Druidical monuments, or some such thing. If I engage to sit primly beside Fanny in the barouche, will you escort us?"

He agreed very readily, promised to discover the exact whereabouts of the place, and soon after took his leave. Serena said, as soon as he had left the house: "I would not read you the rest of my aunt's letter while Hector was with us, for he is unacquainted with the people she writes of, and I daresay it would have bored him excessively. My dear, where *did* he learn his antiquated notions? From his mother, I should judge – the very picture of provincial respectability! Poor woman! I pity her – but not more than she pities herself, I fancy! It must be a trial to have such a *volage* creature as I am foisted upon her!"

Fanny, her tender heart wrung by the difficulties she clearly perceived to lie in the Major's path, said: "Indeed, Serena, you did not behave as you ought! I could not but think that his feelings upon this occasion did him honour!"

"Could you not?" Serena said, surprised. "I thought they showed him to be imbued with some pretty Gothic notions! But never mind that! My aunt writes me an enchanting description of the Laleham-woman's progress – or regress! I don't know which it may be! Only listen!" She picked up Lady Theresa's letter, and read aloud: *"It is now impossible to avoid meeting that Laleham-Creature, who is everywhere to be seen. You would have been diverted to have been a spectator of the comedy enacted last week at Mrs Egerton's party. The Creature was there, with Miss Laleham – who, though well enough, is not, in my opinion, pretty* au fait de beauté *and in high croak. The D. of Devonshire coming in, she took care to place herself in his way, claiming to have made his acquaintance at the Salmesburys' Cotillion-ball, and overwhelming him with simpering civilities. But he, not hearing a word, as you may suppose, favoured her with no more than a bow, and some indifferent response, and passed on. She was obliged to fall back upon a mere Marquis – Rotherham, who was so complaisant as to remain by her for some ten minutes, and to take notice of Miss Laleham. His attention then being claimed by Mrs Martindale, the descent of the Creature down the social ladder was rapid, not a single Earl being present, and the only Viscount Lord Castlereagh, whom she did not attempt,* pour cause. *A handful of paltry barons, all of them married, reduced her to the level of an Esquire, after which, she retired, I must suppose, disconsolate.* A propos, *Cordelia Monksleigh is thrown into rage by the Creature's having dropped her, she says, because her usefulness ended with her procuring for the Creature the invitation-card to the Rotherham ball; but I suspect the cause is farther to seek, Master Gerard having become vastly* épris *during the Easter vacation. Reason enough!* That *connection would by no means suit the Creature's ambition, nor Cordelia's either, if she had but the wit to perceive it."* Serena lowered the sheet. "You will own that my aunt, whatever may be her faults, is the most entertaining correspondent, Fanny! What would I not have given to have been at that party -! You know, if the Laleham-woman should have written to Mrs Floore, boasting of her friendship with Devonshire, I doubt if I shall be able to convince the dear old lady that although his Grace may be as deaf as a post, he is neither cross-eyed nor an octogenarian! As for attempting to persuade her that the Creature might as well lay siege to one of the Royal Dukes as to him, or to Rotherham, for that matter, I shall not do it! It would be too unkind! She believes there does not exist a man who would not fall instantly in love with Emily! Would you not have liked to have seen Rotherham caught in the toils? I think it no more than his just desert, for having attended that Quenbury Assembly!"

Fanny assented to it, but absently. Serena put up the letter, saying: "I must think of some way of stopping Rotherham's projected visit to us. A pity! After the insipidities of Bath, his caustic tongue would come as a relief. However, in the mood Hector is in, it will not do. I shall be obliged to write an excuse so thin as to put him in a passion."

She went away, not perceiving the expression of startled reproach in Fanny's face. What, in fact, she wrote to Rotherham she did not disclose; but a few days later she received a brief note from him, read it with raised brows, and said: "Well! I have succeeded in my object. Rotherham does not come."

Fanny could almost have believed her to be disappointed. The note was torn up, and Serena began to talk of something else.

Fanny herself was profoundly relieved. If Rotherham should dislike the match, as she feared he would, he would not scruple, she thought, to treat the Major with wounding contempt. Her imagination quailed at the scene; she felt that she could almost have interposed her own shrinking person between the Marquis and his prey; and was thankful that for the present, at any rate, this deed of heroism would not be necessary. She did not know that Fate had another trial in store for her. Her father arrived in Bath, without invitation or advertisement.

He was ushered into the drawing-room in Laura Place when, as ill-luck would have it, Major Kirkby was with her. She was not precisely discomposed, but she was certainly startled, and jumped up with a cry of: "Papa!"

He embraced her kindly enough, but his countenance was severe, and the glance he cast at the Major repulsive.

"Papa, I had no notion I was to have this pleasure! Oh, is there something amiss at home? Mama? My sisters?"

"All perfectly stout!" he replied. "I have been spending a few days with my friend, Abberley, at Cheltenham, and while I was in the west I thought I would come to see how you go on."

"How very much obliged to you I am! Very comfortably, I assure you! Oh, I must introduce Major Kirkby! My father, Sir William Claypole, Major!"

The Major bowed; Sir William nodded, in no very encouraging style, saying briefly: "How d'ye do?"

"The Major," said Fanny perseveringly, "has spent some years in the Peninsula, Papa. Only fancy! He thinks he once met my cousin Harry, when they were both in Lisbon!"

"Ay, did you so? Very likely! Are you on furlough, sir?"

"I've sold out, sir."

This information appeared to displease Sir William. He said: "Ha!" and turned to ask Fanny how she liked her situation in Laura Place. She was distressed by his evident dislike of her visitor, and could not forbear looking at the Major, to see whether he was as much offended as she feared he must be. She encountered such a rueful smile, so much amused understanding in his eyes, that she was at once reassured and embarrassed. Within a few minutes, he recollected an engagement, and took his leave, saying in an undervoice, as she gave him her hand: "It will be better if I don't ride with Serena tomorrow."

He went away, and she turned to face her father. He broke in immediately upon her enquiries after the other members of her family. "Fanny, how is this? I promise you I thought the whole tale a Banbury story, but, upon my soul, what do I find but that fellow closeted with you!"

"The whole tale?" she repeated. "What tale, if you please?"

"Why, that there is some half-pay officer dangling after you, and making you the talk of the town!"

"It is untrue!"

"Very well, very well, it appears he has sold out, but that's mere quibbling!" he said testily.

"He is not dangling after me."

The quiet dignity of her tone seemed to strike him. She had, indeed, never looked more the great lady. He said, in a milder voice: "Well, I am happy to receive your assurance on that head, my dear, but I did not expect to find you entertaining a young man tête-à-tête."

"Papa, I think you must forget my condition! I am not a girl! If my widowhood -"

"The fact is, my dear, your widowhood is no protection!" he interrupted bluntly. "I don't say, if you were older – But you're little more than a child, and a deal too pretty to rely upon that cap you wear to save you from having advances made to you! I knew how it would be, the instant you informed us you were removing to Bath!"

"Pray, Papa, will you tell me, if you please, who has had the monstrous impertinence to tell such stories about me?"

"I had it from that old fool, Dorrington, and you may suppose I did not enquire who might be his informant. I daresay he may have friends in Bath. I gave him a pretty sharp set-down, and let him see I did not relish his style of humour."

"Oh, how right Serena is!" she cried, pressing her hands to her hot cheeks. "Of all the odious people in the world there can be none so detestable as the Bath quizzes! I wonder you have not been told that General Hendy is dangling after me!

"What, is he staying here? Well, he always had an eye for a pretty female, but as for dangling after you – Good God, Fanny, he must be sixty if he's a day! It's a different matter, my dear, when a young jackanapes like this Major Kirkby of yours throws out lures! Now, don't put yourself in a fuss! I daresay there's no harm done but what may be put right very easily. I told Mama that if you had been indiscreet it must have been all in innocence. The thing is it won't do for you to be living here with no better chaperon than Lady Serena. We must decide what is best to be done."

In the greatest dismay, she stammered: "Papa, you are quite, quite mistaken! Major Kirkby does not come here to see me!"

He gave a low whistle. "You don't mean to tell me Lady Serena is the object of his gallantry?" She nodded. "Well! So it *was* true! Neither your mama nor I would credit it! I should have thought the young lady too high in the instep to have encouraged the attentions of a mere nobody! She must be the most outrageous flirt!"

"Oh, no, no!" she uttered, almost extinguished.

"Well, I won't argue with you, but I can tell you this, Fanny, if she should get into a scrape you will be blamed for it!"

"Who told you *this* story?" she asked faintly.

"Your Aunt Charlotte had it in a letter from Mrs Holroyd, and told your mama. *She* said your Major was for ever in Laura Place, and careering all over the countryside with Lady Serena besides. I need not tell you that was coming a bit too strong for me, my dear! It made your mama and me disbelieve the whole."

Fanny sat limply down, and covered her face with her hands. "Oh, how careless I have been! I should not have allowed – I should have gone with them!"

Sir William regarded her in the liveliest consternation. "You don't mean to tell me it's true? Upon my word, Fanny!"

"No, no, it is not what you think! Papa, you must not spread it about – Serena does not wish it to be known while she is in mourning – but they are *engaged*!"

"What?" he demanded. "Lady Serena engaged to a Major Kirkby?"

"Yes!" she said, and, for no very apparent reason, burst into tears.

CHAPTER TWELVE

BEYOND SAYING: "Well, well, there is nothing for you to cry about, my dear!" Sir William paid very little heed to Fanny's sudden spring of tears. Women, in his view, were always bursting into tears for no reason comprehensible to the sterner sex. He was very much taken aback by the news she had confided to him, and, at first, inclined to dislike it almost as much as he would have disliked the news of her own engagement. But Fanny, quickly wiping her eyes, soon contrived to talk him out of his disapproval. He was not much impressed by the touching picture she painted of a seven-year attachment. "Very fine talking!" he said. "It may be so with *him*, though I take leave to doubt it! He may *think* he never fancied another female, but all I can say, if he found no little love-bird to entertain him in seven years, is that he must be a nincompoop! No, no, my dear, that's doing it too brown! As for Lady Serena, all this constancy didn't prevent her from becoming engaged to Rotherham! But what you tell me of his having come into property puts a different complexion on the matter. Not that I think the Carlows will take kindly to the match, but that's no concern of mine!"

Guiltily aware of having conveyed to him the impression that the Major's estate was extensive, and his fortune handsome, Fanny devoutly trusted that he would not question her too closely on the subject. He did ask her in what part of the country the estate was situated, but the timely entrance of Lybster, with wine and glasses on a large silver tray, made it unnecessary for her to say more than: "In Kent, Papa." His attention was drawn off; he poured himself a glass of sherry; was agreeably surprised at its quality; and for some minutes was more interested to learn where it had been procured than in the size or whereabouts of the Major's property.

By the time Lybster, after discussing with Sir William the respective merits of Bristol Milk, Oloroso, and Manzanilla, had departed, Sir William had refilled his glass, and was feeling in charity with the world. He told his daughter that she had a good butler; bored her very much by recalling how in his youth Mountain-Malaga had been much drunk; what he had paid for a tun in the '80s; how one was rarely offered it in these degenerate days; and at last came back to the subject of Serena's engagement. The more he thought of it the more he liked it, for if Serena were to be married before the end of the year the way would be clear for Agnes to pay her sister a prolonged visit. "That is to say, if she doesn't go off this Season, and although your mama is making every effort I need not scruple to tell you, my dear, that I entertain very few hopes. She does not take. It's a pity you cannot give her a little of your beauty! Though to my mind handsome is as handsome does, and a spoonful of honey on her tongue would get her a respectable husband sooner than a bushel of strawberries squashed on her face. Yes, Mama is determined to clear her complexion, and they say strawberries will do the trick. I hope they may, but so far it seems to me a great waste of good fruit. Kitty, now, is another thing. You would be surprised at the improvement in her since you saw her last! She is not unlike what you were at her age, and should go off easily, Mama thinks."

He continued in this strain for some minutes, so well-pleased with his scheme for foisting an unmarriageable sister on to Fanny that her marked absence of enthusiasm quite escaped his notice. Over his third glass of sherry he once more returned to Serena's engagement, but this time it was to warn Fanny against allowing the Major to be too particular in his attentions. "It won't do to set tongues wagging, if the engagement is not to be announced until the autumn," he said. "Ten to one, it will come to the ears of her family that *one* man is dancing attendance on her. If I were you, Fanny, I would relax a trifle: permit people to call, you know! It is more than six months now since Spenborough died, and although I should not wish you to be leaving off your mourning, or going to public parties, I think there could be no impropriety in your entertaining – quite quietly, of course! – select company in your own house. A card-party, perhaps, or a dinner or two. No doubt there are plenty of other gentlemen in Bath who would be happy to be given the opportunity of dancing attendance on your daughter-in-law, for she's a fine-looking girl, and an heiress besides. I suppose there's no fear of Rotherham's thrusting a spoke into the wheel?"

"We do not know how he will like it, Papa, but he has no power to prevent it."

"No power! I should call the strings of the purse power enough!"

"Neither Serena nor Major Kirkby would do so, however."

"More fools they! But it's not my business, after all. What I am concerned with is that there shan't be any more gossip about it, for that must draw *you* in, my dear. A good thing if the young man were to remove from Bath, but I suppose there's no chance of his doing that. The next best thing is to render him less conspicuous, and that you may achieve by allowing others to visit you."

"If you think it right, Papa," she said obediently. "I own, it would be agreeable if I might go out a little sometimes, and it was on that subject that I was talking to Major Kirkby when you arrived. You must know that the Masters of Ceremonies here have been most civil to us, and in particular have frequently been begging us to go to lectures or concerts. It so happens that there is to be a concert at the Lower Rooms which I should very much like to hear. Mr Guynette came to tell me of it yesterday, and to promise, if we would go, that we should have seats in a retired place. Do you think we might? Major Kirkby sees no harm in it, and if he does not I feel there can be none."

"None at all," replied Sir William. "A concert is not the same thing as a ball, you know. But if the Major means to escort you, take along some other gentleman as well! I dare say you are acquainted with some?"

"Oh, yes!" Fanny said, rather doubtfully.

"You could invite old Hendy!" said Sir William, laughing heartily.

"Yes – except that I don't think he likes the Major very much," said Fanny.

"Jealous of him, no doubt! Thinks he will be cut out by a fine, upstanding young man!" said Sir William, still much amused, and apparently forgetting his earlier and less flattering description of the Major.

If Fanny felt that her father's scheme was not very likely to achieve his object, she did not say so. She was more concerned to know how Serena would receive the news that her secret had been betrayed. But Serena, when she came in pleasantly refreshed by a seven mile walk with a similarly energetic acquaintance, took it in very good part, merely begging Fanny to adjure Sir William not to mention her engagement to anyone but his wife. She came down to dinner looking so handsome in dove-gray with black ribbons that Sir William was quite captivated. Knowing that it would please Fanny, she laid herself out to amuse him, and succeeded so well that when he took up his candle to go to bed he declared he had seldom enjoyed an evening more. In his own home, no one regaled him with lively conversation, or encouraged him to recount anecdotes of his youth. He would not, in fact, have approved of it had any of his daughters talked in the Lady Serena's racy fashion; and he would certainly not have played piquet with them for penny points, for that, win or lose, could have done him no good at all.

So well pleased with his entertainment was he that he decided to remain in Bath for another night. He told Fanny that it would do no harm for the Major to be seen in his company, and said that he would go with both ladies to the Pump Room, and promenade with them there. It did not seem to Fanny that the sight of her father lending his countenance to the Major would be very likely to allay the suspicions of the Pump Room gossips, but having a strong disposition to think anyone's judgment more to be trusted than her own, and being, besides, still a good deal in awe of him, she made no demur. It was by no means certain that the Major would visit the Pump

Room, for ever since the daily rides with Serena had become the rule he had taken care not to go there too often.

But the Major, wishing to discover from Fanny the probable length of Sir William's stay, did visit it, and was considerably taken aback to find himself being shaken warmly by the hand, and greeted in much the same way as he could fancy Sir William greeting a favourite nephew.

And, after all, Fanny perceived, Sir William did not manage so badly. He discovered several acquaintances in the room, and to each one he contrived to convey the impression that Major Kirkby, an old and valued friend, had been devoting himself to Lady Spenborough and her daughter-in-law at his express entreaty. The Major's quickness in following this lead pleased him so much that he began to think him a very good sort of a man, and invited him to dine in Laura Place that evening, and to play a rubber or two of whist afterwards. Fanny, an indifferent cardplayer, was too thankful to have prevailed upon Serena not to introduce her father to Mrs Floore to protest.

At dinner, Sir William continued to be pleased both with the Major and with Fanny's cook, some Spanish fritters earning his special commendation. The port was very tolerable too; and he sat down presently to the card-table in a mood of great good-humour. This, however, did not long endure, for he cut his daughter for partner, and if he was the most skilled of the four players, she was by far the least. The first rubber reduced Fanny almost to tears, so acid and incessant were the criticisms made by her parent of her mistakes. By good fortune, she cut next with the Major, and he smiled at her so reassuringly when she said, with a nervous little laugh, that he was to be pitied, that she quite plucked up courage, and, in consequence, played very much better. Sir William continued to point out her errors to her, but since these were now to his advantage, he did so in a tolerant spirit which did not much discompose her. The Major encouraged her with as much praise as he could, without absurdity, bestow, found ingenious excuses for her blunders, and, when the rubber ended in their defeat, said: "Lady Spenborough, shall we challenge these expert gamesters to a return? Do let us have our revenge on them!"

She was very willing; and as Serena was a skilled player Sir William raised no objection. Serena was so grateful to the Major for shielding Fanny from assault that she gave him both her hands and her lips at parting, a thing that she was not very prone to do, and said warmly: "You are quite the kindest man alive, Hector! *Thank you!*"

Sir William went back to London next day, and his daughter did her best to carry out his instructions to her. Rather to her surprise, Serena approved of them. So a very respectable and correspondingly dull gentleman of their acquaintance was invited to accompany them to the concert; and Fanny wrote careful notes to a number of persons, bidding them to a small evening reception. Life settled down into a slightly more variegated pattern, enlivened by morning visitors, and an occasional party. Several expeditions were made to places of historic interest in the vicinity of Bath, and if the Major rode behind the barouche, so too did some other gentleman. There was no difficulty in finding a suitable fourth to these parties: the only difficulty lay in deciding whose turn it was to be honoured with an invitation. Every unattached gentleman who had cudgelled his brains for weeks to hit upon a way of becoming acquainted with the most beautiful woman in Bath no sooner heard that the bereaved ladies were now receiving visitors than he scoured the town for some common acquaintance who could be persuaded to perform the coveted introduction. One or two lost their hearts to Fanny, but these were in the minority, Serena's admirers far outnumbering them, and behaving with an ardency and a devotion which made Fanny fear that the Major might be hurt. He seemed, however, to be rather amused; and whenever one of her flirts contrived to draw Serena away from her mama-in-law, to show her a very fine view, or to conduct her to the top of a ruined keep, he made no attempt to go after the truants, but walked with Fanny instead, concealing whatever chagrin he might have felt.

Fanny, incapable herself of conducting the sort of light flirtation of which Serena was an accomplished exponent, was distressed, and ventured to remonstrate. But Serena only laughed, and said that she was following out the spirit of Sir William's advice. "The Bath quizzes will *now* say of me that so far from being violently attached to one man I am shockingly *volage*!"

Fanny could only hope that the Major would not share this opinion. She told him once, when she saw Serena positively encouraging the gallantry of young Mr Nantwich, that Serena had a great deal of vivacity. "In her set, you know," she said, trying for an airy note, "that sort of – of liveliness is quite the thing! It doesn't denote the *least* want of delicacy, or – or unsteadiness!"

He glanced down into her perturbed countenance, smiling a little. "I am not jealous, I promise you," he said.

"Oh, no! I am persuaded you could not be!"

His eyes followed Serena and her admirer. "If all these moonstruck swains flatter themselves that she has any other intention than to enjoy a little sport they must be a set of ninnyhammers," he remarked. "I own, it is not a sport I like, but there is no particular harm in it when the lady is as skilled in it as I perceive Serena to be."

She thought that she could detect a note of reserve in his voice, and said something about funning humours and openness of temper. He agreed to this; and she had the happy thought of adding that by dispensing her favours amongst several Serena was throwing sand in the eyes of those who suspected her of a single attachment. That made him laugh. He said: "Lady Spenborough, are you trying to bamboozle me, or has Serena been bamboozling you? She is enjoying herself hugely! Don't look so anxious! Do you care to stroll in the wood? May I give you my arm?"

Her conscience told her that it was her duty to follow Serena, but since to do that would entail bringing the Major once more within sight and hearing of what could not (for all his brave words) but give him pain, she yielded to inclination. Nothing was more comfortable than a walk with Major Kirkby! He moderated his pace to hers, handed her carefully over the smallest obstacle, warned her of damp patches, and always chose a smooth path for her to tread. They were on the cosiest of terms, Fanny having very soon lost her shyness, and the Major discovering in her so sympathetic a listener that before very long he had put her in possession of nearly every detail of his career. In return, she told him all about her home, and her family and how much she dreaded having her sister Agnes sent to live with her. He entered fully into her sentiments upon this; and although she never spoke of Mama except with respect, or mentioned her marriage, it did not take him long to arrive at a pretty fair understanding of why she had accepted the hand of a man old enough to have been her father. His reflections upon this subject he kept to himself.

Nothing occurred to disturb the harmony of these summer days until one morning in June the *Morning Post*, when opened at the only page that interested Fanny, was found to contain a bomb-shell. She had just read aloud to Serena the news of the Princess Charlotte's indisposition, and was about to speculate on the probable nature of the malady, when her eyes alighted on another item of social intelligence. A sharp gasp broke from her, and she cried out impulsively: "Good God! Oh, *no*! Impossible!"

"Well, what now?" enquired Serena, engaged in arranging roses in a bowl.

"Rotherham!" uttered Fanny, in a strangled voice.

Serena turned quickly to look at her. "Rotherham? What has happened to him?" she said sharply. "Is he ill too? Fanny, he's not *dead*?"

"Oh, no, no!" Fanny said. "*Betrothed!*"

"Betrothed!"

"Yes! The most shocking thing! To Emily Laleham!"

"It's not true!"

"It must be, Serena, for here it is, *published*! I don't wonder at your amazement! That poor child! Oh, what a wicked, abominable woman Lady Laleham is! *A marriage has been arranged* – yes, and well do I know who arranged it! – *between Ivo Spencer Barrasford, Marquis of Rotherham, and Emily Mary, eldest daughter of Sir Walter Laleham, Bart* – You see, there *can* be no mistake! Oh, I don't know when I have been more distressed!"

She looked up from the paper to Serena, standing like a stone in the middle of the room, two roses held in her hand, her cheeks perfectly white, and in her eyes an expression of blank horror.

"What have I done?" Serena said, in a queer, hoarse voice. "O God, what have I done?"

"Dearest, *you* are not to blame!" Fanny cried. "He met her in my house, not in yours! Not that I feel I am to blame either, for heaven knows I never invited Lady Laleham to visit me on that fatal day! And from all we hear of the horrid, encroaching way she has been thrusting herself into the highest circles, he must have met her somewhere, even if not in *my* house! Though, to be sure, it would not have been in that style, just seated round the table, as we were, conversing without the least formality. Oh, if I had known what would come of it, I would have been *uncivil* to Lady Laleham rather than have admitted her into the breakfast-parlour!" She saw that Serena was staring at her in a fixed, blank way, and then that a trickle of blood was running down one of her fingers. "Oh, you have scratched your hand with those thorns! Take care you don't smear your gown, dearest!"

Her words seemed to recall Serena to herself. She gave a slight start, and glanced down at her hand. Her fingers unclenched themselves from about the rose-stems; she laid the flowers down, saying quietly: "So I have! How stupid! Pray, Fanny, attend to these! I must go and wash my hands."

She went quickly from the room, and was gone for some time. When she returned, it was with some tale of having been obliged to mend the torn gathers of one of the flounces round the hem of her gown. Fanny, who knew that she never set a stitch, might, had her mind not been taken up with the news of Rotherham's engagement, have felt considerable surprise at this unprecedented happening. As it was, she merely said absently: "How vexing! Have you sent your woman out? You know, Serena, the more I think of it the more I am convinced Lady Laleham had *this* in mind when she forced herself upon us that day!"

"Very likely. I put nothing beyond her!" Serena said lightly.

"I should never have thought Emily the kind of girl to take his fancy!"

"There is no telling what a man will fancy."

"No, very true! But she is quite as silly as I am, and I thought he held silly females in the greatest contempt! Only think of that impatient, sarcastic way he speaks when one has said something he thinks stupid! He did seem to be amused by the droll things she said, not in the least meaning to be droll, but I thought he was quizzing her, and not very kindly!"

"So did I, but it appears that we were mistaken."

"Yes, indeed! The Quenbury Assembly, too! *That* was why he chose to take his wards to it! But the way he spoke of Emily that very night, when you quarrelled with him about his having stood up only with her – how could he have done so, if he had felt the smallest *tendre* for her? Do you remember his telling us how he could get nothing out of her but Yes, and No, and so had *drawn no more coverts*, but had come to take his leave of us instead?"

"Very clearly. Also my own words on that occasion! I imagine her behaviour must have piqued him, and what began as an idle amusement became a serious pursuit. I daresay he can never before have tossed his handkerchief and not seen it picked up! I admire Emily very much, I did not think she had it in her to bring the odious Marquis so tamely to heel!"

"Oh, Serena, I am sure such a thought was never in her head! She did not like him! Indeed, I believe she was afraid of him! That is what makes this news so particularly dreadful!"

"If he loves her, she will have nothing to fear," Serena said, a slight constriction in her throat.

"If -! I cannot credit it!"

"Whatever else you cannot credit, that at least is sure!" Serena said. "No other reason can possibly exist for his having asked her to marry him! She has nothing to recommend her, neither birth nor fortune, but a pretty face and the artlessness of a kitten!"

"Then he is infatuated, which is worse than all, for you may depend upon it he will soon recover from that, and grow bored with her, and make her miserable!"

"You take a gloomy view of her prospects!"

"Yes, for I know what a harsh temper he has, and how unfeeling he is, besides being proud and overbearing! And I know she has been forced into this by her hateful mother!"

Serena shrugged her shoulders. "Why put yourself in this passion, my dear? It is no concern of yours, after all!"

"Oh, no! But if you knew what it means to a girl to be forced into marriage with a man more than twice her age you would not -" She stopped, aghast at her own words. The colour flooded her cheeks; she looked stricken and blurted out "I beg your pardon! I didn't mean – I would not for the world – I don't know how I came to say such a thing!"

"There is no need to beg my pardon. I always thought it atrocious, and sincerely pitied you."

"No, no, don't say so! Your papa – no one could have been kinder – more considerate! You mustn't think that I meant to compare him for one moment with Rotherham!"

"I don't. There, Fanny, don't cry! It is all very sad, but there's no use in becoming agitated over it. We have nothing to do with Emily's troubles."

Fanny dried her tears, but said: "I didn't think you could be so unfeeling! It ought to be stopped!"

"Stopped! No, that it cannot be!" Serena said. "Put that out of your head, Fanny! It has been announced, and must go forward!"

She spoke so sternly that Fanny was quite startled. "But, Serena, *you* did not think so!" she could not help saying.

"No! I did not, and so the more reason this engagement should not be broken! It will not be: we may trust the Laleham-woman for that!" She paused, and then said: "Well! I must not delay to send him my felicitations. It had better be done immediately, in fact."

"Serena, if I ought to do the same, I am sorry, but nothing would prevail upon me to felicitate either of them on an event of which I most deeply disapprove!" Fanny said, with unwonted vehemence.

Serena had already seated herself at the writing table, and spoke without turning her head. "Unnecessary! I will say on your behalf everything that is proper to the occasion."

"I wish very much that you would not!" Fanny said.

No answer was vouchsafed to this decidedly pettish remark, but after a moment Serena said: "After all, it turns out very well for *me*! No moment than this could be better for the announcement *I* have to make! He will be much too absorbed in his own affairs to cavil at *my* engagement."

"Yes, indeed!" Fanny said, brightening a little.

Silence fell, broken only by the scratch of Serena's quill. Fanny, seated in the window, and leaning her chin in her hand, remained lost in melancholy thought until her attention was attracted by the sight of an old-fashioned landaulette drawing up immediately beneath the window. The next instant she uttered a sharp exclamation. "Serena! Mrs Floore! She must be coming to tell you the news! Good gracious, what a figure she is, in that hat! My love, some gentleman is handing her out, and I vow and declare to you the carriage is within an ace of tipping over under her weight! Quick! shall I tell Lybster to say we are gone out?"

"Certainly not! Why should you?" replied Serena shaking the sand from her letter, and pulling open the little drawer in which Fanny kept her wafers.

"Oh, I don't know, but I wish she had not come here! I shall not know what to say to her!"

"Nonsense! You will say all that is proper."

"Perhaps she will not be able to mount the stairs!" said Fanny, with a nervous giggle.

But although the performance of this feat took time it proved to be not beyond Mrs Floore's powers. With the aid of the baluster-rail and Mr Goring's stalwart arm she arrived, panting but triumphant, on the first floor, and paused to take breath. Observing that Lybster was about to throw open the door into the drawing-room, she stopped him by the simple expedient of grasping his sleeve. Affronted, he gazed at her with much hauteur, and said in freezing accents: "Madam!"

"Looby!" enunciated Mrs Floore, between gasps. "You wait! Trying to push me in – like a landed salmon!"

"One moment, if you please!" said Mr Goring, quite unperturbed either by his old friend's unconventional behaviour or by the butler's evident disgust. He removed the fan from Mrs Floore's clutch, and opened it, and began to ply it briskly.

"Thank you, Ned!" she said presently. "Lord, how the heat does draw one out!"

Concluding that she now felt ready to meet her hostess, Lybster opened the door, and announced in the voice of one refraining from comment: "Mrs Floore, Mr Goring, my lady!"

Fanny came forward, with her hand out. "How do you do? I am so glad you have come to visit us, ma'am: pray, will you not be seated? Lybster, some wine, if you please!"

He bowed, and withdrew; but as his gait was stately he was not gone from the room in time to escape hearing Mrs Floore say gratefully: "Bless your sweet face! Your butler was all for having me believe he didn't know but what you'd stepped out, for which I'm sure I don't blame him, but, 'Lord,' I said, 'you've no need to be scared! Her ladyship will see me fast enough, take my word for it!' Which he did, so here I am. And I brought Mr Goring along with me, just in case I should be overcome by the heat, which is a thing that happened to me once, right in the middle of the South Parade, and caused as much excitement as if a circus had come to town. Ned! Make your bow to Lady Spenborough! "

Mr Goring, who had been shaking hands with Serena, showed no signs of resenting this peremptory command, but turned to greet his hostess. She made him politely welcome, but had scarcely time to offer him her hand before Mrs Floore was again claiming her attention.

"If you've seen the newspapers this morning, my lady, you won't wonder what brings me here!"

"No, indeed: most – most interesting news, ma'am! You must be excessively pleased, I am sure!"

"Well," said Mrs Floore, "I don't deny it's a fine thing to be marrying a Marquis, for I daresay they don't grow on every tree, and a very odd sort of a woman I'd be if I didn't feel puffed-up enough at this moment to burst my staylaces. If Emma likes him, I'm very glad he *is* a Marquis; but if she don't, he might be fifty Marquises, and still I'd say she'd be better off with a plain man she *could* like!"

"We must suppose that she does like him, ma'am," Serena said smiling.

"Begging your pardon, my dear, we don't have to suppose anything of the kind!" said Mrs Floore bluntly. "You know that daughter of mine, and so, I'll be bound, does her ladyship! What poor little Emma might like is the last thing in the world she'd trouble her head about, and that's the truth, small pleasure though it is to me to say such a thing of my own flesh and blood!"

Fortunately, since Fanny knew not what to reply to this forthright speech,

Lybster came back into the room at that moment, so that she was able to create a diversion by supplying her guests with refreshment. Serena said: "No doubt you have had letters from them, ma'am?"

"I've had one from Sukey, my dear, but Emma's not one for writing letters. And if she had written to me I wouldn't know any more than I do now, because it's my belief that Prawle made her learn off by heart a set of letters out of the *Complete Letter-Writer*, and told her never to use any other ones. As for Sukey, naturally she's in high delight! In fact, anyone would think she was in love with this precious Marquis herself, for she gives him such a character that if I credited the half of what she writes I should very likely think he was an Archangel. So, since Ned, who happened to be with me when Roger came in with the newspaper and the letters, couldn't tell me any more about him than that he was a famous sportsman, I made up my mind I'd come straight round to see *you*, Lady Serena, for, 'Mark my words,' I said to Ned, 'her ladyship will know all about him!' And you needn't mind speaking out in front of him, my dear, any more than if he was my son, which I'm sorry to say he isn't! What's more, he's pretty well acquainted with Emma, for he saw a great deal of her when she was staying with me, and went with us to the Assemblies, and the theatre, and such-like."

Serena glanced at Mr Goring, but his countenance gave nothing away.

"Yes, Lord Rotherham is very well known in the world of sport, I believe," Fanny said, in a colourless voice.

Mr Goring raised his eyes from the contemplation of the wine in his glass, and directed a level look at her.

"Well, I don't know that I like the sound of that, to start with!" said Mrs Floore dubiously. "If he's a racing man, that means betting, and I've got one gamester on my hands already, and I don't want another!"

Fanny was too overcome by the thought of Rotherham's being on Mrs Floore's hands to venture on a response. Serena laughed out, and said: "Don't be alarmed, ma'am! Rotherham's fortune is extremely large, and he is a great deal more addicted to boxing, and shooting, and hunting than to gaming!"

"Well, I'm glad to hear you say so, my dear. Not that I hold with boxing, because it's low, and not the sort of thing I should expect a Marquis to be fond of. However, Ned tells me it's quite the established mode amongst the smart beaux, and at all events he won't go dragging Emma into boxing-saloons. But if he thinks to make her go out shooting and hunting with him it won't do at all! Why, she'd be frightened to death!"

"I expect, ma'am, that he must be aware that – she doesn't share his tastes in that direction."

"If he don't know it now he will the very first time he sees her crying her eyes out all because the cat's got hold of a mouse!" said Mrs Floore. She looked piercingly at Serena. "Tell me this, my dear! How old is he?"

"He is thirty-eight," replied Serena calmly.

"Thirty-eight! Lord, that's more than twenty years older than she is!" cried Mrs Floore, aghast.

"True. He is not cross-eyed, however," Serena said, with a faint smile.

"Well, if he isn't, I should like to know how it comes about he wasn't snapped up years ago!" said Mrs Floore tartly. "He isn't queer in his attic, is he?"

"Far from it! His understanding is excellent, and he does not suffer from any infirmity whatsoever."

"Come, that's better!" said Mrs Floore, relieved. "Is he handsome?"

"No. I should rather call him striking, ma'am. Certainly not handsome."

"Do you know him well, my dear?"

Fanny cast an anxious glance at Serena. After a moment's hesitation, Serena replied: "Very well. I have known him all my life."

"There! What did I tell you?" Mrs Floore demanded of her escort. "*I* knew which shop to come to! So now you answer me this, my lady, if you'll be so good, and that I know you are! – Is he the sort of man that'll make my Emma a good husband?"

"Indeed, I hope so, ma'am! He can give her – a great position, wealth, consequence -"

"I know that," interrupted Mrs Floore grimly. "And it ain't what I asked you, my dear!"

Aware that not only Mrs Floore's gaze was fixed upon her but Mr Goring's also, Serena said: "Dear ma'am, you must not question me so closely, if you please! I think you cannot be aware that I was once engaged to Lord Rotherham myself!"

Mr Goring's gaze now became intent; Mrs Floore was so much surprised that she nearly dropped her wineglass. "You?" she gasped. "Lord bless my soul! Goodness gracious! Well, I declare! That's *one* thing Sukey didn't see fit to tell me – if she knows it!"

"The engagement – and its termination – were in all the newspapers, ma'am," Serena replied, her colour heightened.

"Ay, they would be," nodded Mrs Floore. "It's a lesson to me to read the Court page, which I don't mind telling you I'm not in the habit of doing. Well, I'm sure I beg your pardon, my dear – not but what if I *had* known of it I'd still have asked you for your opinion of the gentleman, though I wouldn't have done so but in private. Certainly not with Ned Goring sitting in the room, as I hope you'll believe!"

"I don't see that my being in the room makes any difference at all," said Mr Goring unexpectedly. "I'll go away, if you like, but, whether I go or whether I stay, don't ask her ladyship any more questions, ma'am!"

"Thank you!" Serena said, smiling at him. "But it is very natural that Mrs Floore should wish to know why I cried off from the engagement. It was for no reason, ma'am, that precludes him from making some other female a perfectly respectable husband. The truth is that we found we did not suit. Our dispositions were too alike. Each of us, in fact, is autocratic, and neither of us has the sweetest of tempers. But a gentler woman than I am would not provoke Rotherham as I did, and might, I daresay, be very content to be his wife."

"Yes, and I daresay this carpet is content to be trodden on!" retorted Mrs Floore. "A man should be master in his own house: I've got nothing to say against that, as long as he don't interfere in what's no business of his! But if I find this Marquis don't know the difference between master and tyrant, not one penny will I settle on Emma, and we'll see what he and Sukey have to say to *that*!"

"I'm afraid, ma'am, that Emily's fortune is a matter of indifference to him."

"Oh, it is, is it? Well, if Emily's been pushed into this against her will, I'll go up to London, and tell his lordship who I am, and what I mean to do, which is to hire a house in the best part of the town, and set up as his grandma! And we'll see if *that's* a matter of indifference to him!" declared the old lady triumphantly.

CHAPTER THIRTEEN

A LETTER from Lady Theresa followed hard upon the announcement in the *Gazette*. It was unfranked, so that Serena was obliged to pay for the privilege of reading two crossed pages of lament and recrimination. Not even his sister could have felt Rotherham's engagement more keenly. Lady Theresa took it as a personal insult, and laid the blame at her niece's door. As for Lady Laleham, no words could describe the shameless vulgarity of her conduct. From the moment of her having brought her chit of a daughter to town, she had lost no opportunity to throw her in Rotherham's way – but who would have supposed that a man of his age would succumb to mere prettiness and an ingenuous tongue? Lady Theresa prophesied disaster for all concerned, and hoped that when Serena was dying an old maid she would remember these words, and be sorry. Meanwhile she remained her affectionate aunt.

Two days later Mrs Floore was the recipient of a letter from London. She met Serena in the Pump Room, her face wreathed in smiles, and pressed upon her a letter from Emily, begging her to read it. "Bless her heart, I've never had such a letter from her before, never!" she declared. "So excited as she is – why, she's in downright transports! But you'll see for yourself!"

Serena took the letter with some reluctance, but the old lady was obviously so anxious that she should read it that she made no demur.

It was neither well written nor well expressed, but it owed nothing to any manual: the voice of Emily spoke in every incoherent but ecstatic sentence. Serena thought it the effusion of a child; and could almost have supposed that she was reading a description of a promised treat rather than a girl's account of her betrothal. Although Rotherham's name occurred over and over again, it was always in connection with his rank, his riches, the fine houses he owned, the splendid horses he drove, and the envy the conquest of him had aroused in other ladies' breasts. He had driven with her in the Park, in his curricle, which had made everyone stare, because he was said never to drive females. When he took them to the opera it was like going out with a Prince, because he had his own box in the best place imaginable, and everyone knew him, and there was never any delay in getting into his carriage, because as soon as the lackeys saw him coming they ran out to call to the coachman, and so they had not to wait in the vestibule, or to say who they were. Rotherham House, too! When Grandma saw it, she would be astonished, and wonder to think of her little Emily the mistress of such an establishment, giving parties in it, and standing at the head of the staircase with a tiara on her head. There were *hundreds* of servants, some of them so genteel you would take them for visitors, and all the footmen in black satin knee-breeches. Then there was Delford Park, which she had not yet seen, but she believed it to be grander even than Milverley, and how she would go on in such a place she couldn't think.

So it went on, conveying to Serena the picture of an unsophisticated child, dazzled by riches, breathless at finding herself suddenly the heroine of a fantastic dream, intoxicated by her own staggering success. There was not a word to indicate that she had formed an attachment; she was concerned not with Ivo Barrasford, but with the Marquis of Rotherham.

Serena hardly dared look up from these pages, so clearly did they convey to her the knowledge that affection had played no part in one side at least of this contract. It seemed impossible that Mrs Floore could detect anything in the letter but the excitement of a flattered child; and it was a hard case to know what to say of so disquieting a communication.

"Well?" Mrs Floore said. "What do you think of *that*, my dear?"

Serena gave her back the folded sheets. "She is a little carried away, ma'am, which is not to be marvelled at. Perhaps -"

"Ay, that she is!" chuckled Mrs Floore. "So excited and happy as she is! Lord, he's regularly swept her off her feet, hasn't he? Lord Rotherham this, and Lord Rotherham that till you'd think there wasn't another soul in London! Which you can see there isn't, not in her eyes! Well, I don't know when I've been in higher croak myself, and the relief it is to me, my dear, you wouldn't credit!" She dived into her reticule for her handkerchief, and unashamedly wiped her eyes. "You see what she writes, my lady, about me visiting her in her grand house! Bless her sweet heart! I shan't do it, but only to know she wants me to makes up for everything!"

Serena said all that was suitable, and left the old lady in a blissful dream of vicarious grandeur. She did not mention the letter to Fanny, and tried to put it out of her own mind. It recurred too often for her comfort; again and again she found herself dwelling upon all its implications, foreseeing nothing but disillusionment in store for such an ill-assorted couple, and wondering, in astonished disgust, how Rotherham could have been fool enough not to have perceived the feather-brain behind a charming face.

It was a week before she received an answer to her letter to him. The London mail reached Bath every morning between the hours of ten and twelve, and the letter was brought up from the receiving-office half an hour after she had set forth on a picnic expedition under the nominal chaperonage of a young matron of her acquaintance. Fanny could not think it proper to make one of a party of merry-makers. She would not go herself, and tried timidly to dissuade Serena. But Serena seemed to be fast recovering the tone of her mind, and was bent on amusement. She might almost have been said to have been in outrageous spirits, gay to dissipation. Fanny lived in dread of her suddenly deciding to go to balls again, and impressed upon Major Kirkby the necessity of his preventing so imprudent a start. He made a hopeless gesture: "What can I do?"

"She must mind what *you* say!"

He shook his head.

"Oh, yes, yes!" Fanny cried. "If you were to forbid her -"

"Forbid her! I?" he exclaimed. "She would most hotly resent it! Indeed, Lady Spenborough, I dare not!"

"She could not resent it from you!"

He flushed, and stammered: "I have no right – When we are married – Not that I could ever seek to interfere with her pleasure! And surely," he added, in an imploring tone, "it cannot be wrong, if she does it?"

She saw that he shrank from arousing Serena's temper, and was too deeply sympathetic to press him further. She could only pray that Serena would stop short of public balls, and beg her to behave with discretion while under Mrs Osborne's casual chaperonage. Serena, setting upon her copper curls the most fetching of flat-crowned villager-hats of white satin-straw with a cluster of white roses, cast her a wicked look out of the corners of her eyes, and said meekly: "Yes, Mama!"

So Serena, squired by her Major, sallied forth on a picnic expedition; and Fanny, presently glancing through the day's mail and seeing one letter with Rotherham's name on the cover, was obliged to contain her soul in patience until such time as Serena should return to Laura Place. This was not until dinner-time, and then, instead of immediately reading the letter, she put it aside, saying: "Fanny, have I kept you waiting? I do beg your pardon! Order them to serve dinner immediately: I'll be with you in five minutes!"

"Oh, no! Do read your letters first! I could not but notice that one has Rotherham's frank upon the cover, and you must be anxious to know how he receives the news of your engagement!"

"I am more anxious that you should not be kept waiting another moment for your dinner. I don't think it's of the least consequence whether Rotherham likes it or not: he cannot reasonably refuse his consent to it. I'll read what he has to say after we've dined."

Fanny could almost have boxed her ears.

But when Serena at last broke the wafer, and spread open the single sheet, the Marquis's message proved to be a disappointment. Fanny watched Serena read it, herself quite breathless with anxiety, and could not forbear saying eagerly: "Well? What does he say? He does not forbid it?"

"My dear, how should he? He makes no comment upon it, merely that he will be at Claycross next week, and will visit Bath on Thursday, for one night, to discuss with me the winding up of the Trust. We will invite him to dine here, and Hector too."

"But is that all he has to say?" demanded Fanny incredulously.

"You don't know his style of letter-writing! This is a typical example of it. Oh, he thanks me for my felicitations, of course, and says that it will be proper for him to make the acquaintance of Major Kirkby before giving his formal consent to my marriage."

"Then at least he doesn't mean to be disagreeable about it!" said Fanny, considerably relieved.

But when, on the following Thursday, Rotherham was ushered into the drawing-room, this comfortable conviction left her. He looked to be in anything but a complaisant mood. The sardonic lines about his mouth were marked, and a frown drew his black brows into a bar across his face. He was dressed with propriety, in an evening coat and knee breeches, but, as usual, there was a hint of carelessness about his appearance, as though the pattern of his waistcoat or the set of his neckcloth was a matter of indifference to him. He greeted her unsmilingly, and turned to meet Serena.

She had chosen to dignify the occasion by arraying herself in a gown which had been made for her by Bath's leading modiste, and never before worn. It was a striking creation, of black figured lace over a robe of white satin, the bodice cut low, and the train long. With it she wore her diamond earrings, and the triple necklace of pearls her father had given her at her coming-of-age. She looked magnificent, but the comment she evoked from the Marquis was scarcely flattering. "Good God, Serena!" he said, as he briefly shook her hand. "Setting up as a magpie?"

"Just so! I collect it doesn't find favour with you?" she retorted, a spark in her eye.

He shrugged. "I know nothing of such matters."

"No one, my dear Rotherham, having once clapped eyes on you, could doubt *that*!"

With nervous haste, Fanny interrupted this promising start to one of the interchanges she dreaded. "Lord Rotherham, I must introduce Major Kirkby to you!"

He turned to confront the Major, whom he had not previously seemed to notice. His hard eyes surveyed him unrecognizingly. He put out his hand, saying curtly: "How do you do?"

Never, thought Fanny, could two men have formed a stronger contrast to each other! They might have served as models for Apollo and Vulcan, the one so tall and graceful, classically featured, and golden-haired, the other swarthy and harsh faced, with massive shoulders, his whole person suggesting power rather than grace. In looks, in deportment, in manners there could be no comparison: the Major far outshone the Marquis.

"We have met before, sir," the Major said.

"Have we?" said Rotherham, the bar of his brows lifting slightly. "I've no recollection of it. When, and where?"

"Upon more than one occasion!" replied the Major, steadily meeting that hard stare. "In London – seven years ago!"

"Indeed? If it is seven years since we met, I must hold that to be a sufficient excuse for having forgotten the circumstance. Did you form one of Serena's court?"

"Yes. I did," said the Major.

"Ah, no wonder, then! I never disintegrated the mass into its component parts."

This time it was Serena who intervened. "I informed you, Rotherham, that the attachment between us was of long-standing date."

"Certainly you did, but you can hardly have expected me to have known that it was of such long-standing date as that. I had, on the contrary, every reason to suppose otherwise."

Serena flushed vividly; the Major held his lips firmly compressed over hard-clenched teeth; Fanny flung herself once more into the breach. "I have not felicitated you yet, Lord Rotherham, upon your engagement. I hope you left Miss Laleham well?"

"Well, and in great beauty," he replied. "You remind me that she desired me to convey all sorts of messages to you both. Also that I stand in your debt."

"In my debt?" she repeated doubtfully.

"So I must think. I owe my first introduction to Miss Laleham to you, and consider myself much obliged to you."

She could not bring herself to say more than: "I wish you both very happy."

"Thank you! You are a notable matchmaker, Lady Spenborough: accept my compliments!"

She had never been more thankful to hear dinner announced.

While the servants were in the room, only indifferent subjects were discussed. It was second nature to Serena to promote conversation, and to set a party going on the right lines. No matter how vexed she might be, she could not fail in her duties as a hostess. Fanny, seated opposite to her, nervous and oppressed, wondered and admired, and did her best to appear at ease. She had never yet been so in Rotherham's presence, however. At his most mellow, he made her feel stupid; when he sparred with Serena for an opening, she felt quite sick with apprehension. The Major saw it, and, chancing to meet her eye, smiled reassuringly at her, and took the earliest opportunity that offered of sliding out of a discussion of the restored King of Spain's despotic conduct, and turned to ask her quietly if she had succeeded in her search for a birthday-present likely to appeal to the taste of her youngest sister. She responded gratefully, feeling herself protected; and Serena, seeing her happily engaged in abusing the Bath shops, and describing her hunt for a certain type of work-box, was content to let drop the subject of Spain, which she had chosen because it was one on which the Major could speak with authority. Rotherham sat for a moment, listening to Fanny but surveying the Major from under his frowning brows; then he turned his head towards Serena, and said: "I imagine Lady Theresa will have told you of Buckingham's duel with Sir Thomas Hardy? An odd business! The cause is said to be some offensive letters written to and about Lady Hardy. Anonymous, of course, but Hardy held Buckingham to be the author."

"Persuaded by her ladyship! Of *that* I am in no doubt! I don't credit a word of it! Does anyone?"

"Only the inveterate scandalmongers. The character of a gentleman protects Buckingham, or should."

"I think so indeed! But tell me, Ivo! how does the *antiquated* courtship progress? My aunt wrote of having seen their Senilities flirting away at some party or other!"

He replied, with a caustic comment which made her burst out laughing; and in another moment they were in the thick of the sort of conversation Fanny had hoped might be averted. Rotherham seemed to have recovered from his ill-humour: he was regaling Serena with a salted anecdote. Names and nicknames were tossed to and fro; it was Rotherham now who had taken charge of the conversation, Fanny thought, and once again she was labouring to keep pace with it. There was something about the Duke of Devonshire dining at Carlton House, and sitting between the Chancellor and Lord Caithness: what was there in that to make Serena exclaim? Ponsonby too idle, Tierney too unwell, Lord George Cavendish too insolent for leadership: what leader-ship ?

"I *thought* they had made no way this session!" Serena said.

"The reverse! Brougham threw the cat among the pigeons, of course. By the by, Croker came out admirably over the attack on the Navy Estimates: he was offered a Privy Councillor's office as a result, but declined it."

"Are you interested in politics, Major Kirkby?" said Fanny despairingly.

"Not in the least!" he replied, in cheerful accents.

"For shame, Hector!" Serena rallied him.

He smiled at her, but shook his head. "You will have to instruct me!"

"You have been interested in more important matters, Major," said Rotherham, leaning back in his chair, the fingers of one hand crooked round the stem of his wineglass.

"I don't know that. Certainly politics have not come in my way yet."

"You must bring him in, Serena. The Party needs new blood."

"Not I!" she returned lightly. "How odious it would be of me to try to push him into what he does not care for!"

"You will do it, nevertheless."

"Do you care to wager on that chance?"

"It would be robbing you. You will never be able to keep your talents buried." He raised his glass to his lips, and over it looked at the Major. "Serena was made to be a political hostess, you know. Can you subdue her? I doubt it."

"She knows I would never try to do so."

"Good God!" said Rotherham. "I hope you are not serious! The picture you conjure up is quite horrifying, believe me!"

"And *I* hope that Hector knows that you are talking nonsense!" Serena said, stretching out her hand to the Major, and bestowing her most brilliant smile upon him.

He took the hand, and kissed it. "Of course I do! And *you* know that whatever you wish me to do I shall like to do!" he said laughingly.

Rotherham sipped his wine, watching this by-play with unexpected approval in his face. The second course had come to an end, and, in obedience to a sign from Serena, the servants had left the room. Fanny picked up her fan, but before she could rise, Serena said: "Have I your consent and approval, Ivo?"

"Certainly – unless I discover that the Major has a wife in Spain, or some other such trifling impediment. When do you propose to be married?"

"It cannot be until I am out of mourning. I don't feel it would be proper even to announce the engagement at this present."

"Most improper. It will be as well, however, since the control of your fortune will pass from my hands to his, if I have some talk with him on this subject."

"Yes, pray do!" she said cordially. "And I wish you will tell me what I may count on, Ivo! I never made the least enquiry, you know, because to know the precise sum I *might* have enjoyed, but for that abominable Trust, would have made my situation the more insupportable."

"About ten thousand a year," he replied indifferently.

"Ten thousand a *year*?" repeated the Major, in an appalled voice.

Rotherham glanced at him across the table. "You may call it that. It is not possible to be quite exact. It is derived from several sources, which I shall presently explain to you."

"But – Good God, how can this be? I knew, of course, that some disparity between our fortunes there must be, but *this*!"

"I own, *I* had not thought it would be as much," said Serena, mildly surprised.

"But there must have been an entail!" the Major exclaimed, as though snatching at a straw of hope. "Such an income as that represents -" He broke off, in the throes of calculation.

"Something in the region of two hundred thousand," supplied Rotherham helpfully. "All that belongs to the Carlow family naturally goes with the title. This fortune was inherited by the late Earl from his mother, and belonged absolutely to himself."

"Yes, I knew *that*," said Serena. "Papa always told me I should inherit my grandmother's property, but I supposed it to be a comfortable independence merely. I call this a very respectable fortune, don't you, Fanny?"

"I should not know what to do with the half of it!" Fanny said, awed.

Rotherham smiled. "Serena will know. The strongest likelihood is that she will run into debt."

"I should wish it to be tied up!"

These words, vehemently uttered, made Serena look at the Major in great surprise. "Why, what can you mean, love? You can't suppose I shall do anything so absurd as to run into debt! I assure you I am not so improvident! Rotherham, I have not the remotest guess why you should laugh in that detestable way! I was never in debt in my life!"

He threw her a glance of mockery. "You must forgive me, Serena! I wish you will tell me how you contrived, on the seven hundred pounds a year which I, in my ignorance, thought you spent on your attire, to maintain that expensive stable of yours."

"You know very well that Papa bought all my horses!" she said.

"Just so," he agreed. "Now you will be obliged to buy your own."

"Which I can well afford to do, and remain excellently mounted!"

"Certainly you can, but you will have to take care, you know! It won't do to be paying nine hundred guineas for some showy-looking bay you are glad to part with on any terms at the end of your first day out on him."

Wrath flamed in her eyes and her cheeks. "Were you never taken-in over a horse?" she demanded.

"Yes," he said reflectively. "But I can't recall that I ever paid a fancy price for an animal which -"

"Be quiet!" she shot at him. "All those years ago – when I was still green -! Only *you* would cast it up at me still, Rotherham! Do I make mistakes now? Do I?"

"Oh, not as bad as that one!" he said. "I'm prepared to bet a large sum on your having paid too much for that mare I saw at Milverley, but -"

She was on her feet. "If you dare – if you *dare* tell me again she's too short in the back -!"

"Serena, for heavens' sake!" begged the Major. "You are distressing Lady Spenborough! What the deuce does it matter if Lord Rotherham chooses to criticize the mare?"

She paid not the slightest heed, but drove home her challenge. "Well, my lord? Well?"

"Don't try to browbeat me, my girl!" he replied. "I tell you again, too short in the back!" He looked at her, his eyes glinting. "And you know it!"

She bit her lip. Her eyes strove with his for a moment or two, but suddenly she burst into laughter, and sat down again. "Of all the *odious* creatures -! Perhaps she is a trifle too short in the back – but only a trifle! You need not have been so unhandsome as to provoke me into exposing myself to my betrothed!"

The glint was still in his eyes, but he said: "The temptation was irresistible to see whether you would take the fly. Console yourself with the reflection that you never look more magnificent than when in a rage!"

"Thank you! I don't admire myself in that state! What were we saying, before we fell into this foolish dispute?"

"Major Kirkby had expressed a desire that your fortune should be tied up. If I am not to provoke you again, I will refrain from applauding so wise a suggestion."

"You are mistaken," the Major said. "There was no thought in my head of keeping Serena out of debt! I should wish it – or the better part of it, at all events! – to be tied up in such a way that neither she nor I can benefit by it!"

"But, my dearest Hector!" cried Serena. "You must be mad!"

"I am not mad. You haven't considered, my darling! Do you realize that your fortune is almost ten times the size of mine?"

"Is it?" she said. "Does that signify? Are you afraid that people will say you married me for my money? Why should you care for that, when you know it to be untrue?"

"Not only that! Serena, cannot you see how intolerable my position must be?"

"No, how should it be so? If I used it to alter your way of life, of course it would be quite horrid for you, but I promise you I shall not! It will be in your hands, not in mine, so if I should run mad suddenly, and wish to purchase a palace, or some such thing, it will be out of my power to do so."

He gave a laugh that had something of a groan in it. "Oh, my dear, you *don't* see! But Lord Rotherham must!"

"Oh, yes! Shall I refuse my consent to your marriage?"

"I wish to God you would!"

"Well, so do not I!" said Serena. "Hector, I *do* see, but indeed you are too quixotic! I daresay we shan't spend it – not all of it, I mean – but why should I give it up? Besides, who is to have it if we don't? Rotherham? My cousin? You can't expect me to do anything so crackbrained as to abandon what is my own to them or to anyone!"

"That was not in my head. Of course I would not ask you to give your fortune away! I don't even ask you to tie up the whole. But when it comes to the settlements, could we not create a new Trust, Serena?"

She was puzzled. "I see no sense in that. What sort of a Trust had you in mind?"

"Not – not an unusual one!" he stammered, thrown off his balance by her entire lack of comprehension. He saw that Fanny was looking at him in innocent enquiry, and said hastily: "This is not the place – or the occasion! I believe that when I have talked the matter over with Lord Rotherham he will agree as to the propriety of what I have to suggest."

"But it has nothing whatsoever to do with Rotherham!" Serena said indignantly. "What *are* you suggesting?"

"Don't be so bird-witted, Serena!" said Rotherham impatiently. "What I understand Major Kirkby to mean, is that your fortune should be tied up in your children."

"In my children!" she exclaimed. "Is that what you indeed meant, Hector? Good gracious, why could you not say so?"

"Because this is neither the place nor the occasion," said Rotherham. "He told you so."

"Well, if it is not, *you* did not seem to think so!"

"No, but that was because I lack delicacy."

She laughed. "Or would waste none upon me? You know, Hector, I think I would rather *not* tie up all my fortune in my children."

"Not all! I'm not so unreasonable as that! But if you kept for yourself a tenth - Serena, could you not be content with that, with what you have now, and what I can give you?" the Major said pleadingly.

She said without hesitation: "With that, or far less, if I was obliged to, my love! But - but I am *not* obliged to, and I do think that it would be quite ridiculous of us to *choose* to live on a smaller income than we need! Suppose I did get into debt, or that we had a sudden need for a large sum of money? My dear, it would drive us *both* into a frenzy to think we had been so foolish as to put it out of our power to draw upon my fortune!"

Rotherham gave a crack of laughter. "Admirable common sense, Serena! I trust for both your sakes you will succeed in bringing Major Kirkby round to your way of thinking. You have, after all, several months in which to argue the matter."

"Oh, yes, let us not talk of it any more tonight!" Fanny begged, getting up from her chair. "It is so very difficult for you both!"

The Major moved to the door, and opened it. Fanny paused beside him, looking up into his face, and saying with a wistful smile: "You will find an answer to the problem – I am quite certain that you will!"

His grave face relaxed; he returned the smile, but with an effort. She and Serena went out of the room, and he shut the door behind them, and turned to confront Rotherham.

CHAPTER FOURTEEN

ROTHERHAM sat down again, and refilled both his own and the Major's glass. The Major returned to his chair, but stood behind it, his hands gripping its back. He said jerkily: "She must be persuaded to do that!"

"I don't know what your powers of persuasion are," replied Rotherham, "but I should doubt whether you will succeed."

"If she knew that you were in agreement with me -"

"Nothing would more surely set up her back. Moreover, I am not in agreement with you. I fail to see why Serena should be deprived of what she has every right to enjoy." He picked up his wineglass, and lounged back in his chair, one leg stretched out before him, and his hand thrust into the pocket of his breeches. He surveyed the Major somewhat satirically. "Serena, my dear sir, is the daughter of an extremely wealthy man, and has lived her whole life, until Spenborough's death, in the first style of affluence. I know of no reason why she should be obliged to spend the rest of it in reduced circumstances. I should doubt very much her ability to do so. However, it is no concern of mine. By all means persuade her, if you think you can do it, and believe yourself able to support her when you have done it!"

There was a long silence. The Major sat down rather heavily, and for some time remained staring blindly at his wineglass, which he kept on twisting round and round, a finger and thumb gripping its stem. At last he drew a long breath, and looked up with an air of resolution. "Lord Rotherham, when I asked Serena to marry me, it was in the belief that although her fortune might be larger than my own, it was not so immense as to render my proposal an effrontery! I am astonished that you should behave with such – I must call it forbearance! I am well aware in what a light I must appear to anyone not familiar with the circumstances! In justice to myself, I wish to tell you that I have loved her the memory of her – ever since I first saw her! She, too, formed an attachment. She would have married me then, but my suit was considered to be ineligible – which, indeed, it was! I was a mere lad, a younger son! We were parted. I never hoped to see her again, but forget her I could not! She was to me – an unattainable dream, a beautiful goddess beyond my reach!" He stopped, flushing, and said with some difficulty: "But I need not try to explain *that* to you, I fancy. I am aware – Serena has told me -"

"If Serena has told you that I ever thought her a goddess, she's either an unconscionable liar, or she's hoaxing you!" interrupted Rotherham tartly.

"She did not – I only thought -"

"Then think it no longer! I collect that when you succeeded to the property you now possess, you decided she was no longer above your touch?"

The Major shook his head. "It never entered my head. I didn't suppose even that she could remember me. But we met – here in Bath – neither of us dreaming of such a thing." He raised his eyes fleetingly to that harsh face, and said, colouring as he spoke: "It was as though the years rolled back – for both of us!"

"I see." Rotherham smiled slightly. "Your dream, in fact, had come true."

"It sounds foolish, I daresay. I had not meant to tell you all this! But what has happened tonight -"

"Not at all. You are singularly fortunate, Major Kirkby. In my experience, the embodiment of such a dream is frequently a severe disappointment. So Serena is just what you had imagined her to be! You must have been far better acquainted with her than I had supposed possible!"

"How could I – how *could* I be disappointed in her?" demanded the Major, with unnecessary violence.

"Evidently you are not."

"No! Unthinkable!"

"Then we need not think of it. I am obliged to you for honouring me with your confidence, but it was unnecessary. I had not imagined that you wished to marry Serena for the sake of her fortune: she's not such a fool as to be taken in by a fortune-hunter! Nor is she answerable to me for her actions."

"Was it not – to guard her from just such a fortune hunter as I must appear that her father appointed you to be her Trustee?"

Rotherham's mouth twisted rather wryly. "No. It was not. No doubt he hoped, at the least, that I should prevent her marriage to some obviously undesirable person. Mere disparity of fortune would not, I fancy, constitute undesirability in the eyes of the Law. She would marry whom she chose, even though I swore she shouldn't touch a penny more than the pin money she now enjoys." He gave a short laugh. "And fight me afterwards to the Courts of Appeal!" he added. He got up. "There is really no more to say. Shall we go?"

"Yes. That is – I must think! Before I knew the size of this appalling fortune, I had qualms that I had no business to – Had it not been for Lady Spenborough, I believe I must have torn myself away!"

Rotherham had strolled towards the door, but he paused, and looked at the Major. "Did Lady Spenborough encourage you to declare yourself?"

"Yes. I was in miserable uncertainty! I felt she was the most proper person to be consulted!"

"Good God!"

"You are thinking of her youth! But I knew her to be devoted to Serena! Her kindness, her sympathy I can find no words to describe! To lose Serena must be such a blow to her, but I believe she never spares a thought for herself. I think I never knew one so young and so timid to have so much strength of character, so much understanding!"

"An excellent woman," agreed Rotherham. "Serena's marriage will no doubt be a sad loss to her. She is really quite unfitted to live alone."

"Exactly so! One cannot but feel that she needs to be protected from – But I fear she will have her sister thrust upon her, and from all I can discover a more disagreeable, censorious girl never existed!"

"Indeed? A gloomy prospect, certainly. However, I dare say she will marry again."

"Marry!" The Major sounded thunderstruck, but said quickly, after a blank moment: "Why, yes! Of course! We must hope she may."

"I do hope it," said Rotherham cryptically, and opened the door.

The sound of music met them, as they mounted the stairs. They found Fanny seated by the open window, gazing out into the gathering dusk, and Serena at the piano in the back half of the drawing-room. She stopped playing when she saw that the gentlemen had come in, but the Major went to her, saying: "Ah, don't get up! You were playing the Haydn sonata I recommended to you!"

"Attempting to play it! It is not fit yet to be heard!"

"Try it once more!" he coaxed her. "I'll turn for you."

She allowed herself to be persuaded. Rotherham walked over to the window, and sat down beside Fanny. For a few moments he watched the couple at the far end of the room, his face expressionless. Then he turned his head to look at Fanny. He said, his voice a little lowered: "I understand that this marriage has your approval, Lady Spenborough."

"Yes, I – I feel so sure that he will make Serena happy!"

"Do you?"

"It couldn't be otherwise!" she said wistfully. "He is so very kind, and – and has loved her so devotedly!"

"So I am informed."

"Indeed, it is quite true! He worships her: I think there is nothing he would not do to please her!"

"Excellent! Does he quarrel with her?"

"No, no! His temper is of the sweetest, and he is so patient! I cannot but feel that his tenderness and forbearance must put it out of her power to quarrel with him." She saw the sardonic smile curl his lips, and faltered: "You do not dislike him, Lord Rotherham?"

He shrugged. "I see nothing to dislike."

"I am so glad you have not withheld your consent."

"It would have been useless."

She looked anxiously at him, and nerved herself to say: "I am afraid you are not quite pleased. He is not her equal in rank or fortune, but in worth, I do assure you -"

He interrupted her, in his brusque way. "On the contrary! I am much better pleased than I expected to be. Had I known -" He broke off. She saw that the smile had quite vanished, and that his brows were lowering again. He sat in a brown study for several minutes. It seemed to her that his face hardened as she watched him. As though he felt her eyes upon him, he came out of his reverie, and turned his head to meet her enquiring look. "Such persons as you and Major Kirkby are to be envied!" he said abruptly. "You make mistakes, but you will not make the crass mistakes that spring from a temper never brought under control! I must go. Don't get up!"

She was wholly bewildered, and could only say: "You will stay for tea!"

"Thank you, no! It is not yet dark, and there will be a full moon presently: I mean to start for London tonight." He shook hands with her, and strode away to take his leave of Serena and the Major.

"Going so soon!" Serena exclaimed, rising quickly from the piano-stool. "Good God, have I driven you away by my lamentable performance?"

"I wasn't listening to it. I am sleeping at Marlborough, or Newbury, tonight, and must not stay."

She smiled, but retained his hand. "You have not wished me happy."

There was a moment's silence, while each stared into the other's eyes. "Have I not? I do wish you happy, Serena." His grasp on her hand tightened rather painfully for an instant. He released it, and turned to shake hands with the Major. "I wish you happy too. I fancy you will be."

A brief goodbye, and he was gone. Serena shut the piano. The Major waited for a moment, watching her, as she gathered her music together. "No more?" he asked gently.

She looked as though she did not realize what she had been doing. Then she put the music into a cabinet, and replied. "Not tonight. I must practise it before I play it to you again." She turned, and laid her hand on his arm, walking with him into the front half of the room. "Well, that went off pretty tolerably, didn't it? I wish I had not flown into a rage, but he made me do so. Did you hate him?"

"I didn't love him," he confessed. "But I thought he treated my pretensions with a degree of kindness I had no right to expect."

"Your pretensions! I wish you will not talk in that absurd way!" she said impatiently. He was silent, and she pressed his arm, saying, in a lighter tone: "Do you know I am close on twenty-six years of age? I am very much obliged to you for offering for me! I had quite given up hope of achieving a respectable alliance."

He smiled, but said: "It won't do, Serena. You must not try to turn it off! This matter must be seriously discussed between us."

"Not now! I don't know how it is, but I have the headache. Don't tease me, Hector!"

"My darling! I will rather beg you to go up to bed! You should not have let me keep you at the piano! Have you any fever?"

She pulled her hand away. "No, no! It's nothing – the heat! Ah, here is the tea-tray at last!"

He looked at her in concern, which was not lessened by Fanny's saying: "A headache? *You*, dearest? I never knew you to complain of such a thing before! Oh, I hope you may not have a touch of the sun! I wish you will go to bed! Lybster, desire her ladyship's woman to fetch some vinegar to her room directly, if you please!"

"No!" almost shrieked Serena. "For heaven's sake, let me alone! Of all things in the world I most abominate being -" She clipped the word off short, and gave a gasp. "I beg your pardon!" she said, forcing a smile. "You are both of you very kind, but pray believe I don't wish to have my temples bathed with vinegar, or to have such a rout made over nothing! I shall be better when I have drunk some tea."

It seemed as if the Major was going to say something, but even as he opened his mouth to speak Fanny caught his eye, and very slightly shook her head. "Will you take this cup to Serena, Major?" she said calmly.

But he had first to hover over Serena, while she disposed herself in a wing-chair, to place a cushion behind her head, and a stool at her feet. Her hands gripped the arms of her chair till her knuckles gleamed, and her lips were tightly compressed. But when he set her cup down on a table beside her, she smiled again, and thanked him. Fanny began to talk to him, in her soft voice, distracting his attention from Serena. In a minute or two, Serena sat up, allowing the cushion to slide down behind her, and sipped her tea. When she spoke, it was in her usual manner, but when she had finished the tea in her cup she went away to bed, saying, however, that her headache was gone, and she was merely sleepy.

The Major turned an anxious gaze upon Fanny. "Do you think her seriously unwell, Lady Spenborough?"

"Oh, I hope not!" she replied. "I think, perhaps, Lord Rotherham vexed her. If she is not better in the morning, I will try to persuade her to let me send for the doctor. But it never answers to pay any heed if she is not quite well." She smiled at him consolingly. "She cannot bear anyone to be in a fuss about her, you see. Indeed, I quite thought she would have flown out at you for trying to make her comfortable. Will you have some more tea?"

"No, thank you. I must go. I shall call tomorrow morning, if I may, to see how she goes on," he said.

But when he presented himself in Laura Place at ten o'clock next day, he found the ladies breakfasting, Serena in her riding-dress. She greeted him with mock abuse, demanding to be told why he had broken faith with her. "Ten whole minutes did I wait for you to come trotting over the bridge, and that, let me tell you, is longer than I have waited for any man before! Well for you you did *not* appear by that time, for I should certainly have sworn at you! Fanny, I forbid you to give him that coffee! He has *slighted* me!"

"I never dreamed you would ride this morning!" he exclaimed. "I came only to see how you did! Are you sure you are quite well? You didn't go alone?"

"No, with Fobbing."

"It is too hot for riding: I wish you will not!"

"On the contrary, it was delightful. I don't gallop Maid Marian, of course."

"I was thinking of you, not the mare!"

"Oh, hush!" Fanny said laughing. "You could not say anything she would think more shocking!"

"No, indeed! And not one word of apology, note!"

"My repentance is too deep to be expressed! You won't go out again, will you? At least not in the heat of the day!"

"Yes, I've persuaded Fanny to forgo the drinking of her horrid waters, and to drive with me instead to Melksham Forest. I hope you give her credit for heroism!"

"What, you don't mean to drive in your phaeton?"

"Most certainly I do!"

"Serena, not alone, I do implore you!"

"You and Fobbing will ride behind us, to protect us from highwaymen, and to set the phaeton on its wheels again when I have overturned it. I won't do so above twice!"

There was nothing but nonsense to be got out of her, then or thereafter. She was in the gayest of moods all day, and at her most affectionate, yet when he parted from her he felt that he had not once come within touching distance of her.

He thought it wisest not to revert immediately to the vexed question of her inheritance, and when, after ten days, he ventured to raise the subject, she surprised him by listening without interruption to his carefully considered arguments, and by saying, when he had done: "Very well: let it be as you wish, my dear! After all, I don't greatly care. Not enough, at all events, to make you uncomfortable. When the time comes, arrange it as you think proper!"

She would have banished the matter there; he could not. No sooner did she yield than he was torn by doubt. Rotherham's words echoed in his mind: what right had he to insist on her relinquishing the means whereby she might live as she had always done? She listened with what patience she could muster, but exclaimed at last: "Oh, Hector, what are you at? You told me you cannot bear it if I use my fortune, and I submitted! Now you tell me you cannot bear to deprive me of it!"

"Do I seem absurd? I suppose I must. I don't wish you to *submit*, now or ever! I couldn't do it on such terms as that. Only if you too desired it!"

"No, that is asking too much of me!" she cried. "I must have less than common sense if I *desired* anything so foolish!"

"Oh, my dear, if it seems foolish to you, how could I let you make a sacrifice to my pride?"

She looked at him strangely. "Ask yourself how I could let you sacrifice your pride to my extravagant habits. I could tell you how easily I might do that! Don't – don't encourage me to rule you! I shall try to, you know. There! you are warned! Handsome of me, wasn't it? Don't let us speak of this again! Only tell me when you have decided what to do!"

They did not speak of it again. He thought of it continually; she seemed to have put it quite out of her mind. If her indifference was a mask, she never let it slip. She seemed to him to be in the best of health and spirits, so full of unflagging energy that it was he who sometimes felt tired, keeping pace with her. He told Fanny once, half in jest, half in earnest, that he never knew from one moment to the next where she would be, or what she might be doing. "I think," Fanny said, "that it is perhaps because she is very happy. She has always a great deal of energy, but I never saw her so restless before. She can't be still!"

Mrs Floore noticed it, and drew her own conclusions. She bore down upon Fanny one day in the Pump Room, and, ruthlessly ousting young Mr Ryde, her most fervent admirer, from her side, lowered herself into the chair he had been obliged to offer her. "Well, I don't doubt that's one enemy I've made!" she remarked cheerfully. "Between you, my lady, you and Lady Serena have got the men in this town so love-lorn that it's a wonder the other young females ain't all gone off into declines!"

Fanny laughed, but shook her head. "It is Lady Serena they admire, not me, ma'am!"

"I don't deny anyone would take her for a jam-jar, the way all these silly bumble-bees keep buzzing round her," agreed Mrs Floore, "but there's some that like you better, if you'll pardon my saying so! As for that young sprig that gave up his chair to me with the worst grace I ever did see, he makes a bigger cake of himself than ever the Major did, when he used to come day after day into this room, looking for her ladyship."

"Mr Ryde is only a boy, and dreadfully stupid!" Fanny said hastily.

"He's stupid enough, I grant you. Which the Major is not," said Mrs Floore, cocking a shrewd eye at Fanny. "What I thought at first, my lady, was that *that* was just a Bath-flirtation. But, lord bless me, Lady Serena wouldn't be in such a fine flow of spirits if that's all it is! When is it to be, that's what I'd like to know?"

Fanny, anything but appreciative of the wink so roguishly bestowed upon her, said as coldly as her tender heart would permit: "I am afraid I don't know what you mean, ma'am."

"Keeping it a secret, are they?" Mrs Floore shook with fat chuckles. "As though it wasn't plain enough for a blind man to see! Well, if that's how it is, I won't ask any questions, my lady. I can't help watching them, and having my own notions, though!"

The very thought of being watched by Mrs Floore was so objectionable to Fanny that she almost summoned up enough resolution to remonstrate with Serena on her imprudence. But before she had quite succeeded in doing so something happened to give the old lady's thoughts another direction. Midway through July she once more had herself driven to Laura Place, announcing on arrival that such a piece of news as she had she couldn't keep to herself, not if she died of it.

"Which I very likely would have done, through going off pop, like a gingerbeer bottle," she said. "Who do you think will be staying with me before I'm more than a day older?"

Neither lady could hazard a guess, though Serena hugely delighted Mrs Floore by saying promptly: "The Prince Regent!"

"Better than him!" Mrs Floore declared, when she had recovered from the paroxysm into which this sally threw her. "Emma!"

"Emily!" Serena exclaimed. "Delightful, indeed! How pleased you must be! The Lalehams are in Gloucestershire again, then?"

"No, that's the best of it!" said Mrs Floore. "Though heaven knows I shouldn't be saying so, for the other poor little things – three of them, that is – are so full of the measles as never was! So Sukey stayed in London, with Emma, because there wasn't a house to be had in Brighton, which she had a fancy for. Only it seems the Marquis don't care for Brighton, so it was just as well, I daresay. Not that I'd ever want Emma to go and get ill with this nasty influenza that's going about in London, which is what she did do, poor little soul! Not four days after they came back from this place, Delford, which Sukey tells me is the Marquis's country home. Seat, she calls it, and I'm bound to say it don't sound like a *home* to me. Well, it's all according to taste, but you mark my words, my dear, when he gets to be as fat as I am – which I'm sure I hope he won't – this Marquis will wish he hadn't got to walk a quarter of a mile from his bedroom to get to his dinner! I shouldn't wonder at it if that's how poor Emma came to get ill, for she's never been much of a one for long walks."

"Delford is very large, but Lady Laleham exaggerates a little, ma'am," Serena said, faintly smiling.

"You can lay your life to that, my dear! Well, the long and the short of it is that she did take ill, and very sick she must have been, because Sukey writes that the doctor says she must go out of London, on account of her being regularly knocked up, and her nerves quite upset besides."

"I am so sorry!" Fanny said. "So Lady Laleham is to bring her on a visit to you, ma'am?"

"No!" said Mrs Floore, a smile of delight spreading over her large face.

"Depend upon it, Sukey would have taken her to Jericho rather than come to me! But *she's* got the influenza now, so there's no help for it but for her to send Emma down with her maid tomorrow! She's coming post, of course, and see if I don't have her blooming again in a trice!"

CHAPTER FIFTEEN

EMILY, when encountered a few days later, certainly bore all the appearance of a young lady lately risen from a sickbed. The delicate bloom had faded from her cheeks; she was thinner; and jumped at sudden noises. Mrs Floore ascribed her condition to the rigours of a London season, and told Serena that she could willingly box her daughter's ears for having allowed poor little Emma to become so fagged. Serena thought the explanation reasonable, but Fanny declared that some other cause than late nights must be sought to account for the hunted look in Emily's wide eyes. "And it is not far to seek!" she added significantly. "That wicked woman compelled her to accept Rotherham's offer, and she is terrified of him!"

"How can you be so absurd?" said Serena impatiently. "Rotherham is not an ogre!"

But gentle Fanny for once refused to be overborne. "Yes, he is," she asserted. "I don't scruple to tell you, dearest, that he frightens *me*, and I am not seventeen!"

"I know you are never at ease with him, and a great piece of nonsense that is, Fanny! Pray, what cause has he given you to fear him?"

"Oh, none! It is just – You cannot understand, Serena, because you are not at all shy, and were never afraid of anything in your life, I suppose!"

"Certainly not of Rotherham! You should consider that if there is anything in his manner that makes you nervous he is not in love with you."

Fanny shuddered. "Oh, that would be more terrifying than anything!" she exclaimed.

"You are being foolish beyond permission. I daresay the marriage was arranged by the Laleham-woman, and that Emily is in love with Ivo I most strongly doubt; but, after all, such marriages are quite common, and often succeed to admiration. If he loves her, he will very soon teach her to return his sentiments."

"Serena, I *cannot* believe that he loves her! No two persons could be less suited!"

Serena shrugged her shoulders, saying, in a hard voice: "Good God, Fanny, how many times has one seen a clever man wedded to a pretty simpleton, and wondered what could have made him choose her? Emily will not dispute with Rotherham; she will be docile; she will think him infallible – and that should suit him perfectly!"

"Him! Very likely, but what of her? If he frightens her now, what will it be when they are married?"

"Let me recommend you, Fanny, not to put yourself into high fidgets over what is nothing but conjecture! You do not know that he has frightened Emily. If she is a little nervous, depend upon it he has been making love to her. He is a man of strong passions, and she is such an innocent baby that I should not marvel at it if she had been scared. She will very soon overcome such prudery, I assure you!" She saw Fanny shake her head, and fold her lips, and said sharply: "This will not do! If there was any truth in these freakish notions of yours, she need not have accepted his offer!"

Fanny looked up quickly. "Ah, you cannot know you don't understand, Serena!"

"Oh, you mean that she dare not disobey her mother! Well, my love, however strictly Lady Laleham may rule her, it is not in her power to force her into a disagreeable marriage. And if she is in such dread of her, she must welcome any chance to escape from her tyranny!"

Fanny gazed at her wonderingly, and then bent over her embroidery again. "I don't think you would *ever* understand," she said mournfully. "You see, dearest, you grew up under such different circumstances! You never held my lord in awe. Indeed, I was used to think you were his companion rather than his daughter, and I am persuaded neither of you had the least notion of filial obedience! It quite astonished me to hear how he would consult you, and how boldly you maintained your own opinions and went your own way! I should never have dared to have talked so to my parents, you know. Habits of strict obedience, I think, are not readily overcome. It seems impossible to you that Lady Laleham could force Emily into a distasteful marriage, but it is not impossible. To some girls – to most girls, indeed – the thought of setting up one's own will does not even occur."

"You encourage me to think that Emily will be the very wife for Rotherham!" Serena replied. "And if you imagine, my dear, that he will give her any reason to be afraid of him, you are doing him an injustice. Though his manners are not conciliatory, he is, I must remind you, a gentleman!"

No more was said; nor did Emily, walking with Serena in the Sydney Gardens, appear to regret her engagement. In the intervals of exclaiming rapturously at the various amenities of this miniature Vauxhall, she chattered about the parties she had been to in London, and seemed to be full of such items of information as that the Queen had smiled at her upon her presentation, and that one of the Princesses had actually spoken to her.

"Did you enjoy yourself?" Serena asked.

"Oh, yes, indeed! And we went several times to Vauxhall Gardens, and to the theatre, and a Review in Hyde Park, and Almack's – oh, I am sure we must have been to *everything*!" Emily declared.

"No wonder you became so worn out!"

"No, for I am not quite accustomed to so many parties. When one is tired, one doesn't care for anything very much, and – and one gets into stupid humours – Mama says. And I had influenza. Have you ever had it, Lady

Serena? It is the horridest thing, for it makes you excessively miserable, so that the least thing makes you cry. But Mama was very kind to me, and she let me come to stay with Grandmama, and, oh, it is so comfortable!"

"I hope you are making a long stay with her?"

At this, the frightened look returned. Emma stammered: "Oh, I wish – I don't know – Mama said . . ."

"Your Mama will be thinking of your bride-clothes soon, no doubt," Serena said lightly.

"Yes. I mean – Oh, not *yet*!"

"When is the wedding-date to be?"

"I – we – it is not decided! Lord Rotherham spoke of September, but – but I would like not to be married until I am eighteen! I shall be eighteen in November, you know, and I shall know how to go on better, don't you think?"

"What, because you are eighteen?" Serena laughed. "Will it make such a difference to you?"

"I don't know. It is only that I seem not to know the things I should, to be a Marchioness, and I think I should try to learn how to be a great lady, and – and if I am not married till November perhaps I may do so."

"I cannot suppose that Lord Rotherham desires you to be in any way other than you are now, my dear Emily."

There was no reply to this. Glancing at her, Serena saw that Emily was deeply flushed, her eyes downcast. She said, after a pause: "Do you expect to see Lord Rotherham in Bath?"

The eyes were quickly raised; the colour receded. "In Bath! Oh, *no*! The doctor said I must not be excited! Mama said she would explain to him. Besides – he must not meet Grandmama!"

"Indeed!" Serena said dryly. "May I ask if he is never to meet Mrs Floore?"

"No, no! I could not *endure* it!"

"I don't wish to seem to criticize your mama, Emily, but you are making a mistake. You must not despise your grandmama."

Emily burst into tears. Fortunately, one of the shady arbours with which the gardens were liberally provided was close at hand, and unoccupied. Having no desire to walk through a public place in company with a gustily sobbing girl, Serena guided Emily into the arbour, commanding her, in stringent accents, to compose herself. It was a little time before she could do this, and when her tears ceased to flow they left her face so much blotched that Serena kept her sitting in the arbour until these traces of emotion had faded. By way of diverting her mind, she asked her if she had enjoyed her visit to Delford. From the disjointed account Emily gave her of this, she gathered that it had not been wholly delightful. Emily seemed to waver between a glorious vision of herself ruling over the vast pile, and terror of its servants. She was sure that the housekeeper held her in contempt; she would never dare to give an order to the steward; and she had mistaken Lady Silchester's dresser for a fellow-guest, which had made Mama cross. Yes, Lady Silchester had been acting as hostess for her brother. She was very proud, wasn't she? There had been a great many people staying at Delford: dreadfully alarming people, who all looked at her, and all knew one another. There had been a huge dinner-party, too: over forty persons invited, and so many courses that she had lost count of them. Lord Rotherham had said that when next such a dinner-party was held at Delford she would be the hostess.

This was said with so frightened a look up into Serena's face, the pansy-brown eyes dilating a little, that Serena was satisfied that it was not her bridegroom but his circumstances which had thrown Emily into such alarm. She wondered that Rotherham should not have realized that to introduce this inexperienced child to Delford under such conditions must make her miserably aware of her shortcomings. What could have induced him to have filled his house with exalted guests? He might have guessed that he was subjecting her to a severe ordeal; while as for summoning, apparently, half the county to a state dinner-party, and then telling the poor girl that in future she would be expected to preside over just such gatherings, Serena could think of nothing so ill-judged. Plainly, he had wanted to show off his chosen bride, but he should have known better than to have done it in such a way.

She found that Mrs Floore shared this opinion. She was hugely gratified to know that his lordship was so proud of her little Emma, but thought him a zany not to have realized how shy and retiring she was. Mrs Floore was in a triumphant mood, having routed her daughter in one swift engagement. Unfortunately for Lady Laleham, who wished to remove Emily from her grandmother's charge as soon as she herself was restored to health, Sir Walter had suffered severe reverses, and these, coupled with the accumulated bills for her own and Emily's expensive gowns, had made it necessary for her to apply to her mother for relief. Mrs Floore was perfectly ready to send her as much money as she wanted, but she made it a condition that Emily should be left in her charge until her own doctor pronounced her to be perfectly well again. Lady Laleham was obliged to accede to these terms, and Emily's spirits immediately improved. A suggestion, put forward by her ladyship, that she should join her daughter in Beaufort Square was so bluntly vetoed by Mrs Floore that she did not repeat it.

"Which I knew she wouldn't," Mrs Floore told Serena. "She's welcome to play off her airs in her own house, but I won't have her doing it in mine, and so she knows! Well, my dear, I don't deny Sukey's been a rare disappointment to me, to put it no higher, but there's a bright side to everything, and at least I have the whip hand of her. Offend me, she daren't, for fear I might stop paying her the allowance I do, let alone cut her out of my Will. So now we must think how to put Emma in spirits again! I'll take her to the Dress Ball on Monday, at the New Assembly Rooms, and Ned Goring shall gallant us to it. There'll be nothing for Sukey to take exception to in that, nor his lordship neither, even if they was to know of it, which there's no reason they should, because there's no waltzing, you know, and not even a cotillion on the Monday night balls."

"But I thought Emily was to be very quiet!" said Serena, laughing. "Was she not knocked up by balls in London?"

"Ay, so she was, but it's one thing to be going to them night after night, and never in bed till two or three in the morning, and quite another to be going to one of the Assemblies here now and then! Why, they never go on beyond eleven o'clock at the New Rooms, my dear, and only till midnight at the Lower Rooms, on Tuesdays! What's more, it won't do the poor little soul any good to be hipped, and to sit moping here with only me for company!

I'll take her to the next Gala night at the Sydney Gardens, too, which is a thing I've never done yet, because this is the first time she's visited me during the summer. I'll be bound she'll enjoy watching the fireworks, and so I shall myself."

Serena, looking at that fat, jolly countenance, did not doubt it. Mrs Floore was in a rollicking humour, determined to make the most of her beloved granddaughter's visit. "For it's not likely she'll ever stay with me again," she said, with a sigh. "However, she shall do what the doctor tells her she should, never fear! And one thing he says is that she mustn't sit cooped up within doors this lovely weather, so if you would let her go walking with you sometimes, my lady, it would be a great kindness, and what she'd like a deal better than driving in the landaulet with me, I daresay, for that's mighty dull work for a girl."

"Certainly: I shall be glad of her company," Serena replied. "Perhaps she would like to ride with me."

This suggestion found instant favour with Mrs Floore, who at once made plans for the hire of a quiet hack. Emily herself was torn between gratification at being asked to ride with such a horsewoman as Lady Serena, and fear that she might be expected to leap all sorts of obstacles, or find herself mounted on a refractory horse. However, the animal provided for her proved to be of placid, not to say sluggish, disposition, and Serena, knowing her limitations, took her for just the sort of expeditions that would have suited Fanny. Whenever opportunity offered, she did her best to instruct Emily in the duties of the mistress of a noble household; but the questions shyly put to her by the girl, and the dismay which many of her answers provoked, did not augur very well for the future. She supposed that Rotherham, himself careless of appearances, disliking the formality that still obtained in many families of *ton*, was indifferent to Emily's ignorance of so much that any girl of his own rank would have known from her birth.

August came, and still Emily remained in Bath. To any impartial observer, she seemed quite to have regained her bloom, but Mrs Floore, looking her physician firmly in the eye, said that she was still far from well. He was so obliging as to agree with her; and upon Emily's happening to give a little cough, shook his head, spoke of the unwisdom of neglecting coughs, and prescribed magnesia and breadpudding as a cure.

Major Kirkby, finding that he was frequently expected to squire Emily as well as Serena, told Fanny that he was in a puzzle to discover what there was in the girl to endear her to Serena. A pretty little creature, he acknowledged, but gooseish. Fanny explained that it was all kindness: Emily had always looked up to Serena, and that was why Serena took pity on her. But the Major was not satisfied. "That is all very well," he objected, "but she seems to believe herself to be in some sort responsible for Miss Laleham! She is for ever telling her how she should conduct herself in this or that circumstance!"

"I wish she would not!" Fanny said impulsively. "I would like Emily to conduct herself so awkwardly as to give Lord Rotherham a disgust of her, for I am persuaded she will be miserable if she marries him! How Serena can fail to see that, I know not!"

"I don't think Serena cares for that," he said slowly. "She appears to me to be wholly bent on training Miss Laleham to make Rotherham a conformable wife. I can tell you this, Lady Spenborough: she does not mean *this* engagement of his to be broken off."

"But what concern is it of hers?" cried Fanny. "Surely you must be mistaken!"

"I asked her very much that question myself. She replied that it had been no very pleasant thing for him when she jilted him, and she would not for the world have him subjected to another such slight."

Fanny looked very much surprised, but when she had thought it over for a minute, she said: "She has known him all her life, of course, and no matter how bitterly they quarrel they always seem to contrive to remain on terms with each other. But it is very wrong of her to interfere in this! I don't believe Emily wants to marry Rotherham. She would not dare to tell Serena so, I daresay, and Serena takes care not to leave her alone with me, because she knows what my feelings are on that head."

He smiled. "So if Serena interferes in one direction, you would be happy to do so in the other?"

"Oh, no, no! Only if Emily confided in me – if she should ask my advice – I would counsel her most strongly not to marry a man for whom she feels no decided preference! A man, too, so much older than herself, and of such a harsh disposition! She cannot be aware – even if he were as kind, as considerate as -" Her voice failed; she turned away her head, colouring painfully.

Unconsciously, he placed his hand over hers, as it lay on the arm of her chair, and pressed it reassuringly. It seemed to flutter under his. After a moment, it was gently withdrawn, and Fanny said, a little breathlessly: "I should not have spoken so. I don't wish you to think that I was not most sincerely attached to Lord Spenborough. My memories of him must always be grateful, and affectionate."

"You need say no more," he replied, in a low voice. "I understand you perfectly." There was a brief pause; then he said, with a resumption of his usual manner: "I am afraid you must sometimes be lonely now that Serena is so often with her tiresome protégée. I have a very good mind to give her a scold for neglecting you!"

"Indeed, you must do no such thing! I assure you, she doesn't neglect me, and I am not at all lonely."

It was true. Since she had emerged from her strict seclusion she had never lacked for company, and had by this time many acquaintances in Bath. She received and returned morning visits, attended one or two concerts, dined out several times, and even consented to appear at a few select rout-parties. She felt herself adventurous indeed, for she had never before gone alone into society. Before her marriage, she had dwelt in her mother's shadow; after it, in her husband's, or her stepdaughter's. She was too well-accustomed to every sort of social gathering to feel the want of support, and only one circumstance marred her quiet enjoyment of Bath's mild social life. Protected as she had been, she had never learnt how to hold her many admirers at a distance. She was not naturally flirtatious, and an elderly and fond husband, who knew his world, had taken care not to expose her to the temptations of fashionable London. Would-be cicisbeos, throwing out lures, had made haste to seek easier game after encountering one look from my Lord Spenborough;

and Fanny had continued in serene unconsciousness that she was either sought or guarded. But so young and so divinely fair a widow exercised a powerful fascination over the susceptible, and she soon found herself in small difficulties. A shocked look was enough to check the advances of her more elderly admirers, but several love-lorn youths seriously discomposed her by the assiduity of their attentions, and their apparent determination to make her and themselves conspicuous. Serena would have known just how to depress pretensions, but Fanny lacked her lightness of touch, and, moreover, could never bring herself to snub a young gentleman who bashfully presented her with an elegant posy, or ran all over town to procure for her some elusive commodity which she had been heard to express a wish to possess. She believed that her circumstances protected her from receiving unwanted proposals, and comforted herself with the thought that the more violent of her adorers were too young to nourish serious intentions. It came as a severe shock to her, therefore, when Mr Augustus Ryde, the son of an old acquaintance of her mother's, so far forgot himself as to cast himself at her feet, and to utter an impassioned declaration.

He had gained admittance to her drawing-room by offering to be the bearer to Fanny of a note from his gratified parent. He found Fanny alone, looking so pretty and so fairy-like in her clinging black robe and veil, that he lost his head. Fanny, having read Mrs Ryde's note, said: "Excuse me, if you please, while I write an answer to Mrs Ryde's kind invitation! Perhaps you will be so obliging as to deliver it to her." She made as if to rise from her chair, but was prevented by Mr Ryde's throwing himself on to his knees before her, and imploring her to hear him.

Startled, Fanny stammered: "Mr Ryde! I beg you – get up! You forget yourself! Oh, *pray* –!"

It was to no avail. Her hands were seized, and covered with kisses, and upon her outraged ears fell a tumultuous torrent of words. Desperate attempts to check this outpouring were unheeded, possibly unheard. Mr Ryde, not content with laying his heart at her feet, gave her an incoherent account of his present circumstances and future expectations, swore eternal devotion, and declared his intention of plunging into the Avon if denied hope. Perceiving that she shrank back in alarm, shocked tears in her eyes, he begged her not to be frightened, and contrived to get an arm round her slim waist.

Into this ridiculous scene walked Major Kirkby, unannounced. He checked on the threshold, considerably astonished. One glance sufficed to put him in tolerably accurate possession of the facts. He trod briskly across the floor, as the disconcerted lover turned a startled face towards him, and Fanny gave a thankful cry. A hand grasping his coat-collar assisted Mr Ryde to rise swiftly to his feet. "You had best beg Lady Spenborough's pardon before you go," said the Major cheerfully. "And another time don't come to pay a morning visit when you're foxed!"

Confused, and indignant, Mr Ryde hotly refuted this suggestion, and tried somewhat incoherently to assure both Fanny and the Major of the honourable nature of his proposal. But Fanny merely hid her scarlet face in her hands, and the Major propelled him to the door, saying: "When you are five years older you may make proposals, and by that time you will know better than to force your attentions upon a lady whose circumstances should be enough to protect her from annoyance. Take yourself off! If you oblige me to escort you downstairs, I shall do so in a way you won't care for."

With these damping words, he pushed Mr Ryde out of the room, and shut the door upon him. "Stupid young coxcomb!" he remarked, turning again into the room. When he saw that Fanny was by no means inclined to laugh the matter off, but was, in fact, excessively distressed and agitated, and he went quickly towards her, exclaiming in concern: "You must not take it so to heart! The devil! I wish I *had* kicked him downstairs!"

She tried to overcome her emotion, but as fast as she wiped the tears from her cheeks her eyes filled again. The novelty of the experience had upset her as much as its impropriety. She was trembling pitiably, and as pale as she had before been red. "How could he? How *could* he insult me so?" she sobbed.

"It was very bad, but he didn't mean to insult you!" the Major assured her. "To be sure, he deserves to be flogged for impertinence, but it was nothing more than a silly boy's infatuation!"

"Oh, what must *my* conduct have been to have allowed him to suppose that such *dreadful* advances could be welcome to me?" wept Fanny. "Not one year widowed, and this – I never dreamed – it never occurred to me -!"

"No, no, of course it did not!" said the Major soothingly, dropping on one knee in precisely the spot vacated by Mr Ryde, and taking the widow's hand in a comforting clasp. "*You* are not to be blamed! Your conduct has been irreproachable! Don't -! I can't bear to see you so unhappy, my – Lady Spenborough!"

"I beg your pardon – it is very silly!" Fanny choked, making heroic efforts to compose herself, and succeeding only in uttering a stifled sob. "I didn't know how to stop him, and he kept on kissing my hands, and saying such things, and frightening me so! Indeed, I am very sorry to be so foolish! I am s-so very m-much obliged to you for s-sending him away! I can't think w-what I should have done if you had not c-come in, for he – oh, Major Kirkby, he actually put his arm round me! I am so much ashamed, but *indeed* I never gave him the least encouragement!"

At this point, the Major, going one better than Mr Ryde, put both his own arms round the drooping figure, cradling it protectively, and saying involuntarily: "Fanny, Fanny! There, my darling, there, then! Don't cry! I'll see to it the young cub doesn't come near you again! There's nothing now to be frightened of!"

Quite how it happened, neither knew. The outraged widow, finding an inviting shoulder so close, sank instinctively against it, and the next instant was locked in a far more alarming embrace than she had been subjected to by the unlucky Mr Ryde. The impropriety of it did not seem to strike her. Her heart leaped in her bosom; she clung tightly to the Major; and put up her face to receive his kiss.

For a long moment they stayed thus, then, as though realization dawned simultaneously on each of them, Fanny made a convulsive movement to free herself, and the Major's arms dropped from about her, and he sprang up, exclaiming: "Fanny! Oh, my God, my God, what have I done?"

They stared at one another, pale as death, horror in their faces. "I I beg your pardon!" the Major stammered. "I didn't mean – Oh, my darling, what are we to do?"

The colour came rushing back to her cheeks; so tender a glow shone in her eyes that it was all he could do not to take her back into his arms. But she said in a constricted voice: "You were only trying to comfort me. I know you did not mean -"

"Fanny, Fanny, don't say it! We could not help ourselves!" he interrupted, striding over to the window, as though he dared not trust himself to look at her. "The fool that I have been!"

Such bitter anguish throbbed in his voice that she winced, and bowed her head to hide a fresh spring of tears. A long silence fell. Fanny surreptitiously wiped her eyes, and said faintly: "It was my fault. You must forget – how silly I was. I don't regard it. I know you cannot have meant it."

"I think I must have loved you from the moment I saw you."

"Oh, no, no! Hector, think what you are saying! You love Serena! All these years you have loved her!"

"I have loved a dream. A sickly, sentimental dream which only a moonstruck fool could have created! The vision I cherished it was not of Serena! She was never like it!"

"No, not like your dream, but better by far!" she said quickly.

"Yes, better by far! She is a grand creature! I admire her, I honour her, I think her the most beautiful woman I ever beheld – but I do not love her!"

She pressed a hand to her temple. "How can this be? Oh, no it is not possible! It *could* not be!"

"Do you believe me to be mad?" he asked, coming away from the window. "How can I make you understand?" He sat down opposite to her, and dropped his head into his hands. "It wasn't madness, but folly! When I knew her first – oh, I was head over ears in love with her! as ridiculous an object, I suppose, as that wretched boy I found with you just now! Separated from her, joining my regiment, as I did, in the Peninsula, seeing no women other than camp-followers and Spanish peasants for months, there was nothing to banish Serena's image from my memory. It was not enough to remember her: insensibly I laid coat upon coat of new and more dazzling paint upon my image! Her face I could not alter; her *self* I did! Perhaps I never knew it!" He looked up, a painful smile twisting his lips. "Were you ever given laudanum for an aching tooth, Fanny? Enough to make you believe your dreams were real? That was what Serena's image was to me. Then – I met her again." He paused, and sank his head in his hands again, and groaned. "Her face, more lovely even than I remembered it! her smiling eyelids, the music in her voice, her witchery, the very grace of her every movement – all, all as I had remembered them! I was in love again, but still in that insane dream! The woman beneath what blinded my eyes was a stranger to me. My image I had endowed with my own thoughts, my own tastes: Serena and I have scarcely a thought in common, and our tastes -" He broke off, with a mirthless laugh. "Well, you must know how widely divergent they are!"

"I know that you have sometimes been surprised – even disappointed, but you have been happy! Surely you have been happy?" Fanny said imploringly.

"I have been happy because of *you*," he replied. "Today I know that. I did not before. I was like a man dazzled by strong sunlight, and when my eyes grew accustomed, and I saw a landscape less perfect than I had imagined it, I shut them. I didn't think it possible that my feeling for Serena could change. That *you* were the woman I loved I never knew until I had you in my arms, and realized that to let you go would be to tear the heart out of my chest."

She rose quickly, and knelt beside him, putting her arms round him. "And mine! Oh, Hector, Hector, and mine! Oh, how wicked I have been! For *I* knew how much I loved you!"

They clung together, her head on his shoulder, his hand holding it there. Her tears fell silently; when she spoke again her voice had a resolute calm. "It cannot be, my dearest."

"No. I know it. Well for you to be saved from such a contemptible clodpole as I have proved myself to be!" he said bitterly.

She drew his hand from her cheek, and held it. "You must not talk so. Or speak to me of what might have been. We must neither of us think of that ever again. Hector, we *could* not –!"

"You need not tell me so. In me, it would be infamous!"

"You will learn to be happy with Serena – indeed, you will, dearest! Just now it seems as though – but we shall grow accustomed, both of us! Where there is no question of *dislike*, one does, you see. I-I *know* that. Serena must never so much as suspect this!"

"No," he said hopelessly.

She could not forbear to put her hand up, lightly stroking his waving fair hair. "There is so much in Serena that is true, not a part of your image! Her courage, and her kindness, and her generosity – oh, a thousand things!" She tried to smile. "You will forget you were ever so foolish as to love me, even a little. Serena is cleverer than I am, and so much more beautiful!"

He took her face between his hands, and looked deep into her eyes. "Cleverer, and more beautiful, but so much less dear!" he said, in an aching voice. He let her go. "Don't be afraid! I have been a fool, but I hope I am a man of honour."

"I know, oh, I know! You have been a little shocked to find that Serena is not quite what you thought her, but you will recover, and you will wonder at yourself for not having perceived at once how much more worth loving she is than that stupid image you made! And she loves you, Hector!"

He was silent for a moment, staring at his clenched hands, but presently he raised his eyes to Fanny's again, in a searching, questioning look. "Does she?" he asked.

She was amazed. "But, Hector -! Oh, how can you doubt it, when she has even said she will relinquish her fortune only to please you?"

He sighed. "Yes. I was forgetting. But it has sometimes seemed to me – Fanny, are you sure it is not Rotherham whom she really loves?"

"Rotherham?" The blankest incredulity sounded in Fanny's voice. "Good God, what makes you think such a thing?"

"I didn't think it. But when he came here – afterwards – the suspicion crossed my mind that it was so."

"No, no, she could not! Oh, if you had ever heard what she says of her engagement to him you would not entertain such thoughts! They cannot meet without falling out! And he! Did you think he loved her still?"

"No," he said heavily. "I saw no sign – it did not occur to me. He made no attempt to prevent our engagement. On the contrary! He behaved to me with a forbearance, indeed, a kindness, which I neither expected nor felt that I deserved! And his own engagement was announced before he knew of Serena's."

There was another long silence. Fanny rose to her feet. "She doesn't care for him. Oh, I am sure she could not! It is the feeling for a man who was her father's friend! If it were so – and you too -!"

He too rose. "She shall never, God helping me, know the truth! I must go. How I am to face her I know not! Fanny, I cannot do it immediately! There is some business at home which I should have attended to long since. I'll go away. Inform her that I called to tell her I had a letter from my agent, that I mean to leave by the mail-coach this afternoon!" He glanced at the gilded clock on the mantelshelf. "It leaves Bath at five o'clock, does it not? I have just time to pack my portmanteau, and to catch it."

"It will not do!" she cried. "If you go away like this, what must she think?"

"I shall come back. Tell her that it is only for a few days! I must have time to collect myself! Just at this moment -" He broke off, caught her hands, and kissed them passionately, uttering: "My darling, my darling! *Forgive* me!" Then, without another word, or a backward look, he strode quickly out of the room.

CHAPTER SIXTEEN

WHEN SERENA returned to Laura Place, it was nearly three hours later, and Fanny had had time to compose herself. She had fled to the security of her bedchamber as soon as she had heard the front door slam behind the Major, and had given way to uncontrollable despair. The violence of her feelings left her so exhausted that even in the midst of her agitating reflections, she fell asleep. She awoke not much refreshed, but calm, and if her spirits could not be other than low and oppressed and her cheeks wan, there were no longer signs to be seen in her face of a prolonged bout of crying.

Serena came in to find her seated in the window-embrasure, with a book lying open on her knee. "Fanny, have you been picturing me kidnapped, or lost, or dead on the road? I am filled with remorse, and why I ever consented to go to Wells with that stupid party I cannot imagine! I might have known it would be too far for comfort or enjoyment! Indeed, I did know it, and allowed myself *and* you to be victimized merely because Emily wanted to go, and could not unless I took her. Or so I thought, but, upon my soul, I fancy Mrs Beaulieu would have accepted her with complaisance even though she had met her but once before in her life! Her good-nature is really excessive: such a parcel of ramshackle people as she had permitted to join the party I never companied with in my life before! I assure you, Fanny, that with the exception of her own family, the Aylshams, young Thormanby, and myself, Mr Goring was the most creditable member of the expedition!"

"Good heavens, did *he* go with you?"

"He did, upon Mrs Floore's suggestion. It was out of my power to refuse to sponsor him, and by the time I had run my eye over the rest of the party I was glad of it! He is not, perhaps, the most enlivening of companions, but he may be depended upon to maintain a stolid sobriety, and his joining us enabled me to dispense with Fobbing's escort, for which I was thankful! I should have been in disgrace with Fobbing for a week, had he seen our cavalcade! I am well served, you will tell me, for not attending to Hector! He told me how it would be – though I *don't* think he foresaw that I should spend the better part of my time in Wells in giving set-downs to one dashing blade, and foiling the attempts of another to withdraw me from the rest of the party!"

"Dearest, how disagreeable it must have been! I *wish* you had not gone!"

"Yes, so did I! It was a dead bore. We didn't reach Wells until noon, for in spite of all the fine tales I was told it is a three-hour drive; and we spent four interminable hours there, resting the horses, eating a nuncheon, looking at the Cathedral, and dawdling about the town. And, that nothing might be lacking to crown my day, I allowed Emily to drive to Wells in a landaulet with the young Aylshams and no chaperon to check the sort of high spirits that inevitably attack a party of children of whom not one is over eighteen years of age! By the time she had reached Wells she was by far too full of liveliness for propriety, and ready to maintain an *à suivie* flirtation with the court-card who had ridden close to the landaulet all the way to Wells."

"Serena, you did not permit it? For *either* of you to be in a chain with such vulgar persons is shocking!"

"Exactly so! I formed an instant alliance with the respectable Mr Goring, and between us we kept her under close guard. To do her justice, once away from the wilder members of the party she soon became sober again. But I gave her a tremendous scold on the way home, I promise you!"

"Did you consider what Lord Rotherham would say to all this?" Fanny asked, glancing fleetingly at her.

"It was unnecessary: I knew! *That* was the gist of my scold, and it brought upon me a flood of tears, and entreaties not to tell him, or Mama."

"Tears and entreaties! Do you still say that she is not afraid of him, Serena?"

"No, she is a good deal in awe of him, and I fancy he has frightened her," Serena replied coolly.

"If he has done that, you will scarcely persist in believing that he loves her!"

Serena turned away to pick up her gloves. "I have every reason to believe, my dear Fanny, that he loves her *à corps perdu*," she said, in a dry voice. "Unless I much mistake the matter, it is the violence of his passion which has put her in a fright, not his withering tongue! Of *that* she stands in awe merely, and it is as well she should, for she is too giddy, and too often betrayed into some piece of hoydenish conduct. She was not thrown into a panic by rebuke, I'll swear! She is too well-accustomed to it. For a man of experience, Rotherham has handled her very ill. If I did not suspect that he has realized it already, I should be strongly tempted to tell him so."

"*Serena!*" Fanny protested, quite scandalized.

"Don't distress yourself! I fancy that is why he has not come to Bath to see Emily. No doubt Lady Laleham hinted him away: she at least is clever enough to know that with such a shy little innocent as Emily it would be fatal to set too hot a pace to courtship. I wonder she ever left them alone together except that I collect he was at first careful not to alarm a filly he must have known was as shy as she could stare, ready to bolt at one false move." Her lip curled. "He's impatient, but I never knew him to be so on the box or in the saddle. I own, I am astonished that a man with such fine, light hands could have blundered so!"

"Serena, I do beseech you not to talk in that horrid way!" broke in Fanny. "Emily is not a *horse*!"

"Filly, my love, filly!"

"*No,* Serena! And whatever you may choose to imagine, it's my belief he hasn't come to Bath because he doesn't know Emily is here. Recollect that Lady Laleham would not let him set eyes on Mrs Floore for the world! Depend upon it, she has fobbed him off – if it was necessary, which I don't at all believe! – with some lie."

"Rotherham is well aware of Emily's direction. She received a letter from him yesterday, written from Claycross," replied Serena. "Lady Laleham found another means of keeping him away from Bath, you see. I don't doubt he will handle Emily with far more discretion when he meets her again – though I cannot think it wise of him to write, pressing for an early marriage, before he has soothed her maidenly fears. However, I trust I have to some extent performed that office for him."

"He is pressing for an early marriage?" Fanny repeated.

"Yes, why not?" Serena said evenly. "He is very right, though he had better have seen her first. Once she is his wife, he will very soon teach her not to shrink from his embraces."

"How can you? Oh, how can you?" Fanny exclaimed, shuddering. "When you know that she neither loves nor trusts him!"

"She will rapidly do both. She is amazingly persuadable I assure you!" Serena retorted. She glanced at the clock. "Do we dine at eight? How *tonnish* we become! I must go and make myself tidy. Does Hector dine with us tonight, or is he vexed with me for having flouted his extremely wise advice?"

"You know he is never vexed," Fanny said. "But he doesn't come to us tonight. He called this afternoon, to desire me to tell you that he was obliged to go into Kent for a few days, and meant to catch the mail, at five o'clock."

"Good heavens, what a sudden start! Has some disaster befallen?"

"Oh, no! That is, I did not question him, naturally! But he said something about business which he had neglected, and his agent's having written to tell him that it had become most urgent."

"Oh, I see! Very likely, I daresay. I recall that he told me once that he had come to Bath for a few weeks only. The weeks have turned into months! I hope he will despatch his business swiftly: how moped we shall be without him!"

"Yes, indeed!" Fanny agreed. Her voice sounded hollow in her own ears; she fancied Serena had noticed it, and made haste to change the subject. "Serena, if Rotherham comes to see Emily – and if he is now at Claycross you cannot doubt that he will! -"

"I doubt it very much," Serena interrupted. "I understand he has been there for a fortnight, or more! He has neither visited Emily, nor suggested to her that he should. If you won't allow my first answer to that riddle to be correct, perhaps he is trying to pique her. How good for him to be kept champing at the bit! I wish I might see it!"

"Can it be that he has guests staying with him?" said Fanny.

"I have not the remotest conjecture, my dear!" replied Serena. "Perhaps, since Lady Laleham is at Cherrifield Place again, he finds her company sufficiently amusing!"

But his lordship, although alone at Claycross, showed no disposition to fraternize with his future mother-in-law. He even omitted to pay her the compliment of leaving cards at Cherrifield Place, a circumstance which made her so uneasy that she bullied Sir Walter into riding over to Claycross to discover whether Rotherham had taken offence at Emily's prolonged stay in Bath, and to reassure him if he had.

Sir Walter was a man of placid temperament, but he was also strongly opposed to any form of activity that seemed likely to cast the least rub in the way of his quite remarkable hedonism, and he resented this effort to compel him to enter into his wife's matrimonial schemes. It was his practice to abandon home and children entirely to her management, partly because he was indifferent to both, and partly because argument was abhorrent to him. Having long outlived his fondness for his wife, he spent as little time in her vicinity as was possible, and was inclined to be aggrieved that his only reward for being so obliging as to spend a week under his own roof was to be hunted out on an embarrassing errand.

"I sometimes wonder," declared Lady Laleham acidly, "whether you have a spark of affection for your children, Sir Walter!"

He was stung by the injustice of this speech, and replied indignantly: "Very pretty talking, upon my soul, when I've let you drag me down to this damned lazar-house! If coming to see the brats when they're covered all over with spots isn't being affectionate, I should like to know what is!"

"Have you *no* desire to see your eldest daughter creditably established?" she demanded.

"Yes, I have!" he retorted. "It's a damned expense, puffing her off all over town, and the sooner she's off my hands the better pleased I shall be."

"Expense!" she gasped. "*Your* hands! And who, pray, paid the London bills?"

"Your mother did, and that's what I complain of. I'm not unreasonable, and if you choose to persuade the old lady to fritter away a fortune on presentation-gowns, and balls, and the rest of it, I'm not surprised she hasn't sent me that draft."

"Mama has promised to send it when Emily is well again," Lady Laleham said, controlling herself with some difficulty.

"Yes, provided you don't take the girl away from her! A rare bargain, that! I shouldn't be surprised if Emily never does get well, and then where shall we be?"

"What nonsense!" she said scornfully. "Emily shall come home the instant we are rid of these vexatious measles. Mama cannot withhold our daughter from us for ever!"

"No, but she can withhold her money, which is a deal more to the point! If you weren't stuffed so full of senseless ambition, Susan, you'd see whether the old lady wouldn't be prepared to pay us a handsome sum to let her keep Emily for good!"

"Emily," said his wife coldly, "will return to us precisely when I desire her to, and she will be married as soon afterwards as Rotherham chooses."

"Well, the odds are he won't choose to marry her at all, if I get a clap on the shoulder, so take care you don't out-jockey yourself, my lady!" said Sir Walter.

"You will not be arrested for debt, if that is what you mean, while your daughter is known to be betrothed to one of the richest peers in the land," she replied. "If the engagement were to be declared off, it would be another matter, no doubt. You will oblige me, therefore, by going to Claycross, and setting Rotherham's mind at ease – if any suspicion lurks in it that Emily is reluctant to marry him!"

"I don't mind going to Claycross, because Rotherham has a devilish good sherry in his cellars; but if Emily bolted to your mother because she didn't want to marry Rotherham it stands to reason she'll come home if he cries off, and as soon as she does that the old lady will hand over the blunt. Which will be all the same to me. In fact, if she don't like him, I'd as lief she didn't marry him, for I've nothing against her, and I don't like him myself."

"She does like him!" Lady Laleham said swiftly. "She is very young, however, and his ardour frightened her. It was nothing but a piece of nonsense, I assure you! I blame myself for having allowed them out of my sight: it shan't happen again."

"Well, you can make yourself easy on one count: Rotherham won't cry off."

"I wish I might be certain of that!"

Sir Walter shook his head. "Ah, it's one of the things I never could teach you!" he said regretfully. "You will just have to take my word for it: a gentleman, my dear, doesn't cry off from a betrothal."

She bit her lip, but refrained from speech. Sir Walter was so much pleased with his triumph that he rode over to Claycross the very next day.

He was ushered into Rotherham's library twenty minutes after Lord Spenborough, paying a ceremonial visit, had left it: a circumstance which possibly accounted for the expression of impatient boredom on his host's face. He was accorded a civil, if unenthusiastic, welcome, and for half an hour sat talking of sporting events. Since this was his favourite subject, he might have continued to discuss for the remainder of his visit the form of various race-horses, and the respective chances of Scroggins, and Church, a reputedly tiresome customer, in a forthcoming encounter at Moulseyhurst.

But when Rotherham rose to refill the glasses he said: "What news have you to give me of Miss Laleham?"

Reminded of his errand, Sir Walter replied: "Oh, tol-lol, you know! Better: decidedly better! In fact, she's fretting to come home."

"What prevents her?"

"Measles. Can't have the poor girl coming out in spots! However, it won't be long now! There aren't any more of them to catch 'em. William was the last – no, not William! Wilfred? Well, I've no head for names, but the youngest of them, at all events."

"Is Miss Laleham well enough to receive a visit from me?" asked Rotherham.

"Nothing she'd like better, I daresay, but the deuce is in it that her grandmother's not well. Not receiving visitors at present. Well, she can't: she's in bed," said Sir Walter, surprising himself by his own inventiveness.

He found to his discomfort that his host was looking at him in a disagreeably piercing way. "Tell me, Laleham!" said Rotherham. "Is Miss Laleham regretting her engagement to me? The truth, if you please!"

This, thought Sir Walter bitterly, was just the sort of thing that made one dislike Rotherham. Flinging damned abrupt questions at one's head, no matter whether one happened to be swallowing sherry at the moment, or not! No manners, not a particle of proper feeling! "God bless my soul!" he ejaculated, still choking a little. "Of course she isn't! Nothing of the sort, Marquis, nothing of the sort! Lord, what a notion to take into your head! Regretting it, indeed!"

He laughed heartily, but saw that there was not so much as the flicker of a smile on Rotherham's somewhat grim mouth. His curiously brilliant eyes had narrowed, in a measuring look, and he kept them fixed on his visitor's face for much longer than Sir Walter thought necessary or mannerly.

"Talks of nothing but her bride clothes!" produced Sir Walter, feeling impelled to say something.

"Gratifying!"

Sir Walter decided that his visit had lasted long enough.

Returning from attending his guest to where his horse was being held for him, Rotherham walked into the house, a heavy frown on his face. His butler, waiting by the front-door, observed this with a sinking heart. He had cherished hopes that a visit from his prospective father-in-law might alleviate his lordship's distemper, but it was evident that it had not done so. More up in the boughs than ever! thought Mr Peaslake, his countenance wholly impassive.

Rotherham stopped. Peaslake, enduring that disconcerting stare, rapidly searched his conscience, found it clean, and registered a silent vow to send the new footman packing if he had dared yet again to alter the position of so much as a pen on my lord's desk.

"Peaslake!"

"My lord?"

"If anyone else should come to visit me while I remain under this roof, I have ridden out, and you don't know when I mean to return!"

"Very good, my lord!" said Peaslake, not betraying by the faintest quiver of a muscle his heartfelt relief.

There was never anything at all equivocal about his lordship's orders, and no one in his employment would have dreamt of deviating from them by a hairsbreadth, but this particular order cast the household, two days later, into a quandary. After a good deal of argument, some maintaining that it was not meant to apply to the unexpected visitor left by the head footman to cool his heels in one of the saloons, and others asserting that it most certainly was, Peaslake fixed the head footman with a commanding eye, and recommended him to go and discover what his lordship's pleasure might be.

"Not me, Mr Peaslake!" said Charles emphatically.

"You heard me!" said Peaslake awfully.

"I won't do it! I don't mind hearing you, and I'm sorry to be disobliging, but what I don't want to hear is *him* asking me if I'm deaf, or can't understand plain English, thanking you all the same! And it ain't right for you to tell Robert to go," he added, as the butler's eye fell on his colleague, "not after what happened this morning!"

"I will ask Mr Wilton's advice," said Peaslake.

This announcement met with unanimous approval. If any member of the establishment could expect to come off scatheless when his lordship was in raging ill-humour, that one was his steward, who had come to Claycross before his lordship had been born.

He listened to the problem, and said, after a moment's thought: "I fear he will not be pleased, but I am of the opinion that he should be told of it."

"Yes, Mr Wilton. Such is my own view," agreed Peaslake. He added dispassionately: "Except that he said he did not wish to be disturbed."

"I see," said Mr Wilton, carefully laying his pen down in the tray provided for it. "In that case, I will myself carry the message to him, if you would prefer it?"

"Thank you, Mr Wilton, I would!" said Peaslake gratefully, following him out of his office, and watching with respect his intrepid advance upon the library.

Rotherham was seated at his desk, a litter of papers round him. When the door opened, he spoke without raising his eyes from the document he was perusing. "When I say I don't wish to be disturbed, I mean exactly that! Out!" he snapped.

"I beg your lordship's pardon," said the steward, with unshaken calm.

Rotherham looked up, his scowl lifting a little. "Oh, it's you, Wilton! What is it?"

"I came to inform you, my lord, that Mr Monksleigh wishes to see you."

"Write and tell him I'm ruralizing, and will see no one."

"Mr Monksleigh is already here, my lord."

Rotherham flung down the paper he was holding. "Oh, hell and the devil confound it!" he exclaimed. "*Now* what?"

Mr Wilton did not reply, but waited placidly.

"I shall have to see him, I suppose," Rotherham said irritably. "Tell him to come in! – and warn him he isn't staying here more than one night!"

Mr Wilton bowed, and turned to leave the room.

"One moment!" said Rotherham, struck by a sudden thought. "Why the devil are you being employed to announce visitors, Wilton? I keep a butler and four foot men in this house, and I fail to see why it should be necessary for you to perform their duties! Where's Peaslake?"

"He is here, my lord," responded Mr Wilton calmly.

"Then why didn't he come to inform me of Mr Monksleigh's arrival?"

Mr Wilton neither blenched at the dangerous note in that harsh voice, nor answered the question. He merely looked at his master very steadily.

Suddenly a twisted grin dawned. "Pigeon-hearted imbecile! No, I don't mean you, and you know I don't! Wilton, I'm blue-devilled!"

"Yes, my lord. It has been noticed that you are a trifle out of sorts."

Rotherham burst out laughing. "Why don't you say as sulky as a bear, and be done with it? I give you leave! *You* don't exasperate me by shaking like a blancmanger merely because I look at you!"

"Oh, no, my lord! But, then, I have known you for a very long time, and have become quite accustomed to your fits of the sullens," said Mr Wilton reassuringly.

Rotherham's eyes gleamed appreciation. "Wilton, are you *never* out of temper?"

"In my position, my lord, one is obliged to master one's ill-humour," said Mr Wilton.

Rotherham flung up a hand. "*Touché*! *Damn* you, how dare you?"

Mr Wilton smiled at him. "Shall I bring Mr Monksleigh to you here, my lord?"

"No, certainly not! Send Peaslake to do so! You can tell him I won't snap his nose off, if you like!"

"Very well, my lord," said Mr Wilton, and withdrew.

A few minutes later, the butler opened the door, and announced Mr Monksleigh, and Rotherham's eldest ward strode resolutely into the room.

A slender young gentleman, dressed in the extreme of fashion, with skin-tight pantaloons of bright yellow, and starched shirt-points so high that they obscured his cheek-bones, he was plainly struggling with conflicting emotions. Wrath sparkled in his eyes, but trepidation had caused his cheeks to assume a somewhat pallid hue. He came to a halt in the middle of the room, gulped, drew an audible breath, and uttered explosively: "Cousin Rotherham! I must and will speak to you!"

"Where the *devil* did you get that abominable waistcoat?" demanded Rotherham.

CHAPTER SEVENTEEN

SINCE MR MONKSLEIGH had occupied himself, while left to wait in the Green Saloon, in composing and silently rehearsing his opening speech, this entirely unexpected question threw him off his balance. He blinked, and stammered: "It isn't ab-bominable! It's all the c-crack!"

"Don't let me see it again! What do you want?"

Mr Monksleigh, touched on the raw, hesitated. On the one hand, he was strongly tempted to defend his taste in waistcoats; on the other, he had been given the cue for his opening speech. He decided to respond to it, drew another deep breath, and said, in rather too highpitched a voice, and much more rapidly than he had intended: "Cousin Rotherham! Little though you may relish my visit, little though you may like what I have to say, reluctant though you may be to reply to me, I will not submit to being turned away from your door! It is imperative -"

"You haven't been turned away from my door."

"It is imperative that I should have speech with you!" said Mr Monksleigh.

"You are having speech with me – a vast deal of speech! How much?"

Choking with indignation, Mr Monksleigh said: "I didn't come to ask you for money! I don't want any money!"

"Good God! Aren't you in debt?"

"No, I am not! Well, nothing to signify!" he amended. "And if I hadn't had to come all the way to Claycross to find you I should be quite plump in the pocket, what's more! Naturally, I didn't bargain for that! There's no way of living economically if one is obliged to dash all over the country, but that wasn't my fault! First there was the hack, to carry me to Aldersgate; then there was my ticket on the mail coach; and the tip to the guard; and another to the coachman, of course; and then I had to hire a chaise-and-pair to bring me here from Gloucester; and as a matter of fact I *shall* have to ask you to for an advance on next quarter's allowance, unless you prefer to *lend* me some blunt. I daresay you think I ought to have travelled on the stage, but -"

"Have I said so?"

"No, but -"

"Then wait until I do! What have you come to say to me?"

"Cousin Rotherham!" began Mr Monksleigh again.

"I'm not a public meeting!" said Rotherham irascibly. "Don't say *Cousin Rotherham!* every time you open your mouth! Say what you have to say like a reasonable being! And sit down!"

Mr Monksleigh flushed scarlet, and obeyed, biting his over-sensitive lip. He stared resentfully at his guardian, lounging behind his desk, and watching him with faint scorn in his eyes. He had arrived at Claycross so burning with the sense of his wrongs that had Rotherham met him on the doorstep he felt sure that he could have discharged his errand with fluency, dignity, and forcefulness. But first he had been kept waiting for twenty minutes; next he had been obliged to suspend his oratory to admit that a monetary advance would be welcome indeed, necessary, if the post-boys were to be paid; and now he had been sharply called to order as though he had been a schoolboy. All these things had a damping effect upon him, but, as he stared at Rotherham, every ill he had suffered at his hands, every malicious spoke that had been thrust into his ambitions, and every cruel set-down he had received, came into his mind, and a sense of injury gave him courage to speak. "It is of a piece with all the rest!" he said suddenly, kneading his hands together between his knees.

"What is?"

"You know very well! Perhaps you thought I shouldn't dare speak to you! But -"

"If I thought that, I've learnt my mistake!" interpolated Rotherham. "What the devil are you accusing me of?" He perceived that his ward was labouring under strong emotion, and said, with a good deal of authority in his voice, but much less asperity: "Come, Gerard, don't be a gudgeon! What am I supposed to have done?"

"Everything you could, to blight every ambition I ever had!" Gerard replied, with suppressed violence.

Rotherham looked considerably taken aback. "Comprehensive!" he said dryly.

"It's true! You never liked me! Just because I didn't wish to hunt, or box, or play cricket, or shoot, or – or any of the things you like, except fishing, and it's no thanks to you I *do* like fishing, because you forbade me to borrow your rods, as though I had *intended* to break it – I mean -"

"What you mean," said Rotherham ruthlessly, "is that I taught you in one sharp lesson not to take my rods without leave! If this is a sample of the various ways in which I have blighted your ambition -"

"Well, it isn't! I only – Well, anyway, I shouldn't care for that if it weren't for all the rest! It has been one thing after another! When I was at Eton, and had the chance to spend the summer holidays sailing with friends, could I prevail upon you to give your consent? No! You sent me to that miserable grinder, just because my tutor told you I shouldn't pass Little-Go. Much he knew about it! But of course you chose to believe him, and not me, because you have always taken a – a malicious delight in thwarting me! Ay! and when you *knew* that I wanted to go up to Oxford, with my particular friends, you sent me to Cambridge! If that was not malice, *what* was it?"

Rotherham, who had stretched both legs out, was lying back in his chair, with his ankles crossed, and his hands in the pockets of his buckskin breeches, regarding his incensed ward with a look of sardonic amusement. He said: "A desire to separate you from your particular friends. Go on!"

This answer not unnaturally fanned the flames of Mr Monksleigh's fury. "You *admit it*! I guessed as much! All of a piece! Yes, and you refused to lend me the money to get my poems published, and not content with that, you insulted me!"

"Did I?" said Rotherham, faintly surprised.

"You know you did! You said you liked better security for your investments!"

"That was certainly unkind. You must blame my unfortunate manner! I've never had the least finesse, I fear. However, I can't feel that I blighted *that* ambition. You'll be of age in little more than a year, and then you can pay to have the poems published yourself."

"And I shall do so! And also," said Gerard belligerently, "I shall choose what friends I like, and go where I like, and do what I like!"

"Rake's Progress. Have I chosen any friends for you, by the way?"

"No, you haven't! All you do is to *object* to my friends! Would you permit me to visit Brighton, that time, when Lord Grosmont asked me to go along with him? No, you would not! But that wasn't the worst! Last year! When I came down in the middle of term, after Boney escaped from Elba, and *begged* you to give me permission to enrol as a volunteer! Did you listen to a word I said? Did you *consider* the matter? Did you give me permission? Did -"

"No," interrupted Rotherham unexpectedly. "I did not."

Disconcerted by this sudden answer to his rhetorical questions Gerard glared at him. "And very poor-spirited I thought you, to submit so tamely to my decree," Rotherham added.

A vivid flush rose to Gerard's face. He said hotly: "I was forced to submit! You have always had the whip-hand! I have been obliged to do as you ordered me, because *you* paid for my education, and for my brothers', and Cambridge too, and if ever I had dared to -"

"Stop!" Such molten rage sounded in the one rapped-out word that Gerard quailed. Rotherham was no longer lounging in his chair, and there was no vestige of amusement in his face. It wore instead so unpleasant an expression that Gerard's heart began to thud violently, and he felt rather sick. Rotherham was leaning forward, one hand on his desk, and clenched hard. "Have I ever held that threat over your head?" he demanded. "Answer me!"

"No!" Gerard said, his voice jumping nervously. "No, but – but I knew it was you who sent me to Eton, and now Ch-Charlie as well, and -"

"Did I tell you so?"

"No," Gerard muttered, quite unable to meet those brilliant, angry eyes. "My mother...."

"Then how *dare* you speak to me like that, you insufferable cub?" Rotherham said sternly.

Scarlet-faced, Gerard faltered: "I – I beg your pardon! didn't mean – Of course, I am excessively grateful to you, C-Cousin Rotherham!"

"If I had wanted your damned gratitude I should have told you that I had taken upon myself the charge of your education! I don't want it!"

Gerard cast a fleeting look up at him. "I'm glad you don't! To know that I'm beholden to you – *now*!"

"Make yourself easy! You owe me nothing – any of you! I have done nothing for you!" Gerard looked up again, startled. "That surprises you, does it? Do you imagine that I cared the snap of my fingers how or where you were educated? You were wonderfully wrong! All I cared for was that your father's sons should be educated as he was, and as he would have wished them to be! Anything I've chosen to do has been for him, not for you!"

Crestfallen, and considerably shaken, Gerard stammered: "I – I didn't know! I beg your pardon! I didn't mean to say – to say what I *did* say, precisely!"

"Very well," Rotherham said curtly.

"I didn't really think you would -"

"Oh, that will do, that will do!"

"Yes, but I lost my temper! I shouldn't have -"

Rotherham gave a short laugh. "Well, I must be the last man alive not to pardon you for that! Have you come to the end of your catalogue of my past crimes? What is my present offence?"

Mr Monksleigh, having been obliged to offer his guardian an apology, now found it extremely difficult to hurl his culminating accusation at him with anything approaching the passion requisite to convince him of the magnitude of the charge, and of his own desperate sincerity. He had been forced into a position of disadvantage, and the knowledge of this filled him with annoyance rather than with noble rage. He said sulkily: "You have ruined my life!"

It had sounded better, when he had uttered it in the Green Saloon. If Rotherham had been privileged to have heard it then, it would have shocked him out of his scornful indifference, and might even have penetrated his marble heart, and touched him with remorse. It certainly would not have amused him, which was the only effect it appeared now to have upon him. Venturing to steal a glance at him, Gerard saw that he was faintly smiling. The relaxing of his face from its appalling grimness, the quenching of the menacing glitter in his eyes, enabled Gerard to breathe much more easily, but did nothing to endear his guardian to him. Flushing angrily, he said: "You think that ridiculous, I dare say!"

"Damned ridiculous!"

"Yes! Because you have no more sensibility yourself than – than a stone, you think others have none!"

"On the contrary! I am continually being sickened by the excessive sensibility displayed by so many persons of my acquaintance. But that is beside the point! Don't keep me in suspense! How have I so unexpectedly achieved what you are persuaded has been my object for years?"

"I never said that! I daresay you may not have intended to destroy all my hopes! I can readily believe you never so much as thought of what must be *my* sensations when I heard when I discovered -"

"Do try to cultivate a more orderly mind!" interposed Rotherham. "The very fact that I take a malicious pleasure in thwarting you shows intention. I ought to have sent you to Oxford, after all. Clearly, they don't make you study Logic at Cambridge."

"Oh, *damn* you, be quiet!" exclaimed Gerard. "You think me a child, to be roasted and sneered at, but I am not!" His underlip quivered; angry tears sprang to his eyes. He brushed them away, saying in a breaking voice: "You did not even *tell* me -! You left me to discover it, *weeks* afterwards, when you must have known – you *must* have known the shock – the c-crushing blow – it would be to me!" His pent-up emotions choked him. He gave a gasp, and buried his face in his hands.

Rotherham's brows snapped together. He stared at Gerard for a moment, and then rose, and walked across the room to where a side-table stood, bearing upon it several decanters and glasses. He filled two of the glasses, and returned with them, setting one down upon his desk. He dropped a hand on Gerard's shoulder, gripping it not unkindly. "Enough! Come, now! I've told you I don't like an excess of sensibility! No, I am not roasting you: I see that things are more serious than I had supposed. Here's some wine for you! Drink it, and then tell me without any more nonsense what it is that I have done to upset you so much!"

The words were scarcely sympathetic, but the voice, although unemotional, was no longer derisive. Gerard said thickly: "I don't want it! I -"

"Do as I bid you!"

The voice had sharpened. Gerard responded to it involuntarily, starting a little. He took the glass in his unsteady hand, and gulped down some of its contents. Rotherham retired again to his chair behind the large desk, and picked up his own glass. "Now, in as few words as possible, what is it?"

"You know what it is," Gerard said bitterly. "You used your rank – and your wealth – to steal from me the only girl I could *ever* care for!" He perceived that Rotherham was staring at him with sudden intentness, and added: "Miss Laleham!"

"Good God!"

The ejaculation held blank astonishment, but Gerard said: "You knew very well – must have known! – that I – that she -"

"No doubt! – had I half the interest in your affairs with which you credit me! As it is, I did not know." He paused, and sipped his wine, looking at Gerard over the rim of the glass, his brows frowning again, the eyes beneath them narrowed, very hard and bright. "It would have made no difference, except that I should have informed you of the event. I am sorry, if the news came as a blow to you, but at your age you will very speedily recover from it."

This speech, uttered, as it was, in a cold voice, was anything but soothing to a young gentleman suffering the pangs of his first love-affair. It was evident that Rotherham thought his passion a thing of very little account; and his suggestion that it would soon be forgotten, instead of consoling Gerard, made his bosom swell with indignation.

"So that is all you have to say! I might have known how it would be! *Recover* from it!"

"Yes, recover from it," said Rotherham. His lips curled. "I should be more impressed by these tragedy-airs if it had not taken you so long to make up your mind to enact me an affecting scene! I know not how many weeks it is since the engagement was announced, but -"

"I came into Gloucestershire the instant I knew of it!" Gerard said, half starting from his chair. "I never saw the announcement! When I'm up at Cambridge, very often I don't look at a newspaper for days on end! No one told me until only the other day, when Mrs Maldon asked me – asked *me*! – if I was acquainted with the future Lady Rotherham! I was astonished, as may be supposed, to learn that you were engaged, but that was as nothing to the – the horror and stupefaction which held me s-speechless, when Em – Miss Laleham's name was disclosed!"

"I wish to God you were still suffering from horror and stupefaction, if that is the effect such feelings have upon you!" broke in Rotherham. "Be damned to these periods of yours! If you would play-act less, I might believe more! As it is -!" He shrugged. "You came down at the beginning of June, it is now August, your mother is well aware of my engagement, and you say you heard no mention of it until a few days ago? Coming it too strong, Gerard! The truth is that you've talked yourself into this fine frenzy – putting on airs to be interesting!"

Gerard was on his feet, colour flaming in his cheeks. "You shall unsay that! How dare you give me the lie? I have not seen my mother that is, I had not done so until yesterday! I went with the Maldons to Scarborough! When I learned of the engagement, I posted south immediately!"

"What the devil for?"

"To put a stop to it!" Gerard said fiercely.

"To do *what*?"

"Yes! It did not occur to you that *I* might thrust a spoke into *your* wheel, did it?"

"No, and it still does not."

"We shall see! I know, as surely as I stand here -"

"Which won't be very surely, if I have to listen to much more of this rodomontade!"

"You cannot silence me by threats, my lord!"

"It seems improbable that you could be silenced by anything short of a gag. And don't call me *my lord!* It makes you appear even more absurd than you do already."

"I care nothing for what you may think of me, or for your jibes! Emily does not love you – *cannot* love you! You have forced her into this horrible engagement! You and her mother between you! And I say it shall not be!"

Rotherham was once more lying back in his chair, the derisive smile on his lips. "Indeed? And how do you propose to stop it?"

"I am going to see Emily!"

"Oh, no, you are not!"

"Nothing – *nothing* will prevent me! I know well how the business was accomplished! *I* was out of the way, *she*, so gentle, so timid, so friendless, a a dove, fluttering unavailingly in – in the clutches of a *vulture* (for so I think of Lady Laleham, curse her!) and of a – a *wolf*! She, I say -" He broke off, for Rotherham had given a shout of laughter.

"Oh, I don't think the dove would do much fluttering in such a situation as that!" he said.

Gerard, white with fury, hammered his fist on the desk between them. "Ay, a splendid jest, isn't it? Almost as droll as to lead to the altar a girl whose heart you know to be given to another! But you will not do it!"

"I probably shouldn't. Are you asking me to believe that her heart has been given to you?"

"It is true, for all your sneers! From the moment I first saw her, at the Assembly, last Christmas, we became attached!"

"Very likely. *She* is a beautiful girl, and *you* were the first young man to come in her way. You both enjoyed an agreeable flirtation. I've no objection."

"It was not a flirtation! It endured! When she came to London, before *you* had cast your – your predatory eye in her direction, the attachment between us had been confirmed! Had it not been for the odious pretensions of her mother, who would not listen to my offer, it would not have been your engagement that was announced, but mine!"

"Rid your mind of that illusion at least! I should not have permitted you to become engaged to Miss Laleham, or to anyone else."

"I can believe it! But I do not admit your right to interfere in what concerns me so nearly!"

"What you admit doesn't signify. Until you come of age, I have rights over you of which you don't appear to have the smallest conception. I have not chosen to exercise very many of these, but I will tell you now that I shall allow you neither to entangle yourself in an engagement, nor to embarrass my affianced wife by obtruding yourself upon her."

"Obtruding -! Ha! So you fancy she would be embarrassed, do you, cousin?"

"If you subjected her to such a scene as this, I imagine she would be thrown into a fever. She is recovering from a severe attack of influenza."

"Is she?" said Gerard, with awful sarcasm. "Or was it a severe attack of the Marquis of Rotherham? I know that she has been hidden from me: *that* I learned at Cherrifield Place, this very day! From Lady Laleham I expected to hear nothing of Emily's present whereabouts! She would take good care not to let me come near Emily! Now it appears that you too are afraid to disclose her direction! That tells its own tale, Cousin Rotherham!"

"I have not the smallest objection to disclosing her direction," replied Rotherham. "She is visiting her grandmother, in Bath."

"In Bath!" cried Gerard, his face lighting up.

"Yes, in Bath. But you, my dear Gerard, will not go to Bath. When you leave this house, you will return to London, or to Scarborough, if you like: that's all one to me!"

"Oh, no, I shall not!" countered Gerard. "It is not in your power to compel me! You have told me where I may find Emily, and find her I will! She must tell me with her own lips that her feelings have undergone a change, that she is happy in her engagement, before I will believe it! I tell you this because I scorn to deceive you! You shall never say that I went without informing you of my intention!"

"I shall never say that you went at all," said Rotherham, thrusting back his chair, and rising suddenly to his feet. "And I will tell you why, cockerel! You dare not! For just so long as I will bear with you, you crow a puny defiance! But when my patience cracks, you have done with crowing! Beneath all this bombast, you are so much afraid of me that one look is enough make you cringe!" He gave a bark of laughter. "*You* disobey my commands! I wish I may see it! You haven't enough spirit to do so much as keep your knees from knocking together when I comb you down! I know exactly what you will do in this case. You will boast of what you have a very good mind to do, play the broken-hearted lover to gain the sympathy of the credulous, whine to your mother about my tyranny, and give as an excuse for your chickenheartedness the fear that if you failed to respond to my hand on your bridle I should wreak my vengeance on your brothers! What you will not say is that you fear my spurs! But that is the truth!"

He paused, scanning his ward. Gerard was as white as his preposterous shirt-points, trembling a little, and breathing jerkily, but his burning eyes were fixed on Rotherham's face, and did not flinch from the piercing challenge of those contemptuous gray ones. His hands were clenched at his sides; he whispered: "I would like to *kill* you!"

"I don't doubt it. You would probably like to hit me too, but you won't do it. Nor will you treat me to any more of your heroics. You may remain here tonight, but tomorrow you will return whence you came."

"I wouldn't remain another instant under your roof for anything you might offer me!" Gerard gasped.

"Gerard, I said I would have no more heroics!"

"I am leaving Claycross *now*!" Gerard spat at him, and plunged towards the door.

"Not so fast! You are forgetting something!" Gerard paused, and looked over his shoulder. "You told me that your pockets were to let, which is not surprising, after all this posting about the country. How much do you want?"

Gerard stood irresolute. To spurn this offer would be a splendid gesture, and one which he longed to make; on the other hand, there were the post-charges to be paid, and more than a month to be lived through before he received the next quarter's allowance. His sense of dramatic value was outraged by what he perceived to be an anticlimax of a particularly galling nature, and it was in anything but a grateful tone that he said: "I shall be obliged to you if you will advance me fifty pounds, cousin!"

"Oh, you will, will you? And what shall I be expected to advance midway through the next quarter?"

"Rest assured that I shall not ask you to advance me a penny!" said Gerard grandly.

"You wouldn't dare to, would you?" said Rotherham, opening a court-cupboard at the end of the room, and taking from it a strong-box. "You would apply to your mother. Well, since it appears to be entirely my fault that you are at a standstill, I'll let you have your fifty pounds. Next time you wish to upbraid me, do it by letter!"

"If you refuse to advance me my own money, I will only accept *yours* as a loan!" declared Gerard. "I shall repay you the instant I come of age!"

"As you please," shrugged Rotherham, unlocking the strong-box.

"And I will give you my note-of-hand!"

"By all means. You'll find a pen on my desk."

Gerard cast him a look of acute loathing, snatched up a quill, dragged a sheet of paper at random from a sheaf, and in trembling haste wrote a promise to pay. He then flung the quill down, and said: "I shall meet that on the day I gain possession of my principal at latest! And, if I can contrive it, much sooner! I'm obliged to you! Goodbye!"

He then crammed the bills held out to him into his pocket, and hurried out of the room, slamming the door behind him. Rotherham put his strong-box away, and walked slowly back to his desk. He picked up the note-of hand, and began, abstractedly, to tear it into small shreds, his brows lowering, and his lips compressed. The door opened again, and he glanced up quickly.

It was his steward who had entered, and who said in a quiet but resolute voice: "My lord, you will please allow me to have speech with you!"

"Well?"

"I saw Mr Gerard as he left the house, my lord. It is not for me to remonstrate with you, but since there is no one else to do it, I must! You must not let him go like that!"

"I'm damned glad he has gone. My temper will stand no more of him!"

"My lord, this will not do! He is your ward, remember! I have never seen such a look on his face before. What did you do to him, to make him as white as his shirt?"

"What the devil do you suppose I did to a whey-faced weakling I could control with my right hand tied behind me?" demanded Rotherham wrathfully.

"Not that you used your strength, my lord, but your tongue!"

"Yes, I used that to some purpose," said Rotherham, with a grim smile.

"My lord, whatever he may have done -"

"He has done nothing. I doubt if he has the spirit to do anything but nauseate me with his gasconades and his fustian theatrics!"

"Let me fetch him back!" Wilton begged. "You should not frighten him so!"

"I should not be able to frighten him so!"

"You frighten many people, my lord. It has sometimes seemed to me that when your black mood is on you it is your wish to frighten people. But I am sure I don't know why, for you can never tolerate anyone who fears you."

Rotherham looked up quickly, a reluctant laugh escaping him. "True!"

"It is not too late: let me fetch Mr Gerard back!"

"No. I should not have flayed him, I acknowledge, but the temptation to do so was irresistible. It will do him no harm, and may do him a great deal of good."

"My lord -!

"Wilton, I have a considerable regard for you, but you have not the power to make me change my mind!"

"I know that, my lord," Wilton said. "There was only one person who ever had that power."

Danger flickered in Rotherham's eyes, but he did not speak. The steward looked steadily at him for a moment, and then turned, and walked out of the room.

CHAPTER EIGHTEEN

MR MONKSLEIGH reached Bath after dark, and in a Thrasonical mood. When he had given the order to the post-boy to take the Bath road, he had done so in the white heat of his rage, but with a quake of fear in his heart. The experience he had passed through had set every nerve in his slight body quivering, for although he had been stung to fury by the lash of Rotherham's tongue only pride had kept him from breaking down, and betraying the terror beneath his bravado. He was both timid and abnormally sensitive; and from having a keen and often morbid imagination was apt to fancy that persons who, in fact, never gave him a thought were criticizing him unkindly. Anticipation was more dreadful to him than performance; and to be harshly rated turned him sick. A wish to appear to be of consequence was unhappily allied to a lack of self-confidence which he tried to conceal under a boastful manner; and nothing could more surely have won for him the contempt of his guardian. There was never a more ill-assorted pair; and if Gerard was the last boy alive to appeal to Rotherham, no worse guardian than Rotherham could well have been found for a boy compact of timidity and vainglory. A much younger Gerard, at once anxious to impress an almost unknown guardian and afraid that he would be despised by him, encountered a look from those hard, bright eyes, and wilted under it. It was neither angry nor disdainful; it was almost incurious, but it utterly disconcerted Gerard. He had the feeling that it pierced right into his mind, and saw everything that he most wished to hide; and he never recovered from that first, disastrous meeting. Rotherham indifferent made him feel ill-at-ease; when, later, he saw Rotherham angry, he was terrified. A natural abruptness he mistook for a sign of dislike; he read a threat into every curt command; and if he was reprimanded, he was always sure that the brief but shattering scold was but the prelude to hideous retribution. The fact that on the only occasion when condign retribution had fallen upon him it was neither hideous nor even particularly severe quite irrationally failed to reassure him. He thought it a miracle that he had been let off lightly, just as he was convinced, every time he annoyed Rotherham, that he had escaped chastisement by no more than a hairs-breadth.

It was doubtful if Rotherham, with his nerves of steel, his tireless strength, and his impatience of weakness, would ever have felt much liking for so delicate and nervous a boy as Gerard; but he would not have been intolerant of him had it not been for Gerard's unfortunate tendency to brag about himself. In the early days of his guardianship, he had frequently invited him to one or other of his country seats, feeling that however great a nuisance a schoolboy might be to him it was clearly his duty to take an interest in him, giving him a day's hunting, teaching him how to handle a gun, or cast a line, and how to keep a straight left. He very soon realized that Gerard, so far from being grateful, regarded these benefits in the light of severe ordeals, and would have become merely bored had he not heard Gerard, after an ignominious day in the saddle, during the course of which he had contrived to evade all but the easiest of jumps, boasting to one of the servants of the regular raspers he had taken. Rotherham, caring nothing for anyone's admiration or disapproval, and contemptuous of shams, was violently exasperated, and thereafter regarded his ward not with indifference but with scorn. Even Gerard's docility irritated him. He preferred the more resilient Charles, whose predilection for getting into all the more damaging and perilous forms of mischief had made him declare that never again would he have the whelp to stay with him. But as soon as Charles had outgrown his destructive puppyhood he had every intention of opening his doors to him, and of taking him in hand. Charles provoked him to anger, but never to contempt. Severely castigated for setting a booby trap for the butler, which resulted in a splendid breakage of crockery, the chances were that he would bounce into the room not half an hour later, announcing in conscience-stricken accents that he feared he had killed one of the peacocks with his bow and arrow. He found nothing unnerving in the look that made his elder brother shake in his shoes; and when threatened with frightful penalties he grinned. He was outrageously mischievous, maddeningly obstinate, and wholly averse from respecting prohibitions; and since these characteristics never failed to rouse his guardian to wrath neither Gerard nor Mrs Monksleigh could understand why he was quite unafraid of Rotherham, or why Rotherham, however angry, never withered him with the remarks which made Gerard writhe.

"Cousin Rotherham likes people who square up to him," said Charles. "He's a great gun!"

But Rotherham today had shown no signs of liking it, thought Gerard bitterly, unable to perceive the gulf that lay between his rehearsed defiance, and his graceless brother's innate pugnacity. It had angered him into uttering words so scathing that for several stark minutes Gerard had been thrown into such a storm of shocked fury that he was jerked out of his shams, and hurled his defiance at Rotherham without the smallest thought of impressing him. He was angry, and frightened, and deeply mortified; and for quite some time continued in this frame of mind. But as the distance increased between himself and Claycross the tone of his mind became gradually restored, and from quaking at the realization that he was flatly disobeying Rotherham, and wondering what the result would be, he began to believe that he had acquitted himself well in his distressing interview with him. From thinking of all the retorts he might have made was a very short step to imagining that he really had made them; and by the time he reached Bath he was almost set up again in his own conceit, and much inclined to think that he had taught Rotherham a lesson.

Since nothing would be more disagreeable than to be obliged to apply to Rotherham for more funds, he prudently sought out a modest hostelry in the less fashionable part of the town, and installed himself there with every intention of discovering Emily's whereabouts on the following morning. In the event, it was not until two days later that he saw her entering the Pump Room with her grandmother, and was at last able to approach her. The task of locating the house of a lady whose name he had never been told had proved to be unexpectedly difficult.

Emily was very much surprised to see him, and accorded him an ingenuously delighted welcome. He was a pretty youth, with pleasing manners, and such an air of fashion that his company could not but add to her consequence. His passion for her, moreover, was expressed with the greatest decorum, and took the form of humble worship, which was quite unalarming. Upon her first going to London, he had been assiduous in his attentions, and she had enjoyed with him her first flirtation. Not a profound thinker, if she remembered the vows she had exchanged with him, she supposed that he had meant them no more seriously than she had. She did recollect that she had felt very low for quite a week after Mama had forbidden him to visit them again, but Mama had assured her that she would soon recover from her disappointment, which, in fact, she had. Amongst the crowd of Pinks, Tulips, Blades, Beaux, and High Sticklers with whom she rapidly became acquainted, Gerard was to a great extent forgotten.

But she liked him very well, and was happy to meet him again, and at once presented him to Mrs Floore.

Mrs Floore came as a shock to him, for although he had frequently heard his mama stigmatize Lady Laleham as a vulgar creature he had paid very little heed to a stricture he had heard often before, and which generally denoted merely that Mrs Monksleigh had quarrelled with whichever lady was in question. He had expected nothing as unrefined as Mrs Floore, who was arrayed in a gown of such a powerful shade of purple that he almost blinked. However, he had very good manners, and he quickly concealed his astonishment, and made her a civil bow.

Mrs Floore was inclined to favour him. She liked young persons, and Gerard struck her as a pretty-behaved beau, dressed as fine as fivepence, and plainly of the first respectability. But her shrewd gaze had not failed to perceive the ardour in his face when he had come hurrying up to Emily, and she determined not to encourage him. It would never do, she thought, for him to be dangling after Emily in a love-lorn way calculated to set Bath tongues wagging. There was no saying but what Emily's grand Marquis might not like it above half, if it came to his ears. So when she heard him asking Emily if she would be at the Lower Rooms that evening, she interposed, saying that Emily must stay at home to recruit her strength for the Gala night at the Sydney Gardens on the following evening. Gerard, on his guard from the instant he realized this amazing old lady's relationship to his adored, took this with perfect propriety. It was Emily who exclaimed against the prohibition, but so much more in the manner of a child denied a treat than in that of a damsel bent on flirting with a personable admirer, that Mrs Floore relented a little, and said that they would see. It naturally did not occur to her that Emily could have a *tendre* for any other man than her betrothed, but she was well aware that Emily was apt (in the most innocent way) to give rather more encouragement than was seemly in her situation to her admirers. It was all very well for the chit to talk in that misleadingly confiding way of hers to a steady young fellow like Ned Goring, whom one could trust to take no liberties; quite another for her to be giving this smart town sprig to think that she would welcome a flirtation.

But when, after Gerard had escorted the two ladies back to Beaufort

Square, very politely giving Mrs Floore his arm, she told Emily that it would not do for her to be too friendly with such a handsome young beau, Emily looked surprised, and said: "But he is such a splendid dancer, Grandmama! Must I not stand up with him? Why ought I not? He is quite the thing, you know!"

"I daresay he's of the first stare, pet, but would his lordship like it? That's what you ought to think of, only you're such a flighty little puss – well, there!"

"Oh, but Lord Rotherham could have not the least objection!" Emily assured her. "Gerard is his ward. They are cousins.

That, of course, put a very different complexion on the matter, and made Mrs Floore exclaim against Emily for not having told her so in time for her to have invited Mr Monksleigh to dine with them. But that was soon rectified. She took Emily to the ball, and there was Mr Monksleigh, nattier than ever in evening dress, his ordered locks glistening with Russia Oil, and the many swathes of his neckcloth obliging him to hold his head very much up. Several young ladies watched his progress across the room with approval, most of the gentlemen with tolerant amusement, and Mr Guynette, who had attempted unavailingly to present him to a lady lacking a partner for the boulanger, with strong disapprobation.

Gerard was in no mood for dancing, but since there seemed to be no other way of detaching Emily from her grandmother, he led her into the set that was just forming, saving urgently: "I must see you alone! How may it be contrived?"

She shook her head wonderingly. "Grandmama would not like it! Besides, everyone would stare!"

"Not here! But we must meet! Emily, I have only just learnt of this – this engagement you have entered into! Have been forced into! I know you cannot – I have come all the way from Scarborough to see you! Quickly, where may we meet?"

Her hand trembled in his; she whispered: "Oh -! I don't know! It is so dreadful! I am very unhappy!"

He caught his breath. "I knew it!"

There was no time for more; they were obliged to take their places in the set; to school their countenances; and to exchange such conversation as was suitable to the occasion. When the movement of the dance brought them together, Gerard said: "Will your grandmama permit me to visit her?"

"Yes, but pray take care! She said I must not be too friendly, only then I told her you were Lord Rotherham's ward, and so she will ask you to dine with us, and go to the Sydney Gardens tomorrow. Oh, Gerard, I do not know what to do!"

He squeezed her fingers. "I have come to save you!"

She found nothing to smile at in this announcement, but threw him a look brimful of gratitude and admiration as they parted again, and waited hopefully to know how her rescue was to be accomplished.

She had to remain in suspense until the following evening; and when he was at last able to disclose his plans to her, she found them disappointing.

After dining in Beaufort Square, and taking immense pains to ingratiate himself with Mrs Floore, Gerard accompanied the ladies to the Sydney

Gardens, where various entertainments, ranging from illuminations to dancing, were provided for Bath's visitors. Here, by great good fortune, a crony of Mrs Floore's was encountered, who had been staying at Lyme Regis for some weeks. The two ladies naturally had much gossip to exchange; and when they were fairly launched in intimate conversation, Gerard seized the opportunity to beg permission to take Emily to look at the waterfalls, which had all been illuminated for the occasion. "I will take good care of her, ma'am!" he promised.

Mrs Floore nodded indulgently. She still thought him an agreeable youth, but he would have been affronted had he known how swiftly and how accurately she had summed him up. He was, in her estimation, a harmless boy, scarcely fledged as yet, but anxious to convince everyone that he was a buck of the first head. She had been much amused, at dinner, by the carelessness with which he related anecdotes of *ton;* and when, encouraged by a good-nature which he mistook for respect, he played off a few of the airs of an exquisite, her eyes twinkled appreciatively, and she decided that however much pride and sensibility the Marquis might have he could scarcely take exception to Emily's accepting the escort of so callow a young gentleman.

Since two or three thousand persons were in the Gardens, it was some little time before Gerard could find a vacant and sufficiently secluded nook to appropriate. All his mind was concentrated on this, but Emily, who possessed the faculty of living only in the immediate present, kept on stopping to exclaim at Merlin grottoes, or cascades, or festoons of coloured lanterns. However, he eventually discovered a discreet arbour, persuaded her to enter it, and to sit down upon the rustic bench there. Seating himself beside her, he clasped her mittened hand, and uttered: "Tell me the whole!"

She was not articulate, and found this command hard to obey. Her account of her engagement was neither fluent nor coherent, but by dint of frequently interpolated questions he was able to piece the story together, if not entirely to understand the circumstances which had induced her to enter into an engagement with a man for whom she felt not a scrap of affection. He believed that her mother's tyranny accounted for all, and failed to perceive that the prospect of becoming a Marchioness had strongly attracted her. Nor had he the smallest suspicion that her sentiments towards himself had undergone a change.

She had been taken quite by surprise. She had had no notion that Rotherham had a decided preference for her, for although he had been her host at the Rotherham House ball, it had been Mrs Monksleigh whose name had figured on the invitation-card, and she had quite thought that he had had nothing to say in the matter.

"He never troubled himself at all, *that* you may be sure of!" said Gerard. "*I* made Mama invite you!"

"Oh, did you? How *very* kind that was of you! I never enjoyed anything half as much, did you? It was a *magnificent* ball! I had no notion how grand Rotherham House is! So many handsome saloons, and *hundreds* of footmen, and that huge crystal chandelier in the ballroom, sparkling like diamonds, and your Mama standing at the head of the great staircase -"

"Yes, yes, I know!" Gerard said, a trifle impatiently. "But Rotherham didn't even solicit you to dance, did he?"

"Oh, no! He only said how do you do to me, and of course I had no expectation of his asking me to stand up with him, with so many grand people there! In fact, until we – we became engaged, I never did dance with him, except that once, at Quenbury. We were for ever meeting, at parties, you know, and he was always very civil to me, and sometimes he paid me a compliment, only – only I don't know how it is, but when he says a thing that sounds pretty, he does so in a way that – well, in a way that makes one feel that he is being satirical!"

"You need not tell *me* that!" said Gerard, with a darkling look. "When did he commence making up to you?"

"Oh, never! In fact, I had no notion he was disposed to like me, for whenever he talked to me it was in a quizzing way, which put me quite out of countenance. So you may imagine my astonishment when Mama told me had offered for me! Mama says he behaved with the greatest propriety, exactly as he ought."

"Behaved with the greatest propriety?" echoed Gerard incredulously. "*Cousin Rotherham*? Why, he doesn't give a groat for such stuff! He always does just as he chooses, and doesn't care for ceremony, or for having distinguished manners, or for showing people proper observance, or any thing like that!"

"Oh, yes, Gerard, he does!" Emily said earnestly, raising her eyes to his face. "He becomes dreadfully vexed if one does not behave just as he says one ought, or – or if one is shy, and does not know how to talk to people! He says very cutting things, d-doesn't he? If one angers him!"

"So he has treated you to his devilish ill-humour already, has he?" demanded Gerard, his eyes kindling. "Pretty conduct towards his betrothed, upon my word! It is just as I thought! He does not love you! I believe he wishes to marry you only to spite me!"

She shook her head, turning away her face. "No, no! He *does* love me, only – Oh, I don't want to be married to him!"

"Good God, you shall not be!" he said vehemently, seizing her hand, and kissing it. "I cannot think how you could have consented! That he should have behaved to you in such a way -!"

"Oh, no! Not *then*!" she explained. "How could I say I would not, when Mama had arranged it, and was so pleased with me? It is *very* wrong not to obey one's parents, and even Papa was pleased, too, for he said that after all I was not such a complete zero as he had thought. And Mama said I should learn to love Lord Rotherham, and he would give me everything I could possibly desire, besides making me a great lady, with all those houses, and my own carriage, and a Marchioness's robes, if there should happen to be a Coronation, which, of course, there must be, mustn't there? Because the poor King -"

"But, Emily, all that is *nothing*!" protested Gerard. "You would not sell yourself for a Marchioness's coronet!"

"No," agreed Emily, rather doubtfully. "I did think at first that perhaps – But that was when Lord Rotherham was behaving with propriety."

Aghast, and quite thunderstruck, Gerard demanded: "Do you mean to tell me that Rotherham – that Rotherham used you *improperly*? It is worse even than I guessed! Good God, I would never have believed -"

"No, no!" stammered Emily, blushing fierily, and hanging down her head. "It was only that he is a man of strong passions! Mama explained it to me, and she said I must be flattered by – by the violence of his feelings. But – I don't like to be k-kissed so roughly, and that m-makes him angry, and – Oh, Gerard, I am *afraid* of him!"

"He is the greatest beast in nature!" Gerard said, his voice shaking with indignation. "You must tell him at once that you cannot marry him!"

Her eyes widened in startled dismay. "*C-cry off*? I can't! M-mama would not allow me to!"

"Emily, dearest Emily, she cannot compel you to marry *anyone* against your will! You have only to be firm!"

Anything less firm than the appearance Emily presented as she listened to these brave words would have been hard to find. Her face was as pale as it had a moment earlier been red, her eyes charged with apprehension, and her whole frame trembling. Nothing that he could urge seemed to convince her that it would be possible to withstand the combined assault of her mother and Lord Rotherham. The very thought of being forced to confront two such formidable persons made her feel faint and sick. Moreover, the alternative to marriage, little though Gerard might think it, was almost worse, since it would carry with it no such alleviations as coronets and consequence. Mama had said that ladies who cried off from engagements were left to wear the willow all their days, and she was quite right, for only think of Lady Serena, so beautiful and clever, and still single! She would have to live at home, with Miss Prawle and the children, and be in disgrace, and see her sisters all married, and going to parties, and – oh no, impossible! Gerard did not understand!

But Gerard assured her that none of these ills would come to pass – or, at any rate, only for a short time. For Gerard had evolved a cunning scheme, and he rather fancied that when he had explained it to her his adored Emily would perceive that nothing could better have served their ends than her engagement to Rotherham and its rupture. "For if you had not become engaged, dear love, your Mama would continue scheming to marry you to some man of rank and fortune, and I daresay she could never have been brought to listen to my suit. But when you have declared off with Rotherham, she will think it useless to persist, and she will very likely bring out Anne next season, and leave you in Gloucestershire."

"Anne?" exclaimed Anne's elder sister indignantly. "She will only be sixteen, and I could not *endure* it!"

"Yes, yes, only listen!" begged Gerard, alight with eagerness. "I come of age in November of 1817 – very little more than a year from now! *Then* Rotherham will be obliged to put me in possession of my fortune – well, it is not precisely a *fortune*, but it brings me close on three hundred pounds a year, which is an independence, at least. I am not perfectly sure whether Rotherham would be obliged to pay it to me *now*, if I left Cambridge, because my father left it to me – well, to Cousin Rotherham in trust for me, until I am twenty-one – so that it should provide for my schooling and maintenance. Only Rotherham gives it to me for my allowance, and chose to pay for my education himself. *I* did not ask him to, and, in fact, I would liefer he did not, because to be under an obligation to him is of all things what I most dislike! I daresay he sent me to Eton just to get me into his power! However, never mind that! The thing is that I fear he can compel me to finish my time at Cambridge – and, you know, I do think perhaps I should, because I mean to embrace a political career, and to get my degree would be helpful, I expect. One of my particular friends is related to Lord Liverpool, and has interest with him, and he is very ready to oblige me. So you see that I have excellent prospects *besides* my poetry! Rotherham may not think that writing poetry is a gainful occupation, but only consider Lord Byron! Why, he must have made a fortune, Emily, and if he could do so, why should not I?"

Emily, a little dazed by all this eloquence, could think of no reason why he should not, and shook her head wonderingly.

"No! Well, we shall see!" said Gerard. "I do not count upon it, mind, for public taste is so bad – But we needn't concern ourselves with that at this present! This is what we must do! *You* must cry off from this *wicked* engagement: that's certain! *I* will go up to Cambridge for my Third Year, and the instant I come down, which will be next June, I shall seek an introduction to Liverpool – there will be no difficulty about *that!* and establish myself in the way to a successful career. *Then*, in November, when I come of age, and your Mama has despaired of finding what *she* thinks an eligible husband for you – only, if you *should* receive an offer, you must be resolute in declining it, you know! – I shall offer for you again, and she will be only too thankful! What do you think of *that*, dearest?"

She did not tell him. She was a very softhearted girl, besides being almost wholly deficient in moral courage, and she shrank from giving him her opinion of a scheme which in no way recommended itself to her. She perceived that he entertained no doubts that her sentiments towards him were the same as they had been in the spring; and to break it to him that although she still liked him very well she had no desire to marry him seemed to her to be an impossible task. She sought refuge in evasions, talked of filial duty, and said that Lady Serena had told her that she was a goose to be afraid of Lord Rotherham.

"Lady Serena!" he ejaculated. "Pray, why did *she* jilt him? I should very much like to ask her that home question!"

"Well, she is residing in Laura Place, with Lady Spenborough," said Emily doubtfully, "but do you think you ought? She might think it an impertinence. Besides, she told me herself that she cried off because she and Lord Rotherham didn't suit. They quarrelled so frequently that she became quite exhausted, but I can't think she was afraid of him! She is afraid of *nothing*!"

"Lady Serena in Bath?" said Gerard, in a tone of considerably less elation. "Lord, I wish she were not!"

"Don't you like her?" asked Emily, shocked.

"Oh, yes! Well – yes, I like her well enough! I wish she may not tell Rotherham I am here, though! You know, for all she jilted him they are still wondrous great, and there's no telling what she might take it into her head to do, for I am sure she is very odd and unaccountable. On no account, Emily, must you divulge to her the attachment between us!"

"Oh, no!" she said, glad to be able to accede to one at least of his demands.

"If I should chance to meet her, I shall say that I came to Bath to visit a friend of mine. The only thing is, Cousin Rotherham forbade me to come here, so -"

"He forbade you?" she cried, cast into renewed dismay. "You have not seen him, surely?"

"Certainly I have seen him!" he replied, throwing out his chest a little. "When Lady Laleham refused to disclose your whereabouts -"

She interrupted with a tiny shriek. "You have been to Cherrifield Place? Oh, Gerard, how *could* you? Whatever shall I do? If Mama knew -"

"Well, it can't be helped," he said, rather sulkily. "How else was I to find you? And if I leave Bath immediately – as soon as we are agreed upon what we should both do, I mean – very likely she won't think anything of my visit. If she does, I think you should tell her that you would not listen to my suit, and that will make all right."

"Does Lord Rotherham know that you are here?" she asked anxiously.

"Well, I told him that I *should* come here, but ten to one he didn't believe I should dare to disobey him. Indeed, I know he did not! He is so set up in conceit of himself – But I fancy I have shown him that he cannot browbeat *me*! I'm not afraid of him! Though I should wish not to be in Bath, if he should take it into his head to visit you," said Gerard, with perfect sincerity. "I don't mean, of course, that I shouldn't prefer to face him *now*, man to man, but the thing is that it would very likely ruin all if I did," he added, lapsing slightly.

Emily, both hands to her cheeks in a distracted gesture, paid very little heed to this. "Oh, heavens, what shall I do? Oh, how could you, Gerard?"

"But I have *told* you what you must do!" he pointed out. "You have only to be resolute in refusing to continue in the engagement, and, although it may be a trifle unpleasant at first, I daresay, there is nothing either your mama or Rotherham can do to compel you to yield, recollect! Of course, it would not do, if you were to disclose that you are betrothed to me. It is the shabbiest thing that I'm not of age! If I *were*, and Rotherham had no legal power over me, I need not tell you that I should remain at your side, and see to it you were not scolded or bullied! But it is only for a little time, dearest, and then we shall be married!"

But Emily, deriving no comfort from this prospect, merely begged him to take her back to her grandmother, and declared herself to be incapable of deciding, without reflection, upon any course of action. She was so much agitated that Gerard saw that it would be useless to press her for an immediate promise. He could perceive no flaw in his plan, but he knew that females were easily alarmed by anything unexpected, besides not being possessed of superior intellects capable of grappling in a flash with all the aspects of a problem. So he said soothingly that she must consider all he had said, and tell him the result of her lucubrations on the following day. Where should they meet?

Emily was at first inclined to think that they ought not to meet at all, but since he persisted in his determination, she said at last: "Oh, dear! I'm sure I shan't – Oh, I don't know how it may be contrived, unless Grandmama will let me go to Meyler's Library, while she is in the Pump Room, which I frequently do, because it adjoins it, you know, and -"

"But we can't talk in a crowded library!" objected Gerard. "I'll tell you what, Emily! You must pretend that you wish to change your book, but instead slip away to the Abbey! I shall be there, and it is only a very little way!"

CHAPTER NINETEEN

EMILY KEPT the appointment, but little was gained by the clandestine interview. She arrived at the Abbey doors in a flutter, because she had caught sight of one of Mrs Floore's acquaintances on the way, and could not be sure that she had not herself been seen. It was in vain that Gerard assured her that the sight of an unattended damsel traversing the short distance between the Pump Room and the Abbey would not shock the most prudish person: Emily could not be easy. He drew her into the Abbey, but, as might have been foreseen, this was found to be over-full of visitors, wandering about it, and looking at its beauties and antiquities. Even Gerard could not feel that he had chosen an ideal spot for the assignation; and as for Emily, she could lend him no more than half an ear, so much occupied was she in keeping a look-out for any more of Mrs Floore's friends. In any event, it was only too plain that she was still in a state of miserable indecision, and the end of it was that they parted with nothing settled but that they should meet again that evening at the theatre. Mr Goring was coming to Bath later in the day, and had invited Mrs Floore and Emily to go with him to the box he had procured. This was just the sort of evening's entertainment which exactly suited Mrs Floore, for not only did she enjoy any kind of spectacle, but the New Theatre being situated on the south side of Beaufort Square, she could go to it without being obliged to order out her carriage. When people marvelled at her choosing to live in Beaufort Square, she pointed this advantage out to them, adding that on such evenings as she was alone she was able to sit in the window of her drawing-room, and watch who was attending the theatre, and thus avoid being moped to death.

Emily acquiesced in Gerard's suggestion that he should obtain a seat in the house, but she showed no enthusiasm at the prospect of being again urged to make up her mind. It was an exercise to which she was not at all accustomed. However, Gerard was insistent, and she gave way, reflecting that it was unlikely that he would find an opportunity to be private with her.

She then sped back to the Pump Room, and Gerard, who had not journeyed into the west country prepared to make a prolonged stay, went off to purchase a shirt, and some additional neckcloths. It would have been too much to have said that his inamorata had disappointed him, but she had certainly disconcerted him. When he was himself behaving with what he considered to be amazing resolution, it was a little hard to find that the person for whom he had made his brilliant plan showed so Laodicean a spirit. Moreover, he had hoped to have left Bath by midday, and to be kept kicking his heels indefinitely in such a dangerous locality was not at all what he liked. At any moment, Rotherham, suspicious of his intentions, might take it into his head to come to Bath, just to make sure he was not there; and then, thought Gerard, where would they be?

It was as he emerged from a shop in Bond Street that he had the misfortune to encounter one of the perils which beset him. He heard himself hailed, in surprised accents, and looked round to see Lady Serena, escorted by a tall man of very upright bearing, waving to him. There was nothing for it but to cross the street towards her, summoning to his lips what he hoped was a delighted smile.

"Why, Gerard, how comes this about?" Serena said, giving him her hand. "What brings you to Bath?"

"A friend – a college friend of mine, ma'am!" he replied. "Has been begging me for ever to pay him a visit! He lives here, you see, with his family. At least, not here, but just beyond the town!"

"Indeed! Do you mean to make a long stay?" she asked kindly.

"No, oh, no! In fact, I am going back to London tomorrow." He then thought that she must wonder at his having come over a hundred miles only to spend a couple of days with his friends, and at once created another friend, living in Wiltshire, with whom he said he had been staying for several weeks.

Serena, taking only a casual interest in this, introduced him to Major Kirkby. They all three walked on to the end of the street, where Gerard took his leave, saying that he was pledged to meet his host in Westgate Street. He then walked quickly away down Parsonage Lane, and the Major and Serena, turning to the left, strolled along in the direction of Bridge Street.

"And who is that young fribble?" enquired the Major.

She laughed. "Rotherham's eldest ward. He is guardian to all his cousin's children, and a very bad guardian, too! He takes not the least interest in them, and *this* boy he holds in contempt, and is often, I think, very unkind to him. For there is no harm in Gerard, even if, in his efforts to be taken for a Bond Street beau, he does contrive to look very like a counter-coxcomb. I can see you thought him one!"

"Oh, no!" said the Major. "I have seen too many boys of his age trying to come the dandy! Most of them outgrow it quite speedily. He wasn't at all glad to meet you, was he?"

"Did you think he was not?" she said. "He's very shy, you know. I daresay you overawed him with your height and your grave countenance!"

"My grave countenance!" he repeated, a tinge of red creeping into it. "Is it so grave?"

"It has been grave since you returned to Bath," she told him. "Did you find something amiss at home?"

"Not exactly amiss – some tiresome business, too long neglected! My mother is rather unwell!" said the Major, snatching at this excuse, and thankful for the first time in his life that his parent's chief diversion was to detect in herself unmistakable symptoms of some deepseated disorder.

"I am so sorry!" Serena said, with quick sympathy. "I hope no serious illness?"

"No, I believe – that is, I trust not! The doctor was to visit her this morning."

"I shouldn't wonder at it if Bath is to blame. It was tolerable in the spring, but I know of no more enervating town to be in during the summer. It does not agree with Fanny, I know. Have you noticed how hagged she is looking? She says this heavy, windless weather we've endured now for a week makes her feel stuffed to death. I know exactly what she means, don't you? I am conscious of it myself. Everything seems to be an abominable fag, and one becomes languid in spirit, and rather cross. That is to say, I become rather cross! Fanny was never cross in her life."

"Cross you may be, but not languid in spirit!" he said, smiling.

"Hipped, then, and on the fidgets!" She glanced up at him as she spoke, and saw that he was regarding her with a little trouble in his eyes. She slid her hand in his arm, and said, in her funning voice: "You may take that as a compliment, if you please! Five days you were away! The only marvel is that I did not fall into a lethargy. I daresay I must have done so, had I not been occupied in thinking how shabbily I was used, and how best I should punish you!"

"Did you miss me?" he asked.

"Very much: it was a dreadful bore! I hope you missed me: it would be too bad if I were the only sufferer!"

He responded in kind; and spent the rest of the walk to Laura Place in telling her of the alterations to his house he meant to put in hand. He parted from her on her doorstep. She invited him to come in, and to partake of a nuncheon, but although he longed to see Fanny he knew that he must see her as seldom as possible, and he declined, saying that he had promised his mother to come home within the hour.

"I won't press you, then. Pray, give my love to Mrs Kirkby, and tell her how sorry I am to hear that she is out of sorts!"

"Thank you, I will. Do we ride tomorrow, Serena?"

"Yes, indeed! Will you – Oh, confound it! Is not tomorrow Wednesday? Then I cannot. I promised I would ride with Emily to Farley Castle. Drive with me instead, later in the day!"

"Willingly! At what time?"

"A little before three o'clock? That is, if Mrs Kirkby will spare you to me."

"Of course she will. I shall be here!" he promised.

She went into the house, and up the stairs to the drawing room, where Fanny was seated, with her embroidery frame in front of her. She looked up, and smiled, as Serena came in, but her eyes were heavy, and her cheeks rather wan. Serena said quickly: "Fanny, have you the headache again?"

"It's nothing! Only a very little headache. I shall lie down presently, and soon be quite cured of it."

Serena stood looking down at her in some concern. "You look worn to a bone! Tell me, my dear, wouldn't you like to go away from Bath? I don't know how anyone can escape being invalidish here, it is so oppressive! Shall we go back to the Dower House?"

"No, no!" Fanny said. "Indeed, I'm not ill, dearest! I daresay if the sun would but shine I should be in a capital way again. I don't know how it is, but these hot, dull days always give me the headache."

"We only hired this house until the end of August," persisted Serena. "Why not leave it now? Do you say no because you think I don't wish to leave Hector? Tell me truthfully, Fanny! I'll go with you tomorrow, if you would like it."

"Dear, dear Serena!" Fanny said, catching Serena's hand, and nursing it to her cheek. "So good to me! so *very* good to me!"

"Now, what in the world is this?" Serena rallied her. "I begin to think that you must be more sickly than I had guessed! I warn you, if you talk to me of my *goodness* – and in such a melancholy voice! – I shall send for a doctor. Or shall it be the Dower House?"

"It shall be neither," Fanny said, with determined cheerfulness. "I don't at all wish to leave Bath before I must. Don't let us prose about my health! Next you will be telling me I look hagged and *ridée*! Did you hear any news in the town?"

"No news, but I saw a new face: Gerard Monksleigh's! I wish you might have seen him! Very much the Pink of the *Ton*, with shirt-points serving as blinkers, and a very dashing waistcoat!"

"Good gracious, I wonder what brings him here? Is Mrs Monksleigh here too?"

"No, he said he was staying with friends in the neighbourhood. Hector thought he wasn't pleased to see me, but *my* guess is that -" She broke off suddenly, and a laugh sprang to her eyes. "Oh, I wonder if Hector was right after all? Fanny, do you recall my aunt's writing to me once that Gerard had been very much smitten with Emily? Can it be that the foolish boy has come here to dangle after her?"

"He would be a more suitable match for her than Lord Rotherham," said Fanny.

"He would be the worst possible match for her, my dear, for, setting aside the fact that he has no fortune, he is very nearly as silly as she is, and has not yet outgrown the schoolboy. However, it is not all likely that he will be a danger to Ivo, even if he has come to Bath in a love-lorn state. I notice that Emily's flirtations are always with men a good deal older than herself: her youthful admirers she considers stupid. It won't do, of course, if Gerard makes a cake of himself by enacting the disappointed lover for the entertainment of the Bath quizzes. I do wonder whether he was telling me a whisker when he said he was visiting friends, or whether he is lurking somewhere in Bath. It will be well, perhaps, if I drop a hint to Emily not to encourage him to dangle after her. She is riding to Farley Castle with me tomorrow."

She spoke lightly, unaware of the fact that all recollection of this engagement had been banished from Emily's mind. The four o'clock mail had brought her shocking tidings. Lady Laleham and Lord Rotherham were coming to Bath.

Lady Laleham was so obliging as to disclose the day of her arrival; Lord Rotherham, more alarmingly still, wrote at the end of a brief letter which all too clearly showed impatience, gathering wrath, and a determination to claim his reluctant bride, merely that he proposed to come to Bath immediately, and expected to find Emily not only ready to receive him, but prepared to come to a point. He made no mention of Mr Monksleigh; Lady Laleham, on the other hand, telling her daughter of Gerard's abortive call at Cherrifield Place, warned her that if, by some chance, he had succeeded in discovering her direction, and was even now in Bath, he must be sent instantly to the rightabout. If Lord Rotherham were to find out that although he had been refused permission to visit his betrothed Mr Monksleigh (who appeared to think himself a rival) was making up to her, he would be very (heavily underscored) and justifiably angry. So, too, would be Emily's affectionate Mama.

The combined effect of these two missives was to throw Emily into a fever of apprehension. Converging upon her, each filled with rage and determination, were two dread figures, one of whom would certainly arrive on the following afternoon, the other perhaps even sooner. Between them she would inevitably be crushed. She saw herself being dragged by her mother to the altar, and there delivered into the power of one who by this time figured in her distorted imagination as a merciless ogre. That her grandmother might intervene to save her from this hideous fate never occurred to her, partly because Mrs Floore, not unnaturally, had refrained from expressing to her her opinion of her only daughter; and partly because it was incredible to Emily that her vulgar, goodnatured grandmama could exercise the smallest influence over the far more formidable Lady Laleham. Her only hope of support seemed to lie in Mr Monksleigh's slender person. Terrifying under any circumstances though the approaching ordeal must be, she felt that if he would only remain at her side to protect her there might be a very faint chance of her surviving it. Or he might be able to think of a way of escape. It was true that the only plan he had so far evolved would not serve the purpose at all, since it depended for its success on the resolution she was well aware that she lacked; but when he learned of the imminent peril in which she stood he might, perhaps, be inspired with further schemes.

Her hope was not misplaced. After looking round the theatre, and perceiving, with a start of surprise, that Mrs Floore was in one of the boxes, Gerard hurried upstairs in the first interval, encountering Mr Goring's party on their way to the foyer. He received a friendly greeting from Mrs Floore, a slight bow from Mr Goring, and from Emily a look so full of meaning that he at once realized that something of an appalling nature must have happened since the morning. Mr Goring being occupied in guiding Mrs Floore to a seat against the wall, it was an easy matter for Gerard to whisk Emily to the other end of the foyer, where in an urgent undervoice she told him of the letters she had received, and besought his counsel and support.

He showed no tendency to minimize the danger. Indeed, he was more inclined to magnify it. The intelligence that his guardian was coming, like Nemesis, to Bath, transfixed him with dismay, and set his wits working faster than ever before in his life. Emily's timid suggestion that he should come to Beaufort Square to confront Rotherham at her side, he dismissed hastily, saying with great vehemence: "Useless!"

Emily wrung her hands. "They will make me do just as they say, then! I can't – I *can't* tell them I w-won't, Gerard! Oh, do you think Mama and Lady Serena may be right, and it won't be so very dreadful to be married to Lord Rotherham?"

"No," said Gerard positively. "It would be far worse than you dream of! I tell you this, Emily, Rotherham is a tyrant! He will make you wholly subservient to his will. *I* have cause to know! *You* cannot yet have seen him in one of his rages, my poor darling! They are quite ungoverned! His servants are all terrified of him, and with good cause!" He saw that her face was perfectly white, and pressed home his advantage. "You must not meet him! All will be lost, if you come within reach of that – that ruthless despotism! Emily, we must elope!"

It was not to be expected that she would instantly perceive the advantages of this course. She was, in fact, shocked by such a suggestion, but by the time Gerard had regaled her with an account of his own sufferings at Rotherham's hands, and some liberal prophecies of the horrors in store for her; and had declared himself to be incapable of imagining the extent or effects of the Marquis's wrath, when he discovered – as discover he would – what had been going on in Bath, she was ready to consent to any measure that would rescue her from her Andromeda-like plight. People were beginning to leave the foyer; Gerard had only time, before Mrs Floore bore down upon them, to warn her not to breathe a word to her, but to meet him in Queen's Square at ten o'clock on the following morning. "Leave everything to me!" he ordered. "Once in my care you are safe!"

These somewhat grandiloquent words were music to her ears. Naturally dependent, she was only too thankful to be able to cast her cares on to his shoulders; and now that he had ceased to counsel her to face her tyrants with resolution she began to think that she might like him very well as a husband. At least he was kind, and gentle, and loved her very much; and although he was not her ideal she supposed that they might live very contentedly together.

Her mind relieved of its paramount dread, she was able to listen to the rest of the play with tolerable enjoyment, but she did not recover her vivacity, her attitude being languid and listless enough to make Mrs Floore say, as soon as Mr Goring had escorted them home: "Now, Emma-love, you just tell Grandma what's the matter, and no nonsense! If you're looking like a drowned mouse all because your ma is coming to stay with me tomorrow, you're a goosecap! Now, ain't you?"

"I-I am afraid Mama means to take me away from you, Grandmama!" faltered Emily.

"Bless your sweet heart!" exclaimed Mrs Floore, planting a smacking kiss upon her cheek. "So you don't want to leave your grandma! Well, I don't deny I love to hear you say so, my pet, but there's reason in all things, and I can't say that I'm surprised your ma's got to be a trifle impatient. I'll be bound she's got her head full of your bride-clothes by this time – and so will you have before you are very much older! Lord, how I do look forward to reading all about you when you're a Marchioness! You think about what's before you, pet, and never mind about your old grandma!"

This bracing speech, excellent in intention though it was, shut the door on confidence. Grandmama, as much as Mama, wished to see Emily a Marchioness. Emily kissed her, and went upstairs to bed, planning her escape on the morrow, praying that it might not be frustrated by the arrival of her betrothed, and wondering where Gerard meant to take her.

CHAPTER TWENTY

SERENA, ARRIVING in Beaufort Square at eleven o'clock on the following morning, mounted on her good-looking mare, and attended by her groom, was a little surprised not to see a livery horse waiting outside Mrs Floore's house. Fully alive to the honour of being invited to ride with so noted a horsewoman, Emily had formed the practice, on these occasions, of ordering her hired hack to be brought round quite twenty minutes too soon, and of running out of the house, the instant she saw, from her look-out in the dining-room window, that neat figure rounding the corner of the square.

"You had better knock on the door, Fobbing," Serena said, holding out her hand for his bridle.

He gave it to her, but before he had reached the front door, it opened, and Mr Goring stepped out. He came up to the mare, and, looking gravely into the beautiful face above him, said: "Lady Serena, Mrs Floore desires me to ask you if you will be so good as to come into the house for a moment."

Her brows rose swiftly. "I will do so, certainly. Is anything amiss?"

"I am afraid very much amiss," he replied, in a heavy tone. He held up his hand. "May I assist you to -"

"No, I thank you." One deft, practised movement, and her voluminous skirt was clear of the pommels. The next instant she was on the ground, and giving her bridle into Fobbing's hand. She caught up her skirt, swinging it over her arm, and went with Mr Goring into the house. "Is Emily ill?" she asked.

"No, not ill. It will be better, I daresay, if you learn from Mrs Floore what has occurred. I myself arrived here only a short time ago, and – But I will take you up to Mrs Floore! I should warn you that you will find her in considerable distress, Lady Serena."

Good God, what can have happened?" she exclaimed, hurrying towards the stairs, her whip still in her hand.

He followed close on her booted heels, and on the first floor slid in front of her, to open the door into the drawing-room. Serena went in, with her free stride, but checked in astonished dismay at the spectacle that met her eyes. The redoubtable Mrs Floore, still attired in her dressing-gown, was lying back in a deep wing-chair, her housekeeper holding burnt feathers to her nose, and her maid kneeling before her and chafing her hands.

"My dear ma'am -! For heaven's sake, what dreadful accident has befallen?" Serena demanded.

The housekeeper, shedding tears, sobbed: "It's her poor heart, my lady! The shock gave her such palpitations as was like to have carried her off! Years ago, the doctor told me she should take care, and now see what's come of it! Oh, my lady, what a serpent's tooth she has nourished in her bosom!"

The maid, much moved, began to sob in sympathy. Mrs Floore, whose usually rubicund countenance Serena saw to have assumed an alarmingly gray tinge, opened her eyes, and said faintly: "Oh, my dear! What shall I do? Why didn't she *tell* me? Oh, what a silly, blind fool I have been! I thought – What am I to do?"

Serena, casting her whip on to the table, and stripping off her elegant gauntlets, said, in her authoritative way: "You shall remain perfectly quiet, dear ma'am, until you are a little restored. Get up off the floor, woman, and fetch some hartshorn, or a cordial, to your mistress immediately! And take those feathers away, you idiot! Mr Goring, be so good as to help me move her on to the sofa!"

He was very willing, but a little doubtful, and said in a low voice: "I had better call up the butler: she is too heavy for you, ma'am!"

Serena, who had quickly arranged some cushions at the head of the sofa, merely replied briefly: "Take her shoulders, and do not talk nonsense!"

Once disposed at full length on the sofa, Mrs Floore moaned, but soon began to look less gray. She tried to speak, but Serena hushed her, saying: "Presently, ma'am!" When the maid came back, bearing a glass containing a dose of some cordial in her trembling hand, Serena took it from her, and, raising the sufferer's head, obliged her to swallow it. In a very short space of time the colour began to come back into Mrs Floore's cheeks, and her breathing became more regular. The housekeeper, bereft of her evil-smelling feathers, waved a vinaigrette about under her nose, and her maid, still much affected, fanned her with a copy of the *Morning Post*.

Serena moved away to the window, where Mr Goring was standing. "The less she tries to talk the better it will be for her," she said, in an undervoice. "Now, tell me, if you please, what has happened to overset her like this?"

"Emily – Miss Laleham, I should say has left the house," he responded, still in that heavy tone. He saw that she was staring at him with knit brows, and added: "She has run away, ma'am. Leaving behind her a letter for her grandmother."

"Good heavens! Where is it?"

"Give it to her, Ned!" commanded Mrs Floore, struggling to sit up. "Drat you, Stoke, don't keep pushing me back! Give me those smelling-salts, and go away, do! I don't need you any more, nor you neither, Betsey, crying all over me! No, don't you go, Ned! If there's anything to be done, there's no one else to do it for me, for I can't go careering all over the country – not that it would do a mite of good if I could, for who's to say where she's gone to? Oh, Emma, why ever didn't you tell your grandma?"

Mr Goring had picked up a sheet of paper from the table, and had in silence handed it to Serena.

Dearest Grandmama, it began, in Emily's unformed writing, I am so very sorry and I do not like to grieve you but I cannot bear it and I cannot marry Lord R. in spite of coronets, because he frightens me, and I did not tell you but he has written me a dreadful letter and is coming here and he and Mama will make me do just what they want, and indeed I cannot bear it, though I hate excessively to leave you without saying goodbye. Pray do not be angry with me, my dear, dearest Grandmama. Your loving Emma. P.S. Pray, pray do not tell Mama or Lord R. where I have gone.

"You would certainly be in a puzzle to do so!" said Serena, reaching the postscript. "Of all the bird-witted little idiots -! My dear ma'am, I beg your pardon, but she deserves to be slapped for such folly! What the *devil* does she mean by writing such stuff? Rotherham write her a 'dreadful letter'? What nonsense! If he has grown impatient, it is not to be wondered at, but to write of him as though he were an ogre is quite abominable!"

"But she is afraid of him, Lady Serena," said Mr Goring.

"I ought to have known it was Sukey's doing!" said Mrs Floore, in an agony of remorse. "Right at the start, didn't I suspect it? Only then Emma wrote me such a letter, so happy it seemed to me, that I thought – Poor little lamb, if I'd only had the sense to tell her what I think of Sukey, which I never did, not thinking it seemly, she wouldn't have been afraid to tell me! And now there's Sukey coming here this very day, and how to face her I don't know, for there's no denying I haven't taken proper care of Emma. Not that I care a fig for Sukey, and so I shall tell her! And as for this precious Marquis, let him dare show his face here! Let him dare, that's all I ask! Scaring the dear little soul out of her senses, which nobody can tell me he hasn't done, because I know better! And last night – Oh, Ned, I thought she was moped because she didn't want Sukey to take her away from me, and all I did was to tell her to think about her bride-clothes, so I daresay she took it into her head I was as set on this nasty marriage as her ma! And now what am I to do? When I think of my little Emma, running off all alone, to hide herself heaven knows where -"

"You may be certain of one thing at least, ma'am!" interrupted Serena. "She has not run away alone!"

Mr Goring directed a steady look at her. "Is there an attachment between her and young Monksleigh, ma'am?"

She shrugged. "On her side, I should very much doubt it; on his, evidently! I shall be sorry for him if it ever comes to Rotherham's ears that he persuaded Emily into this escapade! It is the most disgraceful thing to have done, and if he comes off with a whole skin he may think himself fortunate! Mrs Floore, pray don't cry! The matter is not past mending, I assure you. I collect that Gerard came to Bath to see Emily, not to stay with friends: has he been to this house? Had you no suspicion of what was in the wind?"

"No, my dear, because Emma said he was the Marquis's ward, which made it seem right to me, and besides which I thought he was such a twiddle-poop there wasn't the least harm in letting him go with us to the Gala night, which I did."

Serena smiled, but said: "Depend upon it, this dramatic flight was his notion, not Emily's, ma'am! What is more, I would wager my pearls all this nonsense about Rotherham was put into her silly head by him! But let us not waste time in discussing that! What we have to do is to get her back. Mr

Goring, I shall need your help!"

"I shall be happy to do everything in my power, Lady Serena, to restore Miss Laleham to Mrs Floore, but I will have no hand in forcing her into marriage with a man whom she fears," he replied bluntly.

"Let me see anyone dare!" said Mrs Floore. "Only fetch her back to me, and trust me to send this Marquis to the rightabout, and Sukey too!"

"There is no question of forcing her to marry Rotherham," said Serena. "When she meets him again, I fancy she will discover that the extremely unamiable portrait she has painted of him is wide of the mark. Is it known when she left the house?"

"No, because no one saw her go, only she wasn't gone before ten o'clock, that Betsey swears to, for she heard her moving about in her bedroom when she passed the door. And she ate a bite of bread and butter, and drank a cup of coffee, before she went, and Stoke says the tray was taken up to her at a quarter to ten, just as usual. For I don't get up to breakfast myself, so Emma has hers in bed too."

"Come, this is much better!" said Serena. "I feared she might have left overnight, in which case we should have had something to do indeed. Mr Goring, have you met Gerard Monksleigh?"

"I met him at the theatre last night, ma'am."

"Then you will be able to describe him," said Serena briskly. "We may be sure of this: they are not lurking in Bath! I do Gerard the justice to think that he means to marry Emily though how he imagines he may do so, when each of them is under age, is more than I can tell! It would be in keeping with all the rest if he is bearing her off to Gretna Green, but where he found the money for such a journey is again more than I can tell! He may, of course, be taking her to London, with some hopeful notion of procuring a special licence there."

"Oh, my dear, supposing he has it in his pocket already?" exclaimed Mrs Floore. "Supposing he went to Wells, or Bristol, and has married her? Oh, I don't want her to go throwing herself away on that young fellow!"

"Don't distress yourself, ma'am! He would find it difficult to induce anyone to believe he is of age."

"Lady Serena is right, ma'am," interpolated Mr Goring. "He would be required to bring proof of his age, for he looks a stripling. What do you wish me to do, Lady Serena?"

"To visit the posting-houses here, of course. I imagine you must know them well. Discover if Gerard hired a chaise, and where it was to take him. Did you ride here from Bristol? Is your horse in Bath?"

"I drove here, ma'am, in my curricle. If I should be able to discover the road they took, I can have the horses put to in a trice," he replied. "I'll set out immediately."

"Ned Goring, I'll go all the way to Land's End for Emma, but I'll do it decently!" declared Mrs Floore. "Don't you think to hoist me into any nasty, open carriage! A chaise-and-four, that's what you'll hire!"

"My dear ma'am, you are going to remain quietly here," said Serena. "It would be quite unfit for you to be rocked and jolted for heaven knows how many hours! Moreover, if this exploit is to be kept secret, it is most necessary that you should be here. If Rotherham is indeed on his way to Bath, he will have to be fobbed off, you know. Whatever be the issue between him and Emily, you cannot wish him to know how scandalously she is behaving – or Lady Laleham either, for that matter! You must tell them both that Emily has gone with a party on an expedition of pleasure. And as for your curricle, Mr Goring, leave it where it is! We shall catch our runaways very much more speedily if we ride, and we shan't advertise to every pike-keeper, and every chance traveller, that we are racing in pursuit of someone. That is a thing we should do our best to avoid."

He stared at her. "You do not mean to go, ma'am!"

"Of course I mean to go!" she replied impatiently. "How in the world do you think you could manage without me? You are quite unrelated to Emily; you cannot compel her to return with you! All that would happen, I dare swear, is that you and Gerard would be fighting it out, with the post-boys as seconds, and then there *would* be the devil to pay!"

He was too much surprised to hear such an expression on her lips to smile at the absurdity of the picture she conjured up. "But you will not *ride*, ma'am? You cannot have considered! They must be many miles ahead of us already! It would not do for you: you would be fatigued to death!"

"Mr Goring, have you ever hunted with the Cottesmore?" she demanded.

"No, ma'am, I have not, but -"

"Well, I have done so every year!" she said. "There is no country like it for long and fast runs. It is said to be the wildest and the roughest of the Shires, you know. So don't waste solicitude on me, I beg of you! My mare was bred to stay, and she's as fresh as she can stare. The only difficulty will be *your* mount."

His sense of decorum, which was strong, was shocked by the thought of a lady's setting out, quite unchaperoned, on a chase that might lead her many miles from Bath, but he attempted no further remonstrance. He was conscious of the same sensation which had more than once assailed Major Kirkby, of being swept along irresistibly by an impetuous, vigorous will, against which it was impossible to fight. It was plain to him that the Lady Serena was going to assume the control of the chase. He wondered whether she had considered the possibility of finding herself, at nightfall, out of reach of her home, unprovided with so much as a hairbrush, and escorted by a single gentleman, but he did not venture to put the question to her. He said instead: "I know where I may procure a good horse, Lady Serena."

"Excellent! Then will you go now, and see what you can discover? Inform my groom, if you please, that my plans have been altered. I am going with Miss Laleham to join a picnic party, and since we do not set out immediately he must walk the mare a little, till I am ready for her."

"You will not take him with you?" he suggested tentatively.

"No, certainly not: he would be a confounded nuisance, for ever trying to persuade me to turn back! I had rather have your escort, Mr Goring!" she replied, with the flash of a smile.

He stammered that he would be honoured to serve her, and went away to obey her various commands.

Mrs Floore, who had been sitting limply on the sofa, listening to this exchange, a gleam of hope in her eyes, but the lines on her face deeply carven all at once, said, with an effort: "I ought not to let you go, my lady. I know I ought not. Whatever will Lady Spenborough say to me?"

Serena laughed. "Why, nothing, ma'am! I am going to write to her, and Fobbing shall take the letter to her. I must tell her what has taken me away, I am afraid, but you may rest assured the story is safe with her. May I write at your desk?"

"Oh, yes, my lady!" Mrs Floore answered mechanically. She sat plucking restlessly at a fold of her dressing-gown, and suddenly demanded: "What did he do to her? Why did he scare her out of her senses? Why did he want to offer for her, if he didn't love her?"

"Exactly!" said Serena dryly. "An unanswerable question, is it not? I believe the truth is, ma'am, that he is more in love with her than she can as yet understand. She is very young – quite childish, in fact! – and not, I think, of a passionate disposition. It is otherwise with him, and that, unless I much mistake the matter, is what alarmed her. What can she have known of love, after all? A few discreet flirtations, the homage of a boy like Gerard, protestations, compliments, respectful hand kissings! She would not get such tepid stuff from Rotherham! No doubt her shrinking provoked him! I can believe that he let her see that he is not a man to be trifled with, but as for giving her cause to fly from him, in this outrageous fashion, stuff and nonsense! Of course he should have guessed that it would be necessary to handle her at first with the greatest gentleness! It is unfortunate that he did not, but we may suppose that he has learnt his lesson. He has been careful to keep away from her: another mistake, but from what she has told me I collect he has allowed himself to be ruled in this by Lady Laleham. He would have done better to have visited Emily long since. She would not then have built up this ridiculous picture of him! However, if he is indeed coming here, he will very soon set matters to rights. He has only to show her tenderness, and she will wonder how she came to be such a goose."

"There's a great deal in what you say, my dear," agreed Mrs Floore. "But it's as plain as a pikestaff she don't love him!"

"She loves no one else," Serena replied. "It is not unusual, ma'am, for a bride to start with no more than liking."

"Well, it don't appear she likes him either!" said Mrs Floore, reviving a little. "What's more, my dear, those ways may do very well for *tonnish* people, but they don't do for me! If Emma don't love him, she shan't marry him!"

Serena looked up from the letter she was writing. "It would not be well for her to cry off, ma'am, believe me!"

"*You* did so!" Mrs Floore pointed out.

"Yes, I did," agreed Serena, dipping the pen in the standish again.

Mrs Floore digested this. "Sukey and her dratted ambition!" she said, suddenly and bitterly. "You needn't tell me, my dear! *I* know the world! *You* could cry off, and no one to say more than that you were rid of a bad bargain; but if Emma did it, there'd be plenty to say that, if the truth was known, it was him, and not her, that really did the crying off!"

"I did not say it was well for me either, ma'am," Serena replied quietly.

Mrs Floore heaved a large sigh. "I don't know what to do for the best, and that's a fact! If you're right, my lady, and Emma finds she likes him after all, I wouldn't want to spoil her chances, because there's no doubt she has got a fancy to be a Marchioness. At the same time – Well, one thing is certain, and that's that I'm not letting the Marquis into the house until I have Emma safe and sound here again! The servants shall tell him she's gone off for a picnic, and very likely won't be home till late – Oh, lor', whatever's to be done if you and Ned don't find them today? If they go putting up at a posting-house for the night, it'll be no use finding them at all!"

"If I know Gerard," retorted Serena, "he will insist on driving through the night, ma'am! He will wish to put as much ground as possible between himself and Rotherham – and with good reason! But if Mr Goring can discover the road they took, I have no doubt we shall catch them long before nightfall."

Mr Goring returned to Beaufort Square just before twelve o'clock, and came running up the stairs, with a look of triumph on his face. Serena said, as soon as he entered the drawing-room: "You have found out where they went! My compliments, Mr Goring! You have been very much quicker than I had dared to hope."

"It was just a piece of good luck," he said, colouring. "I might as well have gone to half a dozen houses before hitting upon the right one. As it chanced, I got certain news at the second one I visited. There seems to be no doubt that it was Monksleigh who hired a post-chaise early this morning, and ordered it to be in Queen's Square at ten o'clock. A yellow-bodied chaise, drawn by a single pair of horses."

"Well, I must say!" exclaimed Mrs Floore indignantly. "If he had to make off with poor little Emma, he might have done it stylishly! One pair of horses only! I call it downright shabby!"

"I fancy Master Gerard is none too plump in the pocket, ma'am," said Serena, amused.

"Then he's got no business to elope with my granddaughter!" said Mrs Floore.

"Very true! Where are they off to, Mr Goring?"

"The chaise was booked to Wolverhampton, ma'am, which makes it seem as though your guess was correct."

"*Wolverhampton?*" demanded Mrs Floore. "Why, that's where all the locks and keys come from! Very good they are, too, but what maggot's got into the boy's head to take Emma there? It's all of a piece! Whoever heard of going to a manufacturing town for a wedding trip?"

"No, no, ma'am, I don't think you need fear that!" Serena said, laughing. "It's as I told you: Gerard is husbanding his resources! Depend upon it, they mean to go on by stagecoach, or perhaps mail, to the Border. Never mind!" she added soothingly, seeing signs of gathering wrath in Mrs Floore's countenance. "They are not going to reach Wolverhampton, or any place near it, ma'am."

Mr Goring, who had spread open a map upon the table, said: "I bought this, for although I know the country here-abouts pretty well, if we are obliged to ride much beyond Gloucester I might find myself at a loss."

"Very well done of you!" Serena approved, going to his side, and leaning one hand on the table, while she studied the map. "They will have taken the Bristol pike road, though it's longer. We came into Bath from Milverley by way of Nailsworth, but the road is very bad: brings the horses down to a walk in places. How far is it to Bristol?"

"Twelve and a half miles. They should have reached it in an hour. Bristol to Gloucester is about thirty-four miles: a good pike-road. They must change horses ten miles out of Bristol, at the Ship Inn, or go on to Falfield, fifteen miles out."

"They won't do that, travelling with one pair."

"No. The next change, then, will be at the Cambridge Inn, here, about a mile short of the Church End turnpike, and ten miles from Gloucester. If we knew when they set out from Bath -!"

"We have a fair notion. Gerard ordered the chaise to be in Queen's Square at ten, and at ten Emily was still in her bedroom which one can't but feel is precisely what would happen in such an absurd adventure as this. When did you know that she was missing, ma'am?"

Mrs Floore shook her head helplessly, but Mr Goring, thinking the matter over, said: "I arrived here about a quarter of an hour before you rode up, Lady Serena, and it had been known then for several minutes, I think."

"Then we may take it that they started between – ten or fifteen minutes after ten, and half past ten. My dear sir, we are only an hour and a half behind them! What I wish to do is to overtake them before they reach Gloucester. We can't but run true on the line up to that point, but once in Gloucester we might be obliged to make several casts. We will take the Nailsworth road as far as Badminton, and the ride cross-country to Dursley – a nice point, that! – and join the Bristol-Gloucester Road *here*!"

He nodded. "Ay, the road comes out at the Cambridge Inn."

"Where the scent should be hot!" she said, her eyes dancing. "Come, let's be off!"

"I am ready, but – it will be a twenty-five mile ride, Lady Serena! Do you think -"

"Oh, the mare will do it!" she said cheerfully, pulling on her gauntlets. "All we have to do now is to get rid of Fobbing! The worst of a groom who ran beside one on one's first pony is that he can't be ordered off without explanation. I'll tell him our picnic party doesn't assemble until half past twelve, but that I want my letter carried to Lady Spenborough at once, in case she should be uneasy. Mrs Floore, you will have Emma under your wing again before nightfall, I promise you! Pray don't tease yourself any more!"

Mr Goring opened the door, and held it for her, but before he followed her out of the room, he looked at Mrs Floore and said: "I'll do my best to bring her back, ma'am, but – don't let them push her into marriage with Lord Rotherham!"

"You may depend upon it I won't!" said Mrs Floore grimly.

"She isn't old enough to marry anyone yet!" he said, and hesitated, as though he would have said more. Then he seemed to think better of it, bade Mrs Floore a curt good bye, and departed in Serena's wake.

CHAPTER TWENTY ONE

THE START to the elopement was not altogether auspicious, for the bride was tardy, and the groom harassed. What had seemed to Gerard, after watching the first act of a romantic drama, a splendid scheme, he found, upon more sober reflection, to present several disagreeable aspects to his view. For one thing, he had no idea whether the marriage of two minors was any more legal in Scotland than in England, or whether it would be possible for it to be set aside. He told himself that once the knot was tied neither Rotherham nor his mother would choose to cause a scandal by intervening; and tried to think no more of the possibility. Instead, he reckoned up his resources, made a vague guess at the distance to be travelled, totted up post-charges, and, at the end of all these calculations, decided to sell his watch. Elopements to Gretna Green, he realized bitterly, were luxuries to be afforded only by men of substance, for not merely was one obliged to journey over three hundred miles to reach the Border: one was obliged to come all the way back again. This reflection brought another difficulty before him: how, if his pockets were to let, was he to support a wife during the month that must elapse before he received the following quarter's allowance? The only solution that presented itself to him was that he should convey Emily to his mother's house, and he could not but see that, fond parent though she was, his mother might not accord his clandestine bride a very warm welcome. And if Rotherham (out of revenge) insisted on his spending another year at Cambridge, Emily would have to remain under his mother's roof until he came down for good, and it was just possible that she might not like such an arrangement. He wondered if he could instal her in rooms in Cambridge, and decided that if he exercised the most stringent economy it could be managed.

These problems nagged at him, but they were for the future, which he was much in the habit of leaving to take care of itself. A far more pressing anxiety was the fear that Rotherham, arriving in Bath to find Emily gone, might guess her destination, and follow her. He had warned her not to tell anyone of her flight, and he could not think that he had given Mrs Floore the least cause to suspect him of being implicated in it; but if she mentioned his name Rotherham would know at once that the flight was an elopement. And then what would he do? Perhaps he would be too proud to chase after an unwilling bride. Gerard could picture his look of contempt, the curl of his lip, the shrug of his powerful shoulders. Unfortunately he could even more clearly picture his look of blazing anger; and when he at last fell asleep his dreams were haunted by the sound of hooves, relentlessly drawing nearer and ever nearer, and by lurid, muddled scenes, in which he was always looking down the barrel of a duelling-pistol. Waking in a sweat, it was a little time before he could throw off the impression of the dream, and realize that whatever else Rotherham might do, he would not challenge his ward to a duel. But Rotherham was a boxer, and whether he would consider himself debarred by his guardianship from wreaking a pugilistic vengeance on his ward was a question to which Gerard could find no answer. Of the two fates he thought he would prefer to be shot.

That Rotherham would be very angry with him, he had no doubt; that Rotherham (and, indeed, several other interested persons) would have every right to be angry, scarcely occurred to him. In general, of course, elopements were condemned; in his case, only an insensate person could fail to perceive the purity of his motive. The thing was not so much an elopement as a rescue. Indeed, only as a last resort had he planned it, when he had failed to induce Emily to be resolute.

He was up betimes in the morning, for he had much to do. The sale of his watch was disappointing; he was obliged, regretfully, to part with his second-best fob, and a very pretty tie-pin as well; and even when these sacrifices had been made the hire of a chaise-and-four to the Border was quite out of the reach of his purse. With post-charges as high as one shilling and twopence per mile for each horse, the hire of a chaise-and-pair only for a journey of over three hundred miles would, he realized, leave him in extremely straitened circumstances. Like Mrs Floore, he felt that to elope in anything less than a chaise and four was odiously shabby, but there was no help for it. Then it occurred to him that to pay off the chaise at some point along the road, and to continue by stage, or mail, would not only be a vast saving, but would throw Rotherham (if he pursued them) off the scent. So he booked a chaise to Wolverhampton, and began to think that in so doing he had performed a masterly stroke.

This mood of elation was of brief duration. He and the yellow-bodied chaise arrived in Queen's Square precisely at five minutes to ten, in case Emily should be early, which meant that for twenty-five tense minutes he had nothing to do but walk up and down one side of the square, in fretting impatience, a prey to every gloomy foreboding. And when Emily did appear, carrying two bandboxes, and looking perfectly distracted, she exclaimed breathlessly, and in total disregard of the post-boy: "Oh, I am so sorry! I could not escape before, because Betsey was for ever in and out of Grandmama's room, and she must have seen me! Pray don't be vexed! Indeed, it was not my fault!"

Nothing could have been more unfortunate, as Gerard was immediately to discover. The postilion, ejecting the straw from his mouth, indicated in unmistakable terms that, being possessed of strong scruples, he could not bring himself, unless greased in the fist, to assist in a runaway marriage. His manner was amiability itself, and a broad grin adorned his homely countenance, but Gerard, grinding his teeth, thought it well to comply with his suggestion, and to untie the strings of his purse. Amongst the incidental expenses of the journey he had not foreseen the need to bribe the post-boys, so it was not surprising that his first words to Emily, when he climbed up into the chaise, and sat down beside her, were more aggrieved than lover-like. "What in thunder made you say all that in that fellow's hearing?" he demanded. "When I had taken care to tell them at the stables that you were my sister! Of course, if you mean to blurt out the truth in that fashion, I shall have no money left to pay the post-boys, or the tolls, or anything!"

"Oh, I am sorry! Oh, don't be vexed!" she replied imploringly.

"No, no!" he assured her. "Good God, how could I be vexed with you, dearest, sweetest Emily? I only said – well, you must own it was the most totty-headed thing to do!"

Her lip trembled. "*Oh* -!"

"No, not that!" Gerard said hastily, slipping his arm round her waist. "Just a dear little goose! But do take care, my darling! Setting aside all else, if it were known along the road that we were eloping, we should be easily traced, and we don't want that, do we?"

No, decidedly Emily did not want that. The mere thought of being pursued made her shiver, and turn saucer-like eyes towards him. "D-do you suppose M-mama will come after me?" she faltered.

"Good God!" he ejaculated. "I had not thought of that! Yes, very likely she might, only I daresay she will not find it convenient to drop as much blunt as a chaise-and-four would need, because you told me yourself your papa don't often find himself with the dibs in tune, and you've no notion what it costs to hire four horses, Emily! You may depend upon it she'd hire a pair only!"

"Yes, but Grandmama has a great deal of money!"

"Well, it doesn't signify. If she isn't expected to arrive in Bath until the afternoon, we shall have several hours' start of her. She'd never catch us – even if she knew the way we had gone, which she won't. The person I was thinking of is Rotherham."

"Oh, no! Oh, Gerard, no!"

He patted her shoulder soothingly. "Don't be afraid! Even if he did catch us, I shall not permit him to alarm you," he said stoutly. "The only thing is that I'd as lief he didn't come up with us, because of this dashed business of my being his ward. It's bound to make things awkward. However, there's no reason to suppose he means to come to Bath today, and in any event I've got a precious good scheme for throwing him off the scent! If he's devilish clever, he might be able to follow us as far as to Wolverhampton, but I flatter myself he'll throw-up there, because I've provided him with a regular stopper! We shall pay off the chaise, Emily, and go on by stage-coach! Depend upon it, he will never think of *that*, particularly as we shall have to change stages at one or two places. I think there are no stages running direct from there to Carlisle, which is where I thought we should change into a chaise again."

"But it is horridly uncomfortable on the stage!" objected Emily.

She was still unconvinced that she would find a complicated journey by stage-coach entertaining when they reached Bristol, and changed horses for the first time. Gerard kept a sharp eye on the extortionate post-boy, alighting from the chaise, and engaging him in talk to prevent his passing the word to the new postilion that he was helping an eloping couple to reach the Border. Meanwhile, the ostlers, adjured to fig out two lively ones, poled up the two most lethargic animals in the stables, and assured Gerard (with a wink at the post boy) that they would be found to be prime steppers. After a very short distance, it became obvious that they were prime stumblers, and Gerard, letting down the window in the front of the chaise, angrily scolded the postilion, who at once pulled up, and, slewing himself round in the saddle, hotly defended himself. Emily tugged at Gerard's sleeve, begging him not to argue with the man, and pointing out, very sensibly, that since there was no possibility of changing the undesirable steeds until the next posting-house was reached, it was wasting precious time to quarrel with the postilion. Gerard sat back again, fuming with wrath, and the chaise was set in motion with a sudden jerk that almost flung the passengers on to its floor.

To persons anxious to put as much space between themselves and Bath as possible, and in the shortest time, the slow progress over the next nine miles was agonizing. Emily soon became a prey to agitating reflections. Against all reason, she fancied that they were already being pursued, and every time an imperative blast on a horn gave notice that some faster vehicle was about to pass the chaise, she clutched Gerard's arm, and uttered a shriek. However, at the Ship Inn they fared better, being supplied with two strengthy beasts, and a youthful post-boy, who, on being urged to spring 'em a bit, obeyed with such enthusiasm that the body of the chaise rocked and lurched so violently that Emily began to feel sick. Gerard had to request the postboy to abate the pace, but he felt that a good deal of lost time had been made up, and applied himself to the task of assuaging Emily's fears, and directing her thoughts towards a halcyon future. By dint of skimming lightly over the next year or two, and dwelling on the time when he should have become an important member of Lord Liverpool's administration, he succeeded pretty well. By the time the Cambridge Inn was reached, twenty-three miles out of Bristol, Emily had temporarily forgotten her fears in discussing the rival merits of Green Street and Grosvenor Square as possible localities for the house of a rising politician.

A couple of miles farther on, a slight contretemps occurred, at the Church End turnpike, where the pike-keeper made a spirited attempt to overcharge one whom he took to be a greenhorn. But from this encounter Gerard came off triumphant, which pleased him so much that he began to feel more confident; and for the next four miles boasted to Emily of all the occasions when ugly customers, trying to cheat him, had found themselves powerfully set down.

It was at about this time that Serena and Mr Goring, after a splendid cross-country gallop, dropped into a narrow lane, leading to the village of Dursley from the Bristol to Gloucester pike-road.

"By Jove, Lady Serena, you're a devil to go!" Mr Goring exclaimed, in involuntary admiration.

She laughed, leaning forward to pat the mare's steaming neck. "I like a slapping pace, don't you?"

"I should have called it a *splitting* pace!" he retorted. "Neck or nothing! My heart was in my mouth when you rode straight for that drop fence!"

"Was it indeed? It didn't seem to me that you were precisely hanging back, Mr Goring!"

He smiled. "Why, if *you* chose to take the fence, what could I do but follow?"

"Very true! Pitting that peacocky bay of yours against my mare, you could do nothing else – but you did your best to get ahead of me, I thought!" she said, throwing him a quizzical look. "Confess that you enjoyed that last point as much as I did! For myself, I could almost forgive Gerard and Emily their iniquities: I haven't liked anything so well since I came to Bath. What is the time?"

He pulled out his watch. "Twenty minutes to two. We should come up with them before they reach Gloucester, I think."

In another few minutes they were on the pike-road, and with the Cambridge Inn in sight. Here, Serena permitted Mr Goring, who knew the house well, to make the necessary enquiries. He returned to her presently with the intelligence that the yellow chaise had changed horses there about twenty minutes previously. "They were sweating badly," he added, as he hoisted himself into the saddle again, "so no doubt young Monksleigh is making the best speed he can."

"In that case, we won't jaunter along either," said Serena.

"What do you mean to do when we sight the chaise?" asked Mr Goring. "Am I to hold it up?"

"Good God, no! We want no dramatic scenes upon the high-road! We shall follow discreetly behind, to see which inn they mean to patronize. Leave it to me, then! I know Gloucester as you know Bristol. I shall be better able to carry it off smoothly than you. Yes, I know you would like to have a turn-up with Gerard, but it's my ambition to emerge from this imbroglio without kicking up any dust!"

Thus it was that Gerard, jumping down from the chaise at the Bell Inn, Gloucester, to inspect the horses that were being led out, received an extremely unpleasant shock. "How glad I am to have caught you!" said an affable voice. "You need not have the horses put to!"

Gerard spun round, hardly believing his ears. But they had not deceived him: it was the Lady Serena who had spoken. She was standing just behind him, a pleasant smile on her lips, but her eyes glinting. His own eyes starting at her, he stood transfixed, and could only stammer: "L-Lady Serena!"

"I knew you would be surprised!" she said, still with that horrid affability. "It is not necessary, after all, for Emily to hurry north: her brother is very much better! Famous news, isn't it? The letter came too late for anyone to be able to stop you before you left Bath, so I told her grandmother I would ride after you. Mr Goring – do you know Mr Goring? – was so obliging as to give me his escort, and here we are!"

He uttered in a choked voice: "It's no concern of yours, ma'am! I -"

"Oh, no, but I was happy to be of service!" She nodded smilingly at the elderly ostler, who was touching his forelock to her. "Good-day to you, Runcorn! It is some time since you stabled my horses for me, isn't it? I am glad you are still here, for I want you to take charge of my mare, and Mr Goring's horse too. Ah, I see Emily staring at me! I must instantly tell her the good news, Gerard! Do you go into the house, and bespeak refreshment for us all! Tell the landlord it is for me, and that I should like a private parlour!"

"Lady Serena!" he said furiously. "I must make it plain to you -"

"Indeed, yes! We have so much to say to one another! *I* in particular! But not, do you think, in the courtyard?"

She turned away, and walked towards the chaise, where Mr Goring, having relinquished the bridles he had been holding into the ostler's hands, was already persuading Emily to alight. She seemed to be on the point of bursting into tears, but he took her hand in a firm clasp, and said gravely, but with great kindness: "Come, Miss Laleham! There is nothing to be afraid of: you must not go any farther! Let me help you down, and then we will talk the matter over sensibly, shall we?"

"You don't understand!" she said, trying to pull her hand away. "I can't – I won't -"

"Yes, I do understand, but you are making a mistake you would bitterly regret, my child. Rest assured that your grandmama won't permit anyone to compel you to do what you don't like!"

She looked unconvinced, but his tone, which was much that of a man bent on soothing a frightened baby, calmed her a little, and made her feel a sense of protection. She stopped trying to free her hand, and only made a faint protest when he lifted her down from the chaise. She found herself confronting Serena, and hung her head guiltily, not daring to look up into her face.

"That's right!" said Serena, in a heartening voice. "Now, before we go home again, we'll drink some coffee, my dear. Mr Goring, I shall leave it to you to see that the horses are properly bestowed. Tell old Runcorn that Fobbing will ride over to fetch home my mare in a couple of days' time, if you please, and arrange for four good horses to be put to half an-hour from now. I know I may safely depend upon you."

She then swept Emily irresistibly into the inn, encountering Gerard in the doorway, and saying: "Well, have you done as I bade you?"

This question, calculated as it was to reduce Mr Monksleigh to the status of a schoolboy, made him flush angrily, and say in a sulky voice: "I am willing to break our journey for a few minutes, ma'am, but pray do not imagine that I shall permit you to dictate to me, or to tyrannize over Miss Laleham! In future, Miss Laleham's welfare -"

He stopped, not because he was interrupted, but because it was abundantly plain that she was not attending to him. The landlord was bustling up, and she walked past Gerard to meet him, saying, in her friendly way: "Well, Shere, and how are you?"

"Pretty stout, my lady, I thank you! And how is your ladyship? And my Lady Spenborough? Now, if I had but known we was to have the honour of serving your ladyship with a nuncheon today -!"

"Just some coffee and cold meat will do excellently for us. I daresay Mr Monksleigh will have told you that he was escorting Miss Laleham here on what was feared to be a sad errand. One of her brothers took ill suddenly, and the worst was apprehended, so that nothing would do but she must post to Wolverhampton, where he is staying. However, better tidings have been received, I am happy to say, and so I have come galloping after her, to save her a tedious and most anxious journey! Dear Emily, you are still quite overset, and I am sure it is not to be wondered at! You shall rest quietly for a while, before returning to Bath."

The landlord at once, and in the most solicitous fashion, begged them both to come into his best private parlour; and Emily, dazed by Serena's eloquence, and incapable of resisting her, allowed herself to be shepherded into the parlour, and tenderly deposited in a chair. Mr Monksleigh brought up the rear, not knowing what else to do. Self-confidence was rapidly deserting him, but as soon as the landlord had bowed himself out of the room, he made another attempt to assert himself, saying, in a blustering voice: "Let it be understood, ma'am, that we are not to be turned from our purpose! You do not know the circumstances which have led to our taking what no doubt seems to you a rash step! Not that it signifies in the least! Upon my word, I shall be interested to learn by what right you -" The speech ended here somewhat abruptly, for Serena rounded on him, an alarming flash in her eyes. "Are you out of your senses?" she demanded. "What the *deuce* do you mean by daring to address me in such terms?"

He blenched, but muttered: "Well, I don't see what business it is of yours! You need not think -"

"Let me remind you, Gerard, that you are not talking to one of your college friends!" she interrupted. "I don't take that tone from anyone alive, and least of all from a cub of your age! I have previously thought that Rotherham was too severe with you, but I am fast reaching the conclusion he has been too easy! What you need, and what I am strongly tempted to see that you receive, is a sharp lesson in civility! Do not stand there glowering at me in that stupid, ill-bred style! And do not waste your time talking fustian to me about the circumstances which led you to take what you call a rash step, but which you know very well to be a disgraceful and a dishonourable prank!"

Mr Goring, who had entered the room at the start of this masterly trimming, and had listened to it with deep appreciation, said very politely: "I shall be happy to be of service to you, Lady Serena."

Her eyes twinkled. "I don't doubt it – or that you are an excellent teacher, sir! but I hope not to put you to so much trouble."

"It would be a pleasure, ma'am."

Mr Monksleigh, finding himself between an avenging goddess on the one hand, and a stocky and determined gentleman on the other, thought it prudent to retreat from his dangerous position. He begged pardon, and said that he had not meant to be uncivil. The landlord, accompanied by a waiter, then came back into the room, to set the table, a mundane business which seemed to Gerard quite out of keeping with the romantic nature of his escapade. And when they were alone again, Lady Serena sat down at the head of the table, and began to pour out the coffee, commanding the star-crossed lovers to come and take their places, as though she were presiding over a nursery meal.

"Oh, I could not swallow anything!" Emily said, in lachrymose accents.

"I daresay you will find, when you make the attempt, that you are mistaken," replied Serena. "For my part, I am excessively hungry, and so, I don't doubt, is Mr Goring. So come and sit down to the table, if you please! Mr Goring, if you will take the foot, and carve the ham, Gerard may sit on my other hand, and so we shall be comfortable."

Anything less comfortable than the attitudes assumed by the lovers could scarcely have been imagined. Mr Goring, glancing up from his task, was hard put to it not to laugh.

"I won't go back! I *won't*!" Emily declared, tearfully. "Oh, no one was ever so unhappy as I am!"

"Well, you know, I think you deserve to be unhappy," said Serena. "You have caused Mr Goring and me a great deal of trouble; you have behaved in a way that must, if ever it were to be known, sink you quite beneath reproach; and, which is worst of all, you have made your grandmama ill. Really, Emily, you are quite old enough to know better than to be so outrageously thoughtless! When I arrived in Beaufort Square this morning, it was to find Mrs Floore recovering from a heart attack, and in such distress that I don't know when I have been more shocked."

Emily burst into tears. "Lady Serena, it is useless to seek to interfere!" said Gerard. "This step has not been lightly taken! And as for being dishonourable, it's no such thing! If you think I acted behind Rotherham's back, you are much mistaken! Before ever I came to Bath I went to Claycross, and told my cousin what I should do!"

Lady Serena lowered her cup. "You told Rotherham you were going to elope with Emily?" she repeated.

He reddened. "No, not that! Well, I didn't mean *then* to elope! I told him I should go to Bath, *whatever* he said, and if he didn't choose to believe me, I'm sure it was not my fault!"

"Are we to understand that Rotherham, in fact, forbade you to approach Emily?" asked Serena. "My poor Gerard! What a fortunate thing it is that I was able to catch you! We must *hope* that this escapade doesn't reach his ears, but there's no saying that it won't, and I am strongly of the opinion that you should book yourself a seat on the next London-bound coach."

"*I'm* not afraid of Rotherham!" stated Gerard.

"Then I know just what you should do!" said Serena cordially. "Take the bull by the horns, my dear Gerard! You know what Rotherham is! Seek him out, and make a clean breast of it, and he won't be *nearly* as angry!"

He cast her a look of intense dislike. "I've no desire to see him at all, ma'am!"

Serena spread mustard on a mouthful of ham, and said thoughtfully: "Well, I can't but feel that if I stood in your shoes I had rather seek him than have him seek me. However, that is quite your own affair! But put this absurd Gretna Green idea out of your head, I do beg of you! If I fail to persuade you to abandon your project, I shall have no choice but to inform Rotherham immediately, and then you will see him somewhere on the road to Scotland. I shan't envy you *that* meeting."

Emily shrieked: "You would not! Oh, you would not do so cruel a thing!"

"Of course I should! It would be far more cruel to let you ruin yourself in Gerard's company. And talking of ruin, pray how did you come by the money to pay for this trip, Gerard?"

"I suppose you think I stole it!" he said furiously. "If you must know, I borrowed it!"

"Who in the world was fool enough to lend you enough money to get to Gretna Green and back?" she demanded, quite astonished.

"I shall pay it back on the day I come of age! In fact, he holds my note-of-hand!"

"Who does? You know, this becomes more and more serious!" Serena said. "I fear Rotherham will be quite out of patience with you."

"Well, he will not, because it was he who lent me the money!" retorted Gerard.

Mr Goring choked over a mouthful of bread and butter; Serena, after gazing in an awed way at Gerard for a few moments, said unsteadily: "You borrowed money from Rotherham to enable you to elope with the girl to whom he is betrothed? No doubt he gave you his blessing as well!"

"No, he did not! Of course I didn't tell him I wanted it for – Well, I *didn't* want it for that! I mean, I hadn't thought of eloping then, or I shouldn't have – though it isn't as if I asked him to *give* me the money, after all!" he added defensively.

Mr Goring, listening to him in grim amusement, remarked dispassionately: "You're certainly an original, Monksleigh!"

"Oh, Gerard, how could you?" said Emily. "Oh, dear, how dreadful everything is! I'm sure it would be *very* wrong of us to let Lord Rotherham pay for my marriage to *you*! Now I shall have to go back to Bath, and I wish I were *dead*!"

Gerard, who, to do him justice, had not until now considered this particular aspect of his exploit, flushed scarlet, and said in a deeply mortified voice: "Well, if it was wrong, at least I did it for your sake!"

Serena refilled her cup. "I daresay it may prove to be a blessing," she observed. "His worst enemy never said of Rotherham that he had no sense of humour, and the chances are he would laugh so much that he would forget to be angry with you, Gerard."

He did not appear to derive much comfort from this, but before he could speak, Emily said, tightly clasping her hands: "Lady Serena, I don't want to marry Lord Rotherham! Oh, pray do not try to persuade me! I cannot love him!"

"Then I suggest that you tell him so," replied Serena calmly.

"T-tell him so -?" repeated Emily, her eyes widening in horror.

"Yes, tell him so," said Serena. "When a gentleman, my dear Emily, does you the honour to offer for your hand, and you accept his offer, the barest civility demands that if you should afterwards wish to cry off you must at least inform him of the alteration in your sentiments."

Emily began to cry again. Mr Goring said: "Miss Laleham, pray don't distress yourself! What Lady Serena says is true, but she should have told you also that you have nothing to fear in returning to Mrs Floore's house! I can assure you that you will find in her a stout supporter! Had you informed her of your dislike of Rotherham, this unfortunate affair need never have been!"

She raised her wet eyes to his face in an incredulous look. "Oh, but Mama -!"

"Believe me," he said earnestly, "Mrs Floore is more than a match for your mama! Indeed, my poor child, you must return with us! You have allowed the irritation of your nerves to overset your judgment: I have never met Lord Rotherham, but it is inconceivable to me that he, or any other man, could wish to marry a lady who held him in such aversion!"

"Mr Goring," said Serena, "it is a happiness to have become acquainted with you! Your common sense is admirable! I can think of no one more unlikely than Rotherham to hold a reluctant female to her engagement to him, and you will own that I have reason to know what I am talking about!" A murmur from Emily caused her to whip round, saying sharply: "If you bleat 'Mama' just once more, Emily, you will find that I have a temper quite as much to be dreaded as Rotherham's! Why, you little ninnyhammer, if it is Mama you fear, marry Rotherham tomorrow! You could not have found any man more capable of protecting you from her! Or, I dare swear, more willing to do so! Yes, you may stare! That had not occurred to you, had it? There is another thing that has not occurred to you! We have heard a great deal from you about the terror with which he has inspired you, but I have yet to hear you acknowledge that he has treated you during these weeks you have skulked in Bath with a forbearance of which I did not believe a man of his temper to have been capable! Why he should love such a sapskull as you, I know not, but it is clearly seen that he does! His reward is that when at he last tells you that it is time you came to a point, rather than summon up the courage to face him, and to tell him the truth, you elope with a silly schoolboy for whom you do not care the snap of your fingers! His own ward, too! Did you plan it, between the pair of you, to make him appear ridiculous? Of you, Gerard, I can believe it! After this day's disclosures, it is not in your power to surprise me! You are an ill-conditioned puppy, without gratitude, without propriety, without a thought in your head for anything but what may happen to suit your pleasure!" Her scorching gaze swept to Emily's horrified countenance. "You I acquit of all but childish folly, but I will tell you this, my girl: but for that saving grace – if grace you call it! – I should think you the most contemptible and vulgar of jilts!"

These flaming words not unnaturally left both the persons to whom they were addressed speechless and shaken. Gerard was red to the roots of his hair, Emily paper-white, and almost cowering in her chair. Mr Goring rose, and went to her, laying a hand on her shoulder. Over her head he spoke to Serena. "No more, ma'am, I beg of you! You have said enough! She has indeed behaved ill, but you forget what you yourself have said! – She is the merest child: one, moreover, who is timid, and has felt herself to be alone, and has never known the sympathy and support which girls more fortunately circumstanced than herself enjoy!"

"Yes!" burst in Gerard. "But when *I* rescue her, and try to protect her -"

"If you have the slightest regard for your skin, be silent!" interrupted Mr Goring, his voice losing some of its deliberate calm. "No man who wishes to *protect* an ignorant girl persuades her into taking a step that must expose her to the censure and the contempt of the world!"

The storm vanished from Serena's face, and she gave an involuntary laugh. "You set us all to rights, Mr Goring! There is really no more to be said, and if we are to be in Bath again by dinner-time we should set forward immediately. You need not look so scared, Emily! I shan't scold you any more – and I hope you will not, because I once lost my temper with you, imagine me to be an ogress!"

"Oh, no, no!" Emily stammered. "How *could* I? I never meant – I didn't think -"

"But you have turned Rotherham into an ogre, have you not?" Serena said, arching her brows. "Come! I think you would do well to wait until you have seen him again before you decide to jilt him, my dear. It may be, you know, that you will find that the picture you have painted is a false one. If he still seems terrible to you, why, then, tell him you wish to cry off!" She held out her hand, but spoke to Mr Goring. "Do you come with us, sir?"

"I shall ride behind the chaise, ma'am."

"Emily!" exclaimed Gerard. "Will you permit yourself to be dragged from my side?"

"I am so very sorry!" she said, trembling. "Pray forgive me! I didn't mean to behave so wickedly!"

"My dear Gerard, if you wish to remain at Emily's side, you have only to hire a horse!" said Serena. "Then, when Rotherham comes to Bath, you may confront him together."

"No. no!" cried Emily, clutching her arm. "Oh, don't let him! Lord Rotherham and Mama would know what I did, and I couldn't *bear* it!"

"If my love means so little to you, go!" said Gerard nobly. "I see that the coronet has won!"

CHAPTER TWENTY TWO

WHEN MAJOR Kirkby rode over the Bridge into Laura Place shortly before three o'clock, he was surprised not to see Fobbing waiting there with Serena's phaeton, and still more surprised to be informed by Lybster that the Lady Serena had gone off on a picnic expedition. Lady Spenborough, added Lybster, was in the drawing-room, and had desired him to show the Major upstairs. He observed that the Major had hitched his horse's bridle over the railings, and said that he would send my lady's footman to take charge of the animal.

He then led the Major upstairs, announced him, and went away, shaking his head. In his view, there was something smoky going on, some undergame of which he could not approve.

Fanny jumped up from the sofa, as the door shut behind Lybster, and moved impulsively towards the Major, exclaiming: "Oh, Hector, I am so glad you have come! I am in the most dreadful worry!"

"My dear, what is it?" he asked quickly, catching her hands. "Fanny, you are trembling! My darling -!"

She gave a gasp, and disengaged her hands, casting an imploring look up at him. "Hector – no! You must not – I should not have -! Oh, my love, *remember*!"

He walked away to the window, and stood staring out. "Yes, I beg your pardon! What has happened to distress you, my dear?"

She blew her nose, and said rather huskily: "It's Serena. She has quite taken leave of her senses, Hector!"

He turned his head. "Good heavens, what has she done? Where is she?"

"That," said Fanny distractedly, "is what is so agitating, for I don't know! I mean, *anything* might have happened to her, and if she has not been murdered by footpads, or kidnapped by Mr Goring – for what, after all, do we know of him? she may be halfway to Wolverhampton by this time!"

"Halfway to *Wolverhampton*?" he repeated, startled. "Fanny, for heavens' sake -! Why should Serena go to Wolverhampton? Who is Mr Goring?"

"Oh, he is Mrs Floore's godson, or some such thing! I daresay a very worthy young man, but so *very* dull and respectable!"

He could not help laughing. "Well, if he is dull and respectable, he will hardly have kidnapped Serena!"

"No, I don't suppose it is as bad as that, but what if she *doesn't* catch them before they reach Gloucester? She can't ride all night, and there she will be, miles and miles from Bath, and no luggage, but only Mr Goring, and her reputation quite lost! You had better read her letter!"

"Indeed, I think I had!" he said.

She dragged it from her reticule, and gave it to him. "She says I am to tell you what has happened, so you may as well see just what she says. Hector, I am quite *vexed* with Serena!"

He had unfolded the sheet of paper, and was rapidly running his eyes down it. "Emily – Gerard – Gretna Green! Good God! What's this? Oh, I see! Monksleigh hired the chaise to take him to Wolverhampton. My dear, Serena doesn't say *she* means to go there!"

"She is equal to anything!" said Fanny despairingly.

He went on reading the letter, frowning a little. When he reached the end of it, he folded it, and gave it back to Fanny without a word.

"What am I to do?" she asked. "What *can* I do?"

"I don't think either of us can do anything," he replied. "If I thought it would be of the least use, I would ride after her, but either she is already on her way back, or she must be far beyond my reach. Fanny, does she *often* do things like this?"

"Oh, thank goodness, no! In fact, I've never before known her to ride off with a strange man – well, the merest acquaintance, at all events! and not even take Fobbing with her! Of course, it is very wrong of Gerard and Emily to elope, but it is not Serena's business to take care of Emily! And, I must say, if the wretched girl fears that her odious mother will push her into marrying Lord Rotherham unless she runs away with Gerard, I cannot wholly blame her! How Serena can believe that Emily could ever be happy with such a man as Rotherham is something that quite baffles me, Hector!"

"Do you think that Serena is greatly concerned with Emily's happiness?" he asked slowly. "It seems to me that it is *Rotherham's* happiness which interests her." He took the letter out of her hand, and unfolded it again. "*I can't and I won't allow them to serve Ivo such a trick! It is unthinkable that he should be twice jilted, and this time for such a Bartholomew baby as Gerard – a silly boy that is half flash and half foolish, and his own ward besides!*" He lowered the paper, and looked at Fanny. "If you ask me, my love, Emily might have eloped with Serena's blessing had Rotherham not been in question! Lord, what a tangle!"

She stared up at him. "But, Hector, it isn't possible! She told me months before she met you again that she had only once cared for anyone, and that it was you! And when you met – oh, Hector, you cannot doubt that she was in love with you again on that instant!"

He said ruefully: "I did not doubt it any more than I doubted my own feelings, Fanny."

"Hector, I am persuaded you are mistaken! She *could* not love Rotherham! As for him, I have never seen a sign that he regretted the breaking of the engagement: indeed, far otherwise! He doesn't care the snap of his fingers for her – well, has he not shown that he doesn't, if we had needed showing? He has no tenderness for her, not even solicitude! He -"

"Do you think that Serena desires to be treated with solicitude, Fanny?" he asked. "It has sometimes seemed to me that nothing vexes her more."

"Oh, no, no!" she protested. "Not *vexes* her! She doesn't like one to *cosset* her, but -" She stopped uncertainly. "Well, perhaps – But Rotherham does not even admire her beauty! Do you recall what he said when he dined here, and she was looking quite ravishing? He said she looked like a magpie and that is precisely the sort of thing he always does say to her! Indeed, I am sure you are refining too much upon what she has written in that letter! Though she does not regret it, I believe she thinks that she didn't use him well, which is why she must feel it so particularly, now that it seems as though he will be jilted a second time. For, of course, it *was* quite shocking to have cried off almost at the last moment. I can't think how she had the courage to do it!"

"She doesn't lack courage, Fanny," he replied. He glanced at Serena's letter again, and then laid it down on the table at Fanny's elbow. "I suppose she will bring that foolish girl back. If they outwit her – I wonder? But they won't! To own the truth, I can't imagine her being outwitted by anyone!" He sighed faintly, but said with determined cheerfulness: "There is nothing to be done, my dear. We can only trust to this man, Goring, to take care of her. I had better leave you. If she returns in time for dinner, as she promises, will you send me word by your footman? If she does not -"

"If she does not," said Fanny resolutely, "I shall set out myself!"

"Fanny, Fanny!" he said, half laughing. "No, my darling, you will not!"

"I must!" said Fanny tragically. "It is my duty, Hector! I know I shan't find Serena, but as long as I am not in this house, I can *prevaricate*, and say I was with her! And I beg of you, Hector, don't leave me here alone! I *know* Lord Rotherham will come here, and even when there is *nothing* on my conscience he puts me in a flutter! He will fix his eyes on my face, and ask me the most stabbing questions, and I shall betray all!"

"But, Fanny -!"

"Don't – *don't*, I implore you, say that I have only to decide what I shall tell him!" Fanny begged. "You must know that I am not at all clever, and when Rotherham bends that *look* upon me I become utterly bird-witted! Hector, I cannot be your wife, but I shall be your mother-in-law, and you *cannot* leave me to Rotherham's mercy!"

He dropped on his knees beside her chair, gathering her hands in his, and kissing them again and again. "Fanny, Fanny, don't!" he said unsteadily. "If you look at me like that, how can I -? Dearest, most foolish Fanny, there is no reason to think Rotherham will come to Bath today! I ought not to remain! Besides, I can't keep your footman walking my horse up and down outside for the rest of the day!"

"Tell John to take him back to the stables!" she urged him. "Pray, love, don't take away your support! If I must remain alone here, wondering what has become of Serena, and thinking every knock on the door to be Rotherham's, my senses will become wholly disordered!"

He was not proof against such an appeal. He thought it not very likely that Rotherham would arrive in Bath that day, but he remained with Fanny, with a backgammon-board as chaperon.

And Fanny was quite right. Not very long after five o'clock, Lybster opened the drawing room door, and announced Lord Rotherham.

Fanny was taken by surprise, neither she nor the Major having heard a knock on the street-door. She had just lifted a pile of backgammon pieces, and she gave such a violent start that she dropped them, and they went rolling over the floor in several directions. The Major met her agonized look with a reassuring smile, and was near to bursting into laughter, so comical was her expression of dismay.

Rotherham, pausing halfway across the room, glanced keenly from one to the other of them, bent to pick up a piece that had come to rest against his foot, and said: "How do you do? I am afraid I have startled you, Lady Spenborough!"

"No – oh, no!" Fanny said, blushing, and rising to her feet. "That is, yes! I wasn't expecting to see you! Oh, pray don't trouble about those stupid pieces!"

He dropped three of them on to the board, and shook hands. "I understand Serena is out," he said, turning to offer his hand to the Major. "When does she return?"

The look Fanny cast at the Major was eloquent. *I told you so*! said her eyes. He came at once to the rescue. "It would be a bold man who would dare to prophesy!" he said smilingly. "She has gone off on an expedition, with a party of her friends, and there's no saying when they will get back to Bath."

"Where has she gone to?"

To Fanny's deep admiration, the Major replied without hesitation: "I believe there was some notion of trying to get as far as to the Wookey Hole."

"I wonder you let her."

This remark, though it sounded more of a comment than a criticism, shook the Major slightly. Fanny sprang loyally into the breach. "She will be sorry to have missed you. What a pity you did not advise us of your coming to Bath!"

"Oh, she won't miss me!" said Rotherham. "I'll wait for her – if I shall not be in your way?"

"No, no, not at all!" said Fanny, in a hollow voice. "Pray, won't you sit down?"

"Thank you." He chose a chair opposite to the sofa. "Don't let me interrupt your game!"

"We had just finished. Do you – do you make a long stay in Bath?"

"I can't tell. Has Miss Laleham also gone to the Wookey Hole?"

"I don't know – that is, I forget whether – Oh, I expect she has!" said

Fanny, feeling herself being driven into a corner. She knew that that unnerving gaze was fixed on her, and began with slightly trembling hands to put the backgammon pieces into their box.

"By the by, has my eldest ward been seen in Bath?" asked Rotherham abruptly.

The Major was just in time to catch one of the pieces which, slipping from between Fanny's fingers, rolled across the board to the edge. "Oh, thank you! So clumsy! G-Gerard, Lord Rotherham? *I* haven't seen him. Did you expect to find him here?"

"I wasn't sure. That's why I asked you."

Fanny found herself obliged to look up, and was lost. The compelling eyes held hers, but they were not frowning, she noticed. A rather mocking smile lurked in them. "I accept without question that you haven't seen him, Lady Spenborough. Has anyone?"

"Are you talking of a boy called Monksleigh?" interposed the Major. "Yes, I've seen him. Serena introduced him to me. He said he was staying with friends outside the town."

"He lied, then. Has he too gone to the Wookey Hole?"

"No, indeed he hasn't!" Fanny said quickly. "He – he has left Bath, I believe!"

"Oh, my God, why did I never thrust some jumping powder down his throat while there was still time to cure him of cowheartedness?" exclaimed Rotherham, in accents of extreme exasperation. He got up abruptly. "He heard I was coming, and fled, did he? I wish you will stop fencing with me, Lady Spenborough! Sooner or later I am bound to discover what has been going on here, and I'd as lief it was sooner! I've already been refused admittance in Beaufort Square, where I learned that Miss Laleham will not be in until late this evening, that Mrs Floore is out, visiting friends, and that Lady Laleham is expected in Bath this afternoon. Now I find that Serena too is not expected back until late, and that that ward of mine has taken himself off in a hurry, which makes nonsense of the whole! Having had the spirit to come here, why the devil couldn't he -" He stopped suddenly, his brows snapping together: "Good God, did she send him packing?"

Fanny cast another of her imploring looks at the Major, but he too had risen, and his eyes were on Rotherham's face. "Am I to understand that you knew young Monksleigh to be in love with Miss Laleham?" he asked bluntly.

"Knew it?" Rotherham gave a short laugh, and strode over to the window. "What can one *know* of a bag of wind? He enacted me a ranting tragedy, but as to discovering whether there is one grain of sincerity amongst the fustian, you might as well try to milk a pigeon! Just playing off his tricks, was he?" He shrugged. "I should have guessed it!"

"No," said the Major deliberately. "Far from it!"

"Hector!" The cry was startled out of Fanny.

Rotherham swung round. One swift glance at Fanny's horrified face, and his eyes went to the Major's, in a hard, questioning stare. "Well? Out with it!"

Fanny sprang up, with a rustle of silken skirts, and clasped her hands about the Major's arm. "Hector, you must not! Oh, pray -!"

He laid his hand over her clutching fingers. "But I think I should," he said gently. "Haven't you said from the outset that nothing but misery could come of the marriage? Your ward, Marquis, according to our information, eloped this morning with your betrothed."

"What?" Rotherham thundered, making Fanny wince. "Are you trying to hoax me?"

"On *such* a subject? Certainly not! They set out in a chaise and pair, and were bound, it is presumed, for Gretna Green."

"By God, I've wronged that boy!" exclaimed Rotherham. "So that's why I wasn't permitted to enter Mrs Floore's house! Gretna Green, indeed!" His brows drew together again. "Good God, they will never get there! I'll swear all the money the young fool had was the fifty pounds I gave him! Why the devil couldn't he have asked me for a hundred while he was about it? Of all the addle-brained cawkers -! *Now* he'll find himself aground before he reaches Carlisle!"

Fanny's hands fell from the Major's arm. Fascinated, she stared at Rotherham.

"He appears only to have booked the chaise as far as to Wolverhampton," said the Major, contriving by a superhuman effort to preserve his countenance. "Possibly – he has foreseen that he might find himself without a feather to fly with, and means to proceed thence by stage-coach."

"God grant me patience!" ejaculated Rotherham wrathfully. "If ever I knew such a slow top -! Does he know no better than to take a girl to Wolverhampton – *Wolverhampton*, my God! – and then to push her into a stage-coach? And I don't doubt *I* shall be blamed for it, if all comes to ruin! How the devil could I guess he was such a cod's head that he wouldn't know better unless I told him?"

"Perhaps," said the Major, who had sat down again, and was giving way to his emotion, "he f-felt there might be a little – awkwardness in applying to you for instruction!"

One of his sharp cracks of laughter broke from Rotherham. "He might, of course!" he acknowledged. Another thought brought back the frown to his brow. "What's Serena doing in this?" he demanded. "You're not going to tell me she has gone along to chaperon Emily?"

"No: to bring her back!" said the Major. "She has ridden in pursuit of them."

"And you let her?"

"It was not in my power to attempt to stop her. I only learned of it this afternoon. It was far too late to try to catch her. I can only trust she'll come to no harm."

"Serena?" Rotherham's lip curled. "You needn't be anxious on her account! It isn't she who will come to harm. So she means to bring Emily back, does she? I am obliged to her!"

He came slowly away from the window, a brooding look in his harsh face, his lips tightly gripped together. He saw that Fanny was watching him, and said curtly: "No doubt she will be home presently. I shouldn't tease yourself about her, Lady Spenborough, if I were you: she's very well able to take care of herself. I won't wait to see her."

He held out his hand, but before she could take it the Major had risen, and picked up from the table Serena's letter. "You had better read what she wrote to Lady Spenborough," he said. "I fancy it makes the matter tolerably plain."

Rotherham took the paper from him, directing a searching glance at him from under his brows. Then he bent his gaze upon the letter, and began to read it, his face very grim. But he had not proceeded far before his expression changed. The set look disappeared, to be succeeded by one of mingled wrath and astonishment. He did not speak, until he came to the end, but he seemed to find it difficult to control himself. At last he looked up, and Fanny's heart instantly jumped into her mouth, such a blaze of anger was there in his eyes. "I *will* wait to see Serena!" he said. "I must certainly thank her in person! So busy as she has been on my behalf!" He rounded suddenly on the Major: "And who the devil is this Goring she writes of?" he demanded.

"I have never met him, but Lady Spenborough tells me he is Mrs Floore's godson, and a most – er – sober and respectable young man," replied the Major. "We must depend on him to bring her safely back."

"Oh, we must, must we?" said Rotherham savagely. "She is a great deal more likely to bring him back – on a hurdle! Any man who lets Serena lead him into one of her damned May Games can't be other than a bottlehead!" He broke off, jerking up his head, his eyes going swiftly to the window. The clop of a horse's hooves, which had been growing steadily louder, ceased suddenly. Two quick strides took Rotherham back to the window. He flung it up, and looked down at the vehicle drawn up outside the house. There was a tense pause; then Rotherham said, leaning his hands on the window-sill, Serena's letter crushed in one of them: "Her ladyship – in a hired hack!"

He shut the window with a slam, and turned. Fanny sprang up. "Serena? Oh, thank God! Oh, what a relief!"

She then shrank instinctively towards the Major, for the look Rotherham turned on her was bright and menacing. "Don't thank God too soon, Lady Spenborough! Serena is in a great deal more danger now than she has been all day, believe me!"

"No, no, stop!" she cried. "What are you going to do to her?"

"Murder her!" he said, through shut teeth, and went hastily out of the room.

Fanny started forward, but the Major caught her arm. "No, my dear! Let be!"

"Hector, go after him!" she said urgently. "His face – Oh, he looked like a *fiend*! Heaven only knows what he may do in such a wicked passion! You *must* do something! Hector, it is your duty to protect Serena!"

"So I might, if I thought she stood in peril of her life," he replied, laughing. "What I do think is that I should make a very bad third in *that* quarrel!"

Meanwhile, Rotherham, running down the stairs, reached the entrance floor just as Serena walked past Lybster into the house. Under the stiff, curling brim of her tall hat, her face was a little pale, and her eyes frowning in a look of fatigue. She laid her whip down on the table, and began to strip off her gauntlets. "Is her ladyship in, Lybster?"

"In the drawing-room, my lady. Also -"

"Ridden that short-backed mare of yours to a standstill, Serena?"

She looked round quickly. "Ivo! You here?"

"Yes, Serena, as you see!" he said, advancing upon her. "Not only here, but extremely anxious to have a few words with you!"

"Dear me, in the sullens again?" she asked, her voice light, but her eyes watchful. "Are you vexed because Emily did not abandon our expedition on the chance that you might arrive in Bath today? How absurd of you!"

"My girl," said Rotherham dangerously, "it will be just as well for you if you stop thinking me a bleater, whom you can gull by pitching me your damned gammon! Come in here!" He pushed open the door into the dining-room, and to Lybster's intense disappointment pulled Serena into the room, and shut the door in the butler's face. "Now, Serena! *Now*!" he said. "What the *devil* have you been doing? Don't lie to me! I know what expedition yours was!" He unclenched his left hand, and showed her the crushed letter. "Do you recognize that? Then tell me the truth!"

She said indignantly: "So, not content with browbeating Emily, you have bullied Fanny into giving you my letter, have you? Well, if I find you've upset her, you will very speedily wish you had remembered with whom you would have to deal, if you came raging into this house! *I* am not a wretched schoolgirl, wilting under your frown!"

"You are a meddlesome vixen!" he told her angrily.

Her eyes flashed, but she choked back a pungent retort, struggled for a moment with herself, and finally said, in a voice of determined calm: "No. This is no moment for a turn-up, Rotherham. If you have read my letter, it may be for the best. Of course you are angry – though why you should make *me* your scapegoat God knows! Never mind that! I can stand a knock or two. Ivo, what a *fool* you have been! You may blame yourself for what happened today! Don't vent your wrath on Gerard! I've sent him back to London with such a flea in his ear as he will not soon forget, I assure you!"

"You have, have you? How much – how *very* much – I am obliged to you! Go on!"

"You are more obliged to me than you know! You may dismiss Gerard from your mind: Emily is no more in love with him than I am! Had you had enough sense to have come to Bath, without heralding your arrival in a letter anyone but an *idiot* would have known must scare the child out of what little wit – out of her wits! – she would never have spared Gerard a thought! She seized on him merely as a means of escape. Really, Ivo, you have handled this like the veriest whipster! *You*! You have the vilest temper in creation, but I've never known you lose it with a nervous young 'un! Couldn't you guess that if you let Emily see it, she would behave exactly as would a filly you had spurred? She turned you into a positive ogre – and you could have made her adore you! Instead, you frightened her – and the devil's own task I have had, all the way from Gloucester, to convince her she has been a goose! I can't tell whether I've succeeded, but I can't do any more! The rest is with you! Be gentle with her, and I think all may be well!"

"O *God*!" uttered Rotherham, in a strangled voice. "What have I ever done to be cursed with such a marplot as you, Serena? So you've convinced her that I'm not such a devil as I made her think! I thank you! And I thought that if there was *one* person I could depend upon to urge the wretched girl on no account to marry me, it was you! I might have guessed you would bullfinch me if you could!"

"*Rotherham!*" exclaimed Serena, grasping a chairback. "Are you telling me – are you *daring* to tell me – you *meant* to scare Emily into jilting you?"

"Of course I meant it!" he said furiously. "You think I'm clever in the saddle, do you? Much obliged to you! A pity you didn't remember it earlier! Good God, Serena, you can't have supposed that I wanted to marry that hen-witted girl?"

"Then why the *devil* did you offer for her?" she demanded.

"It only needed that!" he said. "Serena, I could break your damned neck!"

She stared at him in bewilderment. "Why? How was I to guess you had run mad? Anyone would think it was *my* fault you lost your head over a pretty face!"

"I never lost my head over any but *one* face, God help me! My temper, yes – once too often! I offered for Emily because *you* had become engaged to Kirkby! And if you were not a paperskull, you would have guessed it!"

"It's a lie! I only wrote to tell you of my engagement after the notice of yours had appeared in the *Gazette*!" she said swiftly.

"And you thought that because you hadn't told me of it I didn't know? Well, I did know! You cannot live in a man's pocket here, my girl, without setting tongues wagging! From three separate sources did I hear of your doings!"

"If you choose to listen to gossip -"

"No, I didn't listen to it – until I knew who it was who had appeared in Bath! *Then* I did more than listen! I got the truth out of Claypole!"

"You didn't so much as remember Hector!" she stammered.

"Of course I remembered him!" he said scornfully. "I remembered something else too! – that unknown person whose name you refused to divulge, when I first visited you here!"

"Unknown person?" she repeated blankly. "Oh, good God! Mrs Floore! I had not *seen* Hector then! Ivo, what a *fool* you were!"

"I was a fool," he said grimly, "but not in believing that Claypole spoke the truth!"

"And you became engaged to Emily merely because *I* – Ivo, it is beyond words! To use a child very nearly young enough to be your daughter as a weapon of revenge on me – I wonder that you dare to stand there and tell me of such an *iniquity*!" Serena said hotly.

"It wasn't as bad as that!" he said, flushing. "I meant *then* to marry her! If that curst Adonis of yours had won you, what did it signify whom I married? I must marry *someone,* and Emily was as good as another – better! I knew I could mould her into whatever shape I pleased; I knew she would be happy enough with what I could give her; I knew the Laleham-harpy would jump at my offer. And I knew you would hate it, Serena! Oh, yes, infamous, wasn't it? I did it because I was mad with anger – but I never meant to play the child false!"

"And what, most noble Marquis," enquired Serena scathingly, "made you change your mind, and decide instead to be rid of her?"

He set his hands on her shoulders, and gripped them, holding her eyes with his. "Years ago, Serena, you fancied yourself head over ears in love with a devilish handsome lad! I didn't think then that he was the man for you –

and when I saw you both together here, I was even more certain of it! But when I heard of his reappearance, and of the reception he got from you, I was shaken as I never was before, and hope to God I never shall be again! But the instant I saw the pair of you I knew that I had rolled myself up to no purpose at all! I don't know what madness seized you, but I do know that you don't love Kirkby, and never did, or will!"

She wrenched herself away. "Did you? Did you, indeed? Perhaps you thought I loved you!"

"No – but I knew that I still loved you! I could see you would break with Kirkby – Lord, Serena, if I hadn't been in such a damned tangle myself I should have laughed myself into stitches! My poor girl, did you really think you could be happy with a man that would let you walk rough-shod over him? For how long did you enjoy having your own, undisputed way? When did you begin to feel bored?"

"Let me tell you this, Rotherham!" she flung at him. "Hector is worth a dozen of you!"

"Oh, probably two or three dozen! What has that to say to anything?"

"It has this to say! I am pledged to him, and I shall marry him, so let me recommend you to lose no time in reinstating yourself in Emily's good graces! How *dare* you talk to me like this? And to think I didn't believe the things Emily poured out to me today!" She paused, almost choking. "You deliberately tried to make that girl cry off!"

"Well, how the devil else was I to get out of a marriage that was going to wreck the pair of us – and Emily, too, for that matter?"

"*You* made your bed –"

"– and we could all of us lie on it, I suppose?" he interjected witheringly.

She drew a breath. "Good God, had you no compunction? You had offered her a great position, a -"

"Yes, I had! And if you fancy that her mother forced her to accept my offer, you're out, my girl! I never tampered with her affections: don't think it! Had I thought she cared one jot for me it would have been a different story, but she didn't! She wanted nothing from me but rank and fortune, and she made that abundantly plain!"

"Ivo, did you, or did you not make violent love to her, and tell her that if she played the coquette with you after you were married it would be very much the worse for her?" Serena demanded.

"Oh, not then!" he replied coolly. "That was later! God knows what she thought I had in store for her, little fool!"

"Oh, how I wish she had slapped your face!" raged Serena.

"So did I wish it!" he retorted. "Lord, Serena, I even made her think I should be such a jealous husband that she would do better to marry a Bluebeard! I ran the gamut of impatience, jealousy, intemperate passion, veiled threats, and nothing I could do or say outweighed my coronet!"

"In her mother's eyes!"

"Oh, yes! I don't deny that woman had a good deal to do with it! But make no mistake about it, Serena! – until I convinced Emily that she would not enjoy all that stuff by half as much as she had thought she would, I could have been as brutal as I chose, and she would still have married me!"

She gave a gasp. "Delford! Ivo, you – you *fiend*! When she told me about that visit – the pomp and the ceremony you overwhelmed her with – the *people* you filled the house with – the formality you insisted on – I thought that either she was exaggerating to impress me, or that you had run mad!"

He grinned at her. "You never saw such a party! I had the state apartments opened, and shut my own rooms up, and dug out the gold plate, and -"

"How you can stand there and *boast* to me -! No wonder Emily stared at me when I told her you had no turn for ceremony!"

"Grandeur she wanted, and grandeur I gave her – full measure, and brimming over! Lady Laleham revelled in it, but Emily didn't. That was when I saw the scales begin to tip. Then she was ill – by the bye, Serena, that was the best thing I've ever heard Gerard say! I told him Emily had been suffering from an attack of influenza, and damme if he didn't rip back at me that it was more likely an attack of the Marquis of Rotherham! I never thought the boy had it in him to land me such a doubler!"

"Or to elope with Emily?" she demanded. "Was that your doing too? I can believe you capable even of that!"

"No, it never entered my head that he had enough spirit for such a stroke as that. All I did was to try whether I could sting him into coming here, and enacting his tragedy to Emily. He prated about the attachment that had existed between them, and for anything I knew it might have been true. If it was true, and he had enough courage to come here in defiance of me, I thought he might be the very thing that was wanted to weigh the scales completely down against that damned coronet. I gave him a couple of day's grace, and then sent Emily a letter, calculated – as you so correctly pointed out to me, my clever one! – to scare her out of her wits. I can't say I expected an elopement, though."

"And if you had? Do you expect me to believe that you would not still have used the wretched boy in that unprincipled way?"

To her seething anger, he appeared to consider this quite dispassionately for a moment or two. "No, I couldn't have helped him to a Gretna Green marriage," he decided.

"This is something indeed! No doubt, if I had not frustrated that crazy scheme, *you* would now be posting north to do it yourself!"

"What I should be doing at this moment, if you had not wrecked everything with your damned meddling, would be thanking God for deliverance!" he returned trenchantly. "What I *thought* to find here was Emily playing Juliet to Gerard's Romeo! His heroics may not appeal to me, but they are just the thing to put a little spirit into her! All she needed to make her cry off by the time her mother sent her here, was someone to support her! The fool that I was, I believed I could rely on *you* to scotch what you must have seen was the worst marriage ever planned! Very free you are with your condemnations of what *I* did, you shrew! Reserve some of your censure for your own behaviour! Instead of telling the chit she had better go hang herself than cling like a damned limpet to a man you knew would make her a hellish husband, you did all you could to persuade her I had all the amiable qualities which no one knows better than you I have *not*! By the time Gerard burst in on me, I knew you were failing me, but that you were ranged on the side of the Laleham-harpy I never dreamed! What was in that red head of yours, my sweetest scold? Spite?"

Quick as a flash she struck at him, but he was quicker still, and caught her wrist in mid-air. "Oh, no, you don't! You'll hit me when I choose to let you, and at no other time, Serena! Why did you try to push me into that marriage? Answer me, *damn* you!"

"I never pushed you into anything!" she replied pantingly. "Wiser men than you have fallen in love with pretty feather heads! You to talk to *me* of spite! It never entered my head that you had offered for Emily because you wanted to be revenged on me, and hoped I should be hurt! You have gone your length, Rotherham! I may be every one of the things you are so obliging as to call me, but the only thought I had was to save you from the humiliation of being twice jilted! You may let me go: I would not *touch* you, any more than I would touch a toad!"

He laughed. "Wouldn't you? We'll see that! Now, you listen to me, my girl! There's nothing I should like better than to continue quarrelling with you, but thanks to your well-meant but corkbrained efforts on my behalf the tangle is now past unravelling, and must be cut! When I've done that, I'll come back, and you may revile me to your heart's content!"

"Don't you dare set foot inside this house again!" she said.

"Try if you can keep me out!" he advised her, and let her wrist go, and strode out of the room, a little too quickly for Lybster, hovering in a disinterested fashion in the narrow hall. "What a rare day's entertainment for you!" he said sardonically.

"I beg your lordship's pardon?" said Lybster, the picture of bewildered dignity.

"You may well! Inform Lady Spenborough that I shall be dining here tonight!"

"Yes, my lord."

Serena was in the doorway, her eyes flashing green fire. "You will on no account admit Lord Rotherham into this house, Lybster!"

"No, my lady," said Lybster, moving to the street door, and opening it for Rotherham.

Serena turned towards the stairs. Fanny, on the first landing, whisked herself back into the drawing-room, and softly closed the door. "There! You heard what she said!" she whispered to Major Kirkby.

"Yes, and I heard what he said," he replied.

Serena's hasty steps sounded outside. Fanny looked anxiously towards the door, but Serena passed on, and up the next flight. "Oh, dear, I fear she is in one of her rages!" said Fanny. "What shall I do? Oh, what a dreadful day this is!"

He smiled. "No, I think not, love. If I were you, I would do what I am going to do: retire to change for dinner!"

"Hector, you don't mean to leave me to dine with those two?" she cried, aghast.

"Not I! Do you think I have no interest in the outcome of this battle? I too am dining with you, my love!" he said.

CHAPTER TWENTY THREE

ADMITTED INTO Mrs Floore's house, Rotherham had barely time to hand his hat to the butler before a door opened at the back of the hall, and Lady Laleham came out, dressed in all the elegance of figured silk and lace, and wreathed in smiles. "Ah, dear Lord Rotherham!" she pronounced. "I knew you might be depended upon to call again! Such a sad mischance that you should have found no one at home when you came this afternoon! But you must not blame us, you know, for you forgot to tell Emily which day you meant to arrive in Bath! I hope I see you well?"

"My health, I thank you, ma'am, is excellent. I cannot, however, say as much for my temper, which has been exasperated beyond anything which I am prepared to endure!" he replied, in his harshest voice.

She laid the tips of her fingers on his arm, in a fleeting gesture of sympathy. "I know," she said, considerably to his surprise. "Will you come into the morning-room? You will, I know, forgive my mother for not receiving you: she is elderly, and, alas, not capable of exertion!"

"The person I wish to see, Lady Laleham, is not your mother, but your daughter!"

"Exactly so!" she smiled, preceding him into the morning room. "And here she is!"

He strode into the room, and paused, looking grimly at his prospective bride. She was standing beside a large wing chair, one trembling hand resting on its back, her eyes huge in her white face, and her breathing uneven. She looked very young, very pretty, and very apprehensive, and she showed no disposition to come forward to greet her betrothed until her mother said, in a voice of honeyed reproof: "Emily-dear!" After that, she advanced, and said: "How do you do?" putting out her hand.

"Effusive!" said Rotherham. "You must not behave as though I were your whole dependence and delight, you know!"

"She is a little tired," explained Lady Laleham, "and she has been a very silly, naughty child, which she knows she must confess to you."

His eyes went to her face, an arrested expression in them.

"L-Lady Serena said I n-need not t-tell, Mama!"

"We are very much indebted to Lady Serena, my love," Lady Laleham returned smoothly, "but you will allow Mama to know best what you should do." She met Rotherham's fierce stare with perfect coolness, a faint smile on her painted lips. "The poor child is afraid that you will be very angry with her, Lord Rotherham, but I have assured her that where there is full confession there must always be forgiveness, particularly when it is accompanied by deep repentance."

The wretched Emily, perceiving that her betrothed was looking like a thundercloud, began to feel faint. But Rotherham was not thinking about her. He was seeing the ground being cut from beneath his feet by a stratagem which he recognized, in a cold fury, to be masterly. And he could think of no way to prevent Emily from casting herself upon his mercy. Out it all came, in halting, shamefaced sentences from Emily, skilfully embroidered by her mother. She had thought he was very angry with her, when she had received his letter; he had stayed away from her for so long that she feared he no longer loved her; Gerard had told her such dreadful things that she had taken fright. But Lady Serena had come to the rescue just when she was wishing she had not done such a wicked thing; and Lady Serena had assured her that she had nothing to fear from Lord Rotherham. So she had come home and had been crying her eyes out ever since because she was so very, very sorry. Finally, would he forgive her, and believe that she would never do it again?

He became aware that she had finished speaking, and saw that her eyes were fixed on his face in a look of painful enquiry. He said abruptly: "Emily, do you love Gerard?"

"Oh, *no*!" she said, and there was no mistaking the sincerity in her voice.

No way of escape there. There was only one way out, and that was to play the outraged lover, and repudiate the engagement. It could not be done. To push her into flinging that handsome diamond ring he had given her in his face was one thing; to push her into eloping with his ward, and then to round on her, was quite another. He wondered what pressure her mother had brought to bear to make her so anxious to marry him. She was no longer thinking of riches and position. If he could get rid of Lady Laleham, he might be able to reach an understanding with Emily – if she was capable of understanding anything, which she did not look to be.

"I think it would be as well if we talked this over alone," he said.

Lady Laleham had no intention of allowing this. Unfortunately, Emily's terror of him was greater than her dread of her mother, and she gave him no support, but shrank towards Lady Laleham.

At which moment the door opened, and a startling vision surged into the room. "I thought as much!" said Mrs Floore ominously. "And who gave you leave to entertain guests in my house, Sukey?" She retained her clutch on Mr Goring's supporting arm, and added: "No, you stay here, Ned! There's nothing that's happened here this day you don't know, and a true friend you've been, like your father would have been before you!"

Rotherham, with difficulty withdrawing his eyes from the magnificence before him, glanced at Lady Laleham. What he saw in her face afforded him considerable solace. Fury and chagrin were writ large in it, and beneath these emotions, unless he much mistook the matter, fear. So this was the mysterious grandmother about whom he had quizzed Emily on his first meeting with her! He bent his penetrating stare upon her again, as she settled herself in the chair of her choice, and directed Mr Goring to pull forward a footstool.

Mrs Floore was doing justice to the occasion in a staggering gown of lustring, with tobine stripes of a rich ruby, and a quantity of floss trimming. This splendid robe was draped over panniers, fashionable in her youth, and was worn over an underdress of satin. A medley of brooches adorned the low-cut corsage, and round her short neck she had clasped several strings of remarkably large pearls. A turban of ruby silk and tinsel was embellished with a cluster of ostrich plumes, and from the lobes of her ears hung two large rubies.

"That's right," nodded Mrs Floore, shifting the position of the stool a trifle with one red heeled and buckled shoe. "Now let me take a look at this precious Marquis I've heard so much about!"

Lady Laleham, with an unconvincing smile pinned to her mouth, murmured to Rotherham: "Dear Mama is quite an eccentric!"

"I'm not an eccentric, and I'm not deaf!" said her dear Mama sharply. "I'm a plain woman that came of good merchant stock, which, though I may not have your fine-lady airs and graces, my dear, I've got more sense than to be ashamed of! And another thing I'll tell you is that you'd do better to introduce this Marquis to me than to stand there biting your lips, and wondering what he must be thinking of your ma! He can think what he likes, and if Emma means to marry him – which, however, isn't by any means a settled thing! – the sooner he gets used to her grandma the better it will be for him!"

"How do you do?" said Rotherham, slightly bowing, his tone indifferent, but his eyes keenly surveying this amazing old lady.

She gave him back stare for stare, taking him in from the heels of his boots to the crown of his black locks. "Good gracious, you're a regular blackamoor!" she exclaimed. "Well, they say handsome is as handsome does, but from all I can make out, my lord, you haven't done very handsome yet."

"You must not mind Mama: she is so droll!" said Lady Laleham.

"It'll be more to the point if I don't mind him," observed Mrs Floore, who was clearly in a belligerent mood. "You must excuse me staring at you, my lord, but I never did see such peculiar eyebrows! Now, I shouldn't wonder at it, Emma, my pet, if half the time you thought he was scowling at you it was nothing but the way his eyebrows grow, which he can't help, though, of course, it's a pity."

Rotherham kept his countenance set in its forbidding lines. At any other moment, he would have exerted himself to please Mrs Floore, for he was strongly attracted to her, but since her attitude appeared to be hostile he saw in her his one hope of salvation, and began to consider how best to annoy her.

"Dear Mama, you know that Emily wished to see Lord Rotherham in private!" said Lady Laleham. "Don't you think, perhaps -"

"No, I don't," replied Mrs Floore bluntly. "What's more, it wasn't Emma that wanted to be private with him, and if she had done, I don't see much privacy for her with you standing over her, Sukey!"

"You forget, Mama, that I am her mother."

"Well, and if I do, whose fault is that?" demanded Mrs Floore. "You act motherly, and maybe I *won't* forget! From the look on poor little Emma's face, you've been bullying her, the pair of you. That's right, Ned, you give her a chair, and don't you be afraid, my pet, because you haven't any need to be!"

"None at all!" said Lady Laleham. "Lord Rotherham has been most forbearing, just as I knew he would be, and has not uttered one word of censure, has he, Emily?"

"No, Mama," said Emily, in a small, scared voice.

"It's to be hoped he hasn't!" said Mrs Floore, her eyes snapping. "That's not to say he won't hear a word of censure from me – in fact, a good many words! Yes, it's all very well to be high in the instep, my lord, and to look at me as though I was a spider, and very likely you're thinking I'm just a vulgar old woman, but what I say is that if anyone's to blame for what's happened it's you!"

"I've no objection to vulgarity," replied Rotherham. "What, however, I do not tolerate is interference. That had better be understood immediately."

Mrs Floore seemed to swell. "Ho! So when I tell you I won't have my granddaughter made miserable, that's interference, is it"

"If Emily is made miserable by me, the remedy is in her own hands."

"Mama, pray be quiet!" cried Lady Laleham. "Such nonsense! As though she has not every reason to be the happiest girl alive!"

"You may toad-eat his lordship as much as you like, Sukey, but don't you run away with the idea you can tell me to be quiet, or you and me will fall out, which would *not* suit your book! Ever since Emma got herself engaged to this Marquis, she's looked downright seedy, and she's been no more her merry self -"

"My dear Mama, I have told you a score of times that London, and all the gaieties she enjoyed, were too much for her!"

"Then there is no need for you to feel any further anxiety about her health," said Rotherham. "We are not going to live in London."

This pronouncement, uttered as it was in a curt, matter-of-fact voice, surprised Emily into uplifting her voice: "Not going to live in London?" she repeated.

"No."

"Dear child, Lord Rotherham means that you will mostly be at Delford, or at Claycross!" interposed Lady Laleham. "Naturally, you will be in London for a few months during the spring!"

"I mean nothing of the sort," said Rotherham, without heat, but with finality. "I am closing Rotherham House."

"Closing Rotherham House?" exclaimed Lady Laleham, as though she could not believe her ears. "But – but why?"

He shrugged. "I dislike living in town, and abominate *ton* parties."

Emily's eyes darkened in dismay. "N-no parties at all?" she asked.

He glanced down at her. "We shall entertain at Delford, of course."

"Oh, no!" she said involuntarily. "I-I couldn't!" She flushed, and added pleadingly: "I would rather live in London! At least, *some* part of the year! Delford is so very big, and – and – I don't like it!"

"I am afraid, since it is my home, you will have to overcome your dislike of it."

"Of course she will!" said Lady Laleham. "But surely you cannot mean to keep her there throughout the year!"

"Why not?"

"I'll soon tell you why not!" interrupted Mrs Floore, who had been listening in gathering wrath. "If Delford is the place where poor little Emma had to walk half a mile from her bedroom to the dining-room, it isn't the kind of house that'll suit her at all! Besides, from what she tells me, it's stuck right out in the country, and she's had enough of that kind of thing at Cherrifield Place! What's she going to do with herself all day long?"

"She will find plenty to do, I imagine. She will have first to learn what is expected of Lady Rotherham, which is likely to keep her pretty fully occupied for some months. She will hunt, of course -"

"Hunt?" cried Emily. "Oh, no, please! I never do so!"

"You will," he said.

"J-jump over those *dreadful* fences you showed me?" Emily said, horror in her voice. "I *couldn't*!"

"We shall see!"

"Well, if ever I heard anything to equal it!" gasped Mrs Floore. "First, she's to learn a lot of lessons, and next she's to be made to break her neck!"

"Oh, she won't break her neck!" said Rotherham. "A few tumbles won't hurt her! I shall have some fairly easy jumps put up, and school her over them."

"*No!*" almost shrieked Emily. "I won't, I won't!"

"No more you shall, lovey!" hotly declared Mrs Floore.

"It will be as well, Emily, if you realize that when you are Lady Rotherham I shall expect obedience from you. I warn you, it will not do if you say 'I won't' to me."

Mr Goring, who had been seated rather in the background got up, and said in his level tone: "We've heard a great deal of what *you* expect, and what *you* like, my lord, but we haven't yet heard you ask Miss Laleham what *she* would like!"

"She'll learn to like what I like – if she's wise! I did not choose a bride out of the schoolroom, sir, to have her setting up her will against mine!"

Mr Goring's jaw was becoming momentarily more aggressive. "It seems to me, Lord Rotherham, that what you want is a slave, not a wife!"

Mrs Floore, unable to contain herself another instant, said forcefully: "And he's not getting a slave in my Emma! Why, the man's a downright monster! A fine husband you caught for Emma, Sukey! I wonder you aren't ashamed to look me in the face! If I didn't say to Lady Serena that it wouldn't matter to you if a man was cross-eyed, and had one foot in the grave! Not so long as he was a Duke, which is all you care for! And this Choctaw Indian here isn't even a Duke!"

There was the faintest tremor at the corners of Rotherham's mouth, but it went unnoticed. Lady Laleham said: "I cannot believe that Lord Rotherham means all he says! I am sure he means to make Emily very happy!"

"Certainly," said Rotherham, bored. "She has only to adapt herself to my wishes, and I see no reason why she should not be perfectly happy."

Suddenly Emily sprang up, and fled to her grandmother's chair. "I can't, I can't! I don't care if I am ruined! *I can't!* Oh, Grandmama, don't let Mama make me!"

"Emily!" There was a red spot on each of Lady Laleham's cheeks. "How dare you say such a thing? As though I should dream -"

"You keep your distance, Sukey!" commanded Mrs Floore.

Mr Goring, stepping up to Rotherham, his chin now well out-thrust, said: "Perhaps your lordship will do me the favour of stepping outside for a few minutes!"

"No, you fool!" said Rotherham, very softly.

"Emily, think what you are doing!" Lady Laleham was saying urgently. "You'll never get a husband, if you play the jilt! Particularly after your folly today! The whole world will think it was *you* who were jilted! You'll have to stay at home, for *I* shan't take you to town again, and you'll end your days an old maid -"

"You're wrong, ma'am!" said Mr Goring. "There's time and to spare before she need think of being married, but you needn't fear she won't get another offer, because I can tell you that she will!"

"You can lay your life she will!" said Mrs Floore. "Now, don't you cry, my pretty, because your ma isn't going to make you do anything!"

"What shall I do?" sobbed Emily. "I don't w-want to go home in d-disgrace, and I don't w-want to have n-no reputation!"

"Emma, would you like to stay with your old grandma? Now, think, lovey! It ain't very lively, living here, and nothing but the Assemblies, and the Sydney Gardens, and if it's the *ton* parties you want, I can't give them to you, because if I was to take you to London I couldn't chaperon you, my pet, because there's no getting round it, I'm not a fine lady, and I never will be! Myself, I think you'd be a deal happier if you was to forget all these Marquises and things, but it's for you to say."

"Live with you *always*?" Emily cried, lifting a flushed, tear-stained face from Mrs Floore's lap. "Oh, *Grandmama!*"

"Bless you, my precious! said Mrs Floore, giving her a smacking kiss.

"Have you taken leave of your senses?" demanded Lady Laleham. "I'll have you know Emily is *my* daughter, Mama!"

"And I'll have you know, Sukey, that if I have one more word out of you, you can pay your own bills from now on, and so can Sir Walter!"

There was a pregnant silence. Mrs Floore patted Emily's shoulder. "You dry your eyes, love, and give the Marquis back his ring!"

"When you see your sisters all married before you, I hope you will remember this day, Emily!" said Lady Laleham. "For my part, I wash my hands of you!"

"And a very good thing too," commented Mrs Floore. "Go on, love! The sooner we're rid of this Marquis of yours the sooner we can have our dinner, which I'm sure we all need!"

The door shut with a slam behind Lady Laleham. Emily shyly held out the ring to Rotherham. "If you please – I beg your pardon, – but we should not *suit!*"

"Thank you," he said, taking the ring. "You have no need to beg my pardon: I will beg yours instead. The truth is that we both made a mistake. I wish you extremely happy, and I feel sure you will be – but Mr Goring is quite right: there's plenty of time before you need think of marriage. As for your reputation, and your sisters, and all the rest of that nonsense, you needn't regard it!" He glanced at the ring in his hand, and said: "I think you had better keep this – but wear it on another finger!"

"Oh, *thank* you!" gasped Emily naïvely.

He turned from her, to confront Mrs Floore, who had heaved herself up out of her chair, and was eyeing him with sharp suspicion. He grinned at her. "Don't worry, ma'am! All that you would like to say to me, and a great deal more, has already been hurled at my head, and I fancy there is more to come. I am delighted to have made your acquaintance, and I trust that – next year, perhaps – I shall have the pleasure of entertaining you, and Emily, of course, at Rotherham House! By the way, don't send a notice to the papers! I shall be sending one that will obviate the necessity, and will convince the world that I have treated Emily abominably – which, I own, I have!"

"So that's it, is it?" said Mrs Floore. "Of all the impudence! Well, I'm sorry for her, that's all! And I hope with all my heart that she'll lead you such a dance as will put you in your place once and for all!"

"She will do her best. Pay me a visit when you come to town, Goring, and we'll put the gloves on. You shall tell me, too, how you enjoyed taking care of Lady Serena: you had my sympathy!"

A brief bow, and he was gone. Half an hour later, he was being admitted to the house in Laura Place by Fanny's footman. He found the butler in the drawing-room, engaged in lighting the candles in the wall-sconces. "Masterly, Lybster!" he said. "Go and tell the Lady Serena that although you did not let me in I am nevertheless here, and should like to see her immediately!"

"Her ladyship, my lord," said Lybster, with an apologetic cough, "informed me that if your lordship *should* happen to cross the threshold, she would partake of dinner in her bedchamber."

"Did she, by God? Go and tell her ladyship that if she does not come down to me, I shall go up to her!"

"Yes, my lord – if your lordship insists!" said Lybster, and departed.

He did not return, but within five minutes Serena swept into the room, her cheeks flushed, and her eyes far too fierce to suit the dove gray gown she was wearing. "How – *dare* – you send me insolent messages by my own servants?" she demanded.

"I thought that would fetch you down," he remarked, walking forward.

"Yes, and you will be shortly extremely sorry that it did! If you think, Ivo -"

This speech ended abruptly. Not only was she roughly jerked into Rotherham's arms, but her mouth was crushed under his. For a moment or two, she strained every muscle to break free, and then, quite suddenly, the fight went out of her, and she seemed to melt into his embrace. It tightened ruthlessly, and only relaxed sufficiently to allow her to get her breath when Rotherham at last raised his head, and looked down into her eyes. "Well, you beautiful, bad-tempered thorn in my flesh? Well? Have you done scolding yet?"

She lay against his arm, her head flung back on his shoulder her eyes glinting at him under their curved lids. "Detestable creature! Mannerless, conscienceless, overbearing, selfish, arrogant – oh, how much I dislike you!" she sighed. "And how much you dislike me! I'd as lief be mauled by a tiger! You're mad, too. Never were you more thankful to be rid of anything than of me! Own it! All these years -!"

"Never!" he assented fervently. "I swore then that never again would I put it in your power to drive me to the brink of insanity with your obstinate, headstrong, wilful, *intolerable* conduct! But it's no use, Serena! don't you *know* that? I thought I had torn you out of my heart – I thought you were nothing to me but an old friend's daughter – until – What made you do it, Serena? What crazy folly made you do it?"

The smile vanished from her eyes. "O God, I don't know! I *meant* it, Ivo! When I saw him again – oh, I felt I was a girl – a nineteen-year-old! Perhaps it was because I was so lonely, perhaps because he still loved me so much, thought me a goddess, flattered me – oh, Ivo, *worshipped* me as you never did, I'll swear!"

"No, I don't worship you," he said, mocking her. "I know you for what you are, you enchanting termagant! And what you are I can't exist without! I saw him worshipping you, poor devil, and shutting his eyes to your imperfections! I pitied him, but I held him in contempt as well, because what is most admirable in you he liked least! *I'll* open no gates for you, my girl! you'll take any fence I take, and we'll clear it neck and neck!" He felt the response in the quiver that ran through her, and laughed, and kissed her again. "You may set the county alight, if you choose, but ride rough-shod over me you will not, if we fight from cockcrow to sundown!"

"Ivo, Ivo!" she whispered, turning her face into his shoulder. She seemed to struggle with herself, and looked up at last, to say: "I cannot – I *must* not! It is too base – and oh, what would Papa say to me for behaving *ungentlemanly*? Ivo, I have been Hector's *dream*!"

"It's a dream he has awakened from, believe me!" he said dryly. "Lord, Serena, the clever fool that you are! Stop mouthing fustian to me, or I'll shake some sense into you! Haven't you *seen* what has been going on under your nose? Your calf-love doesn't want to be your husband! He is hoping to God he may become your father-in-law!"

She stared at him with knit brows; then she began to laugh. He kissed her again, heard a slight sound, and looked over her head towards the door. Major Kirkby, quietly entering the room, was standing with one hand on the door, watching them.

"I don't beg your pardon, Kirkby," Rotherham said. "I am reclaiming my own property."

Serena pulled herself out of his arms, and went towards the Major, her hands held out: "Hector, forgive me! I have used you so shamefully: I think I must be the most fickle wretch alive!"

He took her hands and kissed them. "Not as fickle as I! Nor such a crass fool! My dear, I wish you happy with all my heart! You are a grander creature than any I ever dreamed of."

She smiled. "Only I am not your dear. And you are the kindest and best of men, but not my love!"

He was still holding her hands, rather flushed, a rueful look in his eye. "There is something – I don't know how to tell you! I must appear worse than a fool!"

"I've told her already," interposed Rotherham. "I see no need to wish you happy: you will both be extremely happy!" He held out his hand, and gripped the Major's, saying, with his derisive smile: "Do you own at last that

I was right, when I told Spenborough seven years ago that you and Serena would never suit? When I met you again, in this house, I came prepared to dislike you profoundly: I ended the evening most sincerely pitying you! You are too good a man for such a termagant, Kirkby!"

"How like you – how *very* like you!" Serena said. Her eyes went to the door. "Fanny! Oh, foolish Fanny, why didn't you tell me to take my claws out of Hector weeks ago? My dear, you were made for one another!"

"Oh, Serena, I feel a traitress!" Fanny said, her eyes brimming over.

"No, why should you? I'm afraid you will be shocked, my dear, but I am going to marry the odious Marquis after all!"

"Hector said it would be so," Fanny said, sighing. "I do so much *hope* that you will be happy, dearest!"

"You don't depend upon it, however, Lady Spenborough?"

She blushed rosily. "Oh, no, no! I mean, yes! Only it has always seemed to me that you held one another in positive aversion!"

"Acute of you!"

She had never known how to take his abrupt, incomprehensible remarks, and was always flurried by them. She said quickly: "I am so very glad you have made up your differences! My lord would have been so happy!" She saw Serena's face quiver, and added at once: "Only, how very awkward it will be for you! How shall you advertise it? For you will be dreadfully roasted, you know, if you announce your engagement for the *second* time!"

Serena turned laughing eyes towards Rotherham. "Fanny is perfectly right! Shall we say that the engagement between the Marquis of Rotherham and the Lady Serena Carlow has been *resumed*?"

"No, intolerable! I will never be engaged to you again, Serena! The advertisement which I propose to send to the *Gazette* will state that the marriage between the Marquis of Rotherham and the Lady Serena Carlow took place, privately, at Bath."

Her eyes lit, but she said: "Ivo, how can I? It is not yet a year "

"No, it is not a year, but even your Aunt Theresa will not think it improper if I add to the notice the information that we are spending our honeymoon abroad, and do not expect to be in England again until November. There will be no wedding festivities, and no bride-visits. What we may choose to do while touring the Continent will offend no one." He stretched out his hand imperatively, and she laid hers in it. His fingers closed on hers. "We will do better this time, Serena."

"Yes," she said, holding tightly to his hand. "We will do better, Ivo!"

THE NONESUCH

CHAPTER ONE

THERE WAS a twinkle in the Nonesuch's eye as he scanned the countenances of his assembled relations, but his voice was perfectly grave, even a trifle apologetic. "I am afraid it is quite true, ma'am," he said, addressing himself to his Aunt Sophia. "I *am* the heir."

Since the question, so indignantly posed by Lady Lindeth, had been rhetorical, this very frank and manly confession surprised no one. They all knew that old Cousin Joseph Calver had left his fortune to Waldo; and when Lady Lindeth had summoned him to account for himself she had acted on the impulse of the moment, and with no expectation of hearing the news denied. Nor had she had any very real expectation of Waldo's renouncing the bequest in favour of her only child. She naturally felt that no worthier heir to eccentric Cousin Joseph's estate existed than Julian; and she had done her best to introduce the noble orphan to him, even enduring the rigours of a week spent at Harrogate, when Julian had been an engaging child in nankeens and a frilled shirt, and she had tried (quite unavailingly) to gain entrance to Broom Hall. Three times had she driven out from Harrogate, the bored but docile little boy beside her, only to be told, twice, by Cousin Joseph's butler, that the Master was not feeling clever enough to receive visitors; and, once, that the Master would thank her not to come pestering him, because he didn't want to see her, nor her son, nor anyone else. Enquiry had elicited the information that the only visitor ever admitted into the house was the doctor. Local opinion was divided, charitable persons maintaining that a disappointment suffered in his youth was responsible for this churlishness; others asserting that he was a muckworm who grudged every groat he was obliged to spend. Having had the opportunity to perceive the neglected condition of the grounds of Broom Hall, Lady Lindeth had ranged herself with the majority. A suspicion that Cousin Joseph might not be as plump in the pocket as was supposed had occurred only to be dismissed: Broom Hall, though greatly inferior in style and size to young Lord Lindeth's seat in the Midlands, was a very respectable house, with probably as many as thirty bedrooms. It did not stand in a park, but its gardens appeared to be extensive; and she was credibly informed that most of the surrounding land belonged to the estate. She had left Harrogate much inclined to think that Cousin Joseph's fortune was considerably larger than had previously been supposed. She did not grudge it to him, but she would have thought herself a very unnatural parent had she not made a push to secure it for her son. So she had swallowed her resentment at the treatment she had received, and had continued, throughout the succeeding years, to send Joseph small Christmas gifts, and periodical letters, affectionately enquiring after the state of his health, and regaling him with accounts of Julian's virtues, beauty, and scholastic progress. And after all her pains he had left his entire estate to Waldo, who was neither the most senior of his relations nor the one who bore his name!

The most senior of the three cousins gathered together in Lady Lindeth's drawing-room was George Wingham, the son of her ladyship's eldest sister. He was a very worthy man, however prosy; she was not particularly fond of him, but she thought she could have borne it better had Cousin Joseph made him his heir, for she was obliged to acknowledge that his seniority gave him a certain amount of right to the bequest. Not, of course, so good a right as Laurence Calver. Lady Lindeth held Laurence, the youngest of her nephews, in contempt and dislike, but she hoped she was a just woman, and she felt she could have supported with equanimity his succession to a fortune which he would have lost no time in dissipating.

But that Cousin Joseph, ignoring the claims of George, and Laurence, and her beloved Julian, should have named Waldo Hawkridge as his heir was so intolerable that had she been of a nervous disposition she thought she must have succumbed to Spasms when she had first heard the incredible news. As it was, she had been unable to speak for a full minute; and when she did she had merely uttered Waldo's name, in a voice so vibrant with loathing that Julian, the bearer of the tidings, had been startled. "But, Mama --" he had expostulated. "You *like* Waldo!"

That was perfectly true, but quite beside the point, as she crossly told her son. She was, in fact, much attached to Waldo, but neither her fondness for him nor her gratitude for his unfailing kindness to Julian prevented her from feeling positively unwell whenever she thought of his enormous wealth. To learn that Cousin Joseph's estate was to be added to an already indecently large fortune did make her feel for a few minutes that so far from liking him she detested him.

She said now, in a peevish tone: "I can't conceive what should have induced that disagreeable old man to choose you for his heir!"

"There is no understanding it at all," Sir Waldo replied sympathetically.

"I don't believe you ever so much as *saw* him, either!"

"No, I never did."

"Well, I must own," said George, "that it was an odd sort of a thing to do. One would have thought – However, none of us had the least claim on the old fellow, and I'm sure he had a perfect right to leave his money where he chose!"

At this, Laurence Calver, who had been lounging on the sofa, and moodily playing with an ornate quizzing-glass, let the glass fall on the end of its ribbon, and jerked himself up, saying angrily: "*You* had no claim to it – or Waldo – or Lindeth! But *I'm* a Calver! I-I think it *damnable*!"

"Very possibly!" snapped his aunt. "But you will be good enough not to use such language in my presence, if you please!"

He coloured, and mumbled an apology, but the reproof did nothing to improve his temper, and he embarked on a long and incoherent diatribe, which ranged stammeringly over a wide ground, embracing all the real and fancied causes of his sense of ill-usage, the malevolence of Joseph Calver, and the suspected duplicity of Waldo Hawkridge.

Until George Wingham intervened, he was heard in unresponsive silence. His oblique animadversions on Sir Waldo's character did indeed bring a flash into Lord Lindeth's eyes, but he folded his lips tightly on a retort. Laurence had always been jealous of Waldo: everyone knew that; and very ludicrous it was to watch his attempts to outshine his cousin. He was several years younger than Waldo, and he possessed none of the attributes which Nature had so generously bestowed on the Nonesuch. Failing to excel in any of the sports which had won for Waldo his title, he had lately turned towards the dandy-set, abandoning the sporting attire of the Corinthian for all the extravagances of fashion popular amongst the young dandies. Julian, three years his junior, thought that he looked ridiculous in any guise; and instinctively turned his eyes towards Waldo. They warmed as they looked, for to Julian Sir Waldo was at once a magnificent personage in whose company it was an honour to be seen, the big cousin who had taught him to ride, drive, shoot, fish, and box; a fount of wisdom; and the surest refuge in times of stress. He had even taught him something of his own way with the starched folds of a neckcloth: not the intricacies of the Mathematical or the Oriental Tie, but an elegant fashion of his own, as unobtrusive as it was exquisite. Laurence would do well to imitate the quiet neatness of Waldo's dress, Julian thought, not realizing that the plain, close-fitting coats which so admirably became Waldo could only be worn to advantage by men of splendid physique. Less fortunate aspirants to high fashion were obliged to adopt a more florid style, with padding to disguise sloping shoulders, and huge, laid-back lapels to widen a narrow chest.

He glanced again at Laurence, not so much folding his lips as gripping them tightly together, to keep back the retort he knew Waldo didn't wish him to utter. From vapourings about the injustice of fate, Laurence, working himself into a passion, was becoming more particular in his complaints. Any stranger listening to him would have supposed that Waldo was wealthy at his expense, Julian thought indignantly: certainly that Waldo had always treated him shabbily. Well, whether Waldo liked it or not, he was not going to sit meekly silent any longer!

But before he could speak George had intervened, saying in a voice of grim warning: "Take care! If anyone has cause to be grateful to Waldo, you have, you distempered young Jack-at-warts!"

"Oh, George, don't be a fool!" begged Sir Waldo.

His stolid senior paid no heed to this, but kept his stern gaze on Laurence. "Who paid your Oxford debts?" he demanded. "Who gets you out of sponging-houses? Who saved you from the devil's own mess, not a month ago? *I* know to what tune you were bit at that hell in Pall Mall! – no, it wasn't Waldo who told me, so you needn't cast any of your black looks at him! The Sharps tried on the grand mace with you, didn't they? Lord, it was all hollow for them! You were *born* a bleater!"

"That's enough!" Waldo interrupted.

"It is! More than enough!" said George rebelliously.

"Tell me, Laurie," said Waldo, ignoring this interpolation, "do you *want* a house in Yorkshire?"

"No, but – what do *you* want with it? *Why* should you have it? You've got Manifold – you've got a town house – you've got that place in Leicestershire – and – you ain't even a Calver!"

"And what the devil has that to say to anything?" struck in George. "What have the Calvers to do with Manifold, pray? Or with the house in Charles Street? Or with -"

"George, if you don't hold your tongue we shall be at outs, you and I!"

"Oh, very well!" growled George. "But when that ramshackle court-card starts talking as though he thought *he* ought to own Manifold, which has been in your family since the lord knows when -!"

"He doesn't think anything of the sort. He thinks merely that he ought to own Broom Hall. But what would you do with it if you did own it, Laurie? I haven't seen it, but I collect it's a small estate, subsisting on the rents of various farms and holdings. Have you a fancy for setting up as an agriculturist?"

"No, I have not!" replied Laurence angrily. "If that sneaking screw had left it to me, I'd have sold it – which I don't doubt *you'll* do – as though you weren't *swimming* in riches already!"

"Yes, you would have sold it, and wasted its price within six months. Well, I can put it to better use than that." The smile crept back into his eyes; he said consolingly: "Does it comfort you to know that it won't add to my riches? It won't: quite the reverse, I daresay!"

Mr Wingham directed a sharply suspicious look at him, but it was Lady Lindeth who spoke, exclaiming incredulously: "What? Do you mean to tell me that that detestable old man wasn't possessed of a handsome fortune after all?"

"Doing it rather too brown!" said Laurence, his not uncomely features marred by a sneer.

"I can't tell you yet what he was possessed of, ma'am, but I've been given no reason to suppose that he's made me heir to more than a competence – deriving, I collect, from the estate. And as you and George have both frequently described to me the deplorable state of decay into which the place has fallen I should imagine that the task of bringing it into order is likely to swallow the revenue, and a good deal more besides."

"Is that what you mean to do?" asked Julian curiously. "Bring it into order?"

"Possibly: I can't tell, until I've seen it."

"No, of course – Waldo, you know *I* don't want it, but what the dooce do *you* – Oh!" He broke off, laughing, and said mischievously: "I'll swear I know, but I won't tell George – word of a Lindeth!"

"*Tell* me?" said George, with a scornful snort. "Do you take me for a flat, young sauce-box? He wants it for another Orphan Asylum, of course!"

"An Orphan Asylum!" Laurence jerked himself to his feet, staring at Sir Waldo with narrowed, glittering eyes. "So that's it, is it? What ought to be mine is to be squandered on the scaff and raff of the back-slums! You don't want it yourself, but you'd rather by far benefit a set of dirty, worthless brats than your own kith and kin!"

"I don't think you are concerned with any of my kith and kin other than yourself, Laurie," replied Sir Waldo. "That being so – yes, I would."

"You – you – By God, you make me sick!" Laurence said, trembling with fury.

"Well, take yourself off!" recommended Julian, as flushed as Laurence was pale. "You only came here to nose out what you might, and you've done that! And if you think you're at liberty to insult Waldo under any roof of mine I'll have you know you're much mistaken!"

"Make yourself easy: I'm going, toad-eater!" Laurence flung at him. "And you need not put yourself to the trouble of escorting me downstairs! Ma'am, your very obedient servant!"

"Tragedy Jack!" remarked George, as the door slammed behind the outraged dandy. "Well-done, young 'un!" He added, with a grin that suddenly lightened his rather heavy countenance: "You and your roofs! Try telling me *I* came to nose out what I might – and see what I'll do to you!"

Julian laughed, relaxing. "Well, you did, but that's different! You don't grudge Cousin Joseph's property to Waldo any more than I do!"

"No, but that ain't to say I don't grudge it to those curst brats of his!" said George frankly. He was himself a man of substance, but he was also the father of a large and hopeful family, and although he would have repudiated with indignation any suggestion that he was not very well able to provide for his children, he had for years been unable to consider his unknown and remote cousin's problematical fortune without thinking that it would furnish him with a useful addition to his own estate. He was neither an unkindly nor an ungenerous man; he subscribed what was proper to Charity; but he did feel that Waldo carried the thing to excess. That, of course, was largely the fault of his upbringing: his father, the late Sir Thurstan Hawkridge, had been a considerable philanthropist; but George could not remember that he had ever gone to such absurd lengths as to succour and educate the lord only knew how many of the nameless and gallows-born waifs with which every city was ridden.

He looked up, to find that Waldo was watching him, the faintest hint of a question in his eyes. He reddened, saying roughly: "No, I don't want Broom Hall, and I hope I know better than to waste my time recommending you not to drop your blunt providing for a parcel of paupers who won't thank you for it, and, you may depend upon it, won't grow up to be the respectable citizens *you* think they will, either! But I must say I do wonder what made that old miser leave his money to you!"

Sir Waldo could have enlightened him, but thought it more tactful to refrain from divulging that he figured in his eccentric relative's Will as "the only member of my family who has paid no more heed to me than I have to him."

"Well, for my part I think it very unsatisfactory," said Lady Lindeth. "And not at all what poor Cousin Joseph would have wished!"

"You do mean to do that, Waldo?" Julian asked.

"Yes, I think so, if I find the place at all suitable. It may not be – and in any event I don't want it prattled about, so just you keep your tongue, young man!"

"Well, of all the abominable injustices! *I* didn't prattle about your horrid brats: it was George! Waldo, if you mean to go north, may I go with you?"

"Why, yes, if you wish, but you'll find it a dead bore, you know. There will be a good deal of business to be settled with Cousin Joseph's attorney, which will keep me busy in Leeds; and whatever I decide to do with Broom Hall I must look into things there, and set about putting them in order. Dull work! In the middle of the Season, too!"

"Much I care! That's what *I* think a dead bore: going from one horrible squeeze to another; doing the pretty to people I'd as lief never see again; showing-off in the Grand Strut -"

"You know, you're spoilt, Julian!" interrupted George severely.

"No, I'm not. I never did like going to parties, and I never shall – not these insipid *ton* parties, at all events. I like living in the country. I say, Waldo, I wonder if there's any fishing to be had near Broom Hall?" He saw that Sir Waldo was looking at Lady Lindeth, and added: "Oh, Mama don't object! Do you, Mama?"

"No," she answered. "You must do as you please – though it seems a pity you should go out of town just now. There's the Aveburys' Dress-party, and – However, if you prefer to go to Yorkshire with Waldo I am sure I have nothing to say!"

There was a good deal of reluctance in her voice, which one at least of her audience recognized and appreciated. She was a devoted but not a foolish parent; and while, on the one hand, she was bent on thrusting her son into the heart of the *ton*, and (if possible) arranging an advantageous marriage for him; on the other, she had far too much wisdom either to try to drive him against his inclination, or to cast the least rub in the way of his allegiance to his cousin Waldo. It stood greatly to her credit that almost from the hour of her widowhood she had made up her mind that she must never keep Julian tied to her apron-strings. But although she had adhered strictly to this resolve she had suffered many qualms, fearing that the very sweetness of his disposition might be his undoing. He was a handsome boy, and one who had come into the world hosed and shod, as the saying was; and her dread was that he might be flattered and coaxed into such company as Laurence kept, with disastrous results. With Waldo he was not only safe but fortunate as well, since Waldo, taking him into his own circle, was introducing him to men of the first rank and character. That most of these gentlemen were addicted to the more dangerous, and (in her view) more degrading forms of sport, she did not allow to weigh with her. It was incomprehensible to her why any man should wish to risk his neck in the hunting field, or in a curricle race; or should derive the smallest satisfaction from *planting a flush hit* in the face of some unoffending acquaintance, encountered in Jackson's Boxing Saloon; but she was fortified in her acceptance of these peculiar activities by the knowledge that no female was fitted to be a judge of such matters; and by the realization that nothing was farther from her ambition than to see her son joining the ranks of those who abjured violent sports. Furthermore, however many pangs of jealousy she might have been made to suffer when, having failed to turn Julian from some adolescent and ill-judged start, she had seen Waldo blight it by the mere lifting of an eyebrow, she could still be thankful to him. His ideas might not coincide with hers; she might resent Julian's devotion to him; but while she knew his influence over her darling to be strong no maternal apprehensions seriously troubled her.

She met his eyes, and saw the understanding smile in them. He said: "I know, ma'am – but where's the use? I'll take good care of him!"

The annoying thing about him was that he did know, though never had she confided in him her ambition to see Julian achieve the social success to which his birth, his looks, and his fortune entitled him. She responded tartly: "He is of age, and very well able, I trust, to take care of himself! A very odd idea of me you must have, my dear Waldo, if you think he is obliged to ask my permission for anything he may wish to do!"

The smile touched his lips; he murmured: "No! the only idea I have of you, ma'am, is that you are a woman of great good sense."

As he turned away from her, Julian, whose attention had been diverted by a question addressed to him by Mr Wingham, demanded gaily: "Are you talking secrets? When do you mean to go to Yorkshire?"

"I haven't decided the precise date, but sometime next week. I shall be travelling post, of course."

The expression of disappointment on Julian's face was ludicrous enough to make even his ruffled mother smile. He exclaimed impulsively: "Oh, *no*! You can't wish to be shut up in a stuffy chaise for – Oh, you're trying to gammon me, are you? Waldo, you're a – you're a -"

"Gull-catcher," supplied George, on the broad grin.

Julian accepted this blithely. "Yes, *and* a regular dryboots! Curricle, Waldo, or phaeton?"

"I don't see how we can go by either when I've no horses stabled on the Great North Road," objected Waldo.

But Julian was not to be hoaxed twice. He retorted that if his cousin was such a nip-farthing as to grudge the expense of sending his cattle forward they would either hire job-horses, or proceed by such easy stages as could be managed by one team.

"I like young Lindeth," said George, when, presently, he walked with his cousin in the direction of Bond Street. "A very good sort of a boy: nothing of the rum 'un about *him*! But as for Laurence -! Upon my word, Waldo, I wonder that you should bear with him as you do! Well, I was used to think him more flash than foolish, but after listening to his damned insolence today I think him the most buffleheaded clunch I ever saw in my life! If there's *one* person anybody but a sapskull would have taken precious care not to rub against, it's you! Good God, where does he think he'd be, if you was to abandon him? Don't you tell me he hasn't cost you a small fortune, because *I'm* not a gapeseed! Why you didn't lose your temper and tell him he'd had his last groat from you I shall never know!"

"Yes, you will," responded Sir Waldo calmly. "I didn't lose my temper because that is precisely what I *had* told him."

George was so much surprised that he halted in his tracks. "You had? Waldo, you don't mean it!"

"No, probably not, but today's outburst shows that Laurie thinks I do. So now you know why I hadn't the smallest inclination to lose my temper. For how much longer do you mean to stand like a stock, attracting the attention of the vulgar? *Do* come out of your trance, George!"

Thus adjured, Mr Wingham fell into step again beside his tall cousin, saying earnestly: "I was never more glad of anything in my life! Now, don't waver from it, I beg of you! Damme if I wouldn't prefer to see you wasting the ready on a pack of ragged brats than on that young once-a-week man!"

"Oh, George, no!" expostulated Sir Waldo. "Coming it *too* strong!"

"Oh, no, I ain't!" said George obstinately. "When I think of the things he said today, and the gratitude he owes you -"

"He owes me none."

"*What*?" George gasped, once more coming to a sudden halt.

His cousin's hand, gripping his arm, forced him onward. "No, George: not again!" said Sir Waldo firmly. "I've done very badly by Laurie. If you don't know that, I do."

"Well, I don't!" George declared. "From the time he was at Harrow you've positively *lavished* money on him! You never did so for Julian!"

"Oh, I've never done more for Julian than send him a guinea under the seal, when he was a schoolboy!" said Sir Waldo, laughing.

"So I knew! Of course, you may say he was pretty wellbreeched, but -"

"I shan't say anything of the sort. I should have done no more for him whatever his circumstances might have been. By the time he went to Harrow I wasn't such a cawker as I was when Laurie was a boy." He paused, slightly frowning, and then said abruptly: "You know, George, when my father died, I was too young for my inheritance!"

"Well, I own we all thought so – made sure you'd play ducks and drakes with it! but you never did so, and --"

"No, I did worse: I ruined Laurie."

"Oh, come now, Waldo --" George protested, adding after a moment's reflection: "Encouraged him to depend on you, you mean. I suppose you did and I'm damned if I know why, for you never liked him above half, did you?"

"I didn't. But when I was – what did he call it? *swimming in riches*, and my uncle was possessed of no more than an independance – besides being as big a screw as our cousin Joseph, and keeping Laurie devilish short – it seemed so hard-fisted not to come to Laurie's rescue!"

"Yes, I see," said George slowly. "And having once begun to frank him you couldn't stop."

"I might have done so, but I didn't. What, after all, did it signify to me? By the time I'd acquired enough sense to know what it signified to *him*, the mischief had been done."

"Oh!" George turned this over in his mind. "Ay, very likely! But if you think the fault is yours, all I can say is that it ain't like you to leave him to sink or swim now! What's more, I don't believe you would!"

"No, I was afraid he wouldn't believe it either," admitted Sir Waldo. "He seems to have done so, however, which makes me hopeful that the mischief has not gone beyond repair."

George uttered a bark of sceptical laughter. "He'll be gapped in some hell before the week's out – and don't tell me you've tied him up, because he ain't such a bottlehead that he don't know you'd never compel him to pay the forfeit!"

"I haven't, but I paid his gaming debts only on his promise that he would incur no more of them."

"His promise -! Good God, Waldo, you don't depend on that, do you?"

"But I do. Laurie won't go back on his word: witness his rage today, only because I've compelled him to pledge it!"

"Once a gamester always a gamester!"

"My dear George, Laurie is no more a gamester than I am!" replied Sir Waldo, amused. "All he wishes to do is to sport a figure in the world. Do believe that I know him much better than you do, and take that frown off your face!" He slipped his hand within his cousin's arm, grasping it lightly. "Instead, tell me this, old chap! Do you want Broom Hall? Because, if you do – and you need not fly up into the boughs! – I hope you know you've only to -"

"I do not!" interrupted George, with unnecessary violence. "Merely because I said I thought it an odd start in Cousin Joseph to have left his property to you – By the bye, my aunt didn't like it above half, did she?"

"No – most understandable I But I really can't feel that Lindeth stands in the least need of Broom Hall."

"Oh, lord, no! any more than I do! Bless the boy, he never gave it a thought! You know, Waldo, it's my belief he's going to cut up all her hopes! Ever since he came down from Oxford she's been trying to push him into the first style of fashion – *and* into an eligible marriage – and then, when there isn't a *ton* party he ain't invited to attend, what does he do but beg you to let him go with you into the wilds of Yorkshire! I promise you, I was hard put to it not to burst out laughing at the look in her face when young Julian said the Season was a dead bore! Mark me if she don't prevent his going with you!"

"She won't even make the attempt. She's by far too fond of him to try to thrust him down any path he doesn't wish to follow – and has too much commonsense as well. Poor Aunt Lindeth! I do most sincerely pity her! She was obliged to abandon her efforts to bring her husband into fashion, for he despised nothing more; and to discover now that Julian, who has all in his favour to blossom into a Pink of the *Ton*, is as bored by such stuff as ever his father was is really very hard."

"I think the better of him for it," declared George. "To own the truth, I always looked to see him trying to follow in *your* steps! Well, if she does let him go with you next week, take care he don't fall into mischief – unless you have a fancy for getting your eyes scratched out!"

"None at all! Are you apprehensive that he will form an attachment to a milkmaid? Or set the countryside by the ears? You terrify me, George!"

"No, no!" George said, chuckling. "It's you who will do that! Well, I don't mean you'll set 'em all by the ears precisely, but, lord, what a flutter there will be when they find the Nonesuch amongst 'em!"

"Oh, for God's sake, George!" said Sir Waldo, withdrawing his hand abruptly from his cousin's arm. "Don't talk such nonsense! If I were a betting man, I'd lay you odds against the chance that anyone at Oversett has ever heard of me!"

CHAPTER TWO

NEITHER PROPHECY hit the mark, but, in the event, Mr Wingham came nearer to it than Sir Waldo. Broom Hall belonged to a country parish whose centre was the village of Oversett, situated in the West Riding, rather closer to Leeds than to Harrogate, and not above twenty miles from York; and although the majority of the Reverend John Chartley's parishioners knew nothing about Sir Waldo, and several elderly gentlemen, such as Squire Mickleby, took very little interest in any member of the Corinthian set, amongst the ladies, and the younger gentlemen, a good deal of excitement was felt. No one was acquainted with Sir Waldo; but several ladies had at some time or another spent a few weeks in London, and had had him pointed out to them in the Park or at the Opera as one of the leaders of the *ton;* and every budding young whip who prided himself on his light hands and the prime nature of his turn-out was torn between longing to see just how Sir Waldo did the trick and dread lest such an out-and-out top-sawyer should regard with contempt the efforts of his admirers to emulate his skill.

The first person to learn the news was the Rector, and it was his daughter who carried it to Staples, the most considerable house in the neighbourhood, where it was variously received. Mrs Underhill, who knew no more of Sir Waldo than the Rector's most illiterate parishioner, but understood, from the awe in Miss Chartley's face, that the news was remarkable, said, in a placid voice: "Fancy!" Miss Charlotte, a bouncing fifteen-year-old, looked for guidance at Miss Trent, her adolescent adoration of her young preceptress having led her to regard that lady as an authority on any subject which came under discussion; and Mrs Underhill's niece, Miss Theophania Wield, fixed her large, suddenly sparkling eyes on Miss Chartley's face, and uttered breathlessly: "Is it true? Coming to Broom Hall? Oh, you're shamming it, Patience – I know you are!"

Miss Trent, though the announcement had caused her to look up from her stitchery, her brows raised in momentary surprise, resumed her work, volunteering no remark; but Mr Courtenay Underhill, who had lounged in to pay his respects to his mama's visitor, exclaimed in the liveliest astonishment: "Sir Waldo Hawkridge? Old Calver's heir? Good God! Mama, did you hear? Sir Waldo Hawkridge!"

"Yes, dear. Well, I'm sure I hope he'll find it to his liking, though it will be wonderful if he does, the way Mr Calver let all go to rack and ruin! I don't seem able to recall him at the moment, but there! I never was one for remembering names – not but what you'd think I should keep that one in my head, for I never heard such a funny one!"

"They call him the Nonesuch!" said Courtenay reverently.

"Do they, love? That would be a nickname, I daresay. Depend upon it, it was given him for some silly reason, like the way your grandfather was used to call your poor Aunt Jane Muffin, all because -"

"Oh!" cried her niece, impatiently interrupting these amiable meanderings, "as though anyone was ever called that for a stupid joke! It means – it means *perfection*! Doesn't it, Ancilla?"

Miss Trent, selecting a length of silk from her skein, replied, in her cool, well-bred voice: "A paragon, certainly."

"Fudge! It means being the greatest Go among all the Goers!" stated Courtenay. "*Particularly* on the roads – though they say the Nonesuch is a clipping rider to hounds too. Gregory Ash – and he knows *all* the Melton men! – told me that in harness and out no man can do more with a horse than the Nonesuch. Well, if he is coming here, I won't be seen driving that chestnut I had from old Skeeby, that's certain! Mama, Mr Badgworth has a neatish bay he'd be willing to sell: beautiful stepper – carries a good head – just the right stamp!"

"Oh, pooh! As though anyone cares a rush for such stuff!" broke in Miss Wield scornfully. "Sir Waldo is first in *consequence* with the *ton*, and of the first style of elegance, besides being very handsome, and *hugely* wealthy!"

"Elegant! Handsome!" jeered Courtenay, mimicking her. "Much you know about it!"

"I do know!" she flashed. "When I was at my uncle's house in Portland Place -"

"Yes, you were as thick as inkle-weavers with him, of course! What miff-maff you do talk! I don't suppose you've ever so much as clapped eyes on him!"

"I have, I *have*! Frequently! Well, *several* times! And he is handsome and elegant! Ancilla, he is, isn't he?"

Miss Chartley, who was a very gentle, prettily behaved girl, seized the opportunity to intervene in what promised to develop into a shrill quarrel, turning towards Miss Trent, and saying in her soft, shy voice: "I expect you know more about Sir Waldo than any of us, for you were used to live in London, were you not? Perhaps you may even have met him?"

"No, indeed I have not," Miss Trent replied. "I never saw him, to my knowledge, and know no more of him than the rest of the world." She added, with the glimmer of a smile: "The company he keeps was quite above my touch!"

"I daresay you didn't wish for his acquaintance," said Charlotte. "I'm sure *I* don't: I hate beaux! And if he is coming here to hold up his nose at us all I hope he will go away again!"

"I expect he will," said Miss Trent, threading her needle.

"Yes, that is what Papa says," agreed Miss Chartley. "He thinks he can only be coming to settle with the lawyers, and perhaps to sell Broom Hall, for he can't wish to live in it, can he? Papa says he has a very beautiful house in Gloucestershire, which has been in his family for generations. And if he is so very fine and fashionable he must think this a dull place, I daresay –

though it is quite close to Harrogate, of course."

"Harrogate!" said Courtenay contemptuously. "*That* won't fadge! He won't remain at Broom Hall above a sennight I'll be bound! There's nothing to make him wish to stay, after all."

"No?" said his cousin, a provocative smile on her exquisite countenance.

"No!" he stated, revolted by this odious self-satisfaction. "And if you think he has only to see you to fall in love with you you much mistake the matter! I dare swear he is acquainted with a score of girls prettier by far than you!"

"Oh, no!" she said, adding simply: "He couldn't be!"

Miss Chartley protested involuntarily: "Oh, Tiffany, how can you? I beg your pardon, but indeed you shouldn't -!"

"It's perfectly true!" argued Miss Wield. "*I* didn't make my face, so why shouldn't I say it's beautiful? Everyone else does!"

Young Mr Underhill instantly entered a caveat, but Miss Chartley was silenced. Herself a modest girl, she was deeply shocked, but however much she might deprecate such vainglory honesty compelled her to acknowledge that Tiffany Wield was the most beautiful creature she had ever seen or imagined. Everything about her was perfection. Not the most spiteful critic could say of her that it was a pity she was too tall, or too short, or that her nose spoiled her loveliness, or that she was not so beautiful in profile: she was beautiful from every angle, thought Miss Chartley. Even her dusky locks, springing so prettily from a wide brow, curled naturally; and if attention was first attracted by her deep and intensely blue eyes, fringed by their long black lashes, closer scrutiny revealed that a little, straight nose, enchantingly curved lips, and a complexion like the bloom on a peach were equally worthy of admiration. She was only seventeen years of age, but her figure betrayed neither puppy-fat nor awkward angles; and when she opened her mouth it was seen that her teeth were like matched pearls. Until her return, a short time since, to Staples, where her childhood had been spent, Patience Chartley had been generally held to be the prettiest girl in the neighbourhood, but Tiffany had quite eclipsed her. Patience had been brought up to believe that one's appearance was a matter of no importance, but when the parent who had inculcated one with this dictum said that it gave him pleasure merely to rest his eyes on Tiffany's lovely face one might perhaps be pardoned for feeling just a trifle wistful. No one, thought Patience, observing herself in the mirror when she dressed her soft brown hair, was going to look twice at her when Tiffany was present. She accepted her inferiority meekly, so free from jealousy that she wished very much that Tiffany would not say such things as must surely repel her most devout admirers.

Apparently sharing her views, Mrs Underhill expostulated, saying in a voice which held more of pleading than censure: "Now, Tiffany-love! You shouldn't talk like that! Whatever would people think if they was to hear you? It's not becoming – and so, I'll be bound, Miss Trent will tell you!"

"Much I care!"

"Well, that shows what a pea-goose you are!" struck in Charlotte, firing up in defence of her idol. "Because Miss Trent is much more genteel than you are, or any of us, and -"

"Thank you, Charlotte, that will do!"

"Well, it's true!" muttered Charlotte rebelliously.

Ignoring her, Miss Trent smiled at Mrs Underhill, saying: "No, ma'am; not at all becoming, and not at all wise either."

"Why not?" Tiffany demanded.

Miss Trent regarded her thoughtfully. "Well, it's an odd circumstance, but I've frequently observed that whenever you boast of your beauty you seem to lose some of it. I expect it must be the change in your expression."

Startled, Tiffany flew to gaze anxiously into the ornate looking-glass which hung above the fireplace. "*Do* I?" she asked naïvely. "*Really* do I, Ancilla?"

"Yes, decidedly," replied Miss Trent, perjuring her soul without the least hesitation. "Besides, when a female is seen to admire herself it sets up people's backs, and she finds very soon that she is paid fewer compliments than any girl of her acquaintance. And nothing is more agreeable than a prettily turned compliment!"

"That's true!" exclaimed Tiffany, much struck. She broke into laughter, flitting across the room to bestow a brief embrace upon Miss Trent. "I *do* love you, you horrid thing, because however odious you may be you are never *stuffy*! I won't admire myself any more: I'll beg pardon for being an antidote instead! Oh, Patience, are you positively sure Sir Waldo is coming?"

"Yes, for Wedmore told Papa that he had received orders from Mr Calver's lawyer to have all in readiness for Sir Waldo by next week. And also that he is bringing another gentleman with him, and several servants. The poor Wedmores! Papa said all he might to soothe them, but they have been thrown into such a quake! Mr Smeeth seems to have told them how rich and grand Sir Waldo is, so, of course, they are in dread that he will expect a degree of comfort it is not in their power to provide for him."

"Now, that," suddenly interjected Mrs Underhill, "puts me in mind of something I *should* like to know, my dear! For when my Matlock told me I couldn't credit it, for all she had it from Mrs Wedmore herself. Is it true that Mr Calver left them nothing but twenty pounds, and his gold watch?"

Patience nodded sorrowfully. "Yes, ma'am, I'm afraid it is. I know one shouldn't speak ill of the dead, but one can't help feeling that it was very wrong and ungrateful, after so many years of faithful service!

"Well, for my part, I never did see, and no more I ever shall, that being dead makes a scrap of difference to what you was like when you were alive!" said Mrs Underhill, with unwonted energy. "A nasty, disagreeable clutchfist he was, and you may depend upon it that's what he is still! And not in heaven either! If you can tell me who ever said one should speak respectfully of those who have gone to the other place, you'll have told me something I never heard before, my dear!"

Patience was obliged to laugh, but she said: "No, indeed, but perhaps one ought not to judge, without knowing all the circumstances. Mama, I own, feels as you do, but Papa says we can't know what may have been at the root of poor Mr Calver's churlishness, and that we should rather pity him. He must have been very unhappy!"

"Well, your Papa is bound to say something Christian, being a Reverend," replied Mrs Underhill, in a reasonable spirit. "The ones *I* pity are the Wedmores – not but what they'd have left that old screw years ago, if they'd had a mite of sense, instead of believing he'd leave them well provided for, which anyone could have guessed he wouldn't, whatever he may have promised them! How are they going to find another situation at their time of life? Tell me that!"

But as Miss Chartley was quite unable to tell her she only sighed, and shook her head, thus affording Tiffany an opportunity to turn the conversation into another, and, in her view, far more important channel. She asked her aunt how soon after his arrival she meant to call on Sir Waldo.

Mrs Underhill's origins were humble; with the best will in the world to conduct herself like a lady of quality she had never managed to grasp all the intricacies of the social code. But some things she did know. She exclaimed: "Good gracious, Tiffany, whatever next? As though I didn't know better than go calling on a gentleman! If your uncle were alive it would have been for him to do, if he'd thought fit, which I daresay he wouldn't have, any more than I do myself, because what's the use of leaving cards on this Sir Waldo if he don't mean to stay at Broom Hall?"

"Then Courtenay must do so!" said Tiffany, paying no heed to the latter part of this speech.

But Courtenay, to her considerable indignation, refused to do anything of the sort. Modesty was not one of his outstanding characteristics, nor were his manners, in his own home, distinguished by propriety; but the suggestion that he, at the age of nineteen, should have the effrontery to thrust himself on Sir Waldo affected him so profoundly that he turned quite pale, and told his cousin that she must be mad to suppose that he would be so impudent.

The urgency with which Miss Wield conducted the ensuing argument, and the burst of angry tears which ended it made Mrs Underhill feel very uneasy. She confided, later, to Miss Trent that she did hope Sir Waldo wasn't going to upset them all. "I'm sure I don't know why anyone should be in a fuss over him, but there's Tiffany as mad as fire, all because Courtenay don't feel it would be the thing for him to call! Well, my dear, I don't scruple to own that that's put me a trifle on the fidgets, for you know what she is!"

Miss Trent did know. She owed her present position to the knowledge, which had made it possible for her, in the past, to manage the wayward Beauty rather more successfully than had anyone else.

Miss Wield was the sole surviving child of Mrs Underhill's brother, and an orphan. The late Mr Wield had been a wool merchant of considerable affluence. He was generally considered to have married above his station; but if he had done so with social advancement as his goal he must have been disappointed, since Mrs Wield's brothers showed little disposition to treat him with anything more than indifferent civility, and the lady herself was too shy and too sickly to make any attempt to climb the social ladder. She had died during Tiffany's infancy, and the widower had been glad to accept his sister's offer to rear the child with her own son. Mr Underhill had already retired from trade with a genteel fortune, and had bought Staples, where his gentlemanly manners and sporting tastes were rapidly making him acceptable to all but the highest sticklers in the neighbourhood. Rejecting his elder brother-in-law's tepid offer to admit the little girl into his own London household, Mr Wield consigned her to his sister's care, thinking that if she and Courtenay, two years her senior, were one day to make a match of it he would not be ill-pleased. Contrary to expectation he had not married again; nor did he outlive Mr Underhill by more than a year. He died when Tiffany was fourteen, leaving his fortune, of which she was the sole heiress, in the hands of trustees, and his daughter to the joint guardianship of her two maternal uncles, the younger of these gentlemen having been substituted for the deceased Mr Underhill.

Mrs Underhill had naturally been much affronted by this arrangement. Like her brother, she had looked forward to a marriage between Tiffany and her son. Mr Underhill had left his family very comfortably provided for; no one could have said she was a mercenary woman; but just as Lady Lindeth coveted Joseph Calver's supposed fortune for Julian, so did she covet Tiffany's very real fortune for Courtenay. She said, as soon as she knew the terms of Mr Wield's Will, that she knew how it would be: mark her words if those Burfords didn't snatch the child away before the cat had time to lick its ear! She was right. Mr James Burford, a bachelor, certainly made no attempt to take charge of his niece; but Mr Henry Burford, a banker, residing in very good style in Portland Place, lost no time in removing Tiffany from Staples, and installing her in his daughters' school-room. The heiress to a considerable fortune was a very different matter from the motherless child whom Mr Burford had expected to see superseded by a half-brother: besides his two daughters he had three sons.

Mrs Underhill was an easy-going woman, but she might have roused herself to struggle for possession of the heiress if she had been able to suppress a feeling of relief at the prospect of being rid of a damsel crudely described by the rougher members of her household as a proper varmint. Neither she nor a succession of governesses had ever known how to control Tiffany, who, at fourteen, had been as headstrong as she was fearless. Her exploits had scandalized the county, and given her aunt severe palpitations; she led Courtenay and little Charlotte into hair-raising situations; she drove three of her governesses from the house in a state of nervous prostration; already as pretty as a picture, she could change in the twinkling of an eye from an engagingly affectionate child into a positive termagant. Mrs Underhill surrendered her without protest, saying that Mrs Burford little knew what she had undertaken.

It did not take Mrs Burford long to find this out. She said (with perfect truth) that Tiffany had been ruined by indulgence; there was nothing for it but to send her to school.

So Tiffany was packed off to Miss Climping's Seminary in Bath, to be tamed, and transformed from a tomboy into an accomplished young lady.

Unfortunately, Miss Climping's establishment included a number of day-pupils, with whom Tiffany soon struck up friendships. She was permitted to visit them, and once outside the seminary considerably extended her circle of acquaintances. It was not until a billet from a love-lorn youth, addressed to Tiffany, and smuggled into the house by a venial servant, fell into Miss Climping's hands that the good lady realized that the unexceptionable visits to schoolfriends masked far from desirable excursions; or that a girl not yet sixteen could embark on a clandestine love-affair. Tiffany was a valuable pupil, her trustees paying for every extra on the curriculum without a blink; but had it not been for one circumstance Miss Climping would have requested Mr Burford to remove from her select establishment a firebrand who threatened to ruin its reputation. That was the arrival, to assume the duties of a junior teacher, of Ancilla Trent, herself a one-time pupil at the school. Bored by the reproaches and the homilies of what she called a parcel of old dowdies, Tiffany took an instant fancy to the new teacher, who was only eight years older than herself, and in whose clear gray eyes she was swift to detect a twinkle. It did not take her long to discover that however straitened her circumstances might be Ancilla came of a good family, and had been used to move in unquestionably genteel circles. She recognized, and was a little awed by, a certain elegance which owed nothing to Ancilla's simple dresses; and bit by bit she began to lend an ear to such scraps of worldly advice as Ancilla let fall at seasonable moments. It was no part of Ancilla's duty to admonish the older pupils, nor did she do so. She appreciated the humour of certain outrageous pranks, but managed to convey to the heiress that they were perhaps a little childish; and when informed of Tiffany's determination to marry into the peerage not only accepted this as a praiseworthy ambition, but entered with gratifying enthusiasm into various schemes for furthering it. As these were solely concerned with the preparation of the future peeress for her exalted estate, Tiffany was induced to pay attention to lessons in Deportment, to practise her music, and even, occasionally, to read a book; so that when she left school she had ceased to be a tomboy, and had even acquired a few accomplishments and a smattering of learning.

But she was harder than ever to manage, and nothing was farther from her intention than to submit to her Aunt Burford's plans for her. Mrs Burford, launching her eldest daughter into society, said that Tiffany was too young to be brought out. She might sometimes be allowed to join a small, informal party, or be included in an expedition of pleasure, but she was to consider herself still a schoolroom miss. She would attend concerts and dancing-lessons under the chaperonage of her cousins' governess; and she must spend a part of her time trying to improve her French, and learning to play the harp.

Mrs Burford had reckoned without her host. Tiffany did none of these things; and at the end of three months Mrs Burford informed her lord that unless he wished to be plunged into some shocking scandal, and to see the wife of his bosom dwindle into the grave, he would be so obliging as to send his niece back to Yorkshire. Not only was she so lost to all sense of propriety as to escape from the house when she was believed to be in bed and asleep, and to attend a masquerade at Vauxhall Gardens, escorted by a besotted youth she had met heaven only knew where or how: she was utterly destroying her cousin Bella's chances of forming an eligible connection. No sooner did a possible suitor catch sight of Bella's abominable cousin, said Mrs Burford bitterly, than he had eyes for no one else. As for a marriage between her and Jack, or William, even had she shown herself willing (which she most certainly had not), Mrs Burford would prefer to see any of her sons beggared than married to such a dreadful girl.

Mr Burford was ready enough to be rid of his tiresome ward, but he was a man of scruples, and he could not think it right to consign Tiffany to the care of Mrs Underhill, who had already shown herself to be incapable of controlling her. It was Mrs Burford who had the happy notion of writing to beg Miss Climping to give them the benefit of her advice. And Miss Climping, perceiving an opportunity to advance the interests of Ancilla Trent, of whom she was extremely fond, suggested that Mrs Burford should try to persuade Miss Trent to accept the post of governess-companion in Mrs Underhill's household. Miss Trent, besides being a most superior female (no doubt Mrs Burford was acquainted with her uncle, General Sir Mordaunt Trent), had also the distinction of being the only person who had ever been known to exercise the smallest influence over Miss Wield.

Thus it was that Ancilla became an inmate of Staples, and, within a surprisingly short time, Mrs Underhill's principal confidante.

Mrs Underhill had not previously confided in any of the governesses she had employed, for although she was a good-natured woman, she was quite understandably jealous of her dignity; and in her anxiety not to betray her origins she was prone to adopt towards her dependants a manner so stiff as to border on the top-lofty. She had been too much delighted to regain possession of her niece to raise any objection to the proviso that Miss Trent must accompany Tiffany; but she had deeply resented it, and had privately resolved to make it plain to Miss Trent that however many Generals might be members of her family any attempt on her part to come the lady of Quality over them at Staples would be severely snubbed. But as Miss Trent, far from doing any such thing, treated her with a civil deference not usually accorded to her by her children Mrs Underhill's repressive haughtiness was abandoned within a week; and it was not long before she was telling her acquaintance that they wouldn't believe what a comfort to her was the despised governess.

She said now, developing her theme: "She's no more than a child, when all's said, but with *that* face, and the things one hears about these smart town-beaux – Well, it does put me quite in a worry, my dear, and I don't deny it!"

"But I don't think it need, ma'am: indeed I don't!" Miss Trent responded. "She may set her cap at him – in fact, I'm tolerably certain that she will, just to show us all that she can bring any man to his knees! – and he might flirt with her, perhaps. But as for doing her any harm no, no, there can't be the least cause for you to be in a worry! Only consider, dear ma'am! She's not a little serving-maid with no one at her back to protect her!"

"No," agreed Mrs Underhill doubtfully. "That's true enough, but – he might want to *marry* her, and a pretty piece of business that would be!"

"If he shows any such disposition," said Miss Trent, laughter warming her eyes, "we must take care to remind her that he is not a member of the peerage!"

Mrs Underhill smiled, but she sighed too, saying that she wished to goodness Sir Waldo wasn't coming to Broom Hall.

The wish was echoed, a few days later, by the Squire, who told Miss Trent that he heartily wished the Nonesuch at Jericho.

He had overtaken her on her way back to Staples from the village, and had very civilly dismounted from his hack to walk with her down the lane. He was thought by many to be rather an alarming man, for besides being a trifle testy he had an abrupt manner, and a disconcerting way of staring very hard at people from under his bristling eyebrows. Mrs Underhill always became flustered in his presence, but Miss Trent was not of a nervous disposition. She met his fierce gaze calmly, and answered the questions he shot at her without starting or stammering, thus winning his rare approval. He said she was a sensible woman: no nambypamby nonsense about her! He wished he could say the same of some others he might mention.

In this instance Miss Trent responded only with a slight smile, which caused him to say, in a threatening tone: "Don't tell me *you* are in raptures over this Pink of the *Ton*!"

That drew a laugh from her. "No, how should I be? I am past the age of falling into raptures, sir!"

"Gammon! Chit of a girl!" he growled.

"Six-and-twenty!"

"Ay, so you may be: exactly what I thought! Wouldn't signify if you was six-and-fifty, either. Look at my wife! Killed with delight because this chuckfarthing fellow is coming amongst us! Means to give a party in his honour, if you please! None of your pot-luck, mind! Oh, no! Shouldn't wonder if she sends out her cards for a turtle-dinner, and has a waltzing-ball to round the thing off in style! Ay, you may laugh, miss! Don't blame you! *I* shall laugh when the fellow sends his regrets – which he will do, if I know anything about these Town Tulips! I shall call on him, of course: can't but do the civil, though I'd as lief give him the go-by."

"Never mind, sir!" said Miss Trent encouragingly. "I daresay he will be gone again within a sennight, and he can't break any hearts in such a short time, surely?"

"Break any hearts? Oh, you're thinking of the girls! *They* don't bother me! It's our boys. Damme if I wouldn't be better pleased if he was a Bond Street fribble, for *that* wouldn't send 'em mad after him! The mischief is that he's a Top-of-the-Trees Corinthian – and I've seen what harm they can do to silly young greenheads!"

The amusement left her face; she replied, after a moment: "Yes, sir: so too have I. In my own family – But that was in London! I can't think that here, in such a quiet neighbourhood, the silliest greenhead could find the means to run into a ruinous course."

"Oh, I don't fear they'll do that!" he said impatiently. "Merely break their necks, trying to outdo their precious Nonesuch! Would you believe it? – even my Arthur, slow-top though he is, has smashed my phaeton, trying to drive through my west farm-gate with never a check – nor any precision of eye neither! As for Banningham's cub, riding that goose-rumped gray of his up the stairs at Brent Lodge, and your Courtenay hunting the squirrel on the Harrogate road – but mum for that! No harm done, and a rare trimming he got from old Adstock – for it was the wheels of *his* carriage the young chucklehead was trying to graze! Driving to an inch! 'You can't drive to an ell!' Adcock told him. But you won't repeat that!"

She assured him that she would not; and as they had by this time reached the main gates of Staples he took his leave of her saying sardonically, as he hoisted himself into the saddle, that they might think themselves fortunate Joseph Calver hadn't gone to roost in the middle of the hunting season, when every cawker for miles round, after first pledging his father's credit for white-topped boots, would have crammed his horse at a stake-and-bound, and would have been brought home on a hurdle. "Mark my words!" he admonished Miss Trent. "You'll see Underhill rigged out in a coat with a dozen shoulder-capes, and buttons the size of saucers before you're much older! I told Arthur not to think I'd help him to make a cake of himself, aping the out-and-outers, but I don't doubt Courtenay will get what he wants out of his mother! All the same, you females!"

CHAPTER THREE

IT WAS perhaps inevitable that the Nonesuch's arrival at Broom Hall should fall a long way short of expectation. Young Mr Mickleby, the Squire's son, was able to report to his cronies that Sir Waldo had sent his horses on ahead, for he had himself seen two grooms turn in at the gates of Broom Hall. But the horses they led were only coverhacks: goodlooking prads, but nothing marvellous, and no more than two of them. They were followed by a travelling-carriage, which was later discovered to contain only a couple of soberly-clad servants, and a disappointingly small amount of baggage. It soon became known that Sir Waldo was driving himself from London, by easy stages; and although this accorded, in the main, with the younger gentlemen's ideas of how a noted whip should travel, *easy stages* fell tamely on their ears, spoiling visions of some sporting vehicle, slap up to the echo, swirling through the village in a cloud of dust.

No one of more note than the ostler at the Crown witnessed Sir Waldo's arrival in Oversett, and his account of this momentous event was discouraging. Instead of a curricle-and-four, which even provincials knew to be the highest kick of fashion, Sir Waldo was driving a phaeton; and so far from swirling through the village he had entered it at a sedate trot, and had pulled up his team outside the Crown, to ask the way to Broom Hall. No, said Tom Ostler, it wasn't a high-perch-phaeton: just an ordinary perch-phaeton, drawn by four proper good 'uns – a bang-up set-out of blood and bone! There was another gentleman with Sir Waldo, and a groom riding behind. Very pleasant-spoken, Sir Waldo, but not at all the regular dash Tom Ostler had been led to expect: he wasn't rigged out half as fine as Mr Ash, for instance, or even Mr Underhill.

This was dispiriting, and worse was to follow. The Squire, paying his promised call, was agreeably surprised by Sir Waldo: a circumstance which might please the Squire's contemporaries but which conjured up in the minds of Mr Underhill, Mr Banningham, and, indeed, Mr Arthur Mickleby as well, a sadly dull picture. No buck of the first head, it was gloomily felt, would have met with the Squire's approval. Arthur ventured to ask if he was a great swell. "How the devil should I know?" said his father irascibly. "He ain't all daintification, if that's what you mean." He eyed Arthur's exquisitely starched shirt-points, and the wonderful arrangement of his neckcloth, and added, with awful sarcasm: "*You'll* cast him quite into the shade! Lord, he'll be like a farthing-candle held to the sun!"

To his wife he was rather more forthcoming. Mrs Mickleby was as eager as her son to learn what Sir Waldo was like, and far less easy to snub. Goaded, the Squire said: "Fashionable? Nothing of the sort! Turns out in excellent style, and looks the gentleman – which is more than Arthur does, since he took to aping the smarts!"

"Oh, don't be so provoking!" exclaimed Mrs Mickleby. "My cousin told me he was of the first style of elegance – *bang-up to the nines*, he said! You know his droll way!"

"Well, he ain't bang-up to the nines. Not the kind of man to be cutting a dash amongst a set of quiet folk like us, my dear!"

Mrs Mickleby opened her mouth to utter a retort, saw the malicious gleam in the Squire's eye, and shut it again.

Pleased with this success, the Squire relented. "It's of no use to ask me what sort of coat he was wearing, or how he ties his neckcloth, because I didn't take any note of such frippery nonsense – which I *should* have done if he'd been sporting a waistcoat like that Jack-a-dandy one Ash was wearing the last time I saw him! Seemed to me he looked just as he ought. Nothing out of the ordinary!" He paused, considering the matter. "Got a certain sort of something about him," he pronounced. "I don't know what it is! You'd better ask him to dinner, and see for yourself. Told him I hoped he'd come and eat his mutton with us one day."

"Told him – Mr Mickleby! You did not! *Eat his mutton with us*! Of all the vulgar, shabby-genteel – What did he say?"

"Said he'd be very happy to do so," replied the Squire, enjoying his triumph.

"Very civil of him! I shall hope to show him, my dear Ned, that although we may be *quiet folk* we are not precisely *savages*! Who is the young man he brought with him?"

But the Squire, beyond saying that Sir Waldo had mentioned that his cousin was bearing him company, was unable to enlighten her. He had not seen the young man, and it had not seemed proper to him to enquire more particularly into his identity. Indeed, as his wife told Mrs Chartley, in some exasperation, it had apparently not seemed proper to him to find out anything whatsoever about Sir Waldo. She was perfectly at a loss to guess what the pair of them had found to talk about for a whole hour.

The next person to see Sir Waldo was Courtenay Underhill, and in circumstances which set all doubts to rest. By a stroke of rare good fortune, Courtenay was privileged to witness the Nonesuch perform just such a piece of driving skill as he had yearned to see; and was thus able to reassure his friends. He had been riding along the road when he had seen Sir Waldo's phaeton approaching. He had known at once that it must be his, for he did not recognize the horses. "*Such* a team! I never saw such perfect movers!

Matched to a hair, and beautifully put-together! I had a capital view, for it was on that long stretch half a mile short of the pike-road to Leeds. Well, the Nonesuch was coming along at a spanking pace, overtaking a farm-cart, which I'd just met. The fellow that was leading the horse made as much room as he could, but you know how narrow the lane is, and ditched too; I must say I thought the Nonesuch would be pretty well bound to check, but he kept on, so when he went past me I stopped, and looked back well, to own the truth I thought he'd either lock his wheels, or topple into the ditch!"

"He gave the cart the go-by? On *that* road?" demanded Mr Banningham, awed.

Young Mr Mickleby shook his head. "I wouldn't have cared to attempt it: not just there!"

"I should rather think you wouldn't!" said Mr Banningham, with a crack of rude laughter.

This unkind reference to his late mishap made Arthur flush angrily; but before he could utter a suitable retort Courtenay said impatiently: "Oh, sneck up! He gave it the go-by just as though – just as though he had yards to spare! More like inches! I never saw anything like it in my life! I'll tell you another thing: he catches the thong of his whip over his head. I mean to practise that."

"Ah!" said Mr Banningham knowledgeably. "Nervous wheelers! Cousin of mine says it's the quietest way, but there ain't many people that can do it. Shouldn't think you could. Was the Nonesuch wearing FHC toggery?"

"No – at least, I don't know, for he had on a white drab box coat. Looked as trim as a trencher, but nothing to make one stare. Greg says the out-and-outers all have as many as a dozen or more capes to their box coats, but I didn't notice anything like that. No nosegay in his buttonhole, either: just a few whip-points thrust through it."

Meanwhile, the Nonesuch, as yet unaware of the interest he was creating, had found enough to do at Broom Hall to keep him in Yorkshire for much longer than he had anticipated. The house itself was in better repair than he had been led to expect, the main part of it, though sadly in need of renovation, being, as Wedmore anxiously assured him, quite dry. Wedmore made no such claim either for the eastern wing, which contained a number of rooms bare of furnishings, or for the servants' wing. Of late years, he said, the Master hadn't taken much account of them. There were slates missing from the roofs: they did the best they could with pails set to catch the worst leaks, but there was no denying those parts of the house were a trifle damp. "I only hope dry-rot may not have set in," said Sir Waldo. "We must get a surveyor to come and inspect it immediately. Did your master employ a bailiff?"

"Well, sir, no!" Wedmore replied apologetically. "There used to be one – Mr Hucking, a very respectable man – but – but -"

"Not of late years?" suggested Sir Waldo.

Neither the defective roofs nor the lack of a bailiff was any concern of the old butler's; but he was a meek, nervous man, and was so much in the habit of bearing the blame for every shortcoming in the establishment that it was several moments before he could believe that Sir Waldo really was smiling. Much relieved, he responded with an answering smile, and said: "The

Master got to be very eccentric, sir, if you'll pardon the expression. Mr Hucking thought there were things that needed doing, but he couldn't prevail upon the Master to lay out any money, and he quite lost heart. He was used to say that bad landlords make bad tenants, and I'm bound to own – Well, sir, I daresay you'll see for yourself how things are!"

"I've already seen enough to prove to me that I shall be kept pretty busy for the next few weeks," said Sir Waldo, rather grimly. "Now I should like to discuss with Mrs Wedmore what are the most pressing needs here: will you desire her to come to me, if you please?"

"Waldo, you're never going to lay out *your* blunt, bringing this rackety place into order?" demanded Lord Lindeth, as Wedmore departed. "I may be a green 'un, and I know I haven't sat in my own saddle for very long yet, but I'm not a *widgeon*, and only a widgeon could fail to see that this old lickpenny of a cousin of ours has let the estate go to rack! It's true we haven't had time to do more than throw a glance over it, but don't you tell me that old Joseph ever spent a groat on his land that wasn't wrenched from him, *or* that he hasn't let out the farms on short leases to a set of ramshackle rascals that dragged what they might from the land, and never ploughed a penny back! *I* don't blame them! Why – why if *one* of my tenants was living in the sort of tumbledown ruin I saw when we rode round the place yesterday, I'd – I'd lord, I'd never hold up my head again!"

"Very true: I hope you wouldn't! But with good management I see no reason why the estate shouldn't become tolerably profitable: profitable enough to pay for itself, at all events."

"Not without your tipping over the dibs in style!" countered Julian.

"No, Master Nestor! But do you imagine that I mean to throw the place on the market in its present state? What a very poor opinion you must hold of me!"

"Yes!" Julian said, laughing at him. "For thinking you can gammon me into believing you mean to bring the place into order so that you may presently sell it at a handsome profit! Don't throw your cap after *that* one: I know you much too well to be bamboozled! You are going to bring it into order so that it will support some more of your wretched orphans. I daresay it may, but I'd lay you long odds that it won't also give you back what you'll spend on it!"

"If only old Joseph had known how much after his own heart you were, Julian -!" said Sir Waldo, shaking his head. "No, no, don't try to mill me down! You know you can't do it – and we shall have Mrs Wedmore upon us at any moment! Take comfort from the thought that I haven't yet decided whether the place is what I want for my wretched orphans: all I *have* decided is that it would go too much against the pluck with me to shrug off this – er honeyfall!"

"Honeyfall? An obligation, more like!" exclaimed Julian.

"Just so!" agreed Sir Waldo, quizzing him. "You've nicked the nick – as usual, of course! *No*, you pretentious young miller! Most certainly not!"

Lord Lindeth, his spirited attempt at reprisals foiled, said hopefully: "No, but I dashed nearly popped in a hit over your guard, didn't I?"

"Country work!" mocked Sir Waldo, releasing his wrists as the door opened. "Ah, Mrs Wedmore! Come in!"

"Yes, sir," said the housekeeper, dropping a curtsy. "And if it is about the sheet which his lordship put his foot through last night, I'm very sorry, sir, but they're worn so thin, the linen ones -"

"About that, and a great many other things," he interrupted, smiling reassuringly down at her. "Why didn't you confess like a man, Lindeth? Afraid to give your head to Mrs Wedmore for washing, no doubt! Go away, and I'll try what I can do to make your peace with her!"

"Oh, *sir* -!" protested Mrs Wedmore, much flustered. "As though I would think of such a thing! I was only wishful to explain to you –"

"Of course you were! It's quite unnecessary, however. What I wish is that you will tell me what must be purchased to make this house habitable, and where it may be most quickly obtained."

Mrs Wedmore could not remember when more welcome words had fallen on her ears. She gave a gasp, and said in a strangled voice that quite failed to conceal her emotions: "Yes, sir! I shall be most happy to – if you *mean* it, sir!" She read confirmation in his face, drew a deep breath, and launched into a catalogue of her more pressing needs.

The outcome of this interview would have vexed him very much, had he known of it; but as his staff at Manifold had always taken it for granted that whatever was needed in the house might instantly be ordered, and none of his neighbours considered anything less than the installation (by his mother) of the very newest and most revolutionary of closed kitchen-stoves to be worthy of interest, he had no idea that the *carte blanche* he gave the Wedmores would instantly become a topic for wonder and discussion in the district.

It was Mrs Underhill who brought the news back to Staples, after visiting the Rectory one day for a comfortable gossip with Mrs Chartley. Mrs Wedmore, of Broom Hall, and Mrs Honeywick, of the Rectory, were old cronies, and into her friend's receptive ear had Mrs Wedmore poured forth every detail of a never-to-be-forgotten orgy of spending in Leeds.

"And let alone all the linen, and the china, and such, he's got the builders at Broom Hall as well, looking to see what must be done to the roof, and inspecting every bit of timber in the house, so it looks as though he means to stay, doesn't it, my dear?" said Mrs Underhill.

Miss Trent agreed that it did.

"Yes, but on the other hand," argued Mrs Underhill, "he told Wedmore he wouldn't be entertaining guests, so he didn't want any smart footmen hired. Well, of course, he *is* a single man, but you'd expect him to be inviting his friends to stay with him, wouldn't you?"

Not having considered the matter, Miss Trent had formed no expectations, but again she agreed.

"Yes," nodded Mrs Underhill. Her face clouded. "But there's something I don't like, Miss Trent not above half I don't! He's got a lord with him!"

"Has he, indeed?" said Miss Trent, trying to preserve her countenance. "What sort of a – I mean, *which* lord, ma'am?"

"That I can't tell you, for Mrs Honeywick couldn't remember his name, so she wasn't able to tell her mistress: only that he's Sir Waldo's cousin, and very young and handsome. Well! The Squire's lady may be in high croak – which I don't doubt she is, for, you know, my dear, she does think herself the pink of gentility – but for my part I had as lief we hadn't got any handsome young lords strutting about the neighbourhood! Not that I don't care for modish company. When Mr Underhill was alive we were for ever increasing our covers for guests, not to mention going to the Assemblies in Harrogate, and the York Races, and I'm sure if I've passed the time of day with one lord I've done so with a dozen. What's more, my dear, for all the airs she gives herself, Mrs Mickleby won't set such a dinner before this one as I shall, *that* you may depend on! Yes, and that puts me in mind of another thing! She's sent out her dinner-cards, and not a word on mine about Tiffany! She told Mrs Chartley that she knew I shouldn't wish her to invite Tiffany to a formal party, her not being, properly speaking, out yet. Well, if that's what she thinks she's never seen Tiffany in one of her tantrums! It isn't, of course: she don't want Tiffany to be there, shining down her daughters, and I can't say I blame her, for a plainer pair of girls you'd be hard put to it to find!"

It was evident that she was torn between her hope of securing the heiress for her son, and a strong desire to out-do the Squire's wife. Her intelligence was not of a high order, but she had a certain shrewdness which informed her that the graciousness of Mrs Mickleby's manners was an expression not of civility but of condescension. Mrs Mickleby, in fact, was coming the great lady over her, and that (as she had once, in an expansive moment, told Miss Trent) was something she wouldn't put up with, not if it was ever so! Mrs Mickleby might be related to persons of consequence, and she certainly was the Squire's wife, but Staples was a far larger house than the Manor, and Mrs Underhill, however inferior her breeding, knew better than to employ a Female to cook for herself or her guests.

Miss Trent did not for a moment suppose that the issue was in doubt; so she was not surprised when Mrs Underhill launched immediately into a discussion on the number of persons to be invited to dinner; how many courses should be served; and whether or not the dinner should be followed by a dance. The question was, which would Sir Waldo prefer? What did Miss Trent think?

"I think that Sir Waldo's preferences don't signify, ma'am," replied Ancilla frankly. "It is rather which would *you* prefer!"

"Well, if ever I thought to hear you say such a nonsensical thing!" exclaimed Mrs Underhill. "When the party's to be given in his honour! Not that I should be consulting my own tastes however it might be, for you don't give parties to please yourself – at least, *I* don't!"

"No, indeed you don't, ma'am!" Ancilla said affectionately. The smile which made her look younger, and decidedly mischievous, danced in her eyes. "In general, you give them to please Tiffany! You should not, you know."

"Yes, it's all very well to talk like that, my dear, but I'm sure it's natural she should want a bit of gaiety, even though her Aunt Burford didn't see fit to bring her out this year. What's more, my dear – and I don't scruple to own it, for well I know I can say what I choose to you, and no harm done! – if Tiffany was to find it too slow for her here there's no saying but what she'd beg her uncle to fetch her away, which he *would* do, because it's my belief he didn't like sending her back to me above half – and no wonder!"

Ancilla hesitated for a moment; and then, raising her eyes to Mrs

Underhill's face, said, a little diffidently: "I understand you, ma'am – of course! but but do you think that Mr Courtenay Underhill shows the least disposition to – to fix his interest with his cousin? And could you be comfortable with her as your daughter-in-law?"

"No, but that's no matter. It was the wish of both their fathers – and she's young yet! I daresay she'll grow to be more conformable," said Mrs Underhill optimistically. Her mind reverted to the more immediate problem; after pondering deeply for a few moments, she said: "Twenty-four couples could stand up in my drawing-room, and very likely more, but the thing is there *ain't* as many young persons in the district: not without I was to invite a set of company, like the Butterlaws, which I wouldn't for my life do! It might be that Sir Waldo would as lief sit down to a rubber of whist, but then there's this young lord of his! It has me quite in a worry to decide what to do for the best!"

"How would it be, ma'am, if you were to make no decision, but to leave it to chance? Then, if you thought your guests would like to get up a set or two, I can play the music for them."

But Mrs Underhill would have none of this. "If I give a dance, I'll hire the musicians from Harrogate, like I did at Christmas," she declared. "There's never been anything nip-cheese about my parties, and nor there ever will be! What's more, I won't have you demean yourself, as if you was of no more account than that fubsy-faced creature that was here before you came to us! No: you'll take your place at the table, and help me to entertain my guests, like you were one of the family, which I'm sure I often feel you are, so kind and obliging as you've always been to me, my dear!"

Ancilla blushed rosily, but shook her head. "Thank you! You are a great deal too good, ma'am. But it would never do! Only think how Mrs Mickleby would stare! Charlotte and I will eat our dinners in the schoolroom, and I'll bring her down to the drawing-room afterwards, as a good governess should."

"Now, don't you talk flummery to me!" begged Mrs Underhill. "You was hired to be a governess-*companion* to Tiffany, and that's a very different matter, for all you've been so kind as to teach my Charlotte. And very grateful I am to you. I promise you."

"I don't feel I deserve any gratitude!" said Ancilla ruefully. "I haven't succeeded in teaching her very much."

"Oh, well!" said Mrs Underhill tolerantly. "I don't hold with keeping girls cooped up in the schoolroom; and to my way of thinking they don't need to have their heads stuffed full of learning. You teach her to be pretty-behaved, and you'll hear no complaints from me! And as for the Squire's wife, let her stare! Not that I think she would, for she's always very civil to you, on account of your uncle being a General. In fact, it wouldn't have astonished me if she'd invited you to her party." She stopped, the most pressing problem of all evoked by her own words. "That party! Oh, dear, whatever's to be done, Miss Trent? Tiffany will be as mad as Bedlam when she knows she's not to go! Such a dust as she'll raise! I own it puts me in a quake only to think of it!"

"She's bound to fly into a passion," admitted Ancilla, "but I believe I may be able to reconcile her. In a very improper way, of course, but it is never of the least use to appeal to her sense of what is right, because I don't think she has any – or any regard for the sensibilities of others either."

Mrs Underhill uttered a faint protest; but she found it impossible to deny that Tiffany, for all her caressing ways, had never yet shown the smallest consideration for anyone. She did not enquire into the methods Miss Trent meant to employ to keep that volatile damsel in good spirits; and Miss Trent volunteered no explanation. Her methods were certainly unorthodox, and must have earned the censure of any mother anxious to see her daughter grow into a modest female, with delicacy of character as well as prettiness of person. But Miss Trent had long since realized that her lovely charge was governed by self-interest. Perhaps, if she were to be deeply in love one day, her nature might undergo a change; meanwhile, the best that the most conscientious preceptress could do for her was to instil into her head the belief that elegant manners were as essential for social success as an enchanting face; to keep her from passing the line; and to prevent her setting everyone in the house by the ears whenever her will was crossed.

So when Tiffany came tempestuously into the schoolroom (as Ancilla had known she would), to pour out the tale of Mrs Mickleby's infamous conduct, she listened to her with an air of blank amazement, and exclaimed: "But --! Good heavens, Tiffany, you don't mean to tell me that you *wish* to go to that party? You cannot be serious!"

Tiffany's bosom was heaving stormily, but an arrested, questioning look came into her eyes as she stared at Miss Trent. "What do you mean?"

Miss Trent arched her brows incredulously. "*You* at such an insipid squeeze? Oh, dear, how *very* improper in me to say that! Charlotte, don't sit with your mouth at half-cock! You were not listening – and if you dare to repeat what I said I shall drag you through fields full of cows!"

Charlotte giggled, but Tiffany stamped her foot angrily. "It is a party for Sir Waldo and his cousin, and *everybody* will be there!"

"Exactly so! Now, don't eat me! If you indeed wished for it I'm sorry but I must own it is not at all the sort of party at which I should wish you to make an appearance. You would be the youngest lady present, and you may depend upon it that Mrs Mickleby, if she had asked you, would have taken care to have your place set as far from her distinguished guests as possible. I imagine you would have had Humphrey Colebatch to squire you, perfectly tongue-tied, poor boy! Another thing – which I know one ought not to consider, of course! – is that you couldn't wear the dress that becomes you better than any of the others: – I mean the one with the knots of ribbon and the sash exactly the colour of your eyes."

"Yes, I could!"

"Not in Mrs Mickleby's drawing-room!" Ancilla said. "Only think of all those green curtains and chairs! the effect would be ruined!"

Tiffany was beginning to look thoughtful; but she said, with a slight pout: "Yes, but I don't see why Mary Mickleby should be at the party, or Sophia Banningham, and not me! They aren't out either at least, they haven't had a London season!"

"No, and I wouldn't wager a groat on the chance that when they get up from dinner Mrs Mickleby won't pack all the young people off to the morning-room, to play speculation, or some such thing. There is to be no dancing, you know: just a chattery evening, with a little whist for the gentlemen, I daresay."

"Oh, no! How shabby! Do you think it will be like that indeed? How bored Sir Waldo and his cousin will be!"

"No doubt they will be. And how agreeably surprised when they come to your aunt's party!"

"Yes, very true!" Tiffany said, brightening.

"Sir Waldo!" exclaimed Charlotte scornfully. "I think it's the stupidest thing! Everybody running wild over him, except Miss Trent and me! You don't want to meet him, do you, ma'am?"

"No, not particularly, which is a fortunate circumstance, for I can't suppose that he would think me any more interesting than I think him," responded Ancilla cheerfully.

CHAPTER FOUR

IRONICALLY ENOUGH, the two persons who least desired the introduction were the first of the Staples household to meet Sir Waldo. Charlotte and Miss Trent, driving into the village in the one-horse phaeton originally bestowed on Mrs Underhill by her husband in the mistaken belief that it would afford her amusement to tool herself about the neighbourhood, were bound for the Church, with a basket full of flowers. Leaving the phaeton in the stableyard of the Rectory, they carried the basket through the wicket-gate into the Churchyard, and were employed in arranging lilies and delphiniums in two vases set on the altar when they were startled by a man's voice, saying: "But how charming!"

"Oh, how you made me jump!" exclaimed Charlotte involuntarily.

"Did I? I beg your pardon!"

Miss Trent turned her head, and saw that a stranger had entered the Church, accompanied by the Rector, who said: "Well met, Miss Trent! How do you do, Charlotte? Charming indeed, is it not, Sir Waldo? And, I think, unusual. We are indebted to Miss Trent both for the notion and for the execution of it. But you are not yet acquainted! Sir Waldo Hawkridge – Miss Trent, Miss Charlotte Underhill!"

Charlotte bobbed a schoolgirl's curtsy; Miss Trent, bowing slightly, critically watched the advance up the aisle towards her of this representative of a set she held in poor esteem. He carried himself with the natural grace of the athlete; he was certainly good-looking; and she was obliged to acknowledge that although it was evident that no provincial tailor was responsible for the cut of his coat he adopted none of the extravagances of fashion. He was dressed for riding, in buckskins and topboots, and he carried his hat and crop in one hand. The other, a shapely member, bare of rings, he held out to her, saying: "How do you do? May I compliment you? I have recently seen saloons and ballrooms decorated in this style, but not, I believe, a Church. It is altogether delightful!"

Their eyes met, both pairs gray, hers very cool and clear, his faintly smiling; she gave him her hand, and was aware of the strength latent in the clasp of his. She was a tall woman, but she had to look up to his face; and, as she did so, she became conscious of a tug of attraction. The thought flashed into her mind that she beheld the embodiment of her ideal. It was as instantly banished; she said, as he released her hand: "You are too good, sir. Mine was not the inspiration, however. In the parish where I was used to reside it has been the custom for some years."

It would have been too much to have said that Miss Trent's instinctive recognition of the ideal was reciprocated. The Nonesuch had been for too many years the target at which ambitious females had aimed their arrows to be any longer impressionable; and certain painful disillusionments suffered in his youth had hardened his heart against feminine wiles. He was not so much cynical as armoured; and at the age of five-and-thirty believed that he was past the age of falling in love. What he saw in Miss Trent he liked: the fine eyes which looked so directly into his, the graceful carriage, the indefinably well-bred air which distinguished her, and the absence of any affectation in her manners. He liked her voice, too, and the civil indifference with which she had received his compliment. It was refreshing to meet a marriageable female who did not instantly exert herself to win his admiration; it might be pleasant to pursue her acquaintance; but if he were never to see her again it would not cost him any pang of regret.

She turned her head away, to attend to the Rector, who was gently quizzing Charlotte. "I saw your phaeton in the yard, and was told by my good James that *Miss Charlotte* had driven in. Now, that I *didn't* see, which is a severe disappointment!"

"Oh, Mr Chartley, you *know* -!" protested Charlotte, overcome by blushes and giggles. "It was Miss Trent!"

He laughed, and glanced at Sir Waldo. "Not even Miss Trent, who, I must tell you, is a very pretty whip, and a pattern-card of patience besides, has succeeded in curing this foolish child of a profound mistrust of even the sleepiest cart-horse! Eh, Charlotte?"

"Well, I *don't* like horses!" she said boldly. She cast a defiant look at Sir Waldo, and added: "And I won't pretend I do, because I hate shams! You can never tell what they mean to do next! And if you pat them, they – they *twitch*!"

This was rather too much for the Rector's and Miss Trent's gravity, but Sir Waldo, though there was a laugh in his eye, replied gravely: "Very true! And when you stretch out your hand only to stroke their noses they toss up their heads, as though they supposed you meant to do them an injury!"

Encouraged, Charlotte said: "Yes! Though my brother says you should take hold of the bridle before you do so. But if they think you mean to hurt them, when they are for ever being cosseted and cared-for, they must be perfectly addle-brained!"

"I'm afraid they haven't very much intelligence," he admitted.

She opened her eyes at that. "But *you* like them, don't you, sir?"

"Yes, but there is never any accounting for tastes, you know." He smiled at Ancilla. "I collect that we share that particular taste, ma'am?"

"Mr Chartley has misled you, sir. I'm the merest whipster. Charlotte, we must not stand dawdling any longer!"

"But you will take a look in at the Rectory before you go, won't you?" said the Rector. "Sir Waldo has been admiring our little Church, and I have promised to show him the twelfth-century piscina – our greatest pride, is it not?"

He moved away, and Sir Waldo, with a smile and a bow to the ladies, followed him. But when the flowers were arranged to Ancilla's satisfaction, and she picked up her basket, nodding to Charlotte to come away with her, the Rector joined her, and the whole party left the Church together. Ancilla found herself walking beside Sir Waldo down the path leading to the Rectory; declined his offer to carry the basket; and asked him civilly how he liked the Yorkshire scene.

"Very well – as much as I have seen of it," he replied. "As yet, that's not very much: I have been spending most of my time in Leeds. I hope presently to see more of the countryside. My young cousin has been exploring far and wide, and is enthusiastic; says it is finer by far than his own county. That's because the Squire has put him in the way of getting some excellent fishing."

She laughed. "I hope he will enjoy good sport – though my small experience informs me that *catching* fish is not necessary for your true angler's enjoyment."

"Oh, no! But to *lose* a fish is quite another matter!"

"Certainly! One cannot wonder that it should cast even the most cheerful person into gloom, for it is always such an enormous one that escapes!"

"I begin to think you are yourself an angler, ma'am: you are so exactly right!"

"Indeed I am not! I was used to accompany my brothers sometimes, when I was a girl, but I very soon discovered that it was not at all the sport for me. When I caught nothing – which was in general the case – I found it a dead bore, and when a fish did get on my hook I was at a loss to know what to do with it, because I can't bear handling fish! They wriggle so!"

They had reached the wicket-gate; he held it open for her, saying gravely: "They do, don't they? So slimy, too! Almost as disagreeable as Miss Charlotte's twitching horses!"

She stepped past him into the garden, but paused there, waiting for Charlotte and the Rector to join them. "Poor Charlotte! It was too bad of Mr Chartley to poke fun at her, for she has tried so hard to overcome her fear of horses, and is secretly much ashamed of it. Pray don't laugh at her!"

"You may be sure I shan't. I should be far more likely to recommend her not to give the matter another thought. Now, why do you look surprised, ma'am?"

She coloured faintly. "Did I do so? Perhaps because it *did* surprise me a little to hear you say that – being yourself, so I'm told, such a notable horseman."

He raised his brows. "But must I therefore despise those who don't care for horses?"

"No – but I have frequently observed that gentlemen who are addicted to sporting pursuits are prone to despise those whose interests are quite different." She added quickly: "It is very understandable, I daresay!"

"I should rather call it intolerably conceited," he replied. He regarded her quizzically. "Furthermore, ma'am, I have a notion that it is *you* who despise those of *us* who are addicted to sport!"

"That's to say I'm intolerably conceited," she countered, smiling. "I am afraid I deserved it!"

They were interrupted by the Rector, who came up with Charlotte at that moment. He suggested that Sir Waldo should return to the house with them, but this was declined. Sir Waldo took his leave of the ladies, and went off with the Rector towards the stables.

Charlotte was plainly bursting to discuss the unexpected encounter, but Ancilla checked her, begging her to reserve her remarks until they should be out of earshot of her very penetrating voice. She was obedient, and listened docilely enough to a warning against any indiscreet utterance; but Ancilla knew her too well to place much reliance on her assurance that she would mind her tongue. As soon as she became excited, she would blurt out whatever thought came into her head, infallibly incurring Mrs Chartley's deep, if unexpressed, disapproval. Mrs Chartley was a kindly woman, but her sense of propriety was strict. It was with relief that Ancilla saw her charge carried off by her friend and contemporary, Miss Jane Chartley, who came running down the stairs as soon as they had entered the house. No doubt the Rectory schoolroom would be regaled with Charlotte's opinion of the Nonesuch, but at least her governess would not be put to the blush by her forthright speech and far from retiring manners.

In the event, when she was ushered into the parlour, Ancilla found Patience alone. She was busy with some white work, hemming a seam with the tiniest of stitches, but she gladly laid it aside when she saw Ancilla. She was quite as eager to discuss the Nonesuch as Charlotte, but being a very well brought-up girl she was much less precipitate, and spent as much as five minutes talking on indifferent topics before saying: "I must tell you that we have had such an interesting visitor this morning, Miss Trent. Papa took him to see the Church: I wonder, did you meet him there?"

"Sir Waldo? Yes, we did. Indeed, we walked back together, all four of us, and parted at the gate. Your papa went off with him then to the stables."

"Oh, yes! He rode over to call on Papa, and then Papa brought him in to introduce him to Mama and me, and he was with us for quite half-an-hour. What did you think of him? Were you surprised? I own, I was – and Mama too, I think! All the gentlemen have been talking so much about his being such an out-and-out Corinthian that I had pictured something quite different – though I've never *seen* a Corinthian, of course. You have, I expect: is that what they are really like? Do you think he *is* one?"

"There can be no doubt he is: a very famous one! As for whether all Corinthians are like him, I can't tell, for I was never acquainted with one."

Patience said shyly: "I fancy you don't care for that set, and I must say I never thought I should either, for one hears *such* things about them! But he is not in the least what I had imagined! Not proud, or or what Dick calls a *dashing blade*! He was so easy, and unaffected, and well-informed; and he seems to feel just as he ought about serious matters: he and Papa talked a little of the dreadful hardships the poor people have been suffering, and I could see how pleased Papa was with him. What did *you* think of him, Miss Trent?"

"Oh, a diamond of the first water!" replied Ancilla promptly. "His air, one of decided fashion; his manners most polished; his address – perfection!"

Patience looked at her. "You didn't like him?"

"On the contrary! I thought him very amiable."

"Ah, that signifies that you think his *manners* amiable, but not – not his disposition!"

"My dear Miss Chartley, I know nothing about his disposition!"

"No, but – Oh, I think I must tell you! It can't be wrong to do so! Sir Waldo hasn't mentioned the matter, even to Papa, and we believe he would as lief it were not known, because he told Wedmore that Mr Calver had privately desired him, when the precise state of his affairs should have been ascertained, to make provision for his old servants. Even Papa doesn't believe Mr Calver did anything of the sort! The Wedmores are to have a pension which will make them comfortable beyond anything they had hoped for: Mrs Wedmore came to tell Honeywick yesterday! You may imagine how much she was overcome – how thankful!"

"Indeed! I am very glad to know that Sir Waldo has done what he should."

"Yes, and of course it was expected that he would. You may say that he is so wealthy that it means no more to him than it would mean to me to give a penny to a beggar, but what strikes one so particularly is the *manner* of it. It was done with a delicacy that shows Sir Waldo to be a man of sensibility, not above considering what must have been the feelings of two such faithful people when they discovered how little their service had been valued!"

Ancilla acknowledged it; but murmured wickedly: "He has won your heart, I see! He has *great* address!"

"Oh, *no*! " cried Patience, quite shocked. "How can you? Oh, you are funning, but indeed you should not! I hope my heart is not so easily won!"

Ancilla smiled at her. "I hope it may not be – and certainly not by a Corinthian! Don't look distressed! I was only funning, of course: I don't fear for you!"

Recovering her complexion, Patience said: "We shall none of us have time to lose our hearts: he doesn't mean to settle at Broom Hall, you know."

"I should suppose not: he would find it very slow. Does he mean to sell the place?"

"We don't know. He didn't tell us what he means to do; and, naturally, one would not ask prying questions." She looked up, as her mother came into the room, and smiled, saying: "I have been telling Miss Trent how agreeable we think Sir Waldo Hawkridge, Mama: gossiping, you will say!"

"I suppose we all gossip about him," Mrs Chartley replied, shaking hands with Ancilla. "How do you do, Miss Trent? Yes, I must own that I was very pleasantly surprised in Sir Waldo. After the tales we have heard about *the Nonesuch* I had not expected to find that this Tulip of the *Ton*, instead of being a great coxcomb, is a man who wants neither sense nor feeling. I thought his manners particularly good, too: he has an air of well-bred ease, and no pretension – and as for his leading our sons astray, nonsense! I hope they *may* copy him! Indeed, I find myself regretting that Dick is at school, for he would be all the better for a little polish!"

"Town bronze, ma'am? Oh, no!" Ancilla protested.

"Oh, not à la modality! I meant only that it would do him a great deal of good to perceive that a man may be sporting-mad without advertizing the circumstance."

She said no more about Sir Waldo, and Ancilla made no attempt to bring the conversation back to him. His name was not mentioned again until Charlotte, seated beside her in the phaeton, uttered in awed accents: "Well! To think we should have been the first to meet Sir Waldo, and to talk to him! Oh, Miss Trent, wasn't it nuts for us?"

Ancilla burst out laughing, but protested as well. "Charlotte! Do you wish to see me turned off without a character, you abominable girl? *Nuts for us*, indeed!"

"As though Mama would! No, but *wasn't it*? Tiffany will be as angry as a wasp!"

Knowing that it would be useless to expect Charlotte to refrain from exulting over her cousin, Ancilla held her peace. She was justified by the result: Tiffany received the news with indifference; for while Charlotte had been making the acquaintance of the Nonesuch she had met and dazzled Lord Lindeth.

Whether the encounter had been by accident or by her own design was a point she left undisclosed. She had refused to accompany her cousin and governess that morning, voting the object of the expedition slow work, and declaring that nothing would prevail upon her to sit bodkin in a carriage designed to carry no more than two persons. Instead, she had had her pretty bay mare saddled, and had ridden out alone, declining the escort of the groom expressly hired to attend her. Since there was nothing unusual about this he made no attempt to dissuade her from conduct unbefitting her years and station, merely remarking to Courtenay's groom that one of these days, mark his words, Miss would be brought home with her neck broke, ramming her horses along the way she did, and thinking herself at home to a peg, which the lord knew she wasn't.

The latter part of this criticism Tiffany would have much resented; but she would have been rather pleased than annoyed at the accusation of ramming her horses along, which she considered to be exactly the style to be expected of one who took pride in being a hard-goer. Accustomed, as a little girl, to career all over the countryside on her pony, she had not as yet learnt to accept chaperonage; and although she was willing to ride with Courtenay, or with Ancilla, she found the presence of her groom irksome, and dispensed with it whenever she could. On this occasion she had an excellent reason for doing so: the Squire had let fall the information that young Lord Lindeth was going to fish the stream that ran through the grounds of the Manor; and Tiffany, by no means reconciled to her exclusion from Mrs Mickleby's dinner-party, had every intention of making his acquaintance. Miss Trent might be right in thinking that the party would not suit her; but even less did it suit her to be the last lady of consequence in the neighbourhood to meet the distinguished newcomers. No more than her aunt did she doubt that Mrs Mickleby's omission of her name from the elegant dinner-card sent to Mrs Underhill sprang from a jealous fear that her own two daughters would be cast into the shade by the appearance on the scene of an accredited beauty. Well! Mrs Mickleby, no doubt hopeful that Mary or Caroline would contrive to attract the interest of a titled gentleman, should discover that one at least of her exalted guests was in no mood to make either of these damsels the object of his gallantry. Lord Lindeth, if the beautiful Miss Wield could contrive it, was going to think the party very flat, when he looked in vain for her amongst the guests.

It was an easy matter to find Lord Lindeth. The stream he was fishing wound through a stretch of open country. Tiffany saw him from a distance, and cantered easily in his direction, neither so close to the stream as to make it apparent that she wished to attract his attention, nor so far from it that he would not hear the thud of the mare's hooves. It was a little unfortunate that his back should be turned towards her, but she felt sure that he would look round when he heard her approach. She reckoned without her host: Lord Lindeth was casting into a likely pool; he had got a rise; and he gave not the smallest sign of having heard the sound of a ridden horse. For a moment it seemed as though Miss Wield's careful strategy must be thrown away. She was a resourceful girl, however, and as soon as she realized that he was wholly absorbed in his sport she let her whip fall, and reined in, uttering a distressful exclamation.

That did make him look round, not so much interested as vexed. It was on the tip of his tongue to request the intruder to make less noise when he perceived that the rude interruption had come from a lady.

"Oh, I beg your pardon!" Tiffany called. "But would you be so very obliging, sir, as to give me my whip again? I can't think how I came to be so stupid, but I've dropped it!"

He reeled in his line, saying: "Yes, of course – with pleasure, ma'am!"

She sat still, serenely awaiting his approach. He laid his rod down, and came towards her. There was a slight look of impatience on his face, but this speedily vanished when he was near enough to see what a vision of beauty had accosted him. Instead of picking up the whip he stood staring up at Tiffany, frank admiration in his gaze.

She was dressed in a flowing habit of sapphire-blue velvet, a lace cravat round her neck, and a curled ostrich plume caressing her cheek. It did not occur to Julian that this undeniably becoming costume was scarcely the established country-mode; he thought only that never in his life had he beheld a more staggeringly lovely girl.

An enchanting smile made him blink; Tiffany said contritely: "I *am* so sorry! I interrupted you – but I can't mount without a block, so you see .... !"

He found his tongue, saying quickly: "No, no, you didn't, I assure you!"

A gleam shone in her eyes. "But I know very well I did!"

He laughed, flushing a little: "Well, yes! But you needn't be sorry: *I'm* not!"

"Oh, and you looked so vexed!"

"That was before I saw who had interrupted me," he retorted audaciously.

"But you don't know who I am!"

"Oh, yes, I do. Diana!"

"No, I'm not!" she said innocently. "I'm Tiffany Wield!"

"Tiffany! How pretty! But you make me remember an old poem: *Queen and huntress, chaste and fair* – though I rather fancy it was about the moon, not the goddess. But I know the title is *To Diana*, and the refrain, or whatever it's called, is *Goddess, excellently bright*! So -!"

"I don't think I ought to listen to you," she said demurely. "After all, sir, we haven't been regularly introduced yet!"

"There's no one to perform that office for us," he pointed out. "Do you care for such stuff?"

"No, not a scrap, but my aunt thinks I should! And also that I should *never* converse with strange gentlemen!"

"Very true!" he answered promptly. "May I present Lord Lindeth to you, Miss Wield? – he is most anxious to make your acquaintance!"

She gave a trill of laughter. "How do you do? How absurd you are!"

"I know – but what else was to be done in such a case? I was afraid you would gallop away!"

"So I shall if you will be so very obliging as to pick up my whip for me, sir!"

He did so, but stood holding it. "I'm tempted to keep it from you!"

She held out her hand. "No, please!"

He gave it to her. "Only funning!" It struck him that it was strange that so young and lovely a girl should be quite unattended, and he said, glancing about him in a puzzled way: "Is no one with you, Miss Wield? Your groom, or – or -"

"No one! It's so *stuffy* to have a groom at one's heels! Do you think it very improper?"

"No, indeed! But if anything were to happen – some accident -"

"I'm not afraid of that!" She shortened the bridle. "I must go now. Thank you for coming to my rescue!"

"Oh, wait!" he begged. "You haven't told me where you live, or when I shall see you again!"

"I live at Staples – and who knows when you will see me again?" she replied, her eyes glinting down into his. "I'm sure *I* don't!"

"Staples," he said, committing it to memory. "I think I know – oh, I should have told you that I'm at Broom Hall, with my cousin, Waldo Hawkridge! Yes, and we are to dine at the Manor the day after tomorrow – some sort of a party, I believe! Shall I see you there?"

"Perhaps – perhaps not!" she said mischievously, and was off before he could demand a more positive answer.

CHAPTER FIVE

LORD LINDETH, who had greeted with disapprobation the news that he was to be dragged out to a dinner-party, returned to Broom Hall after his encounter with Miss Wield in quite a different frame of mind. The first thing he did was to run through the various visiting-cards which had been bestowed upon his cousin; the next was to burst into the library, where Sir Waldo was frowning over his deceased cousin's rent-books, demanding: "Waldo, are you acquainted with anyone called Wield?"

"No, I don't think so," replied Sir Waldo, rather absently.

"Do pay attention!" begged Julian. "From Staples! Isn't that the place with the wrought-iron gates, beyond the village? They *must* have called, but I can't find any card!"

"Presumably they haven't called, then.

"No, but – of course, the name might not be Wield: she spoke of her *aunt*, and I suppose – But there's no card bearing that direction that I can find!"

Sir Waldo looked up at this, a laugh in his eye. "Oho! *She*?"

"Oh, Waldo, I've met the most *ravishing* girl!" disclosed his lordship. "Now, think! Who lives at Staples?"

"Miss Wield, I collect."

"Yes, but – Oh, don't be so provoking! Surely you must know who *owns* the place."

"I can see not the smallest reason why I must know and I don't."

"I wish you may not have lost the card! You would suppose her uncle must have called, wouldn't you?"

"Well, I haven't so far given the matter any consideration," said Sir Waldo apologetically. "Perhaps he doesn't approve of me?"

Julian stared at him. "Nonsense! Why shouldn't he?"

"I can't imagine."

"No, nor anyone else! Do stop talking slum, and try to be serious!"

"I am serious!" protested Sir Waldo. "Quite perturbed, in fact! I have sustained an introduction to someone who, unless I am much mistaken, *does* disapprove of me."

"Who?" demanded Julian.

"A female whose name I can't recall. A remarkably good-looking one, too," he added reflectively. "And not just in the common style, either."

"She sounds a maggotty creature to me!" said Julian frankly. "Not but what I think you're shamming it! Why should she disapprove of you?"

"I rather fear, my fatal addiction to sport."

"What a ninnyhammer! No, but, Waldo, do think! Are you perfectly sure no one from Staples has been here?"

"Not to my knowledge. Which leaves us quite at a stand, doesn't it?"

"Well, it does – except that she may be at the party. She didn't precisely say so, but – Lord, what a fortunate thing it was that we stayed with the Arkendales on our way here! I might not else have brought my evening rig with me!"

This ingenuous observation made Sir Waldo's lips twitch, for Julian's reception of the news that his journey north was to be broken by a visit to the home of one of the highest sticklers in the country would not have led anyone to foresee that he would presently think himself fortunate to have undergone a stay which he had stigmatized as an intolerable bore. Similarly, when he knew that he had been included in Mrs Mickleby's invitation to Waldo he had denied any expectation of enjoyment, saying that if he had guessed that he had fled from the London scene only to be plunged into a succession of country dinner-parties he would not have accompanied his cousin.

But all such unsociable ideas were now at an end; it was not he but Sir Waldo who deplored the necessity of attending a dinner-party on a wet evening: Julian had no doubt of its being a delightful party; and as for the ancient vehicle brought round from the coach-house for their conveyance, he told his cousin, who was eyeing it with fastidious dislike, that he was a great deal too nice, and would find it perfectly comfortable.

Miss Wield would have been pleased, though not at all surprised, to have known how eagerly his lordship looked forward to meeting her at the Manor, and how disappointed he was not to see her there; but if she had been an invisible spectator she would not have guessed from his demeanour that he was at all disappointed. He was far too polite to betray himself; and of too cheerful and friendly a disposition to show the least want of cordiality. It was a great shame that his ravishing girl was absent; but he had discovered her aunt's name, and had formed various plans for putting himself in this lady's way. Meanwhile, there were several pretty girls to be seen, and he was perfectly ready to make himself agreeable to them.

A quick survey of the drawing-room was enough to inform Sir Waldo that the beautiful Miss Wield was not present. Miss Chartley and Miss Colebatch were the best-looking ladies, the one angelically fair, the other a handsome redhead, but neither corresponded to the lyrical description Julian had given him of Miss Wield's surpassing beauty. He glanced towards Julian, and was amused to see that he was being very well entertained amongst the younger members of the party. He was not surprised, for he had not taken Julian's raptures very seriously: Julian had begun to develop an interest in the fair sex, but he was still at the experimental stage, and during the past year had discovered at least half-a-dozen goddesses worthy of his enthusiastic admiration. His cousin saw no need to feel any apprehension: Julian was enjoying the flirtations proper to his calf-time, and was some way yet from forming a lasting passion.

For himself, Sir Waldo was resigned to an evening's boredom, denied even the amusement of pursuing his acquaintance with the lady who disapproved of him. He had looked in vain for her, and was conscious of disappointment. He could not recall her name, but he did remember that he had been attracted by her air of cool distinction, and the smile which leaped so suddenly into her eyes. She was intelligent, too, and had a sense of humour: a rare thing, he thought, amongst females. He would have liked to have known her better, and had looked forward to meeting her again. But she was not present, and he was provided instead with a number of middle-aged persons, as dull as they were worthy, and with a sprinkling of boys and girls. Amongst the girls, he awarded the palm to Miss Chartley, with whom he exchanged a few words. He liked, as much as the sweetness of her expression, the unaffected manners which, in spite of a not unbecoming shyness, enabled her to respond to his greeting without blushing, nervously giggling, or assuming a worldly air to impress him. As for the boys, he would have had to be extremely dull-witted not to have realized, within a very few moments of entering the room, that most of them were taking in every detail of his dress, and, while too bashful to put themselves forward, were hoping that before the evening was out they would be able to boast of having talked to the Nonesuch. He was well-accustomed to being the object of any aspiring young sportsman's hero-worship, but he neither sought nor valued such adulation. Mr Underhill, Mr Arthur Mickleby, Mr Jack Banningham, and Mr Gregory Ash, bowing deeply, and uttering reverently *Sir*! and *Honoured*! would have been stunned to know that the only young gentleman to engage Sir Waldo's amused interest was Humphrey Colebatch, a redheaded youth (like his sister), afflicted with an appalling stutter. Presented by his fond father somewhat dauntingly as *this silly chub of mine*, and further stigmatized by the rider: *not of your cut, I'm sorry to say!* he had disclosed, in the explosive manner of those suffering an impediment of speech, that he was not interested in sport.

"He's bookish," explained Sir Ralph, torn between pride in his son's scholastic attainments and the horrid fear that he had fathered a miscreature. "Worst seat in the county! But there! No accounting for tastes, eh? Take my daughter, Lizzie! Never opened a book in her life, but rides with a light hand and an easy bit, and handles the reins in form."

"Does she?" Sir Waldo said politely. He smiled encouragingly at Humphrey. "Oxford?"

"Cam-Cam-Cambridge!" He added, after a brief struggle: Magdalene. J-just d-down. Th-third year."

"Magdalene! So was I – Magdalen, Oxford, though. What do you mean to do next?"

"G-go up for a fourth year!" replied Humphrey doggedly, and with a challenging look at his father.

"Fellowship?"

"Yes, sir. I *hope*!"

But at this point Sir Ralph intervened, testily adjuring him not to keep boring on about his affairs; so he bowed awkwardly to Sir Waldo, and walked away. Upon which Sir Ralph said that scholarship was all very well in its way, but that if he had guessed that his heir was going to run mad after it he would never have let him go up to Cambridge at all. He showed a disposition to become even more confidential, asking to be told what Sir Waldo would do in such a case; but as Sir Waldo did not feel himself to be qualified to advise harassed parents, and was too little interested to bend his mind to the problem, he speedily extricated himself from this tête-à-tête. It spoke volumes for his social address that he contrived to do it without in any way offending Sir Ralph.

Meanwhile, those of Humphrey's contemporaries who had jealously observed his encounter with the Nonesuch pounced upon him, demanding to be told what Sir Waldo had said to him.

"W-wouldn't interest you!" responded Humphrey, with odious loftiness. "N-nothing about sport! We talked ab-about Cam-Cambridge."

This disclosure stunned his audience. Mr Banningham was the first to recover his power of speech; he expressed the sentiments of his boon companions by saying: "He *must* have thought you a slow-top!"

"N-not at all!" retorted Humphrey, curling his lip. "W-what's m-more, he's not such a c-c-cod's head as you l-led me to think him!"

At any other time so insufferable a speech must have goaded his childhood's playmates into punitive action. A sense of propriety, however, restrained them, and enabled Humphrey to saunter away, not only unmolested, but filled with the comfortable conviction of having, in a few heaven-sent moments, paid off all the scores of a short lifetime.

Since Mrs Mickleby seated the Nonesuch between herself and Lady Colebatch at her extended dining-table, it was not until much later in the evening that he made the acquaintance of Mrs Underhill. In the welter of introductions he had scarcely distinguished her amongst so many matrons; but Lord Lindeth had not been so careless. Undismayed by a gown of puce satin, lavishly adorned with lace and diamonds, and by a headdress supporting a plume of curled feathers clasped by a glittering brooch of opulent dimensions, he had seized the first opportunity that offered of approaching Mrs Underhill, when the gentlemen joined the ladies after dinner; and it was he who made Sir Waldo known to her. Obedient to the summons telegraphed to him by his young cousin, Sir Waldo came across the room, and was immediately made aware of his duty.

"Oh, here is my cousin!" said his lordship artlessly. "Waldo, I fancy you have already been presented to Mrs Underhill!"

"Yes, indeed!" responded Sir Waldo, rising nobly to the occasion.

"Well, we were introduced," conceded Mrs Underhill, "but it wouldn't surprise me if you didn't happen to catch my name. I'm sure there's nothing more confusing than to be introduced to a score of strangers. Many's the time I've been in a regular hobble, trying to set the right names to the right faces!"

"But in this instance, ma'am, I have something to assist my memory!" said Sir Waldo, with admirable aplomb. "Did I not have the pleasure of meeting your daughter not so many days since? Miss – Miss Charlotte Underhill? She was helping another lady – a tall lady, older than herself – to deck the Church with flowers."

"That's right!" said Mrs Underhill, pleased with him. "And mightily puffed-up she's been ever since, you talking to her so kindly, as she tells me you did! As for the tall lady, that would be Miss Trent: her governess. Well, properly speaking, she's my niece's companion, and a very superior young female. Her uncle is General Sir Mordaunt Trent!"

"Indeed!" murmured Sir Waldo.

"Waldo!" interrupted Julian, "Mrs Underhill has been so kind as to invite us to attend the party she is holding on Wednesday next! I believe we have no other engagement?"

"None that I know of. How delightful! We are very much obliged to you, ma'am!" said Sir Waldo, with the courtesy for which he was renowned.

But afterwards, jolting back to Broom Hall in the late Mr Calver's ill-sprung carriage, he expressed the acid hope that his cousin was properly grateful to him for accepting the invitation.

"Yes, very grateful!" replied Julian blithely. "Not but what I knew you would!"

"Having thrust me into an impossible position I imagine you might!"

Julian chuckled. "I know, but – She's that glorious creature's aunt, Waldo!"

"I am aware! It remains only for you to discover that your glorious creature is engaged to one of the local blades, and you will have come by your deserts."

"Oh, no! I'm tolerably sure she's not!" said Julian confidently. "Her cousin must have mentioned the circumstance, if – Besides, -"

"Do you mean Charlotte? Was she there tonight?"

"Charlotte? No – who's she? Courtenay Underhill!"

"Oh, a male cousin! What is *he* like?"

"Oh – oh, very agreeable!" said Julian. He hesitated, and then said: "Yes, I know what you're thinking, and I suppose he is inclined to be what you'd call a coxcomb, but he's very young: hardly more than a schoolboy!"

"Quoth the graybeard!" said Sir Waldo lazily.

"Now, Waldo -! I only meant that I shouldn't think he could be twenty yet, and I'm *three*-and-twenty, after all!"

"No, are you? I'll say this for you then: you're wearing *very* well!"

The infectious chuckle broke from Julian again. He retorted: "I'm too old, at all events, to ape *your* modes!"

"Is that what Master Underhill does?"

"Corinthian fashions, anyway. He was looking you over so closely that I wouldn't bet a groat on the chance that he won't turn out in your sort of rig within the week. He asked me all manner of questions about you, too."

"Julian!" said Sir Waldo, with deep foreboding. "Tell me at once just *how* rum you pitched it to that wretched youth?"

"I didn't! I said *I* didn't know what larks you was used to engage in – which was true, though I know more now than I did yesterday! Waldo, *did* you once win five guineas by flooring the bruiser at some Fair in the second round?"

"Good God! How the devil did that story reach Yorkshire? I did: and if *that's* the sort of folly this chuckleheaded new friend of yours admires I hope you told him it was a fudge!"

"No, how could I? I told him to ask *you* for the truth of it. He didn't like to approach you tonight, but I daresay he will, when we go to Staples next week."

"Before then – long before then! – I shall have sent you packing, you hell-born brat!"

"Not you! I'd rack up at the Crown if you cast me out! Only wait until you have seen Miss Wield! *Then* you'll understand!"

Sir Waldo returned a light answer, but he was beginning to feel a little uneasy. There was a certain rapt note in Julian's voice which was new to him; and he had not previously known his young cousin to pursue a fair object with a determination that brushed aside such obvious disadvantages as a vulgar aunt, and a cousin whom he frankly acknowledged to be a coxcomb. He set little store by his consequence, but Sir Waldo had never yet seen him either encouraging the advances of led-captains, or seeking the company of those whom he would himself have described as being not fit to go; and it seemed highly improbable that he would try to fix his interest with any girl, be she never so beautiful, who was sprung from the mushroom-class he instinctively avoided. At the same time, it would be unlike him to be thinking of mere dalliance. Under his gaiety, Sir Waldo knew, ran a vein of seriousness, and strong principles: he might (though his experienced cousin doubted it) look for amusement amongst the muslin-company, but it would be wholly foreign to his nature deliberately to raise in any virtuous breast expectations which he had no intention of fulfilling. He had once or twice fancied himself in love, and had paid court to the chosen fair; but these affairs had dwindled, and had died perfectly natural deaths. He had never dangled after any marriageable girl in the cynical spirit of the rake: his youthful adventures in love might be transient, but he had embarked on them in all sincerity.

"I like the Squire, don't you?" remarked Julian idly.

"Better than I like his wife!"

"Oh, lord, yes! All pretension, ain't she? The girls are very unaffected and jolly, too: nothing to look at, of course! I suppose the most striking, *au fait de beauté,* as Mama would say, was the redheaded dasher, with the quiz of a brother, but, for my part, I prefer Miss Chartley's style – *and* her parents! No pretensions *there,* but I don't know how to express it!"

"A touch of quality?" suggested Sir Waldo.

"Ay, that's it!" agreed Julian, yawning, and relapsing into sleepy silence.

He made no further reference to Miss Wield, either then or during the succeeding days; and so far from showing any of the signs of the love-lorn entered with enthusiasm on a search for a likely hunter, under the aegis of Mr Gregory Ash; struck up a friendship with Jack Banningham's elder brother, and went flapper-shooting with him; dragged his cousin twenty miles to watch a disappointing mill; and in general seemed to be more interested in sport than in ravishing beauties. Sir Waldo did not quite banish his uneasy suspicion that he was harder-hit than his mother would like, but he relegated it to the back of his mind, thinking that he might well have been mistaken.

On Wednesday, when he saw Miss Wield at the Staples party, he knew that he had not been mistaken.

The hall at Staples was very large and lofty, with the main staircase rising from it in a graceful curve. Just as the cousins, having relinquished their hats and cloaks into the care of a powdered footman, were about to cross the floor in the wake of the butler, Miss Wield came lightly down the stairs, checking at sight of the guests, and exclaiming: "Oh! Oh, dear, I didn't know anyone had arrived yet! I'm late, and my aunt will scold! Oh, how do you do, Lord Lindeth!"

As conduct befitting one who was to all intents and purposes a daughter of the house this belated arrival on the scene might leave much to be desired; but as an entrance it was superb. Sir Waldo was not at all surprised to hear Lord Lindeth catch his breath; he himself thought that he had never beheld a lovelier vision, and he was neither impressionable nor three-and-twenty. The velvet ribbons which embellished a ball dress of celestial blue crape and silver gauze were of an intense blue, but not more brilliant than Tiffany's eyes, to which they seemed to draw attention. Pausing on the stairway, one gloved hand resting on the baluster-rail, her pretty lips parting in a smile which showed her white teeth, Tiffany presented a picture to gladden most men's hearts.

O my God! thought Sir Waldo. *Now we* are *in the basket!*

She resumed her floating descent of the stairs, as Julian stood spellbound. Recovering, he started forward to meet her, stammering: "M-Miss Wield! We meet again – at last!"

Enchanting dimples peeped as she gave him her hand. "At last? But it's hardly more than a sennight since I disturbed you at your fishing! You were vexed, too – horridly vexed!"

"Never!" he declared, laughing. "Only when I looked in vain for you at the Manor last week and I wasn't *vexed* then: that's too small a word!" He ventured to press her hand before releasing it, and turning to introduce his cousin to her.

Sir Waldo, who strongly (and quite correctly) suspected that Tiffany had been lying in wait on the upper landing, and had thus been able exactly to time her appearance on the scene, bowed, and said How-do-you-do, his manner a nice blend of civility and indifference. Tiffany, accustomed to meet with blatant admiration, was piqued. She had not sojourned for long under her uncle Burford's roof in Portland Place, but she had not wasted her time there, and she was well aware that, notwithstanding his rank, Lord Lindeth was a nonentity, when compared with his splendid cousin. To attach the Nonesuch, however temporarily, would be enough to confer distinction on any lady; to inspire him with a lasting passion would be a resounding triumph; for although he was said to have many flirts these seemed always to be married ladies, and the decided preferences he showed from time to time had led neither to scandal nor to any belief that his affections had been seriously engaged.

Dropping a demure curtsy, Tiffany raised her eyes to his face, favouring him with a wide, innocent gaze. She had previously only seen him from a distance, and she now perceived that he was very good-looking, and even more elegant than she had supposed. But instead of showing admiration he was looking rather amused, and that displeased her very much. She smiled at Lord Lindeth, and said: "I'll take you to my aunt, shall I? Then perhaps she won't scold after all!"

Mrs Underhill showed no disposition to scold, though she was quite shocked to think that two such distinguished guests should have entered her drawing-room unannounced. When, much later, she learned from her offended butler that Miss Tiffany had waved him aside, like a straw, she was aghast, and exclaimed: "Whatever must they have thought?"

Totton shuddered; but Tiffany, reproached for her social lapse, only laughed, and declared, on the authority of one who had lived for three months on the fringe of the *ton*, that a want of ceremony was just what such persons as Lord Lindeth and the Nonesuch preferred.

Lord Lindeth, too much dazzled to question the propriety of Tiffany's conduct in impulsively seizing his hand, and leading him up to his hostess, would have endorsed this pronouncement; Sir Waldo, following in their wake, reflected that he would have thought Tiffany's artlessness amusing, if only some other young man than Julian had been enthralled by it. He was in no way responsible for Julian; but he was fond of the boy, and he knew very well that his aunt Lindeth implicitly trusted him to keep her darling out of mischief. This duty had not, so far, imposed any great tax on his ingenuity: Tiffany would have been flattered to know that one glance at her had been enough to convince Sir Waldo that she represented the first real danger Julian had encountered.

A swift look round the room informed Sir Waldo that the company consisted of the same persons whom he had met at the Squire's dinner-party, and he resigned himself to an evening's boredom, exactly as his hostess had foretold. "Because you can't conjure up persons which don't exist, not with the best will in the world you can't," she had said to Miss Trent. "Mrs Mickleby took care to invite all the genteel families she could lay her hands on, drat her! I daresay, if we only knew it, she thinks I'll make up my numbers with the Shilbottles, and the Tumbys, and the Wrangles, which is where she'll find herself mightily mistaken."

Miss Trent suggested mildly that the Shilbottles were very agreeable people, but was overborne. "Agreeable they may be," said Mrs Underhill, "but they're not genteel. Mr Shilbottle goes to Leeds every day to his manufactory, and I hope I know better than to invite him to meet a lord! Why, next you'll be telling me I ought to send a card to the Badgers! No! His lordship and Sir Waldo had better be bored than disgusted!" She added, on a hopeful note: "*One* thing you may depend on: they'll find nothing amiss with their dinner!"

The repast which she set before her guests was certainly enormous, consisting of two courses, with four removes, and a score of side-dishes, ranging from a rump of beef à la Mantua, wax baskets of prawns and crayfish, to orange soufflés and asparagus, and some atlets of palates: a delicacy for which her cook was famous.

Miss Trent was not present at dinner, but she brought Charlotte down to the drawing-room afterwards, and was instantly seen by Sir Waldo, when he came into the room with the rest of the gentlemen. She was wearing a dress of crape with lilac ribbons, with long sleeves, and the bodice cut rather high, as befitted a governess, but he thought she looked the most distinguished lady present, and very soon made his way to her side.

The room had been cleared for dancing, and the musicians from Harrogate were tuning their instruments. Mrs Underhill, explaining that she thought the young people would like to dance, had begged Sir Waldo not to think himself obliged to take part, if he did not care for it, which had made it easy for him to range himself amongst the elders of the party. He might be noted for his courtesy but he had not the remotest intention of standing up with a dozen provincial girls through a succession of country dances. But when the first set was forming he went up to Miss Trent, and solicited the honour of leading her into it. She declined it, but could not help feeling gratified.

"That's a set-down!" remarked Sir Waldo. "Are you going to tell me that you *don't* dance, ma'am?"

She was thrown into a little natural confusion by this unexpected rejoinder, and said with less than her usual calm: "No, thank you. That is, yes, of course I do, but not – I mean -"

"Go on!" he said encouragingly, as she stopped, vexed with herself for being suddenly so *gauche*. "You do dance, but not with – er – *gentlemen who are addicted to sporting pursuits*! Have I that correctly?"

She looked quickly at him. "Did I say that?"

"Yes, and in a tone of severe disapprobation. You did not *then* tell me you preferred not to dance with me, of course: the occasion hadn't arisen."

"I haven't told you so now, sir!" she replied, with spirit. "I said – I hope civilly! – that I don't dance at all!"

"After which," he reminded her, "you said that you *do* dance, *but not*! Civility then overcame you, I collect! Quite tied your tongue, in fact! So I came to your rescue. I wish you will tell me what I've done to earn your disapproval."

"You are quite mistaken, sir. You must know that you have done nothing. I assure you I don't disapprove of you!"

"Just my imagination, Miss Trent? I don't believe it, but I'm very ready to be convinced. Shall we join this set?"

"Sir Waldo, you are labouring under a misapprehension! It would be most improper in me to stand up with you, or with anyone! I'm not a guest here: I am the governess!"

"Yes, but a *most* superior female!" he murmured.

She looked at him in some astonishment. "Did you know it, then? And asked me to dance? Well, I'm very much obliged to you, but I think it shows a strange want of conduct in you! To ask the governess rather than Miss Wield -!"

"My cousin was before me. Now, don't recite me a catalogue of the girls I *might* have asked to stand up with me! I daresay they are very amiable, I can see that one or two are pretty, and I know that I should find them all dead bores. I'm glad you won't dance: I had rather by far talk to you!"

"Well, it won't do!" she said resolutely. "I am quite beneath your touch, sir!"

"No, no, that's coming it much too strong!" he said. "When I have it on excellent authority that your uncle is a General!"

For a moment she suspected him of mockery; then she met his eyes, and realized that the laughter in them was at a joke he believed she would appreciate. She said, with a quivering lip: "D-did Mrs Underhill say that? Oh, dear! I shouldn't think you could possibly believe that she didn't learn about my uncle from me, but I promise you she didn't!"

"Another of my misapprehensions! I had naturally supposed that you introduced him into every conversation, and had been wondering how it came about that you forgot to mention him when we first met."

She choked. "I wish you will stop trying to make me laugh! Do, pray, Sir Waldo, go and talk to Mrs Mickleby, or Lady Colebatch, or someone! I might have twenty generals in my family, but I should still be the governess, and you must know that governesses remain discreetly in the background."

"That sounds like fustian," he remarked.

"Well, it isn't! It – it is a matter of social usage. It will be thought most unbecoming in me to put myself forward. I can see that already Mrs Banningham is wondering what can possess you to stand talking to me like this! Just the thing to set people in a bustle! *You* may stand on too high a form to care for the World's opinion, but I can assure you *I* don't!"

"Oh, I'm not nearly as arrogant as you think!" he assured her. "Setting people in a bustle is the last thing I wish to do! But I find it hard to believe that even the most deplorably top-lofty matron could think it remarkable that I should engage in conversation the niece of one of my acquaintances. I should rather suppose that she would think it abominably uncivil of me *not* to do so!"

"Are you acquainted with my uncle?" she demanded.

"Of course I am: we are members of the same club! I don't mean to boast, however! He is an older and by far more distinguished man than I am, and *acquaintance* is all I claim."

She smiled, but looked rather searchingly at him. "Are you also acquainted with his son, sir? My cousin, Mr Bernard Trent?"

"Not to my knowledge. Ought I to be?"

"Oh, no! He is very young. But he has a number of friends amongst the Corinthian set. I thought perhaps you might have encountered him."

He shook his head; and as Sir Ralph Colebatch came up at that moment she excused herself, and moved away to find Charlotte. She soon saw her, going down the dance with Arthur Mickleby; and realized ruefully, but with a little amusement, that while she had been engaged with the Nonesuch her enterprising pupil had contrived to induce Arthur to lead her into the set. Some mothers, she reflected, would have censured her pretty severely for not having kept a stricter chaperonage over a schoolgirl admitted to the drawing-room merely to watch the dancing for an hour, before going demurely upstairs to bed; but she was not surprised to find Mrs Underhill complacently eyeing her daughter's performance, or to learn that she had given Charlotte leave to dance.

"Well, I daresay I ought to have said no," she admitted, "but I like to see young people enjoying themselves, which it's plain she is, bless her! I'm sure there's no harm in her taking her place in a country-dance or two, for it's not as if there was to be any waltzing, *that* you may depend on! Nor it isn't a formal ball, which would be a very different matter, of course." She withdrew her gaze from Charlotte, and said kindly: "And if any gentleman was to ask you to stand up with him, my dear, I hope you'll do so! There's no one will wonder at it, not after seeing Sir Waldo going smash up to you, the way he did, and stand talking to you as though you was old friends!"

"He was speaking to me of my uncle, ma'am!" said Miss Trent, snatching at the excuse offered her by the Nonesuch, but flushing a little. "They are acquainted, you see."

"Ay, that's just what I said to Mrs Banningham!" nodded Mrs Underhill. "'Oh,' I said, 'you may depend upon it Sir Waldo is acquainted with the General, and they are chatting away about him, and all their London friends! I'm sure nothing could be more natural,' I said, 'for Miss Trent is very well-connected,' I said. That made her look yellow, I can tell you! Well, I hope I'm not one to take an affront into my head where none's intended, but I've had a score to settle with Mrs B. ever since she behaved so uppish to me at the Lord-Lieutenant's party!" A cloud descended on her brow; she said: "However, there's always something to spoil one's pleasure, and I don't scruple to own to *you*, Miss Trent, that the way his lordship looks at Tiffany has put me in a regular fidget! Mark me if we don't have him sitting in her pocket now, for anyone can see he's nutty upon her!"

This was undeniable. Miss Trent thought it would have been wonderful if he had not been looking at Tiffany with that glow of admiration in his eyes; for Tiffany, always responsive to flattery, was at her most radiant: a delicate flush in her cheeks, her eyes sparkling like sapphires, and a lovely, provocative smile on her lips. Half-a-dozen young gentlemen had begged for the honour of leading her into the first set; she had scattered promises amongst them, and had bestowed her hand on Lord Lindeth, taking her place with him while three less fortunate damsels were still unprovided with partners. But that was a circumstance she was unlikely to notice.

"Miss Trent, if he thinks to stand up with her more than twice that's something I won't allow!" said Mrs Underhill suddenly. "You must tell her she's not to do so, for she'll pay no heed to me, and it's you her uncle looked to, after all!"

Ancilla smiled, but said: "She wouldn't flout you publicly, ma'am. I'll take care, of course – but I fancy Lord Lindeth won't ask her for a third dance."

"Lord, my dear, what he'd like to do is to stand up with her for *every* dance!"

"Yes, but he knows he can't do so, and has too much propriety of taste, I'm persuaded, to make the attempt. And, to own the truth, ma'am, I think Tiffany wouldn't grant him more than two dances in any event."

"Tiffany?" exclaimed Mrs Underhill incredulously. "Why, she's got no more notion of propriety than the kitchen cat!"

"No, alas! But she is a most accomplished flirt, ma'am!" She could not help laughing at Mrs Underhill's face of horror. "I beg your pardon! Of course it is very wrong – shockingly precocious, too! but you will own that a mere flirtation with Lindeth need not throw you into a quake."

"Yes, but he's a lord!" objected Mrs Underhill. "You know how she says she means to marry one!"

"We must convince her that she would be throwing herself away on anyone under the rank of a Viscount!" said Ancilla lightly.

The dance came to an end, and she soon had the satisfaction of seeing that she had prophesied correctly: Tiffany stood up for the next one with Arthur Mickleby, and went on to dance the boulanger with Jack Banningham. Lord Lindeth, meanwhile, did his duty by Miss Colebatch and Miss Chartley; and Miss Trent extricated Charlotte from a group of slightly noisy young people, and inexorably bore her off to bed. Charlotte thought herself abominably ill-used to be compelled to withdraw before supper: she had been looking forward to drinking her very first glass of champagne. Miss Trent, barely repressing a shudder, handed her over to her old nurse, and returned to the drawing-room.

She entered it to find that the musicians were enjoying a respite. She could not see Mrs Underhill, and guessed that she had gone into the adjoining saloon, where some of the more elderly guests were playing whist. Nor could she see Tiffany: a circumstance which filled her with foreboding. Just as she had realized that Lindeth was another absentee, and was wondering where first to search for them, a voice spoke at her elbow.

"Looking for your other charge, Miss Trent?"

She turned her head quickly, to find that Sir Waldo was somewhat quizzically regarding her. He flicked open his snuff-box with one deft finger, and helped himself to a delicate pinch. "On the terrace," he said.

"Oh, no!" she said involuntarily.

"Well, of course, they may have been tempted to take a stroll about the gardens," he conceded. "The terrace, however, was the declared objective."

"I collect it was Lord Lindeth who took her on to the terrace!"

"Do you? *My* reading of the matter was that it was rather Miss Wield who took Lindeth on to it!"

She bit her lip. "She is very young – hardly out of the schoolroom!"

"A reflection which must cause her relations to feel grave concern," he said, in a tone of affable agreement.

She found herself to be so much in accord with him that it was difficult to think of anything to say in extenuation of Tiffany's conduct. "She – she is inclined to be headstrong, and quite ignorant of – of – And since it was your cousin who *most* improperly escorted her I think you should have prevented him!"

"My dear Miss Trent, I'm not Lindeth's keeper! I'm not Miss Wield's keeper either, I thank God!"

"You may well!" she said, with considerable asperity. Then, as she saw the amusement in his face, she added: "Yes, you may laugh, sir, but I *am* Miss Wield's keeper – or, at any rate, I am responsible for her! – and it's no laughing matter to me! I must *do* something!"

She looked round the room as she spoke, a furrow between her brows. It was a warm June night, and the drawing-room was hot and airless. More than one unbecomingly flushed young lady was fanning herself, and several shirt-points were beginning to wilt. Miss Trent's brow cleared; she went up to a little group which included Miss Chartley, the dashing Miss Colebatch, and the younger of the Squire's daughters, with their attendant swains, and said, with her charming smile: "Dreadfully hot, isn't it? I dare not open the windows: you know what an outcry there would be! Would you like to come out for a little while? It is such a beautiful moonlight night, with not a breeze stirring, that I have ventured to direct the servants to bring some lemonade on to the terrace. But you must put on your shawls, mind!"

The suggestion was thankfully acclaimed by the gentlemen, and by the Squire's jolly daughter, who clapped her hands together, exclaiming: "Oh, famous fun! Do let us go!" Miss Chartley, wondering what Mama would say, looked a little doubtful, but decided that if Miss Trent was sponsoring this interlude it must be unexceptionable; and in a very few minutes that resourceful lady had assembled some four or five couples, dropped an urgent word in Totton's astonished ear, and had informed several matrons, with smiling assurance, that she had yielded to the persuasions of their various offspring, and was permitting them (under her chaperonage) to take a turn on the terrace, before resuming their exertions on the floor. She would take good care that none of the young ladies caught chills; and, indeed, must hurry away to be sure that they had put on their shawls.

Sir Waldo was an appreciative spectator of this talented performance; and when Miss Trent, having shepherded her flock on to the terrace, was about to follow them, she found him once more at her elbow, smiling at her in a way which was oddly disturbing. "Well done!" he said, holding back the heavy curtain that hung beside the long window of the saloon that gave on to the terrace.

"Thank you! I hope it may answer, but I'm afraid it will be thought very odd conduct in a respectable governess," she replied, passing out into the moonlight.

"Not at all: you carried it off to admiration," he said, following her. He raised his quizzing-glass, and through it scanned the scene. "I realize, of course, that if the truants have gone farther afield it will be my unenviable task to discover them, and – No, they have not been so imprudent. How fortunate! Now we may both be easy!"

"Yes, indeed!" she responded, with the utmost cordiality. "I was shocked to see you in *such* a worry, sir!"

He laughed, but before he could answer her she had stepped away from him to put a scarf round Tiffany's shoulders. Courtenay, who had been awaiting his moment, seized the opportunity afforded by the Nonesuch's being alone for the first time during the evening to approach him, asking very respectfully if he might procure a glass of champagne for him. He then added, in case the great man should snub him for presuming to address him: "I'm Underhill, you know, sir!"

Sir Waldo declined the champagne, but in a friendly manner which gave the lie to Mr Jack Banningham, who had prophesied that any attempt on Courtenay's part to engage him in conversation would be met with a severe setdown. He said: "We met at the Manor, didn't we? I rather fancy I saw you on the Harrogate road the other day, driving a well ribbed-up bay."

No more encouragement was needed. Within a very few minutes Courtenay was subjecting him to a stringent cross-examination on his real and imagined exploits. He bore it very well, but interrupted at last to say: "But must you throw *all* my youthful follies in my face? I thought I had lived them down!"

Courtenay was shocked; but Miss Trent, standing within earshot, felt that her first favourable impression of the Nonesuch had not been entirely erroneous.

CHAPTER SIX

IT HAD been Mrs Mickleby who had first had the honour of entertaining the Nonesuch and his cousin; but it was generally acknowledged that the event which started the succession of gaieties which made that summer memorable was Mrs Underhill's informal ball. Hostesses who had previously vied with one another only in the mildest ways became suddenly imbued with the spirit of fierce competition; and the invitation cards which showered upon the district promised treats which ranged from turtle-dinners to Venetian breakfasts. Assemblies and picnics became everyday occurrences, even Mrs Chartley succumbing to the prevailing rage, and organizing a select party to partake of an al fresco meal by the ruins of Kirkstall Abbey. This unpretentious expedition achieved a greater degree of success than attended many of the more resplendent entertainments which enlivened the month; for not only did the skies smile upon it, but the Nonesuch graced it with his presence. Mrs Banningham, whose daring Cotillion Ball had fallen sadly flat, for many days found it hard to meet the Rector's wife with even the semblance of cordiality; and it was no consolation to know that she had only herself to blame for the failure of a party designed to outshine all others. She was imprudent enough to exclude the Staples family from the ball, informing her dear friend, Mrs Syston, (in the strictest confidence) that Tiffany Wield should be given no opportunity to flirt with Lord Lindeth under her roof. Mrs Syston told no one the secret, except Mrs Winkleigh, whom she felt sure she could trust not to repeat it; but in some mysterious way Mrs Underhill got wind of Mrs Banningham's fell intention, and nipped in with some invitations of her own before ever Mrs Banningham's gilt-edged cards had been procured from Leeds. One of the under-grooms was sent off with a note to Sir Waldo Hawkridge, inviting him and his cousin to dine at Staples on the fatal day; and no sooner had his acceptance been received than the Chartleys and the Colebatches were also bidden to dine. Not a party, wrote Mrs Underhill to all these persons: just a conversable evening with a few friends.

"And if that don't take Mrs B. at fault, you may call me a wetgoose!" she told Miss Trent. "Done to a cow's thumb, that's what she'll be! She and her Cotillion Balls!"

Great was Mrs Banningham's chagrin when she received Sir Waldo's polite regrets; and greater still her rage when she discovered that all the absentees had been at Staples, eating dinner on the terrace, and then, when the light began to fail, going indoors, either to chat, or to play such childish games as Cross-questions, and Jackstraws. Her own party had been distinguished by a certain languor. Everyone had been disappointed by the absence of the Nonesuch; and if the ladies were glad to find Tiffany absent, almost all the younger gentlemen, including Mrs Banningham's son Jack, considered any ball at which she was not present an intolerable bore. Mrs Banningham was even denied the solace of picturing the Nonesuch's boredom at Staples, for Courtenay told Jack that the party had not broken up till past midnight, and that when it came to playing Jackstraws the Nonesuch had them all beat to flinders, even Miss Trent, who had such deft fingers. It seemed that he had challenged Miss Trent to a match, when he discovered how good she was at the game. Capital sport it had been, too, with Sir Ralph Colebatch offering odds on Miss Trent, and even the Rector wagering a coachwheel on the issue. Mrs Banningham could not delude herself, or anyone else, into thinking that the Nonesuch had been bored.

He had not been at all bored; nor had Julian found it difficult to persuade him to accept Mrs Underhill's invitation. The Nonesuch, who had meant to spend no more time in Yorkshire than might be necessary for setting in train certain repairs and alterations to Broom Hall, was lingering on, and under conditions of some discomfort, since the builders were already at work in the house. He had his own reasons for remaining; but if he could have placed the slightest dependance on Julian's going back with him to London he would have subordinated these (temporarily, at all events), for the sake of conveying that besotted young man out of danger. But when he had thrown out a feeler Julian had said, with studied airiness: "Do you know, I rather fancy I shall remove to Harrogate for a while, if you mean to go back to London? I like Yorkshire, and I've made certain engagements – and more than half promised to go with Edward Banningham to some races next month."

So he remained at Broom Hall, steering an intricate course between his own interests and Julian's. His trusting young cousin would have been astonished, and deeply shocked, had he known that Waldo's lazy complaisance masked a grim determination to thrust a spoke into the wheel of his courtship. His allegiance to Waldo was too strong to be easily shaken; he did not for a moment wish him otherwhere; but he was often troubled by vague discomfort; and although Waldo had not uttered a word in her dispraise he could not rid himself of the suspicion that he regarded Tiffany a little contemptuously, and too often treated her as though she had been an importunate child, to be tolerated but given a few salutory set-downs. And then, having infuriated her, he would relent, charming her out of her sullens with his glinting smile, and a word or two spoken in a voice that held a tantalizing mixture of amusement and admiration. Even Julian could not decide whether he was sincere, or merely mocking; Julian only knew that Tiffany was never at her best when he was present. He thought that perhaps she too felt that Waldo did not like her, which made her nervous and selfconscious. And when you were very young, and shy, and anxious to make a good impression on someone of whom you stood in awe it was fatally easy to behave like a show-off character in your efforts to conceal your shyness. It did not occur to Julian that there was not a particle of shyness in Tiffany's nature; still less that Waldo was deliberately provoking her to betray the least amiable side of her disposition.

But Sir Waldo, with fifteen years' experience at his back, had taken Tiffany's measure almost at a glance. It was not his custom to trifle with the affections of fledglings, but within a week of having made Tiffany's acquaintance he set himself, without compunction, to the task of intriguing her to the point of pursuing him in preference to Julian. He had had too many lures cast out to him not to recognize the signs of a lady desirous of engaging his interest; and he knew that for some reason beyond his understanding he possessed the wholly unwanted gift of inspiring débutantes with romantic but misplaced *tendres* for him. He had been on his guard ever since he had been (as he had supposed) paternally kind to the niece of an old friend. She had tumbled into love with him; and from this embarrassing situation he had learnt also to recognize the signs of a maiden on the verge of losing her heart to him. Since he had nothing but contempt for the man of the world who amused himself at the expense of a pretty girl's sensibility, it was his practice to discourage any such tendency. Had he detected in Tiffany the least indication of a romantic disposition he would have adhered to his rule; but he saw nothing in her but a determination to add his name to the roll of her conquests, and strongly doubted that she had a heart to lose. If he was wrong, he thought, cynically, that it would do her no harm to experience some of the pangs of unrequited love with which her numerous suitors were afflicted. He believed her to be as selfish as she was conceited; and, while it was possible that time might improve her, he was persuaded that neither her disposition nor her breeding made her an eligible wife for young Lord Lindeth.

He had told Miss Trent that he was not Lindeth's keeper, and that, in the strictest sense, was true. Julian's father had left him to the guardianship of his mother, and had appointed two middle-aged legal gentlemen as his trustees; but Sir Waldo's shrewd Aunt Sophia had enlisted his aid in rearing the noble orphan at a very early stage in Julian's career, and he had progressed, by imperceptible degrees, from the splendid cousin who initiated his protégé into every manly form of sport (besides sending him guineas under the seals of his occasional letters, and from time to time descending in a blaze of real dapper-dog magnificence on Eton, driving a team of sixteen-mile-an-hour tits, and treating half-a-dozen of his cousin's cons to such sock as made them the envy of every Oppidan and Tug in the College) to the social mentor who introduced Julian into select circles, and steered him past the shoals in which many a green navigator had wallowed and foundered. He had come to regard Julian as his especial charge; and although Julian's years now numbered three-and-twenty he still so regarded him: Lady Lindeth could not blame him more than he would blame himself if he allowed Julian to be trapped into a disastrous marriage without raising a finger to prevent it.

To cut out a young cousin who reposed complete trust in him might go very much against the pluck with him, but it presented few difficulties to a man of his address and experience. Indulged almost from the hour of her birth; endowed not only with beauty but with a considerable independance as well; encouraged to think herself a matrimonial prize of the first stare, Tiffany had come to regard every unattached man's homage as her due. Sir Waldo had watched her at the Staples ball, playing off her cajolery in an attempt to attach Humphrey Colebatch; and he had not the smallest doubt that she did it only because that scholarly but unprepossessing youth was patently impervious to her charms. He was well aware, too, that while she would look upon his own capture as a resounding triumph he ranked in her eyes amongst the graybeards who had outlived the age of gallantry. There had been speculation, and a hint of doubt, in the swift glance she had first thrown him. She had certainly set her cap at him, but he could have nipped her tentative advances in the bud with the utmost ease. He would have done it had he not seen the glow in Julian's eyes as they rested on her ravishing countenance, and realized that that guileless young man was wholly dazzled.

Sir Waldo was neither dazzled by Tiffany's beauty, nor so stupid as to suppose that any good purpose would be served by his pointing out to Julian those defects in the lovely creature which were perfectly plain to him, but to which Julian was obviously blind. But Julian, under his compliance, had a sensibility, and a delicacy of principle, to which virtues Sir Waldo judged Tiffany to be a stranger; and nothing could more effectually cool his ardour than the discovery that in their stead she had vanity, and a sublime disregard for the comfort or the susceptibilities of anyone but herself. Julian might ignore, and indignantly resent, warnings uttered by even so revered a mentor as his Top-of-the-Trees cousin, but he would not disbelieve the evidence of his own eyes. So the Nonesuch, instead of damping the beautiful Miss Wield's pretensions, blew hot and cold on her, encouraging her one day to believe that she had awakened his interest, and the next devoting himself to some other lady. He paid her occasional compliments, but was just as likely to utter a lazy set-down; and when he engaged her in a little mild flirtation he did it so lightly that she could never be quite sure that he was not merely being playful, in the manner of a man amusing a child. She had not previously encountered his like, for her admirers were all much younger men, quite lacking in subtlety. Either they languished for love of her, or (like Humphrey Colebatch) paid no attention to her at all. But the Nonesuch, by turns fascinating and detestable, was maddeningly elusive; and so far from showing a disposition to languish he laughed at her suitors, and said that they were making great cakes of themselves. Tiffany took that as an insult, and determined to bring him to her feet. He saw the flash of anger in her eyes, and smiled. "No, no! You'd be gapped, you know."

"I don't know what you mean!"

"Why, that you're wondering whether you might not make me a great cake. I shouldn't attempt it, if I were you: I never dangle – not even after quite pretty girls."

"Quite pretty?" she gasped. *"M-me?"*

"Oh, decidedly!" he said, perfectly gravely. "Or so I think, but, then, I've no prejudice against dark girls. I daresay others might not agree with me."

"They do!" she asserted, pink with indignation. "They say – *everyone* says I'm *beautiful!*"

He managed to preserve his countenance, but his lips twitched slightly. "Yes, of course," he replied. "It's well known that *all heiresses are beautiful!*"

She stared up at him incredulously. "But-but don't you think I'm beautiful?"

"Very!"

"Well, I know I am," she said candidly. "Ancilla thinks I shouldn't say so – and I meant not to, on account of losing some of my beauty when I do. At least, that's what Ancilla said, but I don't see how it could be so, do you?"

"No, indeed: quite absurd! You do very right to mention the matter."

She thought this over, darkly suspicious, and finally demanded: "Why?"

"People are so unobservant!" he answered in dulcet accents.

She broke into a trill of delicious laughter. "Oh, abominable! You are the *horridest* creature! I'll have no more to do with you!"

He waved a careless farewell as she flitted away, but he thought privately that when she forgot her affectations, and laughed out suddenly, acknowledging a hit, she was disastrously engaging.

Miss Trent, who had approached them in time to hear these last sallies, observed in a dispassionate voice: "*Quite* abominable!"

He smiled, his eyes dwelling appreciatively on her. She was always very simply attired; but she wore the inexpensive muslins and cambrics which she fashioned for herself with an air of elegance; and never had he seen her, even on the hottest day, presenting anything but a cool and uncrumpled appearance.

Sir Waldo, having cleared up one small misunderstanding, had contrived to get upon excellent terms with Miss Trent. His ear had been quick to catch the note of constraint in her voice when she had asked him if he was acquainted with her cousin; he fancied that she was pleased when he disclaimed any knowledge of Mr Bernard Trent; and he presently sought enlightenment of Julian.

"Bernard Trent?" said Julian. "No, I don't think – oh, yes, I do, though! You mean General Trent's son, don't you? I've only seen him by scraps: the sort of cawker who talks flash, and is buckish about horses!" He broke off, as a thought occurred to him, and exclaimed: "Good God, is he related to Miss Trent?"

"Her cousin, I collect."

"Lord! Well, he's the greatest gull that ever was!" said Julian frankly. "Crony of Mountsorrel's – at Harrow together, I fancy – and you know what a Peep o' Day boy *he* is, Waldo! Always kicking up larks, and thinking himself at home to a peg, which the lord knows he ain't, and going about town accompanied by the worst barnacles you ever clapped eyes on!"

"Yes, I know young Mountsorrel: one of the newer Tulips!"

"Tulips!" snorted Julian, with all the scorn of one who had been introduced, at his first coming-out, into the pink of Corinthian society. "Smatterers, more like! A set of roly-poly fellows who think it makes them regular dashes to box the Watch, or get swine-drunk at the Field of Blood! And as for being of the Corinthian-cut – why, most of 'em ain't even fit to go!"

"You're very severe!" said Sir Waldo, amused.

"Well, it was you who taught me to be!" Julian retorted. "Mountsorrel is nothing but a cod's head, I own, but only think of the ramshackle fellows he's in a string with! There's Watchett, for instance: he wears more capes to his driving-coat than you do, but you'll none of you admit him to the Four-Horse Club! Stone, too! *His* notion of sport is bull-baiting, and going on the spree in Tothill Fields. Then there's Elstead: he knocks-up more horses in a season than you would in a lifetime, and flies at anything in the shape of gaming. Thinks himself slap up to the echo. Why, when were you ever seen rubbing shoulders in one of the Pall Mall hells with a set of Greek banditti?"

"Is that what young Trent does?"

"I don't know: not a friend of mine. I haven't seen him lately: rusticating, I daresay. He didn't look to me like a downy one, so you may depend upon it he found himself in Tow Street."

Armed with this information, Sir Waldo very soon found the opportunity to set himself right with Miss Trent. Wasting no subtlety, he told her cheerfully that she had misjudged him.

They were riding side by side, Julian and Tiffany a little way ahead. Mrs Underhill felt herself powerless to prevent the almost daily rides of this couple, but she did insist on Ancilla's accompanying them, and was sometimes able to persuade her son to join the party. Occasionally Patience Chartley went with them; and, quite frequently, Sir Waldo.

Ancilla turned her head to look at him, raising her brows. "In what way, sir?"

"In laying your cousin's follies at my door." He smiled at her startled look, and betraying flush. "What happened to him? Lindeth tells me he's in a string with young Mountsorrel, and his set."

"He was used to be – he and Lord Mountsorrel were at school together – but no longer, I hope. His connection with him was ruinous."

"Ran into Dun territory, did he? The younger men don't come much in my way, but I've always understood that Mountsorrel has more money than sense, which makes him dangerous company for other greenhorns. Too many gull-catchers hang about him – not to mention the Bloods, and the Dashers, and the Care-for-Nobodies."

"Yes. My uncle said that, or something like it. But indeed I never laid Bernard's follies at your door, sir!"

"Didn't you? That's discouraging: I believed I had solved the riddle of your dislike of me."

"I don't dislike you. If-if you thought me stiff when we first met it was because I dislike the set you represent!"

"I don't think you know anything about the set I represent," he responded coolly. "Let me assure you that it is very far removed from Mountsorrel's, ma'am!"

"Of course but you are – oh, the Nonesuch!" she said with a quick smile. "Mountsorrel and his friends copy you as far as they are able -"

"I beg your pardon!" he interrupted. "They don't – being *un*able! Dear me, I sound just like the Beautiful Miss Wield, don't I? Some of them copy the Corinthian rig in the exaggerated form I *don't* affect; but *my* set, Miss Trent, is composed of men who were born with a natural aptitude for athletic sports. We *do* the thing; Mountsorrel, and his kind, are lookers-on. Don't ask me why they should ape our fashions, when there is nothing more distasteful to them, I daresay, than the sports we enjoy, for I can't tell you! But you may believe that the youngster anxious to excel in sporting exercises is safer amongst the Corinthians than amongst the Bond Street beaux."

"Ah, yes, but – does it not lead to more dangerous things? To gaming, for instance?"

"Gaming, Miss Trent, is not confined to any one class of society," he said dryly. "It won't lead him to haunt the wine-shops in Tothill Fields, to wake the night-music, or to pursue the – er – West-end comets, to his destruction." He laughed suddenly. "You foolish girl! Don't you know that if he did so it would be bellows to mend with him within five minutes of his engaging in a little sparring exercise at Jackson's?"

"To own the truth, I had never considered the matter," she confessed. "Though I do recall, now you put me in mind of it, that whenever my brother Harry was engaged to play in a cricket-match, or some such thing, he was used to take the greatest pains not to put himself out of frame, as he called it."

"Wise youth! Is he too a budding Corinthian?"

"Oh, no! He is a soldier."

"Like your uncle!"

"Yes, and my father, too."

"Indeed? Tell me about him! Was he engaged at Waterloo?"

"Yes – that is, my brother was, but not my father. My father was killed at Ciudad Rodrigo."

"I am sorry." His tone was grave; but he did not pursue the subject, asking her instead, after a moment or two, if her brother was with the Army of Occupation. She was grateful to him for respecting her reserve, and answered far more readily than she might have done. She seldom mentioned her family, for Mrs Underhill was interested only in the General; and although Mrs Chartley sometimes enquired kindly after her mother, and her brothers, she rarely allowed herself to be lured into giving more than civil responses, feeling that Mrs Chartley could have little interest in persons with whom she was unacquainted.

Sir Waldo was much more successful in winning her out of her reticence; and it was not many days before he knew more about Miss Trent's family than Mrs Chartley, preoccupied with her own family and her husband's parish, had even guessed. He knew that Will – the best of all sons and brothers! – was the incumbent of a parish in Derbyshire, and already the father of a hopeful family. He had married the daughter of one of Papa's oldest friends, a dear, good girl, beloved of them all. Mama and Sally lived with him and Mary, and in the greatest harmony. Sally was the youngest of the family: only a schoolroom child yet, but already remarkably accomplished, and bidding fair to become a very pretty girl. Christopher joined them during the holidays, except when his uncle invited him to stay in London, and indulged him with all manner of high treats, from snipeshooting in Regent's Park, or skating on the Serpentine, to Astley's Amphitheatre, and pugilistic displays at the Fives Court. Uncle Mordaunt had taken upon his shoulders the whole charge of Kit's education at Harrow. Nothing could exceed Uncle Mordaunt's goodness and generosity: in spite of possessing a fortune that was genteel rather than handsome he had been almost at outs with them all for refusing to live upon his bounty! But with Will so comfortably situated; and Harry now able (since he got his Company) to contribute towards the family funds; and Mama teaching Sally herself, which she was well qualified to do, being the daughter of a Professor of Greek, and (as they told her when they wanted to joke her) very *blue*! It would be shocking to be so much beholden.

"And the elder Miss Trent, I collect, doesn't choose to be in any way beholden?"

"No more than I need. But you mustn't suppose that I am not already very much obliged to my uncle and aunt, if you please! My aunt was so kind as to bring me out, as the saying is – and to spare no pains to get me eligibly riveted!" she added, a gurgle of laughter in her throat. "She had a strong persuasion that even though I've no fortune a respectable alliance might have been achieved for me would I but *apply* myself to the business! Oh, dear! I ought not to laugh at her, for she bore with me most patiently, but she *is* such a funny one!"

His eyes gleamed appreciatively, but he said: "Poor lady! Were you never tempted to apply yourself?"

"No, I was always old cattish," she replied cheerfully.

"Were you indeed? Did you remain with your uncle for only one season?"

She nodded. "Yes, but pray don't imagine that I might not have stayed had I wished to do so! To have done so when he has three daughters of his own to bring out would have been rather too strong, I thought – particularly when Bernard had got so shockingly into debt."

"So you became a governess! Not without opposition, I should suppose!"

"Oh, no! Will and Harry made a great dust, and even Mary said she took it very unkind in me not to wish to live at their expense. They all pictured me eking out a miserable existence on a pittance – and used as if I had been a slave into the bargain! The only comfort they could find was in the thought that I could return to them if I found my lot insupportable."

"Have you never done so?" he asked, looking rather searchingly at her.

"No, never. No doubt I might have done so, but I've been singularly fortunate. Miss Climping, dear creature, treated me as though I had been her niece rather than the junior mistress; and it was she who recommended me to Mrs Burford, to take charge of Tiffany."

"Good God, do you count that good fortune?"

"Most certainly I do! My dear sir, if I were to tell you what an enormous wage I'm paid it would make you stare!"

"I know very little about such matters, but I seem to have heard that an upper man can command a bigger wage than a governess."

"Ah, but I am a very superior governess!" she said, putting on an air of large consequence. "Only fancy! Besides such commonplace subjects as water-colour sketching and the use of the globes, I instruct my pupils in music – both pianoforte and harp; and can speak and read French *and* Italian!"

"I have no doubt at all that you earn every penny of your hire," he said, smiling.

She laughed. "The mischief is that I don't! My conscience pricks me very often, I promise you, for Charlotte has neither inclination nor aptitude; and

Tiffany will do no more than commit to memory the words of an Italian song. I've convinced her that *some* skill on the pianoforte is an indispensable accomplishment for a lady with social ambitions; but nothing will prevail upon her to play the harp. She complains that it breaks her nails, and says that it is better to have pretty nails than to be able to perform upon the harp."

"I still maintain that you earn your hire, ma'am!"

He was thinking of this interchange when she joined him on the terrace, saying: "*Quite* abominable!" He was well aware by this time that her position was far more that of guardian than governess; and as he believed that she had too much intelligence not to have realized what was the end to which his dealings with Tiffany were directed he lived in daily expectation of being called to book. It seemed to him that Mrs Underhill viewed Julian's infatuation with complaisance. Far from demurring at his frequent visits she had begged them both to treat Staples as their own, standing upon no ceremony. "For very uncomfortable it must be at Broom Hall, with builders working there, and plaster-dust in everything, as well I know it is!" she had said. "So take your pot-luck with us, Sir Waldo, whenever you fancy, and be sure you'll be very welcome!"

He said now, leading Miss Trent to one of the rustic seats on the terrace: "Very true! But do you think it will do your ravishing charge any harm to receive a few set-downs?"

"Oh, no!" she replied calmly. "I fear it won't do her any good either – but that, after all, is not your object, is it?"

He checked her, as she was about to sit down, saying: "One moment! You will have the sun in your eyes: I'll turn the seat a little."

She let him do so, but said, smiling faintly: "Trying to change the subject, sir?"

"No, no! Just sparring for wind, ma'am!"

"I imagine that to be some horrid boxing cant," she observed, seating herself. "I trust, however, that you don't think me such a ninny as to be blind to what *is* your object?"

He sat down beside her. "No, I don't," he confessed. "I'll own to you that I've been torn between the hope that you did know, and the dread of having a peal rung over me!"

If she blushed it was so slightly that he was unaware of it. She replied, ignoring the first part of his sentence: "Oh, I don't mean to scold!"

"Now you *have* surprised me!" he remarked.

"I suppose, under certain circumstances I might scold," she said thoughtfully. "But my situation is rather difficult. The thing is, you see, that Mrs Underhill doesn't wish Tiffany to marry your cousin any more than you do."

"In that case, it is a little astonishing that she should encourage Julian to run tame here," he said sceptically.

"I daresay it may seem so to you, not knowing Tiffany as well as I – we – do. I can assure you that if her mind is set on anything the least hint of opposition is enough to goad her into going her length, however outrageous that may be. And in general it *is* outrageous," she added candidly. "You will allow that an *à suivie* flirtation, conducted in my presence, or her aunt's, is by far less dangerous than clandestine meetings would be. For one thing, it is not so romantic; and, for another, such meetings would of necessity be infrequent, as well as brief, and that, you know, would preclude her becoming bored with Lord Lindeth."

He could not help smiling at her matter-of-factness, but he said: "Yes, I will allow that, ma'am. I will even concede that the girl might prevail upon Lindeth to meet her in such a way. But when you talk of her becoming *bored* with him I think you are wide of the mark. I daresay she may be – but Lindeth would be a big prize for her to win."

She wrinkled her brow. "Well,it is very natural that you should think that, but *she* doesn't. She means to marry a Marquis."

"Means to – *Which* Marquis?"

"*Any* Marquis," Ancilla replied.

"Of all the absurdities!"

"I don't know that. When you consider that besides beauty she is possessed of a handsome fortune you must surely own that a brilliant match is by no means impossible. In any event, I beg you won't depress *that* one of her pretensions! I have suggested to her that to form a connection with a mere baron and before she is even out! – would be perfectly bird-witted!"

He regarded her in some amusement. "Have you, indeed? What a very odd sort of a governess you are, ma'am!"

"Yes, and you can't imagine what a worry I have been in, trying to decide what I ought to do in this troublesome situation," she said seriously. "I *think* I am right to scotch the affair, if I can; for while, on the one hand, the Burfords might welcome the match; on the other, Mrs Underhill would not, and Tiffany is too young to be contracted to anyone."

"Why wouldn't Mrs Underhill welcome the match?"

"Because she wants Tiffany to marry her cousin, of course."

"Good God! I should have said that the boy holds her in contempt and dislike!"

"Mrs Underwood thinks they will learn to love one another."

"Foolish beyond permission! Isn't he dangling after the pretty redhead?"

"Yes, and I should think they will make a match of it one day," she agreed. "Which would be a very good thing, for they suit wonderfully. And once Tiffany has left Staples, which will be next year, when her aunt Burford is pledged to bring her out, Mrs Underhill will very soon become reconciled. In the meantime, I do believe it to be my duty to do my possible to keep Tiffany quite – quite unattached!" She smiled kindly upon him, and added: "So I am very grateful to you for your assistance, Sir Waldo!"

"Even though – if the little minx has made up her mind to marry a Marquis! – it must be thought superfluous!"

"Oh, no! We can't foretell what *might* happen, you know. Tiffany is only a precocious child, and although she may indulge dreams of grandeur she doesn't *scheme*. Would you care to say that she won't take just enough fancy to Lord Lindeth to imagine herself in love? I promise you I wouldn't! He is very good-looking, you know, besides having such engaging manners! Indeed, I am more than half in love with him myself!"

"Now, that I utterly forbid!" he declared.

She laughed. "I should rather think you might! I must be several years his senior. But in all seriousness, sir, a marriage between him and Tiffany would not do!"

"I am well aware of it."

"Even if her birth matched his!" she said earnestly. "It must seem shocking in me to say such a thing of her, but I feel it would be quite wicked of me not to put you on your guard!"

"You believe it to be necessary?"

"I don't know. I've seen how she can bring people round her thumb, and how charming she can be, when she chooses. But she hasn't a particle of that sweetness of disposition which is in your cousin, and nothing but misery could be the outcome of a marriage between them!"

"Let me assure you, ma'am, since you seem to think I might succumb to her wiles, that my taste runs to females of quite another complexion!"

"I am glad of it," she said, thinking, however, that he might well be courting more danger than he was yet aware of.

"That's the kindest thing you have yet said to me," he murmured.

She glanced at him, a puzzled expression in her eyes. They met his, and saw that they were quizzically smiling; and the suspicion flashed into her mind that he was trying to beguile her into flirtation. It was swiftly succeeded by the startling realization that she could very easily be so beguiled. That would never do, of course; so she said lightly: "I should be sorry to see anyone in Tiffany's toils. Which puts me in mind of something I had to say to you! Tell me, Sir Waldo, what do you think of this proposed expedition to Knaresborough?"

"Too far, and the weather too sultry," he replied, tacitly accepting her rebuff. He thought she sighed faintly, and said: "Do you wish for it, then?"

"I own I should like to go, if it were possible. Your cousin's description of the Dripping Well made me long to see it. Tiffany, too. No sooner had Lord Lindeth told us of the wild, ragged rocks, and the cavern which was once the lair of bandits than she became mad after it!"

He smiled. "*Mysteries of Udolpho*?"

"Naturally! And I must own that it sounds most romantic. Isn't it odd that it should be Lord Lindeth, a stranger to the district, who should have told us about it?"

"Oh, no! Natives are never enraptured by their surroundings. *Over great familiarity*, you know, *genders despite*."

"Very true. I wish it were not too far to make an expedition eligible. I had not thought it above sixteen miles."

"Which would mean a ride of thirty-two miles."

"Nothing of the sort! Two rides of sixteen miles, with a long rest between for repose and refreshment! That's a very different matter."

"Out again, Miss Trent! Refreshment, certainly; but instead of reposing yourself you would spend your time clambering up rocky crags, and exploring caverns. Why don't you go by carriage, if go you must?"

"Because nothing would prevail upon Tiffany to sit beside me in a carriage, driving sedately along the road when she might be on horseback, enjoying a canter over the moor. To be honest with you, I should think it sadly flat myself! Do you picture us being quite knocked up? I know my own powers, and as for Tiffany, she is the most indefatigable girl imaginable. However, it *is* very hot, so I'll say no more."

"*You* may say no more, but if the Beautiful Baggage is indeed mad after it there will be not the least need for you to do so, will there?"

She choked, but replied awfully: "Sir Waldo, you go too far! Besides, you have only to drop a word in your cousin's ear to make him cry off, which will end the matter."

"My dear Miss Trent, if it would give you pleasure to go I withdraw my objection. In fact, I'll accompany you."

There could be no denying that it was very agreeable to be talked to in such a manner. Miss Trent was no self-deceiver, and she did not deny it; but she was uneasily aware of running the risk of forming far too strong an attachment to the Nonesuch. Commonsense told her that he was merely alleviating boredom with a little dalliance, probably thinking (for she was persuaded he would not wantonly trifle with any female's affections) that she was past the age of being taken in by his light advances; but although there was often a laugh in his eyes there was also a certain warmth, and, in his voice, a note of sincerity hard to withstand. She remembered that her aunt had told her once, in a moment of exasperation, that she was a great deal too nice in her requirements; and she thought, wryly, that poor Lady Trent had spoken more truly than she knew, and would have been as much surprised as dismayed to have learnt that her provoking niece, having repulsed two very eligible suitors, had discovered that no less a personage than the Nonesuch would do for her.

It would be fatal to indulge a *tendre* for him; and the wisest course to pursue would be to avoid his company; but as this, in the circumstances, was impossible, the next best thing would be to maintain a cool friendliness. So she said, with all the composure at her command: "Yes, it would be prudent in you to do so, no doubt. *Your* presence will divert Tiffany far more surely than mine."

"Oh, I've another reason than that!" he said.

She put up her brows, saying frigidly: "Indeed?"

The disarming twinkle was in his eyes. "Four is a more comfortable number than three, don't you think?" he suggested blandly.

She agreed to it, but with a quivering lip. Sir Waldo, duly noting this circumstance, continued to expatiate on the advantages of adding a second gentleman to the expedition, producing several which made it quite impossible for Miss Trent to keep her countenance. He was interrupted in this unchivalrous assault upon her defences by the reappearance on the scene of Tiffany, who came dancing out on to the terrace with Julian and Courtenay at her heels, and disclosed that the party of four had become a party of six.

"We have settled it between us to go to Knaresborough on Friday!" she announced, sparkling with delight. "It is to be a regular cavalcade, which will be such good fun! Lizzie Colebatch is to go with us, and Courtenay too, of course. And you, Sir Waldo – if you please?"

It was said so prettily, and with such an appealing smile, that he thought it no wonder that Julian should watch her in blatant admiration. He replied: "Thank you: I do please!"

"Miss Colebatch!" Ancilla exclaimed, taken aback. "Tiffany, I don't think Lady Colebatch will permit her to go!"

"Yes, yes, she will!" Tiffany asserted, with a trill of laughter. "Lindeth and Courtenay have persuaded her, promising that *you* will be with us, you dear dragon!"

"Yes, but that's not what I mean," said Ancilla. "Miss Colebatch dislikes the hot weather so much that I should have thought her mama must have forbidden her to go on such an expedition. Does she perfectly understand where it is you mean to go?"

She was reassured on this point; but although Lady Colebatch's sanction made it improper for her to raise any further objection she could not feel at ease. Lady Colebatch was an indolent, good-natured woman who was much inclined to let her children overrule her judgment, but Ancilla knew how quickly Elizabeth wilted in the heat, and began to wish that the expedition had never been projected. Courtenay was confident that all would be well, for they meant to make an early start, so that they would have reached Knaresborough long before midday; and Tiffany said gaily that Lizzie only disliked the heat because it made her skin so red.

The three younger members of the party then began to discuss the route they should follow, the hour at which they should assemble, and the rival merits of the various inns in Knaresborough, Julian inviting the company to partake of a nuncheon at the Crown and Bell, and Courtenay asserting that the Bay Horse was superior.

"Well, as you wish!" Julian said. "You must know better than I do! Shall we ask Miss Chartley to go with us? Would she care for it?"

"Patience! Good gracious, no!" exclaimed Tiffany. "What put such a notion as that into your head?"

"You don't think she would like it? But she's an excellent horsewoman, and I know she loves exploring ancient places, for she told me so."

"Told you so? When?" demanded Tiffany.

"At Kirkstall, when we were wandering about the ruins. She knows almost as much as her father – do let us invite her to go with us!"

Miss Trent found herself digging her nails into the palms of her hands. It was irrational, but little as she wanted Tiffany to captivate Lindeth she could not help dreading the threatened tantrum. Since Courtenay was the one marriageable man whose devotion Tiffany neither desired nor demanded she was perfectly happy to include Miss Colebatch in the party, but that any one of her admirers should betray even the smallest interest in another lady invariably roused a demon of jealousy in her breast. She said now, with a glittering smile, well-known to her family: "Why? Do you like her so much?"

He looked at her in a little surprise. "Yes – that is, I *like* her, of course! I should think everyone must."

"Oh, if you have a fancy for insipid girls -!" she said, shrugging.

"Do you think her insipid?" he asked. "She doesn't seem so to me. She is very gentle, and persuadable, I agree, but not *insipid*, surely! She doesn't want for sense, you know."

"Oh, she has *every* virtue, and *every* amiable quality! For my part, I find her prosy propriety a dead bore – but that's of no consequence! Do, pray, invite her! I daresay she will be able to recite you the whole history of the Dripping Well!"

Even Julian could not mistake the rancour behind the smile. Miss Trent saw the slight look of shock in his face, and decided that she could not bear to hear her charge expose herself any more. She said quietly: "I am afraid it would be useless to invite Miss Chartley, sir. I know that Mrs Chartley wouldn't permit her to go with us on such a long, fatiguing expedition. Indeed, I begin to wonder whether we should any of us attempt it."

This alarming apostasy caused an instant throw-up. Miss Chartley was forgotten in the more urgent necessity of alternately abusing Miss Trent for chickenheartedness, and cajoling her into unsaying her words. But before he left Staples Julian had received from Tiffany an explanation of her spiteful outburst which quite cleared the cloud from his brow. She owned her fault so contritely that he longed to take her in his arms and kiss away her troubled look. He perfectly understood how provoking it must be to have Patience Chartley held up to her continually as a model; and he thought her penitence so candid and so humble that by the time he took his leave he had not only assured her that she was not in the least to be blamed for flying into a pet, but also that he didn't care a rush whether or not Patience went with them to Knaresborough. Later, he tried to disabuse his cousin's mind of whatever unjust thoughts it might harbour: not because Waldo referred to the matter, but because it seemed to him that he carefully avoided doing so. He said rather haltingly: "I daresay it may have seemed odd to you that Miss Wield was – that she shouldn't wish for Miss Chartley to accompany us on Friday."

"What, after such a slip-slop as you made?" said Sir Waldo, laughing. "Not in the least odd! You *did* grass yourself, didn't you? I hadn't believed you could be such a greenhorn."

Flushing, Julian said stiffly: "I don't understand what you mean! If you imagine that Miss Wield was – was cross because I wished to invite Miss Chartley – it wasn't so at all!"

"Wasn't it?" said Sir Waldo, amusement lurking beneath his too-obviously assumed gravity. "Well, take my advice, you young cawker, and never praise one woman to another!"

"You are quite mistaken!" said Julian, more stiffly than ever.

"Yes, yes, of course I am – being so green myself!" agreed Sir Waldo soothingly. "So, for God's sake, don't stir any more coals to convince me of it! I am convinced – wholly! – and I detest brangles!"

CHAPTER SEVEN

MR UNDERHILL'S optimistic plan of making an early start on Friday morning was not realized. He was certainly up betimes; but in spite of his having hammered on his cousin's door at an early hour, warning her to make haste, since it was going to be a scorching day, the rest of the breakfast-party, which included Sir Waldo and Lord Lindeth, had finished the handsome repast provided for them before Tiffany came floating into the parlour, artlessly enquiring whether she was late.

"Yes, you are!" growled Courtenay. "We've been waiting for you this age! What the deuce have you been about? You have had time enough to rig yourself out a dozen times!"

"That's just what she does," said Charlotte impishly. "First she puts one dress on, and decides it don't become her, and so then she tries another – don't you, cousin?"

"Well, I'm sure you look very becoming in that habit, love," interposed Mrs Underhill hastily. "Though if I was you I wouldn't choose to wear velvet, not in this weather!"

By the time Tiffany had eaten her breakfast, put on her hat to her satisfaction, and found such unaccountably mislaid articles as her gloves, and her riding-whip, the hour was considerably advanced, and Courtenay in a fret of impatience, saying that Lizzie must be supposing by now that they had forgotten all about her. However, when they reached Colby Place they found the family just getting up from the breakfast-table, and Lizzie by no means ready to set out. There was thus a further delay while Lizzie ran upstairs to complete her toilet, accompanied by her two younger sisters, who were presently heard demanding of some apparently remote person what she had done with Miss Lizzie's boots.

During this period Lindeth and Tiffany enjoyed a quiet flirtation, Sir Ralph gave the Nonesuch a long and involved account of his triumph over someone who had tried to get the better of him in a bargain, Courtenay fidgeted about the room, and Lady Colebatch prosed to Miss Trent with all the placidity of one to whom time meant nothing.

"Only two hours later than was planned," remarked Sir Waldo, when the calvacade at last set forth. "Very good!"

Miss Trent, who had been regretting for nearly as long that she had ever expressed a wish to see the Dripping Well, replied: "I suppose it might have been expected!"

"Yes, and I did expect it," he said cheerfully.

"I wonder then that you should have lent yourself to this expedition."

"One becomes inured to the unpunctuality of your sex, ma'am," he responded.

Incensed by this unjust animadversion, she said tartly: "Let me inform you, sir, that *I* kept no one waiting!"

"But you are a very exceptional female," he pointed out.

"I assure you, I am nothing of the sort."

"I shall not allow you to be a judge of that. Oh, no, don't look at me so crossly! What can I possibly have said to vex you?"

"I beg your pardon! Nothing, of course: merely, I'm not in the mood for nonsense, Sir Waldo!"

"That's no reason for scowling at me!" he objected. "I haven't been boring you to death for the past half-hour! Of course, I may bore you before the day is out, but it won't be with vapid commonplaces, I promise you."

"Take care!" she warned him, glancing significantly towards Miss Colebatch, who was riding ahead of them, with Courtenay.

"Neither of them is paying the least heed to us. Do you always ride that straightshouldered cocktail?"

"Yes – Mrs Underhill having bought him for my use. He does very well for me."

"I wish I had the mounting of you. Do you hunt?"

"No. When Tiffany goes out with the hounds she is her cousin's responsibility, not mine."

"Thank God for that! You would certainly come to grief if you attempted to hunt that animal. I only hope you may not be saddle-sick before ever we reach Knaresborough."

"Indeed, so do I! I don't know why you should think me such a poor creature!"

"I don't: I think your horse a poor creature, and a most uncomfortable ride."

"Oh, no, I assure you -" She broke off, checked by a lifted eyebrow. "Well, perhaps he is not very – very easy-paced! In any event, I don't mean to argue with you about him, for I am persuaded it would be very stupid in me to do so."

"It would," he agreed. "I collect it didn't occur to your amiable charge to lend you her other hack? By the bye, what made your resolution fail the other day?"

She did not pretend to misunderstand him, but answered frankly: "I *couldn't* allow her to expose herself!"

He smiled. "Couldn't you? Never mind! I fancy she contrived to charm Lindeth out of his disapproval, but the image became just a trifle smudged, nevertheless. I added my mite later in the day – which is why I am being treated with a little reserve."

"Are you? Oh, dear, how horrid it is, and how very difficult to know what my duty is! Odious to be scheming against the child!"

"Is that what you are doing? I had no notion of it, and thought the scheming was all on my side."

"Not precisely scheming, but – but *conniving*, by allowing you to bamboozle her!"

"My dear girl, how do you imagine you could stop me?"

Miss Trent toyed with the idea of objecting to this mode of address, and then decided that it would be wiser to ignore it. "I don't know, but -"

"Nor anyone else. Don't tease yourself to no purpose! You are really quite helpless in the matter, you know."

She turned her head, gravely regarding him. "Don't you feel some compunction, Sir Waldo?"

"None at all. I should feel much more than compunction if I did not do my utmost to prevent Lindeth's falling a victim to as vain and heartless a minx as I have yet had the ill-fortune to encounter. Do I seem to you a villain? I promise you I am not!"

"No, no! But you do make her show her worst side!"

"True! Does it occur to you that if I employed such tactics against oh, Miss Chartley – Miss Colebatch there – yourself – I should be taken completely at fault? You would none of you show a side you don't possess. What's more, ma'am, I don't *make* the chit coquet with me, or boast of her looks and her conquests to impress me: I merely offer her the opportunity to do so – and much good that would do me if she had as much elegance of mind as of person! All I should win by casting out such lures to a girl of character would be a well-deserved set-down."

She could not deny it, and rode on in silence. He saw that she was still looking rather troubled, and said: "Take comfort, you over-anxious creature! I may encourage her to betray her tantrums and her selfishness but I would no more *create* a situation to conjure up these faults than I would compromise her." He laughed suddenly. "A work of supererogation! If she could fly into a passion merely because Julian expressed a mild desire to include Miss Chartley in this party we shan't suffer from a want of such situations! Who knows! He may feel it incumbent upon him to pay a little attention to Miss Colebatch presently, in which case we shall find ourselves in the centre of a vortex!"

She was obliged to laugh, but she shuddered too, begging him not to raise such hideous spectres. "Though I've no real apprehension in this instance," she added. "Miss Colebatch is the one girl with whom Tiffany has struck up a friendship."

"Yes, I have observed that the redhead regards her with enormous admiration."

"I shall take leave to tell you, Sir Waldo," said Miss Trent severely, "that that remark had better have been left unspoken!"

"It would have been, had I been talking to anyone but yourself."

Fortunately, since she could not think what to say in reply to this, Courtenay came trotting back to them at that moment, to inform them of a slight change of plan. By skirting the cornfield that lay beyond the hedge to their right they could cut a corner, and so be the sooner out of the lane, and on to open ground, he said. The only thing was that there was no gate on the farther side: did Miss Trent feel she could jump the hedge?

"What, on that collection of bad points? Certainly not!" said Sir Waldo.

Courtenay grinned, but said: "I know, but there's nothing to it, sir! He'll brush through it easily enough – or she could *pull* him through it, if she chooses!"

"Oh, could she?" said Miss Trent, her eye kindling. "Well, she *don't* choose! By all means let us escape as soon as we may from this stuffy lane!"

"*I* knew you were a right one!" said Courtenay. "There is a gate on this side, where the others are waiting, and I'll have it open in a trice."

He wheeled his hack, and trotted off again. Miss Trent turned her fulminating gaze upon the Nonesuch, but he disarmed her by throwing up his hand in the gesture of a fencer acknowledging a hit, saying hastily: "No, no, don't snap my nose off! I cry craven!"

"So I should hope, sir!" she said, moving off in Courtenay's wake. She said over her shoulder, sudden mischief in her face: "I wish that handsome thoroughbred of yours may not make you look no-how by refusing!"

An answering gleam shone in his eyes. "You mean you wish he *may*! But I'm on my guard, and shall wait for you to show me the way!"

The hedge proved, however, to be much as Courtenay had described it, presenting no particular difficulty to even the sorriest steed, but Tiffany, who was leading the procession round the side of the field, approached it at a slapping pace, and soared over it with inches to spare. Miss Colebatch exclaimed: "Oh, one would think that lovely mare had wings! I wish I could ride like that!"

"I'm glad *you* don't ride like that!" said Courtenay. "Wings! She's more like to end with a broken leg!" He reined his horse aside, saying politely to Sir Waldo: "Will you go, sir?"

"Yes, if you wish – but rather more tamely! Your cousin is an intrepid horsewoman, and might become an accomplished one, but you should teach her not to ride at a hedge as if she had a stretch of water to clear. She'll take a rattling fall one of these days."

"Lord, sir, I've told her over and over again to ride *fast* at water, and *slow* at timber, but she never pays the least heed to what anyone says! She's a show-off – though I'll say this for her! – she don't care a rush for a tumble!"

"And rides with a light hand," said Julian, with a challenging look at Sir Waldo.

"Yes, and such a picture as she presents!" said Miss Colebatch.

Miss Trent, following Sir Waldo over the hedge, observed, as she reined in beside him, that that at least was true. He shrugged, but did not reply. The rest of the party joined them; and as they were now upon uncultivated ground they rode on in a body for some way, and the opportunity for private conversation was lost.

It was when they had covered perhaps half the distance to Knaresborough that Miss Trent, herself uncomfortably hot, noticed that Miss Colebatch, who had started out in tearing spirits, had become unusually silent. Watching her, she saw her sag in the saddle, and then jerk herself upright again; and she edged her horse alongside her, saying quietly: "Are you feeling quite the thing, Miss Colebatch?"

A rather piteous glance was cast at her, but Elizabeth, trying to smile, replied: "Oh yes! That is, I-I have the headache a little, but *pray* don't regard it! I shall be better directly, and I would not for the world – It is just the excessive heat!"

Miss Trent now perceived that under the sun's scorch she was looking very sickly. She said: "No wonder! I find it insufferably hot myself, and shall be thankful to call a halt to this expedition."

"Oh, no, no!" gasped Elizabeth imploringly. "Don't say anything *pray*!" Her chest heaved suddenly, and her mouth went awry. "Oh, Miss Trent, I d-do feel so s-sick!" she disclosed, tears starting to her eyes.

Miss Trent leaned forward to catch her slack bridle, bringing both their horses to a halt. She had not come unprepared for such an emergency, and, thrusting a hand into her pocket, produced a bottle of smelling-salts. By this time the rest of the party had seen that something was wrong, and had gathered round them. Miss Trent, dropping her own bridle, supported Elizabeth's wilting frame with one arm while she held the vinaigrette under her nose with her other hand. She said: "Miss Colebatch is overcome by the heat. Lift her down, Mr Underhill!"

He dismounted quickly, very much concerned, and, with a little assistance from Lindeth, soon had poor Elizabeth out of the saddle. Miss Trent was already on the ground, and after directing them to lay their burden on the turf desired them to retire to a distance.

Elizabeth was not sick, but she retched distressingly for some minutes; and felt so faint and dizzy that she was presently glad to obey Miss Trent's command to lie still, and to keep her eyes shut. Ancilla remained beside her, shielding her as much as possible from the sun, and fanning her with her own hat. The gentlemen, meanwhile, conferred apart, while Tiffany stood watching her friend, and enquiring from time to time if Ancilla thought she would soon be better.

After a few moments the Nonesuch detached himself from the male group, and came towards Ancilla. He made a sign to her that he wished to speak to her; she nodded, and, leaving Tiffany to take her place, got up, and went to him.

"Just as you foretold, eh?" he said. "How is she?"

"Better, but in no cause to go on, poor girl! I have been racking my brains to think what were best to do, and can hit upon nothing. I think, if she could but get out of the sun she would revive, but there are no trees, and not even a bush to afford her some shade!"

"Do you think, if her horse were led, she could go on for half a mile? Underhill tells us that there's a village, and an inn: no more than a small alehouse, I collect, but he says the woman who keeps it is respectable, and the immediate need, as you say, is to bring Miss Colebatch out of the sun. What do you think?"

"An excellent suggestion!" she replied decidedly. "We must at all events make the attempt to get her there, for she can't remain here, on the open moor. I believe that if she could rest in the cool, and we could get some water for her, she will soon recover – but she must not go any farther, Sir Waldo!"

"Oh, no! There can be no question of that," he agreed. "We'll take her to the inn, and decide then how best to convey her home."

She nodded, and went back to the sufferer, who had revived sufficiently to think herself well enough to resume the journey. She was encouraged by Tiffany, who greeted Miss Trent with the news that Lizzie was much better, and needed only a rest to make her perfectly ready to ride on. When she learned that they were to go to Courtenay's inn she said enthusiastically that it was the very thing. "We may all of us refresh there, and get cool!" she said. "You will like that, won't you, Lizzie?"

Miss Colebatch agreed to it, saying valiantly that she knew she would soon feel as well as any of them; but when she was helped to her feet her head swam so sickeningly that she reeled, and would have fallen but for the support of Miss Trent's arm around her. She was lifted on to her saddle, and was told by Courtenay, in a heartening voice, that she had nothing to do but hold on to the pommel, and sniff the vinaigrette if she felt faint. "No, you don't want the bridle: I'm going to lead White Star," he said. "And no need to be afraid of falling off, because I shan't let you!"

"Thank you – so very sorry – so stupid of me!" she managed to say.

"No such thing! Here, Tiffany, you know the way to Moor Cross! Lindeth is going to ride ahead to warn old Mrs Rowsely, so you'd best go with him!"

She was very willing to do this, announcing gaily that they would form the advance guard, and cantered off with Lindeth. When the rest of the party reached the village, she came dancing out of the little stone inn, crying: "Oh, it is the prettiest place imaginable! Do make haste and come into the taproom! Only fancy, I had never been in a taproom before, but there's no parlour, so I was obliged to! It is so diverting! You'll be enchanted, Lizzie!"

Miss Colebatch, whose headache had developed into a severe migraine, was only dimly aware of being addressed, and she did not attempt to respond. Courtenay's hand, which had been grasping her elbow, was removed, and she almost toppled into the arms of the Nonesuch, who was waiting to receive her. He carried her into the inn, where an elderly landlady, over-awed by this unprecedented invasion, dropped a nervous curtsy, and begged him to lay Miss down on the settle. She had placed a folded blanket over its uncompromising wooden seat, and fetched down a flock pillow: two circumstances to which Tiffany proudly drew his attention, saying that it was she who had directed Mrs Rowsely to do so.

"And while Lizzie rests we are going to sit on the benches outside, just as if we were rustics!" she said, laughing. "Lindeth has ordered *home-brewed* for you, but I am going to drink a glass of milk, because Mrs Rowsely has no lemons. It seems very odd to me, and I detest milk, but I don't mean to complain! Do come out! Ancilla will look after poor Lizzie."

She flitted away again, but he lingered for a few moments, while Miss Trent desired the landlady to bring a bowl of water, and some vinegar. The door of the inn opened directly into the taproom, but there was no other ventilation, the tiny latticed windows resisting Sir Waldo's efforts to force them open. The room was low-pitched and stuffy, and a strong aroma of spirituous liquors pervaded the air. Sir Waldo said abruptly: "This won't do. I collect there's no other room than the kitchen on this floor, but there must be a bedchamber abovestairs. Shall I arrange to have her moved to it?"

"If I could be sure that no one will come in, I believe it would be better to remain here," she replied, in a low tone. "It would be far hotter, immediately under the roof, you know."

"Very well; I'll attend to it," he said.

Half-an-hour later she emerged from the inn. Three empty tankards and a milkstained glass stood on one of the benches against the wall of the house;

of Tiffany and Sir Waldo there was no sign, but she saw Lindeth and Courtenay walking down the street. They hastened their steps when they caught sight of her, and came up, anxiously asking how Elizabeth did.

"Asleep," she answered. "Where is Tiffany?"

"Oh, she has gone off to look at the Church with Sir Waldo!" said Courtenay. "Lindeth and I have been enquiring all over for some sort of a carriage, but there's nothing to be had, so we've decided – that is, if you agree! – that I'd best ride to Bardsey, and see what I can come by there. Do you think Lizzie will be well enough to be driven home when she wakes, ma'am?"

"I hope so. I expect she will pluck up when she has had some tea." She smiled at Julian. "Poor girl, she is so much distressed at having spoilt your party! She made me promise to beg your pardon, and even suggested that we should continue without her!"

"What, abandon her in a common alehouse? I should rather think not!" exclaimed Courtenay.

"There's no question of that, of course," Julian said. "I am only sorry she should be feeling so poorly. I wish we might bring a doctor to her!"

Miss Trent assured him that matters were not very serious, and recommended Courtenay to saddle up. He went off to the small stableyard to do this, just as Tiffany and the Nonesuch came strolling down the street. Tiffany had caught the sweeping skirt of her velvet habit over her arm, and from the sparkling countenance she had upturned to Sir Waldo's Miss Trent judged that he had been entertaining her very agreeably.

"Oh, is Lizzie better now?" she demanded, running up to Miss Trent. "Is she ready to go on?"

"Well, she's asleep at the moment, but I am afraid she won't be stout enough to ride any farther."

"Then what's to be done?" asked Tiffany blankly. "How can you say she won't be stout enough? I'm persuaded she would wish to do so!"

"Even if she did wish it, it would be very imprudent," Ancilla said. "Indeed, Tiffany, I couldn't permit it! You wouldn't wish her to run the risk of making herself really ill!"

"No, of course I shouldn't!" Tiffany said impatiently. "But what a fuss for nothing more than a headache! I should have thought she would have *tried* to be better!"

"My dear, she is quite determined to be better, not because she wishes to ride any more, but because she is so much distressed at the thought of spoiling the expedition. I have assured her that we are all agreed that it is a great deal too sultry -"

"You can't mean that it must be given up!" cried Tiffany, looking in dismay from Ancilla to Lindeth.

It was he who answered her, saying gently: "You wouldn't care to go without her. None of us would! Another day, when it isn't so hot -"

"Oh, *no*!" Tiffany interrupted imploringly. "I hate put-offs! I know what it would be – we should never go to the Dripping Well, and I *want* to!"

"Yes, we will go, I promise you," he said. "It is very disappointing that we can't go today, but -"

"We *can* go today!" she insisted. "Not Lizzie, if she doesn't care for it, but the rest of us!"

He looked slightly taken aback for an instant, but a moment later smiled, and said: "You don't mean that, I know. In any event, we can't go, because we've settled that your cousin is to ride to Bardsey, to see if he can come by a carriage there."

Her face cleared at that; she said eagerly: "So that Lizzie can drive the rest of the way? Oh, that's a capital scheme!"

"So that she can be driven home," he corrected.

"Oh! Yes, well, perhaps that would be best. I daresay he would much *prefer* to drive Lizzie home, too, and it will make Lizzie feel much more comfortable to know she hasn't spoilt the day for us after all. Only consider! She will be perfectly safe with Courtenay, and so we may be easy! *Do* say you will go, Lindeth! Ancilla? Sir Waldo?"

Ancilla shook her head, trying to frown her down; but Sir Waldo, apparently divorced from the scene, was pensively observing through his quizzing-glass the gyrations of a large white butterfly, and evinced no sign of having heard the appeal. But Courtenay, leading his horse out of the yard, did hear it, and it was he who answered.

"Go where? To Knaresborough? Of course not! We are none of us going there. I wonder you should think of such a thing!"

"Why shouldn't I? I don't mean *you*, either: you are to drive Lizzie home! We need not *all* go with her!"

"Miss Trent must! Ma'am, you surely won't leave Lizzie?"

"Of course not," she replied. "Don't say any more, Tiffany! You must know you cannot go without me, and that I cannot under any circumstances leave Miss Colebatch."

"I could go if Courtenay went," Tiffany argued.

"Well, I'm not going," said Courtenay. "I'm going to Bardsey, to try if I can find some sort of a vehicle there. But it ain't on a pike-road, so the odds are I shan't be able to get anything better than a gig. Would a gig serve, ma'am?"

"No, no, of course it wouldn't!" interposed Tiffany. "She would have the sun beating down upon her head, and that would never do! I don't think she should attempt the journey until it is cooler, do you, Ancilla? Poor Lizzie, I daresay she would liefer stay in this delightful inn! Then we can all ride home together, when the rest of us come back from Knaresborough! She will be quite well by that time, and Ancilla won't object to staying with her, will you, Ancilla?"

Lindeth, who was beginning to look extremely troubled, said: "I don't think you can have considered. It would be quite improper for two ladies to spend the day in a taproom!"

"Oh, fudge! *I* shouldn't care a rush, so why should Lizzie? She will have Ancilla to bear her company!"

"But you could not enjoy the expedition, knowing that they were so uncomfortably situated!" he suggested.

"Oh, couldn't she?" said Courtenay, with a crack of rude laughter. "You don't know her! I can tell you this, Tiffany! you may as well stop scheming, because you won't cozen me into going to Knaresborough, and that's my last word!"

A flush rose to her cheeks; her eyes blazed. "I think you are the horridest, most disobliging *toad*!" she said passionately. "I *want* to go to Knaresborough, I *will* go!"

"Tiffany!" uttered Miss Trent, in despairing accents. "For heaven's sake -!"

Tiffany rounded on her. "Yes, and I think you're as disagreeable and unkind as he is, Ancilla! You ought to do what *I* want, not what Lizzie wants! She shouldn't have come with us if she meant to be ill!"

"Take a damper!" said Courtenay sharply, looking towards the door of the inn. "Hallo, Lizzie! Are you feeling more the thing now?"

Miss Colebatch, steadying herself with a hand on the doorframe smiled waveringly, and said: "Yes, thank you. I'm much better – quite well! Only so very sorry to have been such a bother!"

Tiffany ran to her. "Oh, you *are* better! I can see you are! I knew you would be! You don't wish to go home, do you? Only think how flat it would be!"

"Miss Colebatch, don't come out into the sun!" interposed Miss Trent, taking her hand. "I am going to ask the landlady to make some tea for us, so come and sit down again!"

"Yes, some tea will refresh you," agreed Tiffany. "You'll be as right as a trivet then!"

"Oh, yes! Only I don't think – I'm afraid if I tried to ride -"

"But you're not going to ride, Miss Colebatch," said Julian. "Underhill is to fetch a carriage for you, and we are none of us going to Knaresborough. It's far too hot!"

"Yes, that's right, Lizzie," corroborated Courtenay. "I'm just off – and I'll tell you what! I'll get an umbrella to shield you from the sun, even if I have to steal one! So just you stay quietly in the taproom with Miss Trent until I return! I shan't be gone much above an hour, I hope."

"An hour?" exclaimed Tiffany. "And what am *I* to do, pray? Do you imagine I'm going to sit in that odious, stuffy taproom for a whole hour? I won't!"

"Oh, so it's odious and stuffy now, is it?" said Courtenay. "I thought you said you wouldn't care a rush if you were obliged to spend the rest of the day in it? Yes, you can look daggers at me if you choose, but *I* know what you are, and that's a selfish little cat! You never did care a button for anyone but yourself, and it's my belief you never will!"

Tiffany burst into tears; and Miss Colebatch, sympathetic tears starting to her own eyes, cried: "Oh, Courtenay, no! You mustn't – It is all my fault for being so stupid! Oh, Tiffany, I *beg* your pardon!"

"*You* beg *her* pardon?" ejaculated Courtenay.

"Mr Underhill, will you please mind your tongue?" said Miss Trent, with all the authority of her calling. "Stop crying, Tiffany! If you don't care to stay here, I suggest you ride into Bardsey with your cousin. Then you may enjoy your quarrel without making the rest of us uncomfortable!"

Courtenay opened his mouth, encountered a quelling look, and shut it again.

"I won't!" sobbed Tiffany. "I hate Courtenay, and I don't want to go to Bardsey!"

Miss Trent, well aware of the ease with which Tiffany could lash herself into a fit of hysterics, cast a harassed look round in search of support.

Lindeth, his lips rather firmly compressed, and his eyes lowered, neither spoke nor moved; but the Nonesuch, amusement in his face, strolled up to Tiffany, and said: "Come, come, my child! The beautiful Miss Wield with swollen red eyes? Oh, no, I beseech you! I couldn't bear to see it!"

She looked up involuntarily, hiccuping on a sob, but with her tears suddenly checked. "Swollen – Oh, *no*! Oh, Sir Waldo, are they?"

He put a finger under her chin, tilting up her face, and scrutinizing it with the glinting smile so many females had found fascinating. "Thank God, no! Just like bluebells drenched with dew!"

She revived as though by magic. "*Are* they? Oh, how pretty!"

"Ravishing, I promise you."

She gave a delighted little trill of laughter. "I mean how prettily *said*!"

"Yes, wasn't it?" he agreed, carefully drying her cheeks with his own handkerchief. "What very long eyelashes you have! Do they ever become tangled?"

"No! Of course they don't! How can you be so foolish? You are trying to flatter me!"

"Impossible! *Don't* you wish to ride to Bardsey?"

Her face clouded instantly. "With Courtenay? No, I thank you!"

"With me?"

"With you! But – but you are not going – are you?"

"Not unless you do."

A provocative smile lilted on her lips. "Ancilla wouldn't permit it!" she said, with a challenging glance cast at her preceptress.

"What, even though Courtenay goes with us?" He turned towards Miss Trent, interrogating her with one quizzical eyebrow. "What do you say, ma'am?"

She had been listening to this interchange with mixed feelings, torn between gratitude to him for averting a storm, and indignation at the unscrupulous methods he employed. Her answering look spoke volumes, but all she said was: "I am persuaded Mrs Underhill would raise no objection, if her cousin is to go with Tiffany."

"Then I'll go and saddle the horses again," he said. "You, Julian, will remain to keep watch and ward over the ladies!"

"Of course," Julian replied quietly.

"Unless you should choose instead to accompany us?" suggested Tiffany, blithely forgetting that it had been agreed that two defenceless females could not be abandoned in an alehouse.

"No, I thank you," he said, and turned from her to persuade Miss Colebatch, with his sweetest smile, to retire again into the taproom.

Miss Trent had seen the look of shocked dismay in his face when it had been so forcibly borne in upon him that his goddess had feet of clay; and her heart was wrung with pity. She might tell herself that his well-wishers might rejoice in his disillusionment, but she was conscious of an irrational and almost overpowering impulse to find excuses for Tiffany. She subdued it, strengthened by the saucy look her artless charge cast at Julian before she tripped off in Sir Waldo's wake. It was abundantly plain to her that Tiffany saw nothing in Julian's refusal to ride to Bardsey but an expression of jealousy, which in no way displeased her. Tiffany delighted in setting her admirers at loggerheads, and never wasted a thought on the pain she inflicted; and had she been told that Julian was as much hurt by his cousin's behaviour as by hers she would have been as incredulous as she was uncaring. But Miss Trent's heart had more than once been wrung by the puzzled look in Julian's eyes when he had watched Sir Waldo flirting with Tiffany, and she could not help longing to reassure him.

She stayed to see the riding-party off before joining Miss Colebatch and Julian in the taproom. She found them already discussing a pot of tea, Elizabeth reclining on the settle and looking rather more cheerful, and Lindeth not seeming to be in need of reassurance. Miss Trent warmly, if silently, applauded the good manners which prompted him to appear very well satisfied with his situation; and at once seconded his efforts to divert Elizabeth. She, poor girl, was still far from being her usually lively self, for, in addition to an aching head, she was suffering the mortification of knowing that she had ruined what should have been a day of pleasure, and had made her dear friend cry. She could not help laughing when Julian, amongst other schemes for ensuring her privacy, announced his intention of borrowing an apron from the landlady, and carrying tankards out to any thirsty patrons of the Bird in Hand; but a moment later she was wondering whether Tiffany would ever forgive her, and saying, for perhaps the fiftieth time, that she could not conceive what had come over her, or how she could have been so stupid.

"Well, for my part," said Miss Trent, "I am glad that something did come over you! I was wishing I had never expressed a desire to visit the Dripping Well, and was never more thankful than when it was decided to abandon the scheme."

"You are always so kind! But Tiffany was so set on it!"

"My dear Miss Colebatch, if Tiffany suffers no worse disappointments than today's she may count herself fortunate!" replied Ancilla lightly. "I wish you won't tease yourself merely because she flew into one of her tantrums! You must know what a spoilt child she is!"

"It *is* that, isn't it?" Julian said eagerly. "Just – just childishness! She is so lovely, and – and engaging that it's no wonder she should be a trifle spoilt."

"No, indeed!" she said, adding with what she felt to be odious duplicity: "You must not blame Mrs Underhill, however. I daresay she should have been stricter, but her own nature is so gentle and yielding that she is no match for Tiffany. And she *does* so much dread her passions! I must own I do too! No one can be more enchanting than Tiffany, and no one that ever met can more easily throw an entire household into discomfort! I can't tell you, sir, how very much obliged I am to your cousin for coming to our rescue as he did!"

He responded only with a quick, constrained smile, and she said no more, hoping that she had given him enough to digest for the present; and had perhaps made him wonder whether Sir Waldo's conduct had not sprung rather from a laudable impulse to nip a painful scene in the bud than from any desire to cut out his young cousin.

CHAPTER EIGHT

"I DON'T dey that I was thankful to be spared a fit of strong hysterics," Miss Trent told the Nonesuch, when, at the end of that memorable day, Miss Colebatch had been safely restored to her parents, "and I can't doubt that *you* don't deny, sir, that your conduct was utterly unscrupulous!"

"Yes, I shall," he replied coolly. "I did nothing to promote the scene; I refrained from adding as much as one twig to the flames; and when I did intervene it was from motives of chivalry."

"From *what*?" she gasped.

"Motives of chivalry," he repeated, meeting her astonished gaze with a grave countenance, but with such a twinkle in his eyes that she was hard put to it not to laugh. "A look of such piteous entreaty was cast at me -"

"No!" protested Miss Trent. "Not *piteous*! I didn't!"

"Piteous!" said the Nonesuch remorselessly. "Your eyes, ma'am as well you know!! – cried *Help me*! What could I do but respond to the appeal?"

"Next you will say that it went much against the pluck with you!" said Miss Trent, justly incensed.

"No service I could render you, ma'am, would go against the pluck!"

Her colour mounted, but she said: "I should have guessed you would have a glib answer ready!"

"You might also have guessed that I meant it."

She found herself suddenly a little breathless; and wished, for the first time, that she was more experienced in the art of dalliance. There was a note of sincerity in his voice; but caution warned her not to allow herself to be taken in by a man of the world whom she judged to be expert in flirtation. She managed to laugh, although rather shakily, and to say: "Very prettily said. Sir Waldo! I must give you credit too for having brought Tiffany back to us all compliance and good humour. A triumph indeed!"

"Fencing with me, Miss Trent?"

She was silent for a moment or two, and when she did speak it was with a good deal of constraint. "I think you forget my situation, sir."

"On the contrary: your situation chafes me too much to be forgotten."

She looked at him in astonishment. "Chafes you!"

"Beyond endurance! You stare! Does it seem so strange to you that I should very much dislike seeing you in such a position?"

"Good heavens!" she exclaimed. "One would suppose I was one of those unfortunate governesses who, for £24 a year, become drudges! But I'm no such thing! I'm excessively expensive, in fact."

"So you once told me."

"Well, it's true. I don't like to boast, but I can't allow you to suppose that I eke out a miserable existence on a pittance. I am paid *£150 a year*!"

"My dear girl, it would make no difference if you were paid ten times that sum!"

"That shows how little you know! It makes a great deal of difference, I promise you. Females who are paid very high wages are never used like drudges."

"You are at the beck and call of a woman I could more readily suppose to be your housekeeper than your mistress; you are obliged to endure impertinence from that abominable chit any time she is out of temper, and patronage from such mushrooms as -"

"Nonsense!" she interrupted. "Mrs Underhill treats me as if I were one of her family, and I won't have her abused! I think myself very fortunate, and if *I* don't dislike my position there can be no reason for anyone else to do so!"

"Oh, yes, there can be!" he retorted.

They had reached the gates of Staples, where the others had pulled up to wait for them. Miss Trent hardly knew whether to be glad or sorry that her tête-à-tête with the Nonesuch had come to an abrupt end; and when he and Lindeth had taken their leave she rode up the avenue to the house so lost in her own thoughts that Courtenay had to speak her name twice before she realized that she was being addressed. He supposed her to be tired; and Tiffany, at her most caressing, was instantly all solicitude. Miss Trent was obliged to take herself to task for harbouring the uncharitable suspicion that her engaging manner sprang from a wish to avert a scold for her previous conduct.

Mrs Underhill said she was quite shocked to think of poor Lizzie's indisposition, but not at all surprised. She and Charlotte had taken a turn in the shrubbery, which had regularly exhausted her, so hot as it had been. Miss Trent made no mention of Tiffany's outburst, but when Courtenay came in he gave his mother a full and indignant account of it, stigmatizing his lovely cousin as a devil's daughter whom he was ashamed to own, and adding that she might as well stop setting her cap at Lindeth, since the veriest clodpole could have seen how outrageous he thought her behaviour.

This was all very dreadful, but, as Mrs Underhill presently confided to Miss Trent, every cloud had a silver lining. "For Courtenay told me, my dear, that his lordship was downright shocked, so I shouldn't wonder at it if he began to hedge off. Very likely it will have given him a disgust of her, for there's nothing gentlemen hate more than the sort of dust Tiffany kicks up when she flies into one of her miffs. Don't you think so?"

Miss Trent agreed. She also thought that Courtenay's disgust was considerably stronger than Lindeth's, but this she did not say.

"And it was Sir Waldo that stopped her from going her length, and took her off to Bardsey, which I'll be bound you were glad of, my dear, though whether it was what *he* wanted to do is another matter!"

The arch note in the good lady's voice was unmistakeable. Miss Trent's fine eyes turned towards her involuntarily, asking a startled question.

"Lor', my dear, as if I was such a nodcock as not to know it's you he's got a preference for!" said Mrs Underhill, with a fat chuckle. "To be sure, I did think at first that he was making up to Tiffany, but for all I haven't got book-learning I hope I've enough rumgumption to know he's trying to fix his interest with you!"

"You are mistaken, ma'am – you *must* be mistaken!" stammered Ancilla.

"Well, that's what I thought myself, when I first took the notion into my head," conceded Mrs Underhill. "Not that I mean you ain't genteel, as I hope I don't need to tell you, for I'm sure anyone would take you for a lady of quality, such distinguished ways as you have, which even Mrs Mickleby has remarked to me more than once. But there's no denying it isn't to be expected that such a smart as Sir Waldo wouldn't be looking a great deal higher if he was hanging out for a wife, for from what Mrs M. tells me he's a gentleman of the first consequence, let alone being as rich as a new-shorn lamb, and has goodness knows how many fine ladies on the catch for him!"

"Ma'am!" interrupted Ancilla, in a stifled voice, "I am neither a fine lady, nor am I on the catch for Sir Waldo!"

"No, my dear, and well do I know it! I shouldn't wonder at it if it was that which took his fancy. If you was to ask me, I should say that there's nothing will make a gentleman sheer off quicker than the feel that he's being hunted! Lord! the females that set their caps at Mr Underhill! Of course, he wasn't a grand town-beau, like Sir Waldo, but he was thought to be a great catch, and might have had his pick of all the girls in Huddersfield. And what must he do but set his fancy on me, just because I didn't pay any more heed to him than I did to any of my beaux!"

Miss Trent, only too glad to encourage this divagation, said: "I don't think *that* was why he set his fancy on you, ma'am, but I can readily believe that you had any number of beaux!"

"Well, I had," admitted Mrs Underhill, gratified. "You wouldn't think it, to look at me now, but, though it don't become me to say so, I was used to be a very pretty girl, and had so many compliments paid me – But *that's* not what I was wanting to say to you!"

Miss Trent, having learnt by experience that however far her employer might wander from the point she rarely lost sight of it, resigned herself.

"You won't take it amiss when I tell you, my dear, that when I saw the look in Sir Waldo's eyes whenever he had them fixed on you, which nobody could mistake, though I'd be hard put to it to describe it to you, if you was to ask me, it cast me into quite a quake, thinking that he was intending to give you a slip on the shoulder, as the saying is."

"Dear ma'am, I am – I am very much obliged to you for your concern, but indeed you have no need to be in a quake!"

"No, that's just what I think myself," said Mrs Underhill, nodding wisely. "I'd have dropped a hint in your ear otherwise, you being so young, for all you try to gammon everyone into thinking you an old maid! But, 'no,' I said to myself, 'a libertine he may be' – not that I've any reason to suppose he is, mind! – 'but he ain't making up to Miss Trent meaning nothing more than marriage with the left hand: not with her uncle being General Sir Mordaunt Trent, as he is!' Well, it stands to reason, doesn't it?" She paused, eyeing Ancilla in some bewilderment. "Now, whatever have I said to throw you into whoops?" she demanded.

"Oh, I beg your pardon, ma'am!" Ancilla said, wiping her streaming eyes. "But it is so – so absurd -!"

"Exactly so! But don't you tell me he ain't making up to you, because I'm not as blind as a beetle, which I'd have to be not to see what's going on under my nose!"

Ancilla had stopped laughing. She was rather flushed, and she said haltingly: "I think, ma'am I think you refine too much on Sir Waldo's gallantry. I am persuaded he has no other intention than to amuse himself with a little flirtation."

Mrs Underhill's face fell; but after thinking it over for a minute, she brightened, saying: "No, you're out there, my dear. It's Tiffany he flirts with, which, of course, he oughtn't to do, but, lord, they all do it, even the Squire, and you can't blame them, so pretty and saucy as she is! But he don't look at her the way he looks at you – no, and he don't talk to you as he does to her either! What's more, if she ain't in the room he don't look up every time the door opens, hoping she's going to come in!"

Her cool composure seriously disturbed, Ancilla said involuntarily: "Oh, Mrs Underhill, *d-does* he do so when – Oh, no! *Surely* not?"

"Lord bless you, my dear, of course he does!" replied Mrs Underhill, with an indulgent laugh. "And if it *is* you – well, often and often I've thought to myself that if he was to smile at me the way he does at you I should be cast into a regular flutter, as old as I am!"

Miss Trent felt her cheeks burning, and pressed her slim hands to them. "He-he has a very charming smile, I know!"

"I'll be bound you do!" retorted Mrs Underhill. "Mark my words if we don't have him popping the question before we've had time to turn round! And this I will say, my dear: I couldn't be better pleased if you was my own daughter! Not that he'd do for Charlotte, even if she was old enough, which, of course, she isn't, because, from all I can discover, he's nutty upon horses, and well you know that she can't abide 'em!"

Miss Trent gave a shaky laugh. "Yes, indeed I know it. But – Dear Mrs Underhill, *pray* don't say any more! You mustn't encourage me to to indulge ridiculous dreams! Sir Waldo knows exactly how to make himself very – very agreeable to females, and, I daresay, has broken many hearts. I am determined he shall not break mine! To suppose that he – a matrimonial prize of the first stare! – would entertain for as much as one moment the notion of contracting so unequal a match . . ." Her voice failed; she recovered it again to say, with an attempt at a smile: "You won't speak of this to anyone, I know!"

"Certainly not!" said Mrs Underhill. "But don't you behave missish, my dear, and start hinting him away because you think you ain't good enough for him! That's for him to decide, and you may depend upon it that a man of five – or six-and-thirty knows what will suit him. It would be a splendid thing for you, let alone making the Squire's lady and Mrs Banningham as mad as fire!"

On this invigorating thought she took her departure, leaving Miss Trent to her own reflections.

It was long before she fell asleep that night. Mrs Underhill's blunt words had forced her to confront the truth she had hitherto refused to acknowledge: she had been in love with the Nonesuch for weeks.

Like a stupidly romantic schoolgirl, she thought, dazzled by the aura of magnificence that hung about a Top-of-the-Trees Corinthian, and foolishly endowing him with heroic qualities because he had a handsome face and splendid figure, rode and drove his high-couraged horses with such effortless mastery, and bore himself with an unconscious assurance which cozened ninnyhammers like herself into thinking he was a demigod. Not that she was quite as idiotish as that, of course. She could scarcely help admiring his appearance, but she had not fallen in love with his face, or his figure, and certainly not with his air of elegance. He had considerable charm of manner, but she decided that it was not that either. She thought it might be the humour that lurked in his eyes, or perhaps his smile. But Lindeth had a delightful smile too, and she was not in the least in love with him. In fact, she didn't know why she loved the Nonesuch, but only that from the moment of first setting eyes on him she had felt so strong an attraction that it had shocked her, because he was clearly the exemplar of a set of persons whom she held in abhorrence.

Caution warned her not to place overmuch reliance on what Mrs Underhill had said. Far better than Mrs Underhill did she know how very unlikely it was that a man of Sir Waldo's eligibility, who could look as high as he pleased for a wife and must be thought to be past the age of contracting a rash engagement, should entertain the smallest intention of offering marriage to an obscure female who had neither consequence nor any extraordinary degree of beauty to recommend her. On the other hand, the things he had said to her that day, before they had parted at the gates of Staples, seemed to indicate that he had something other than mere flirtation in mind. If that had been all he sought she could not conceive why her inferior situation should chafe him, or why, if he had not been sincere, he should have told her that it did. Pondering the matter, she was obliged to own that she knew very little about the art of flirtation; and hard upon this thought came the realization that she knew very little about Sir Waldo either. He had shown himself to be most truly the gentleman, never above his company, nor betraying his boredom, and never seeking to impress the neighbourhood by playing off the airs of an exquisite. As for exerting an evil influence over his young admirers, she had it on the authority of the Squire that his coming to Broom Hall had done them all a great deal of good. Together with their extravagant waistcoats and their monstrous neckcloths they had abandoned such dare-devil sports as Hunting the Squirrel or riding their cover-hacks up the stairs of their parents' houses: the Nonesuch never wore startling raiment, and he let it be seen that he thought the Dashes and the Neck-or-Nothings not at all the thing. So instead of rushing into wild excesses as a result of his coming amongst them the youthful aspirants to Corinthian fame (said the Squire, with a chuckle) had now run mad over achieving what their hero would think a proper mode.

It was possible, however, that in his own element Sir Waldo might show another side to his character. Not for a moment did Ancilla believe that he would lead greenhorns astray; but she was bound to acknowledge that for anything she knew his path might be littered with wounded hearts. She could not doubt that he was a master of the art of flirtation; and she was only too well aware of his fatal fascination. She decided that her wisest course would be to put him out of her mind. After reaching this conclusion she lay thinking about him until at last she fell asleep.

Upon the following day she was driven over to Colby Place in Mrs Underhill's smart new barouche to enquire after Elizabeth. Charlotte had been her companion designate, but as soon as Tiffany heard of the scheme she said that it was exactly what she had been meaning to do herself, and very prettily begged Miss Trent to grant her a place in the carriage. Forthright Charlotte, who suffered from few illusions, instantly cried off, saying that she preferred to bear Mama company at home than to occupy the forward seat in the barouche. So Tiffany went with Miss Trent, looking a picture of lovely innocence in a gown of sprig muslin, and a charming hat of chip straw, tied under her chin with blue ribbons. A parasol protected her complexion from the sun; and upon the forward seat reposed a basket of grapes. These were an offering from Mrs Underhill, whose succession-houses were the envy of her acquaintances; but Miss Trent, labouring under even fewer illusions than Charlotte, would not have hazarded a groat against the chance that Tiffany would not present them as the fruits of her own solicitude. Any doubts she might have cherished were dispelled by that damsel's disarmingly naïve explanation.

"So *no one* could think I was unkind to poor Lizzie, could they? And *also*, Ancilla, I have invited Patience to go with us to Leeds on Friday, because she wants to purchase new gloves and sandals for the Colebatches' ball next week, just as I do, and was in quite a puzzle to know how to manage, on account of Mrs Chartley's being laid up with one of her colicky disorders!"

"That *was* kind of you, Tiffany!" said Miss Trent admiringly.

"Well, I think it was," said Tiffany. "For there's nothing so uncomfortable as having a third person in one's carriage! It means you will be obliged to sit forward – But I knew you wouldn't care a button!"

"No, indeed!" agreed Miss Trent, with great cordiality. "I am only too happy to be allowed to contribute my mite to your generosity."

"Yes," said Tiffany, sublimely unconscious of satire, "I was persuaded you would say I had done just as I ought!"

When they reached Colby Place they perceived that they were not the only visitors. A glossy phaeton, to which was harnessed a team once described by Courtenay as a bang-up set-out of blood and bone, was drawn up in the shade of a large elm tree. A groom in plain livery touched his hat to the ladies; and Tiffany exclaimed: "Oh, Sir Waldo is here!"

But it was not Sir Waldo, as they discovered when they entered the house, and found Lord Lindeth chatting to Lady Colebatch in her morning-parlour. He jumped up as they were ushered into the room, and when he saw Tiffany a warm light sprang to his eyes, and he said, in a low tone, as soon as she had greeted her hostess and turned to hold out her hand to him: "That's right! I knew you would come!"

"But of course!" she said, opening her eyes to their widest. "Poor Lizzie! Is she better, Lady Colebatch? I have brought some grapes for her."

Lady Colebatch, accepting the basket with thanks, replied placidly that there was nothing the matter with Lizzie that would not be amended by a day's repose, and invited Tiffany to run upstairs to join Miss Chartley at her bedside.

"Patience? Why, what brings her here?" demanded Tiffany, astonished, and by no means pleased to discover that the Rector's daughter had been before her in paying a visit of condolence.

Still less was she pleased when she learned that Patience, hearing the news of her friend's collapse through the mysterious but inevitable village-channels, had set out to walk the three miles that separated Colby Place from the village, but had been overtaken by Lindeth, driving his cousin's phaeton, and bent upon the same charitable errand. He had naturally taken her up beside him, which, said Lady Colebatch, with unruffled serenity, she was excessively relieved to know, because although she knew Patience to be an indefatigable walker it would have cast her into high fidgets to have thought of her having trudged so far in such warm weather.

Lindeth did not seem to have wasted his time during the short drive. Miss Chartley had chanced to mention the forthcoming shopping expedition to Leeds, and he had instantly proposed a capital plan to her, which he now propounded to Miss Trent. "I know my cousin has business in Leeds on Friday, so I am hereby issuing an invitation to you all to partake of a nuncheon at the King's Head!" he said gaily. "Do say you will come, ma'am! I've extracted a promise from Miss Chartley that *she* will, if her mama should not object!"

"*I* see!" said Miss Trent, quizzing him. "She *would* object if I were not there to chaperon the party! My dear Lord Lindeth, how can I find the words to thank you for your *very* flattering invitation? I am quite overcome!"

He laughed, blushing. "No, no, I didn't mean it so! You know I didn't! Miss Wield, what do you say?" He smiled at her, adding softly: "Instead of the nuncheon we *didn't* eat at Knaresborough! You won't be so cruel as to refuse!"

It piqued her to be the last to receive his invitation, but she was on her best behaviour, and she replied at once: "Oh, no! A delightful scheme! The very thing to revive us after all our shopping!"

She then went off, with every appearance of alacrity, to visit Elizabeth; and Lady Colebatch remarked that she didn't know what Lizzie had done to deserve such kind friends.

When Tiffany came down again she was accompanied by Miss Chartley, and the whole party took their leave. Miss Trent wondered whether his infatuation would prompt Lindeth to offer to take Tiffany up in place of Patience, and hardly knew whether to be glad or sorry when he made no such suggestion. It was Patience who hesitated, as he stood waiting to hand her up into the carriage, glancing towards Tiffany with a question in her eyes, and saying in her gentle way: "Wouldn't you prefer to go in the phaeton, Tiffany?"

Tiffany would infinitely have preferred it, and had Julian invited her she would have accepted, after a graceful show of reluctance. But Julian had not invited her, and he did not now add his voice to Miss Chartley's. That it would have been scarcely civil of him to have done so never occurred to Tiffany; if it had, she would have brushed such an excuse aside: he had chosen to be civil to Patience at *her* expense, and that, in her eyes, was an unpardonable offence. As for accepting a seat in the phaeton at Patience's hands, she would have chosen rather to walk back to Staples. She uttered a brittle laugh, and said: "No, I thank you! I detest riding in phaetons, and am in a constant quake – unless they are being driven by someone I know won't overturn them!"

Miss Trent, who had been stroking one of the leaders, said, in a voice that had in the past more than once abashed a pert pupil: "My dear Tiffany, surely you are able to distinguish between perch-phaeton and a *high*-perch phaeton?" She paid no further heed to Tiffany, but smiled at Lindeth: "The fact that you are driving your cousin's team tells me that you're no whipster, Lord Lindeth! Or did you steal them when his back was turned?"

He laughed. "No, I shouldn't dare! Waldo always lets me drive his horses. He must, you know, for it was he who taught me to handle the reins in form. Only think of the wound his pride would suffer if he had to own that his pupil was not fit to be trusted with his horses! Don't be afraid, Miss Chartley! I'm not a top-sawyer, but I shan't overturn you!"

"Indeed, I haven't the smallest fear of that," she replied, glancing shyly up at him. "You drove me here so comfortably!"

"Thank you!" He saw that Tiffany was preparing to get into the barouche, and walked across to her, to hand her in. "I mean to make you unsay those words one of these days!" he said playfully. "The grossest injustice! I wish we hadn't to part so soon: I've scarcely exchanged half-a-dozen sentences with you. Did you find Miss Colebatch better? Her mama assured me we need not be afraid of a put-off of their ball next week. Will you dance the waltz with me?"

"*What?*" she exclaimed, her sulks instantly forgotten. "Lindeth, you can't mean we are to *waltz*? Oh, you're hoaxing me!"

He shook his head. "I'm not! Dashing, isn't it?"

"Oh, yes, and such fun!" she cried, clapping her hands. "I declare I'm ready to *dote* on Lady Colebatch! But how does she dare to be so dreadfully fast? Only think how Mrs Mickleby will look!"

"It has her sanction – almost her blessing!"

"Impossible!"

"I assure you!" His eyes danced. "Lady Colebatch sought her counsel, and she – naturally! – applied to those *tonnish* London cousins of hers. They informed her that the waltz is now all the crack, and is even permitted at Almack's. Only rustics, they wrote, still frowned on it. *So* -!"

"Oh, famous, famous!" she giggled. "The great Mrs Mickleby *a rustic*? *Now* I understand!"

"And you'll stand up with me?"

"If my aunt permits!" she replied demurely.

He smiled, pressed her hand fleetingly, and went back to the phaeton. Tiffany was so much delighted with his news that she was not only able to bear with equanimity the sight of him driving off with Patience beside him, but to chat merrily to Miss Trent about the treat in store all the way back to Staples.

CHAPTER NINE

MEANWHILE, LORD Lindeth, driving Miss Chartley home at an easy pace, naturally told her that the waltz would be danced at the Colby Place ball. She was quite as much surprised as Tiffany had been, but she received the news very differently, saying wistfully: "I have never learnt to waltz, but I shall enjoy watching it."

"You could learn the steps in a trice," he assured her. "*I* know how well you dance, Miss Chartley! Any caper-merchant could teach you in one lesson! Why, I could do so myself – though I'm no dab at it! Do let me!"

She smiled gratefully at him, but said simply: "I don't think Mama would permit it."

"Wouldn't she? Not even when she knows Mrs Mickleby sanctions it?"

She shook her head, but closed her lips on speech. A lady of true quality, said Mama, did not puff off her consequence: anything of that nature belonged to the mushroom class! Mama never mentioned the matter, but she was far better bred than the Squire's wife, and well did Patience know that she would be considerably affronted by any suggestion that she should accept Mrs Mickleby as a model.

"Does she believe it to be an improper dance?" asked Lindeth. "So too did my own mother, until she saw that it was no such thing. I shall see if I can't persuade Mrs Chartley to relent! It would be too bad if you were obliged merely to *watch* it!"

"I'm afraid you wouldn't succeed," she said, thinking there was no real intention behind his words.

She was mistaken. When they reached the Rectory Lindeth entered it with her, and was soon engaged in coaxing Mrs Chartley, recovering from her indisposition on the sofa in her drawing-room, to revise her opinion of the fast German dance which had become the rage in London.

She was by no means impervious to his charm, but her sense of propriety was strict, and it is doubtful whether he would have prevailed upon her to relax it had he not received support from an unexpected quarter. The Rector, coming into the room and learning what was the subject under discussion, said that since the world began each generation had condemned the manners and customs of the next. For himself, he would not judge a dance he had never seen performed. Smiling kindly upon Julian, he invited him to show them the steps.

"Mr Chartley!" protested his wife, in half-laughing reproach.

"I was very fond of dancing when I was young," said the Rector reminiscently. "Dear me, what dashers we were! Always up to the knocker, as you young people would say!"

That made them all laugh; and when he told his wife that while he hoped no child of his would ever pass the line he found he could not wish his daughter to be a dowdy, Mrs Chartley flung up her hands in mock dismay, and consented to postpone judgment. The end of it was that Julian was persuaded to give Patience her first lesson, ably assisted by Miss Jane Chartley, who not only bullied her shrinking elder sister into standing up with him, but volunteered to play the music. This she did with great aplomb, strongly marking the time, in a manner which made her startled mama wonder who had taught her to play waltzes. It was certainly not her rather prim governess.

Patience (like her father) was very fond of dancing, and as soon as she had overcome her nervousness she showed herself to be an apt pupil, a trifle stiff, when she found Lindeth's arm round her for the first time, but quickly mastering the steps and the rhythm of the dance.

"Bravo!" applauded the Rector, gently clapping his hands. "Very pretty! Very pretty indeed!"

"Oh, do you think so, Papa?" Patience said eagerly. "I was dreadfully awkward, and kept missing my step! But, if you don't think it indecorous, I-I should like to learn to do it correctly. It *is* so exhilarating!"

It was this impulsive utterance which made Mrs Chartley say, later: "My dear John, I marvel at your countenancing this most improper dance! When they went down the room together, with his left hand holding her right one above their heads, *his* right hand was *clasping her waist*!"

"For guidance, my love!" said the Rector. "Lindeth had no *amorous* intention! I saw nothing improper. Indeed, I should have wished to see Patience a trifle less unyielding – but I daresay she was awkward from ignorance!"

"It's my belief," said Mrs Chartley severely, "that you would like to dance the waltz yourself!"

"No, no, not at my age!" he said guiltily. A smile crept into his eyes. "But if it had been in fashion when I was a young man, and not, of course, in orders, I *should* have danced it – and with you, my love! Would *you* have disliked it?"

A dimple quivered in her cheek, but she said: "My mother would never have permitted such a thing. Do you, in all sincerity, expect me to permit Patience to – to twirl round a ballroom in a male embrace – for I can call it nothing less than that!"

"You are the best judge of what she should do, my dear, and I must leave it to you to decide. I must own, however, that I should not wish to see Patience sitting against the wall while her friends are, as you phrase it, twirling round the room."

"No," agreed Mrs Chartley, forcibly struck by this aspect. "No, indeed!"

"Far be it from me to desire her to outshine her friends," said the Rector unconvincingly, "but I have sometimes thought that although she cannot rival little Tiffany's beauty she is by far the more graceful dancer."

These words afforded his wife food for considerable thought. She could not be perfectly reconciled, but her resolution wavered. The reference to Tiffany, little though the Rector knew it, had operated powerfully upon her. She was not, she hoped, a worldly woman, but neither was she so saintly (or so unnatural a parent) as to be unmoved by the spectacle of her daughter's being cast into the shade by an odiously precocious little baggage who was wild to a fault, as vain as she was beautiful, and wholly wanting in character and disposition. Mrs Chartley, in fact, did not like Tiffany Wield; and she had been thinking for some time that it was sad to see such a delightful young man as Lindeth in her toils. Heaven knew she was no matchmaking mother! Unlike certain of her husband's parishioners, she had made not the smallest attempt to throw her child in his lordship's way; but when she had watched him dancing with Patience the thought had flashed across her mind that they were a remarkably well-suited couple. Lindeth was just the sort of young man she would have chosen for Patience. It was one thing to make no push to engage his interest in the child, but quite another to throw obstacles in the way of his becoming better acquainted with her.

She was still in a state of indecision when the matter was clinched by an invitation to Patience from Mrs Underhill, to attend one or two morning dances at Staples, to practise the waltz.

"Morning dances!" she exclaimed. "Good gracious, what next?"

Patience, her eyes shining, and her cheeks in a glow, said: "It was Tiffany's suggestion, Mama, and Miss Trent says it is quite true that they have become the fashion in London. Just to enable people to practise waltzes and quadrilles, you know. And she has undertaken to play for us, and tell us all how to waltz in the correct manner. Mama, nearly all my friends are going! And even Courtenay Underhill, and the Banninghams, and Arthur Mickleby are determined to learn! And Lord Lindeth and Mr Ash have been so obliging as to promise to come too, to show us the way. And Mrs Underhill will be present, and -"

"My dear, how you do run on!"

"I beg your pardon, ma'am! Only, may I go? Not if you dislike it – but I *should* like to so very much!"

Mrs Chartley could not withstand such an appeal. "Well, my love, since your papa sees no harm in it, and the ball is to be a private one, not a public assembly, "

"Oh, *thank you*, Mama!" breathed Patience. "Now I can look forward to it, which I didn't when I thought I should be obliged to sit down when the others were all dancing!"

"No, that would never do," agreed Mrs Chartley, visualizing such a scene with profound disapprobation.

"It is going to be a beautiful party!" confided Patience. "There are to be coloured lamps in the garden, and – but this is a great secret, Mama, which Lizzie whispered to me! – a firework display at midnight!"

"It's to be hoped, then, that it doesn't rain," said Mrs Chartley.

"Oh, don't suggest such a thing!" begged Patience. "Mama, would you think it very extravagant if I were to purchase a new reticule for it? I've been to so many parties that mine is looking sadly shabby."

"No, not at all. You know, my dear, I have been thinking that if you were to bring back a length of satin from Leeds on Friday we could very easily make a fresh underdress for your gauze ball-dress. I never did like the green we chose. A soft shade of pink would become you. And if you can find some velvet ribbon to match it – How vexatious it is that I can't go with you! But Dr Wibsey threatens me with all manner of evil consequences if I don't continue to be invalidish until the end of the week at least, so if I am to take you to this ball next week I suppose I must do what he tells me. Well, you will have Miss Trent to advise you! Let yourself be guided by her: she has excellent taste!"

What with the dissipation of waltzing at Staples all one rainy morning, and the prospect of an orgy of spending in Leeds, attended by a nuncheon-party, it was in a festive mood that Patience awaited the arrival of the Staples carriage on Friday morning. She had arrayed herself for the occasion in her best walking-dress of figured muslin, with long sleeves, and a double flounce round the hem; on her head she wore a pretty straw bonnet, trimmed with flowers; on her feet sandals of tan kid; in one hand she held a small parasol; and in the other (very tightly) a stocking-purse containing the enormous largesse bestowed on her by her Mama. It seemed quite profligate to spend so much money on her adornment, for although the Rector had been born to an independance which enabled him to command the elegancies of life he had reared his children in habits of economy, and in the belief that it was wrong to set store by one's appearance. "Going to waste your money on *more* finery?" he had said, smiling, but disapproving too. "My dear sir," had said Mama, "you would not wish your daughter to be seen in worn-out slippers and soiled gloves, I hope!" Afterwards she had explained the suppression of the pink satin and the velvet ribbon, saying in a confidential tone which made Patience feel suddenly very much more grown-up, that it was better not to talk to men about frills and furbelows, because they had no understanding of such things, and were merely bored by feminine chatter.

Miss Trent thought that she had seldom seen Patience in such good looks, and reflected that nothing became a girl so well as a glow of pleasurable excitement. She was inevitably dimmed by Tiffany, who was in great beauty, and wearing a dashing bonnet with a very high crown and a huge, upstanding poke framing her face, but there was something very taking about her countenance; and her eyes, though lacking the brilliance of Tiffany's, held a particularly sweet expression.

The drive into Leeds, once Patience had won a spirited argument with Miss Trent on which of them really *preferred* to sit with her back to the horses, was accomplished in perfect amity. Tiffany took no part in a dispute which she felt to be no concern of hers, but she was very ready to discuss with her companions the various purchases she meant to make in the town, and to show a civil, if fleeting, interest in Patience's more modest requirements. Being a considerable heiress she had a great deal of pin-money allowed her; and as, unlike Patience, she had not the smallest notion of economy, it was enough for her to see something that took her fancy to make her buy it immediately. Her drawers were crammed with the expensive spoils of her visits to Leeds or Harrogate, most of which she had decided did not become her, or which were not as pretty as she had at first thought them. They ranged from innumerable pairs of rosettes for slippers to a Spartan diadem which (mercifully) was found to make her look positively haggish; and included such diverse items as an Angola shawl suitable for a dowager, a pair of Spanish slippers of sea-green kid, three muffs of spotted ermine, chinchilla, and swansdown, a tangle of spangled ribbon, and a set of head ornaments of silver filigree. She was obliged, at present, to apply to Mrs Underhill whenever she wanted to draw on her allowance. What would happen when she came into full possession of her fortune was a question which conjured up nightmarish visions in the mind of a conscientious governess; and Miss Trent had made persistent and extremely exhausting efforts to instil into her head some glimmerings of the value of money. She had failed, and as she was not one to fling her cap after the impossible there was nothing left for her to do but to check Tiffany's extravagance by whatever means her ingenuity might suggest to her; and to excuse her failure by the reflection that the control of that volatile damsel's inheritance would pass into the hands of her unknown but inevitable husband.

When they reached Leeds they alighted from the carriage at the King's Arms, and set forth on foot down the main shopping street. Leeds was a thriving and rapidly expanding town, numbering amongst its public edifices two Cloth Halls (one of which was of impressive dimensions, and was divided into six covered streets); five Churches; a Moot Hall; the Exchange (a handsome building of octangular design); an Infirmary; a House of Recovery for persons afflicted with infectious diseases; a Charity school, clothing and educating upwards of a hundred children, and over which (had they but known it) Sir Waldo Hawkridge was, at the time of their arrival in the town, being escorted by several of the Governors; a number of cloth and carpet manufactories; several cotton mills, and foundries; inns innumerable; and half-a-dozen excellent posting-houses. The buildings were for the most part of red brick, beginning to be blackened by the smoke of industry; and while none could be thought magnificent there were several Squares and Parades which contained private residences of considerable elegance. There were some very good shops and silk warehouses; and it was not long before Miss Trent's ingenuity was put to the test, Tiffany falling in love first with a pair of gold French shoebuckles ornamented with paste; and next with a Surprise fan of crape, lavishly embellished with purple and gold devices. Miss Trent had never seen anything so exquisite as the buckles, and bemoaned the change in fashion which had made it impossible for anyone to wear them now without appearing perfectly Gothic. As for the fan, she agreed that it was a most amusing trifle: just what she would wish to buy for herself, if it had not been so excessively ugly!

These hazards successfully skirted, she steered her charges into a large and entrancing establishment, where both young ladies bought some gloves and some ribbons, and Tiffany several pairs of silk stockings, which aroused such envy in Miss Chartley's gentle bosom that she determined to save twelve shillings from the sum reposing in her purse so that she could buy just one pair to wear at the Colebatches' ball.

After this they visited the silk warehouse which enjoyed Mrs Chartley's patronage; and while Tiffany, who soon lost interest in the choice of a satin to furnish a new underdress for Patience's gauze ball-gown, wandered about, inspecting silks and velvets, with a dazed and slavishly admiring young shopman in attendance, Miss Trent placed her taste and experience at her young friend's disposal. A very reasonably priced satin of a charming shade of pink; having been discovered, there was only enough time left before the ladies' assignation with Lord Lindeth for the purchase of Patience's new dancing-sandals. This was soon accomplished, and although it took several minutes to dissuade Tiffany from investing in a pair of pale blue silk sandals, they returned to the King's Arms before their host had begun to entertain any very serious fear that some accident must have overtaken them.

He was awaiting them in a private parlour, and it was evident from the array of cold meats, fruit, jellies, and creams on the table that he had taken great pains over their entertainment. Only one thing, in Miss Trent's view, was wanting. For no persuasion would she have betrayed the smallest interest in the whereabouts of the Nonesuch; but when Tiffany, who had few reserves, demanded to know why he was not present, she felt, for once, no desire to censure this unbecoming pertness.

"He'll be here presently," Lindeth answered. "We won't wait for him, however: he warned me not to – said I was to make his apologies, if he was detained. I daresay he is still interviewing bailiffs! From what I saw, that lawyer – what's his name? – Smeeth! – had a score of 'em drawn up in line for his inspection!"

"Oh!" Tiffany said, pouting. "Dull work!"

"Well -" He hesitated, and then said: "Yes, of course it is – dull work for a lady, I mean."

"I should suppose it must be very difficult," said Patience thoughtfully. "In particular, if you mean to leave the bailiff in sole charge. One hears of such shocking instances of tyranny, and neglect – though my father says the fault too often lies at the landlord's door."

"Yes, very true," he agreed. "Screws like old Joseph Calver, wringing every groat it will yield out of his land, and leasing his farms on short terms to thriftless get-pennies, because -" He stopped, seeing, the frown that creased Tiffany's brow. "But I don't know why we should be talking about such things, and boring Miss Wield!"

"No, nor do I!" she said, all demure mischief. "*Tell* me why?"

He laughed. "Not for the world! I'll invite you to the table instead! I hope you are very hungry! Miss Trent, will you sit here, and may I carve you some chicken?"

"Misuse of language, Lindeth: *hack* is the word!" said Sir Waldo, entering the parlour at that moment. "How do you do, ma'am? Miss Chartley, your very obedient! Miss Wield, yours! I beg all your pardons: I'm late!"

"Now, that puts me in mind of a remark someone once made to me," said Miss Trent, apparently chasing an elusive recollection. "Something about becoming inured to unpunctuality .... Who can have said that, I wonder? I have the wretchedest memory!"

"Then you should not attempt quotation, ma'am!" retorted Sir Waldo, a laugh in his eye. "'To the unpunctuality of your sex' was what I said."

"Oh, no, did he, ma'am?" exclaimed Lindeth. "That's famous. *Hoist with his own petard!*"

"What does that mean, pray?" asked Tiffany.

"You must not ask me," responded Sir Waldo, with a reproving look. "Lindeth shouldn't say such things in the presence of ladies."

"Oh, is it improper?" she said innocently.

"Most improper!" he replied, his gravity unimpaired.

She saw that the others were laughing, and put up her chin, flushing slightly. But as Sir Waldo, taking his seat beside her at the table, asked her to tell him all about the morning's shopping expedition, showing a gratifying interest in her purchases, she very soon mended her temper, and prattled to him throughout the meal in the greatest good humour.

A new reticule for Patience, and velvet ribbon to match the pink satin had still to be found. When they rose from the table, Sir Waldo excused himself, and went away to resume his inspection of bailiffs; but Lindeth, declaring that he had a very good eye for colour, begged to be allowed to escort the ladies. Since the Nonesuch had devoted himself to Tiffany's entertainment at the table, Julian, wondering at this most unusual want of conduct in his cousin, had done his best to keep both his other guests amused; and he had succeeded very well. But Miss Trent, ably seconding his efforts, was assailed by apprehension. The faint suspicion, which had crossed her mind once or twice before, that Miss Chartley was more powerfully attracted to Lindeth than she would have wished anyone to guess was strengthened. The Rector's well-brought up daughter was behaving just as she ought, but the light in her soft eyes when she raised them to his lordship's face was, thought Miss Trent, unmistakeably tender. Like Mrs Chartley, she could not help feeling that they would be very well-suited to one another; but while she knew, on the authority of chroniclers and poets, that it was by no means unusual for a gentleman to transfer his affections almost in the twinkling of an eye (witness the extraordinary revulsion of feeling experienced by young Mr Montague when he first clapped eyes on Miss Capulet!), she did not know whether the Nonesuch would look upon Patience with approbation. Miss Trent could not doubt that if he did not he would contrive to thrust a spoke into the wheel of a possible courtship. That realization, she thought, should have been enough to warn her that he was probably an unscrupulous man of whom she would do well to beware. The mischief was that while she was just able to admit this possibility in his absence she had only to meet his eyes across a room to become instantly convinced of his integrity.

He found an opportunity to exchange a few words with her before he left the King's Arms, asking abruptly: "Shall I see you at the Colebatches' ball?"

"Yes. I have been invited to go, and my kind mistress says I may – or, rather, insists that I must!"

"En chaperon?"

"No, she goes herself, so I am to enjoy a holiday."

"Then I shan't cry off from it."

He did not wait for an answer, but with a smile, and a brief handshake, took his departure.

The next hour was spent very agreeably by the rest of the party in various shops, where not only was a reticule found, and the satin exactly matched, but where Tiffany bought a pair of filigree earrings, and Miss Trent a spray of artificial flowers to wear with her only ball-dress. Lindeth's presence added a good deal of gaiety to the expedition. He took a keen interest in the various purchases, but as he knew very little about feminine fashions he made some wonderful blunders, which rapidly induced a mood of hilarity in his companions. He also discovered a pastrycook's shop advertizing ice-creams; and as the ladies were all feeling hot, and a trifle weary, he experienced no difficulty in persuading them to enter it. Tiffany, puffing off her knowledge, said that it was just like Gunter's: an inaccurate statement, but one which showed her to be in her best humour. Miss Trent thought that she had seldom spent a more pleasant day in her company.

After disposing of several lemon-flavoured ices, they left the pastrycook's, and began to retrace their steps to the King's Arms. The street was a busy one, and there was no room to walk four abreast, so the two girls went ahead, amicably discussing the latest modes, and Lindeth civilly offered his arm to Miss Trent. A picture hanging in the window of a print-shop caught his eye; he recognized the subject, which was the Dripping Well, and at once drew Miss Trent's attention to it. It was while they were studying it that the harmony of the day was suddenly and rudely shattered. Some kind of a stir was taking place further up the street; there were shouts of: "Stop thief!" and as they looked quickly round a ragged urchin came into view, darting towards them with an apple clutched in his hand, and an expression of hunted terror in his starting eyes. He was dodging between the passers-by and had almost reached Patience and Tiffany when a middle-aged citizen thrust his walking-cane between his legs to arrest his progress. A crashing fall was the inevitable result: the child, swerving to avoid the over-zealous citizen, pitched forward, not on the flagway but on to the cobbled street. A cry of protest had burst from Patience; parcels, parasol, and purse were flung away; and under Miss Trent's horrified eyes she sprang into the road, snatching the urchin almost from under the hooves of a high-stepping chestnut harnessed to a tilbury, which was being driven at a spanking pace along the street. For a dreadful moment it seemed as if she must be trampled upon; then the chestnut reared up, snorting, and was miraculously swung to one side; and the driver of the tilbury, a natty young gentleman clad in raiment which, almost as clearly as his handling of the reins, proclaimed him to be a top-sawyer, added his voice to the general hubbub in a furious expletive. The next instant Lindeth had brushed past Miss Trent, racing forward to the rescue, and unceremoniously pushing Tiffany out of the way as he bent over Patience.

"Good God, Miss Chartley -! Are you hurt?"

She had dragged rather than lifted the urchin out of danger, and was on her knees, supporting him in her arms, and gazing down in horror at his face, down which blood was streaming from a gash on the forehead, but she glanced up, saying: "Oh, no, no! But this poor little boy -! Something to stop the bleeding – a handkerchief – *anything* -! Oh, pray, *one* of you -!"

"Here, take mine!" Lindeth said, thrusting it into her hand. "Poor little devil! Knocked himself out!" He looked up at the driver of the tilbury, and said curtly: "I'm sorry, sir, and must thank you for acting so promptly. I trust your horse has suffered no injury."

By this time the natty gentleman had realized that the female kneeling beside the gutter was a young and very pretty girl of obviously gentle birth. Blushing hotly, he stammered: "No, no, not the least in the world! Beg you'll accept my apologies, ma'am! Agitation of the moment – forgot myself! By Jove, though! You might have been killed! Bravest thing I ever saw in my life! By Jove, it was!"

She looked up briefly, to say: "Oh, no! I am so much obliged to you! I don't wonder you were angry – but, you see, I *had* to do it!"

Miss Trent, who had succeeded in pushing her way through the fast-gathering crowd, bent over her, asking anxiously: "How badly is he hurt, my dear?"

"I don't know. His head struck the cobbles. I must take him to the hospital."

"Yes, for I fear this cut must be stitched," said Miss Trent, folding her own handkerchief into a neat pad, and pressing it over the wound. "Do you hold his head so that I can tie Lord Lindeth's handkerchief round it!"

At this point, a fresh voice intruded upon them. The owner of the stolen apple, a stout and breathless shopkeeper, had arrived on the scene, and was loudly announcing his intention of summoning a constable to take the young varmint in charge. He was in a blustering rage, and somewhat roughly told Patience that the gaol was the place for hedge-birds, not the hospital. She said imploringly: "Pray don't give him up to the constable! It was very wrong of him to steal from you, but you see what a little boy he is, and how wretched! And he's badly hurt, too."

"Not he!" retorted the shopkeeper. "Serve him right if he'd broke his neck! It's a shame and a scandal the way him and his like hang about waiting for the chance to prig something! I'll have this young thief made an example of, by God I will!"

"Here, you rascal, that's no way to speak to a lady!" exclaimed the gentleman in the tilbury indignantly. "What's more I'll go bail the brat ain't half as big a thief as you are! *I* know you shopkeepers! All the same: selling farthing-dips for a bull's eye apiece!"

Not unnaturally, the effect of this intervention was far from happy. The injured tradesman appealed to the onlookers for support, and although one or two persons recommended him to pardon the thief, several others ranged themselves on his side. The air was rent with argument; but Lindeth, who had never before found himself in the centre of so embarrassing a scene, collected his wits and his dignity, and in a voice which held a remarkable degree of calm authority bade the shopkeeper declare the worth of the stolen fruit.

The man seemed at first to be determined on revenge, but after some more argument, in which some six or seven members of the crowd took part, he consented to accept the coin held out to him, and withdrew, accompanied by several of his supporters. The crowd now began to disperse; the small thief, coming round from his swoon, started to cry for his home and his Mammy; and while Patience soothed him, assuring him that she would take him to his home directly, and that no one should lock him up in prison, or give him up to the beadle (an official of whom he seemed to stand in terror), Miss Trent, Lord Lindeth, and the gentleman in sporting toggery, who had descended from the tilbury to join in the discussion, held a hurried council.

Throughout this animated scene Tiffany had been standing neglected and alone, rigid with mortification, jostled by such low-bred persons in the crowd as wished to obtain a closer view of the group in the gutter; pushed out of the way by Lord Lindeth; sharply adjured by Miss Trent not to stand like a stock, but to pick up Patience's belongings; and left without chaperonage or male protection by those who should have made her comfort and safety their first concern. Even the sporting gentleman in the tilbury had paid her no heed! Patience – *Patience* – ! – kneeling in the road, with her dress stained with blood, and a ragged and disgusting urchin in her arms, was the heroine of this most revolting piece, while she, the Beautiful Miss Wield, was left to hold as best she might two parasols, two purses, and a load of parcels.

She listened in seething fury to the plans that were being formulated. The sporting gentleman – he said that his name was Baldock, and that he begged to be allowed to place himself at their disposal – was offering to drive Patience and the dirty little boy to the infirmary; Lindeth was assuring her that he would himself convey the pair of them to the boy's home (no doubt a hovel in the back-slums of the town!), and Miss Trent was promising to proceed on foot to the infirmary immediately, there to render Patience all the aid and protection of which she was capable. Not one of them had a thought to spare for *her*! She was tired; she wanted to go home; out of sheer kindness of heart she had agreed to allow Patience (whom she had never liked) to accompany her to Leeds; she had submitted, without a word of protest, to being dragged all over the town in search of some stupid pink satin; her own companion – hired to take care of her! – instead of escorting her away from this degrading scene was merely concerned with Patience's welfare; and now she and Lindeth, without the slightest reference to her, were talking of driving that nasty child to his home in *her* carriage.

"I think I am going to faint!" she announced, in a penetrating voice which lent no colour to this statement.

Lindeth, who was lifting the boy out of Patience's arms, paid no heed; Miss Trent, assisting Patience to her feet, just glanced at her, and said: "I can't attend to you now, Tiffany!" and Mr Baldock, with no more than a cursory look at her, said: "Don't see why *you* should faint, ma'am! Shouldn't have wondered at it if *this* lady had, but not she! Didn't quite catch your name, ma'am, but shall take leave to say you're a regular trump! No – shouldn't have said that! Not the thing to say to a female! Beg your pardon: never been much of a lady's man! What I meant was, you're a – you're a -"

"Heroine!" supplied Lindeth, laughing.

"Ay, so she is! A dashed heroine!"

"Oh, pray -!" Patience protested. "I'm very much obliged to you, but indeed I'm nothing of the sort! If you will be so very good as to drive me to the infirmary, let us go immediately, if you please! He is still bleeding, and I'm afraid he may have injured his leg as well. You can see how it is swelling, and he cries if you touch it!" She looked round. "I don't know what became of my parcels, and my – Oh, Tiffany, you have them all! Thank you! I am so sorry – so disagreeable for you!"

"Oh, *pray* don't mention it!" said Tiffany, quivering with fury. "I *like* picking up parcels and parasols for other people! I *like* being jostled by vulgar persons! *Pray* don't consider me at all! *Or* ask my leave to use *my* carriage for that odious, wicked boy!"

"Well, of all the shrews!" gasped Mr Baldock.

Lindeth, who had been staring at Tiffany, a queer look in his eyes, and his lips rather tightly compressed, turned from her, and said quietly: "Hand Miss Chartley into your tilbury, will you? I'll give the boy to her then, and we can be off."

"Yes, but it will be the deuce of a squeeze," responded Mr Baldock doubtfully.

"No, it won't: I'm going to get up behind." He waited until Patience had climbed into the carriage, and then deposited the whimpering child in her lap, saying gently: "Don't be distressed! There's no need, I promise you."

She was feeling ready to sink, and whispered: "I never thought – I didn't know – Lord Lindeth, stay with her! I shall do very well by myself. Perhaps you could hire a carriage for me? Oh, yes! of course that's what I ought to do! If you would direct the coachman to drive to the infirmary -"

"Stop fretting!" he commanded, smiling up at her. "We'll discuss what's best to be done presently. Meanwhile, Miss Trent will look after Miss Wield: I am coming with you!" He turned, as Miss Trent came up to give Patience her purse, and told her briefly what he meant to do, adding, in an undervoice: "Will you be able to come to the infirmary, ma'am? I think you should, don't you?"

"Of course I shall come," she replied. "Just as soon as I have taken Miss Wield back to the King's Arms!"

He looked relieved. "Yes, if you please. Then I'll find Waldo. He's the man we want in this situation!"

She had been thinking so herself, and although she was surprised that he should have said it she agreed cordially. It was then his lordship's turn to be a little puzzled, for he had spoken more to himself than to her, and (since Waldo very much disliked having his peculiar philanthropy puffed-off) was already regretting it. Before it could be established that they were talking at cross-purposes, Tiffany, almost beside herself with rage at their continued neglect, stalked up to them to demand in a voice vibrant with passion how much longer Miss Trent meant to keep her waiting.

"Not an instant!" replied her preceptress cheerfully, removing from her grasp the parasol and the various packages with which she was still burdened. Over her shoulder, she smiled reassuringly at Patience. "I'll join you at the infirmary directly, Miss Chartley. Now, Tiffany!"

"You will *not* join her at the infirmary!" said Tiffany. "I wish to go home, and it is your duty to stay with me, and if you don't do what *I* want I'll tell my aunt, and have you turned off!"

"Without a character!" nodded Miss Trent, tucking a hand in her arm, and firmly propelling her down the flagway. "And if I were to take you home, abandoning Miss Chartley, her mama would no doubt demand my instant dismissal too, so in either event I must be totally ruined. I am quite sick with apprehension! But if I were you, Tiffany, I would take care how I exposed myself!"

"How *I* exposed myself?" gasped Tiffany. "When it was that odious Patience Chartley, with her insinuating ways, behaving like a hoyden, just to make everyone think her a heroine -"

"Do, Tiffany, strive for a little conduct!" interrupted Miss Trent. "I am not going to bandy words with you in public, so you may as well keep your tongue."

This, however, the outraged beauty was far too angry to do, delivering herself all the way to the King's Arms of a tirade which was as comprehensive as it was absurd. Miss Trent refused to be goaded into retort, but she could willingly have slapped her spoilt charge. She did indeed point out to her that she was attracting the undesirable notice of such passers-by who were privileged to overhear scraps of her diatribe; but although Tiffany lowered her voice she continued to scold.

It might have been supposed that the violence of her emotions would have exhausted her by the time the King's Arms was reached; but she was made of resilient fibre, and the recital of her wrongs and the condemnation of every one of her companions were merely the prelude to a storm which, as experience had taught Miss Trent, would involve her, when it broke, in embarrassment, startle everyone within earshot, and culminate in a fit of shattering hysterics. She knew it to be useless to reason with Tiffany; so when they reached the posting-house she almost dragged her into the parlour which Lindeth had hired for the day, and left her there, saying mendaciously that she was going to procure some hartshorn. Tiffany had already begun to cry in an ominously gusty way, but Miss Trent did not believe that she would work herself into hysterics if no one was present to be shocked or distressed by her passion. She was quite capable, of course, of doing something outrageous when she had lashed herself into one of these fits; but Miss Trent, after rapidly reviewing the circumstances, thought that the worst she could find to do in the middle of Leeds would be to order her aunt's coachman to put the horses to, and to have herself driven back to Staples immediately. When John-Coachman refused to obey this order, as he certainly would, there would really be nothing left for her to do but to smash the china ornaments on the mantelpiece.

Miss Trent might regard the situation in this practical light; but she was much more worried than she had allowed Tiffany to suspect. Her first duty was undoubtedly to that intransigent damsel, and by no stretch of the imagination could this duty be thought to include taking her into the back-slums of the town; but when Mrs Chartley had permitted her daughter to join the expedition she had done so in the belief that she would be respectably chaperoned. Neither she nor Miss Trent, of course, could have foreseen the accident which had made this double chaperonage so difficult; but that she would think it extremely reprehensible of Miss Trent to leave Patience to the sole protection and escort of Lord Lindeth was beyond doubt, or (in Miss Trent's own opinion) censure. Somehow the two conflicting duties must be reconciled. Try as she would, Miss Trent could hit upon no better solution to the problem than to enlist Sir Waldo's support, just as Lindeth had suggested. If he could be induced to keep Tiffany amused until Patience's protégé had been restored to his parents the unfortunate episode might yet end happily.

So it was not to procure hartshorn for Tiffany that Miss Trent hurriedly left the parlour, but to make all speed to the infirmary, whence she meant to send Lindeth off post-haste to find his cousin.

In the event, Sir Waldo entered the King's Arms just as she was about to leave the house. Never had she been more thankful, nor more relieved! She exclaimed impulsively: "Oh, how glad I am to see you! Sir Waldo, you are the *one* person who may be able to help me in this fix, and I do beg that you will!"

"You may be very sure that I will," he replied, looking a little startled, but maintaining his calm. "What fix have you fallen into, and what must I do to extricate you from it?"

She gave a shaky laugh. "Oh, dear! I must seem to you to have flown into alt! I beg your pardon! It wasn't precisely I who fell into a fix, but -"

"Just a moment!" he interrupted. "Do you know that there is blood on your dress?"

She cast a cursory glance down her own person. "Is there? Yes, I see – but it's of no consequence!"

"Well, as you don't appear to have sustained any injury, I'll accept your word for that," he said. "Whose blood is it?"

"I don't know – I mean, I don't know what his name is! A little boy – but I must tell you how it all happened!"

"Do!" he invited.

As concisely as she could, she put him in possession of the facts, making no attempt to conceal from him that it was not the accident which had thrown her into disorder, but Tiffany's obstructive behaviour. "I know it must seem incredible that she should fly into one of her rages at such a moment," she said earnestly, "but you know what she is!"

"Of course I do! It is exactly what I should have expected of her. How could it be otherwise when the rôle of heroine in this stirring drama was snatched from her, and she found herself a mere spectator? Where is she now?"

"Upstairs, in the parlour where we ate nuncheon. That was the reason, of course, and I don't know what enraged her the more: your cousin paying no heed to her, or that absurd Mr Baldock saying he didn't see what cause *she* had to faint! Yes, it's all very well for you to laugh, sir! I own, I should think it very funny myself if it didn't concern me so nearly. Do you see now what a fix I'm in? I can neither leave Tiffany alone here for heaven only knows how long, nor can I abandon Miss Chartley! I never was more distracted! But your cousin said that you were the man to help us in this situation, and, although it surprised me a little that he should say so, I perceived immediately that he was perfectly right! Sir Waldo, will you be so very obliging as to stay with Tiffany – divert her, you know! – while I go with Patience to wherever the boy lives?"

"I don't think that was quite what Lindeth meant," he said dryly, "but certainly I'll take charge of Tiffany. Shall I find her indulging a fit of hysterics?"

"No, for I came away before she had time to throw herself into one. There's no sense in having hysterics, you know, if one is quite by oneself."

He smiled, but said: "It's to be hoped that she doesn't have them for my edification, for I should be quite at a loss to know what to do!"

"She won't," said Miss Trent confidently. "Just flatter her as you very well *do* know how to do!"

"I think that the best service I can render you will be to drive her back to Staples," he said. "You need not then be anxious on her account – I hope!"

The worried crease was smoothed from her brow. She said gratefully: "No, indeed! You know I shouldn't be! And there can be no objection – in an open carriage, and with your groom behind!"

"Yes, those circumstances will compel me to restrain any inclination I may feel to make violent love to her, won't they?" he agreed affably.

She laughed. "Yes – if that was what I had meant to say, which it was not! I know very well you don't feel any such inclination!"

"I imagine you might! Now, I have just one thing to say before we part, ma'am! From what you have told me, this urchin hails from the slums: either in the eastern part of the town, where the dyeing-houses and most of the manufactories are situated, or on the south bank of the river."

"I am afraid so. You are going to say that I shouldn't permit Miss Chartley to go into such districts. I know it, but I don't think I can prevent her."

"No, I am not going to say that. But you must promise me you won't leave the carriage, Miss Trent! So far as I am aware there is no epidemic disease rife there at the moment, but most of the dwellings are little better than hovels, and there is a degree of squalor which makes it excessively imprudent for you – or Miss Chartley, of course – to enter them."

She looked wonderingly at him. "I have never been in the poorer part of the town. Have you, then?"

"Yes, I have, and you may believe that I know what I am saying. Have I your word?"

"Of course: I would not for the world expose Miss Chartley to the least risk!"

"Good girl!" he said, smiling at her. "Tell Julian I've left you in his charge – and that I've removed the worst of your embarrassments!"

He held out his hand, and, when she put hers into it, raised it to his lips, and lightly kissed her fingers.

CHAPTER TEN

TIFFANY DID not greet Sir Waldo with hysterics; but he found her weeping in an angry, uncontrolled way which warned him that a more ticklish task lay before him than he had foreseen. Like a child suffering from over-excitement, she was as miserable as she was cross, and with the slightest encouragement she would have cast herself upon Sir Waldo's chest, and sobbed out her woes into his shoulder. With considerable skill he managed to prevent this without adding to her sense of ill-usage, but he soon saw that it was useless – indeed, perilous – to attempt to bring her to reason. The story she poured out to him bore little resemblance to the unembroidered account furnished earlier by Miss Trent. Tiffany never consciously deviated from the truth, but since she saw everything only as it affected herself the truth was apt to become somewhat distorted. Anyone unacquainted with the facts would have supposed from her version of the accident that Patience, having first, and with incredible selfishness, dragged her companions all over the town in search of her own needs, had next set her cap at Lindeth in a way that would have been diverting had it not been so unbecoming; and finally, in her determination to attract attention to herself, had created a ridiculous scene by dashing into the road to perform a spectacular and quite unnecessary rescue. For her part, Tiffany was persuaded that the nasty boy had been in no danger at all, but Patience, of course, had put on all the airs of a heroine, quite deluding Lindeth, as well as Mr Baldock, who was a very low, vulgar person, with the most disgusting manners of anyone Tiffany had ever met.

There was a good deal more in the same strain, culminating in the iniquity of all concerned in coolly, and without as much as a by-your-leave, appropriating Tiffany's carriage (for even if it did belong to her aunt it had been lent to her, not to Patience) for the conveyance of a dirty and thievish boy who ought rather to have been handed over to the constable. This was the crowning injury, and Tiffany's eyes flashed as she recounted it. She did not deny that she had lost her temper. She had borne everything else without uttering a single complaint, but that had been Too Much.

The Nonesuch, quick to seize opportunity, agreed that such conduct passed all bounds. He was astonished to learn that Lindeth and Miss Trent were so lost to all sense of propriety as to suppose that Tiffany could be left to kick her heels at the King's Arms while they jauntered about the town (with a dirty and thievish boy) in what was undoubtedly her carriage. He said that they would be well served if, when they at last returned to the King's Arms, they were to find that the bird had flown.

"Yes," agreed Tiffany, hiccuping on a sob. "Only, if I were to order John-Coachman to bring the carriage round he wouldn't do it, because he is a detestable old man, and treats me as if I were a child!"

"I'll take you home," said the Nonesuch, with his glinting smile.

She stared at him. "You? In your phaeton? *Now*?" He nodded; and she jumped up, exclaiming ecstatically: "Oh, *yes!* I should like that of all things! And we won't leave a message, either!"

"Oh, that will be quite unnecessary!" he said, with perfect truth.

Her tears ceased abruptly; and if the ill-usage she had suffered still rankled in her bosom it soon became at least temporarily forgotten in the elation of being driven by no less a person than the Nonesuch.

Mrs Underhill was very much shocked when she heard what had happened in Leeds, but although Sir Waldo left Tiffany to tell the story as she pleased the good lady's reception of it was not at all what her niece desired or expected. She said she wouldn't have had such a thing happen for the world. "Not with Mrs Chartley letting Patience go with you, as she did, which quite surprised me, for I never thought she would, and no more she would have, if it hadn't been for Miss Trent being there to take care of her. And what she'll say, when she hears about this – not that Miss Trent could have stopped it, by all I can make out, for it wasn't a thing anyone would *expect* to happen! Well, thank goodness Miss Trent had the sense to stay with Patience! At least Mrs Chartley won't be able to say we didn't do our best, *or* that she was left to be brought home by his lordship, which she wouldn't have liked at all! Not that I mean he wouldn't have kept the line, as I hope I don't need to explain to you, Sir Waldo, for I'm sure I never knew anyone more truly the gentleman – present company excepted, of course – but Mrs Chartley – well, she's nice to a fault, and very strict in her notions!"

This speech was naturally extremely displeasing to Tiffany. There were danger signals in her eyes, which her aunt viewed with apprehension. Mrs Underhill hoped that she was not going to fly into one of her miffs, and she said feebly: "Now, Tiffany-love, there's nothing to put you into high fidgets! To be sure, it was vexatious for you to be obliged to wait, when you was wanting to come home, but you wouldn't have wished to leave poor Miss Chartley with no carriage, now, you know you wouldn't! A very shabby thing that would have been! And Sir Waldo driving you home in his phaeton, which I'll be bound you enjoyed!"

"They should have *asked* me!" said Tiffany obstinately. "If they had done so -"

"*I* see what it is!" suddenly announced Charlotte, whose penetrating gaze had been fixed for some minutes on her cousin's face. "Nobody paid any heed to you! And you might just as easily have rescued the boy as Patience, only you didn't, so it wasn't you that was brave and noble, but *her*, and *that's* why you're in such a pelter!"

"How dare you?" gasped Tiffany, glaring at her.

"Charlotte, *don't*!" begged Mrs Underhill, much agitated.

"*And*," pursued Charlotte, with acute if deplorable insight, "it's my belief the man in the tilbury didn't pay any heed to you either, and that's why you said he was rude and vulgar!"

"Now, that's enough!" said Mrs Underhill, with a very fair assumption of authority. "Whatever must Sir Waldo be thinking of you? I don't know when I've been so mortified! You must please excuse her, sir!"

"I'll excuse them both, ma'am, and leave them to enjoy their quarrel!" he replied, looking amused.

"Oh, dear, and I was going to ask you if you wouldn't stop to eat your dinner with us!" exclaimed Mrs Underhill distressfully.

"Thank you: you are very good, ma'am, but I mustn't stay," he answered, smiling at her in a way which, as she afterwards told Miss Trent, made her feel all of a twitter.

He then took his leave, and went away. He reached Broom Hall as the shadows were lengthening, and strolled into the house, stripping off his gloves. The door leading into the bookroom opened, and a slender sprig of fashion emerged, and paused on the threshold, saying with would-be jauntiness: "Hallo, Waldo!"

At sight of this unexpected visitor Sir Waldo had halted, one glove still only half drawn from his hand, a sudden frown in his eyes. He stood still for an instant; then the frown vanished, and he pulled off his glove, and laid it down on the table. "Dear me!" he said, in a tone of mild surprise. "And what brings you here, Laurie?"

Mr Calver, with the memory of his last encounter with his cousin uncomfortably in mind, was much relieved by the calm friendliness of this greeting. He had not expected to be met with an explosion of wrath, because Waldo never ripped up, or came the ugly; but he had feared that he might cut up a trifle stiff, perhaps. He came forward, saying awkwardly: "I've been visiting friends in York. Thought I'd come over to see how you go on."

"That's very kind of you," said Sir Waldo politely.

"Well, I – well – you know, I don't like to be at outs with you! The last time I saw you – Well, I was in a damned bad skin, and I daresay I may have said things I don't mean! I shouldn't wish you to think -"

"Oh, that's enough, Laurie!" Sir Waldo interrupted, a swift smile banishing the slightly stern look on his face. "Looby! Did you suppose I had taken an affront into my head? What a gudgeon you must think me!"

"No, I don't, but – Well, I thought I'd post over to see you – beg your pardon, you know!"

"I'm much obliged to you. Come into the book-room! Has Wedmore done the honours of the house – such as they are?"

"Oh, yes! Well, I haven't been here much above half-an-hour, but he brought me some sherry, and took Blyth off to unpack my bags." He shot a sidelong look at his cousin, and ventured on a small joke. "I was pretty sure you wouldn't throw me out of doors even if you *had* nabbed the rust!"

"Very unlikely," agreed Sir Waldo, walking over to a sidetable, and pouring himself out a glass of sherry. He drank a little, and stood thoughtfully regarding Laurence.

That exquisite, failing, not for the first time in a somewhat chequered career, to meet that steady, faintly amused gaze, cast himself into a chair, with an assumption of ease, and picked up his own glass from a table at his elbow, saying airily: "I hadn't thought you meant to remain here above a sennight. Everyone is wondering what's become of you! Is Lindeth still with you? Don't he find it devilish slow?"

"Apparently not. Tell me! Who are these friends of yours who live in York?"

"Oh, no one you're acquainted with!"

"I didn't think I was." He picked up the decanter, and walked across the room to refill Laurence's glass. "What is it you want, Laurie?"

"I told you! We came to cuffs, and -"

"No, don't sham it! You haven't travelled all the way from London merely to beg my pardon!"

"I've come from York!" said Laurence, reddening. "If you don't believe me you may enquire at the Black Horse, where I hired a chaise to bring me here!"

"I do believe you. I think you went to York on the Edinburgh mail. Or are you on the rocks again, and was it the stage? Stop trying to make a pigeon of me! You'll only be gapped, you know! What's the matter? Are you in the suds?"

"No, I am not!" replied Laurence angrily. "I may not be flush in the pocket, but I haven't come to ask you to pay any gaming debts!"

"Don't be so ready to sport your canvas! I didn't suppose that was it. There might be other debts which you forgot to mention when you were last down the wind."

"Well, there ain't!" growled Laurence. "Nothing to signify, that is! And if there was, I shouldn't ask you to dub up the possibles! Not after what you said a month ago! I daresay you think I'm a loose screw, but I don't run thin!"

"I wish you will come down from these high ropes! I don't think you a loose screw – though if I were to tell you what I *do* think you you'd be ready to eat me! If you don't want me to dub up the possibles, what *do* you want me to do?"

"It may interest you to know, coz, that it's been make and scrape with me ever since you left London!" said Laurence bitterly. "And when I think of the shifts I've been put to – Well, it's the outside enough for you to be suspecting me of having come to see you only to get you to tip over the dibs! It isn't that at all!" He paused. "At least," he amended, "it ain't debt! If you *must* know, I've hit upon a devilish good scheme – if I can but raise the recruits! Of course, if you don't care to frank me – though it ain't so much franking me, mind, as *investing* your blunt! – there's no more to be said. But considering the times you've offered to buy me a pair of colours -"

"The offer still stands, Laurie."

"Yes, but I don't want it. It wouldn't suit me at all. I haven't any taste for the law, either. I didn't think of it at the time, but if you had suggested the Church to me, when I was up at Oxford, there would have been some sense in it. I daresay I shouldn't have liked it above half, but I wonder you shouldn't have thought of it, if you're so eager to thrust me into some profession or other. After all, I know you've several good livings in your gift! However, it's too late now."

"That's just as well, for I can think of few men less suited to the Church."

"No, very likely I should have found it a dead bore. Not but what a snug parsonage – But it's of no consequence! I fancy I've hit on the very thing, Waldo! What's more, if the thing comes off right there's a fortune in it!"

Concealing his misgivings, Sir Waldo invited him to continue.

"Well, I hadn't meant to broach it to you so soon," said Laurence, rather naïvely. "But since you've asked me to – and there's no reason why you shouldn't care for the scheme: in fact, I'm persuaded you'll think it's the very thing -"

"You are filling me with foreboding, Laurie. Do put me out of suspense!"

"Of course, if you mean to set your face against it from the start I might as well keep my tongue!" said Laurence peevishly.

"We haven't reached the start yet. Cut line!" commanded his cousin.

Laurence looked offended for a moment, but he managed to swallow his spleen. "Yes – Well – well, are you acquainted with Kearney, Waldo?"

"No."

"*Desmond* Kearney!" Sir Waldo shook his head. "Oh! I daresay he may not have come in your way, though I should have thought you must have met him. He's the devil of a man to hounds – a clipping rider! But you high sticklers are so top-lofty -" He broke off, and said hastily: "Not that it signifies! The thing is, Kearney is a friend of mine. Not a feather to fly with, but a first-rate man, and a capital judge of horseflesh! We mean to become partners."

"Partners in what?" asked Sir Waldo blankly.

"Hunters! Selling 'em, I mean."

"O my God!"

"I suppose I might have guessed you would – No, do but listen, Waldo!" begged Laurence, suddenly altering his tone. "Only think of the blunt some of the Melton men drop on their hunters! Well, you're one yourself, so you should know! They say Lord Alvanley gave seven hundred guineas for one of the nags he bought last year, and I could name you a score of men who think nothing of shelling out five or six hundred for horses that were bought originally for no more than eighty or a hundred guineas! Why, if you was to put your own stud under the hammer – just your hunters and your hacks: not your driving-cattle, of course – they wouldn't fetch a penny under five thousand! I daresay you're thinking the scheme might not fadge, but -"

"Might not fadge!" interrupted Sir Waldo. "You'd find yourselves at point non-plus within a twelvemonth!"

"No, that we shouldn't! We have it all planned, and I'd be willing to lay you any odds we shall make an excellent hit. Of course, at first we shall be obliged to spend a good deal of blunt – no need to tell you that! – but -"

"No need at all!"

"Well, there's no doing anything unless one has some capital! The thing is -"

"Thank you, I know what the thing is!" said Sir Waldo acidly. "For God's sake, will you stop trying to tip me a rise? I never in my life listened to such an addle-brained scheme! Do you think me such a flat that I would provide the capital for such a crazy venture? Go into partnership with a man who hasn't a feather to fly with? Oh, no! Laurie! Coming it *too* strong!"

"If you would but *listen* -! Kearney ain't any plumper in the pocket than I am, but he's just come into some property! It was that circumstance which put the notion into his head! He's inherited a place in Ireland, from his uncle – Galway, I think. Sounds to me much like this place: gone to rack, and the house pretty well tumbling down. Seemed to him more of a liability than a honey-fall, for there's no getting rid of it as it stands."

"It seems like that to me too."

"Well, that's where you're out! We mean to put it to dashed good use! Kearney's been to look it over, and he says there's plenty of ground attached, and acres of stabling, which only needs repairing to furnish us with precisely what we need. Now, Waldo, you must know that Ireland's the place for picking up first-rate horses for no more than eighty pounds apiece! No cart-horse blood there! No black drop! A year's schooling, and you sell 'em over here for a couple of hundred at the least!"

"If you think that I'm going to set you up as a horsechanter -"

"No such thing!" exclaimed Laurence indignantly. "They won't be *unsound* horses!"

"They will be if you have anything to do with choosing them."

Laurence struggled with himself, and again managed to suppress his anger. "As a matter of fact, Kearney will attend to that side of the business: he knows the country, and which are the best fairs – and I shouldn't wonder at it if he's as good a judge of a horse as you are! *My* part will be to sell 'em over here."

"Laurie, are you seriously proposing to set up as a dealer?"

"No, of course not! I mean, I'm not going to have a sale-ring, or anything of that kind! I've got a much better notion: I'm going to sell 'em on the hunting-field!"

"*What?*" said Sir Waldo faintly.

"Lord, you know what I mean! You ride a goodlooking hunter of the right stamp with one of the Hunts – the Quorn, for instance – and what happens?"

"You end up in the Whissendine."

"Oh, go to the devil! That's not what I mean! Someone takes a fancy to your horse – asks you if you'd care to sell him, and before you know where you are -"

"Not if he's seen you riding the horse!" interpolated Sir Waldo brutally.

Laurence flushed vividly. "Thank you! Upon my word, coz, of all the damnably unjust things to say! – I collect I'm a slowtop – a skirter – a -"

"No, no, I didn't mean that!" said Sir Waldo, relenting slightly. "You've plenty of pluck, but you sloven your fences, and you don't get the best out of your horses. Also – well, no matter! I'm sorry, but I'll have no hand in this project."

"Waldo, I'm not asking you to *give* it to me!" Laurence urged, rather desperately. "Only to *lend* it and no more than five thousand! I swear I'd pay it back!"

"I doubt it! Oh, I don't doubt you think you would! But I think that so far from your paying me back I should be obliged to tow you out of the River Tick to the tune of a few more thousands. I won't do it."

There was a long silence. Laurence got up jerkily, and went over to stare out of the window. Presently he said: "I know you said when you paid that debt for me last month – that it was the last time, but I never thought you'd refuse to help me when – when I'm trying to do what you've been urging me to for ever!"

Sir Waldo could not help smiling at this. "My dear Laurie, I really don't think I can be said to have urged you to take to horse-coping!"

"You want me to pursue some occupation. And now, when I'm determined not to be idle any longer, or to hang on your sleeve – you make it impossible!"

"Find a respectable occupation, and try me again! You think me a shocking nip-squeeze, but what you are asking me to do is to help you to break your back."

Laurence turned, forcing a smile to his drooping mouth. "No, I don't. You've been devilish generous to me: I know that! Only – Oh, well! I suppose there's no more to be said. I'd best go back to London tomorrow. I know you don't want me here."

"Gammon! Do you wish to stay?"

"Well, I did rather think – I mean, everyone is going out of town now, and you know what Brighton costs in July! You told me I must stop wasting the ready -"

"So it clearly behoves me to house you! Stop playing off your tricks, you incorrigible dryboots! I haven't the smallest objection to your remaining here – but I don't think you'll like it above half! The builders are at work, you know."

"Oh, I don't care a straw for that!" Laurence assured him. "You seem to be pulling the place to bits – all for your ramshackle brats, I collect!"

"That's it," replied Sir Waldo cheerfully. "I must go and tell Wedmore we won't wait dinner for Julian: he's in Leeds, and is likely to be detained. That, by the way, is one of the disadvantages of the house: the only unbroken bell-wire is the one leading from our late lamented cousin's bedroom! There are some other drawbacks, too: your man will tell you all about them! I only hope he won't cut his stick. I live in constant dread of waking one morning to find that Munslow has abandoned me."

Laurence looked rather appalled, but said: "Oh, Blyth wouldn't serve me such a trick! As for your Munslow – I wish I may see him abandoning you! When do you dine? Should I change my rig?"

"Not on my account. We dine at the unfashionable hour of six."

"Oh, yes! country hours!" said Laurence, refusing to be daunted. "I'm glad of it, for, to own the truth, I'm feeling a trifle fagged. Been thinking lately that it was time I went on a repairing lease!"

He maintained this affability until nine o'clock, when, after trying in vain to smother a succession of yawns, he took himself off to bed. Sir Waldo was not in the least deceived. As little as he believed that Laurence had been visiting friends in York did he believe that Laurence either wanted to remain at Broom Hall or was resigned to the frustration of his preposterous scheme. He remembered, with a rueful smile, several previous occasions when, having refused some demand of Laurie's, he had allowed himself to be won over by just such tactics as Laurie was employing now. Laurie remembered them too; probably he had come prepared to meet with an initial rebuff; certainly he had not accepted it as final: that was betrayed by his meekness. When Laurie knew that he could not bring his cousin round his thumb he very rapidly fell into a rage, jealousy and self-pity overcoming his reason, and leading him to rant and complain until he really did believe in his illusionary grievances.

I ought to have sent him packing, Sir Waldo thought, knowing that in yielding to a compassionate impulse he was raising false hopes in Laurie's breast. But he could no more have done it than he could have left him to languish in a debtor's prison. He had little affection for Laurie, and he was well aware that Laurie had as little for him; but when he had told George Wingham that he had ruined Laurie he had spoken in all sincerity. Laurie's idleness, his follies, his reckless extravagance he set at his own door. By his easy, unthinking generosity he had sapped whatever independance Laurie might have had, imposing no check upon his volatility, but rather encouraging him in the conviction that he would never be run quite off his legs because his wealthy cousin would infallibly rescue him from utter disaster. "After all, it means nothing to you!" Laurie had once said to him, when he had been in his first year at Oxford. Sir Waldo, remembering, grimaced at his younger self. Laurie had said bitterly that it was easy for anyone rolling in gold to preach economy; and that younger Waldo, rich beyond most men's dreams, imbued with philanthropic principles imperfectly understood, morbidly anxious never to become clutchfisted, and only too ready to believe, with Laurie, that the difference between their respective circumstances was one of the grosser injustices of fate, had opened wide his purse for that predatory youth to dip into: not once, but so many times that Laurie had come to regard him as one on whom he had a right to depend. Only when he had taken to deep gaming had Sir Waldo put his foot down. He meant to keep it down, strengthened in his resolve by the storm of resentment he had roused in Laurence; but even at the height of exasperation his conscience told him that he was himself much to blame for this. He had often felt sorry for Laurie, but his pity had been mixed with contempt; and because he had never liked him he had given him money, which was an easy thing to do, instead of the very different services he had rendered Julian.

The cases were not, of course, parallel. Laurence was some years older than Julian, and he had not been left fatherless while still in leading-strings. But his father had been a coldhearted man, bored by his children, and grudging every penny he was obliged to spend on them, so that Laurie had naturally enough turned to his cousin for help in any predicament.

It might have been wiser not to have told him that he might remain at Broom Hall, but Sir Waldo had found it impossible to treat him so unkindly. Moreover, Julian was staying at Broom Hall, and that circumstance alone made it imperative that he should also welcome Laurie. Laurie was jealous of his affection for Julian, not because of any fondness for him, but because he was obstinate in the belief that he lavished money on the boy. "If it had been Lindeth who had applied to you, you wouldn't have refused!" Laurie had flung at him once.

"Lindeth doesn't apply to me," he had answered.

"No! he ain't obliged to! Anything he wants he can get from you for the mere lifting of an eyebrow! We all know that!"

"Then you are all wonderfully mistaken," he had said.

But Laurie had not been mistaken in thinking that Julian was his favourite cousin; and just because it was true he would not turn Laurie away from his doors while Julian was at liberty to stay with him for as long as he chose.

He was thinking of Laurie's jealousy, and wondering how many days would pass before he and Julian came to cuffs, when he heard the sound of carriage-wheels, and Julian's voice calling good-night to someone. A few minutes later he came into the room, saying: "Waldo? Oh, there you are! Had you given me up for lost? I beg your pardon, but I knew you wouldn't be in a worry!"

"Not in a worry! When I have been pacing the floor for hours, in the greatest agitation -!"

Julian chuckled. "You look pretty comfortable to me!"

"Merely exhausted. Have you dined?"

"Yes, at the Rectory. They were just sitting down to dinner when we arrived, and Mrs Chartley *would* have me stay. Miss Trent declined it, but the Rector said I need not think I should be obliged to walk home, if I stayed, because his man should drive me here. So I did. I hadn't meant to remain for so long, but we got to talking about everything under the sun – you know how it is! – and I never noticed the time. You didn't wait for me, did you?"

"No, not for a second. Did you restore your young Hemp to his parents?"

"Yes, but as for calling the poor little devil a young Hemp – Good God, he's only six years old, and all he stole was one apple! Miss Trent told you what happened, didn't she? It was the most frightful moment!"

"It must have been. I collect that Miss Chartley showed the greatest presence of mind."

"Yes, and such courage! She made nothing of it: her only concern was for the boy. I could only wonder at her, for she is so quiet and shy that one would never have supposed that she could behave with such intrepidity, or remain so composed! If the danger she had been in had not been enough to overset her you'd have thought that the people who crowded round would have done it! She paid no heed to them – didn't even shrink from the fellow who ranted at her that he was going to hand the boy over to the Law. Lord, Waldo, I never wanted you more in my life!"

"Why? Couldn't you deal with the bloodthirsty citizen without my assistance?"

"That! Of course I could! But I didn't know what the devil ought to be done with the brat. However, Miss Chartley knew – yes, and just what to say to the mother and father, too! The only thing that did overset her – for a few minutes -" He broke off abruptly.

"I can guess," said Sir Waldo helpfully.

Julian shot him a quick, defensive look; but after a slight pause he said, with a forced smile and a mounting colour: "I suppose so – since you drove her back to Staples! I'm very much obliged to you, by the way. Did she – did she rip up to you about it?"

"Oh, yes, but no more than I expected! Accredited beauties, you know, can rarely bear to be eclipsed. It was clearly incumbent upon me to remove her from the scene, but I own I shall always regret that I was denied the privilege of meeting the low, vulgar, and disgustingly ill-mannered young gentleman in the tilbury!"

That drew an involuntary laugh from Julian. "Baldock! First he said he didn't see why *she* should faint, and then he called her a shrew! I don't know why I should laugh, for the lord knows I didn't feel like laughing at the time! But what a clunch!" He was silent again for a minute, and then said, with a little difficulty: "You think I'm a clunch too, don't you? But I've known, ever since that ill-fated expedition to Knaresborough....I thought, at first, that it was just – just because she was so young, and had been so much indulged, but – but, there's no *heart* behind that lovely face, Waldo! Nothing but – oh, well! What a fellow I am to be saying such things! Even to you! But I daresay you may have suspected that she – she did bowl me out, when I first saw her!"

"I should have been astonished if she hadn't," replied Sir Waldo, in an indifferent tone. "I don't recall when I've seen a more beautiful girl. It's a pity she has neither the wits nor the disposition to match her beauty, but I've no doubt she'll do very well without them. If her fortune is sufficiently substantial she may even catch her Marquis!"

"Catch her Marquis?" exclaimed Julian blankly. "Which Marquis?"

"Whichever offers for her. Yes, I know it may seem absurd, but she seems to have set her heart on becoming – at the least! – a Marchioness. It won't surprise me at all if she achieves her ambition. What, by the way, did the Chartleys think of this stirring adventure?"

"*She* was very much shocked, of course," Julian replied, "but the Rector said that Patience – Miss Chartley, I mean! – had done just as she ought! Naturally Mrs Chartley couldn't but wish it hadn't happened: she didn't *blame* anyone! In fact, neither she nor the Rector made much more of it than

Miss Chartley did herself! You may depend upon it that I took care to assure them that she had not entered that dreadful hovel which was the boy's *home*! – Miss Chartley told me there were many worse to be seen, but I swear to you, Waldo, my pigs are better housed! – but Mrs Chartley only said that a clergyman's daughter was used to go amongst the poor. I had thought she would be very much vexed, but not a bit of it! We spent such a comfortable evening! Yes, and only imagine my surprise when I discovered that she was a Yateley! Somehow or other we had got to talking about Timperley, and Mrs Chartley told me that she had been born not so very far from it! Well, in the next county, at all events: Warwick! When she mentioned her previous name, you may guess how I stared!"

"Forgive me!" apologized Sir Waldo. "I'm either very dull, or very forgetful, but I haven't the least guess! Who *are* the Yateleys?"

"Oh, a Warwickshire family! I don't know much about 'em, but you must have heard Mama talk of her great friend, Maria Yateley! She's Lady Stone – a regular fusty mug! – but Mama has known her for ever, and she always speaks of her as Maria Yateley. Well, would you believe it? Mrs Chartley is her first cousin!"

There did not seem to Sir Waldo to be much cause for satisfaction in this discovery, but he responded suitably; and Julian chatted away happily, his sad disillusionment forgotten in telling his cousin all about the very pleasant evening he had spent, and in trying to persuade him that Miss Chartley's protégé, at present domiciled with both his parents and one of his grandmothers, was an eligible candidate for entrance to the Broom Hall Orphanage. Failing in this, he said that he must discuss the matter with the Rector: perhaps the boy could be admitted to the Charity School. "For I feel one ought to do *something*," he said, frowning over the problem. "After Miss Chartley saved him from being trampled on it seems a pity that he should be put to work in one of the manufactories, poor little rat! I daresay if *you* were to speak to the Governors, or the Warden, or whatever they call themselves - "

"No, you talk it over with the Rector!" said Sir Waldo.

"Well, I will." He yawned. "Lord, I am sleepy! I think I'll go to bed, if you've no objection."

"None at all. Oh, by the bye! Laurie is here. He went to bed early too."

Julian had walked over to the door, but he wheeled round at that, exclaiming "*Laurie?* What the devil brings him here?"

"He told me he had been visiting friends in York, and drove over to see how we go on here."

"Gammon!" said Julian scornfully. "What a damned thing! What does he want?"

Sir Waldo raised his brows. "You had better ask him," he replied, a faint chill in his voice.

Julian reddened. "I didn't mean – I know it's your house, and no concern of mine whom you invite to stay in it, but – oh, lord, Waldo, what a dead bore! You didn't invite him, either, did you?"

"No, I didn't," admitted Sir Waldo, with a smile that was a trifle twisted. "I'm sorry, Julian, but I couldn't turn him away, you know!"

"No, I suppose not. Oh, well! As long as he don't start abusing you!"

"I don't think he will. But if he *should* happen to pick out a grievance, oblige me by keeping two circumstances in mind! That he will not be doing so under any roof of yours, and that I am really quite capable of fighting my own battles!"

"Don't I know it!" Julian retorted. "*And* of giving nasty setdowns! Very well! I'll behave with all the propriety in the world – if I can!" He opened the door, but looked over his shoulder, grinning, as a sudden thought assailed him. "Oh, by Jupiter! *Won't* our Bond Street beau stagger the neighbourhood?"

CHAPTER ELEVEN

IF JULIAN'S demeanor, when he met his cousin Laurence on the following morning, put Sir Waldo forcibly in mind of a stiff-legged terrier, not aggressively inclined but giving warning by his slightly raised bristles that he was prepared to repel any attack, this wary hostility soon vanished. Laurence greeted him in the friendliest manner, with apparently no memory of their last stormy encounter; so Julian, naturally sunny-tempered, immediately responded in kind. Laurence was very full of liveliness and wit, giving a droll account of his valet's horror at the privations of life at Broom Hall, and describing the various hazards he had himself encountered. "Not that I mean to complain, coz!" he assured Sir Waldo. "After all, I *know* where the rotten floorboard is now, and even if the ceiling does come down I daresay I may not be lying helpless in bed at the time. I don't regard a few scraps of plaster descending on me as anything to make a dust about! To think that I should have been as cross as crabs because old Joseph left the place to you! You're very welcome to it, Waldo!"

This was clearly so well-intentioned that Julian instantly regaled him with a highly-coloured account of his own first night in the house, when he had put his foot through the sheet; and before very long they were both of them roasting Sir Waldo in lighthearted, if temporary, alliance.

"Jackstraws!" he remarked. "A little more, and you'll find yourselves cast upon the world! Laurie, if you want to ride I can mount you, but if you prefer to drive the matter becomes more complicated. There's my phaeton, and there's a gig, and there's a tub of a coach which I imagine old Joseph must have inherited from his grandfather. We rumble to balls and rout-parties in that: Julian thinks it's just the thing. You won't – and nor, for that matter, do I. You can have the phaeton when I'm not using it myself, but -"

"Oh, lord, no!" Laurence interrupted. "I shouldn't think of taking your horses out! The gig will do well enough, if I should want to drive myself anywhere."

"No, I'll tell you what, Waldo!" said Julian. "The Buffer at the Crown has a whisky, which he lets out on hire: that's the thing for Laurie! He won't like the look of the gig."

"What you mean is that you're afraid he will want it when you do," said Sir Waldo. "Take him into the village, and hire the whisky!"

"I will. I mean to call at the Rectory, too, to see how Miss Chartley does after yesterday's adventure. Are you using the phaeton this morning," Julian asked hopefully.

"No, you may have it."

"Much obliged! Have you driven Waldo's bays, Laurie?"

"Oh, I shall leave driving them to you! *I'm* not a pupil of the great Nonesuch!" said Laurence, with a titter.

"I daresay you are a better fiddler than I am, however," replied Julian, with determined civility.

"Waldo would not say so!"

"Fudge! What do you think, Waldo?"

Sir Waldo was reading one of his letters, and said, without looking up from it: "Think about what?"

"Our handling of the reins. Which of us is the better whip? You are to decide!"

"Impossible! Two halfpennies in a purse!"

"Of all the knaggy things to say!" Julian exclaimed indignantly. "If that's what you think us I wonder at your letting either of us drive your precious bays!"

"Yes, so do I," agreed Sir Waldo, getting up from the breakfast-table. "Have you a fancy to attend a ball, Laurie?"

"Good God, coz, do you have *balls* in these rural parts? What do they dance? minuets?"

"Country-dances and reels – but this one is to be a waltzing-ball, isn't it, Julian?"

Julian laughed. "*Some* waltzing, at all events. You'd be surprised if you knew how gay we've been, Laurie!"

"I think you had better take him to visit Lady Colebatch," said Sir Waldo.

"Puffing him off to the neighbourhood? Very well!"

Laurence was by no means sure that he wished to become acquainted with his cousins' new friends. He was much addicted to *ton* parties, where all the guests were of high fashion, but country entertainments he thought abominably dull. However, when he learned that his cousins were engaged for almost every evening for some time to come he realized that unless he joined them in these rural festivities he would be condemned to solitude, so he yielded, and went away to change the frogged and braided dressing-gown in which he had chosen to breakfast for raiment more suited to paying country morning-visits.

Julian, who had been mischievously looking forward to the effect his dandified cousin's usual costume was likely to have on the neighbourhood, was disappointed to see, when Laurence came strolling into the stableyard, that he was not wearing the town-dress of a Bond Street beau, but had exchanged his delicately hued pantaloons and his mirror-bright Hessian boots for breeches of pale yellow and white-topped riding-boots; and his exaggeratedly long-tailed coat of superfine for a redingote. However, this garment was raised above the ordinary by its stiffly wadded shoulders and its enormous breast flaps; and both the Mathematical Tie which Laurence wore, and the height of his shirt-points, left nothing to be desired. Furthermore, the driving-coat which he tossed negligently into the phaeton bore upwards of a dozen capes. Julian advised him earnestly to put it on, warning him that the roads were very dusty. "You'll be smothered in it!" he prophesied. "It would be too bad, for you look *very* dapper-dog!"

"I regret I can't return the compliment, coz!" said Laurence, surveying him through his quizzing-glass. "If you don't object to my saying so, your rig is more that of a hayseed than of a Nonesuch!"

"Oh, I gave up aping Waldo's fashions when I found I couldn't ape his skill!" retorted Julian, with the blandest of smiles.

Fortunately for the harmony of the day, Laurence recollected that a quarrel with Julian would do nothing to advance his cause with Waldo; so he suppressed a pretty stinging answer, and merely laughed, and said: "How wise!" He then languidly waved aside an offer to yield the reins up to him, and climbed into the phaeton. No conversation was exchanged for the first few minutes; but after critically watching Julian's handling of the mettlesome pair harnessed to the carriage, Laurence said: "You're growing to be a regular dash. Pretty lively, ain't they? What's keeping Waldo here for so long?"

"Why, you know, don't you? He's turning Broom Hall into another orphanage."

"Oh, yes, I know that! He did the same with that place he bought in Surrey, but if he ever spent as much as one night in it it's the first I've heard of it."

"That was different!" objected Julian. "There's the estate to be thought of here, and I can tell you it's in a shocking way! No bailiff, either. Waldo is determined to bring it into good order before he leaves, which means the devil of a lot of work, you know."

"Lord, he must have a dozen men he could employ on that!" Laurence said impatiently.

"Well, he don't choose to. Hallo, here comes the Squire! A very good sort of a man: wife all pretension: one son and two daughters!" explained Julian, in a hurried undervoice, as he pulled up his horses. "Good-morning, sir! Not so hot today, is it? May I present my cousin to you? Mr Calver – Mr Mickleby!"

The Squire, acknowledging Laurence's graceful bow with a brief nod, stared very hard at him, and ejaculated: "Ha! Calver! Ay, you've got a look of old Joseph."

Laurence had never seen Joseph Calver, but he resented this remark: and told Julian, when the Squire had trotted off on his stout cob, that if his manners were a sample of what was to be expected in this uncouth district he would as lief be spared any more introductions. However, when the hire of the whisky had been arranged, he consented to accompany Julian to the Rectory. Leaving the phaeton at the Crown, they walked down the village street, reaching the Rectory just as Mrs Underhill was stepping into her barouche, which was drawn up at the gate.

Mrs Underhill had driven from Staples to enquire after Patience, and to tell Mrs Chartley how sorry she was that such a disagreeable adventure should have befallen her while she had been in Miss Trent's charge; and she had arrived at the Rectory in as flustered a state of mind as was possible in one of her calm temperament, her headstrong niece having flatly refused to accompany her on this visit of reparation. She might know little about fashionable manners, but one thing (she said) she did know, and that was that Tiffany had behaved very badly to Miss Chartley, and owed her an apology. Upon which, Tiffany, after declaring in a torrent of angry words that it was Patience who owed her an apology, for exposing her to a scene of odious embarrassment, had slammed out of the room and locked herself into her bedchamber. So Mrs Underhill, much agitated, had been obliged to excuse her to Mrs Chartley. She said that she was laid down with a headache; but when Patience exclaimed that she was so sorry, because it must have been quite horrid for poor Tiffany to be jostled and stared at by a crowd of people, she had abandoned all pretence, and said bluntly: "It's like you to say so, my dear, but by what I can discover she behaved in a very unbecoming way, and I'm so mortified as never was! And if she won't beg your pardon – which she won't, for bring her to own she's ever at fault you can't, tell her so till Doomsday, – *I* will, and so I do!"

Perceiving that she was very much upset, Mrs Chartley made a sign to Patience to leave them, and applied herself to the task of soothing the poor lady's ruffled sensibilities. She succeeded so well that before long Mrs Underhill was pouring out to her the difficulties and discomforts attached to the guardianship of a spoiled beauty who didn't seem to have a scrap of affection in her. Mrs Chartley listened sympathetically, agreeing that she would have grown up very differently if her uncle had not sent her to school, and encouraging Mrs Underhill's wistfully expressed belief that her tantrums were merely childish, and that she would improve when she was a little older.

Mrs Underhill felt much better after unburdening herself. A glass of ratafia, and a comfortable gossip with her hostess still further restored her; and by the time the two Chartley ladies escorted her to her barouche she was her placid self again, and able to meet Lord Lindeth without suffering any recrudescence of mortification. He performed the introductions, and while Laurence exchanged civilities with the Chartleys he enquired politely after Tiffany, expressing his regret that the previous day's accident should have proved too much for her nerves.

"Nerves!" said Mrs Underhill, rejecting this tactful effort. "She hasn't got any, my lord! A nasty, spiteful temper is what she's got, and wears us all to death with it! Not that she can't be as sweet as a nut when she chooses, but if things don't fall out just the way she wants them to she flies into the boughs directly." She then lowered her voice, and said, with a significant glance cast at Laurence: "Did you say he was your cousin?"

"Yes, ma'am: my cousin Calver."

"Well!" she uttered. "I'm sure we all thought there was never anyone as modish as Sir Waldo, so elegant and trim as he is, but he's nothing to Mr

Calver, is he? Why, he's as fine as a star! I'll be bound he's one of the London smarts?'

"Yes, indeed!" said Julian, his eyes dancing. "A real Pink of the *Ton*!"

"I can see that," she nodded, much impressed. "I hope you'll bring him with you when you come to my turtle-dinner next Friday, if he won't think it a bore."

"He will be very much obliged to you, ma'am," Julian answered promptly. He turned his head towards his cousin. "Laurie, Mrs Underhill has been so kind as to invite you to dine at her house next Friday!"

Laurence, executing one of his exquisite bows, said all that was proper, for he prided himself on his social address, but not even Mrs Underhill's evident admiration reconciled him to the prospect of dining in her house. He described her as a vulgar mushroom, and wondered that his cousins should not have kept her at a proper distance.

"We're not as niffy-naffy as you – or, of course, of such consequence!"

Laurence reddened, and said peevishly: "You needn't ride grub because I don't care for low company! Who *is* the creature?"

"She is a wealthy widow, with a son, a daughter, and a very beautiful niece. She owns the largest house in the neighbourhood, and may be depended on to set a capital dinner before us. She's a cit, but excessively good-natured, and has been particularly kind in giving us an open invitation to dine at Staples whenever we choose – or whenever the builders make Broom Hall intolerable! We have been in the habit of going there quite frequently, so, if you don't want one of Waldo's set-downs, I advise you not to speak of Mrs Underhill to him as a vulgar mushroom!"

"One of Waldo's eccentricities, I collect. Or has he got up a flirtation with the beautiful niece? Is that what's keeping him in Yorkshire?"

"I've told you already what's keeping him. As for Miss Wield, she's no more than seventeen, and if you think Waldo would -"

"Oho!" interrupted Laurence, his curiosity roused. "Have you an interest there yourself?"

Julian flushed, and answered stiffly: "No. I admire her, as everyone must, but I am not one of her suitors. She has dozens of 'em!" He continued, in an easier tone: "She's a diamond of the first water, I promise you! But there are several very pretty girls to be seen – Miss Colebatch is one of them. I hope she may be at home when we get to Colby Place."

"Don't hope it on my account!" said Laurence, yawning. "*I'm* not in the petticoat-line!"

Inasmuch as he was too self-absorbed ever to have contracted even the mildest passion for any lady, this was true; but provided that he was not expected to run errands, or to dance attendance, or, in fact, to put himself out in any way, he was rather fond of feminine society. He was also responsive to flattery, and of this he received full measure at Colby Place. Not only was Miss Colebatch at home, but her two younger sisters were sitting with their mama when the visitors were announced; and from the moment of his entering the room they seemed unable to drag their eyes from the elegant Mr Calver. Awe was writ large on their youthful countenances; and when he was kind enough to address a word or two to one or other of them they showed by their blushes, nervous giggles, and stammering replies how appreciative they were of his condescension. Miss Colebatch, though she did not betray it, was a good deal impressed by his air of _ la modality; and her mama, not content with begging him to honour her ball with his presence, gratified him by asking his advice on various questions concerning it, because she said that she was persuaded he must be familiar with all the latest kicks of high fashion.

He was shortly to be still more gratified. The news that the Nonesuch had another cousin staying with him, and one who was an out-and-out dandy, rapidly spread, and was productive of a spate of notes directed to Sir Waldo, and carrying the assurances of the various hostesses to whom he and Lindeth were engaged that they would be most happy to include Mr Laurence Calver amongst their guests.

Laurence affected unconcern, but he was secretly as much exhilarated as surprised by his sudden and unexpected rise to importance. In London, amongst men of more natural parts and longer purses than his, it was almost impossible to make a hit: particularly (as he had often and resentfully thought) if one had the misfortune to be overshadowed by so magnificent a cousin as the Nonesuch, who, besides being universally acknowledged as Top-of-the-Trees, commanded as much liking as admiration. Far too frequently had Laurence been presented to strangers as Sir Waldo Hawkridge's cousin; and although he had not scrupled to use this relationship to gain the entrance to certain exclusive circles it galled him very much to know that he was accepted merely because of the respect in which Waldo was held. He would have repudiated with scorn any suggestion that he should seek in fame a rural district remote from the hub of fashion; but having been compelled by circumstance to visit his cousin he did not find it at all disagreeable to have become a star in this lesser firmament. Elderly and bucolic gentlemen might look upon him with disfavour; their hard-riding sons were welcome to make Waldo their model: to be admired or despised by dotards and schoolboys were matters of equal indifference to him while he was courted by the ladies, and enjoyed the exquisite satisfaction of knowing that his hair-style, his neckties, and many of his mannerisms were being copied by several aspirants to dandyism. His success made it possible for him to bear, with tolerable equanimity, his cousin's tacit refusal to allow him to reopen the discussion which had brought him to Yorkshire. He had only once attempted to do so. He had been foiled, and he had thought that he had been a trifle too precipitate, perhaps, and must allow Waldo more time for consideration. He meant to have another touch at him after a discreet interval; meanwhile he was very well pleased to bridge the gap with whatever entertainments were offered him.

His appearance at the Colebatches' ball transcended all expectations, and quite eclipsed the local smarts. The beautiful arrangement of his pomaded locks, the height of his shirt-points, the intricacies of his neckcloth, the starched frill which protruded between the lapels of his tightly-fitting coat, with its short front and its extravagantly cutaway tails, the fobs and the seals which hung from his waist, and even the rosettes on his dancing-pumps, proclaimed him to be a Tulip of the first stare. His bow was much admired; if he was not precisely handsome, he was generally held to be goodlooking; and when he led Tiffany Wield on to the floor for the first waltz even the most hostile of his critics acknowledged him to be a most accomplished dancer. The Squire went further, setting Sir Ralph Colebatch off into an alarming choking fit by growling in his ear: "Damned caper-merchant!"

The eyes that followed his progress round the room might have remained fixed in his direction had they not been drawn off by a less agreeable but far more startling sight.

"Look!" ejaculated Mrs Banningham to Mrs Mickleby, in throbbing accents.

The Broom Hall party had arrived just as the opening set of country-dances had come to an end. Having greeted his hostess, Sir Waldo passed on, pausing to exchange a word or two with various acquaintances, unhurried, but scanning the room searchingly as he moved from group to group. His height enabled him to see over many heads, and it was thus that he discovered Miss Trent, who was seated beside Mrs Underhill against the wall on one side of the room. She was wearing a ball-dress of pale orange Italian crape, trimmed with lace, and cut low across the bosom; and instead of the demure braids she considered suitable for a companion-governess she had allowed her natural ringlets to fall becomingly from a knot placed high on her head. She looked very much younger, and, in Sir Waldo's eyes, beautiful.

He made his way towards her, reaching her as the musicians were about to strike up. A smile, and a brief how-do-you-do Mrs Underhill, and he was bowing to Miss Trent, and saying: "May I have the honour, ma'am?"

He had told her that he should ask her for the first waltz, but she had expected him rather to invite her to dance with him later in the evening. She hesitated, feeling that she ought not to be the first lady to stand up with him. "Thank you, but – Miss Colebatch? Should you not -"

"No, certainly not!" he replied. "That's Lindeth's privilege."

"Oh! Yes, of course. But there are many other ladies who have a claim to -"

"No," he interrupted. He smiled down at her, holding out his hand. "With you or no one! Come!"

"That's right, Sir Waldo!" said Mrs Underhill, beaming up at him. "Don't you take no for an answer, that's my advice to you! And as for you, my dear, just you say *thank you kindly, sir*, and no more nonsense!"

Ancilla could not resist. She rose, giving Sir Waldo her hand. Her eyes laughed into his. "Thank you kindly, sir!" she repeated obediently.

His right hand lightly clasped her waist; he said, as he guided her round the room: "That woman is a constant refreshment to me!"

"Indeed!" she said, quizzing him. "How quickly your opinions change, sir! I seem to recall that when you last spoke of her it was in very different terms!"

"I did her an injustice. I now recognize that she is a woman of great good sense. How well you dance l"

It was true, but very few of the onlookers derived any pleasure from the spectacle. Matrons who had brought their daughters to the ball felt their bosoms swell with wrath as they watched Tiffany Wield's companion (or whatever she called herself) gliding over the floor in the Nonesuch's arms, not finding it necessary to mind her steps, but performing the waltz gracefully and easily, and apparently enjoying an amusing conversation with him while she did it.

The Rector was one of those who watched with approval. He said to his wife: "Now, my love, we see how unexceptionable this new dance is! Charming! charming, indeed!"

"Well, I cannot quite like it, but I own that it is very pretty when it is danced correctly," she replied. "I understand that Mr Calver is the best dancer here, but for my part I prefer Sir Waldo's more restrained style. Miss Trent, too, dances as a lady should, but you may depend upon it that as soon as ever they become familiar with the steps Tiffany Wield, and Lizzie Colebatch, and the Mickleby girls will turn it into a romp. I should be sorry indeed to see a daughter of mine led into such impropriety."

He laughed gently. "It would reflect sadly on her upbringing, would it not? I fancy we need feel no apprehension! She is dancing very prettily. It may be my partiality, but I am of the opinion that, saving only Miss Trent, she performs the waltz better than any other lady present."

"Yes," agreed his wife, "but Arthur Mickleby is too clumsy a partner for her."

She saw that Mrs Underhill was quite alone, and went to her, sitting down beside her, and saying: "What do you think of the waltz, Mrs Underhill? My husband is in raptures over it, and thinks me very old-fashioned for not liking it as much as he does!"

"Well, I wouldn't like to be seen dancing it myself," said Mrs Underhill, "but I'm sure I never saw anything so pretty as the way Sir Waldo and Miss Trent glide and twirl about the room so elegantly! What has me in a puzzle is how she knows when he means to go down the room, and when he means to go round and round, for he don't seem to push her or pull her, which you'd think he'd be obliged to, and which he certainly would be, if it was me he had his arm round!"

Mrs Chartley smiled. "They certainly dance very well together."

"Ay, don't they?" nodded Mrs Underhill, watching them complacently. "So well-matched as they are, Miss Trent being so tall, and the both of them so handsome! When she came downstairs this evening, with her hair dressed the way you see it, and that gown on, which she says she's had laid up in lavender ever since she left the General's house, though little would you think it, 'Well,' I said to her, 'I declare I've never seen you in greater beauty!' I said. And no more I have." She lowered her voice, and added conspiratorially: "What's more, Mrs Chartley, I wasn't the only one to be knocked bandy! Oh, no! 'With you or no one!' he said, when she was telling him he should ask another lady to stand up with him!"

"Sir Waldo?" asked Mrs Chartley, startled.

"Sir Waldo!" corroborated Mrs Underhill, with immense satisfaction. "Mind you, it didn't come as any surprise to me! A pea-goose I may be, which Mr Underhill was used to call me – joking me, you understand! – but I've got eyes in my head, and I don't need to wear spectacles either! Nor I'm not such a peagoose as to think it's for the pleasure of *my* company that Sir Waldo comes to Staples as often as he does. I *did* think it was Tiffany he was dangling after, but it ain't. Not but what he flirts with her: that I can't deny. But, to my way of thinking, it's no more than playfulness. It's Miss Trent who brings him to Staples."

Mrs Chartley was disquieted by this confidence; and after a moment's hesitation, said: "That he should feel some degree of preference for Miss Trent is very understandable. To a certain extent they belong to the same world – the London world – and no doubt they have acquaintances in common. Then, too, she is not a girl, but a woman of five or six-and-twenty, with a well-informed mind, and the habits of easy intercourse which come with increasing years. She doesn't want for sense, but when a man of Sir Waldo's address and experience makes a woman the object of his gallantry -"

"Lor', ma'am, whatever are you thinking of?" broke in Mrs Underhill. "It's not marriage with the left hand he has in his mind! Not with her uncle being a General!"

"No, indeed! You mistake me! I meant only to say that it would be unwise to – to encourage Miss Trent to cherish what I am persuaded must be false hopes. Forgive me, dear ma'am, but I feel you are refining too much upon a mere flirtation!"

Mrs Underhill smiled indulgently at her. "Ay, well, he who lives the longest will see the most!" she prophesied.

CHAPTER TWELVE

AS SHE had looked forward to the ball with mixed feelings, so did Ancilla look back upon it. It had been with misgiving that she had accepted Lady Colebatch's invitation, believing, with a sense of guilt, that in doing so she was allowing her desire to overcome the principles she had laid down for herself when she had first stepped deliberately out of her own sphere to become a schoolteacher.

It had been a hard decision to reach, for although her family was not affluent it was respected, and she had been accustomed all her life to move in the first circles of Hertfordshire. Her father's death, coupled as it had been with unlucky investments, had left the family, not in penury, but in uncomfortably straitened circumstances, and no doubt existed in the minds of all those who were acquainted with the Trents that it was incumbent upon Ancilla to relieve her eldest brother of the burden of providing for her by contracting a suitable marriage. It was generally agreed that although she was then in her twenty-fourth year, and had no fortune, her case was not hopeless. She was very goodlooking, with an air of distinction that always attracted attention; she was accomplished; her disposition was charming; though she was not vivacious she had a lively mind, and a witty tongue; and if she had rather too much reserve, and a composure that made her seem sometimes a little cold, her graceful manners always ensured her a welcome at any social function. It was a thousand pities she had not liked any of her admirers well enough to encourage their advances; but it was hoped that now, when she had been out for more than four years and must be fearful of dwindling into an old maid, she would not spurn a respectable offer.

That was what her aunt had hoped, when she had invited her to London for a whole season. Lady Trent, who was sincerely attached to her, had really done her best for her, introducing her to the *ton,* taking her to Almack's, and even presenting her at one of the Queen's Drawing-Rooms, but it had been to no avail. Ancilla would not marry where she did not love; and until she encountered the Nonesuch her heart had never experienced the smallest flutter.

Unwilling to marry, and resolved neither to add to the expenses of her brother's household nor to hang upon her uncle's sleeve, she had made her difficult decision, against the loudly expressed wishes of her family, and in the full realization that if she became a schoolmistress she would, to all intents and purposes, have renounced the world. It had been a hard duty, but she saw it as inescapable; and when she had accepted the post offered her by Miss Climping she had put the social life which she enjoyed behind her, and moulded herself into the form of a governess. By the time she had been fortunate enough to exchange her situation at Bath for the highly paid and privileged one which she now held she had thought herself inured to the disadvantages of her position. It had not been long before that position had become far more agreeable than she had ever supposed possible; but however much her kind employer might urge her to think herself one of the family, discretion, and a strong sense of propriety had prevented her from stepping across the invisible line she had drawn for herself. Her place was in the background, ready to fill a social need, but never putting herself forward. If Mrs Underhill were indisposed, she was perfectly willing to escort Tiffany to a party, where she took her place amongst the chaperons; but when, as had occasionally happened, she had herself received an invitation she had been steadfast in her refusal.

Until the arrival on the scene of the Nonesuch. Within a fortnight of their first meeting – or had it been within a minute? – he had destroyed her calm, undermined her resolution, and utterly demolished her comfort. She had believed herself to be a rational woman, with a well-regulated mind and a temperate disposition; but since his coming into Yorkshire she had swung from breathless happiness to doubt and despondency. Her heart had never previously opposed her mind: they seemed now to be in eternal conflict, the one warning her to take care, the other urging her to throw care and discretion to the wind.

Mind had suffered a severe set-back over the invitation to Lady Colebatch's ball. The correct Miss Trent, who had long since outgrown her love of dancing, desperately wanted to go to the ball. *Just this once!* she pleaded. *What harm can there be in it, when Mrs Underhill particularly wishes me to accept? I have too much sense to let it turn my head!* Her well-regulated mind replied uncompromisingly: *You have none at all. You want to go to this ball because Sir Waldo will be there, and if you had a grain of sense you would hint him away before he has ruined your peace.*

Heart had won. She had gone to the ball, meaning to behave with the utmost circumspection; but no sooner had she dressed her hair in her former style than circumspection fled. She felt young again, as excited as a girl going to her first party, a little reckless.

The recklessness, encouraged by the lights and the laughter, and the music, had grown. She had retained enough prudence to demur when Sir Waldo had asked her to dance the first waltz with him, but none thereafter, she thought. She had felt the exquisite happiness of knowing herself to be sought after by the man of her choice; and when he had asked her to waltz with him a second time she had not hesitated. He had taken her in to supper, too; and when they had gone into the garden to watch the firework-display it had been he who had fetched her shawl, and put it round her shoulders. So heedless had she been, so lost in enchantment, that she had not spared a thought for what might be the opinions of the matrons who watched her so jealously, and was shocked when an acid comment from Mrs Banningham made her realize that she was considered by that lady, and some others too, to be setting her cap at the Nonesuch. She knew it to be spite, but she felt ready to sink; and when Lady Colebatch had said to her, laughingly: "All this dangerous flirting with Sir Waldo -! Fie on you, Miss Trent!" her enjoyment was at an end, and her fears and doubts again assailed her.

She knew herself to be inexperienced in love, and guessed that Sir Waldo was not. It was beyond question that he was strongly attracted to her, but whether he had anything but flirtation in mind she could not tell. When their eyes met, and he smiled, she thought that surely he could not look at her and smile just so if the feeling he had for her was not deeper and more enduring than a mere passing fancy. Then she remembered that she was not the only woman to be charmed by his smile; and wondered if she was flattering herself in believing that that particular smile was one which no one but she had seen. But it was rumoured that he had had many loves: she supposed that a squire of dames must necessarily possess the power of making one believe that he was very much in love with one.

Almost as painful as these doubts was the thought that by allowing the Nonesuch to single her out she, who had so often preached propriety to Tiffany, should herself have set the neighbourhood in a bustle. Her conduct must have been very bad, she thought, for even Courtenay had remarked on it, saying, with a grin: "Lord, ma'am, won't Tiffany be as mad as fire to see the Nonesuch making up to you!"

But it had not entered Tiffany's head that any man, far less a man of Sir Waldo's consequence, could feel the smallest *tendre* for a governess. In talking over the ball she had spoken quite casually of Sir Waldo's having danced two waltzes with Miss Trent, and disclosed, as a very good joke, that some of the old cats had taken snuff at it, because they fancied him to be dangling after her. "You and *Sir Waldo*, Ancilla -!" she gurgled, "I was very nearly in whoops, as you may imagine! Of all the absurdities!"

"I don't think it would be at all absurd!" stated Charlotte belligerently. "Not nearly such an absurdity as for anyone to suppose that he was dangling after *you*! I suppose you're jealous because he didn't ask you to stand up with him first of all!"

"Oh, he couldn't!" said Tiffany, with a saucy look. "Mr Calver was before him! He was obliged to wait for the second waltz with me! And poor Lindeth for the third!"

Miss Trent regarded her thoughtfully for a moment, before lowering her gaze again to the handkerchief she was hemming. She had not been so much absorbed in her own affairs as to have had no leisure to observe Tiffany's behaviour at the ball. Being fairly well conversant with Tiffany's methods of punishing and still further enslaving any member of her court who had displeased her, she had not been surprised when she had seen her at her dazzling best with all the admirers whose noses had been put out of joint by Lord Lindeth, raising melting eyes to Mr Calver's face, and treating Lindeth with careless indifference. Miss Trent had been amused rather than shocked, for these tactics, she thought, betrayed Tiffany's extreme youth. They might answer well enough with callow boys, but they were not at all likely to inspire Lindeth with anything but disgust. She hoped they would do so, but she hoped also that they were not as blatant to others as they were to her.

To one person they were perfectly obvious. Laurence Calver's intellect was not superior, but he had a certain quickness of perception, and a decided talent for discovering scandals and frailties. He went to the ball suspecting that his cousin Lindeth had a considerable interest in the unknown Beauty, and it did not take him long to become convinced of this, or to realize that some tiff had occurred to rupture what had no doubt been a promising *affaire*. That was very interesting, and opened out all sorts of possibilities. The girl was a minx: bang-up to the echo, of course, but not at all the thing for Lindeth. Waldo must know that, so what was he doing to prevent such a shocking alliance? Or was he at a stand? And if so would he be grateful if his other cousin were to intervene? Yes, thought Laurence: if the thing were serious, he would be. It would be very amusing, and not at all difficult: the Beauty had already thrown out unmistakeable lures to him, and he was perfectly ready to accept these. No doubt she was on the catch for Lindeth; and no doubt either that she thought to bring him to the scratch by making him mad with jealousy. Possibly she would succeed in making him jealous – and that would be amusing too – but if she supposed that by flirting outrageously with another man she would goad Lindeth into popping the question she must be as birdwitted as she was beautiful. Too vulgar by half for young Julian!

All this was pleasantly intriguing. It was satisfactory too to have discovered why Waldo was lingering in this God-forsaken district: he had set up a new flirt. Not very like him to make a female who appeared to be some sort of a governess the object of his gallantry, but girls who were just out never took his fancy, and apart from them the only females in the neighbourhood seemed to be fussocks, like Lady Colebatch, or regular worri-crows, like Mrs Banningham and the Squire's wife.

Critically surveying Miss Trent, Laurence doubted whether she would prove a satisfactory flirt. Not striking *au fait de beauté*, and too much of a Long Meg for his taste, but a distinguished-looking woman: nothing of the dasher about her! If Waldo didn't take care he'd find himself riveted, and a rare kettle of fish that would be! The last of the Hawkridges leg-shackled to a nobody who earned her bread by teaching provincial schoolgirls to write and to cipher and to stitch samplers! Devilish funny that would be! But it was odd of Waldo to raise false expectations. Come to think of it, all his flirts were married women of the world, well up to snuff; and he had some pretty Gothic notions about trifling with females on the catch for eligible husbands. Still odder that he shouldn't have seen that this Long Meg of his was badly love-bitten.

Hot on the scent of this really succulent *on-dit*, Laurence sought information of his younger cousin, saying casually: "You didn't tell me that Waldo had set up a new flirt. Who is she?"

Julian stared at him. "New flirt? Waldo?"

"Running rather sly, ain't you?" drawled Laurence. "Tall female – somebody's governess, I collect. Lord, Julian, do you take me for a flat?"

"Miss Trent! Good God, what next? New flirt, indeed! She's Miss Wield's companion: a most agreeable woman, but as for being Waldo's *flirt*! You should know him better!"

"No need to take a pet! All *I* know is that between the pair of 'em they set all the tabbies in an uproar last night!"

"I daresay! They live on scandal-broth!"

"But who is she?" insisted Laurence. "Or is that one of those questions one shouldn't ask?"

"Not in the least. You are probably acquainted with her cousin, Bernard Trent. Her father was killed in the assault on Ciudad Rodrigo, and left the family all to pieces, I fancy. General Trent is her uncle."

"Is he, though?" said Laurence, his eyes widening a little.

He asked no more questions, because he didn't want Waldo to think he was prying into his affairs, and Julian was such a bagpipe that you never knew what he might blurt out, in his artless way. Besides, Julian probably didn't know any more. He had said enough to put quite a different complexion on the matter: it began to look as though Waldo was thinking of becoming a tenant-for-life at last. Nothing wonderful about that: he was bound to marry one day. The wonder was that with the pick of the *ton* to choose from he should throw the handkerchief to a mere Miss Trent, who might be well-enough born, but who was quite unknown, and hadn't rank, fortune, or any extraordinary degree of beauty to recommend her. Lord, what a sensation it would cause! Laurence knew of several top-lofty beauties who would look blue when they heard of it, one of whom had once rudely snubbed him. It would be pleasant to whisper the news in her ear.

Of course, it might not be true; he would be better able to judge when he had seen them together again. He hoped Miss Trent would be present at Mrs Underhill's turtle-dinner: it seemed likely that she would be; and if she was he had every intention of making himself very agreeable to her. If there was the least chance of her becoming Waldo's wife, it was a matter of the highest importance to stand well with her. Really, it was very fortunate that he had come to Yorkshire!

Miss Trent was present at the dinner, but had she been able to do so without disarranging Mrs Underhill's carefully planned table she would have excused herself. She did indeed venture to suggest that since Charlotte was suffering from severe toothache, and would make no appearance in the drawing-room, it would be better if she remained upstairs with her, but Mrs Underhill would not hear of it. Where, she demanded, was she to find a lady to take Miss Trent's place?

"I thought, perhaps, since the Micklebys are coming, ma'am, you might invite the elder Miss Mickleby," suggested Ancilla, but without conviction.

"Don't talk so silly!" begged Mrs Underhill. "As though you didn't know as well as I do that Mrs Mickleby takes an affront into her head if anyone invites one of those dratted girls without t'other! Yes, and so she would if I was to invite either of them at the last minute, like this is, and I can't say I blame her, for a very poor compliment that would be!"

So Miss Trent submitted, and no one could have supposed, observing her cold composure, that she was suffering from acute embarrassment. To a proud woman of her upbringing the imputation of setting her cap at the Nonesuch was so abhorrent that she was nauseated every time she thought of it. Like some vulgar, scheming creature, without delicacy or conduct, throwing out her every lure to snare a husband! Worse! – a husband so wealthy and so distinguished as to be considered one of the biggest prizes to be won! And she the penniless daughter of an officer in a marching regiment! She could not accuse herself of having thrown out lures, but when she looked back over the past month it was upon a vista of rides with the Nonesuch, evenings spent in his company, strolling walks with him in the gardens of Staples, *tête-à-tête*, with him, jokes shared with him: all culminating in that disastrous ball, which she ought never to have attended. How indiscreet she had been! It must have appeared to everyone that she had gone to the ball, breaking her own rule, for no other purpose than to dance with the Nonesuch, and the dreadful truth was that she had. And who, seeing her waltz with him twice, and go in to supper on his arm, and allow him to fetch her shawl, would believe that she had committed these imprudencies unthinkingly, because she loved him, and had been too happy in his company to remember the delicacy of her situation, or even common propriety? She might as well have tied her garter in public!

It was a severe ordeal to be obliged to appear at Mrs Underhill's dinner-party, knowing that Mrs Mickleby's sharp eyes would be watching her: perhaps, even, Mrs Chartley's? She chose from her slender wardrobe the most modest and sober-hued of her few evening-dresses, and set a cap over her tightly braided locks, to which Mrs Underhill took instant exception, exclaiming: "Whatever made you put on a cap, as if you was an old maid of forty? For goodness' sake, go and take it off! There'll be time enough for you to wear caps when you're married!"

"I have no expectation of being married, ma'am, and you know it is customary for a gover-"

"No, and nor you will be if you don't prettify yourself a bit!" interrupted Mrs Underhill tartly. "If you aren't wearing that old, brown dress, too, which is enough to give anyone the dismals! I declare you're as provoking as Tiffany, Miss Trent!"

So Miss Trent went away to remove the offending cap, but she did not change her dress, or come downstairs again until the guests had all arrived, when she slipped unobtrusively into the drawing-room, responding to greetings with smiles and slight curtsies, and sitting down in a chair as far removed from Sir Waldo as was possible.

She was seated at dinner between the Squire and the Rector, and with these two uncritical friends she was able to converse as easily as usual. It was more difficult in the drawing-room, before the gentlemen joined the ladies. Mrs Mickleby talked of nothing but the waltzing-ball, and contrived, with her thin smile, to plant quite a number of tiny daggers in Miss Trent's quivering flesh. Miss Trent met smile with smile, and replied with a calm civility which made Mrs Mickleby's eyes snap angrily. Then Mrs Chartley, taking advantage of a brief pause in these hostilities, moved her seat to one beside Ancilla's, and said: "I am glad of this opportunity to speak to you, Miss Trent. I have been meaning for weeks to ask you if you can recall the details of that way of pickling mushrooms which you once described to me, but whenever I see you I remember about it only when we have parted!"

Ancilla could not but be grateful for the kindness that prompted this intervention, but it brought the colour to her cheeks as Mrs Mickleby's barbs had not. She promised to write down the recipe, and bring it to the Rectory; and wished very much that she could retire to the schoolroom before the gentlemen came in. It was impossible, however: Mrs Underhill expected her to pour out tea later in the evening.

A diversion (but a most unwelcome one) was created by Tiffany, who suddenly exclaimed: "Oh, I have had a famous notion! Do let us play Jackstraws again!"

Since she had broken in not only on what Patience was saying to her, but on what Mrs Mickleby was saying to Mrs Underhill, this lapse from good manners made Miss Trent feel ready to sink, knowing that Mrs Mickleby would set the blame at her door. Worse was to come.

"I was hoping Miss Chartley would give us the pleasure of hearing her sing," said Mrs Underhill. "I'll be bound that's what we should all like best, such a pretty voice as you have, my dear!"

"Oh, no! Jackstraws!"

"Tiffany," said Miss Trent, in a quiet but compelling voice.

The brilliant eyes turned towards her questioningly; she met them with a steady gaze; and Tiffany went into a trill of laughter. "Oh! Oh, I didn't mean to be uncivil! Patience knows I didn't, don't you, Patience?"

"Of course I do!" replied Patience instantly. "I think it would be much more amusing to play Jackstraws. But Miss Trent will beat us all to flinders – even Sir Waldo! If you and he engage in another duel, ma'am, I shan't bet against you this time!"

Miss Trent could only be thankful that at that moment the door opened, and the gentlemen came in. She was able to move away from the group in the middle of the room on the pretext of desiring one of the footmen to open the pianoforte and to light the candles in its brackets; and she remained beside the instrument, looking through a pile of music. After a minute or two she was joined by Laurence, who came up to her, and said very politely: "Can I be of assistance, ma'am? Allow me to lift that for you!"

"Thank you: if you would put it on that table, so that the instrument may be opened -?"

He did so, and then said, with a winning smile: "You must let me tell you how delighted I am to have the pleasure of making your acquaintance, ma'am. With *one* member of your family I'm already acquainted: I believe Bernard Trent is your cousin, is he not?"

Miss Trent inclined her head. It was not encouraging, but Laurence persevered. "A first-rate man! The best of good company! We are quite old friends, he and I."

"Indeed!" said Miss Trent.

He was not unnaturally daunted, for her tone was arctic, and the look in her eyes contemptuous. He wondered what the devil was the matter with her, and felt aggrieved. Anyone would have supposed that she would have been glad to meet someone who knew her cousin, but instead she had snubbed him! Pretty well for a governess! he thought indignantly.

She realized that she had spoken curtly, and added, with a slight smile: "I daresay you are better acquainted with him than I am, sir. He has never come very much in my way."

She turned away, to adjust one of the candles, and as she did so looked up, to find that Sir Waldo was standing within easy earshot. Her eyes met his, and saw that they were alight with amusement, and involuntarily she smiled. It was only for an instant, but Laurence caught the exchange of looks, and was so much pleased to find his suspicion confirmed that he forgot his indignation. If ever two people were head over ears in love! he thought, and tactfully moved away.

Sir Waldo strolled up to the pianoforte, and picked up the snuffers. As he trimmed one of the candlesticks he murmured: "He *meant* well, you know! Of course, I ought to have warned him."

"I'm afraid I was uncivil," she owned.

"No, no, merely quelling!" he assured her.

She could not help laughing, but she was aware of Mrs Mickleby's eyes upon her, and said: "That was very bad! Excuse me – I must speak with Miss Chartley!"

She walked away immediately, and contrived to remain at a distance from him until the tea-tray was brought in. She was ably assisted by Mrs Mickleby, who kept him at her side, and maintained a flow of vivacious small-talk until Patience had been persuaded to sing. After that, Tiffany renewed her demand that they should play at Jackstraws, which enabled Miss Trent to retire into the back drawing-room, where she became busy, finding the straws, and settling the four youngest members of the party round the table. Sir Waldo made no attempt to follow her; but when she was obliged to return to the front drawing-room, to dispense tea, he came up to the table to receive his cup from her, and asked her quietly if he had offended her.

No, but people are saying that I have set my cap at you!

Unthinkable to utter such words! She said: "Offended me? No, indeed! How should you?"

"I don't know. If I did, I should be begging you to forgive me."

Her eyes smarted with sudden tears; she kept them lowered. "How absurd! To own the truth, I have the headache, and should perhaps be begging *your* pardon for being cross and stupid! This is Mr Chartley's cup – would you be kind enough, Sir Waldo, to give it to him?"

He took it from her, but said: "If that's the truth I am sincerely sorry for it, but I don't think it is. What has happened to distress you?"

"Nothing! Sir Waldo, pray -!"

"How intolerable it is that I should be forced to meet you always in public!" he ejaculated under his breath. "I shall drive over tomorrow – and hope to find you, for once, alone!"

That made her look up. "I don't think – I mean, it is not – that is, I cannot conceive, sir, why -"

"I wish for some private conversation with you, Miss Trent. Now, don't freeze me with *Indeed!* as you froze poor Laurie, or tell me that you can't conceive why I should hope to find you alone!"

She forced her lips to smile, but said with a good deal of constraint: "Very well – though it is true! But you must know, sir, that it would be quite improper for me in my situation – to be receiving visitors!"

"Oh, yes! I know that. But mine won't be a *social* call!" He saw the guarded look in her face, and his eyes twinkled. "I have a a certain proposition to lay before you, ma'am! No, I shan't tell you what it is tonight: I can see you would bite my nose off!"

CHAPTER THIRTEEN

BUT WHEN Sir Waldo called at Staples next day he entered upon a scene of disorder. He did not see Miss Trent at all, but he did see Mrs Underhill; and when she had explained why he should have found them all in an uproar, as she phrased it, he made no attempt to see Miss Trent. He had clearly chosen the wrong moment for declaring himself.

Miss Trent, withdrawing from the party as soon as she had poured out tea, had gone upstairs to find Charlotte looking flushed and heavy-eyed, and obviously suffering a good deal of pain. Her old nurse was ministering to her; and she made it plain that while Miss Trent was at liberty to instruct her nursling, neither her advice nor her assistance was required when Miss Charlotte was feeling poorly. She had several infallible remedies for the toothache to hand; and although she was sure it was very obliging of Miss Trent to offer to sit up with Miss Charlotte there was not the least need for her to put herself out.

Correctly understanding this to mean that any attempt on her part to lend Nurse her aid would be regarded by that lady as a gross encroachment, Miss Trent retired, not unthankfully, to her own room, and to bed.

But not to sleep. She was tired, but her brain would not rest. The evening, which was fast assuming the proportions of a nightmare, had culminated in a brief exchange with the Nonesuch which provided her with much food for thought, and was open to more than one interpretation.

It was during the small hours that she was roused from a fitful doze by the creaking of a floor-board. She raised herself on her elbow, thrusting back the curtain round her bed, and listened. A heavy footfall, which she instantly recognized, came to her ears, and the creak of the door that led into the servants' wing; and without troubling to light her candle from the tinder-box that stood on the table by her bed, she got up quickly, groping in the dim dawn light filtering between the blinds for her slippers, and shrugging herself into her dressing-gown. She saw, when she went out on to the broad passage, that the door into Mrs Underhill's room was open; and she went at once to Charlotte's room, where, as she had feared, a most distressing sight confronted her. Charlotte, having stoutly declared when she bade her governess goodnight that she was better, and would be as right as a trivet by morning, was walking up and down the floor in her nightdress, her cap torn off, and tears pouring down her face. Nurse's infallible remedies had failed; Charlotte's toothache had grown steadily worse, until she had been unable to bear it with fortitude any longer. She was obviously almost crazy with pain; and Miss Trent, perceiving that the glands in her neck were swollen, and recalling a hideous night spent in ministering to her brother Christopher in just the same circumstances, had little doubt that an abscess was the cause of her agony. Nurse had tried to apply laudanum to the affected tooth, but Charlotte screamed when she was touched, and behaved so wildly that Nurse had taken fright, and gone away to rouse her mistress.

Mrs Underhill was a devoted parent, but she had very little experience of illness, and could scarcely have been thought an ideal sickroom attendant. Like many fat and naturally placid persons, she became flustered in emergency; and as her sensibility was far greater than her understanding the sight of her daughter's anguish upset her so much that she began to cry almost as much as Charlotte. An attempt to cradle Charlotte in her arms had been fiercely repulsed; her fond soothings had had no other effect than to make Charlotte hysterical; but thankful though she was to see Miss Trent come into the room she was quite indignant with her for showing so little sympathy, and for speaking to Charlotte so sternly.

"However, she did it for the best, and I'm bound to say she made Charlotte sit down in a chair, telling her that to be rampaging about the room, like she was doing, only served to make the pain worse. So then Nurse set a hot brick under her feet, and we wrapped a shawl round her, and Miss Trent told me she thought it was an abscess, and not a bit of use to put laudanum on her poor tooth, but better, if I would permit it, to give her some drops to swallow in a glass of water, so as to make her drowsy. Which it did, after a while, but such a work as it was to get Charlotte to open her lips, or even take the glass in her hand, you wouldn't believe!"

"Poor child!" said Sir Waldo. "I expect she was half mad with pain."

"Yes, and all through her own fault! Well, I hope I'm not unfeeling, but when she owned to Miss Trent that she had had the toothache for close on a sennight, and getting worse all the time, and never a word to a soul, because she was scared to have it drawn, – well, I was so vexed, Sir Waldo, after all that riot and rumpus, that I said to her: 'Let it be a lesson to you, Charlotte!' I said."

"I should think it would be, ma'am. I own I have every sympathy with those who dread having teeth drawn!"

"Yes," agreed Mrs Underhill, shuddering. "But when it comes to letting things get to such a pass as last night, and *still* crying, and saying she wouldn't go to Mr Dishforth, no matter what, it's downright silly! Well, I don't mind saying that it put me in a regular quake only to think of taking her to him, for I can't but cry myself when I see her in such misery, and a nice thing that would have been – the pair of us behaving like watering-pots, and poor Mr Dishforth not knowing what to do, I daresay! Not but what I would have gone with her, only that Miss Trent wouldn't have it, nor Courtenay neither. Miss Trent took her off first thing, and Courtenay went along with them, like the good brother he is. And just as well he did, for they were obliged to hold her down, such a state as she was in, and how Miss Trent would have managed without him I'm sure I don't know. So then they brought her home, and Courtenay's ridden off to fetch Dr Wibsey to her, for she's quite knocked up, and no wonder!"

Decidedly it was not the moment for a declaration. Expressing an entirely sincere hope that Charlotte would soon be herself again, Sir Waldo took his leave.

He was not to see Miss Trent again for five days. Charlotte, instead of making the swift recovery to be expected of such a bouncing girl, returned from Harrogate only to take to her bed. Her feverish condition was ascribed by Dr Wibsey to the poison that had leaked into her system; but Mrs Underhill told Sir Waldo with simple pride that Charlotte was just like she was herself.

"It's seldom I get a screw loose," she said, "for, in general, you know, I go on in a capital way. But if there's the least little thing amiss, such as a colicky disorder, it throws me into such queer stirrups that many's the time when my late husband thought to see me laid by the wall for no more than an epidemic cold!"

Sir Waldo called every day at Staples to enquire after Charlotte, but not until the fifth day was he rewarded by the sight of Miss Trent, and even then it was under inauspicious circumstances. The invalid was taking the air on the terrace, seated in a comfortable chair carried out for her accommodation, with her mother on one side; and her governess, holding up a parasol to protect her from the sun, on the other; and with Mrs Mickleby and her two eldest daughters grouped round her. When Sir Waldo was ushered on to the terrace by Totton Mrs Mickleby had already learnt from her hostess that he had been a regular visitor to Staples. She drew her own conclusions, rejecting without hesitation the ostensible reason of his daily visits.

"So kind as he's been you'd hardly credit!" Mrs Underhill told her, not without complacency. "Never a day passes but what he comes to enquire how Charlotte goes on, and it's seldom that he don't bring with him a book, or some trifle to amuse her, isn't it, love? Well, Charlotte hasn't any more of a fancy for reading than what I have, but she likes Miss Trent to read aloud to her, which she does beautifully, and as good as a play. Well, as I said to Sir Waldo only yesterday, it isn't only Charlotte that's very much obliged to him, for Miss Trent reads it after dinner to us, and I'm sure I couldn't tell you which of us enjoys it the most, me, or Charlotte, or Tiffany. Well, it's so lifelike that I couldn't get to sleep last night for wondering whether that nasty Glossin would get poor Harry Bertram carried off by the smugglers again, or whether the old witch is going to save him – her and the tutor – which Tiffany thinks they're bound to do, on account of its being near the end of the last volume."

"Oh, a novel!" said Mrs Mickleby. "I must confess I am an enemy to that class of literature, but I daresay that you, Miss Trent, are partial to romances."

"When they are as well-written as this one, ma'am, most certainly!" returned Ancilla.

"Oh, and he brought a dissected map!" Charlotte said. "I had never seen one before! It is all made of little pieces which fit into each other, to make a map of Europe!"

The Misses Mickleby had not seen one either, so Miss Trent, feeling that she had a score to pay, advised their mama, very kindly, to procure one for them. "So educational!" she said. "And *quite* unexceptionable!"

Then Sir Waldo arrived, and although he did not single Miss Trent out for any particular attention Mrs Mickleby, who was just as quick as Mr Calver to recognize the signs of an *affaire*, was convinced that if she had not outstayed him he would have found an excuse to take Miss Trent to walk round the gardens, or some such thing.

"And it's my belief, sorry though I am to think it, that she would have gone with him," she told Mrs Banningham later. "I was watching her closely, and I assure you, ma'am, she coloured up the instant his name was announced. I never saw anyone look more conscious!"

"It doesn't astonish me in the least," replied Mrs Banningham. "There was always something about her which I couldn't like. *You*, I know, took quite a fancy to her, but for my part I thought her affected. That excessive reserve, for instance, and her airs of gentility -!"

"Oh, as to that," said Mrs Mickleby, a trifle loftily, "the Trents are a very good family! That is what makes it so distressing to see her showing such a want of delicacy. All those rides! Of course, she was *said* to be playing propriety, but I thought at the time it was very odd, very imprudent!"

"Imprudent!" said Mrs Banningham, with a snort. "Very sly, *I* call it! She has been on the catch for him from the outset. A fine thing it would be for her, without a penny to bless herself with! *If* he makes her an offer, which I don't consider a certain thing at all. A *carte blanche*, possibly; marriage, no!"

"Someone should warn her that he is merely trifling. I should not wish her to be taken in, for however much I may deplore her conduct in luring him on to sit in her pocket, I do not think her *fast*."

"If it isn't fast to dance *twice* with him – the waltz, too! – besides going in to supper with him, and sending him to fetch her shawl, not to mention the way she looked up at him over her shoulder when he put it round her, which quite put *me* to the blush -!"

"Most unbecoming!" agreed Mrs Mickleby. "But you must own that before Sir Waldo came to Broom Hall she behaved with all the propriety in the world. I fear that he may have deceived her into believing that he was hanging out for a wife, merely because he paid her attention; and in her situation, you know, it must have seemed to her worth a push to bring him to the point. One can only pity her!"

Mrs Banningham was easily able to refrain. She said acidly: "I dislike ninnyhammers, and that she must certainly be if she imagines for one moment that a man of his consequences would entertain the thought of *marriage* with her!"

"Very true, but I fancy her experience of the Corinthian set is not large. It would be useless, of course, to suppose that Mrs Underhill would ever give her a hint."

"That vulgar female! She does not give her own niece a hint! I should be sorry to see any daughter of mine behave as Tiffany does. Wild to a fault! There is something very disgusting, too, in her determination to attach every man she meets to her apron-strings. First it was Lord Lindeth, now it is Mr Calver: he, if you please, is teaching her to drive! I saw them with my own eyes. No groom, no Miss Trent to chaperon her! Oh, no! Miss Trent only thinks it her duty to chaperon her when Sir Waldo is with her!"

"I shall be thankful when that wretched girl goes back to her uncle in London! As for Miss Trent, I have always said that she was by far too young for her position, but in this instance it must be allowed that her time has been taken up by Charlotte. If Mrs Underhill preferred her to devote herself to Charlotte rather than to Tiffany, the blame is hers. Far be it from me to suggest that Sir Waldo's daily visits have anything to do with the case! And so Tiffany is playing fast and loose with Lord Lindeth, is she? I daresay Mr Calver is much more in her style. A Macaroni merchant is what Mr Mickleby calls him, but no doubt she thinks him quite up to the nines."

In this she was right: Tiffany was greatly impressed by Laurence, whom she had recognized instantly as belonging to the dandy-set. During her brief sojourn in London she had seen several of these exquisites on the Grand Strut in Hyde Park, and she was well aware that to win the admiration of an out-and-out Pink of the *Ton* added enormously to a lady's consequence. It was not an easy thing to do, because in general the dandies were extremely critical, more likely to survey with boredom, through an insolently lifted quizzing-glass, an accredited beauty than to acclaim her. She was impressed also by his conversation; and flattered by his assumption that she was as familiar with the personalities and the *on-dits* of the *ton* as he was himself. Had it been he, and not Lindeth, who was a Peer, she would have preferred him, because he was so much more fashionable, and because he never bored her by talking about his home in the country, as Lindeth too often did. She would, in any event, have tried to attach him to her apron-strings, because it was torment to her if any young man, even so negligible a one as Humphrey Colebatch, either showed himself to be impervious to her charms, or betrayed a preference for some other girl. In Laurence's case there was an added reason for encouraging his advances: Lindeth, in whom she had detected, since the Leeds adventure, a certain reserve, probably discounted such rivals as Mr Ash, Mr Jack Barmingham, and Mr Arthur Mickleby, but she could not believe that he would be indifferent to the rivalry of his fashionable cousin. She had realized almost immediately that he did not like Laurence: not because he uttered a word in his disparagement, but because, when questioned, he spoke of him in a temperate manner far removed from the eager enthusiasm which any mention of his other cousin kindled in him. Since Tiffany much admired Laurence she had no hesitation in ascribing Lindeth's dislike of him to jealousy; it did not so much as cross her mind that

Lindeth might be contemptuous of Laurence; and had anyone suggested such a solution to her she would have been utterly incredulous.

When Lindeth called at Staples to leave compliment cards, she told him, with a provocative look under her lashes, that his cousin, learning that although she was an accomplished horsewoman in the saddle she had never found anyone capable of teaching her how to handle the reins in form, had begged to be allowed to offer his services.

He stared at her blankly. "Mr Calver says he will teach me to drive to an inch," she added, with one of her sauciest smiles.

"Laurence?" he demanded, the oddest expression on his face.

"Why not?" she countered, lifting an eyebrow at him.

He opened his mouth, shut it again, and turned away to pick up his hat and gloves.

"Well?" persisted Tiffany, pleased with the success of her gambit. "Pray, have you any objection?"

"No, no, not the least in the world!" he said hastily. "How should I? I only – but never mind that!"

That was quite enough to confirm Tiffany in her belief that she had roused a demon of jealousy in his breast. She never knew that his lordship, whom Laurence stigmatized as a bagpipe, snatched the first opportunity that presented itself of admitting his cousin Waldo into a joke which was much too rich to be kept to himself. "I don't know how I contrived to keep my countenance! Laurie! Driving to an inch! Oh, lord, I shall be sick if I laugh any more!"

But Tiffany, with no suspicion that she had afforded Lindeth food for laughter, was very well satisfied. Her former suitors, who had gloomily but unresentfully watched Lindeth's star rise, were roused to violent jealousy by Laurence; and she saw no reason to suppose that Lindeth would not be similarly stirred. For several days she was intoxicated by success, believing herself to be irresistible, and queening it over her court with ever-increasing capriciousness. And since, like Mrs Mickleby, she discarded without hesitation the ostensible reason for the Nonesuch's daily visits, and had never for an instant suspected that he might prefer her companion to her peerless self, she was sure that he too was unable to stay away from her. This seemed so obvious that she did not pause to consider that his behaviour, when he came to Staples, was not in the least that of a man dazzled by her charms. She had always found him incalculable, and if she had thought about it at all she would have supposed that he was content merely to look at her.

Courtenay, revolted by her self-satisfaction and indignant with his friends for making such fools of themselves, told her that she was no better than a vulgar lightskirt, and prophesied that she was riding for a fall; and when she laughed said that Lord Lindeth was only the first man to become disgusted: there would be others soon enough.

"Pooh!"

"Mighty pot-sure, aren't you? But it seems to me that we don't see so much of Lindeth these days!"

"When I want him," boasted Tiffany, smiling in a way which made him want to slap her, "I shall just lift a finger! Then you'll see!"

That sent him off in a rage to represent to his mother the absolute necessity of curbing Tiffany's flirtatious antics. "I tell you, Mama, she's *insufferable*!" he declared.

"Now, Courtenay, for goodness' sake don't go upsetting her!" begged Mrs Underhill, alarmed. "I own I wouldn't wish to see Charlotte being so bold as she is, but she always *was* caper-witted, and it ain't as though she was carrying on with strange gentlemen that mightn't keep the line. If I was to interfere, she wouldn't pay a bit of heed to me – and you know what she is when she's crossed! There's enough trouble in the house, with Charlotte being so poorly, without us having to bear one of Tiffany's tantrums!"

He turned appealingly to Miss Trent, but she shook her head. "I'm afraid the only remedy is for her admirers to grow cool," she said, smiling. "She is too headstrong, and has been allowed to have her own way for too long to submit to restraint. What would you have me do? Lock her in her room? She would climb out of the window, and very likely break her neck. I think, with you, that her behaviour is unbecoming, but she has done nothing scandalous, you know, and I fancy she won't – unless she is goaded to it."

"How Greg, and Jack, and Arthur can make such cakes of themselves -! Lord, it puts me in such a pelter to think they should be such gudgeons that there's no bearing it!"

"I shouldn't let it tease you," she said. "It's the fashion amongst them to worship Tiffany, and fashions don't endure for long."

"Well, I only hope she has a rattling fall!" he said savagely. "And what have you to say to this Calver-fellow? Teaching her to drive indeed! How do we know he ain't a loose screw?"

"We don't, of course, but although I should prefer her not to drive out alone with him every day I have very little apprehension of his taking advantage of her childishness."

"No, indeed!" said Mrs Underhill. "When he asked my permission, and told me I could trust him to take good care of her! He's a very civil young man, and I'm sure I don't know why you should have taken him in dislike!"

"Civil young man! A Bartholomew baby! It's my belief he's a dashed fortune-hunter!"

"Very possibly," agreed Miss Trent, quite unmoved. "But since she's under age we needn't tease ourselves over that. If you imagine that Tiffany would fling her cap over the windmill for a mere commoner you can't know her!"

Oddly enough, at that very moment, Sir Waldo, lifting an eyebrow at Laurence, was saying: "Having a touch at the heiress, Laurie?"

"No, I ain't. If you mean the Wield chit!"

"I do. Just started in the petticoat line, I collect!"

"Well, I haven't. *Is* she an heiress?"

"So I'm given to understand. I rather think she told me so herself."

"Sort of thing she would do," said Laurie. He thought it over for a moment, and then added, "I don't want to be leg-shackled: wouldn't suit me at all! Not but what I may be forced into it."

"I'm reluctant to blight your hopes, Laurie, but I think it only right to warn you that I have reason to suppose that your suit won't prosper. Miss Wield is determined to marry into the Peerage."

"Exactly so!" exclaimed Laurence. "*I* saw at a glance! She means to catch Lindeth, of course. I imagine you wouldn't like that above half!"

"Not as much," said Sir Waldo, in a voice of affable agreement.

"No, and my aunt wouldn't like it either!" said Laurence. "What's more, I wouldn't blame her! No reason why *he* should make a cream-pot marriage: *he* ain't under the hatches!"

"I don't think he has any such intention."

"I know *that*! The silly chub was bowled out by her face. Well, you won't cozen *me* into thinking that young Julian is not your cosset-lamb! You'd give something to see him come safe off, wouldn't you?"

Sir Waldo, who had drawn his snuff-box from his pocket, opened it with an expert flick of one finger, and took a pinch. He looked meditatively at Laurence, amused understanding in his eyes. "Alas, you've missed your tip!" he said.

Laurence stared at him. "If you're trying to bamboozle me into believing that Julian ain't dangling after that girl it's you who have missed your tip, Waldo! You won't tell me that he -"

"The only thing I shall tell you," interposed Sir Waldo, "is that you're after the fair! Oh, don't look so affronted! Console yourself with the reflection that as little as I discuss Julian's business with you do I discuss yours with him!"

He said no more, leaving Laurence puzzled and aggrieved. He had his own reasons for believing that Julian had been cured of his passing infatuation; but if Laurie, bent on detaching Tiffany, had not discovered that his young cousin now had his eyes turned towards a very different quarry so much the better, he thought, profoundly mistrusting Laurie's mischief-making tongue. If Julian's interest in Miss Chartley became fixed, nothing could more surely prejudice his mother against the match than to learn of it from Laurie. The first news of it must come from Julian himself; after which, he reflected wryly, it would be his task to reconcile the widow. She would be bitterly disappointed, but she was no fool, and must already have begun to doubt whether her cherished son would gratify her ambition by offering for any one of the damsels of rank, fortune, and fashion in whose way she had thrown him. She was also a most devoted parent; and once she had recovered from her initial chagrin Sir Waldo believed that she would very soon take the gentle Patience to her bosom. A pungent description of the beautiful Miss Wield would go a long way towards settling her mind.

For himself, he was much inclined to think that after his various tentative excursions Julian had found exactly the wife to suit him. Just as Patience differed from Tiffany, so did Julian's courtship of her differ from his eager pursuit of Tiffany. He had begun with liking; his admiration had been kindled by the Leeds episode; and he was now, in Sir Waldo's judgment, quietly and deeply in love. From such references to Patience as he from time to time let fall, his cousin gathered that she had every amiable quality, a well-informed mind, and a remarkable readiness to meet Julian's ideas, and to share his every sentiment. Sir Waldo guessed that he was a frequent visitor at the Rectory, but there were none of the rides, picnics, and evening parties which had attended his transitory passion for Tiffany. Probably that was why Laurence seemed not to have realized that he had suffered a change of heart; no doubt Laurie supposed him to be in his elder cousin's company when he found him missing from Broom Hall; and was misled by the innate civility which made him continue to call at Staples into thinking him still Tiffany's worshipper.

It was during one of these morning visits that Julian learned that the al fresco ridotto which Tiffany had coaxed her aunt to hold in the gardens was to be postponed. Charlotte still continued to be languid and out of spirits; the doctor recommended a change of air and sea-bathing; so Mrs Underhill was going to take her to Bridlington, where she had a cousin living with his wife in retirement. She explained apologetically to Lindeth, and to Arthur Mickleby, whom Lindeth had found kicking his heels in the Green Saloon, that she hoped they wouldn't be vexed, but she didn't feel able for a ridotto when Charlotte was so poorly. Both young men expressed their regrets, and said everything that was polite; and Arthur reminded Mrs Underhill, in a heartening way, of how he had been taken to Bridlington after the measles, and how quickly he had plucked up there.

In the middle of this speech Tiffany came in wearing her driving-dress, and with Laurence at her heels. "Bridlington? Who is going to *that* stupid place?" she demanded. She extended a careless hand to Lindeth. "How do you do? I haven't seen you this age! Oh, Arthur, have you been waiting for me? Mr Calver has been teaching me how to loop a rein. *You* are not going to Bridlington, are you? It is the dullest, horridest place imaginable! Why don't you go to Scarborough?"

"'Tisn't me, it's Charlotte," explained Arthur. "I was telling Mrs Underhill how much good it did me when *I* was in queer stirrups."

"Oh, Charlotte! *Poor* Charlotte! I daresay it will be the very thing for her. When does she go, ma'am?"

"Well, my dear, I believe I'll take her this week," said Mrs Underhill nervously. "There's no sense in keeping her here, so low and dragged as she is, and Cousin Matty for ever begging me to pay her a visit, and to bring Charlotte along with me. I've been asking his lordship's pardon, and Arthur's too, for being obliged to put off the ridotto."

"Put off my ridotto!" exclaimed Tiffany. "Oh, *no*! you can't mean to be so cruel, ma'am!"

"I'm sure I'm as sorry as I can be, love, but you can't have a party without I'm here, now, can you? It wouldn't be seemly."

"But you must be here, aunt! Send Nurse with Charlotte, or Ancilla! Oh, pray do!"

"I couldn't be easy in my mind, letting the poor lamb go without me, and I wouldn't have the heart for a ridotto, nor any kind of party. But there's no need to get into a fidget, love, for I don't mean to stay above a sennight – that is, not if Charlotte's going on well, and don't dislike to be left with Cousin George and Cousin Matty, which I daresay she won't. But she made me promise her I'd go with her, and so I did. Not that I intended otherwise."

"How can she be so abominably selfish?" cried Tiffany, flushing. "Making you go away when she knows that *I* need you! Depend upon it, she did it for spite, just to spoil my ridotto!"

Arthur looked rather startled, but it was Lindeth who interposed, saying: "It is very natural that she should wish for her mama, don't you think!"

"No!" Tiffany replied crossly. "For she would as lief have Ancilla! Oh, *I* know! Ancilla shall be hostess in your stead, aunt! Famous! We shall do delightfully!"

But Mrs Underhill was steadfast in refusing to entertain this suggestion. Observing the rising storm signals in Tiffany's eyes, she sought to temper the disappointment by promising to hold the ridotto as soon as she returned from Bridlington; but this only made Tiffany stamp her foot, and declare that she hated put-offs, and marvelled that her aunt should be taken in by Charlotte's nonsense. "For my part, I believe she could be perfectly stout if she chose! She is putting on airs to be interesting, which I think quite odious, and so I shall tell her!"

"Here!" protested Arthur, shocked. "That's coming it a bit strong! I beg pardon, but – but you shouldn't say that!" He added haltingly: "And although *I* should have enjoyed it, there – there are several people who don't take to the notion. Well – Mrs Chartley won't permit Patience to come, and, as a matter of fact – Mama won't let my sisters either. Not to a moonlight party in the gardens!"

"There! if I didn't say it wasn't the thing!" exclaimed Mrs Underhill.

"Who cares whether they come or not?" said Tiffany scornfully. "If they choose to be stuffy, I promise you *I* don't!"

Arthur reddened, and got up to take his leave. Mrs Underhill, acutely embarrassed, pressed his hand warmly, and gave him a speaking look; but Tiffany turned her shoulder on him, saying that he was quite as stuffy as his sisters.

"I must be going too, ma'am," Lindeth said. "Pray tell Charlotte how sorry I am to hear that she's so much pulled, and tell her to take care she don't get her toes pinched by a crab when she goes sea-bathing! . . . Are you coming, Laurie?"

"Oh, don't wait for me! I have been thinking, Miss Wield, if we might perhaps get up a party to dance at one of the Assemblies in Harrogate – instead of the ridotto. Would you countenance it, ma'am? With Miss Trent, of course, or some older lady, if any might be persuaded?"

Tiffany's eyes lit up, but Mrs Underhill looked dismayed, and faltered: "Oh, dear! No, no, don't suggest it, Mr Calver, for it's the very thing Mr Burford – that's Tiffany's uncle, and her guardian, you know – don't wish for! Because she ain't out yet, and he won't have her going to public dances, for which, of course, he can't be blamed."

"It wasn't he, but Aunt Burford!" said Tiffany. "The greatest beast in nature! Why shouldn't I go to an Assembly in Harrogate? I *will* go, I *will*!"

Lindeth went quietly away, hearing the storm break behind him. Miss Trent was coming down the stairs, and paused, looking enquiringly at him. "How do you do? Tell me at once! The ridotto?"

He burst out laughing. "Well, yes! Coupled with Mrs Underhill's saying she might not go to a Harrogate Assembly."

Miss Trent closed her eyes for an anguished moment. "I see. How prudent of you to slip away, sir! Would that I could do so too! She will sulk for days!"

CHAPTER FOURTEEN

THAT TIFFANY refrained from sulking was due to Miss Trent, who waited only until they were alone in the room to utter words which provided her with food for reflection. She said cheerfully that she did not wonder at it that Tiffany was bored with her admirers, but that she thought she might have chosen a better way of being rid of them. Tiffany stared at her.

"Nothing, of course, makes a gentleman retire more quickly than a fit of the tantrums; but you should recollect that a reputation for being ill-tempered would be most prejudicial to your success. As for being rude and unkind to your aunt – indeed, Tiffany, I had not thought you such a wet-goose! What will become of you if you drive off *all* your admirers?"

"I *d-don't*! I *c-couldn't*!" Tiffany stammered.

"It can be done more easily than you know," replied Ancilla. "You have accomplished it with Lord Lindeth; and, unless I am much mistaken, we shan't see Arthur Mickleby at Staples for some time to come. Your aunt tells me that you spoke slightingly of his sisters. How *stupid* of you, Tiffany! and how dreadfully ill-bred! How came you to do such a thing?"

"I don't care! I only said they were stuffy, and they are! And I don't care a button for Arthur either! And I didn't drive Lindeth off! I *didn't*! He's jealous, because his cousin is teaching me to drive! I have only to smile at him – How dare you look like that? I tell you -"

"You will be wasting your breath," interrupted Miss Trent. "Try to believe that I am rather more up to snuff than you! I am, you know. Don,t glare at me! When your aunt Burford engaged me to be your companion, she particularly desired me to teach you how to go on in society, and if I didn't warn you that your conduct lately has been such as to give people a disgust of you, I should be failing in my duty."

"Disgust! Of *me*? It's not true!" Tiffany gasped, white with rage.

"If you will stop preening yourself on your beauty, and allow yourself the indulgence of a few moments' reflection, I think you must realize that it *is* true," responded Miss Trent. "Before you began to fancy yourself to be a Nonpareil beyond criticism you were used to take care not to fly into unbecoming rages when any stranger was present; but during these past weeks you have grown to be so puffed up in your own conceit that you seem to think you may go your unbridled length and still command everyone's admiration. Well, you were never more mistaken! That is all I have to say to you and I've said it only because I can't reconcile it with my conscience not to warn you to mend your ways."

She then opened a book, and apparently became so absorbed in it that the furious tirade directed at her did not cause her to betray by the flicker of an eyelid that she heard a word of it. Tiffany slammed out of the room, and was not seen again until she came down to dinner; but as she then seemed to be in her softest mood, even speaking affectionately to Charlotte, and politely to her aunt, Miss Trent was encouraged to suppose that her words had not failed of their intended effect. Towards her, Tiffany adopted a manner of frigid disdain, which had not abated by the following morning, when she refused every offer made by her companion to minister to her entertainment. So Miss Trent, unabashed, left her to her own devices, or (as she suspected) to the attentions of Mr Calver, and seized the opportunity to pay a call on Mrs Chartley, with a copy of the recipe for pickling white mushrooms tucked into her reticule. Charlotte was fretful, and would not go with her, so she went to the village alone, and, having delivered a large parcel at the Crown, to be picked up by the carrier, drove the gig into the Rectory stableyard.

She found Mrs Chartley in her morning-parlour, and received the usual kind welcome from her. Mrs Chartley thanked her for the recipe, enquired after Charlotte, and, when Ancilla would have taken her leave, begged her to sit down for a few minutes.

"I am very glad to see you, Miss Trent," she said, "because I fancy you can perhaps answer a question which is teasing me a good deal." She smiled. "Rather an odd question, you may think – but I know I may depend upon your discretion."

"Certainly you may, ma'am."

Mrs Chartley hesitated. "Yes. If I did not – Miss Trent, I find myself in a quandary! I daresay you are aware that Lord Lindeth is growing extremely particular in his attentions to Patience?"

"I wasn't aware of it, ma'am. I have been constantly with Charlotte, you know. But I am not at all surprised. He always liked her, and I have frequently thought that he and Miss Chartley might have been made for one another. I hope you don't dislike it? I have a great regard for Lord Lindeth – as far as I know him and I believe him to be really worthy of Miss Chartley."

"No. No, I don't dislike it – though I own to some feelings of doubt at the outset. He appeared to me to be violently in love with Tiffany, which argues a volatility I cannot like."

"I had rather say that he was dazzled by her, as so many have been. He might have loved her if her disposition had matched her face, which, alas, it does not! You are thinking that the change in his sentiments was very sudden, but I fancy he began to be disillusioned quite early in their acquaintance. There were several occasions when – But I should not be talking of them!"

"You need not scruple to speak frankly: if her conduct at Leeds is anything to judge by, I can readily understand Lindeth's disillusionment. But to turn so soon from Tiffany to Patience does disquiet me! The Rector, however, sets very little store by it. Indeed, he seems to think it perfectly natural that a young man, when he is *ripe for falling in love* (as he puts it), should transfer his affection to another, when he finds he has mistaken his own heart. It seems very odd to me, but I am well aware, of course, that men *are* odd, even the best of them!"

"And Miss Chartley, ma'am?" Ancilla said, smiling.

"I am very much afraid that she is in danger of forming a lasting attachment," replied Mrs Chartley, with a sigh. "*She* is not volatile, you know, and if he were again to discover that he had mistaken his heart -"

"Forgive me!" Ancilla interposed. "I collect that you believe Lindeth to be fickle. But I have been a great deal in his company, and I have had the opportunity to observe his *infatuation*. As I have said, it might have deepened into *love*, but it never did so. And – I do assure you, ma'am, that it would have been wonderful indeed if an ardent young man, having at that time formed no real attachment, had not succumbed to Tiffany's beauty, and to the encouragement he received from her."

Mrs Chartley's face lightened a little. "So the Rector says. I own, there is no *infatuation* in question now. I don't leave them alone together, I need hardly say, but even if I allowed my daughter the license Tiffany has I am persuaded Lindeth would not *flirt* with her. Indeed, I have been agreeably surprised in him! Under the gaiety which makes his manners so taking, there is a strong vein of seriousness. He feels as he ought on all important subjects, and the tone of his mind is particularly nice."

"But in spite of this you do not wish for the connection, ma'am?" Ancilla asked, a little puzzled.

"My dear, a very strange creature I should be if I did not wish for such an advantageous connection for my daughter! If he is sincere, nothing would please me more than to see her so well established. But although they are not unequal in birth they are unequal in consequence. Nor is Patience an heiress. She will have some four thousand pounds, but that, though it is a respectable portion, might be thought paltry by Lindeth's family. From things he has let fall, about disliking *ton* parties, and being the *despair of his mother* – in his funning way, you know! – I suspect that the family wish him to make what is called a brilliant marriage, and might be strongly opposed to his marriage to a country clergyman's daughter." She paused, and rather aimlessly shifted the position of a book lying on the table at her elbow. "I had fancied that Sir Waldo had been his guardian, but I understand this was not the case. At the same time, there can be no doubt that he has stood in much that position. Nor that his influence over Lindeth is great. That, my dear Miss Trent, is why I have been anxious to have the opportunity of talking to you. If there is any fear that Sir Waldo might exert himself to prevent the marriage – even if he should merely dislike it – I would not upon any account continue to permit Lindeth to visit us as he now does. Neither the Rector nor I would countenance the alliance if it had not the approbation of Lindeth's family. You will understand, I am persuaded, why I am in a quandary, and why I made up my mind to admit you into my confidence. Tell me! What are Sir Waldo's sentiments upon this occasion?"

Miss Trent felt her colour rising, but she responded in a steady voice: "I am honoured by your confidence, ma'am, but Sir Waldo has not taken me into his. I wish I might be able to help you, but it is not in my power."

Mrs Chartley raised her eyes, directing a slightly sceptical look at her. "If that is so, there is no more to be said, of course. I ventured to put the question to you because I know you to be far better acquainted with him than anyone else in the district."

There was silence for a few moments. Then Miss Trent drew a breath, and said: "I have been obliged to be a good deal in his company, ma'am, but I do not stand upon such intimate terms with him as – as you seem to suggest." She managed to smile. "My sins have found me out! I allowed myself to be persuaded to accept Lady Colebatch's invitation, and was imprudent enough to waltz with Sir Waldo, twice. I have been made to regret it. I'm afraid the pleasure of dancing again, after such a long time, went to my head!"

Mrs Chartley's face softened; she leaned forward, and briefly clasped one of Ancilla's hands. "No wonder! I perfectly understand. But – My dear, will you permit me to speak frankly to you? You are a young woman, in spite of your sober ways! And you have not your mama at hand to advise you, have you? I am most sincerely fond of you, so you must forgive me if I seem to you to take too much upon myself. I have been feeling a little anxious about you, for I'm afraid you may be cherishing hopes which are unlikely to be fulfilled. Don't think that I blame you! Sir Waldo's attentions have been marked: it is even common knowledge that not a day has passed since Charlotte has been laid up without his calling on you at Staples."

"To enquire after her progress – to bring her what he thought might entertain her!" Ancilla uttered, her throat constricted.

"My dear!" protested Mrs Chartley, with a slight laugh.

"Ma'am, I only once saw him – and then in company!"

"If you tell me so, I believe you, but it will be a hard task to convince others."

"I am aware of it, ma'am," said Ancilla bitterly. "I am held to be setting my cap at him, am I not?"

"We need not concern ourselves with expressions of spite. That is not at all my opinion. What makes me uneasy is *his* pursuit of *you*. If it had been any other man than Sir Waldo, I should have known it to be a determined courtship, and I should have been expecting every day to be able to wish you happy – for you cannot conceal from me, my dear, that you are by no means indifferent to him. That doesn't surprise me in the least: I fancy there are few women strongminded enough to withstand him. Even I – and he does not make up to me, you know! – am very conscious of his charm. I think him dangerously attractive, and don't for a moment doubt that a great many females have fallen in love with him."

"Did Mrs Mickleby tell you so, ma'am?"

"On the authority of her cousin in London. I should be sorry to place too much reliance on mere gossip, but it has been to some extent borne out by Lindeth – not, you may be sure, with any intention of traducing his cousin. Indeed, the reverse! He often talks about Sir Waldo, and always with admiration – I had almost said, with pride! And one must bear in mind, my dear Miss Trent, that Sir Waldo belongs to a certain set which is considered to be the very height of fashion. In fact, he is its leader, and very much a man of the world. You must know, perhaps better than I do, that the manners and too often the conduct of those who are vulgarly called Top-of-the-Trees are not governed by quite the same principles which are the rule in more modest circles."

"Are you trying to warn me, ma'am, that Sir Waldo is a libertine?" asked

Ancilla bluntly.

"Oh, good gracious! No!" exclaimed Mrs Chartley. "You must not think – my dear, I beg you won't say that I said that! No doubt he has had his – shall we say his adventures? but pray don't imagine that I suspect him of-of -"

"Offering me a *carte blanche*? That, I believe, is the term, is it not? I promise you I should not accept it!"

Mrs Chartley was thrown still more off her balance by this, and said: "No, no! I don't suspect him of meaning to do you the least harm! What I fear is that he may harm you unwittingly, not realizing that you might fall far more deeply in love with him than he knew, or intended. He is accustomed to associate, recollect, with fashionable females who understand the rules of flirtation as you, I am happy to say, do not. Very likely he has been a trifle misled into thinking you are as worldly wise as any of his London flirts: you are *posée* beyond your years, you know! He would not, I am persuaded, tamper with the affections of a girl whom he knew to be inexperienced."

"But you don't hold him in very high esteem, do you, ma'am?" said Ancilla, with a painful smile.

"Oh, you are quite mistaken! In some respects, I hold him in the highest esteem!" Mrs Chartley replied quickly. "I have every reason -" She checked herself, colouring, and added: "All I wish to say to you, my dear, is that you should be on your guard. Don't refine too much upon his gallantry, but recollect that he is a man of five or six-and-thirty, handsome, rich, very much courted and still a bachelor!"

Miss Trent began to pull on her gloves. "I do recollect it," she said, in a low voice. "I am very much obliged to you for your kindness in – in warning me, ma'am, but I beg you to believe that it was unnecessary! You have told me nothing that I haven't told myself." She rose. "I must go. I wish I might have been able to give you the assurance you want. I cannot – but I don't think Sir Waldo would ever stand in the way of what he saw to be Lindeth's happiness."

"Thank you: I hope you may be right. Did you come in the gig? I'll walk with you to the stables. By the bye, what has been the outcome of Mr Calver's Harrogate scheme? I can picture your dismay! We heard of it from Lindeth, and from what he did *not* say I collect that Tiffany was sadly disappointed by her aunt's refusal to countenance it!"

Ancilla laughed. "Not sadly, ma'am! Furiously! Lord Lindeth made good his escape when he saw the storm about to break. I fancy we shall hear no more of the scheme."

"You must be thankful for it! A very rackety suggestion to have put forward! I daresay you will be glad to see the last of that young man."

"Well, I own that I can't like Mr Calver, but I should be doing him less than justice if I didn't tell you that when he saw that Mrs Underhill disliked the scheme he let it drop immediately. I must say, too, that I have felt very much more cordial since he confessed to me that he had spoken without reflection, meaning only to divert Tiffany's mind, and was sincerely sorry for it. He assured me I might depend upon him to discover a hundred reasons, if it should be necessary, why the scheme was ineligible! He was extremely civil as, indeed, he has always been."

They had reached the stables; and they parted on this lighter note. Mrs

Chartley stayed only until Ancilla had stepped up into the gig, and then walked back to the house, along the garden path. Ancilla drove out of the stable-gate, and turned into the village street. Before the cob had broken into a trot a phaeton, drawn by a team of chestnuts, swept round the bend immediately ahead. Knowing herself to be in full view of the Rectory, Miss Trent saw with dismay that Sir Waldo was checking his team, with the evident intention of pulling up alongside the gig. There seemed to be nothing to do but to follow suit, since to urge the cob into a trot at that moment would be so uncivil as to make Sir Waldo think that she was trying to avoid a meeting.

The next instant the phaeton had stopped beside the gig, driven up so close that if she had not known how expert was the driver she would have feared that the wheels would be locked; the groom had jumped down, and run to the wheelers' heads; and Sir Waldo was raising his hat, and smiling at her. "How do you do, ma'am? I must have been born under a lucky star! A moment earlier, and I should have missed you. I have been thinking myself singularly *un*lucky for the past sennight, you know."

She replied, as easily as she could: "So, too, has poor Charlotte. Are you on your way to Leeds?"

"Yes; have you any commissions for me?"

"No, I thank you, none. I must not detain you."

"I have the impression that it's I who am detaining you," he said quizzically.

She smiled, but said: "Well, I certainly ought not to linger: I have been with Mrs Chartley, and stayed longer than I meant to. And you, I expect, have a great deal of business to attend to in Leeds."

"Not so very much. I'm happy to say that I am nearing the end of it."

"You must be heartily tired of it," she agreed. "Have the builders finished their work?"

"No, not yet. I am having – rather extensive alterations made."

She laughed. "No need to tell me that, Sir Waldo! Your alterations are a matter of the greatest interest in the neighbourhood, I promise you!"

"Yes, so I've been told. Speculation is rife, is it? I should have known better than to suppose that no one would care a rush what I did with the house, for my own home is in the country. That's the worst – and sometimes the best – of country-life: intense interest in one's neighbours!"

"Very true. And you, I would remind you, are an exceptionally interesting neighbour in these backward parts! Besides which, you have whetted curiosity by not choosing to disclose whether you mean to sell Broom Hall, or to keep it as a suitable house to stay in when the York Races are run. This reserve, sir, is felt to indicate that there is some mystery attached to your alterations, which you are afraid to make known!"

She spoke in a tone of raillery, and was surprised to see that although he smiled he looked rather rueful. "I think I am," he admitted. "My purpose will be known, but I prefer that it should remain a secret while I remain in the district."

She said: "I was only joking you! Not trying to pry into your concerns!"

"I'm well aware of that. But I have every intention of making a clean breast of the matter to you, Miss Trent. I am afraid that I shall fall under the displeasure of the majority of my neighbours, but I fancy your voice won't swell the chorus of disapproval. You have too liberal a mind. I shall do myself the honour of coming to visit you in the very near future – as I warned you I should, an aeon ago!"

She could not believe that these were the words of a man with nothing but idle dalliance in mind; but she felt obliged to demur. "I should be very happy, but I don't think – Sir Waldo, Mrs Underhill is to take Charlotte to Bridlington, and will be away from home for a sennight, or more!"

He made a sign to his groom, and said, with his glinting smile, as he gave his horses the office: "I know it. I may at last contrive to see you alone, Miss Trent!"

CHAPTER FIFTEEN

MISS TRENT drove home in a happy dream, no longer caring whether her meeting with the Nonesuch had been observed by Mrs Chartley, or not; and able to dismiss that lady's earnest warning with a light heart. Mrs Chartley, she now believed, had misjudged Sir Waldo. So too, indeed, had she: probably they had each of them been prejudiced by their mutual dislike of the Corinthian set; almost certainly (and very strangely) they had been misled by commonsense. Neither she nor Mrs Chartley was of a romantic turn of mind; and she at least had learnt, early in life, the folly of indulging fantastic dreams which belonged only to the realm of fairy-tales. Nothing could be more fantastic than to suppose that the Nonesuch bore the least resemblance to the handsome nursery-prince whose wayward fancy had been fixed on Cinderella, so perhaps they were not so very much to be blamed for their doubts. Inexperienced though she knew herself to be in the art of dalliance, Miss Trent could no longer doubt: she could only wonder. Try as she would she could discover no reason why she should have been preferred to all the noble and lovely ladies hopeful of receiving an offer from the Nonesuch. It seemed so wildly improbable as to be unreal. But when she had tried in vain to place a different construction upon the things he had said to her, it flashed into her mind that nothing, after all, was so wildly improbable as her own headlong tumble into love with the epitome of all that she held in contempt; and that that was precisely what she had done there was no doubt whatsoever.

She returned to Staples treading on air. Even Mrs Underhill, not usually observant, was struck by the bloom in her cheeks, and the glow in her eyes, and declared that she had never seen her in such high beauty. "Never tell me he's popped the question?" she exclaimed.

"No, no, ma'am!" Ancilla replied, blushing and laughing.

"Well, if he hasn't done it now, I'll be bound you know he means to, for what else is there to cast you into alt?" demanded Mrs Underhill reasonably.

"Am I in alt? I didn't know it! Dear Mrs Underhill, pray – *pray* don't ask me questions I cannot answer!"

Mrs Underhill very kindly refrained, but she could not help animadverting on the perversity of fate, which had decreed that she should be away from Staples just as she would have most wished to be at home. "For gentlemen are so unaccountable," she said, "that he may need to be nudged on, and that I *could* have done!"

Miss Trent, albeit profoundly thankful that her employer would not be at hand to perform this office, recognized the kindly intention that had inspired her daunting speech, and thanked her with what gravity she could command, but told her that she would as lief receive no offer from a gentleman who required nudging.

"Yes, that's all very well," retorted Mrs Underhill, "and very easy for you to talk like that, when all you've got to say is yes, or no, as the case may be! As though it didn't stand to reason that a gentleman that's screwed himself up to the point, and very likely hasn't had a wink of sleep all night for making up a pretty speech and learning it off by heart, needs a bit of encouragement, because he's bound to feel bashful, on account of not wishing to make a figure of himself, which gentlemen, my dear, can't abide!"

Miss Trent could not picture the Nonesuch overcome by bashfulness, but she kept this reflection to herself. She had no wish to prolong a discussion which she felt to be unbecoming, so after murmuring an agreement she directed Mrs Underhill's thoughts into a different channel, by producing a list of all the things that must be attended to before that lady could leave Staples with a quiet mind. Fortunately the list was a long one, and included problems of great complexity, chief amongst which loomed the vexed question of the new winter curtains for the drawing-room. These were being made by an indigent widow, living in a village some miles distant from Staples: an arrangement which, owing partly to the dilatory disposition of the widow, and partly to the folly of the silk warehouse in sending silk for the linings which in no way matched the opulent brocade chosen by Mrs Underhill, had already been productive of considerable annoyance.

"If it isn't one thing it's another!" declared Mrs Underhill. "*Faithfully* did they promise to send me another pattern this week! And did they do it? Answer me that!"

"No, ma'am," said Miss Trent obediently. "They sent you a civil letter, explaining why there must be a little delay. Would you perhaps wish me to write to the warehouse, desiring them to send the new pattern to Mrs Tawton, so that she may judge -"

"No, that I wouldn't!" interrupted Mrs Underhill. "*She* judge? She wouldn't know black from white, for a sillier creature I never met! And so slow that – Well, there! I knew how it would be when Mrs Chartley asked me if I'd put some work in her way, for I never yet employed anyone out of kindness but what it cost me more and was worse done than if I'd sent all the way to London to have it made for me! I'd liefer by far have dipped my hand in my pocket, and made her a present of the money, and so I would have done if Mrs Chartley hadn't warned me not, for fear of hurting the silly woman's pride. Which is another thing I don't hold with. Don't you ever, my dear, send out work to anyone that has claims to gentility, for if they don't do it in their time instead of yours ten to one they'll do it wrong, and very likely look as if you'd insulted 'em if you tell 'em it's not been done to your satisfaction!"

"I won't," said Miss Trent. "If you think I may be trusted to judge, I'll take the lining-silk to Mrs Tawton, and look at it beside the brocade. If the pattern is sent before your return, that is. Or would you prefer to let it stand until you can take it yourself?"

"No, that I wouldn't!" said Mrs Underhill. "It's this winter I want my new curtains, not next! Though I don't like to be asking you to run *my* errands, which you might well take offence at!"

"I'm not so genteel, ma'am! So that is settled. Then there is the fruit to be given to -"

"Oh, my goodness, if that hasn't put me in mind of old Matthew!" exclaimed Mrs Underhill. "Well, I'm sure it's no wonder I should have forgot, with all the fuss and worry about Charlotte, and the packing, and such! He's laid up with his rheumatism, and there's a bottle of liniment, and a bit of flannel to be taken to his cottage, which I'll have to find the time to do, because he's a pensioner, and Mr Underhill was always very particular not to neglect any of them."

"I shall be glad of a walk, and I'll go tomorrow morning, as soon as I have seen you and Charlotte safely into the carriage," promised Ancilla.

Since Mrs Underhill, who rarely spent a night away from Staples, was rapidly becoming distracted, this duty proved to be more arduous than might have been expected, and entailed much hurried unpacking to discover whether various indispensable comforts had been included in the numerous trunks and portmanteaux, as Mrs Underhill's maid asserted they had; or whether they had been overlooked, as Mrs Underhill feared they must have been. However, after only one false start, because Charlotte found that she had forgotten her travelling chessboard, the travellers at last drove away, leaving behind them a somewhat breathless and exhausted household.

"Phew!" uttered Courtenay, restoring the handkerchief he had been waving to his pocket. "You'd think they were bound for the Antipodes!" He turned to his giggling cousin, and said, with all the air of a young gentleman virtuously mindful of his mother's parting injunctions: "I'm riding over to Crawshays, and if you care to go with me you may. Only don't keep me kicking my heels for ever while you rig yourself out!"

Having no other engagement, and apprehending that Miss Trent might bear her off to visit the aged Matthew, Tiffany accepted this handsome invitation, and ran into the house to put on her riding-dress. Relieved of responsibility for one morning at least, Miss Trent presently set forth with a basket over her arm, glad of the exercise after her close attendance on Charlotte, and only too happy to be alone with her thoughts.

It was on her way back to Staples that she was overtaken by Lindeth, driving the late Mr Calver's gig. He pulled up beside her, his eyes dancing with amusement. "Good-morning, ma'am! You have missed *such* a capital sight! Do get up beside me, and let me drive you home!"

She smiled up at him. "Why, thank you, but I enjoy walking, you know! What sight have I missed?"

He laughed. "I'll tell you – but you must let me drive you! I think it's going to rain, and you have no umbrella."

"Very well," she replied, taking the hand he stretched down to her, and mounting nimbly into the gig. "Though *I* think the clouds are too high for rain. Don't keep me in suspense another moment! *What* did I miss?"

"Arthur Mickleby, trying to catch the thong of his whip over his head!" he said, still laughing. "I missed it too, but if you'd seen him -! What must he do but practise the trick half-a-mile back on this lane, just where the trees overhang the road! *What* a cawker!"

She began to laugh too. "Oh, no! Did it get caught up?"

"I should rather think it did! By the time I came along he was in such a rage, cursing the tree, and the whip, and that nappy gray of his, that I couldn't have helped laughing if it had been to save my life! Every time he got hold of the butt, and tried to twitch the thong free, the gray took fright, and started forward, so of course Mickleby was obliged to let the whip go while he got the hard-mouthed brute quiet again. So there he was, backing under the tree with the whip swinging like a pendulum, and knocking his hat off!"

Miss Trent, much enjoying this story, said: "To think I should have missed it! Did he succeed in freeing it?"

"Oh, lord, no! It's still there – but I'll lay you odds it won't be for long! Mickleby's gone off home: to fetch a ladder, *I* think! Before anyone comes along and sees the whip dangling, and starts making enquiries! I would, too. He was ready to murder me, but there was nothing I could do about it."

"Poor Arthur! I expect you were perfectly odious!"

"Not a bit of it! I picked up his hat for him! Of course, the whole thing was Waldo's fault: Mickleby must have seen him catch his thong over his head. I tell Waldo that if he stays here much longer he'll get to be so puffed up that there'll be no bearing it! Mickleby, and the rest of them, copy every single thing he does, you know. If he took to wearing his coat inside out they'd do the same!"

"Yes, I think they would," she agreed. "Fortunately, he never does anything extravagant! Indeed, he has exerted a very beneficial influence over his devout worshippers – and has won great popularity amongst their parents in consequence!"

He grinned. "I know he has. He is the most complete hand! But he won't be popular with 'em when they find that he only wanted Broom Hall for his wretched brats!"

"Wretched brats?" repeated Miss Trent, in a queer tone.

"Well, that's what my cousin George calls 'em!" chuckled his lordship. "He don't approve of them at all! He's a very good fellow, but a trifle too full of starch and propriety. Always in the established mode, is George! He told Waldo that to be housing the brats in a respectable neighbourhood is carrying his eccentricity too far. I must say, I wouldn't dare do it myself. Well, even the Rector was pretty taken aback when Waldo broached it to him, and I fancy he's in a bit of a quake over what people like Mrs Mickleby will say to him when they learn that he was in Waldo's confidence!" He became aware suddenly that Miss Trent was curiously silent, and stopped short in the middle of his cheerful rattle, and glanced round to find that her eyes were fixed on his face. There was a blank look in them, which made him say uneasily: "Waldo told you about his children, didn't he, ma'am?"

She looked away, saying stonily: "No. He hasn't mentioned them."

"Oh, lord!" exclaimed Lindeth, in the liveliest dismay. "I had a notion that – Now I am in the suds! For God's sake, ma'am, don't betray me! I don't want one of Waldo's trimmings!"

He spoke half-laughingly; she forced her lips into a faint smile, and replied: "You may be easy on that head, sir. I shall certainly not speak of it."

"He warned me he didn't want it talked of," said Lindeth remorsefully. "He never does himself, you know, except, of course – But I'm not going to say another word!" An alarming thought suddenly assailed him; he said apprehensively: "*You* aren't scandalized, are you, ma'am? I mean, I know all the old tabbies will nab the rust at having brats of that sort planted at Broom Hall, but *you* don't hold up your nose at what you don't think *quite the thing*! After all, most men wouldn't care a straw what became of the poor little devils, much less squander a fortune on housing them, and feeding them, and educating them! You may say that he's so full of juice that it can't signify to him, but -"

Miss Trent, feeling herself to be on the verge of strong hysterics, interrupted him. "My dear Lord Lindeth, I assure you that you have not the smallest need to say more! I collect that you and Sir Waldo will soon be leaving Yorkshire?"

He hesitated, before saying: "Yes – that is, I am not perfectly sure! I must go home, of course, but – I hope to be in Yorkshire again as soon as – well, *soon*!"

"Next month, for the York Races," she agreed. "I daresay you have frequently attended them. This will be the first time I have had that opportunity. Mrs Underhill has the intention of getting up an agreeable party for the event, you know."

He followed this lead readily enough; and the rest of the short drive was beguiled with innocuous chattery, in which his lordship bore decidedly the major part. He would have turned in at the gates of Staples, but Miss Trent would not permit it, saying that if he would set her down at the lodge she would enjoy the walk up the avenue to the house. Her command over both her voice and her countenance was such as to banish from his mind any lingering fear that his indiscreet tongue might have wreaked more mischief than had ever been in his head; and he drove off with a cheerful wave of his beaver.

She walked up the avenue, keeping to the carriageway by instinct rather than by sight, her eyes looking blindly ahead; and the empty basket weighing heavily on her arm. Her thoughts were chaotic; before she could attempt to marshal them into even the semblance of order some period of quiet and solitude would be necessary to enable her to recover from the shock of Lindeth's artless disclosure.

Mercifully, it was granted to her. When she entered the house, it was wrapped in an unusual silence. Tiffany and Courtenay had not returned from their ride; and the servants, all sweeping and dusting finished, were in their own quarters. No one observed her return, and no one disturbed her when she reached the refuge of her bedchamber. She untied the strings of her bonnet, and mechanically smoothed them, before restoring the bonnet to the shelf in her wardrobe. As she turned away she became aware of the trembling of her limbs, and sat down limply, resting her elbows on the dressing-table before her, and sinking her head between her hands. She had not known that shock could affect one in a manner unpleasantly reminiscent of a feverish illness she had suffered years before.

It was long before she could compel her brain to consider rather than to remember. It might be useless to recall everything the Nonesuch had said to her, everything he had done, but there was no helping it. So many of his words had assumed a new significance! He had had a *certain proposition* to lay before her; and *every intention of making a clean breast of the matter* to her; he had known that he would fall under the displeasure of his neighbours, but had fancied that her voice would not swell the chorus of disapproval, because she had *too liberal a mind*. She wondered, in the detachment of despair, what she could have said or done to imbue him, and Lindeth too, with so false an estimate of her character.

The first impulse of her mind had been to reject as incredible the disclosure that Sir Waldo was a hardened libertine; and even when she grew calmer, and was able to think rather than to feel, there still persisted in her brain, beyond reason, the conviction that it could not be true. Had anyone but Lindeth told her that Sir Waldo had fathered nameless children she would not have lent the tale a moment's belief. But Lindeth would never slander his cousin, and what he said could not be scornfully dismissed. She had been amazed that he should speak so lightly of the matter, for she could not doubt that he was himself a young man of principle. Then she thought of what Mrs Chartley had said to her, and realized what strong support her warning gave to Lindeth's words. It was rather dreadful to know that so strict and upright a woman could condone what she had called "adventures". She knew the truth, but she plainly thought little the worse of Sir Waldo. She had uttered her warning not to prevent a marriage, but in the fear that no offer of marriage would be made. She might, like Mrs Mickleby, be scandalized by the arrival in the neighbourhood of Sir Waldo's bastards, but she did not consider them a bar to his marriage with a young woman who was far removed from the wantons with whom he had enjoyed his *adventures*. This attitude of mind would have seemed as incredible to Ancilla as all the rest if she had come to Staples straight from her home, where loose conduct was regarded with abhorrence; but Ancilla had spent some months in London, and she had learnt that in fashionable circles promiscuous conduct was regarded by many with amusement, not with horror. The most surprising people talked openly of the latest *crim. cons.*, and still more surprising were the several haughty ladies of high position who were known to have foisted other men's children on to their husbands. Provided one was discreet in that exclusive world, one might take as many lovers as one chose, and still maintain an accepted respectability. The only unforgiveable crime was to cause a scandal. As for the gentlemen, few people thought the worse of them for rakishness. Even Lady Trent, quite as virtuous as Mrs Chartley, could survey, critically, but without disgust, some Drury Lane vestal well-known to be the latest mistress of a gentleman whom she would entertain in her house that very evening with the greatest cordiality.

But Miss Trent had not been reared in this accommodating morality. She was as much revolted by a libertine as by a prostitute, and she would as soon have contemplated becoming such a man's mistress as his wife.

CHAPTER SIXTEEN

BY THE time Tiffany returned to Staples Miss Trent had regained sufficient command over herself to be able to meet her with at least the semblance of composure. There was a stricken look in her eyes, but Tiffany, very full of her own concerns, did not notice it. She was in sparkling good-humour, for on their way home she and Courtenay had met Lady Colebatch and Lizzie, tooling along the road to the village in a dowdy landaulette. "And Lady Colebatch asked us if we cared to dine at Colby Place this evening – just Courtenay and me! It is not a party – only the Mickleby girls and Arthur, and Jack Banningham! So I may, Ancilla, mayn't I? Oh, she said she would be glad to see you, if you liked to go with us! But I daresay you won't, for all we mean to do is to play games, and there won't be any *strangers* there, so there *can't* be any objection to my going without you! Now, can there?"

"No, none, if Courtenay goes with you."

"*Dear* Ancilla!" Tiffany said, embracing her. "Shall you accompany us? You *need* not, you know!"

"Then I won't," said Miss Trent, faintly smiling.

Courtenay, who had entered the room in Tiffany's wake, cried out at this. Miss Trent pleaded a headache; which made Tiffany say instantly: "I thought you were not looking quite the thing! *Poor* Ancilla! You will be glad of a quiet evening, I daresay: you should go to bed, and I'll bring some lemon peel to put on your temples!"

Miss Trent declined this; so Tiffany, all eager solicitude, offered to find the pastilles her aunt burned whenever she too had the headache; or to mix a glass of hartshorn and water for her to drink.

"Thank you, Tiffany, no!" said Miss Trent firmly. "And I don't want a cataplasm to my feet either! You know I never quack myself!"

Tiffany was rather daunted by this; but after searching her memory for a moment, her brow puckered, she pronounced triumphantly: "Camphorated spirits of lavender!" and ran out of the room, calling to old Nurse.

Miss Trent raised her brows enquiringly at Courtenay. "Why is she so anxious to render me bedfast? If you know of any reason, pray don't keep it from me!"

He grinned. "Well, I don't – except that Lady Colebatch said that she was going to invite Lindeth as well, and I rather fancy Tiffany means to lift her finger. So, of course, she don't want a chaperon!"

"Means to do *what*?" demanded Miss Trent.

His grin broadened. "Lift her finger! That's what she told me she'd do when she wanted to bring Lindeth back to heel; but for my part I think she's mistaken her man! *She* thinks he must be in flat despair because she's been flirting with that court card of a cousin of his, and turning a cold shoulder on him, but I think he don't care a rush! In fact, – but mum for that!"

"Mum indeed for that!" said Miss Trent, roused to speak with unusual earnestness. "I do *beg* of you, -"

"Oh, no need for that!" declared Courtenay virtuously. "I told Mama I wouldn't stir the coals, and no more I will. Unless, of course, *she* comes the ugly," he added, after a thoughtful pause.

Miss Trent could only hope that her charge would refrain. Her humour at the moment seemed sunny, but there was no depending upon its continuance; and although she and her cousin rarely quarrelled when they rode together, each favouring much the same neck-or-nothing style, and Courtenay admitting that with all her faults Tiffany was pluck to the backbone, at all other times they took a delight in vexing one another.

However, they presently set off together in perfect amity, in Courtenay's phaeton, each agreeing that since the party was no dress affair this conveyance was preferable to the rather outdated carriage drawn by a pair of horses kept largely for farmwork which was the only other closed vehicle available during Mrs Underhill's absence from home. Miss Trent, whose opinion of young Mr Underhill's ability to drive a team was not high, noted with relief that he had only a pair harnessed to his phaeton, reflected that the moon was at the full, thus rendering it unlikely that he would drive into a ditch, and retired to grapple with her own melancholy problem.

Not the least perplexing feature of this, as she soon discovered, was her inability to think of the rake whose love-children were to be foisted cynically on to an unsuspecting society and of the delightful man whose smile haunted her dreams as one and the same person. It was in vain that she reminded herself that charm of manner must necessarily form the major part of a rake's stock-in-trade; equally in vain that she lashed herself for having been so stupidly taken in. From this arose the horrifying realization that however tarnished in her eyes might be Sir Waldo's image her love had not withered, as it ought to have done, but persisted strongly enough to make her feel more miserable than ever in her life before.

For on one point her resolution was fixed: there could be no question of marriage with him, even if marriage was what he had in mind, which, in the light of Lindeth's revelations, now seemed doubtful. But when she thought it over she could not believe that he meant to offer her a less honourable alliance. A libertine he might be, but he was no fool, and he must be well aware that she was no female of easy virtue. She wondered why he should wish to marry her; and came to the dreary conclusion that he had probably decided that the time had come for him to marry, and hoped that by choosing a penniless nobody to be his wife he would be at liberty to continue to pursue his present way of life, while she, thankful to be so richly established, turned a blind eye to his *crim. cons.* and herself behaved with all the propriety which he would no doubt demand of the lady who bore his name.

By the time Tiffany and Courtenay returned from Colby Place her headache was no longer feigned. Only a sense of duty kept her from retiring to bed hours earlier; and she could only feel relief when Tiffany, instead of prattling about the party, yawned, shrugged up her shoulders, said that it had been abominably insipid, and that she was fagged to death. An expressive grimace from Courtenay informed Miss Trent that he had a tale to disclose; but as she felt herself to be quite incapable of dealing with Tiffany's problems at that moment she did not stay to hear what the tale was, but went upstairs with her wayward charge.

Tiffany put in no appearance in the breakfast-parlour next morning. Her maid told Miss Trent that she was suffering from a headache: a statement interpreted by Nurse as "in one of her dratted miffs." So Courtenay, cheerfully discussing an enormous breakfast, was able to regale Miss Trent with the history of the previous night's entertainment.

"Lindeth wasn't there," he said, cracking his second egg. "Told Lady Colebatch he was already engaged. Deepest regrets: all that sort of flummery! *But*, ma'am, Patience wasn't there either! *She* had a previous engagement too, and if you can tell me what it could have been but Lindeth's being invited to the Rectory, it's more than anyone else can! Because Arthur Mickleby and his sisters were at Colby Place, and Sophy and Jack Banningham, *and* the Ashes, so where did Lindeth go if it wasn't to the Rectory? Plain as a pikestaff! But what must Mary Mickleby do but – no, it wasn't Mary! it was Jane Mickleby, and just the sort of thing she *would* do! – well, she said, with that silly titter of hers, that she was sure *no one* could give the least guess as to why Patience and Lindeth were both engaged on the same evening. And, if you ask me, ma'am," concluded Courtenay, in a very fairminded spirit, "she didn't say it *only* to pay off a score with Tiffany, but because she's as cross as crabs herself that Lindeth never showed the least preference for *her*! But, however, it may have been, you should have seen Tiffany's face!"

"I am thankful I did not!" responded Miss Trent.

He chuckled. "Ay, so you may be! Lord, what a ninnyhammer she is! It's my belief she'd never had the least suspicion that Lindeth had a *tendre* for Patience – and, I must say, I felt quite *sorry* for her!"

"That was kind of you," said Miss Trent politely.

"Well, I think it was," owned Courtenay. "For I don't like her, and never did! But she's my cousin, after all, and I'm dashed if I wouldn't as lief have her for a cousin as an antidote like Jane Mickleby!" He paused, his fork spearing a vast quantity of ham, halfway to his mouth and said, in portentous accents: "But that wasn't the whole!"

Miss Trent waited with a sinking heart while he masticated this Gargantuan mouthful. "Well?"

"Arthur!" he pronounced, a trifle thickly. He washed down the ham with a gulp of coffee, and handed her his cup to be replenished. "Mighty cool to her!"

"Very likely. She didn't speak of his sisters as she ought."

"I know that, but I've got a notion there was more to it than that. Seemed to me – Well, you know what cakes he, and Jack, and Greg have been making of themselves over that chit, ma'am?"

"Yes?"

"Seemed to me they weren't. Don't know why, but I daresay Jack will tell me, even if Greg don't. Not that they were uncivil, or – or – Dashed if I know what it was! Just struck me that they weren't any of 'em so particular in their attentions. Good thing! For," said Courtenay, about to dig his teeth into a muffin, "they were getting to be dead bores!"

Miss Trent could not share his satisfaction. Since she knew no more than he did what had happened to cause Tiffany's local admirers to grow suddenly cold, she could only hope either that he had been mistaken, or that these ill-used gentlemen were trying a change of tactics in their attempts to attach her.

"Was Mr Calver present?" she asked.

"No, but he wasn't invited," replied Courtenay. "Sir Ralph can't abide him: he told me so. Said he wouldn't have any man-milliners running tame at Colby Place!"

It was in a mood of considerable foreboding that Miss Trent presently went upstairs to visit Tiffany. Never before had that turbulent beauty sustained a rebuff, and what the repercussions might be Miss Trent could only, shudderingly, guess.

She found Tiffany seated, partially clothed, at her dressing-table, while her maid, who was looking aggrieved, brushed out her lustrous black locks. Tiffany made no mention of the previous night's party, but complained of a sleepless night, of a headache, and of unutterable boredom. "I want to go back to London!" she said. "I hate Yorkshire! I declare I had liefer by far be with the Burfords than at Staples, which is dowdy, and slow, and horrid!"

Miss Trent did not think it worth while to remind her that the Burfords were hardly likely to be in Portland Place in the middle of July, or that they had evinced no desire to have their niece restored to them. Instead, she reminded Tiffany that she had the Ashes' party to look forward to, and, not so very far ahead, the York Races. Tiffany disclaimed any interest in either event; so, after trying several more gambits with as little success, Miss Trent left her, hoping that one at least of her admirers would present himself at Staples that day, to restore the discontented beauty to good humour.

At the foot of the staircase she encountered Totton, who informed her that Sir Waldo had called, to enquire if any tidings had yet been received from Mrs Underhill.

"He asked for Miss Tiffany, ma'am, but I told him Miss had the headache," disclosed Totton. "So he said if you was at home he would like to see you instead. I was just coming to find you, ma'am. Sir Waldo is in the Green Saloon."

It was on the tip of her tongue to tell the butler to deny her, but she mastered the impulse. The interview must be faced, since she could not run away from Staples, deserting her post, as she longed to be able to do. She had made up her mind that she must be prepared to meet the Nonesuch, and to conduct herself, when she did so, with calm and dignity.

She entered the Green Saloon to find him standing by the table in the middle of the room, and glancing through the latest issue of the Liverpool *Mercury*. He looked up as the door opened, and at once laid the paper down, saying with the smile that made her heart tremble: "At last!"

"I beg your pardon! Have you been waiting for long?" she returned, determined to maintain an attitude of friendly civility, and desperately hoping that he would understand from this that it would be useless to make her any sort of declaration.

"More than a sennight! Yes, I know you feel that the delicacy of your position makes it ineligible for you to receive visitors, but I have been very discreet, I promise you! I told the butler that I came to enquire after the travellers – and even went so far as to ask first if Miss Wield was at home."

"We have had no news yet."

"You could scarcely have done so, could you? It was the only excuse I could think of." He paused, the laughter arrested in his eyes as they searched her face. "What is it?" he asked, in quite another tone.

She answered with forced lightness: "Why, nothing!"

"No, don't fob me off! Tell me!" he insisted. "Something has happened to distress you: has that spoilt child been plaguing you?"

She had known that it would be a dreadful interview, but not that he would rend her in two by so instantly perceiving the trouble in her face, or by speaking to her in that voice of concern. She managed to summon up a laugh, and to say: "Good gracious, no! Indeed, sir, -"

"Then what?"

How could you ask a man if it was true that he had several love-begotten children? It was wholly impossible: not even the boldest female could do it! Besides, it would be useless: she knew the answer, and her knowledge had not come to her from a doubtful, or a spiteful source: Lindeth had said it, not dreaming of mischief, treating it as only a slightly regrettable commonplace. The thought stiffened her resolution; she said, in a stronger voice: "Nothing more serious than a headache. I fancy there's thunder in the air: it always gives me the headache. Tiffany isn't feeling quite the thing either. Indeed, I should be with her, not talking to morning-visitors! I hope you may not think it uncivil in me to run away, Sir Waldo, but -"

"I don't think you uncivil: merely untruthful! Why do you call me a morning-visitor, when you know very well I've been awaiting the opportunity to see you privately – and certainly not with the object of uttering social inanities?" He smiled at her. "Are you fearful of offending against the proprieties? You're not so missish! And even the most strictly guarded girl, you know, is permitted to receive an offer of marriage unchaperoned!"

She put out her hand, in a repelling gesture, averting her head, and saying imploringly: "No, don't say it! pray don't!"

"But, my dear -!"

"Sir Waldo, I am very much obliged to you – much honoured – but I can't accept your – your very flattering offer!"

"Why not?" he asked quietly.

Dismayed, she realized that she ought to have foreseen that he would say something quite unexpected. She had not, and was betrayed into incoherence. "I don't – I could never – I have no intention of – no thought of marriage!"

He was silent for a moment, a crease between his brows, his eyes, fixed on her profile, a little puzzled. He said at last: "Don't you think that you might perhaps bring yourself to give marriage a thought? It's quite easy, you know! Only consider for how many more years than you *I* never gave it a thought. And then I met you, and loved you, and found that I was thinking of very little else! Forgive me! – I don't mean to sound presumptuous – but I can't believe that you are as indifferent to me as you'd have me think!"

She flushed. "I am aware that I – that I gave you reason to suppose that it would not be disagreeable to me to receive this offer. Even that I have encouraged you! I didn't mean it so. Circumstances have thrown us a good deal together, and – and I found you amusing and conversable, and was led, I am afraid, into – into treating you with a familiarity which you mistook for something warmer than mere liking!"

"You are wrong," he replied. "So far from encouraging me, or treating me with familiarity, you have been at pains to hold me at arm's length. But there has been a look in your eyes – I can't explain, but I couldn't mistake it, unless I were blind, or a green youth, and I'm neither!"

"I don't doubt that you have had a great deal of experience, sir, but in this instance I assure you you have been misled."

"Yes, I have had experience," he said, looking gravely at her. "Is that what's in your mind?"

"No – that is, Sir Waldo, I must be frank with you, and tell you that even if I wished to be married, I could never wish for marriage with a man whose tastes – whose mode of life – is so much opposed to everything which I have been taught to hold in esteem!"

"My dear girl," he said, between hurt and amusement, "I'm really not quite as frippery a fellow as you seem to think! I own that in my grasstime I committed a great many follies and extravagances, but, believe me, I've long since outgrown them! I don't think they were any worse than what nine out of ten youngsters commit, but unfortunately I achieved, through certain circumstances, a notoriety which most young men escape. I was born with a natural aptitude for the sporting pursuits you regard with so much distrust, and I inherited, at far too early an age, a fortune which not only enabled me to indulge my tastes in the most expensive manner imaginable, but which made me an object of such interest that everything I did was noted, and talked of. That's heady stuff for greenhorns, you know! There was a time when I gave the gossips plenty to talk about. But do give me credit for having seen the error of my ways!"

"Yes – oh, yes! But – Sir Waldo, I beg you to say no more! My mind is made up, and discussion can only be painful to us both! I have been very much at fault – I can only ask your forgiveness! If I had known that you were not merely flirting with me -"

"But you did know it," he interposed. "You're not a fool, and you can't have supposed that when I told you I wanted to be private with you, because I had a proposition to lay before you, I was *flirting* with you! You didn't suppose it. Something has occurred since I met you in the village which has brought about this change in you and I fancy I know what it must have been!"

Her eyes lifted quickly to his face, and sank again.

"Tell me!" he said imperatively. "Have you been accused of setting your cap at me? Yes, that's an outrageous question, isn't it? But I know very well that a certain weasel-faced lady of our acquaintance *has* said it, for she did so within my hearing, and I daresay she would not scruple to say it within yours. Has she done so? *Could* you be so absurd as to reject me for such a reason as that?"

"No! If I returned your regard, it would not weigh with me!"

"I see. There doesn't seem to be anything more I can say, does there?"

She could only shake her head, not daring to trust her voice. She saw that he was holding out his hand, and she reluctantly laid her own in it. He lifted it, and kissed her fingers. "I wish you did return my regard," he said. "More than I have ever wished anything in my life! Perhaps you may yet learn to do so: I should warn you that I don't easily despair!"

CHAPTER SEVENTEEN

THE NONESUCH had gone, and Miss Trent's only desire was to reach the refuge of her bedchamber before her overcharged emotions broke their bonds. Sobs, crowding in her chest, threatened to suffocate her; tears, spilling over her eyelids, had to be brushed hastily aside; she crossed the hall blindly, and as she groped for the baluster-rail, setting her foot upon the first stair, Tiffany came tripping down, her good humour restored by the news that Sir Waldo had come to visit her. "Oh, were you coming to find me?" she said blithely. "Totton sent a message up, so you need not have put yourself to that trouble, Ancilla dearest! Is he in the Green Saloon? I have had *such* a capital notion! Now that Mr Calver has taught me to drive so well, I mean to try if I can't coax Sir Waldo to let me drive his chestnuts! Only think what a triumph it would be! Mr Calver says no female has ever driven *any* of his horses!"

It was surprising how swiftly the habit of years could reassert itself. Miss Trent was sick with misery, but her spirit responded automatically to the demands made upon it. She had thought that any attempt to speak must result in a burst of tears, but she heard her own voice say, without a tremor: "He has gone. He came only to discover if we had yet had news of our travellers, and would not stay."

"Would not stay!" Tiffany's expression changed ludicrously. "When I *particularly* wished to see him!"

"I expect he would have done so had he known that," said Ancilla pacifically.

"*You* must have known it! It is too bad of you! I believe you sent him away on purpose to spite me!" said Tiffany, pettishly, but without conviction. "*Now* what is there for me to do?"

Miss Trent pulled herself together. Wisely rejecting such ideas as first occurred to her, which embraced a little much-needed practice on the pianoforte, a sketching expedition, and an hour devoted to the study of the French tongue, she sought in vain for distractions likely to find favour with a damsel determined to pout at every suggestion made to her. Fortunately, an interruption came just in time to save her temper. A carriage drove up to the door, and presently disgorged Elizabeth Colebatch, who came in to beg that Tiffany would accompany her and her mama to Harrogate, where Lady Colebatch was going to consult her favourite practitioner. Elizabeth, still faithful in her allegiance, eagerly described to Tiffany a programme exactly calculated to appeal to her. Besides a survey of the several expensive shops which had sprung up in the town, it included a walk down the New Promenade, and a visit to Hargroves Library, which was the most fashionable lounge in either High or Low Harrogate, and necessitated an instant change of raiment for Tiffany, and the unearthing from a bandbox, where it reposed in a mountain of tissue-paper, of her very best hat. Since the season was in full swing, and all the inns and boarding-houses bursting with company, it was safe to assume that the progress through the town of two modish young ladies, one of whom was a striking redhead, and the other a dazzling brunette, would attract exactly the kind of notice most deprecated by Tiffany's Aunt Burford; but as Miss Trent knew that Mrs Underhill would regard Lady Colebatch's casual chaperonage as a guarantee of propriety she did not feel it incumbent on her to enter a protest. But she did feel it incumbent on her to not to be backward in attention to Lady Colebatch; so, much as she longed for solitude, she went out to beg her to come into the house while Tiffany arrayed herself in her finest feathers. Lady Colebatch declined this, but invited Miss Trent to step into the carriage instead, to indulge in a comfortable coze. Miss Trent bore her part in this with mechanical civility; but little though she relished it, it proved beneficial, in that by the time Elizabeth and Tiffany came out to take their places in the carriage her disordered nerves had grown steadier, and the impulse to sob her heart out had left her.

Her rejected suitor, though in no danger of succumbing to even the mildest fit of hysterics, would also have been glad to have been granted an interval of solitude; but hardly had he entered the book-room at Broom Hall than he was joined by his younger cousin, who came in, asking, as he shut the door: "Are you busy, Waldo? Because, if you're not, there's something I want to say to you. But not if it isn't quite convenient!" he added hastily, perceiving the crease between Sir Waldo's brows.

Mastering the impulse to tell Lord Lindeth that it was extremely inconvenient, Sir Waldo said: "No, I'm not busy. Come and sit down, and tell me all about it!"

The tone was encouraging, and even more so the faint smile in his eyes. It was reflected, a little shyly, in his lordship's innocent orbs. He said simply, but with a rising colour: "I daresay you know – don't you?"

"Well, I have an inkling!" admitted Sir Waldo.

"I thought very likely you had guessed. But I wanted to tell you – and to ask your advice!"

"Ask my advice?" Sir Waldo's brows rose. "Good God, Julian, if you want my advice on whether or not you should offer for Miss Chartley, I can only say that until my advice or my opinion are matters of complete indifference to you -"

"Oh, not *that*!" interrupted Julian impatiently. "I should hope I knew my own mind without your advice, or anyone's! As for your opinion -" He paused, considering, and then said, with a disarmingly apologetic smile: "Well, I *do* care for that, but – but not very much!"

"Very right and proper!" approved Sir Waldo.

"Now you're roasting me! I wish you won't: this is *serious*, Waldo!"

"I'm not roasting you. Why do you need my advice?"

"Well . . ." Julian clasped his hands between his knees, and frowningly regarded them. "The thing is . . . Waldo, when we first came here I daresay you may have guessed – well, I told you, didn't I? that I was pretty well bowled out by Tiffany Wield." He glanced up, crookedly smiling. "You'll say I made a cake of myself, and I suppose I did."

"Not such a cake that you offered for her hand."

Julian looked at him, suddenly surprised. "Do you know, Waldo, I never thought of marriage?" he said naïvely. "I hadn't considered it before, but now you've mentioned it I don't think that I *ever* thought of it until I met Miss Chartley. In fact, I never thought about the future at all. But since I've come to *know* Patience, naturally I've done so, because I wish to spend the rest of my life with her. And, what's more, I'm going to!" he stated, his jaw hardening.

"My blessing on the alliance: she will make you an excellent wife! But wherein do you need my advice? Or are you merely trying to wheedle me into breaking the news to your mama?"

"No, of course not! I shall tell her myself. Though it *would* be helpful if you supported me," he added, after a reflective moment.

"I will."

Julian smiled gratefully at him. "Yes. I know: you *are* such a right one, Waldo!"

"Spare my blushes! And my advice?"

"Well, that's the only thing that has me in a worry!" disclosed his lordship. "I want to come to the point, and although the Chartleys have been as kind and affable as they could be – not hinting me away, or anything of that nature! – I can't but wonder whether it may not be too soon to ask the Rector for permission to propose to Patience! I mean, if he thought I was a regular squire of dames, because I dangled after Miss Wield, he'd be bound to send me packing – and then it would be all holiday with me!"

"I hardly think that he will judge you quite as harshly as that," replied Sir Waldo, with admirable gravity. "After all, you are not entangled with Tiffany, are you?"

"Oh, no!" Julian assured him. "Nothing of that sort! In fact, she brushed me off after what happened in Leeds, so I don't think I need feel myself in any way bound to her, do you?" He chuckled. "Laurie cut me out! I was never more glad of anything! Well, it just *shows* you, doesn't it? Only think of being grateful to Laurie! Lord! But tell me, Waldo! What should I do?"

Sir Waldo, whose private opinion was that the Rector must be living in the hourly expectation of receiving a declaration from Lord Lindeth, had no hesitation in answering this appeal. He recommended his anxious young cousin to make known his intentions at the earliest opportunity, very handsomely offering, at the same time, to reassure the Rector, if he should be misled into believing that his daughter's suitor was a hardened *roué*. Julian grinned appreciatively at this; and for the following half-hour bored Sir Waldo very much by expatiating at length on Miss Chartley's numerous virtues.

He departed at last, but his place was taken within ten minutes by Laurence, who came in, and stood irresolutely on the threshold, eyeing his cousin in some doubt.

Sir Waldo had sat down at the desk. There were several papers spread on it, but he did not seem to be at work on them. His hands were clasped on top of the pile, and his eyes were frowning at the wall in front of him. His expression was unusually grim, and it did not lighten when he turned his head to look at Laurence. Rather, it hardened. "Well?"

If his demeanour had not warned Laurence already that he had chosen an inauspicious moment to seek him out, the uncompromising tone in which this one word was uttered must have done so. Laurence was still holding the door, and he backed himself out of the room, saying hurriedly, as he drew the door to upon himself: "Oh, nothing! I only – Beg pardon! Didn't know you was busy! Some other time!"

"I advise you not to cherish false hopes! At no time!" Sir Waldo said harshly.

Under any ordinary circumstances Laurence would have been provoked into lengthy retort, but on this occasion he did not venture to reply at all, but effaced himself with all possible speed.

The door safely shut between himself and his suddenly formidable cousin, he let his breath go in an astonished: "Phew!" Indignation warred with curiosity in his breast, but curiosity won. After looking speculatively at the door for several moments, as though he could see Waldo's face through its stout panels, he walked away, his somewhat ferret-like brain concentrated on the new and unexpected problem which had presented itself.

It did not take him long to decide that the only possible cause of Waldo's unprecedented behaviour must be a disappointment in love. It was absurd to suppose that he might be faced with pecuniary difficulties; and, in Laurence's view, only love or penury could account for so bleak an aspect. At first glance it seemed equally absurd to suppose that his courtship of Miss Trent could have suffered a setback; but after some moments of reflection Laurence came to the conclusion that this must be the answer. It might seem incredible that a female in her circumstances should rebuff so opulent a suitor, but there could be no doubt that Miss Trent was a very odd creature. But no doubt either that she was as deeply in love with Waldo as he with her. No forbidding frown had marred Waldo's countenance at the breakfast-table: he had been in particularly good spirits. Then he had driven off, tossing a joking remark over his shoulder to Julian; and although he had not disclosed his destination only a lobcock could have doubted that he was bound for Staples. Julian, wrapped up in his own affairs, might not know that Waldo had visited Staples every day for more than a sennight, but his far more astute cousin knew it. It looked very much as if Waldo had popped the question, and had been rejected. But why?

Cudgel his brains as he might, Laurence could arrive at no satisfactory answer to this enigma. Had any man but Waldo been concerned he would have been inclined to think that someone had traduced him to Miss Trent: he rather supposed her to be pretty straitlaced. But so was Waldo straitlaced, and what the devil could the most arrant scandalmonger find to say of him that would disgust any female? And was his Long Meg fool enough to believe a story fabricated by one of the jealous tabbies of the parish?

It was all very perplexing, but an answer there must be, which it might be well worth his while to discover. His first scheme to win his affluent cousin's gratitude had gone awry – it had not taken him very long to realize that no assistance from him had been needed to wean Julian from his attachment to Tiffany Wield – but it might well be that in this new, and very odd, situation lay the means he had been seeking. If, through his agency, the starcrossed lovers became reconciled, it was difficult to see how Waldo – no nip-squeeze, give him his due! – could fail to express his gratitude in a suitable and handsome manner.

Laurence's spirits had been rapidly sinking into gloom, but they now rose. It had been vexatious to find that his admirable plan to detach the Wield chit from Lindeth had been labour wasted. He did not regret it, precisely, for to have stolen the Beauty from under the noses of her ridiculous swains had been amusing, and as good a way as any other of whiling away the time he had been obliged to spend in an excessively boring place. He had even toyed for a day or two with the thought of wooing Tiffany in earnest, but had soon abandoned the scheme. The idea of tying himself up in wedlock was distasteful to him; and although he might have overcome his reluctance for the sake of Tiffany's fortune he could not feel that there was the least likelihood of obtaining her guardians' consent to the match, much less of their relinquishing into his hands the control of her fortune a day before she attained her majority. So however pleasant it might be to flirt elegantly with such an out-and-out beauty the affair was really a waste of time. Its only value was that it now provided him with an excuse for visiting Staples, to see for himself how the land lay there. It might not be easy to coax Miss Trent to confide in him; but although her manner towards him held a good deal of reserve, she had lately begun to show him rather more friendliness; and if she was as bluedevilled as Waldo over the rift between them she might, Laurence considered, be glad to be offered the opportunity to unburden herself. Certainly she would be, if she and Waldo had quarrelled: positively burning to state her grievances, if he knew anything of women! A quarrel, however, seemed highly unlikely: she did not look to be the sort of female to fly into the boughs, or to take affronts into her head; and Waldo's even temper was proverbial. On the whole, Laurence was more inclined to believe that the trouble must be due to some misunderstanding. Very probably each was too proud to seek an explanation of the other, and no one would be more welcome to them than a tactful mediator. Acting as a go-between might prove to be a wearing task, but in the pursuit of his own ends Laurence grudged no expenditure of effort.

Accordingly, he drove over to Staples that very day, ostensibly to visit Tiffany. He was met by the intelligence that Tiffany had gone to Harrogate, and that Miss Trent was laid down on her bed with the headache. He left cards and compliments, and drove off, by no means cast down by this set-back. Laid down with the headache, was she? Promising! That was the excuse females always put forward whenever they had been indulging in a hearty fit of crying: he would have been far more daunted had he found her in excellent spirits.

Waldo's behaviour that evening was satisfactory too: he wasn't exactly cagged, but he wasn't what one could call chirping merry. Agreeable enough when addressed, but for the most part he was in a brown study. Julian had gone off somewhere with Edward Banningham, so there was very little conversation at dinner, Laurence not being such a cawker as to irritate Waldo with idle chatter when it was plain that he didn't want to talk. When they rose from the table, Waldo shut himself up in the book-room, saying that he was sorry to be such bad company, but that a vexatious hitch had occurred in his arrangements for installing a suitable warden at Broom Hall. Humdudgeon, of course, but Laurence replied sympathetically, and said that there was no need for Waldo to trouble his head over him: he would be happy enough with a book.

It was less satisfactory, on the following morning, to find neither Tiffany nor Miss Trent at home, when he called at Staples, but the evening, which was spent by him at the Ashes' house, was more rewarding. Miss Trent had brought Tiffany to the party, and it was easy to see she'd got the hips. She might smile, and converse with her usual tranquillity, but she was suspiciously pale, and there were tell-tale shadows under her eyes. As soon as she could do so, she went to sit beside a mousy little woman whom Laurence presently discovered to be governess to the children of the house. She was taking care not to glance in Waldo's direction: rather too much care, thought Laurence. Out of the tail of his eye he watched Waldo cross the room towards her. He couldn't hear what passed between them, of course, but he was perfectly well able to draw conclusions. He had a pair of sharp eyes, and he saw how tightly her hands were gripping her reticule, and how swiftly the colour rushed into her cheeks and ebbed again. Then Waldo bowed – the bow of a man accepting a rebuff: no question about that! – and went off with Sir William Ash to the card-room. Miss Trent's eyes were downcast, but they lifted as he turned away, and followed him across the room. Lord! thought Laurence, startled, who would have thought that such a cool creature could look like that? Flat despair! But what the devil had happened to set the pair of them at outs?

The sound of a fiddle being tuned obliged him to drag his mind from this intriguing problem. The first set was forming; and as the dance was of an informal nature, Lady Ash having announced that since all the young people knew one another she meant to leave them to choose their own partners, it behoved him to look about him for an unattached lady. He saw Tiffany, talking vivaciously to Miss Banningham, and to Lindeth, who was clearly waiting to lead the eldest daughter of the house into the set. It did vaguely occur to Laurence that it was unusual to find Tiffany without an eager crowd of admirers clamouring for the privilege of dancing with her, but although he bowed, and smirked, and solicited the honour of leading her on to the floor, his mind was still too much preoccupied to allow of his paying more than cursory heed to this circumstance. Nor did he notice that the lady who was being besieged by suppliants was Miss Chartley.

But Miss Trent noticed it, and she thought that it set the seal on an evening of unalleviated misery. Too well did she know that glittering look of Tiffany's, that over-emphatic gaiety; and if she was relieved to see, as the evening progressed, that Tiffany was never left without a partner, her relief was soon tempered by the spectacle of Mr Wilfred Butterlaw, a pimply youth suffering from unrequited adoration of the Beauty, leading her charge into a set. Mercifully for what little peace of mind was left to Miss Trent, she could not know that Mr Butterlaw's evil genius prompted him to blurt out, when he and Tiffany came together in the dance: "I d-don't care a s-straw what anyone says, Miss Wield! I think you're *p-perfect*!"

But although she never knew of this essay in tactlessness she was not at all surprised, during the drive back to Staples, to find that Tiffany was in her most dangerous mood, which found expression, not in one of her stormy outbursts, but in brittle laughter, and the utterance of whatever damaging animadversions on the manners or looks of her acquaintances first occurred to her. Miss Trent preserved a discouraging silence, and devoutly hoped that Courtenay, seated opposite to the ladies, would refrain from adding fuel to the fire. So he did, until Tiffany reached the most galling cause of her discontent, and said, with a trill of laughter: "And Patience Chartley, looking like a dowd in that hideous green dress, and putting on dieaway airs, and pretending to be *so* shy, and *so* modest, and casting down her eyes in that ridiculous way she uses when she wants to persuade everyone that she's a saint!"

"If I were you," interposed Courtenay bluntly, "I wouldn't be quite so spiteful about Patience, miss!"

"Spiteful? Oh, I didn't mean to be! Poor thing, she's close on twenty and has never had an offer! I'm truly sorry for her: it must be odious to be so – so *insipid*!"

"No, you ain't," said Courtenay. "You're as mad as fire because it wasn't you that got all the notice tonight but *her*! And I'll tell you this -!"

"Don't!" said Miss Trent wearily.

The interpolation was unheeded. "If you don't take care," continued Courtenay ruthlessly, "you'll find yourself in the suds – and don't think your precious beauty will save you, because it won't! Lord, if ever I knew such a corkbrained wag-feather as you are! First you drove Lindeth off with your Turkish treatment, then it was Arthur, and to crown all you hadn't even enough sense to keep your tongue about what happened in Leeds, when it was Patience that showed what a game one she is, not you! All you did was to scold like the vixen you are!"

"A game one?" Tiffany said, in a voice shaking with fury. "Patience? She's nothing but a shameless show-off! I collect you had this from Ancilla! She positively *dotes* on dear, demure little Patience – exactly her notion of a well-brought-up girl!"

"Oh, no, I didn't! Miss Trent never told us anything but that Patience had snatched some slum-brat from under the wheels of a carriage, with the greatest pluck and presence of mind! Nor did Lindeth! And as for Patience, she don't talk about it at all! *You* did all the talking! You was afraid one of the others would describe the figure *you* cut, so you set it about that Patience had created an uproar just so that people should think she was a heroine, but that it was all a fudge: no danger to the brat or to herself!"

"Nor was there! If Ancilla says -"

"Wasn't there? Well, *now*, coz, I'll tell you something else! Ned Banningham was in York t'other day, staying with some friends, and who should be one of the people who came to the dinner-party but the fellow who nearly drove over Patience? I don't recall his name, but I daresay you may. Very full of the accident he seems to have been! Told everyone what a trump Patience was, and how she didn't make the least fuss or to-do, and what a stew he was in, thinking she was bound to be trampled on. Described you too. Jack wouldn't tell me what he said, and I'd as lief he didn't, because you *are* my cousin, and I ain't fond of being put to the blush. But Ned told Jack, and of course Jack told Arthur, and then Greg got to hear of it – and *that's* why you got the cold shoulder tonight! I daresay no one would have cared much if you'd said cutting things about Sophy Banningham, because she ain't much liked; but the thing is that everyone likes Patience! What's more, until you came back to Staples, and peacocked all over the neighbourhood, she and Lizzie were the prettiest girls here, *and* the most courted! So take care what you're about, Beautiful Miss Wield!"

CHAPTER EIGHTEEN

BY THE time Miss Trent was at liberty to seek her own bed after that memorable party she was so much exhausted that she fell almost instantly into a deep, yet troubled sleep. The drive back to Staples had ended with Tiffany in floods of tears, which lasted for long after she had been supported upstairs to her bedchamber. Miss Trent, thrusting aside her own troubles, applied herself first to the task of soothing Tiffany, then to that of undressing her, and lastly to the far more difficult duty of trying to point out to her, while she was in a malleable condition, that however brutal Courtenay might have been he had spoken no more than the truth. Bathing Tiffany's temples with Hungary Water, she did her best to mingle sympathy with her unpalatable advice. She thought that Tiffany was attending to her; and found herself pitying the girl. She was vain, and selfish, and unbelievably tiresome, but only a child, after all, and one who had been flattered and spoilt almost from the day of her birth. She had met with a severe check for the first time in her headlong career; it had shocked and frightened her; and perhaps, thought Miss Trent, softly drawing the curtains round her bed, she might profit by so painful a lesson.

She did not come down to breakfast, but when Miss Trent went to visit her she did not find her lying in a darkened room with a damp towel laid over her brow and smelling-salts clasped feebly in her hand, as had happened on a previous and hideous occasion, but sitting up in bed, thoughtfully eating strawberries. She eyed Miss Trent somewhat defensively, but upon being bidden a cheerful good morning responded with perfect amiability.

"No letters yet from Bridlington," said Miss Trent, "but Netley has just brought up a package from the lodge. I couldn't conceive what it might be until I saw the label attached to it, for a more unwieldy parcel you can't imagine! My dear, those idiotish silk merchants haven't sent patterns, but a whole roll of silk! They must have misunderstood Mrs Underhill – and I only hope it may match the brocade! I shall have to take it to Mrs Tawton in the gig. Will you go with me? Do!"

"No, it will take *hours*, and I can't, because I've made a plan of my own."

"Well, that's not very kind! Abandoning me to the company of James, who can never be persuaded to say anything but *Yes, Miss!* and *No, Miss!* What is this plan of yours?"

"I'm going to ride into the village," said Tiffany, a hint of defiance in her voice. She cast a sidelong glance at Miss Trent, and added: "Well, I mean to call at the Rectory! And you know that pink velvet rose I purchased in Harrogate? I am going to wrap it up in silver paper, and give it to Patience! *Especially* to wear with her gauze ball-dress! Do you think that would be a handsome present? It was very expensive, you know, and I haven't worn it, because though I did mean to, last night, I found it didn't become me after all. But Patience frequently wears pink, so I should think she would feel very much obliged to me, shouldn't you? And that will just *show* people! And *also* I shall invite her to go for a walk with us tomorrow – just you and me, you know!"

"That would indeed be a noble gesture!" said Miss Trent admiringly.

"Yes, *wouldn't* it?" said Tiffany naïvely. "It will be horridly dull, and you may depend upon it Patience will be a dead bore, going into raptures over some weed, and saying it's a rare plant, or – But I mean to bear it, even if she moralizes about nature!"

Miss Trent was unable to enter with any marked degree of enthusiasm into these plans, but she acquiesced in them, feeling that they did at least represent a step in the right direction, even though they sprang from the purest self-interest. So she went away to prepare for her long and rather tedious drive to the home of the indigent Mrs Tawton, while Tiffany, tugging at the bell-rope, allowed her imagination to depict various scenes in which her faithless admirers, hearing of her magnanimity, and stricken with remorse at having so wickedly misjudged her, vied with one another in extravagant efforts to win her forgiveness.

It was an agreeable picture, and since she really did feel that she was being magnanimous she rode to the Rectory untroubled by any apprehension that she might not meet with the welcome which she was quite sure she deserved.

The Rector's manservant, who admitted her into the house, seemed to be rather doubtful when she blithely asked to see Miss Chartley, but he ushered her into the drawing-room, and said that he would enquire whether Miss Chartley was at home. He then went away, and Tiffany, after peeping at her reflection in the looking-glass over the fireplace, and rearranging the disposition of the glossy ringlets that clustered under the brim of her hat, wandered over to the window.

The drawing-room looked on to the garden at the rear of the house. It was a very pretty garden, gay with flowers, with a shrubbery, a well-scythed lawn, and several fine trees. Round the trunk of one of these a rustic seat had been built, and in front of it, as though they had just risen from it, Patience and Lindeth were standing side by side, confronting the Rector, who was holding a hand of each.

For a moment Tiffany stood staring, scarcely understanding the significance of what she saw. But when Lindeth looked down at Patience, smiling at her, and she raised her eyes adoringly to his, the truth dawned on her with the blinding effect of a sudden fork of lightning.

She was so totally unprepared that the shock of realization turned her to stone. Incredulity, fury, and chagrin swept over her. *Her* conquest – her most triumphant conquest! – stolen from her by Patience Chartley? It wasn't possible! Patience to receive an offer of marriage from Lindeth? The thought flashed into her mind that he had never so much as hinted at marriage with herself, and she felt suddenly sick with mortification.

The door opened behind her; she heard Mrs Chartley's voice, and turned, pride stiffening her. She never doubted that Mrs Chartley hoped to enjoy her discomfiture, and because the thought uppermost in her mind was that no one should think that she cared a rush for Lindeth she achieved a certain dignity.

She said: "Oh, how do you do, ma'am? I came to bring Patience a trifle I purchased for her in Harrogate. But I must not stay."

She put out her hand rather blindly, proffering the silver-wrapped parcel. Mrs Chartley took it from her, saying in some surprise: "Why, how kind of you, Tiffany! She will be very much obliged to you."

"It's nothing. Only a flower to wear with her gauze dress. I must go!"

Mrs Chartley glanced uncertainly towards the window. "Won't you wait while I see whether I can find her, my dear? I am persuaded she would wish to thank you herself."

"It's of no consequence. The servant said he fancied she was engaged." Tiffany drew in her breath, and said with her most glittering smile: "That's true, isn't it? To Lindeth! Has he offered for her? I-I have been expecting him to do so this age!"

"Well – if you won't spread it about, yes!" admitted Mrs Chartley. "But there must be nothing said, you know, until he has told his mother. So you must not breathe a word, if you please!"

"Oh, no! Though I daresay everyone has guessed! Pray – pray offer her my felicitations, ma'am! I should think they will deal extremely together!"

On this line she took leave of Mrs Chartley, declining her escort to the stableyard, but hurrying out of the house, the flowing skirt of her habit caught over her arm, and one hand clenched tightly on her whip. She was uplifted by the feeling that she had acquitted herself well, but this mood could not last. By the time she reached Staples, all the evils of her situation had been recollected. It no longer mattered that she had behaved so creditably, at the Rectory, for even if Mrs Chartley believed that she was indifferent to the engagement no one else would. Her rivals, Lizzie only excepted, would rejoice in her downfall. She had boasted too freely of being able to bring Lindeth back to her feet by the mere lifting of a finger. She writhed inwardly as she remembered, knowing that it would be said she had been cut out by Patience Chartley. People would laugh at her behind her back, and say sweetly spiteful things to her face; and even her admirers could not be depended on to uphold her.

When she thought of this, and of what had been the cause of their defection, it had the unexpected effect of drying the tears which till then had been flowing fast. Her predicament was too desperate for tears. She could see nothing but humiliation ahead, and by hedge or by stile she must avoid it. In her view there was only one thing to be done, and that was to leave Staples immediately, and to return to London. But London meant Portland Place, and although she could not suppose that even her aunt Burford would send her back to Staples, where she had been unhappy and ill-used, there was no saying that she might not try again to confine her to the schoolroom, until she brought her out in the following spring.

Pacing up and down the floor of her bedroom, Tiffany cudgelled her brains, and not in vain. She remembered all at once the existence of her other guardian, bachelor Uncle James, who lived, with an old housekeeper to look after him, somewhere in the City. That, of course, was undesirable, but might, perhaps, be mended. James Burford, on the few occasions when they had met, had behaved much as all the other elderly gentlemen of her acquaintance did: chuckling at her exploits, pinching her ear, and calling her a naughty little puss. If he should not be instantly delighted to receive his lovely niece he could very easily be brought round her thumb. Either she would remain under his roof until the spring, or he must be persuaded to represent to Aunt Burford the propriety of bringing her out during the Little Season. Far less than Aunt Burford would he be likely to insist on her returning to Staples. Indeed, the more Tiffany thought of the wrongs she had suffered the more convinced did she become that no one could possibly blame her for running away. Aunt Underhill had deserted her, not even inviting her to go to Bridlington too; Courtenay had been unkind and boorish to her from the outset; and Miss Trent, whose sole business it should have been to attend her, had neglected her for Charlotte; and had shown herself to be so wholly wanting in conduct as to have allowed her to be exposed to the Mob in Leeds, going off in *her* carriage with an odious girl to whom she owed no duty at all, and leaving her precious charge alone in a public inn, to be conveyed back to Staples, unchaperoned, by a single gentleman.

The difficulty was to decide how the flight could be achieved. Forgetting for a moment that she had cast Miss Trent for the rôle of villainess in this dramatic piece, Tiffany wondered whether it would be possible to cajole that lady into escorting her to London immediately. Very little consideration sufficed to make her abandon this solution to her problem. Miss Trent was too insensitive to appreciate the necessity of an instant departure; and nothing was more certain than that she would refuse to do anything without first consulting Aunt Underhill. It was even possible that she would advise her charge to live down her humiliation: as though one would not rather die than make the attempt!

No: Miss Trent could only be a hindrance – in fact, it would be wise to be gone from the house before she returned to it. But how was she to get to Leeds? She could ride there: they were too well-accustomed in the stables to her solitary rides to raise any demur; but she thought it would be impossible to carry even the smallest piece of baggage, in which case she would be obliged to drive all the way to London in her habit. Useless to desire the under-coachman to drive her there in the barouche: he would refuse to do it unless she had Miss Trent with her, or her maid. Equally would Courtenay's groom refuse to let her drive herself in his phaeton.

A less determined girl might have been daunted at this point; but it had been truly observed of Miss Wield that there were no lengths to which she would not go to achieve her ends. Rather than have abandoned her project she would have walked to Leeds. Indeed, she was trying to make up her mind whether to pursue this dreary course, carrying a bandbox; or to ride, carrying nothing, when a welcome sound came to her ears. She ran to the window, and saw Mr Calver driving up to the house in his hired whisky.

Tiffany flung up the window, and leaned out to hail him. "Oh, Mr Calver, how do you do? Have you come to take me out? I shall be with you directly!"

He looked up, sweeping off his high-crowned beaver. "Very happy to do so! No need to bustle about, however: I must pay my respects to Miss Trent, you know."

"Oh, she has gone to Nethersett, and won't be home for hours!" Tiffany answered. "Only wait for ten minutes!"

This was not at all what he had hoped to hear; nor had he much desire to sit beside Tiffany while she tooled the whisky round the immediate countryside. There seemed to be no object to be gained by dangling after her any longer; and teaching her to drive was an occupation which had begun to pall on him. However, he could think of no better way of passing the time, so he resigned himself.

He was rather startled, when she came running out of the house some twenty minutes later, to see that she was arrayed in a modish pelisse, with a hat embellished by several curled ostrich plumes on her head, and a large bandbox slung by its ribbons over her arm.

"Here -!" he expostulated. "I mean to say – what the *dooce* -?"

Tiffany handed the bandbox to him, and climbed into the whisky. "You can't think how glad I am that you came!" she said. "I was quite in despair! For I must go to Leeds, and Ancilla set off in the gig quite early, and I don't know where Courtenay may be!"

"Go to Leeds?" he repeated. "But -"

"Yes, it is the most vexatious thing!" she said glibly. "The dressmaker had sent home my new ball-dress, which I particularly wish to wear at the Systons' party, and the stupid creature has made it too tight for me. And how to get to Leeds, with the coachman away, and no one to accompany me, I'd not the least notion, until you came driving up the avenue! You'll take me, won't you? That will make everything right!"

"Well, I don't know," he said dubiously. "I'm not sure I ought. Seems to me Miss Trent might not think it quite the thing."

She laughed. "How can you be so absurd? When I have been driving with you for ever!"

"Yes, but -"

"If you don't escort me, I shall go alone," she warned him. "I shall ride there, and *that* won't be the thing at all. So if you choose to be disobliging -"

"No, no! I suppose I'd better drive you there, if you're so set on it. You can't go alone, at all events," he said, giving his horse the office. "Mind, though! it won't do if you mean to remain for hours with this dressmaker! I should think it will take us close on a couple of hours to get to Leeds and back again. Did you tell anyone where you was off to?"

"Oh, yes!" she assured him mendaciously. "Ancilla won't be in a worry, so you need not be either. And I shan't be with Mrs Walmer above half-an-hour, I promise you!"

He was satisfied with this; and although he had little faith in her ability to emerge from a dressmaker's establishment in so short a space of time, he reflected that he must be certain of finding Miss Trent at home if it was three or more hours before he brought Tiffany back to Staples.

Tiffany beguiled the drive with lighthearted chatter. Having surmounted the first obstacle to her flight, she was in high good-humour, her eyes glowing with excitement, laughter never far from her lips. Already, in her imagination, she was the petted darling of her Uncle James, and had prevailed upon him to remove from the City to a more fashionable quarter of the town. The humiliation of the previous evening's party, and the shock of discovering that Lindeth had become engaged to Patience, were rapidly fading from her mind, and would be wholly forgotten as soon as she had put Yorkshire behind her. Fresh, and far more dazzling conquests lay ahead. She had never cared a button for Lindeth, after all; and as for the rest of her court, they were a set of bumpkins whom she would probably never set eyes on again.

Arrived in Leeds, Laurence, who was unfamiliar with the town, requested her to direct him to a decent posting-house, where the whisky could be left, and the horse baited. "Then I'll escort you to the dressmaker. It won't do for you to be jauntering about this place alone," he said, surveying the crowded street with disfavour.

This put Tiffany in mind of something which, in her large dreams of the future, she had overlooked. Never having travelled except in the company of some older person, who made all the arrangements, she was ignorant of where, and under what conditions, post-chaises were to be hired; or, failing this, the only mode of travel to which she was accustomed, how one obtained a seat on the stage, or the Mail; and at what hour these humbler conveyances left Leeds for London. She stole a glance at Laurence's profile, and decided that it would be necessary to enlist his help. It might require some coaxing to obtain it; but she could not doubt that he was one of her more fervent admirers. Courtenay had jeered at her for being taken in by a fortune-hunter; and if Courtenay was right in thinking that the exquisite Mr Calver was hanging out for a rich wife she thought that it would not be difficult to persuade him to render her a signal service. She directed him to the King's Head, adding that she would like some lemonade, and that there were several private parlours to be hired at this hostelry.

Laurence was perfectly ready to regale her with lemonade, but he thought it quite unnecessary, and even undesirable, to hire a private parlour. However, since she seemed to take it for granted that he would do so, he kept his objections to himself. But when, in the inn's yard, he picked up her bandbox, it occurred to him that it was extraordinarily heavy. When Tiffany had first handed it up to him, he had been too much astonished by her festal raiment to pay any heed to the weight of the bandbox, but he now directed a look at her which was sharp with suspicion, and said: "Very heavy, this dress of yours, ain't it?"

"Well, there are some other things in the box," she confessed.

"I should rather think there must be! Seems to me there's something pretty smokey going on, and if there is -"

"I am going to explain it to you!" she said hastily. "But in private, if you please!"

He regarded her with misgiving; but before he could say more she had flitted away from him, into the inn; and it was not until they had been ushered into the same parlour which Lindeth had hired for his memorable nuncheon-party that he was able to demand the explanation.

Tiffany bestowed upon him her most devastating smile, and said simply: "Well, I told you a bouncer! It isn't a ball-dress. It's – oh, all manner of things! I am going to London!"

"Going to London!" repeated Laurence blankly.

She fixed her glorious eyes to his face in a melting look. "Will you escort me?"

Mr Calver's carefully arranged locks were too lavishly pomaded to rise on end, but his eyes showed a tendency to start from their sockets. He replied, unequivocally: "Good God, no! Of course I won't!"

"Then I must go alone," said Tiffany mournfully.

"Have you taken leave of your senses?" demanded Laurence.

She sighed. "You must know I haven't. I am going to – to seek the protection of my Uncle James Burford."

"What do you want that for?" asked Laurence, unimpressed.

"I am very unhappy," stated Tiffany. "My aunt has not used me as she should. *Or* Ancilla!"

Mr Calver's intelligence was not generally thought to be of a high order, but he had no difficulty in interpreting this tragic utterance. He said gloomily, and with a regrettable want of tact: "Lindeth's offered for the parson's daughter, has he? Oh, well! I guessed as much! No use going to London, though: he wouldn't care a straw!"

"Nor do I care a straw!" declared Tiffany, her eyes flashing. "*That's* not why I am determined – *determined*! – to go to my uncle!"

"Well, it don't signify," said Laurence. "You can't go to London today, that's certain!"

"I can, and I will!"

"Not with my help," said Laurence bluntly.

No one had ever responded thus to Tiffany's demands; and it cost her a severe struggle to keep her temper. "I should be *very* grateful to you!" she suggested.

"I daresay you would," he replied. "Much good that would do me! Lord, what an after-clap there would be if I was to do anything so ramshackle as to drive off to London with a chit of your age and nothing but a dashed bandbox between the pair of us!" he added, looking with profound disapproval at this object.

"I didn't mean we should go in the whisky! How can you be so absurd? A post-chaise, of course!"

"Yes, and four horses as well, no doubt!"

She nodded, surprised that he should have thought it necessary to have asked.

Her innocent look, far from captivating Laurence, exasperated him. "Have you the least notion what it would cost?" he demanded.

"Oh, what can that signify?" she exclaimed impatiently. "My uncle will pay for it!"

"Very likely, but he ain't here," Laurence pointed out.

"He will pay all the charges when I reach London."

"You won't reach London. Who's to pay the first post-boys? Who's to pay for the changes of teams? If it comes to that, who's to pay for your lodging on the road? It's close on two hundred miles to London, you know – at least, I collect you *don't* know! What's more, you can't put up at a posting-house, travelling all by yourself! I shouldn't wonder at it if they refused to take you in. Well, I mean to say, who ever heard of such a thing? Now, do but consider, Miss Wield! You can't do such a jingle-brained thing: take my word for it!"

"Do you care what people may say?" Tiffany asked scornfully.

"Yes," he answered.

"How paltry! I don't!"

"I daresay you don't. You're too young to know what you're talking about. If you're so set on going to London, you ask Miss Trent to take you there!"

"Oh, how *stupid* you are!" she cried passionately. "She wouldn't do it!"

"Well, that quite settles it!" said Laurence. "You drink your lemonade, like a good girl, and I'll drive you back to Staples. No need to tell anyone where we've been: just say we went farther than we intended!"

Curbing the impulse to throw the lemonade in his face, Tiffany said winningly: "I *know* you couldn't be cruel enough to take me back to Staples. I had rather die than go back! Go with me to London! We could pretend we were married, couldn't we? That would make everything right!"

"You know," said Laurence severely, "you've got the most ramshackle notions of anyone I ever met! No, it would not make everything right!"

She looked provocatively at him, under lashes. "What if I *did* marry you? Perhaps I will!"

"Yes, and perhaps you won't!" he retorted. "Of all the outrageous -"

"I am very rich, you know! My cousin says that's why you dangle after me!"

"Oh, does he? Well, you may tell your precious cousin, with my compliments, that I ain't such a gudgeon as to run off with a girl who won't come into her inheritance for four years!" said Laurence, much incensed. "Yes, and another thing! I wouldn't do it if you was of age! For one thing, I don't wish to marry you; and, for another, I ain't a dashed hedge-bird, and I wouldn't run a rig like that even if I were all to pieces!"

"Don't *wish* to marry me?" Tiffany gasped, and suddenly burst into tears.

Horrified, Laurence said: "Not a marrying man! If I were – Oh, lord! For God's sake, don't cry! I didn't mean – that is, any number of men wish to marry you! Shouldn't wonder at it if you became a *duchess*! I assure you – most beautiful girl I ever set eyes on!"

"*Nobody* wants to marry me!" sobbed Tiffany.

"Mickleby! Ash! Young Banningham!" uttered Laurence.

"*Those*!" Tiffany said, with loathing. "Besides, they *don't*! I wish I were dead!"

"You're above their touch!" said Laurence desperately. "Above mine too! You'll marry into the Peerage – see if you don't! But *not*," he added, "if you go beyond the line!"

"I don't care! I want to go to London, and I *will* go to London! If you won't escort me, will you lend me the money for the journey?"

"No – Good God, no! Besides, I haven't got it! And even if I had I wouldn't lend it to you!" Strong indignation rose in his breast. "What do you suppose my cousin Waldo would have to say to me if I was to do anything so cock-brained as to send you off to London in a post-chaise-and-four, with nothing but a dashed bandbox, and not so much as an abigail to take care of you?"

"Sir Waldo?" Tiffany said, her tears arrested. "Do you think he would be vexed?"

"Vexed! Tear me in pieces! What's more," said Laurence fairly, "I wouldn't blame him! A nice mess I should be in! No, I thank you!"

"Very well!" said Tiffany tragically. "Leave me!"

"I do wish," said Laurence, eyeing her with a patent want of admiration, "that you wouldn't talk in that totty-headed fashion! Anyone would think you was regularly dicked in the nob! Leave you, indeed! A pretty figure I should cut!"

She shrugged. "Well, it's no matter to me! If you choose to be disobliging -"

"It may not be any matter to you, but it is to me!" interrupted Laurence. "Seems to me nothing matters to you but yourself!"

"Well, it seems to me that nothing matters to you but *yourself*!" flashed Tiffany. "Go away! Go away, go away, go *away*!"

Her voice rose on every repetition of the command, and Laurence, in the liveliest dread of being precipitated into a scandalous scene, swallowed his spleen, and adopted a conciliatory tone. "Now, listen!" he begged. "You don't want for sense, and you must see that I can't go away, leaving you here alone! What the deuce would you do? Tell me that! And don't say you'll go to London, because for one thing you haven't enough blunt to pay for the hire of a chaise, and for another I'd lay you long odds there ain't a postmaster living that would be such a clunch as to oblige you! If you was to try to tip him a rise, he'd be bound to think you was running away from school, or some such thing, and a rare hobble he'd be in if he aided and abetted you! What *he'd* do would be to send for the constable, and then your tale would be told!" He perceived that her eyes had widened in dismay, and at once enlarged on this theme. "Before you knew where you were you'd be taken before a magistrate, and if you refused to tell him who you was he'd commit you. A pretty piece of business that would be!"

"Oh, no!" she said, shuddering. "He wouldn't – he *couldn't*!"

"Oh, yes, he would!" said Laurence. "So, if you don't want everyone to know you tried to run away, and had to be bailed out of prison, you'd best come home with me now. No need to fear I'll tell a soul what happened! I won't."

She did not answer for a minute or two, but sat staring at him. Miss Trent would instantly have recognized the expression on her face; Laurence was less familiar with it, and waited hopefully for her capitulation. "But if I were to go on the stagecoach, or the Mail," she said thoughtfully, "no one would try to stop me. I know *that*, because several of the girls used to come to Miss Climping's school on the stage. I'm very much obliged to you for warning me! Yes, and the Mail coaches travel all night, so I shan't have to put up at a posting-house! How much will it cost me to buy a ticket, if you please?"

"I don't know, and it don't signify, because I'm not going to let you go to London, post, stage, or Mail!"

She got up, and began to draw on her gloves. "Oh, yes! You can't prevent me. I know just what to do if you try to – and it won't be of the least use to stand leaning against the door like that, because if you don't open it for me *at once* I shall scream for help, and when people come I shall say that you are abducting me!"

"What, in an open carriage, and you hopping down in the yard as merry as a cricket? That won't fadge, you little peagoose!"

"Oh, I shall say that you deceived me, and I never knew what your intentions were until until you made *violent* love to me, just now!" said Tiffany, smiling seraphically.

Laurence moved away from the door. It seemed more than likely that she would put this threat into execution; and although it would be open to him to explain the true circumstances to such persons as came running to her rescue, not only did he shrink from taking any part at all in so vulgar and embarrassing a scene, but he doubted very much whether his story would be believed. He would not have believed it himself, for a more improbable story would have been hard to imagine. On the other hand, Tiffany's story, backed by her youth, her staggering beauty, and the private parlour, was all too probable. He said mildly: "No need to kick up a dust! I ain't stopping you. But the thing is that it will cost you a deal of money to buy a seat on the Mail, and *I* can't frank you – haven't above a couple of guineas in my purse!"

"Then I shall go by the stage. Or even in a *carrier's cart*!" replied Tiffany, her chin mulishly set.

"Wouldn't take you," said Laurence. "Of course, you could go by the stage, but they're deucedly slow, you know. Bound to be overtaken. Nothing that cousin of yours would like better than to go careering after a stage-coach in that phaeton of his!"

"No! How should he guess where I was going? Unless you told him, and *surely* you wouldn't be so wickedly treacherous?"

"Well, I should have to tell him! Dash it all, -"

"Why?" she demanded. "You don't care what becomes of me!"

"No, but I care what becomes of *me*," said Laurence frankly.

Some dim apprehension that she had met her match dawned on Tiffany. She regarded Laurence with a mixture of indignation and unwilling sympathy, annoyed with him for considering no interest but his own, yet perfectly able to appreciate his point of view. After a reflective pause, she said slowly: "People would blame you? *I* see! But you'd help me if no one knew, wouldn't you?"

"Yes, but they're bound to know, so -"

"No, they won't. I've thought of a capital scheme!" interrupted Tiffany. "You must say that I hoaxed you!"

"I shall. It's just what you did do," said Laurence.

"Yes, so it will be *almost* true. Only, you must say that I went off to the dressmaker, and you waited, and waited, but I didn't return, and though you looked all over for me you couldn't find me, and you hadn't the least notion what had happened to me!"

"So I drove back to Broom Hall – just taking a look-in at Staples, to tell Miss Trent I'd lost you in Leeds!"

"Yes," she agreed happily. "For by that time I shall be out of reach. I've quite made up my mind to go by the Mail, and I know precisely what to do about paying for the ticket: I'll sell my pearls – or do you think it would be better to pawn them? I know *all* about that, because when I was at school, in Bath, Mostyn Garrowby, who was my *first* beau, though *much* too young, pawned his watch to take me to a fête in the Sydney Gardens one evening!"

"You don't mean to tell me you was allowed to go to fêtes?" said Laurence, incredulously.

"Oh, no! I had to wait until everyone had gone to bed, of course! Miss Climping never knew."

This artless confidence struck dismay into Laurence's soul. He perceived that Miss Wield was made of bolder stuff than he had guessed; and any hopes he might have cherished of convincing her that her projected journey to London would be fraught with too much impropriety to be undertaken vanished. Such a consideration could not be expected to weigh with a girl audacious enough to steal away from school at dead of night to attend a public fête in the company of a roly-poly youth without a feather to fly with.

"What do you advise?" enquired Tiffany, unclasping the single row of pearls she wore round her neck.

He had been pulling uncertainly at his underlip, but as she turned to the door, shrugging her shoulders, he said: "Here, give 'em to me! If you *must* go to London, I'll pawn 'em for you!"

She paused, eyeing him suspiciously. "I think I'll do it myself – thank you!"

"No, you dashed well won't!" he said, incensed. "You don't suppose I'm going to make off with your pearls, do you?"

"No, but – Well, it wouldn't surprise me in the least if you went galloping back to Staples! Though I must own that if I could trust you – Oh, I know! I'll come with you to the pawnbroker! And then we must discover where to find the Mail, and when it leaves Leeds, and -"

"Very well! You come – but don't blame *me* if we walk smash into someone who knows you!"

The change in her expression was almost ludicrous. She exclaimed: "Oh, no! No, no, surely not?"

"Nothing more likely," he said. "Seems to me the tabbies spend the better part of their time jauntering into Leeds to do some shopping. Not that I care – except that I should be glad if we did meet the Squire's wife, or Mrs Banningham, or -"

She flung up protesting hands. "Oh, how odious you are! You – you would positively *like* to betray me!"

"Well, if that's not the outside of enough!" he said. "When I've warned you -!"

Still rampantly suspicious, she said: "If I let you go alone, and you met one of those horrid creatures, you'd tell them!"

"Give you my word I wouldn't!" he replied promptly.

She was obliged to be satisfied, but it was with obvious reluctance that she dropped her string of pearls into his outstretched hand. He pocketed them, and picked up his hat. "I'll be off, then. You stay here, and don't get into a pucker, mind! I daresay it will take me some little time to arrange matters. I'll tell 'em to send up a nuncheon to you."

He then departed, returning nearly an hour later to find Miss Wield so sick with apprehension that she burst into tears at sight of him. However, when he handed her a ticket, and informed her that he had obtained a seat for her on the next Mail coach bound for London, her tears ceased, and her volatile spirits soared again. They were slightly damped by the news that it was not due to arrive in Leeds, coming from Thirsk, for another two hours, but agreeably diverted by the restoration to her of her pearls. "Thought it best to spout my watch instead," explained Laurence briefly.

She accepted them gratefully, saying, as she clasped them round her neck again: "I am *very* much obliged to you! Only, if I must wait so long for the Mail, perhaps I should travel on the stage, after all."

"Not a seat to be had!" responded Laurence, shaking his head. "Way-bills all made up! Besides, the Mail will overtake the stage – no question about that! You'll be set down at the Bull and Mouth, in St Martin's Lane, by the bye. Plenty of hacks to be had there: nothing for you to do but to give the jarvey your uncle's direction."

"No," she agreed. "But I do wish – Where must I go to meet the Mail?"

"Golden Lion: no need to tease yourself over that! I'll take you there."

The anxious furrow vanished from her brow. "You don't mean to leave me here alone? Then I am most *truly* obliged to you! I misjudged you, Mr Calver!"

He cast her a slightly harried glance. "No, no! That is, told you at the outset I'd have nothing to do with it!"

"Oh, yes but now everything will be right!" she said blithely.

"Well, I hope to God it will be!" said Laurence, with another, and still more harried glance at the clock on the mantelshelf.

CHAPTER NINETEEN

MISS TRENT, returning from a long, dull drive, which had afforded her far too much opportunity to indulge in melancholy reflection, reached Staples in a mood of deep depression. Relinquishing the reins to the monosyllabic groom who had accompanied her on the expedition, she descended from the gig, and rather wearily mounted the broad steps that led to the imposing entrance to the house. The double-doors stood open to the summer sunshine, and she passed through them into the hall, pulling off her gloves, and hoping that she might be granted a respite before being obliged to devise some form of entertainment to keep her exacting charge tolerably well amused during an evening void of any outside attraction. She was momentarily blinded by the transition from bright sunlight to the comparative darkness of the hall, but her vision cleared all too soon; and a lowering presentiment assailed her that no period of repose awaited her. At the foot of the stairs, and engaged in close colloquy, were Mr Courtenay Underhill and Miss Maria Docklow, abigail to Miss Tiffany Wield. Both turned their heads quickly to see who had come into the house, and one glance was enough to confirm Miss Trent's forebodings.

"Oh, dear!" she said, with a faint, rueful smile. "*Now* what's amiss?"

"That damned resty, rackety, caper-witted cousin of mine!" uttered Courtenay explosively. He saw Miss Trent's delicate brows lift slightly, and reddened. "Oh -! Beg pardon, ma'am, but it's enough to make anyone swear, by God it is!"

Miss Trent untied the strings of her straw bonnet, and removed it from her flattened locks. "Well, what has she done to vex you?" she asked, laying the bonnet down on the table.

"Vex me! She's run off with that man-milliner, Calver!" declared Courtenay.

"Nonsense!" said Miss Trent, preserving her calm.

"Well, it ain't nonsense! She's been gone for three hours, let me tell you, and -"

"Has she? Some accident to the carriage, I daresay, or perhaps the horse has gone lame."

"Worse, miss!" announced Miss Docklow, in sepulchral accents.

"Why, how can you know that?" Miss Trent asked, still undismayed.

"Ay! that's what I said!" said Courtenay grimly.

"But," interposed the abigail, determined to hold the centre of the stage, "'if that, sir, is what you think,' I said, 'come upstairs, and see what I have seen, sir!' I said."

"And what did you see?" asked Miss Trent.

Miss Docklow clasped her hands to her spare bosom, and cast up her eyes. "It gave me a Spasm, miss, my constitution being what it is, though far be it from me to utter any word of complaint, which anyone acquainted with me will testify!"

"Oh, never mind that!" said Courtenay angrily. "There's no need for you to put on those die-away airs: no one is blaming *you*! Tiffany has gone off with all her night-gear, and her trinket-box, ma'am!"

"Packed in the box where I had her best hat put away!" said Miss Docklow. "The one she wore to Harrogate, miss; the Waterloo hat, ornamented with feathers! And her China blue *pelisette*, with the silk cords and tassels! And her riding-habit – the *velvet* habit, miss! – left on the floor! Never will it be the same again, do what I will!" Startled at last, yet incredulous, Miss Trent hurried up the stairs, Miss Docklow and Courtenay in her wake. She was brought up short on the threshold of Tiffany's bedchamber, and stood blinking at a scene of the utmost disorder. It bore all the signs of a hasty packing, for drawers were pulled out, the wardrobe doors stood open, and garments had been tossed all over the room. "Good God!" said Miss Trent, stunned.

"*Now*, ma'am, perhaps you'll believe me!" said Courtenay. "Pretty, ain't it? Rare goings-on! Just one of dear little Tiffany's whisky-frisky pranks, eh? By God, it's past all endurance! It ain't enough for her to set us all at odds: oh, no! nothing will do for *her* but to kick up the most infamous scandal -"

"Quiet!" begged Miss Trent. "I do beg of you -!"

"It's all very well for you to say *quiet*," retorted Courtenay savagely, "*I'm* thinking of my mother! And when I consider the way she's cosseted that little viper, and pandered to her -"

"I perfectly understand your feelings," interrupted Miss Trent, "but railing won't mend matters!"

"Nothing can mend *this* matter!"

Looking round the disordered room, her spirit failed for a moment, and she was much inclined to agree with him. She pulled herself together, however, and said: "I can't tell what may be the meaning of this, but I'm certain of one thing: she has not run off with Mr Calver."

"That's where you're out, ma'am! She did go with him! He was seen waiting for her in that carriage he hired from the Crown."

"True it is, miss, though I blush to say it! With his own eyes did Totton see him!"

"He could hardly have seen him with anyone else's eyes!" snapped Miss Trent, her temper fraying. She controlled it, and said in a cooler tone: "You had better put all these garments away, Maria, and make the room tidy again. I am persuaded I need not tell you that we rely upon your discretion. Mr Underhill, pray come downstairs! We must try to think what is best for us to do."

He followed her rather sulkily, saying, as he shut the door of the morning-parlour: "I know what *I* am going to do – and if you hadn't come in just then I should be gone by now, for there's no time to be wasted!"

She had sunk into a chair, her elbows on the table, and her hands pressed to her temples, but she raised her head at this: "Gone where?"

"Harrogate, of course!"

"*Harrogate*? For heaven's sake, why?"

"Lord, ma'am, the fellow can't drive all the way to the Border in a whisky! Depend upon it, he's hired a chaise, and where else could he do that but in Harrogate?"

"Good God, are you suggesting that they are eloping to Gretna Green?" she exclaimed incredulously.

"Of course I am! It's just the sort of thing Tiffany *would* do – you can't deny that!"

"It is not at all the sort of thing Mr Calver would do, however! Nor do I think that Tiffany could by any means be persuaded to elope with a mere commoner! She has far larger plans, I assure you! No, no: *that's* not the answer to this riddle."

"Then what is the answer?" he demanded. "Yes, and why didn't she go with you to Nethersett? You told me at breakfast that you meant to take her along with you!"

"She wished to visit Patience...." Miss Trent's voice faltered, and died.

Courtenay gave a scornful snort. "That's a loud one! Wished to visit Patience, indeed! To beg her pardon, I daresay?"

"To make amends. When you told her that Mr Edward Banningham had spread the true story of what happened in Leeds – Oh, how much I wish you'd kept your tongue! You might have known she would do something outrageous! But so should I have known! I should never have left her: I am shockingly to blame! But she seemed so quiet this morning, scheming how to overcome her set-back -"

"Ay, the sly cat! Scheming how to be rid of you, ma'am, so that she could run off with Calver!"

She was silent, staring with knitted brows straight before her. She said suddenly: "No. She *did* go to the Rectory: recollect that her riding-habit was lying on the floor, with her whip, and her gloves! Something must have happened there. Patience – no, Patience wouldn't rebuff her! But if Mrs Chartley gave her a scold? But what could she have said to drive the child into running away? Mr Underhill, I think I should go to the Rectory immediately, and discover -"

"*No*!" he interrupted forcefully. "I won't have our affairs blabbed all round the district!"

"It's bound to be talked of. And I'm persuaded Mrs Chartley -"

"Not if I fetch her back! Which I promise you I mean to do, for my mother's sake!" He added rather grandly: "I shall be obliged to call that fellow out, of course, but I shall think of some pretext for it."

At any other time she must have laughed, but she was too busy racking her brains to pay much heed to him. "Something must have happened," she repeated. "Something that made her feel she couldn't remain here another instant. Oh, good God, Lindeth! He must have offered for Patience – and she told Tiffany!"

Courtenay gave a whistle of surprise. "So that's serious, is it? Well, by Jove, if ever I expected to see her given her own again! Lord, she'd be as mad as fire! No wonder she ran off with Calver! Trying to hoax everyone into thinking it was him she wanted all along!"

She was momentarily daunted, but she came about again. "Yes, she might do that, in one of her wild fits, but he would not. Wait! Only let me think!" She pressed her hands over her eyes, trying to cast her mind back.

"Well, if she isn't going to Gretna Green, where else can she be going?" he argued.

Her hands dropped. "What a fool I am! To London, of course! That's what she wanted – she begged me to take her back to the Burfords! Of course that's the answer! She must have persuaded Mr Calver to take her to Leeds – perhaps even to escort her to London!" She read disbelief in Courtenay's face, and said: "If she made him believe that she was being hardly used here – you know how she always fancies herself to be illtreated as soon as her will is crossed! Recollect that he doesn't know her as we do! She has shown him her prettiest side, too – and she can be very engaging when she chooses! Or – or perhaps he has done no more than put her on the stage, in charge of the guard."

"Stage!" exclaimed Courtenay contemptuously. "I wish I may see Tiffany condescending to a stage-coach! A post-chaise-and-four is what she'd demand! And much hope I have of catching it!"

"She couldn't go post," said Miss Trent decidedly. "She spent all her pin-money in Harrogate. And I must think it extremely unlikely that Mr Calver could have been able to oblige her with a loan. She would need as much as £25, you know, and how should he be carrying such a sum upon him when all he meant to do was to take her out for a driving-lesson? And I fancy he's not at all beforehand with the world." She thought for a moment, and then said, in a constricted voice: "Mr Underhill, I think – I think you should drive over to Broom Hall, to consult Sir Waldo. He is Mr Calver's cousin, and – and I think he is the person best fitted to handle this matter."

"Well, I won't!" declared Courtenay, reddening. "I'm not a schoolboy, ma'am, and I don't need him to tell me what I should do, or to do it for me, I thank you! I'm going to tell 'em to bring the phaeton up to the house immediately. If that precious pair went to Leeds they must have passed through the village, and someone is bound to have seen them. And if they did, trust me to have Tiffany back by nightfall! If you ask me, I'd say good riddance to her, but I'll be *damned* – begging your pardon! – if I'll let her shab off to the Burfords as if we had made her miserable here!"

Miss Trent had no great faith in his ability to overtake a truant who had had three hours' start; but since she felt quite as strongly as he did that every effort must be made to do it, and realized that to persist in urging that Sir Waldo should be consulted would be a waste of breath and time, she resigned herself to the prospect of an uncomfortable, and possibly nerve-racking drive. He was relieved to learn that she meant to accompany him, but he warned her that he was going to *put 'em along*.

That he would do better to be content with putting his horses well together was an opinion which she kept to herself.

When she found that he had had a team harnessed to the phaeton her heart sank. His leaders were new acquisitions, and he was not yet very expert in pointing them, or, indeed of sticking to them, as she very soon discovered. Observing that there was not a moment to be lost, Courtenay sprang his horses down the avenue to the lodge-gates. Since it was not only rather narrow, but had several bends in it as well, Miss Trent was forced to hold on for dear life. The sharp turn out of the gates was negotiated safely, though not, perhaps, in style, and they were soon bowling along the lane that led to the village. Courtenay, exhilarated by his success in negotiating the difficult turn out of the gate, confided to Miss Trent that he had been practising the use of the whip, and rather thought he could back himself to take a fly off the leader's ear.

"I beg you won't do any such thing!" she replied. "I have no wish to be thrown out into the ditch!"

Nettled, he determined to show her that he was at home to a peg, and it was not long before her worst fears were realized. Within less than a quarter of a mile from Oversett, featheredging a bend in the lane, his front-wheel came into sharp collision with a milestone, partially hidden by rank grass, and the inevitable happened. Miss Trent, picking herself up, more angry than hurt, found that one wheel of the phaeton was lying, a dismal wreck, at some distance from the carriage, that one of the wheelers was down, a trace broken, and both the leaders plunging wildly in a concerted effort to bolt. Blistering words were on the tip of her tongue, but she was a sensible woman, and she realized that there were more urgent things to do than to favour Courtenay with an exact and pithy opinion of his driving-skill. She hurried to his assistance. Between them, they managed to quieten the frightened leaders, backing them gently to relieve the drag on the crippled phaeton from the remaining trace. "Cut it!" she commanded. "I can hold this pair now. Do you get that wheeler on his feet!"

Speechless with rage and chagrin, he had just freed the leaders when, sweeping round the bend towards them, came the Nonesuch, his team of chestnuts well in hand, and his groom seated beside him. The team was pulled up swiftly, every rein holding as true as if it had been single, the groom jumped down, and ran to the wheelers' heads; and the Nonesuch, his amused gaze travelling from Courtenay, beside his struggling wheeler, to Miss Trent, who had led the two sweating leaders to the side of the lane, said: "Dear me! Do what you can, Blyth!"

The groom touched his hat, and went to Courtenay, who was suffering such agonies of mortification at being found in such a situation that he would have been hard put to it to decide whether he wished himself dead or the Nonesuch. He blurted out, scarlet-faced: "It was that curst milestone! I never saw it!"

"Very understandable," agreed Sir Waldo. "But if I were you I would attend to my horses! You really need not explain the circumstances to me." He looked smilingly at Miss Trent. "How do you do, ma'am? Quite a fortunate encounter! I was on my way to visit you – to invite you to go with me to Leeds."

"To Leeds!" The exclamation was surprised out of her; she stood staring up at him, her embarrassment forgotten.

"Yes: on an errand of mercy!" He glanced towards the phaeton, and saw that the fallen wheeler was up. "Very good, Blyth! Now take those leaders in hand!"

The groom, who had been running a hand down one of the unfortunate wheeler's legs, straightened himself, saying: "Yes, sir. Badly strained hock here."

"So I should imagine. Render Mr Underhill all the assistance you can!"

"Sir!" uttered Courtenay, between gritted teeth. "I – we were on our way to Leeds too! That was how it came about that I – I mean, it is a matter of – of great urgency! I *must* get there! I can't tell you why, but if you are going there yourself, would you be so very obliging as to take me with you?"

"Well, no!" said the Nonesuch apologetically. "Phaetons, you know, were not built to carry three persons, and I have been particularly requested to bring Miss Trent with me. Oh, don't look so distressed! Believe me, the matter is not of such great urgency as you think! You may also believe that Miss Trent is far more necessary to the success of my mission than you could hope to be."

Miss Trent, having relinquished the reins she had been holding into Blyth's hands, stepped quickly up to the phaeton, and said, in an undervoice: "You know, then? But how? Where are they?"

"In Leeds, at the King's Head." He leaned across the empty seat beside him, and held down his hand to her. "Come!"

She looked at it, thinking how strong and shapely it was; and then up, meeting his eyes, smiling into hers. She felt helpless, knowing it was her duty to go to Tiffany, longing to be with Sir Waldo, dreading to be with him, afraid, not of his strength but of her own weakness. Before she had made up her mind what to do, Courtenay, whose worshipful regard for the Nonesuch was rapidly diminishing, broke in, saying in a furious voice: "Your pardon, sir! But Miss Trent can't discharge *my* errand, which is of *immediate* urgency, I promise you! I don't care if he *is* your cousin I – I have a very ardent desire to meet Mr Calver!"

"Yes, yes!" said the Nonesuch soothingly. "But you can express your gratitude to him at a more convenient time. Your *immediate* duty is to your horses."

"My *gratitude*?" ejaculated Courtenay, so far forgetful of his immediate duty as to abandon his wheelers, and to stride up to Sir Waldo's phaeton. "That that damned rip makes off with my cousin, and you expect me to be *grateful*? Well, let me tell you, Sir Waldo, -"

"My amiable young cawker," interrupted Sir Waldo, looking down at him in considerable amusement, "you are fair and far off! To whom, do you suppose, do I owe my information?"

Nonplussed, Courtenay glared up at him. "I don't know! I -"

"Well, think!" Sir Waldo advised him. He looked again at Miss Trent, his brows lifting enquiringly.

"Is Tiffany with Mr Calver?" she demanded.

"Well, I trust she may be. She was with him when he sent off his impassioned plea for help, but he seemed to entertain some doubt of his ability to hold her in – er – check for any considerable period. I don't wish to be importunate, ma'am, but are you coming with me, or are you not?"

"I *must* come!" she said, gathering up her skirt in one hand, and holding the other up to him.

He grasped it, drawing her up into the phaeton, and saying softly: "Good girl! Pluck to the backbone! Were you tumbled into the ditch?"

"I collect you've guessed as much from my appearance!" she said, with asperity, and putting up her hands to straighten her bonnet.

"Not a bit of it! A mere knowledge of cause and effect: you are, as ever, precise to a pin – and an enduring delight to me!" He turned his head to address Courtenay once more. "I'll leave Blyth to assist you, Underhill. Indulge no apprehensions! just look to your horses! Miss Wield will very soon be restored to you."

As he spoke, he drew his leaders back gently, and gave the would-be top-sawyer an effortless demonstration of how to turn to the rightabout in a constricted space a sporting vehicle drawn by four high-bred lively ones.

Miss Trent, deeply appreciative of his skill, was moved to say: "You *do* drive to an inch! I wish I could turn a *one*-horse carriage as easily!"

"You will: I'll teach you," he said. "You shall take the shine out of all our fair whips!"

She had no particular desire to take the shine out of anyone, but the implication of these words conjured up a vision of the future so agreeable that it was with great difficulty that she wrenched her mind away from it. Rigidly confining it to the matter in hand, she said: "I hope you mean to explain to me, sir, how it comes about that you are so exactly informed of Tiffany's whereabouts. *I* could only guess what must be her intention, for I have been away from Staples for the better part of the day, and she left no message for me."

"What an abominable girl she is!" he remarked. "My information came, as I told you, from Laurie. He sent off one of the post-boys with a note for me, from the King's Head. As far as I understand the matter – but he wrote in haste, and, to judge from the manner of it, in an extremely harassed state of mind! – Tiffany induced him to drive her to Leeds, by some fetch or wheedle, and only on arrival there divulged her intention of travelling to London. I can't tell you why she should have suddenly taken this notion into her head. All I know is that Laurie has hoaxed her into believing that there is not a place to be had in any of the stage-coaches, and that the Mail doesn't reach Leeds until four o'clock. I should have thought that rather too improbable an hour to have chosen, but Tiffany seems to have accepted it without question."

"Of course it's perfectly ridiculous! But Tiffany knows nothing about Mails or stages. Well! it's some comfort to know that I was right. Mr Underhill *would* have it that she and your cousin had gone off in a post-chaise-and-four, but I couldn't suppose that Mr Calver would be carrying a large enough sum of money on his person."

"Very unlikely," he agreed. "Still more unlikely that he would have disgorged a penny of it for Tiffany's benefit. I'll say this for Laurie: he had her measure from the outset."

"Indeed? It would be interesting to know, then, why he has been so assiduous in his attentions to her!"

He smiled. "Oh, that was to detach her from Julian! He came after the fair, but it was quite a good notion."

"Your own, in fact!" she said, somewhat tartly. "I find it very hard to believe that Mr Calver takes the smallest interest in Lord Lindeth's happiness."

"Oh, he doesn't! He knows, however, that I do; and unless I'm much mistaken his scheme was to win my gratitude. Poor Laurie! It was some time before he realized that his labour was thrown away. Still, it kept him occupied, and did neither of them any harm."

"I think it utterly unscrupulous!" said Miss Trent indignantly. "It would have done a great deal of harm if Tiffany had fallen in love with him!"

"On the contrary, it might have done a great deal of good. It's high time that young woman suffered a shake-up. To own the truth, I rather hoped she might develop just enough *tendre* for him to enable her to bear more easily the shock of finding that Lindeth had offered for Miss Chartley. Not for her sake, but for yours. I can readily imagine what you will be made to suffer, my poor girl!"

She disregarded this, but asked eagerly: "Has he done so? Oh, I am so glad! I hope you don't dislike it, Sir Waldo?"

"Not at all. An unexceptionable girl, and will make him an admirable wife, I daresay."

"I think that too. She has as little worldly ambition as he, and quite as sweet a disposition. But his mother? Will she like it?"

"No, not immediately, but she'll come round to it. She has all the worldly ambition Julian lacks, and has lately been doing her utmost to interest him in various diamonds of the first water. However, I fancy she has begun to realize that it's useless to try to bring him into fashion. In any event, she is by far too fond a parent to cast the least rub in the way of his happiness. Julian informs me, moreover, that Mrs Chartley is related to one of my aunt's oldest friends. His description of this lady – unknown to me, I'm thankful to say! – wouldn't lead one to suppose that my aunt would regard the relationship as an advantage, but he seems to think it will. As far as I remember, he said she was a regular fusty mug – but I daresay he exaggerated!"

A ripple of laughter broke from her. "What a boy he is! Tell me, if you please: when did this event take place, sir?"

"This morning. I had the news from him barely half-an-hour before I received Laurie's message."

"Then I know why Tiffany ran away," said Miss Trent, with a despairing sigh. "She was at the Rectory this morning, and they must have told her. You may say she's abominable – and, of course, very often she *is*! – but one can't but pity her, poor child! So spoiled as she has been all her life, so pretty, and so much petted and admired! – Can't you understand what it must have meant to her, coming, as it did, after the ball last night?"

He glanced down at her. "The ball last night? What happened to overset her then?"

"Good God, surely you must have noticed?" she exclaimed. "All those foolish boys who have been dangling after her ever since I brought her to Staples clustered round Miss Chartley – almost showed Tiffany the cold shoulder!"

"No, I didn't notice," he answered. "I was in the card-room, you know. But I can readily understand her feelings upon being shown a cold shoulder: I was shown one myself, and I assure you I am filled with compassion." Again he glanced down at her, his smile a little wry. "That, Miss Trent, is why I sought refuge in the card-room."

CHAPTER TWENTY

SHE TURNED away her face, aware of her rising colour. He said reflectively: "I can't recall that I was ever so blue-devilled before."

She knew that it was unwise to answer him, but she was stung into saying: "That, Sir Waldo, is – as you would say yourself – doing it rather too brown! You do not appear to me to be suffering from any want of spirits!"

He laughed. "Oh, no! Not since it occurred to me that you were blue-devilled too!"

"To be thrown into a ditch is enough to blue-devil anyone!" she retorted.

"What, *twice*?" he exclaimed. "I had no notion that such an accident had befallen you on the way to the *ball*!"

"It didn't. Last night," she said carefully, "I was not feeling at all the thing. I had the headache."

"Again?" he said, in a voice of deep concern. "My dear Miss Trent, I'm persuaded you should consult a physician about these recurrent headaches of yours!"

She did her best to stifle it, but he caught the sound of the tiny choke of laughter in her throat, and said appreciatively: "Do you know, I think that of all your idiosyncrasies that choke you give, when you are determined not to laugh, is the one that most enchants me. I wish you will do it again!"

Only the recollection that he must of necessity be expert in the art of seduction prevented her from complying with this request. Appalled to discover that in despite of upbringing and principles her every fibre was responsive to the Nonesuch's wicked charm, she said, apparently addressing the ears of his leaders: "Sir Waldo, circumstance compelled me to accept a seat in your carriage. When I consented to go with you to Leeds, I trusted that chivalry – a sense of propriety – would prohibit you from entering again upon this subject."

"Did you?" he said sympathetically. "Only to find your trust misplaced! Well, that is a great deal too bad, and one must naturally shrink from shattering illusions. At the same time – where *did* you pick up such a ridiculous notion?"

The Reverend William Trent, whose mind was of a serious order, had several times warned his elder sister that too lively a sense of humour frequently led to laxity of principle. She now perceived how right he was; and wondered, in dismay, whether it was because he invariably made her laugh that instead of regarding the Nonesuch with revulsion she was obliged to struggle against the impulse to cast every scruple to the winds, and to give her life into his keeping.

"What is it that troubles you, my heart?" he asked gently, after a short pause.

The change of tone almost overset her, but she managed to say, though faintly: "Nothing!"

"No, don't say that. What did I do to bring about this alteration in your sentiments? I've racked my brain to discover the answer searched my memory too, but quite in vain. God knows I'm no saint, but I don't think I'm more of a sinner than any other man. *Tell* me!"

She realized from these words that they must be poles apart. She thought it would be useless to enter upon any discussion, even if she could have brought herself to broach a subject of such delicacy. She said, with as much composure as she could command: "Sir Waldo, pray leave this! I don't wish to be married."

"Why not?"

She ought to have guessed, of course, that he would disconcert her. Casting wildly in her mind for an excuse, she produced, after a betraying pause: "I am an educationist. No doubt it seems strange to you that I should prefer to pursue that profession, but but so it is!"

"My dear girl, so you might, with my goodwill!"

"You would hardly wish your wife to be employed as a teacher in a school!"

"No, certainly not, but if superintending the education of the young is your ambition I can provide you with plenty of material on which to exercise your talents," he said cheerfully.

For a moment she could hardly believe her ears. She turned her head to stare at him; and then, as she saw the familiar glint in his eyes, wrath at his audacity surged up in her, and she gasped: "How *dare* you?"

The words were no sooner uttered than she regretted them; but she had at least the satisfaction of seeing the glint vanish from his eyes. It was succeeded by a look of astonishment. Sir Waldo pulled up his team. "I *beg* your pardon?" he said blankly.

Furiously blushing, she said: "I should not have said it. I didn't intend – Pray forget it, sir!"

"Forget it! How could I possibly do so? What the devil did I say to make you rip up at me? You don't even know what I was talking about, for I haven't yet told you my dark secret! Do you remember that I promised I would do so?"

"I do remember," she replied, in a stifled voice. "You said that you would *make a clean breast* of it, but it is unnecessary. I know what your – your *dark secret* is, Sir Waldo."

"Do you indeed? Which of my cousins took it upon himself to enlighten you?" he asked grimly. "Laurie?"

"No, no! He has never mentioned it to me, I promise you! Don't ask me more!"

"I need not. Julian, of course! I might have known it! If ever there was a prattle-box -! But I can't for the life of me understand why -"

She broke in rather desperately on this. "Oh, pray -! He asked me particularly not to tell you! It was very wrong of me to have said what I did. He thought I knew he meant no harm! I don't think he dreamed that I should not look upon it as – as lightly as he does himself – as *you* do! You told me that you believed I had too liberal a mind to disapprove. You meant it as a compliment, but you were mistaken: my mind is not so liberal. I am aware that in certain circles – the circles to which you belong – such things are scarcely regarded. It is otherwise in my circle. And my family – oh, you would not understand, but you must believe that I *could* not marry a man whose – whose way of life fills me with repugnance!"

He had listened to the first part of this speech in frowning bewilderment, but by the time she reached the end of it the frown had cleared, and a look of intense amusement had taken its place. "So that's it!" he said, a quiver of laughter in his voice. He set his team in motion again. "I'll wring Julian's neck for this! Of all the leaky, chuckleheaded rattles -! Just what *did* he tell you?"

"Indeed, he said nothing more than you told me yourself!" she said earnestly. "Only that people would be bound to disapprove of the use to which you meant to put Broom Hall! He said nothing in your dispraise, I do assure you! In fact, he said that although one of your cousins thinks it not at all the thing to – to house children of that sort in a respectable neighbourhood -"

"George," interpolated Sir Waldo. "Are you sure he didn't refer to them as *Waldo's wretched brats*?"

"I believe he did," she replied stiffly.

"You shouldn't tamper with the text. Go on!"

She eyed his profile with hostility. "There is nothing more to say. I wished merely to make it plain to you that Lord Lindeth spoke of you with as much admiration as affection."

"I daresay. Heaven preserve me from affectionate and admiring relations! Laurie couldn't have served me a worse turn! So you won't help me to set up schools for my wretched brats, Miss Trent?"

"*Schools*?" she repeated, startled.

"In course of time. Oh, don't look so alarmed! Only one at the moment! Those of my brats who are established in Surrey are already provided for."

Dazed, she demanded: "How many children have you?"

"I'm not perfectly sure. I think they numbered fifty when I left London, but there's no saying that there may not be one or two more by now."

"*Fifty*?"

"That's all. I expect shortly to double the number, however," he said affably.

Her eyes kindled. "I collect that you think it a joking matter, Sir Waldo! I do not !"

"I don't think it anything of the sort. It is, in fact, one of the few matters which I take seriously."

"But you cannot possibly have fif-" She broke off abruptly, her eyes widening. "Schools – wretched brats – carrying eccentricity too far – and only the Rector knew -! Oh, what a *fool* I've been!" she cried, between laughter and tears. "And Lindeth said, when we took that child to the infirmary, that *you* were the man we wanted in such a situation! But how *could* I guess that you were interested in *orphans*?"

"Easier to think that I was a loose-screw, was it?" said Sir Waldo, who had once more halted his team. "Let me tell you, my girl, that I'm swallowing no more of your insults! And if I hear another word from you in disparagement of the Corinthian set it will be very much the worse for you!"

Since he palliated this severity by putting his arm round her she was undismayed. Overwhelming relief making her forgetful of the proprieties, she subsided thankfully into his embrace, clutching a fold of his driving-coat, and saying into his shoulder: "Oh, no, you never will! But I *didn't* find it easy to believe! Only people said such things and you talked of making a clean breast of it and then Lindeth! Don't scold me! If you *knew* how unhappy I've been!"

"I do know. But what *you* don't know is that if you don't take your face out of my coat, and look at me, you will be still more unhappy!"

She gave a watery chuckle, and raised her head. The Nonesuch, his arm tightening round her, kissed her. The phaeton jerked forward, and back again, as Sir Waldo, who had transferred the reins to his whip-hand, brought his restive wheelers under control. Miss Trent, emerging somewhat breathlessly from his embrace, said, in shaken accents: "For goodness' sake, take care! If I'm thrown into a ditch a second time I'll never forgive you!"

"You must teach me sometime how to handle my cattle," he said. "I imagine your lessons – Miss Educationist! – will bear a close resemblance to Laurie's efforts to instruct Tiffany."

"Good God! Tiffany!" she exclaimed. "I had quite forgotten her! Waldo, this is *no* time for dalliance – and it isn't the place, either! What William would say if he knew -! You *are* an atrocious person! Since the day I met you I have become steadily more depraved. No, no, don't! We *must* make haste to Leeds: you know we must! There's no saying what Tiffany may do, if she becomes impatient."

"To be honest with you," said Sir Waldo, "I have very little interest in what she may do."

"No, but I cannot cast her off so lightly. She was left to my guardianship, and if anything were to happen to her how dreadfully to blame I should be!"

"Yes, the sooner you're rid of her the better. Is this fast enough for you, or do you wish me to spring 'em?"

"Oh, no! Not that I would venture to dictate to you, dear sir! Tell me about your orphanage! Lindeth said that you squandered a fortune on your wretched brats, and, indeed, I should think you must, if you mean to support a hundred of them. Is it for infants?"

"No, I don't encroach on the Foundling Hospitals. Nor do I squander a fortune on my brats. Broom Hall, for instance, will be largely self-supporting; subsisting on rents, you know."

She smiled. "Don't think me impertinent! – But I am not *wholly* devoid of intelligence! – What will it cost you to bring that estate into order?"

"No more than I can well afford!" he retorted. "Are you fearful of finding yourself in ebb-water if you marry me? You won't! Lindeth misled you: only *half* my fortune is devoted to my favourite charity! My aunt Lindeth will inform you that the whole is *indecent* – if she doesn't describe it in rather stronger terms, which, in moments of stress, she is prone to do."

"My mind now being relieved of care, I wish you will tell me what prompted you to found an orphanage?"

He said reflectively: "I don't know. Tradition, and upbringing, I suppose. My father, and my grandfather before him, were both considerable philanthropists; and my mother was used to be very friendly with Lady Spencer – the one that died a couple of years ago, and was mad after educating the poor. So you may say that I grew up amongst charities! This was one that seemed to me more worth the doing than any other: collecting as many of the homeless waifs you may find in any city as I could, and rearing them to become respectable citizens. My cousin, George Wingham, swears they will all turn into hedge-birds, and, of course, we've had our failures, but not many. The important thing is to enter them to the right trades and to take care they're not bound to bad masters." He stopped, and said, laughing: "What induced you to mount me on my pet hobby-horse? We have matters of more immediate importance to discuss than my wretched brats, my little educationist! – my mother, by the way, will welcome you with open arms, and will very likely egg you on to bully me into starting an asylum for female orphans: she's got about a dozen of 'em already, down at Manifold. How soon may you leave Staples? I warn you, I don't mean to wait on Mrs Underhill's convenience, so if you've any notion of remaining there until Tiffany goes back to London -"

"I haven't!" she interrupted. "Nor, I assure you, would Mrs Underhill ask it of me!"

"I'm happy to hear it. The devil of it is that I must leave with Julian, on Monday: I told the boy I would support his cause with my aunt, and I think I must. I should have wished to have postponed my departure until I could have escorted you to Derbyshire, but as things have fallen out I shall be obliged to leave you here until Julian's affairs are settled, and one or two other matters as well. I'll return as soon as I can, but -"

"I had as lief you did not," she said. "And liefer by far that we should tell no one at Oversett, except Mrs Underhill (whom I hope to heaven I can pledge to secrecy!), of our intentions. Think me foolish if you will, but I don't feel I could bear it! It will be so very much disliked, you know, and – well, I need not tell you what things will be said by certain ladies of our acquaintance! Then there is Tiffany. Waldo, *she* mustn't know until she has recovered a little from Lindeth's engagement! It would be too cruel – when you encouraged the poor child by flirting with her! Besides, I shudder to think of what life at Staples would be if she knew that you had preferred me to her! We should all of us be driven distracted. I must give Mrs Underhill time to fill my post – don't ask me to leave her in the lurch, for I couldn't do it: I have had nothing but kindness from her, remember! But as soon as she has done so I'll go home to Derbyshire, and we may meet there. Oh, how much I long to make you known to Mama and William! But as for *escorts* -! My dear, how can you be so absurd as to suppose that at my age I should need one? The journey will be nothing – no more than fifty miles! I have only to go by the stage to Mansfield, and from there -"

"You will not go by the stage anywhere at all," said Sir Waldo. "I'll send my chaise to fetch you, with my own boys, of course."

"To be sure!" she said instantly. "Outriders, and a courier too, I hope!

Now, do, do be sensible, my dear sir!"

They were still arguing the matter when they reached the King's Head. Leaving the Nonesuch in the stableyard, Miss Trent walked into the inn. She had on several occasions refreshed there with Mrs Underhill, and the first person she encountered was an elderly waiter who was well-known to her. Greeting him with a smile, and speaking with studied coolness, she said: "Good-day to you, John! Are Miss Wield and Mr Calver still here, or have they given me up in despair? I should have been here long since, but was most tiresomely delayed. I hope they may not have left?"

Even as she said it she became aware of tension, and of curious glances cast in her direction, and her heart sank. The waiter coughed in obvious embarrassment, and replied: "No, ma'am. Oh, no, they haven't *left*! The gentleman is in one of the parlours the same one as you was in yourself, ma'am, when you partook of a nuncheon here the other day."

"And Miss Wield?"

"Well, no, ma'am! Miss is in the best bedchamber – being as she is a trifle out of sorts, and the mistress not knowing what else to do but to persuade her to lay down on the bed, with the blinds drawn, till she was more composed, as you might say. Very vapourish, she was – but the mistress will tell you, ma'am!"

Sir Waldo, entering the house at that moment, encountered an anguished look from Miss Trent, and said: "What's amiss?"

"I couldn't take it upon myself to say, sir," responded the waiter, casting down his eyes. "But the gentleman, sir, is in the parlour, the mistress having put some sticking-plaster over the cut, and one of the under-waiters carrying a bottle of cognac up to him – the *best* cognac, sir! – the gentleman, as I understand, having sustained an accident in a manner of speaking!"

"We will go up to him!" said Miss Trent hastily.

"Sinister!" observed Sir Waldo, following her up the narrow stairs. "Where, by the way, is the heroine of this piece?"

"Laid down upon the bed in the best bedchamber," replied Miss Trent, "with the landlady in attendance!"

"Worse and worse! Do you suppose that she stabbed poor Laurie with a carving-knife?"

"Heaven knows! It is quite *appalling* and no laughing matter, let me tell you! Mrs Underhill is very well known here, and it is perfectly obvious to me that that atrocious girl has created a dreadful scandal! The *one* thing I was hopeful of avoiding! Whatever you do, Waldo, don't let her suspect that you regard me even with *tolerance*!"

"Have no fear! I will treat you with civil indifference!" he promised. "I wonder what she *did* do to Laurie?"

He was soon to learn the answer to this. Mr Calver was discovered in the parlour, reclining on a sofa of antiquated and uncomfortable design, a strip of sticking-plaster adorning his brow, his beautifully curled locks sadly dishevelled, a glass in his hand, and a bottle of the King's Head's best cognac standing on the floor beside him. As she stepped over the threshold, Miss Trent trod on splinters of glass; and on the table in the centre of the room was an elegant timepiece, in a slightly battered condition. Miss Wield had not stabbed Mr Calver: she had thrown the clock at his head.

"Snatched it off the mantelpiece and dashed well *hurled* it at me!" said Laurence.

The Nonesuch shook his head. "You must have tried to dodge it," he said. "Really, Laurie, how could you be such a cawker? If you had but stood still it would have missed you by several feet!"

"I should rather think I did try to dodge it!" said Laurence, glaring at him. "So would you have done!"

"Never!" declared the Nonesuch. "When females throw missiles at my head I know better than to budge! Er – would it be indelicate to ask *why* she felt herself impelled to throw the clock at you?"

"Yes, I might have known you would think it vastly amusing!" said Laurence bitterly.

"Well, yes, I think you might!" said Sir Waldo, his eyes dancing.

Miss Trent, perceiving that her beloved had allowed himself to fall into a mood of ill-timed frivolity, directed a quelling frown at him, and said to the injured dandy: "I am so sorry, Mr Calver! I wish you will lie down again: you are not looking at all the thing, and no wonder! Your cousin may think it a jesting matter, but I am excessively grateful to you! Indeed, I cannot conceive how you were able to hold that tiresome child in check for so long!"

Slightly mollified, Laurence said: "It wasn't easy, I can tell you, ma'am. It's my belief she's queer in her attic. Well, would you credit it? – she wanted me to sell her pearl necklet, or put it up the spout, just to pay for the hire of a chaise to carry her to London! I had to gammon her I'd pawned my watch instead!"

"How very wise of you!" said Miss Trent sycophantically. "Pray do sit down, sir! I wish you will tell me – if you feel able – what caused her to to take a sudden pet?"

"To do *what*?" interpolated the Nonesuch.

Miss Trent, turning her back on him in a marked manner, sat down in a chair by the sofa, and smiled at Laurence encouragingly.

"You may well ask, ma'am!" said Laurence. He glanced resentfully at his cousin. "If you are fancying I was trying to make love to her, Waldo, you're no better than a Jack Adams! For one thing, I ain't in the petticoat-line, and for another I wouldn't make love to that devil's daughter if I was!"

"Of course you would not!" said Miss Trent.

"Well, I didn't. What's more, it wasn't *my* fault at all! Mind you, I had the deuce of a task to keep her here! Still, we were going on prosperously enough until she suddenly took it into her head she must drink some tea. Why she should want to maudle her inside with tea at this time of day the lord knows, but *I'd* no objection, as long as it stopped her from riding grub. Which I daresay it would have done if she hadn't asked the jobbernoll who brought in the tray what time the London Mail was expected to arrive in the town. Couldn't catch the fellow's eye – wasn't close enough to give him a nudge! The silly bleater told her there wouldn't be another till tomorrow morning. That brought the trap down! Talk of ringing a peal-! She scolded like a cut-purse! You'd have supposed I was a regular Bermondsey boy! And the waiter standing there with his mouth at half-cock, until I told him to take himself off which I wish I *hadn't* done!" Shuddering at the memory, he recruited his strength with a sip or two of cognac. "The names she called me!

It beats me where she learned 'em, I can tell you that, ma'am!"

"What *did* she call you, Laurie?" enquired Sir Waldo, much interested.

"I wonder," said Miss Trent, in a voice of determined coldness, "if you would be so obliging, sir, as to refrain from asking quite unimportant questions? Mr Calver, what can I say but that I am deeply mortified? As Miss Wield's governess, I must hold myself to blame, but I trust – "

"Learned them from you, did she, ma'am?" said Sir Waldo irrepressibly.

"Very witty!" snapped Laurence. "You wouldn't be so full of fun and gig if *you'd* been in my shoes!"

"Pray don't heed your cousin!" begged Miss Trent. "Only tell me what happened!"

"Well, she twigged I'd been hoaxing her, of course, and it didn't take her above a minute or two to guess *why* I'd kept her kicking her heels here. I give you my word, ma'am, if she'd had a dagger about her she'd have stuck it into me! Not that I cared for that, because I knew she hadn't one. But the next thing was that she said she was going off to spout her pearls that instant, so that she could be gone from the place before you reached us! She'd have done it, too! What's more, I wish I'd let her!"

"I don't wonder at it. But you did not – which was *very* well done of you, sir!"

"I don't know that," he said gloomily. "She wouldn't have raised such a breeze if I'd had the sense to have taken off my bars. The thing was she'd put me in such a tweak by that time that I was hanged if I'd cry craven! Told her that if she tried to shab off I'd squeak beef – what I mean is, tell the landlord who she was, and what she was scheming to do. So then she threw the clock at me. That brought the landlord in on us, and a couple of waiters, and the boots, and a dashed gaggle of chambermaids – and it's my belief they'd had their ears to the door! And before I could utter a word the little hussy was carrying on as though she thought she was Mrs Siddons! Well, she'd threatened to tell everyone I'd been trying to give her a slip on the shoulder if I wouldn't let her leave the room, and, by God, she did it!"

"Oh, *no*!" exclaimed Miss Trent, changing colour. "Oh, how *could* she?"

"If you was to ask me, ma'am, there's precious little she couldn't do! So there was nothing for me to do but tell the landlord she was Mrs Underhill's niece – which he knew – and that she was trying to run off to London, and all I was doing was holding on to her till you arrived to take her in charge. Which he believed, because I'd hired one of the post-boys to carry a message to Waldo. So, as soon as she saw he did believe it, off went her ladyship into hysterics. Lord, you never heard such a commotion in your life!"

"I have frequently heard just such a commotion!" said Miss Trent.

"Where is she, sir?"

"I don't know. The landlady took her off somewhere. No use asking me!"

She got up. "I will go and find the landlady, then. But you must let me thank you, Mr Calver! Indeed, I am so *very* much obliged to you! You have had the most disagreeable time imaginable, and I am astonished you didn't abandon the wretched child!"

"Well, I couldn't do that," said Laurence. "I ain't such a rum touch! Besides – Well, never mind that!"

He watched her cross the room towards the door, and his cousin move to open it for her. In deepening gloom, he observed the punctilious civility of Sir Waldo's slight bow, and the rigidity of Miss Trent's countenance.

Sir Waldo shut the door, and strolled back into the middle of the room. Drawing his snuff-box from his pocket, he tapped it with one long finger, and flicked it open. Taking an infinitesimal pinch, he said, his amused gaze on Laurence's face: "Do tell me, Laurie! Why did you send for me rather than for Underhill?"

Laurence shot him a resentful look. "Thought I could do you a good turn, that's why! And well you know it!"

"But how kind of you!" said Sir Waldo. "I never had the least guess that you had my interests so much at heart."

"Oh, well!" said Laurie awkwardly. "I don't know that I'd say that, precisely, but we're cousins, after all, and it was easy to see your affair was hanging in the hedge, so – "

"What affair?"

Laurence set his empty glass down rather violently. "I know you, coz!" he said angrily. "So don't think to bamboozle me! It's as plain as a pikestaff – "

"And don't *you* think to bamboozle me!" said Sir Waldo, quite pleasantly. "All you wish to do is to put me under an obligation to you, so that I shall be moved to set you up in the horse-coping line. I'm familiar with your tactics."

"Well, damn it, what else can I do?" demanded Laurence in an aggrieved tone. "Who the devil do you suppose is going to dub up the possibles if you don't?"

Sir Waldo's mouth quivered. "I shouldn't think anyone is going to," he replied.

"Yes, that's just like you!" Laurence said, his resentment flaring up. "You're so full of juice you don't know what it is to be bushed – and don't care, either! It wouldn't mean anymore to you to lend me five thousand than it would mean to me to tip over a bull's eye to a waiter. But will you do it? "

"No," said Sir Waldo. "I'm far too hard-fisted. So don't waste any more time or effort in trying to put me under an obligation! You won't do it. You're awake upon some suits, but not on all! And you can't know me as well as you think you do if you imagine I'm not very well able to manage my affairs without your assistance."

"You didn't seem to me to be managing them so very well. No, and even when I threw you and Miss Trent together, you must have made wretched work of it! And you ain't even grateful to me for *trying* to bring you about! When I think of all the trouble I've taken since I came into Yorkshire – let alone being obliged to put up with the infernal racket those builders make – damme if I don't think you *owe* me that paltry five thousand! Because you came the concave suit over me, Waldo, and don't you deny it! Oh, yes, you did! You let me pretty well wear myself out, drawing off that vixen from Lindeth, and it's my belief you knew all along that he was tired of her! And just look what it's led to! Let alone the riot and rumpus I've had to endure, and the blunt I laid out on hiring this parlour, and giving her tea, and lemonade, and buying a ticket for the Mail, my head's been laid open, and I shall very likely carry a scar for the rest of my life!"

"But what have all these misfortunes to do with me?"

"They're got everything to do with you! They'd none of 'em have happened if you hadn't behaved so scaly! Yes, you laugh! It's just what I expected you'd do!"

"You might well!" replied Sir Waldo. "What a hand you are! You know perfectly well that that's nothing but a bag of moonshine!"

"No, I – oh, Waldo, be a good fellow, and oblige me just this once!" Laurence said, with a sudden change of tone. "You wouldn't be so shabby as to refuse, when it was you who made it impossible for me to come by the ready by my own exertions!"

"Now, what in the name of all that's marvellous – "

"You *did*!" insisted Laurence. "You made me give you my word I wouldn't play for more than chicken-stakes! I daresay you think I'll run thin, but that's where you're mistaken!"

"I know very well you won't."

Laurence looked at him in quick surprise, flushing. He said, with a short laugh: "Much obliged to you! It's more than George does!"

"George doesn't mean all he says."

"He can mean it or not for anything I care. Waldo, if I asked you to buy me a cornetcy, would you do it?"

"Tomorrow!"

"Would you expect me to pay it back?"

"Good God, no! Of course I shouldn't!"

"Then why won't you *lend* me the blunt for something I *want*? You'll say a cornetcy wouldn't cost you much above seven or eight hundred pounds, but you wouldn't get it back, remember! Whereas if you was to invest in my scheme you'd make a *profit*!"

Sir Waldo sighed. "I've already told you, Laurie, that – " He broke off as the door opened, and Miss Trent came in, accompanied by Tiffany.

"Oh, so you've recovered, have you?" said Laurence, surveying Tiffany with acute dislike. "In prime twig, I daresay! Never stouter in your life!"

Tiffany was looking rather pale, and decidedly tear-stained, but she was evidently restored to good-humour. Paying no heed to Laurence, she smiled seraphically upon the Nonesuch, and said: "*Thank* you for coming to rescue me! I might have known you would do so, and I'm glad now, though I didn't wish anyone to come after me, at first. But Ancilla says I have made *such* a scandal that there's nothing for it but to take me back to my Uncle Burford, which is exactly what I want! She says she shall write to Aunt Underhill immediately, and as soon as Aunt sends back her consent we shall be off."

"God help your Uncle Burford!" said Laurence.

"You needn't think I have *anything* to say to you, because I haven't!" Tiffany informed him. "And I won't beg your pardon for throwing the clock at you, whatever Ancilla says, because you told lies, and cheated me, and you deserved to have it thrown at you! And, in any event, everything has turned out for the best, and I *am* going to London! So I'm not sorry about anything. When are *you* going to London, Sir Waldo?"

"Almost immediately!" he replied promptly.

For an instant his eyes met Miss Trent's, brimful of laughter. So fleeting was the silent message that passed between them that Tiffany was unaware of it. She looked up at Sir Waldo through her lashes. "I thought you might be," she said demurely.

But Laurence had not missed that swift, revealing exchange of glances, and he ejaculated: "So I *didn't* miss my tip ! Well, I had a notion you was shamming it, coz! Now perhaps you'll own – "

"Laurie!" interrupted Sir Waldo. "I should warn you, perhaps, that if you wish to succeed as a horse-coper you must learn to keep your tongue between your teeth!"

Laurence looked at him. "Are you bamming me?" he asked suspiciously.

"No: merely warning you!"

"I don't understand what you're talking about!" complained Tiffany, by no means pleased at being overlooked.

"Well, who wants you to?" retorted Laurence. "It's coming to something, so it is, if I can't talk to my cousin without having an uppish scrub of a brat prying into what don't concern her!"

"Scrub?" cried Tiffany, colour flaming into her cheeks. "How dare you speak to me like that? I'm not a scrub! I'm not, I'm *not*!"

"A scrub!" repeated Laurence, with relish. "Distempered into the bargain!"

"Quiet!" commanded Sir Waldo.

"Oh, very well!" said Laurence, subsiding.

"I'd liefer be anything but a Bartholomew baby, which is what Courtenay says *you* are! And also a – "

"I said, *Quiet!*"

Tiffany was so much startled by this peremptory reminder that she gasped, and stood staring up at the Nonesuch as though she could not believe that he was speaking not to his cousin, but actually to her. She drew in her breath audibly, and clenched her hands. Miss Trent cast a look of entreaty at Sir Waldo, but he ignored it. He strolled up to the infuriated beauty, and pushed up her chin. "Now, you may listen to me, my child!" he said sternly. "You are becoming a dead bore, and I don't tolerate bores. Neither do I tolerate noisy tantrums. Unless you want to be soundly smacked, enact me no ill-bred scenes!"

There was a moment's astonished silence. Laurence broke it, seizing his cousin's hand, and fervently shaking it. "I *knew* you was a right one!" he declared. "A *great* gun, Waldo! Damme, a *Trojan*!"